The Complete Short Stories

of

L. P. HARTLEY

D1437857

The Complete Short Stories

of

L. P. HARTLEY

WITH AN INTRODUCTION BY

LORD DAVID CECIL

BEAUFORT BOOKS
Publishers
New York

Library of Congress Cataloging-in-Publication Data

Hartley, L.P. (Leslie Poles), 1895–1972.
The complete short stories of L.P. Hartley.

I. Title.
PR6015.A6723A6   1986   823'.912   86-1019

Published in the United States by Beaufort Books Publishers, New York.

Printed in the U.S.A.

CONTENTS

INTRODUCTION

(to *The Collected Short Stories of L. P. Hartley, 1968*)

THE author of *The Go-Between* is one of the most distinguished of modern novelists; and one of the most original. For the world of his creation is composed of such diverse elements. On the one hand he is a keen and accurate observer of the processes of human thought and feeling, especially of its queerer and more whimsical processes: he is also a sharp-eyed chronicler of the social scene. But his picture of both is transformed by the light of a Gothic imagination that reveals itself now in a fanciful reverie, now in the mingled dark and gleam of a mysterious light and a mysterious darkness. Further, both observation and imagination are given significance by the fact that they are made the vehicle of an intense moral vision. It is not a comfortable vision. Man, as seen by Mr. Hartley, is born with a soul that instinctively desires virtue and happiness. But some original sin in himself and in the nature of things is at work to thwart his strivings towards them and brings them, more often than not, to disaster—a disaster he accepts as largely deserved.

Such is the vision of life presented in Mr. Hartley's novels. We find it also in this volume of his collected short stories. With a difference however. In the novels the diverse elements are fused into a single whole; in the stories, one or other tends to dominate. In some the 'Gothic' strain in its author's talent gets it head, as it never does in the novels. Like his eighteenth-century forebears, Mr. Hartley goes in for tales of terror. Sometimes the terror is earthly: *The Island*, *The Killing Bottle*, *The Travelling Grave* are stories of crime. More often the terror is unearthly, an affair of the supernatural. But both earthly and unearthly are steeped in the same atmosphere of eerie and sinister evil. Perhaps this atmosphere suits the unearthly stories best; now and again Mr. Hartley's criminals are too like evil spirits to be wholly convincing as human beings. There is no difficulty, however, in believing in his ghosts. They and their stories assault the imagination with the compelling horror of nightmare. Yet like that of nightmare, their horror is founded on waking experience. For though Mr. Hartley's sense of reality plays a subordinate part in these stories, it is effectively there. The nightmare events are more terrifying because they are interspersed with details drawn from their author's exact and humorous observations of the real world. Rumbold, in *A Visitor from Down-Under*, listens to a programme for children on the wireless, ignorant that it will soon be the medium by which he is brought into communication with the ghost of the man he has murdered.

> '. . . A Children's Party,' the voice announced in an even, neutral tone, nicely balanced between approval and distaste, between enthusiasm and boredom; 'six little girls and six little' (a faint lift in the voice, expressive of tolerant surprise) 'boys. The Broadcasting Company has invited them to tea, and they are anxious that you should share some of their fun.' (At the last word the voice became completely colourless.)

After this it is the ghost's turn to take over: and his intervention is all the more macabre by contrast with what has gone before.

Mr. Hartley's moral preoccupations also have their place in his tales of terror. His ghosts are never inexplicable elementals, but spirits of vengeance or manifestations of spiritual evil. This moral element in his tales give them a disturbing seriousness not to be found in the ordinary ghost story. Like those of Hanry James and Walter De La Mare, they are parables of their authors' profounder beliefs.

Mr. Hartley's Gothic imagination predominates then in one section of his stories; others display his interest in the by-ways of human psychology. He is much concerned with neurotic compulsion and neurotic frustration. Oswald Clayton in *Witheling End* suffers from strong compulsive fits of constraint which have the effect of blighting all his friendships: Mr. Amber in *A Tonic* is possessed by a frustrating fear of death that stops him telling his symptoms to the specialist he has gone to consult, lest they should reveal that his disease is fatal. Akin to these tales, but standing apart from them, is the brief novel called *Simonetta Perkins*, in which is described the gradual steps by which the fastidious and sophisticated Miss Johnson of Boston finds her carefully preserved philosophy of living compulsively undermined by a violent physical passion.

Mr. Hartley's pictures of these different psychological troubles is

wonderfully convincing and his insight into the working of neurosis
alarmingly acute. But it is always the insight of an artist. His interest is
imaginative, not clinical; these stories are not mere efficient studies in
morbid psychology. For we see them through the transfiguring medium
of Mr. Hartley's subtle ironic temperament. Here is the hypochondriac
Mr. Amber waiting to see the specialist.

> Mr. Amber strayed into the waiting-room and sat down in the middle of an
> almost interminable sofa. On either hand it stretched away, a sombre crimson
> expanse figured with rather large fleurs-de-lys and flanked by two tight
> bolsters that matched the sofa, and each other. The room had heavy Oriental
> hangings, indian-red, and gilt French chairs, upholstered in pink. 'A mixture
> of incompatibles,' thought Mr. Amber, 'is contrary to the traditional usages
> of pharmacy, but in practice it may sometimes be not inadmissible.' His mind
> was sensitive to its environment.

Finally Mr. Hartley's sympathetic imagination enables him to endow
his psychological 'cases' with a more universal interest, Clayton and
Amber and the rest of his frustrated heroes are revealed as representa-
tives of the human condition. Their particular quirks may be odd and
even ridiculous, but they are only comical examples of the kind of
weakness that afflicts all of us. As I have said, Mr. Hartley does not take
a hopeful view of the human lot. Most of his dramas end in frustration
if not in anything worse; and if Oswald Clayton and one or two others
do contrive to extract themselves from their troubles, it is through a
chance stroke of luck. The one story in the collection that ends well, in
the full sense of the word, is the delicate little anecdote called *The Price
of the Absolute*. Its last paragraph sees Timothy Carswell going off with
the Celadon vase which he has so recklessly purchased, in a state of
confident rapture; for he feels himself to be the possessor of Absolute
Beauty incarnate. Can this mean, we wonder, that Mr. Hartley thinks
that art is to be trusted even if life is not? that the experience given by a
work of art can be perfect, in a way that an experience given by life
never is? Such an implication seems implicit in the tone with which he
describes the vase.

> Suddenly he stopped, for on a shelf above his head was a vase that arrested his
> attention as sharply as if it had spoken to him. Who can describe perfection?
> I shall not attempt to, nor even indicate the colour; for, like a pearl, the vase
> had its own colour, which floated on its surface more lightly than morning
> mist hangs on a river. . . .
> 'Turn on the light!' commanded the proprietor. So illuminated, the vase

shone as if brightness had been poured over it. It might have been floating in its own essence, so insubstantial did it look. Through layer on layer of soft transparency you seemed to see right into the heart of the vase.

This passage is memorable not only for the light it throws on Mr. Hartley's beliefs, but also as an example of his art at its beautiful best; the precise and exquisite expression of an exquisitely refined sensibility.

D.C.

SIMONETTA PERKINS

Simonetta Perkins *was first published*
in Great Britain in 1925

SIMONETTA PERKINS

'LOVE is the greatest of the passions,' Miss Johnstone read, 'the first and the last.'

She lifted her eyes from the book, and they rested on the grey dome of Santa Maria della Salute, rising like a blister out of the inflamed and suppurating stonework below. The waters of the canal were turbid, bringing the church uncomfortably close. 'How I hate Baroque,' thought Miss Johnstone. 'And this, I am told, is the best example of it. It comes of being born in Boston, I suppose. And yet a Johnstone of Boston should be able to appreciate anything. Anything good, that is.'

She read on.

'Other passions tend to exaggerate and to intensify, but love transforms. The victim of the amorous passion has a holiday from himself. No longer does he discern in the objects he sees before him the pale reflection of his own mediocrity; those objects become the symbols of an inner quickening. An effulgence of the Absolute irradiates his being.'

'How often have I read this sort of thing before,' thought Miss Johnstone, trying to ignore the Salute, and fixing her gaze on the chaster outlines of St. Gregory, across the way. 'Consider the servants here,' she soliloquised, glancing right and left along the sunny terrace whose steps were lapped by the waves; 'has any one of them, for any one moment, been irradiated by an effulgence of the Absolute? I think not.' She met the smirk of a passing concierge with a reproving stare. 'But they are all married, I suppose, or whatever in Venice takes the place of marriage.'

The print rose up at her, and she started once more to read.

'Love is an inheritance that falls to the lot of all mankind. Anger, envy, jealousy, cruelty; pity, charity, humility, courage: these emotions are partial and unequal in their incidence. They visit some, and others they pass by. But man that is born of woman cannot escape love. Of whatsoever age thou art, reader, never believe thyself secure from his fiery dart.'

'Now here,' exclaimed Miss Johnstone, slamming the book face-downwards on the wicker-work table at her side, 'here, among much vapid rhetoric and dreary rubbish is one huge, dangerous, vital, mis-leading falsehood.'

This outburst having caused more than one lorgnette to be directed upon her, Miss Johnstone ceased to testify openly and continued her reflections to herself. But never had her whole consciousness, her whole being, shown itself, to her, so vociferously articulate. From her toes to her hair she was an incarnation of denial. 'It is a lie,' she thought, 'a cruel, useless lie. If I – since the writer, after many meaningless general-izations, now impudently addresses himself to me – if I had been capable of this passion, would not Stephen Seleucis and Michael B. Sprott and Theodore Drakenburg and Walt Watt have awakened it? They awak-ened it in everyone else, even in Mamma.' She looked round: but her mother had not yet appeared.

'The pinnacle of elegibility on which I sat, and to which in a month I must return, was, and no doubt again will be, festooned with offers of marriage. They affected me no more than an invitation to dinner, ex-cept that I was harassed by having to take some of them seriously. I am absolutely immune from love. If I marry, it will be from considerations of convenience.

'Alas that one cannot reply to an author except by making notes in the margin, notes he will never see! And this love-adept has wisely left his margins slender. Let me see what he says now. Aha! a threat!'

'In the case of solipsistical and egocentric natures, the tide of love, long awaited in secret' (Miss Johnstone frowned) 'may find a tortuous and uneasy passage. There is much to be absorbed, much to be over-come. The habit of self-communion must be subdued; all those private delights, the sense, so delicious to some, of retiring into oneself and drawing down the blinds, must be repudiated and foresworn. The un-fortunate egoist must learn to take his pleasure from without; he is no longer his own warehouse and market place, he must go out to buy. No longer may he think, "I will sit in such and such a position, it gives me ease"; or, "I will take a drive to-day and refresh my spirits", or, "to-morrow I will choose a suit of clothes"; for he will no longer find pleasure in the satisfaction of daily needs. Rather he will say, "If I rest my cheek thus upon my finger, how will Chloe regard it?" and, "I will wait upon Melissa with my barouche, though I abhor the motion", and, "since Julia is away I must go ragged and barefoot, for without her sanction I dare not choose either silk or shoe-leather". To such as have been accustomed to give others the first place in their thoughts, the oncoming of love will prove a bloodless revolution; but to the egoists, the epicures of their own sensations, the change will be violent, damaging and bitter.'

'Should I call myself an egoist?' Miss Johnstone mused. 'Others have called me so. They merely meant that I did not care for them. Now if they had said fastidious or discriminating! On the whole it is a pity that Stephen Seleucis is coming next week; but he did once say, "Lavinia, it isn't only your charm that attracts me, it's your refusal to see charm in anyone else. Even in me", he added. How could I contradict him? Certainly I am not selfish. Punctual myself, I am tolerant of unpunctuality in others. It is the mark of a saint, Walt Watt once told me. Why do I recall these foolish compliments? They ought never to have found their way into my diary; and it is no answer to the author of this odious manual (who has somehow contrived to pique me) to urge that idle young men have talked as though they were in love with me. Can it be that I am vain? Why else should I have treasured those insinuating commendations? When Mamma speaks her mind to me, it goes like water off a duck's back.'

At that moment two visitors, both men, walked past her. One tilted his head back, as though his collar chafed him; but Miss Johnstone knew instinctively that he was indicating her, as, with an interrogatory lift of his voice he said,

'Beautiful?'

'Well, no,' his friend replied, 'not really beautiful.' They passed out of ear-shot. Miss Johnstone blinked, and involuntarily caught up the treatise upon Love, in her agitation forgetting to sneer at the opening words.

'Like all great subjects, love has its false prophets. You will hear men say, "I do not know whether I am in love or not"; but *your* heart, reader, will never give you this ambiguous answer. Doubtful symptoms there may be, excitement, irritability, sleeplessness, without cause shown; but uncertainty, when the eye of desire at last has the beloved object in its view, never.'

Miss Johnstone had recovered from her embarrassment. 'What execrable taste!' she exclaimed. 'The eye of desire, pooh!' She raised her own eyes, as though to record a protest to the heavens, but her out-raged glance never climbed to the zenith. An intermediate object arrested it. Posted in front of her, though how it got there unobserved she could not imagine, a gondola lay rocking. At either end it was lashed to those blue posts whose function, apart from picturesqueness, Miss Johnstone for the first time dimly understood; and the gondolier was sitting on the poop and staring at the hotel. No, not at the hotel, decided Miss Johnstone, at me.

She tried to return the stare; it troubled her. It was vivid, abstracted, and unrecognizing. It seemed to be projected up at her out of those fierce blue eyes.

She turned to look behind her, half expecting to see some dumb show, a servant making a face, that would explain the gondolier's in-terest and explain it away. She saw only a blind window and a blank wall. Unwillingly her eyes travelled back, searching vainly in their cir-cuit for some less hazardous haven. Once more they rested on the gon-dolier. Hunched up, he sat, but without any appearance of awkwardness or of constriction; one brown hand drooped over his knee: the gold of his rings glittered against the brown. He was like some black bird that, in settling, had not troubled quite to fold its wings.

'But he can't really fly,' thought Miss Johnstone, meeting his eyes at last, 'and there's the water between us.' Emboldened by the reflection, she scanned his face. Did the twist of his brown moustache make him too predaceous, too piratical? She decided it did not. How did he come by the tawny hair that waved under the gallant curve of the black sombrero? Of course, many Venetians had brown hair. Again she dropped her eyes before the urgency of that stare, and at the same mo-ment was conscious of a change in the demeanour of the loitering servants, and heard a familiar voice.

'Lavinia! Lavinia!' Right and left her mother's summons enfiladed the terrace. 'Am I to wait here all night?'

'Coming!' cried Miss Johnstone in a thin pipe, making her way through the occasional tables to where, nodding and tossing her bold, blonde head, her mother stood while the servants scurried round her.

'Where is my gondola?' that lady demanded, her eye sweeping the Grand Canal with such authority that her daughter thought the craft must rise, like Venus, from the waves. 'I ordered it for eleven. I come down at half-past eleven, and there is no sign of it.'

'Emilio, Emilio,' called a concierge, shrinking so much that his scarlet waistcoat hung quite loosely on him. 'He is here, Madam.'

'Why doesn't he come then, if he's here?' Mrs. Johnstone asked, adding in a gentler tone, 'I see, he's untying himself. What unhandy things these gondolas are. No wonder they are to be abolished.'

Propelled from post to post by Emilio's outstretched hand the deprecated vessel drew up to the steps. With a gesture that just escaped being a flourish, the gondolier took off his hat and held it across his body; his hair blew backwards, caught by the wind. As though in a dream Miss Johnstone saw her mother, poised on the unsteady embarkation board, give him the benefit of that glare before which all Boston quailed; and then, a weakness surely without precedent, she saw her mother's eyelids flicker.

'*Comandi, Signora?*' said the gondolier, whilst Miss Johnstone fitted herself into the space her mother left over.

'What does the man say?' asked Mrs. Johnstone, petulant at being addressed in a foreign tongue.

'He wants to know where to take us,' Lavinia replied.

'Do you mean he doesn't know?' asked her mother, amazed that any wish of hers, however private, should be stillborn.

As though anxious to help, the gondolier came forward a little and leaned over them.

'*La chiesa dei Santi Giovanni e Paolo?*' he suggested. Soft and caressing, his voice lingered over the words as if he loved them.

'They always say that: they always take one there,' pronounced Mrs. Johnstone, implying that every Venetian conversation and destination was included in the gondolier's words. 'No, we will not go there. You have the book, Lavinia; what does it say for the third day?'

'I'm afraid we haven't kept pace with it,' Lavinia said. 'We should have to start out at daybreak. And the churches all shut at twelve. Let's go down the Grand Canal to the Rialto, and back by the little canals.'

'Tell him, then,' said Mrs. Johnstone, settling herself against the cushions.

'*Gondoliere,*' Lavinia began, in a hesitating tone, as if she were about to ask his opinion on some private matter. She turned round to find his face close to hers; the beringed left hand, lying across his knee, was level with her eyes. 'How everyone in Venice seems to strike an attitude,' she thought, and the sentence she had prepared dissolved in her mind. She eked out her order with single words and vague gesticulations. Off sped the gondola; the palaces slid by; now they were under the iron bridge; soon they would be at the great bend. 'This man is a champion, my dear,' remarked Mrs. Johnstone, 'he knows how to put the pace

on.' Never before had Lavinia's mother so cordially approved of anything Venetian. But Lavinia herself·wondered whether such purpose-
fulness was quite in keeping with the spirit of the place. 'He has not
mastered the art of languor,' she murmured. 'Art of what, Lavinia?'
Mrs. Johnstone challenged, stirring under her silks. 'Oh, nothing,
Mamma.' For the thousandth time Lavinia climbed down. Just then
they overtook a barge, piled high with lemons and tomatoes; the barge-
man, impaled as it seemed on his punt-pole and shining with sweat, yet
found it in him to turn and hail, in the sociable Italian fashion, the
Johnstones' gondolier. The gorgeous fruits framed his glittering smile,
and their abundance went well with his loquacity; but Emilio vouchsafed only a mono-syllable in reply, something between a bark and
grunt. 'How taciturn he is,' Lavinia thought. 'I will draw him out; I
will practise my Italian on him; I will ask for information. Questo?'
she demanded, indicating a sombre pile on the left. 'Palazzo Rezzonico,'
he replied, speaking as though the name were heaven-sent, the explosive double z's so tamed and softened they might have fallen from the
lips of an angel. 'That hasn't got us much further,' reflected Lavinia.
'Why does my vocabulary shrivel up directly I have a chance to use it?
If the man had been an Eskimo I could have put the question in
perfect Italian, using the feminine third person singular and all the apparatus of politeness. But one relapses into inarticulateness directly
there is a risk of being understood. And come to that,' Lavinia pondered, frowning at the arabesque of scorpions and centipedes embroidered diagonally up her mother's dress, 'do I ever say what I mean when
there is a likelihood of being understood? Perhaps it is fortunate that
the likelihood is rare.' Association of ideas recalled Stephen Seleucis
and his impending visit. 'If only, in thought, I could bring myself to
call him "Ste",' she mused, 'perhaps I could oblige him and mother.
He cares for culture.'

   Oi!

The sudden bellow startled her. Could Emilio have been responsible
for it? She glanced up; he was staring impassive and unmoved, much
as the campanile must stand after the frightful fracas of its striking midnight. They had left the Grand Canal behind and were elbowing their
way up a narrow waterway; gone was all chance of seeing the Rialto,
the object of their ride. No doubt Mrs. Johnstone had noticed it. 'But
really,' Lavinia reproached herself, 'I must do what I set out to do;
otherwise I shall fall a prey to that anæmia of the will of which my
Venetian compatriots so energetically boast. I shall consider my time

wasted until I have satisfied myself whether Ruskin is right. Mamma thinks he is because her judgments follow her beliefs; my beliefs, if I could entertain any, would follow my judgments, if I could be certain what they were.'

Bui!

That was a good one, and a collision at this perilous corner providentially averted. Emilio and the coal man, *carboniere*, or whatever it is, have words, but without much ill-feeling, to judge from their faces. Emilio would look cross at any time, or is it savage, perhaps, or just stern, incorruptible, fearless, conscious of his Northern blood? He must be descended from the Visigoths I suppose; hence the colouring. How wonderfully he manages the gondola, taking it round these corners as cleanly as if it had a bend in its back. And here we are at the hotel.

The Splendid and Royal came into view, blinking behind its sun-blinds; and the servants, seeing with whom they had to deal, formed a circle on the steps, advertising their anxiety that Mrs. Johnstone should make a successful landing. Even Emilio came down into the hold to give her his arm, stretching it out stiff at an odd impersonal angle, as though it was a bit of ship's furniture. The strength of her clasp left upon his skin a milky stain which faded even as Lavinia, bowed with books and rugs, momentarily laid her hand there. How cool it was, with all that sunshine stored up in it. She heard her mother's voice, raised to the pitch of indignant non-comprehension that had served her so well in life.

'Emilio wants, Emilio who?'

'Emilio Varagnolo, Madam, your gondolier.'

'Well, and what does he want?'

'He wants to be paid.'

'Lavinia,' said her mother, 'you're always wool-gathering. Here, give him this.'

But "this," in all its eloquent parsimony, with all its air of making the foreigner, in his own territory, pay, was precisely what Lavinia could not give him. Already she had suffered much from those uncomfortable partings, from those muttered curses and black looks which were the certain outcome of giving Italians nothing but their due. In this case, it was less than what was due. Mrs. Johnstone's blameless desire that people should not get the better of her generally ended, Lavinia knew, in her getting the better of them. Wondering by how much she should increase the fare she looked across and met the eyes of the gondolier, which also seemed to wonder. Hastily she pulled some

notes out and, scarcely stopping to count them, walked down the little
gangway and put them into his outstretched hand. What she had neglected to do, he did most thoroughly. With an absorption that might
have amused her he reckoned up the sum, and, finding it tally with his
expectations, or perhaps even rise to his hopes, he acknowledged her
generosity with a dazzling smile and a magnificent salute. All the vitality
of which she had been conscious, and whose application to alien activities she had vaguely resented, was suddenly released, let loose upon her
in a flood. She shivered and turned away, only to be recalled.

'Madame! Signorina!'

'What is it?' Lavinia asked.

'Emilio wants to know if he shall return in the afternoon.' Instead of
answering, Lavinia walked back to the steps. Emilio still wore his
smile.

'*Venga qui alle due,–alle due e mezzo*,' she said.

'*Va bene*, Signorina,' he answered, and was gone.

2

'I TOLD the gondolier to come at half-past two,' Lavinia casually mentioned to her mother at luncheon.

'What gondolier, dear?' asked Mrs. Johnstone.

'The one we had this morning.'

'Well, we don't want to encourage the man.'

'How do you mean, "encourage", Mamma?' Lavinia mildly enquired.

'I mean what I say,' said Mrs. Johnstone without attempting further
elucidation.

'Then,' pursued Lavinia, 'we shall be able to see La Madonna dell'
Orto and all those churches on the Northern fringe.'

'Which day are they for?' demanded Mrs. Johnstone, suspicion leaping into her voice.

'They are not all for a day,' confessed Lavinia, reluctantly admitting
the inferior status of the churches on the Northern fringe. 'Tourists
often neglect Sant' Alvise, though it is a gem and well repays a visit,
the guide book says.'

'We are not tourists, whatever it may be,' remarked Mrs. Johnstone.

'And,' continued Lavinia, momentarily elated by the success of her ruse, 'it contains the pseudo-Carpaccios, a notable instance, Mr. Arrantoff says, of Ruskin's faulty *a priori* method and want of true critical sense.'

'Then I am sure I don't want to see them,' Mrs. Johnstone declared. 'And who is Mr. Arrantoff, anyhow?'

'He is quite modern,' said Lavinia feebly.

'All the more reason that he should be wrong,' her mother asserted. 'Ruskin was nearer Carpaccio's date, wasn't he?'

'He wasn't contemporary,' said Lavinia.

'Perhaps not, but no doubt he had the tradition,' Mrs. Johnstone retorted. 'In most cases, as you have told me more times than I can count, the tradition is all we have to go on. Ruskin went on it, I go on it, and you will, if you are sensible. But I am afraid sense is not your strong point, Lavinia. There's something I want to talk to you about. Remind me.'

'Can't you talk to me about it now?' Lavinia asked.

'I don't want everyone in the room to hear me,' her mother replied, raising her voice as though to justify her misgivings. Several people at neighbouring tables turned round in surprise. 'You see,' Mrs. Johnstone commented complacently, 'I was right. They can hear. It will do in the gondola.'

They parted; Mrs. Johnstone to rest, Lavinia to read. The first four volumes of Richardson's masterpiece had yielded little but irritation. Why, she had asked herself a hundred times, if Clarissa really wanted to leave Lovelace, didn't she go? She wasn't a prisoner, but on she stayed, groaning, complaining, fainting, making scenes, when she might have walked out of the front door any hour in the twenty-four. Instead of which she tried to match her wits against the contrivances of a cad, hoping ultimately to charm him into a respectable citizen. But to-day Lavinia found herself more tolerant of Clarissa's voluntary bondage. Where, after all, could Miss Harlowe have gone? Would it be an agreeable home-coming for her, Lavinia, if after a parallel behaviour and a parallel experience she returned to the parental roof? Mrs. Johnstone was not usually tender towards animals, but surely, on that occasion, she could be counted upon to spare the life of the fatted calf. 'Never, my dear Lavinia,' she affectionately admonished herself, 'let any situation get the upper hand of you.' She sighed, realizing from past experience how improbable it was that any situation would put itself to the trouble. 'Not that I should welcome it,' she added, in an access of distaste. 'No Lovelaces for me.' She took up her coffee, which was growing cold, and looking over the brim of the cup she saw Emilio. He had arrived long before his time and was sitting on the low, carved chair, a luxury found only in the best gondolas, reading a newspaper. She watched his hands moving among the sheets, opening and closing. The thought that he could read gave her pleasure, such pleasure as might come from observing an unlooked-for accomplishment in one's own child. She wished he would lean back against the cushions and make himself comfortable: after all, it was his gondola. They cost seven thousand lire, a large sum for a poor man; and yet, as people who keep lodgings must let their best rooms to strangers and live in holes and corners themselves, so he, perhaps, had a scruple about taking the easiest seat. Warm and seductive, an humanitarian mood was visiting her, when the gondolier folded his paper, glanced up, and saw her. His face, she fancied, was friendly behind its glitter, he waved his hat and made a pretty show of activity; but when, in some confusion, she signed to him that she was not ready, he settled down to his paper again. Lavinia also returned to her book, but what she read did not hold her attention; the fact that she knew how to read didn't provide her with a solace, nor Emilio, to judge from his abstraction, with food for pleasurable thought. The dumb show in which she had taken part a moment since repeated itself before the ready auditorium of her mind; she saw his face alight with recognition; she tried to visualize his expression, penetrating, impatient, interrogatory, expectant. He looked as though any moment you might do something that would delight him. Why had she not done it? And yet what could she have done? She had an uneasy feeling that in the exchange of gestures she had not acquitted herself as she should have done, had missed an opportunity. 'Perhaps I can repair the error,' she thought, moving to a chair directly opposite the gondola. A smile rewarded her and she saw to it that this time her own greeting should not lack warmth.

3

DIFFICULT to get at, more difficult to get into, infested outside by noisy children thirsting for money, and inside by sacristans more silent, but no less avaricious, the churches on the Northern fringe were everything that Lavinia had hoped. The September sunshine turned pink into rose, grey into green, danced reflected on the undersides of bridges and lent a healing touch to the cold rococo splendour of the Gesuiti, roofed and walled in gold. Devils at close quarters, at a distance the children with their ash-gold hair looked like angels taken from Bellini's pictures. 'Don't give them anything,' Mrs. Johnstone warned Lavinia, 'we must not encourage beggars.' '*Via, via,*' cried Lavinia, but they only mocked her, repeating the word in high glee, crowding round and pulling at her empty hands till her rings hurt her fingers. Even Emilio, rising in wrath on the poop and fixing them with a glare of unrestrained ferocity, scarcely quelled them. But he was a great help when anything went wrong, when a key couldn't be found, or when a church was hidden round a corner. Personal investigation, poking about on her own, was unthinkable to Mrs. Johnstone. The unknown alarmed her and she never paused to think how she, in her turn, would have alarmed the unknown.

Standing all billowy and large, within a few feet of the fondamenta, she would majestically wave her parasol to Emilio, who, leaving the gondola in charge of a beggar, leapt to do her bidding. Not a single detail of his alacrity was lost upon Lavinia. She wondered how he could walk at all, above all how he could walk so fast; she imagined he would go lop-sided, twisted by the unequal exercise of his profession. But his coming ashore renewed her confidence, she liked to see him striding ahead, and she caught herself abetting her mother in her passion for guidance, even when such guidance clearly was not required.

Never had she felt happier than when, late in the afternoon, they left San Giobbe homeward bound. Or more conscious of virtue. Always a conscientious but rarely an ecstatic sightseer, she had presented to each picture, each sculpture, each tomb, a vitality as persistent as its own. She felt at one with Art. She discriminated, she had her favourites, but her sensibility remained keen and unwearied, never missing an æsthetic intention or misjudging its effectiveness. To what could she attribute this blissful condition? Lavinia did not know, but irrelevantly she turned round and asked the gondolier the name of a church they were passing. 'He will take me for an idiot,' she thought, 'for I have asked him once already.' 'Santa Maria dei Miracoli,' he informed her without a trace of impatience. Lavinia knew it, but she wanted to hear him say it; and she continued to look back at the receding edifice, long after its outlines had been eclipsed and replaced by the figure of Emilio.

Mrs. Johnstone's voice, always startling, made her positively jump. 'Lavinia!'

'Yes, Mamma.'

Mrs. Johnstone generally called her daughter to attention before speaking.

'It was about Ste Seleucis.'

'I knew it was,' Lavinia replied.

'Then why didn't you remind me?' her mother demanded. 'I might easily have forgotten.'

Lavinia was silent.

'Now, when he comes, I want you to be particularly nice to him.'

'I always am, Mamma; that's what he complains of,' Lavinia rejoined.

'Then you must cut the nice part out. Now there were four men in America you might have married, and their names were—'

'I could only have married one,' Lavinia objected.

'Their names were,' Mrs. Johnstone pursued, 'Stephen Seleucis, Theodore Drakenburg, Michael B. Sprott, and Walt Watt. They were not good enough for you.' Mrs. Johnstone paused to let this sink in. 'What did they do? They married someone else.'

'Three other people in all,' Lavinia amended.

'But Stephen didn't,' said Mrs. Johnstone, as though virtue disclaimed the abbreviation that affection craved. 'And next week, I hope you will give him a different answer.'

Lavinia looked upwards at the Bridge of Sighs. 'I should be very inconsistent if I did,' she said at last.

'Who wants you to be consistent?' asked Mrs. Johnstone. 'When you are married you can be as consistent as you like. But not when you are turned twenty-seven and unmarried, and have a grey hair or two, and the reputation of being as forbidding to decent men as the inside of Sing-Sing prison. I could say more, but I will refrain, because you are my daughter and I don't want to hurt your feelings.'

A confession of belated solicitude always rounded off Mrs. Johnstone's harangues on this topic; it had become a formula.

'Decent men?' Lavinia echoed, watching the throng of loungers on the piazzetta. 'You don't think it's their decency that makes me dislike them?' She spoke without irony, reflectively.

'Well, I don't know what else you had to find fault with,' remarked Mrs. Johnstone, 'except their looks. Ste isn't a beauty; but you can't have everything.'

'I am content to have nothing,' muttered Lavinia. In the fuss of landing, for they had reached the hotel, her rebellious utterance escaped censure. Disencumbered, her mother trod heavily upon the fragile gangway, to disappear amid solicitous servants. She herself remained to collect their traps, hidden by the gathering dusk. Some had slipped off Mrs. Johnstone as she rose, her amplitude, as a watershed for these trifles, making the range of search wide, almost incalculable. She knelt, she groped. 'I *will* find them,' thought Lavinia, and then, as her hand closed upon the last, 'why should I find them?' She replaced her mother's smelling-bottle in a crevice of the cushions, and appealed to Emilio with a gesture of despair. Instantly he was on his knees beside her. The search lasted for a full minute. Then '*Ecco, ecco,*' cried the gondolier, delighted by his discovery, holding the smelling-bottle as tenderly as if it had been the relic of a saint. Infected by his high spirits, exalted into a mood she did not recognize, Lavinia stretched out her hand for the bottle and smiled into his eyes. Their exquisite mockery, the overtone of their glitter, annihilated time. Lavinia passed beyond thought into a stellar region where all sensations were one. Then the innumerable demands of life swarmed back and settled upon her, dealing their tiny stings. For one thing Emilio must be paid.

But Emilio had no change. He searched himself, he turned this way and that; he bent forward as though wounded, and backward as though victorious. His hands apologized, his face expressed concern, but not a lira could he find to dilute Lavinia's fifty. So she gave him the note, and then followed the incident which was eventually to cause her much distress and self-reproach. That she didn't, at the time, divine its importance the casual entry in her diary shows.

'The depression I have felt the last few weeks left me to-day; why, I cannot think. Perhaps the homily I gave myself last night in bed has borne fruit. I resolved not to be idle, discontented or inattentive, but to throw myself into life and let the current carry me whither it would. Nothing of the sort seems to have happened; I haven't taken any plunge; but this morning, on the Grand Canal, and still more this afternoon, going round the churches with Mamma (how that bored me at Verona, see August 30th and resolution), I felt extraordinarily happy. (Here the words 'Perhaps I have a capacity for happiness after all,' were deleted). Not quite so happy after dinner when we went out to listen to the piccola serenata; that was with a different gondolier. I think I shall persuade Mamma to stick to the one we had this afternoon, engage him by the day. He wanted to come for us this evening, and I have asked myself since (although it is a trivial matter) why I said we shouldn't need him. I should be sorry if he thought us ungrateful for all his help, but I felt, just at the moment, that I had overpaid him and

it would be disagreeable, with the same man, to reduce the rate in
future; also I wasn't sure whether Mamma might not prefer the Piazza,
and then he would be disappointed of his fare. I don't want to appear
capricious. Emilio didn't take my saying no very well, not as pleasantly
as he took my fifty lire note; I thought he scowled at me, but it was
almost too dark to see. What does it matter? but he had been charming,
and it is so seldom a foreigner takes a genuine interest in one. I hope I
wasn't mean over the money; but it makes it hard for poorer people if
you give too much, and isn't really good for the Italians themselves.
It would be a pity to spoil Emilio. How lovely the false Carpaccios
were—I prefer them to the real ones. Is there anything else? Hiding the
smelling-bottle wasn't the same thing as a lie—just a game, like hunt-
the-thimble.'

4

EVERY prospect in Venice gives the beholder a sense of unworthiness
and of being born out of time; but Lavinia, arrived early on the terrace
next morning, was scarcely at all conscious of inferiority. The sun was
brilliant, the water as still as it would ever be. Incompatibilities did not
trouble her. The great American cruiser moored at the side of the
Bacino, leaning against the land, reassured her by its stability; the
Trieste liner, stealthily revolving on itself, contrasted pleasantly with
the small fry that looked purposeless and stationary, but were no doubt
working hard to get out of the monster's way. The island of St. Giorgio
was evidently the work of a magician; every building fitted into the
cliché that guide-books and tourists had agreed upon for it. 'The Salute
itself,' thought Lavinia, looking her ancient enemy squarely in the face,
'has a decorative quality, and decoration is something, though of course
not the essence of art. Even that ruffianly-looking gondolier is improved
by his crimson sash. Now, if Emilio had one—' And pat to her thought
Emilio appeared, cleaving his way towards her and dressed, not in the
dingy weeds of yesterday, but in a white suit with a sky-blue scarf that
lay like a lake upon his chest, and a sash that poured itself away in a
cascade of flounces from the knot at his side.

Lavinia made up her mind quickly. Espying a high functionary she
took her courage in both hands and addressed him. 'Could she engage
Emilio as Mrs. Johnstone's private gondolier?'

The man's manner, a disagreeable blend of insolence and servility, grew oilier and more offensive.

'No, you cannot have him, he is already engaged; the lady and gentleman who went out with him last night have taken him from day to day.'

'Oh,' said Lavinia, suddenly listless. So this was the meaning of the fine apparel, the meaning of the gondola encrusted with gilt and dripping with fringes? She had been forestalled. Her eyes travelled over the sumptuous vessel and Emilio made her a little salute — the acknowledgment due to a late employer — without much heart in it. She could not go on standing where she was. Despondent she walked back to her chair. The balcony had become a cage, and the day was brilliant, she felt, in spite of her.

'Lavinia!'

'Yes, Mamma.'

'You don't look as though you had slept any too well. Did you?' Tenderness and interest alike were absent from Mrs. Johnstone's enquiry; its tone suggested both certainty and disapproval, and she went on, without waiting for a reply:

'But I've got some good news for you, or what ought to be good news. I give you three guesses.'

Now play up, Lavinia.

'The wordly Elizabeth Templeman is coming here from Rome?'

'Wrong. She is still in bed with the chill she so foolishly caught wandering about the Coliseum after nightfall.'

'The exchange?'

'The exchange is two points worse. Really, Lavinia, you should know these things.' Mrs. Johnstone could make even guessing dangerous.

'Then it must be that Stephen isn't—'

'Isn't! Is, and Monday too. With the Evanses. Now I ought to tell you that Amelia Fielder Evans—'

'My rival?'

'Amelia Fielder Evans,' said Mrs. Johnstone warningly, 'is a very determined woman.'

'Yes,' sighed Lavinia. 'He certainly should be saved from her.'

'Well, you can save him,' Mrs. Johnstone observed, 'and you can do it at dinner on Tuesday. Amelia will be tired from her journey. Now what?'

'Should we bathe?' suggested Lavinia.

'Heavens! But I thought you wanted to go in a gondola. You are changeable, Lavinia.'

'You have always wanted to see the Lido, Mamma.'

'Very well, then.'

'We'll walk to the vaporetto. It's not far.'

Off they went.

5

'How brief is human happiness,' Lavinia wrote that night in her diary. 'My exaltation of yesterday has almost passed away. I loathed the Lido: all those khaki-coloured bodies lying about, half-interred in sand or sprawling over bridge tables, disgusted me inexpressibly. My Puritan blood stirred within me. Why must they make themselves so common? The people who hired our gondolier came out in the afternoon; they were among the worst, perfectly shameless. Mamma was surprised when I went up to speak to them, but one must be civil to people staying in the same hotel. You never know what you may want from them, as Elizabeth Templeman would say. When they heard who we were, they were impressed and showed it; they come from Pittsburg, their speech bewrayeth them. They offered to take us in their gondola whenever we liked. Mamma was for refusing and reproached me afterwards because I said we would. But are we not all God's people? We live too much in a groove, and personalities are more interesting than places, as I have proved in many an essay. Still, even as they left my lips, the gracious words of consent surprised me. Strangers are my abhorrence and my instinct was to dislike these, with their name like a Greek toothpaste, Kolynopulo. America is a nation of hyphens and hybrids.

'How discontented all this sounds. I must make a resolution against exclusiveness, a besetting sin. I have always meant to visit the poor, but Venice is not a good place to begin in. . . . How it would surprise Emilio if I turned up at his home, bringing a tract against profanity! The churches are plastered with notices begging the people not to disgrace the glorious language of Dante, Alfieri, Petrarch, etc. I have an idea what his home is like: it would be fun to see if it is a true one!'

6

'SHAME your mother couldn't come,' said Mr. Kolynopulo, assisting Lavinia, with more gallantry than was necessary, into his gorgeous gondola. 'Does she often have headaches?'

Miss Johnstone wore a harassed air. 'Venice doesn't really suit her,' she replied. 'It's the tiresome sirocco.' She looked wistfully down the lagoon to where that climatic nuisance was wont to assert its presence with an unanswerable visibility; but the air had lost its fever, could not have been clearer. 'The very heavens give me the lie,' she thought; and aloud she said, 'Oh! no, Mr. Kolynopulo, you must let me be selfish and sit here.' To clinch the argument she sank into the half-way seat. 'Venice depends so much on where you sit. Here I can see forwards and sideways and even backwards.' Suiting the action to the word, she gazed earnestly at a point directly in their wake; her scrutiny also included Emilio, who did not return it, but stared angrily at the horizon.

'Good-looking, isn't he?' remarked Mrs. Kolynopulo, indicating Emilio with her thumb.

Lavinia started.

'I suppose he is. I never thought about it,' she said.

'Then you're different from most,' Mrs. Kolynopulo answered. 'I guess he's caused a flutter in many a female breast. We considered ourselves lucky to get him. We've been the subject of congratulation.'

'Not from me,' thought Lavinia, eyeing congratulation's twin subjects with ill-concealed distaste.

'Do you share the flutter?' she presently enquired.

'Bless you, no,' replied his wife. 'We're married. We leave that sort of thing to the single ones.'

The slaves of matrimony exchanged affectionate looks and even, to Lavinia's horror, kissed each other. She wanted to let the subject drop, but instead she asked:

'What sort of thing?'

'What sort of thing which, dear?' Mrs. Kolynopulo playfully asked her.

'What sort of thing do you . . . . . leave?' said Lavinia, with an effort making her meaning clear.

Her temporary hosts looked archly at each other, then laughed long and loud.

'My dear!' protested Mrs. Kolynopulo, still quivering like a jelly.

'You forget, my pretty,' her husband reproved her, 'that Miss John-stone has been properly brought up.'

'Oh dear, you Boston girls, you ingénues!' Mrs. Kolynopulo sighed. 'Ask us another time.'

But Lavinia had had a revulsion. 'May my tongue rot if I do,' she thought, and to change the subject she asked their immediate destination.

'To see the glass made,' Mr. Kolynopulo replied. 'Venetian glass, what?'

'Yes, Venetian, of course,' Lavinia repeated helplessly.

'Well, isn't it one of the recognized sights? We've seen the prison and the pigeons.'

'Oh, perfectly recognized,' Lavinia almost too heartily agreed. 'I see the posters and the man with the leaflets.'

They disembarked.

7

ON their return they found Mrs. Johnstone seated under an awning, a rug across her knees, a bitter-looking cordial at her elbow. The chair beside her was occupied by a mound of American newspapers, and in front of her another chair supported her work—a box of silks and a vast oval frame within which the features of a sylvan scene had begun to disclose themselves. A pale green fountain rose into the air, whose jet, symmetrically bifurcated, played upon a formal cluster of lambs in one corner and a rose-red rock in the other.

The Kolynopulos approached as near as the barricade permitted. Mrs. Johnstone did not dismantle it, nor did she rise.

'I'm glad you took Lavinia to the glass-factory,' she observed, when the conventional expressions of sympathy had exhausted themselves. 'I could never get her to go. She won't take any interest in trade pro-cesses, though I often ask her where she'd be without them.'

'We should still have each other,' said Lavinia.

'Of course we should, darling,' Mrs. Johnstone remarked, greatly pleased. 'What more do we want?' The question hung in the air until the retirement of the Kolynopulos, bowing and smiling, seemed to have answered it.

'Oh, Mamma,' said Lavinia, much concerned. 'I did not know you were ill.'

'You might have done,' her mother replied. 'I told you.'

'Yes,' conceded Lavinia, 'but—'

'You are right in a way,' admitted Mrs. Johnstone. 'It came on afterwards. Providence would not have me a liar. All the same, I don't like your new friends, Lavinia.'

'Nor do I, altogether,' Lavinia confessed.

'Then why let them take you out?'

'Well, we can't both have headaches, for our own sakes,' Lavinia obscurely replied.

'It's not necessary to have them more than once, and mine could have served for both of us, if you'd let it,' Mrs. Johnstone answered. 'You don't understand, Lavinia. Undesirable acquaintances may be kept off in a variety of ways. You saw how I did it just now.'

'But that was very crude, Mamma, you must own, and may have wounded them.'

'If so, I shall have struck oil.' Mrs. Johnstone paused to appreciate her joke. 'No; it's like this. You cannot be too careful. Our station in life is associated with a certain point of view and a certain standard of conduct. Once you get outside it, anything may happen to you. People like that may easily put ideas into your head, and then it'll be no good coming to me to get them out.'

'Would it be any good going to them?' In vision Lavinia saw her mind as an aquarium, in which a couple of unattractive minnows, the gift of the Kolynopulos, eluded Mrs. Johnstone's unpractised hand.

'You'd probably find them more sympathetic,' her mother replied. 'But they couldn't help you, any more than you can help me to get rid of this chill, though you may be said to have given it me, since I caught it bathing with you. But I think you might stay in this afternoon and try.'

After luncheon Lavinia excused herself from accompanying the Kolynopulos on their visit to the Arsenal.

In her diary she wrote:

'Poor Mamma, she hasn't the least notion of what is meant by individualism. She has read Emerson because he was a connection of ours; but she won't cast her bantling on the rocks, as he advised. The Kolynopulos may be carelessly moulded, they are certainly not roughhewn, and they are well above the surface; indeed, they set out to attract all eyes; it would be a silly ship that went aground on them. How can it make any difference to one's soul, that inviolable entity, whom one meets? Milton could not praise a fugitive and cloistered virtue. I welcome whatever little trials the Ks. see fit to put mine to. I have summed them up; I know their tricks and their manners; I can look after myself When their conversation becomes disagreeable, I can always change the subject, as I did this morning. They thought they were working upon my curiosity, whereas all the time I was leading them on. But, to be quite honest (though why I should say that I don't know, since this diary is a record of my most intimate thoughts) I wouldn't have gone with them, but for Emilio. What a contrast he is to them. No wonder people congratulated them, as they might congratulate a toad on its jewel. It must be irksome for him to propel such people about. I hope he distinguishes between us; I hope he knows I only go in their gondola on his account. Do I really want him to know that? Perhaps not; but if you like anyone you can't rest till they know you like them. I didn't realize I liked him until Mrs. Kolynopulo said everyone did; then I saw that they must, and the thought gave me great pleasure. I believe I could stay in Venice for ever. Certainly when the Ks. depart (which is in five days now) I shall engage him. And so to bed, "pillowed on a pleasure", to quote F. W. H. Myers.

'MONDAY.—I am a little uneasy about Mamma. If I hadn't gone to Torcello (and it takes the best part of the day by gondola) she would have stayed in. She didn't want me to go, and perhaps I ought not to have gone; it is dull for her being alone; but she needn't feel so strongly about the Kolynopulos: they are quite amusing in their way, and she might just as well have come with us. Now she has a temperature again, nothing much. I offered to sit up with her the first part of the night, but she wouldn't hear of it. Too late for the Evanses and Stephen to call now; I am glad, rather, that they couldn't get rooms at this hotel. Another scene with Mamma about Stephen. She thinks that if I don't marry him I'll never marry anyone; it is hard for us to make new friends, the choice is so small. The proximity of Amelia goads her into saying more than she means. I told her that Stephen meant nothing to me; since I had been at Venice he had ceased to exist for me. She asked why Venice had made any difference. I couldn't tell her about Emilio, who is the real reason—not that I am in love with him—Heavens! but my thoughts turn on him in a special way; they run on oiled wheels, and if I try to think about Stephen at the same time the reverie breaks up, most painfully. I owe Stephen nothing. He lectures me and domineers over me and the sight of him recalls scenes of my childhood I would much rather forget. The fact that he has loved me for ten years only exasperates me; it is a thought outside my scheme, I don't know how to deal with it. Sufficient unto the day: to-morrow will settle all. Pray heaven he may have fallen in love with Amelia.'

8

BUT he hadn't. Lavinia found him, when she came down next morning, sitting in an arm-chair which he scarcely seemed to touch, poring over a map. He had been waiting an hour, he said, and had already seen her mother, who was much better.

'Yes, a good deal better,' said Lavinia, who had also seen her.

'Very much better,' he repeated, as though the information, coming from his lips, had a peculiar authenticity. 'And now as to plans,' he continued. 'I have worked out two programmes for the next five days — one for Mr. and Mrs. Evans and Amelia, and your mother, if she is well enough to go with them; they don't know Venice. Another, more advanced itinerary for us. Just look here.' He summoned her to the map, and Lavinia, feeling like a map herself, all signs and no substance, complied; but not without a feeble protest.

'But I don't know Venice either.'

'Ah, but you are intelligent, you can learn,' he said. Lavinia resented everything in his remark; the implication that her mother was not intelligent, the readiness to agree that she herself was quick but ignorant.

'I don't know which end the map is up,' she said suddenly.

'What! Not know your compass? We shall have to begin further back than I thought. Now, you're the North. I'll set the map by you. Here is the Piazza: do you see?'

'Yes,' said Lavinia.

'Well, where?'

Lavinia pointed to it.

'Right. Now I've drawn a series of concentric circles, marking on them everything we've got to see. I don't count tourists' tit-bits, like Colleoni and the Frari.'

'I love equestrian statues,' declared Lavinia. 'There are only sixty-four, I believe, in the world. And the Pesaro Madonna is almost my favourite picture in Venice.'

'Well,' said Stephen, 'we'll see what time we've got. Now, here's the first circle of our inferno. What do you put on it? Remember, you've been here nearly a week.' He turned towards Lavinia an acute questioning glance; a pedagogue's glance. His brows were knitted under his thin straight hair; his large prominent features seemed to start from his face and make a dent on Lavinia's mind. Not a mist, not a shadow of diffidence in his impatient eyes; no slightest pre-occupation with her or with himself, only an unabashed anxiety to hear her answer. Lavinia resolved it should be as wrong as she could possibly make it.

'St. Francesco della Vigna,' she suggested, putting her head on one side, a gesture that ordinarily she loathed beyond all others.

He looked at her in consternation; then let the map fall to his knees.

'Why, Lavinia,' he exclaimed. 'You're not trying.'

Tears of mortification came into her eyes.

'I don't think I want to learn,' she confessed.

'Why, of course you don't,' he replied, relieved by this simple explanation of her contumacy. 'No one does. But we've got to. That's what we Americans come here for. Now, try again.'

'Perhaps I could do better outside,' Lavinia temporized. The terrace revealed the Canal, and the Canal, Emilio. He was leaning against a post, expending, it seemed, considerable energy, for the prow of the gondola swung rapidly round. But whatever the exertion, he absorbed it into himself. The economy of movement was complete. There were no ineffective gestures, no effort run to waste; a thousand years of watermanship were expressed in that one manoeuvre. The gondolier saw Lavinia, took off his black hat, and smiled as he draped himself across his platform. There he sat. He smiled when you smiled, generally. He took you where you wanted to go. He forced nothing upon you. He demanded nothing of you. He had no questions, he had no replies. At every moment he was accessible to pleasure; at every moment, unconsciously, he could render pleasure back; it lived in his face, his movements, his whole air, where all the charms of childhood, youth and maturity mingled without losing their identity.

'There's a good-looking man if you like,' Lavinia's companion remarked.

'Yes, he's considered good-looking,' Lavinia concurred.

'I call him very good-looking,' Stephen repeated, as though there was nothing beautiful or ugly but his thinking made it so.

9

'No,' said Miss Evans, speaking, it seemed, for the first time that evening. 'We shall not stay long in Venice.' She rose and stretched herself.

They were sitting, all of them, in the Piazza. Dinner had been a failure, and its sequel, though enlivened by a band and a continual recourse to Florian's refreshments, a disaster.

'Bed-time?' muttered Mr. Evans, brushing his waistcoat with his hands. He jingled his watch-chain which had retained flakes of ash, uncertain in which direction gravity, such was the ambiguity of gradient on Mr. Evans's waistcoat, meant them to go.

'If Amelia wishes,' his wife primly replied.

'I do,' said Amelia.

They parted, Stephen accompanying Lavinia and her mother to their hotel.

'You must take care of that cold, Mrs. Johnstone,' he said, as they stopped at the door. 'And will you lend me Lavinia for half-an-hour? I want her to see the Rialto by moonlight.'

'I always do one or two things for mother before she goes to bed,' Lavinia protested.

'Am I quite helpless?' demanded Mrs. Johnstone. 'Am I utterly infirm? You make me feel an old woman, Lavinia, fussing about after me. Take her, Ste, by all means.'

Lavinia was taken.

On the fondamenta, below the Rialto, they encountered an émeute. Cries rang out; there was a scuffle in which blows were exchanged and blood flowed. Terrified by the sight of men bent on hurting each other, Lavinia tried to draw Stephen away, but he detained her, showing a technical interest in the methods of the combatants.

'Your real Italian,' he said, mimicking the action, 'always stabs from underneath, like this.'

Panic seized Lavinia. She felt vulnerable all over. The malignant light of the moon served only to reveal shadows and darkness; darkness under the great span of the Rialto, darkness in the thick foliage that shrouded the Casa Petrarca, darkness in the antic figures which tripped and rose and struggled with each other in the sheet of pale light that carpeted the fondamenta.

At last Stephen yielded to her entreaties.

'Well, I'm glad I saw that,' he said. But Lavinia felt that something alien, some quality of the night, had entered into her idea of Venice and would persist even in the noonday glare. It was to Stephen she owed this illumination, or rather this obfuscation, and she could not forgive him.

The narrowness of the *mercerie* brought them close together.

'Lavinia,' he said, 'I'm going to ask you a question. I suppose you know what it is.'

She did know, and her unwillingness to hear was aggravated tenfold by his obtuseness in choosing the moment when she liked him less than she had ever done. She was silent.

'Don't you know? Well, what should I be likely to ask?'

Lavinia trembled with obstinacy and rage.

'Well now,' he said, with the air of giving her an easier one. 'What do I generally ask?' He pressed her arm; a thrill of hysteria ran through her. 'Put it another way,' he said. 'In your small but sometimes valuable opinion, Lavinia, what am I most in need of?'

Lavinia's self-control deserted her.

'Consideration, imagination, everything except self-confidence,' she said, and burst into tears.

They walked in silence across the piazza, in silence past St. Moses to Lavinia's hotel.

'Good-night,' he said. There were tears in his voice, and she hated him for that. 'I didn't know you disliked me, Lavinia. I will go away to-morrow, to Verona, I think. Bless you.'

He was gone. Lavinia listened at her mother's door; no sound. She went to bed but her thoughts troubled her, and at about a quarter to four she rose and took out her diary.

'I could never have married Stephen, but I didn't mean to be cruel to him,' she wrote. 'I don't know what came over me. At the time there seemed nothing else to say; but on reflection I can think of a dozen things I might have said, all without wounding him. And he has such deep feelings, like most unselfconscious people, whose interest in a subject blinds them to the fact that they may be boring others with it. He really cares for me, and I ought to have been flattered by his enthusiasm and zeal for my improvement, instead of wanting him to let me go to the devil my own way. Is that where I am bound? I detected a whiff of brimstone this evening and I'm not sure whether the room is clear of it yet. I wasn't really angry with him; that's where he has the advantage over me; I was exasperated and unnerved, whereas he is now plunged, I fear, into real old-fashioned misery, the sort that keeps you awake at nights and is too hard and too heavy to yield to soft analysis. Well, I am awake, too. But that's because I worry about my-self: I am so concerned with self-justification that I whittle away the shame I ought to feel, externalizing it and nibbling bits off it until I grow interested and quite proud of it. If I had a proper nature, instead of this putty-soft putty-coloured affair, my relations towards people would fall into their right places, and not need readjustment at the hands of my sensibility. No one knows where they are with me, be-cause they really aren't anywhere; I am forever making up my mind about myself.

'There, I have succeeded in my discreditable design: I feel easier. But that doesn't mean I am worse than those who don't know in what direction to aim their self-reproaches. Why should stupidity be held the mark of a fine nature? I am not the more bad because I realize where my badness lies. But I do dread to-morrow, with Stephen going away hurt, the Evanses piqued, Mother unwell, and only the Kolynopulos to fall back on—and Emilio, of course. I had almost forgotten him.'

10

LAVINIA's misgivings were not unfounded. In the morning, still keep-ing her bed, Mrs. Johnstone had an audience first of Stephen, then of the Evanses, and, finally, of her daughter, who had gone for refuge and solace to a hairdresser's, where she let herself, half unwillingly, be the subject of successive and extremely time-taking remedial processes, each one imposed upon her with a peculiar affront. It was depressing, this recital of her hair's shortcomings; dry, brittle, under-nourished, split at the ends, it seemed only to stay on, as the buildings of Venice were said to stand, out of politeness. Ploughed, harrowed, sown and reaped, Lavinia's scalp felt like a battlefield. A proposal to exacerbate it further she resisted.

'Does Madam want to lose *all* her hair?'

'No, you idiot, of course I don't.'

Through a film of soapy water Lavinia's eyes tried to blaze; they smarted instead.

'I might just as well cry,' she thought, and seeing the woeful image in the mirror she shed a few tears which didn't show in the general mess.

She appeared before her mother with a false air of freshness.

'Who was it tired her head and was thrown out of a window?' asked Mrs. Johnstone, glaring from the bed.

It is my lot to have to answer stupid questions, Lavinia thought.

'Jezebel, that much-married woman,' she replied.

'Now that's where you're wrong,' Mrs. Johnstone contradicted her. 'She married once; it was the only respectable thing she did.'

'The Psalms say she was all glorious within until she married. Later it says, "So long as the whoredoms of thy mother Jezebel"—I forget what.'

'Lavinia!'

A long silence followed. Miss Johnstone, regardless of her proto-type's defenestration, leaned out of the window. Her own bedroom opened on to an interior court: it must be pleasant to have a room with a view.

'Lavinia,' said her mother at last, 'I don't think Venice is doing you any good. You've sent Ste away broken-hearted; you've offended the Evanses, you've made me ill; and now you address your own mother in the language of the market-place.'

'The language of the Bible,' interposed Lavinia.

'You'll go to the agency now and book places for us in the Orient express. We'll start to-morrow, or Friday at the latest.'

'The Wagons-Lits Company, like the churches,' said Lavinia, 'closes between twelve and two.' The impulse to profanity was new to her, and as she left her mother's room she regarded the intruder with dis-may, an emotion soon overpowered by the realization that in a few hours' time she would have to leave Venice. During her solitary lunch-eon she scoured her mind for a device to circumvent her marching-orders; all the way to the Piazza she asked herself, 'Is there no way out?' She could think of none.

It was the clerk at the counter who, all involuntarily, for he could never willingly have been helpful in his life, showed her the way.

'When do you want to go?' he said, when Lavinia, squashed, elbowed and pounded, at last reached him.

Lavinia pondered. She did not want to go at all. What was the effect, psychologically, of saying you wanted something that you passionately did not want? Did it do you any good? How did the will, thwarted, revenge itself? Where did its energy go, since it was incompressible and must find an outlet somewhere? It might assert itself in some very extravagant fashion. When she spoke, it was with her lips only.

'To-morrow,' she said.

'You can't go to-morrow,' the man replied, his face lighting up with a joy that, contrasted with the ordinary cast of his features, seemed almost innocent.

Lavinia's lips moved again. She would give Providence its chance. 'Friday?'

'Full up, Friday,' said the man, again as though the congestion of the train afforded him immense satisfaction. 'But you can go—'

'Stop,' said Lavinia, running her fingers over the counter and pausing at the third finger of her right hand. 'Will you give me two tickets to Paris for Friday week?'

She walked back, as though in a dream, straight to her mother's room. All the petulance had gone from her manner, and she felt, as she saw Mrs. Johnstone propped on the pillows, with so much that made her formidable either left out or undone, that she could wait upon her mother for ever.

'I am very sorry, Mamma,' she said, 'but all the sleeping-cars to Paris are reserved till next Friday week. So I took tickets for then. I hope you don't mind, and I think it's for the best; you really aren't fit to travel.'

'If I'm fit to stay here I'm fit for anything,' Mrs. Johnstone replied. 'You're sure you went to the right place, Lavinia?'

'Certain, Mamma.'

'Well, I don't imagine it will be much pleasure for you to stay,' Mrs. Johnstone remarked, as though Lavinia were a scapegoat for the sins of the railway company, and that was a comfort.

II

'I NEVER thought,' Lavinia wrote that evening, 'that one result of wrong-doing was to ease the temper. I feel like an angel. It is so long since I did anything I knew to be wrong, I had quite forgotten the taste of it. Certainly I must try again. To do wrong against one's will, as I did last night, how disagreeable! But with the full approval of conscience (it must have approved, or it wouldn't have let me be so nice to Mamma) how intoxicating! Before, when I felt I must only be good, my choice was confined, in fact I had no choice. Now, at last, I see the meaning of free will, which no one can see who has not wil-fully done wrong. Even the people who say they always act for the best, and do so much harm, never get an inkling (it is their punishment) of the pleasure they would have if they knew, as others do, that they are really acting for the worst. The joys of hypocrisy are not self-sufficing, they depend upon the approval of others, whereas deliberate sin can be relished only by oneself; of all pleasures it is the least communicable. Why, I wonder, is that? Let me take an instance. Suppose I saw Emilio beating his mother, because his choice that day happened to be surfeited with good? He would be enjoying himself, just as I enjoyed prolonging our stay by deceiving my mother; but should I enjoy seeing him? Perhaps not, but then cruelty is a thing apart; no one can want to be cruel. Suppose I saw him kissing someone—someone he had no right to kiss? That wouldn't please me either. But if I saw him give alms to a beggar? That would delight me, I know, for I've often wished he would. Well, there's no moral to be drawn from this, except that one should keep one's wickedness within oneself; to look at it from outside seems to dim its lustre. I will not be the spectator of my own mother-beating. Self-examination looks askance upon forbidden delights and morbidity is a force making for righteousness: away with it.'

12

THE regatta of Murano was a sorry affair. Even the Kolynopulos, whose ready response to advertised spectacles had prompted the expedition, confessed disappointment. The dowdy little island was seething with people; the race was conducted with much fuss and continual clearing of the course; but when it actually happened, after a lapse of several hours, excitement had worn itself out and given way to impatience. No gondola, reflected Lavinia, as the first man home was received with shouts and pistol-shots, should ever try to suggest speed. It was like a parody of a boat race, the exhaustion of the performers remaining, the thrill left out, and an air of troubled and unnatural competition hanging over all. On their way back, at Lavinia's request, they visited St. Francesco della Vigna. From across the lagoon the great Campanile had kept catching her eye, its shaft in the purple, its summit in the blue. She promised herself a moment of meditation in the melancholy cloister; but for some reason the church failed her. The ruinous shrine in the centre of the garth assumed a pagan look; the shadows were too thick for comfort; the darkness had nothing to tell her; the heavy doors were locked against her. She purposely outpaced Mrs. Kolynopulo, whose eyes were long in accustoming themselves to the half-light, to seek out a column she remembered — a column which supported a creeper, common enough, and wispy and poor, but lovely from one's consciousness of its rarity in Venice. But its greenness had gone grey, its leaves were falling, and the defeated tendrils, clawing the air, symbolized and reaffirmed her failure to recapture the emotion of her first visit.

Leaving her companion behind, she hastened back to the gondola. Mr. Kolynopulo was asleep, sprawled across the cushions, his head over-weighting the hand that sought to sustain it. Emilio, also, was resting, but as she came he threw himself across the poop into an attitude that absurdly caricatured his fare's. Lavinia laughed and clapped her hands; gone was her sense of isolation, gone her wish to re-create herself by a sentimental communion with the past. The darkness, palpable and unnerving in the cloister, fell into its place, dwindled into a time of day, was absorbed by Emilio and forgotten. Something that had stirred and asserted itself at the back of her mind fell asleep, seemed to die, leaving her spirits free. She resolved to avail herself of a security, a superiority to circumstance, that might vanish as suddenly as it came.

'Mrs. Kolynopulo,' she said, pronouncing the ridiculous name more seriously than ever before, 'you said I might ask you a question: do you remember?'

'No, dear; I can't say that I do.'

'It was about the gondoliers.' Lavinia's buoyancy remained, though she detected a wobble in her flight.

'What about them, dear?' Mrs. Kolynopulo enquired.

Lavinia realized then that her difficulty in putting the question was in itself a partial answer to it; but she had gone too far to draw back.

'You said that married people did not — had not . . . . certain . . . . dealings with the gondoliers that unmarried people had. I wondered what you meant.'

'Why, you've got it, my dear,' Mrs. Kolynopulo chuckled. 'You've said it yourself.'

A sensation of nausea came over Lavinia. She felt degraded and shown up, as though, in a first effort to steal, she had been caught red-handed by a pickpocket of older standing.

'*What* have I said?' she muttered. 'I haven't said anything.'

'Oh yes, you have,' her mentor rejoined. 'You said that certain people had dealings with gondoliers. Well, they do. Relations, it's generally called.'

'Why do they?' Lavinia murmured stupidly.

'Who, dear? The people, or the gondoliers?'

Oh, the agony of answering that question, the effort of bringing her mind to bear upon it. She turned the alternatives over and over, as though playing heads and tails with herself. The words began to have no meaning for her. At last she said:

'The gondoliers.'

'Well,' Mrs. Kolynopulo answered in a tone of considerable relief, 'you may be sure they don't do it for nothing.'

Lavinia said not a word on the way home, and when she went to bed her diary remained unopened. She seemed to have become inarticulate, even to herself.

13

THE following evening, however, she resumed her record. 'I wish I could have left yesterday out of my life, as I left it out of my diary. I didn't mean to refer to it; indeed I didn't mean to add another word to this confession. It is false; it is a sham; there is a lie in every line of it. So, at least, I thought this morning. I have always been, and always shall be, the kind of character the last few days have proved me to be: I am the Lavinia who was cruel to Stephen, who snapped the head off a poor hairdresser, who shocked her mother with an indecent word, and imperilled her health with a lie, who worried two boon companions into disclosing a scandal as untrue as it was vile. This is the house Lavinia has built, and a proper pigsty it is; but real, quite real, unlike the decorous edifice whose pleasing lines are discernible in the pages of this diary and which is a fake, a fallacious façade with nothing behind it. I have lost the power to regulate my life; I feel as though it had suddenly grown too big for me; it fits only where it touches, and it touches only to hurt. I feel that all appeals that are made to me are sent to the wrong address. Lavinia Johnstone passed away early in the week and the person who wears her semblance is a very different creature, who would as soon spit in your eye as speak to you. It is a relief to talk of myself in the third person, I get rid of myself that way: if only I could isolate the new me, and enclose the intruder in a coffin of wax, as bees do! What distressed me in reading Elizabeth's letter this morning was to find that, already, I had ceased to respond to the touches which were meant for me as she knew me; they fell on a dead place. But it will be a long time before my friends notice the change, before I become as strange to them as I am already to myself! And, meanwhile, I can feed their affections with the embalmed Lavinia. It is not a disgusting thought: Mummy was once merchandise — Mizraim cured wounds — Pharaoh was sold for balsams. No doubt many people before me have had to meet the public demand for versions of themselves which, though out of date and superseded, please better than their contemporary personalities could hope to do.'

14

At last the Kolynopulos had gone; gone without leaving Lavinia the reversion of their gondolier. All day she had struggled to put her plea before them; a hundred times she had changed the wording of her request. Elaborately casual it would have to be; she would breathe it as a random gust flutters a flower. It must seem the most natural thing in the world; she would slide it into a sentence without damaging a comma. It must be a favour; well, she would only ask them one. It must be a command; but had she not always commanded them? 'He will be a bond,' Lavinia rehearsed it — 'a visible — a sensible — a tangible memento of your kindness.' But, however she phrased it, she could imagine only one response: Mrs. Kolynopulo's coarse laugh and her husband's complementary wink.

They went before breakfast. Lavinia had no time to lose. The concierges hung about together, in twos, even in threes. She must get one by himself. She must not be haughty with him, she must not let him think her afraid of him. The first one scarcely listened to her and then told her what she wanted was impossible. She withdrew to her bedroom in great agitation. The room looked as if it had slept out all night, and she could not bear to stay in it. The newspapers in the lounge were torn and dog-eared, and three days old. Envelopes, envelopes everywhere, and not a sheet of writing paper. She tried to light a cigarette, but the matches were damp, and the box, though it sprang open as if by magic and revealed a quotation from Spinoza, declined to strike them. One after another she tried, holding each close to the head, wearing a sore place on her finger which the flame, when it at last arrived, immediately cauterized. She gave a little cry which made everyone look at her. She hurried from the room, conscious of everything she did—the pace at which she walked, the way she held her hands, the feel of her clothes. She tried to give her movements an air of resolution; she dropped into a chair as though utterly worn out, she rose the next moment as though a thought had struck her. Then she asked another concierge, only to be told that she must wait until the gondolier came to the hotel and arrange matters with him herself. 'He will never come.' she thought. 'If he does come, someone will snap him up, and if they don't I can never make him understand.' She pictured herself conducting the negotiation, shouting to Emilio across the intervening water, while the servants and the visitors looked on. 'Oh for five minutes of Mamma,' she thought. 'How she would chivvy them! How she would send them about her business! I try to treat them as human beings; there's nothing they hate so much. They are like dogs; they know when one's afraid of them, it's the only intelligence they have.' At that moment she heard a sound at her elbow and looked up; a concierge, a tall melancholy-looking man she had not noticed before, was setting an ash-tray at her side. The simple attention confounded Lavinia; she thanked him through a mist of tears. He still hovered, gravely solicitous. Lavinia cast her line once more. Yes, he would get Emilio for her, he would telephone to the traghetto; there was no difficulty at all.

But there was a difficulty. Emilio had not returned to his station and could not be found. Throughout the day Lavinia's spirits underwent a painful alternation, rising with each effort to trace Emilio, falling when the effort proved vain. A boy was despatched to his home; even that did not bring him. He is having an orgy on the bounty of the Kolyno-pulos, thought Lavinia; or perhaps he has given up being a gondolier and decided to retire. No hypothesis so absurd that she could not entertain it. The explanation of his absence she never knew, but in the evening she heard he had been found and was coming to the hotel to see her.

He came. Lavinia met him in the vestibule. He was talking to the porter who, she thought, should have stood at attention or betrayed by some uneasiness his appreciation of this singular honour. But he went on arranging keys, and talking over his shoulder to Emilio, who stood just inside the street door, as though an imaginary line drawn across the matting forbade him to come further.

Through the glow of her emotion Lavinia realized, for the first time, that he was a poor man. The qualities she had endowed him with had transcended wealth and yet included it. Here, under the electric light, with the gold wall-paper behind his head and the rose-coloured rug at his feet, his poverty became a positive thing. His rings did not disguise it, and the bunch of charms and seals, supported by a gold chain and worn high up on his chest, only emphasized it. He was dressed in his every-day clothes, a sign that his term of private employment was over; they had no shape except the one he gave them. He got them because they were likely to wear well, Lavinia thought. Such a reason for choosing clothes had never occurred to her: suddenly she felt sorry for everyone who had to buy a suit because it was serviceable. But Emilio did not invite pity. He stood a little uneasily, his arms hanging loosely at his sides; he seemed anxious to subdue in himself the electric quality that leaped and glistened and vibrated. But diffidence and deference found a precarious lodging in his face: shrouded and shaded as it was, Lavinia could only glance at it and look away.

She wanted to engage him?

Why, yes, of course.

For how long?

For six days.

And when should he come?

To-night?

No, not to-night. He shook his head as if that was asking too much.

Did she want the gondola de luxe?

Yes, she did.

'Domani, alle dieci e mezzo?'

'Si, signorina. Buona sera.'

Lavinia had to let him go at that. She would have given anything to keep him. Now that he was gone, oddly enough, she could see him much more clearly. The eye of her mind had its hesitations but, it was not intimidated so readily as her physical eye. The vestibule had lost its enchantment, the hotel had reclaimed it; but she would still recall the lustre of his presence, still remember how, as he stood before her, the building at her back, civilization's plaything, had faded from her consciousness, and the tremors and disappointments of the past days had receded with it. The hotel had grown habitable again, the servants were back in their normal stature. She passed the man who had been so helpful to her and hardly recognized him — not out of ingratitude, but because the excitement of meeting Emilio had blotted out her recollection of what went before. But the voice of disillusion whispered to her, the calendar assured her, that her time of exaltation would be short. Could she prolong it? If anyone was a judge of what was practicable,

Elizabeth Templeman was she. She addressed an envelope to Miss Templeman, Hotel Excelsior et Beau Site, Rome.

'My dear Elizabeth,' she wrote,

'I was enchanted to get your letter. What have I to set beside your sick-room adventures? I believe that if you were at the North Pole you could cause jealousy and heart-burning among the very bears. My sick-room experiences (for I have them too) are much more prosaic than yours; poor Mamma is in bed, can't get up for several days, by doctor's orders, and I have to look after her. But strange things happen even in Venice, though not (as you will readily believe) to me. My friend Simonetta Perkins (I don't think you know her—she was recommended to Mamma, who didn't like her, so she devolved upon me) has formed a kind of romantic attachment with a gondolier. She is not in love with him, of course, but she very strongly feels she doesn't want to lose sight of him. Not to see him from time to time would be the death of her, she says. She passionately desires to do him a good turn, but as she has never done one before she doesn't know how to set about it. (She is rather selfish, between ourselves). She has confided her plan to me, and I am passing it on to you to have the benefit of your wordly wisdom, which is renowned in two continents. She meditates transplanting him to America and setting him up near her home, in some attractive occupation, either as a baker, or clerk to a dry goods store, or something like that. She would like it still better if she could get her mother (who is very indulgent) to engage him as footman or chauffeur, or gardener or even furnaceman, if he didn't think that beneath him; then she could look after him, as it were, herself, and see that he wasn't home-sick. She knows a little Italian (very little considering the time she has been here), and is very rich—she could easily transplant St. Mark's, stone by stone, she told me, if the Italian Government would consent to let it go. I said she could do that equally well and at less expense by the exercise of faith; and she replied, quite seriously, that faith only availed to remove inanimate objects like mountains, but it couldn't bring her her gondolier—not a lock of him, not a hair.

'What do you advise her to do? Of course Italians do emigrate, and it would be nicer for him to go as a private servant than settle in the Italian quarter at New York—a most horrible place. I was taken to see it once, with detectives all round me, pointing revolvers.

'I do hope you are better.

Affectionately,
Lavinia Johnstone.'

Lavinia paused, thought for some time, then added a postscript.

'Rome will soon be too hot to hold you; couldn't you flee from the wrath to come and relieve my loneliness in Venice? I am staying till Friday. it is tedious with Mother in bed and no companion but Simonetta and her obsession.'

All the same, Lavinia thought, as she walked upstairs to her mother's room, I hope she won't come.

15

THE mid-day gun boomed, but Lavinia did not hear it.

'You mean he won't come after all,' she said.

The melancholy-looking concierge shook his head.

'He came this morning at seven o'clock and said that he was very sorry, but he could not serve you. He could not hire himself to two families in turn; it would be unfair to the other gondoliers. They must have a chance.'

'I am not a family,' said Lavinia, with a touch of her old spirit.

'No, mademoiselle,' replied the concierge, looking so gravely at her that she wished she had been; her singularity sat heavily upon her. She returned to the terrace where she had been waiting the last two hours. Emilio, too, had arrived; more, he had found a fare. A woman was boarding the gondola. The gangway lurched a little as she crossed it and she turned, giving the man who followed her a smile full of apprehension and affection. She was as lovely as the day. Her companion lengthened his stride and caught her hand, and they stumbled into the gondola together, laughing at their awkwardness. The cluster of servants smiled; Emilio smiled; and Lavinia, charmed out of her wretchedness, smiled too. Into her mind came the Embarkation of St. Ursula; a vision of high hopes, adventure, beauty, pomp, in the morning of the world. Her smile grew wan as it lighted upon Emilio; she did not mean to recognize him, but he spread out his hands so disarmingly that the smile found its way back, flickered up again like a lamp that will burn a moment longer if you shake it.

'Who is that?' she asked at random of the servants who were still congratulating each other in a mysterious, vicarious way.

'Lord Henry de Winton,' someone said. 'They are just married.'

Lavinia went up to her mother's bedroom and stood in front of a pier-glass, studying her reflection.

'Well,' said Mrs. Johnstone from the bed. 'Am I not to see your face?'

'I thought I would look at it myself,' replied Lavinia.

'Shall I tell you what you see there?' asked her mother.

'No,' Lavinia answered, and added, 'you can if you like.'

'Tears,' said Mrs. Johnstone.

'I cry very easily,' Lavinia excused herself.

'As easily as a stone,' her mother rejoined.

That, alas, was only too true. Jack-the-Giant-Killer made the cheese cry by a trick, but the pressure by which the giant squeezed tears out of his stone was genuine and Lavinia could still feel the clasp of his fingers. Emilio had deserted her; he had an instinct for what was gay, what was care-free, what was splendid; a kind of ethical snobbery, she reflected, fingering the pearls that reached to her waist. She was secretive, she wore a hang-dog air, she moved stealthily in her orbit; no wonder people avoided her. She was a liar and a cheat; scratch her and you would find not blood, but a mixture of private toxins. Whereas they went blithely on their way, wearing their happiness in public, anxious that everyone they met should share it. And they had taken Emilio from her — Emilio for whose sake, or at least on whose account, she had foregone her high ironical attitude, the attitude she had spent years in acquiring, which had preserved her from so much if it had given her so little. Her detachment, that had been the marvel of her friends, how could she hope to find it now, its porcelain fragments befouled by slime? Miserably she walked up and down, her inward unrest so intense that the malign or disturbing aspects of what she saw around her contributed nothing to it. Over and over again she traced the stages of her degradation. It began with the hunt for the smelling-bottle; it was still going on: the monster inherited from the Kolyno-pulos had not done growing yet. 'Still,' thought Lavinia, 'if only I had engaged Emilio the first evening, I should have got what I wanted and been satisfied.' She evoked the incident a dozen times, each time saying 'yes,' where before she had said 'no,' almost cheating herself into the belief that she could alter the past. Why had he not told her last night that a trades' union scruple forbade him to enter her service? He must have thought it over, weighed her in the balance and found her wanting. How? Lavinia did not flinch from the mortification of this enquiry. She had overheard someone say she was not really beautiful. But how did her appearance affect the case? *His* appearance had affected it, but then, he was not hiring her. She did not look magnificent, not, like so many Americans, as if she was the principal visitor at Venice. The Johnstones never tried to look like that. He must have taken her meanness over the note at its face value, imagined she would always haggle over a lira. The irrelevance of this consideration, and its ironical inadequacy as the foundation of her sufferings, almost made her scream. But why, she thought, be so cynical? Emilio may not be a liar, if I am. Perhaps he did want to give the other gondoliers a chance. The benison of the thought stole through her, reinstating Emilio, reconciling her to herself. The reverie refreshed her like a sleep.

The servant who interrupted it, bringing her a card, looked as if he had been there a long while.

'To introduce Lord Henry de Winton,' she read, and underneath, the name of an old school-friend.

'Tell him I shall be delighted to see him,' said Lavinia.

He came soon after, his wife with him.

'Ah, Miss Johnstone,' she cried, taking Lavinia's hand, 'you can't think what a pleasure it is to find you. You must overlook the shameless haste with which we take advantage of our introduction.'

'We couldn't help it, you know,' her husband put in, smiling from one to the other. 'We had such accounts of you.'

Lavinia had been for so long seeking rather than sought after that she didn't know what to make of it.

'I hope I shall live up to my reputation,' was all she could think of to say.

If they were chilled they hardly showed it; they continued to look down upon Lavinia, kindling, melting and shining like angelic presences.

'It's hard on you, I own,' said Lady Henry. 'How much pleasanter for you to be like us with no reputation at all, not a rag!' Repudiated virtue triumphed in her eyes; but her husband said:

'You mustn't scare Miss Johnstone. Remember we were warned not to shock her.' They laughed infectiously; but a tiny dart pierced Lavinia's soul and stuck there, quivering.

'You mustn't try me too far,' she said, making an effort.

'You'll take the risk of dining with us, won't you?' Lord Henry begged. He spoke as if it were a tremendous favour, the greatest they could ask. 'And your mother too.'

'I should love to,' said Lavinia. 'Mamma, alas, is in bed.'

Instantly their faces changed, contracted into sympathy and concern. 'Oh, I am so sorry,' Lady Henry murmured. 'Perhaps you'd rather not.'

'Oh, she's not dying,' Lavinia assured them, a faint irony in her tone, partly habitual, but partly, she was ashamed to realize, bitter.

They noticed it, for their eyebrows lifted even as their faces cleared.

'How tiresome for both of you,' Lady Henry said. 'Should we say eight o'clock?'

16

'WHY,' wrote Lavinia, 'when I meet the most charming people in the world should I feel like a fish out of water? The kindness of the de Wintons goes over my head. I feel like a black figure silhouetted against a sunset. The blackness is my will. I have altogether too much of it. This morning I thought it had died. My life seemed dislocated; I did the things I dislike most without minding them at all. Three hours I tramped Venice to find a propitiatory shawl for Mrs. Evans. Malice governed my choice at the last; she will look a fright in it; but as I went from one shop to another, ordering its entire stock to be laid before me, and then going away without buying, I did not feel wretched and distressed, as I used to do. I didn't mind what happened. If I had been struck by lightning I shouldn't have changed colour. Things came to me mechanically, but not in any order or with any sense of choice. Volition was stilled. The de Wintons roused it. They did everything they could to draw me out, to draw me back to their level, their world where I once was, where all desires are at an equipoise, where one wants a thing moderately and forgets it directly one can't get it; where one can leave one's spiritual house, as the dove left the ark, and return to it at will. While they talked, appealing to me now and then, weaving into one fabric the separate threads of our lives, finding common interests, common acquaintances, a hundred similarities of opinion and as many dissimilarities, that should have been just as binding, drawing us to-gether until it seemed our whole existence had passed within a few yards of each other, I felt in the midst of the exquisite witchcraft that each lasso they threw over me dissolved like a rope of sand, leaving me somewhere much lower than the angels, alone with my ungovernable will. It frightenes me; I cannot escape it; I cannot find my way back to that region where diversity is real and inclination nibbles at a million herbs and forgets the wolf, will, that watches him. Emilio is nothing to me; he is the planetary sign, the constellation under which my will is free to do me harm. I have devised a remedy. Cannot I in thought identify myself with the outside world, the world that sees with unimplicated eye Lavinia Johnstone going about her business — notes a feather in her hat as she stands on the terrace, sees her apparently deep in conversation with a rough-looking man, jots down her arrival in a newspaper, thinks she'll be gone in a week, wonders why she doesn't change her clothes oftener, decides after all not to trouble to speak to her? Then I should recover my sense of proportion; I should matter as little to myself as I do to the world.

'I write like a pagan. Perhaps my disorder is more common-place: it is the natural outcome of doing a number of wrong things, letting myself get out of hand. Sin is the reason of my failure with the de Wintons. The Kolynopulos' monster, what exactly is it? It's no use going to Mamma to get rid of it, she said so. I begin to wish that Elizabeth would come.'

Next morning the doctor was due. Lavinia stayed in to hear his report. Each time she sought the sunshine of the terrace she found Emilio there. His presence wounded her; his recognitions, formal and full at first, diminished with each encounter and then ceased. 'He has behaved badly to me,' she thought, injured and yet glad of the injury. Though he avoided her and grudged her his company, he could not take away from her the fact that he, Emilio, acting responsibly with her image in his mind, had wronged her. It was a kind of personal relation, the only one, most likely, she would have. She looked at him again. The sun shone full upon his brown neck. Surely such exposure was dangerous? Suddenly he looked up. With her hand she made a little sweeping motion behind her head. The gondolier smiled, clutched his sailor's collar with both hands and comically pressed it up to his ears, then let it fall. He pointed to the sun, shook his head slowly with an expression of contempt, smiled once more and smoothed away the creases in his collar. The Kolynopulos' monster at last came out of hiding and swam into view. Mechanically Lavinia put out her hand and took a telegram from the waiter's tray.

Earnestly advise Miss Perkins leave Venice immediately. Alas cannot join you. Writing. Elizabeth.

Lavinia crunched up the blue paper and threw it towards the canal.

It was a feeble throw, the wind bore it back; so she took it to the balustrade and hurled it with all her might. It fluttered towards Emilio who
made as though to catch it; but it fell short of him, and she could see it,
just below the water, stealthily uncurling.

The handwriting of Lavinia's diary that night was huddled and uncouth, unlike her usual elegant script. She had been searching Venice,
apparently, for a guide to conduct, or some theological work with a
practical application.

'Of course,' she wrote, 'it's only a Frenchman's view and one can't
put much faith in them. I thought, if the will is corrupt, that is enough
to damn you. Try to thwart the will, try to control it, try to reform it:
I have tried. Faith without works is dead: that is the creed of the Roman
Church and leads to indulgences. If one has faith it follows that one
performs the acts of faith. They are nothing in themselves, have no
value except to illustrate one's faith. Why do them? Because one can't
help it. If the tree is good, so must the fruit be. And if evil? Need it be
altogether evil? There's a danger in arguing from analogy; metaphors
conceal truth. But suppose the tree is evil, at any one time; would it be
logical to say: "You're a bad tree; if you don't bear fruit you'll still be
bad, only not so bad"? The barren fig-tree was cursed for its barren-
ness, not for the quality of its fruit; it may have deliberately refrained
from having figs, because it knew they would be bad, and it didn't
want to be known by its fruit. What I mean is, if the will is corrupt it
will produce corrupt acts, and there is no virtue in refraining from any
particular act, because everything you do will be wrong, wrong before
you do it, wrong when you first think of it, wrong because you think
it. But this man makes a distinction. To want to do wrong without
doing it is concupiscence: it is in the nature of sin, but not sin. Isn't this
a quibble? And it's cold comfort to be told that abstinence is concupiscence, and is in the nature of sin. I wish I could ask someone. After
all, it's an academic point: I can settle it which way I like, it commits
me to nothing. However I argue it I shall still believe that the act does
make a difference; if I wanted to throw myself off the Woolworth
building, and didn't, it would not be the same as if I wanted to and
did.'

'Well, he evidently means us to get out,' said Lady Henry, looking
doubtfully at the deserted campo.

Emilio was offering his arm.

Lord Henry strode ashore without availing himself of the human hand-rail; but his wife and Lavinia accepted its aid in their transit.

'You know,' he said, 'you touch those fellows at your own risk.'

'Nonsense, Henry,' his wife protested. 'Why?'

'Oh, plague, pestilence, dirt, disease,' Lord Henry answered.

'My dear, does he look like it? He will outlive us all. Henry is secretly jealous of our gondolier,' she said, turning to Lavinia. 'Don't you think him an Adonis?'

'He is a genial-looking brigand,' said her husband.

'I was asking Miss Johnstone,' Lady Henry remarked. 'This is a matter for feminine eyes. I dote upon him.' She turned her candid eyes upon her husband with an exquisite pretence of languor.

'Well,' he gently growled, 'what about this palace? I don't see it.'

'*Gondoliere,*' called Lady Henry, '*Dove il palazzo Labia?*' She waved her hand to the grey buildings and the cloudy skies. Emilio climbed out of the boat.

'See how helpful he is,' she commented. 'He knows exactly what I mean.' Walking, Emilio always looked like an upright torpedo, as though he had been released by a mechanical contrivance and would knock down the first obstacle he met, or explode.

'We were fortunate to get him,' she continued. 'We only hold him by a legal fiction; we couldn't hire him, he has been too popular, poor fellow, all the summer, and no doubt fears the stilettos of his friends. I tried my utmost, Henry, didn't I, to shake his resolution. I spoke in every tongue, but he was deaf to them all. So we re-engage him at the end of each ride, which does just as well, and salves his troublesome conscience. To-morrow, alas, we must go.'

They had gone down a passage and reached a door, the sullen solidity of which was impaired by the decay and neglect of centuries. Emilio pulled at the rusty bell and listened.

'Do you think,' Lavinia said suddenly, 'you could ask him to be our gondolier, Mamma's and mine, when you've finished with him? Just for two days; we leave on Friday.'

'Why, of course,' Lady Henry said.

She conducted the negotiation in her voluble broken Italian, pointed at Lavinia, pointed at herself, overrode some objection, made light of some scruple, and finally, out of the welter of questions and replies, drew forth, all raw as it were and quivering, Emilio's consent. Over his fierceness he looked a little sheepish, as though the unusual rapidity of his thoughts had outstripped his expression and left it disconnected, drolly representing an earlier mood.

The door opened and they climbed to the high formal room where Antony and Cleopatra, disembarking, stare at Antony and Cleopatra feasting.

They had tea at Florian's, under a stormy sky.

'Don't you think,' Lady Henry de Winton said, 'Miss Johnstone ought to be told some of those charming things Caroline said about her? Such a rain of dewdrops,' she added turning to Lavinia. 'I think we know you well enough.'

'Perhaps Miss Johnstone doesn't like hearing the truth about herself,' Lord Henry suggested.

'Oh, but such a truth—one could only mind not hearing it. First of all there were the general directions. Do you remember, Henry? We were not to shock her.'

'Caroline thought you were very easily shocked,' said Lord Henry, diffidently.

'She had the Puritan conscience—the only one left in America; she might have stepped out of Mrs. Field's drawing-room.'

'Really, we must talk to Miss Johnstone, not about her,' said Lord Henry, and they pulled up their chairs, turning radiant faces to Lavinia.

'And not Puritan, my dear,' Lord Henry put in. 'Fastidious, choosy.'

'I accept the amendment. Anyhow you would feel a stain like a wound. Then there were your friends.'

'What about them?' Lavinia asked.

'Oh, they were a very compact body, but they agreed in nothing except in liking you. Each one had a pedestal for you, and thought the others did not value you enough. And they were very exacting. They had a special standard for you; if you so much as wobbled, the news was written, telephoned and cabled, in fact universally discussed.'

'And universally denied,' Lord Henry said.

'Of course. But where others might steal a horse, I gathered, you mightn't look over the hedge.'

'That was only because,' Lord Henry gently took her up, 'you never wanted to look over the hedge.'

'Do you recognize yourself in the portrait, Miss Johnstone?' Lady Henry asked.

'Oh, Caroline!' Lavinia groaned.

'There's more to come,' Lady Henry pursued. 'You were inwardly simple, outwardly sophisticated. When you talked about your friends you were never malicious and yet never dull. You were a good judge of character; no one could take you in.'

'She said,' Lord Henry interpolated, with charming solicitude, 'that no one would want to.'

But his wife saw a further meaning in this well-meant gloss and repudiated it.

'Nonsense, Henry: anyone would be delighted to take Miss Johnstone in: she must be the target of all bad characters. Caroline was praising her intelligence. There, you shall pay for interrupting me by completing the catalogue of her virtues: a formidable task.'

'Oh no,' he said, sure of his ground this time, bending upon Lavinia his bright, soft look: 'an easy one. Your poise was what your friends most admired. You took the heat out of controversies; you were a rallying point; you made other people feel at their best; you ingeminated peace.'

'How eloquent he is!' Lady Henry murmured, shaking her head.

'And yet,' he went on, 'you were a great responsibility, the only one they had. They would never let you get married; they would rush to the altar and forbid the banns. You were, you were,' he concluded lamely, 'their criterion of respectability: they couldn't afford to lose you.'

Lavinia got up. Behind her St. Mark's spread out opalescent in the dusk.

'Thank you,' she said, 'and thank you for this afternoon. I must go, but before I go will you tell me what vices Caroline said I had? I know her,' she went on, looking down at them without a smile. 'She must have mentioned some.'

They looked at each other in dismay.

'Be fair,' Lavinia said, turning away. 'Think of the burden I carry, with all those recommendations round my neck.'

'We didn't mean to "give you a character",' Lord Henry's voice stressed the inverted commas.

'Couldn't you,' said Lavinia turning to them again, 'take just a little bit of it away?'

Perhaps Lady Henry was stung by her ungraciousness. 'Caroline did say,' she pronounced judicially, 'that she—that they all—wondered whether, perhaps, you weren't self-deceived: that was what helped you to keep up.'

'Not consciously deceived,' Lord Henry said, 'and they didn't want you undeceived: it was their business to see you weren't.'

They both rose. 'Good-bye,' said Lady Henry. 'It's been delightful meeting you. And may we subscribe to what Caroline said?'

Lavinia said they might.

Without much noticing where she went, she made her way over the iron bridge, past the great church of the Gesuati on to the Fondamenta delle Zattere. The causeway was thronged, chiefly it seemed by old women. Hard-faced but beautiful in the Venetian way, they moved through the mysterious twilight, themselves not mysterious at all. Even their loitering was purposeful. The long low crescent of the Giudecca enfolded the purple waters of the canal, shipping closed it on the east; but at the western end there was a gap which the level sun streamed through, a narrow strait, seeming narrower for the bulwark of a factory that defined its left-hand side. The sense of the open sea, so rare in Venice, came home to Lavinia now; she felt the gap to be a wound in the side of the city, a gash in its completeness, a false word in the incantation of its spell. She fixed her eyes on it hopefully. She was conscious of a sort of drift going by her towards the sea, not a movement of the atmosphere, but an effluence of Venice. It was as though the beauty of the town had nourished itself too long and become its own poison; and at this hour the inflammation sighed itself away. Lavinia longed to let something go from her into the drift, something that also was an inflammation of beauty and would surely join its kind. The healing gale plucked at it, caressed it, and disowned it. The sun, pierced by a gigantic post, disappeared into the sea, and at the same moment the black mass of the Bombay liner detached itself from the wharf, moved slowly across the opening and settled there. The canal was sealed from end to end.

The night was very hot. Lavinia walked to the door of the hotel that opened on the canal and leaned against the door-post, looking out. Voices began to reach her; she recognized the tones, but the intonations seemed different.

'She's like an unlighted candle,' Lady Henry de Winton was saying. 'I can't understand it.'

'An altar-candle?' suggested her husband. 'Well, we did our best to light her.'

'No, not an altar-candle,' Lady Henry said. 'Not so living as that. A candle by a corpse.'

Lavinia tried to move away and could not.

'Didn't you find her a little un-forthcoming,' Lady Henry went on, half-injured, half-perplexed, 'and rather remote, as if she had something on her mind? She didn't seem to be enjoying herself, poor thing. We may have been enjoying ourselves too much, but I don't think it was that. Did you notice how she scarcely ever followed up what one said?'

'Perhaps she was tired,' Lord Henry said. 'She spends a lot of time looking after her mother.'

Does she? thought Lavinia.

'I could see what Caroline meant,' Lady Henry continued. 'The features were there all right, but the face wasn't. I felt so sorry for her, I longed to save her from her depression or whatever it is; I piled it on; I put words into Caroline's mouth; I perjured myself; which reminds me, my darling, that you did dot my "i's" a little too openly.'

'I tried to make what you said seem true,' Lord Henry remarked.

'Of course you did.' There was a pause in which they might have kissed each other.

'Let's forget Miss Johnstone. We've done our kind act for to-day.'

There was a creaking of chairs and Lavinia fled to her room.

'It's no use,' she wrote, after several attempts. 'I cannot say what I think; I do not know what I think. I am intolerably lonely. I am in love with Emilio, I am infatuated by him: that explains me. If I can't be justified, at any rate I can be explained. Why should I hold out any longer? I am unrecognizable to myself, and to my friends. My past life has no claim on me, it doesn't stretch out a hand to me. I believed in it, I lived it as carefully as I could and it has betrayed me. If I invoked it now (I do invoke it) it wouldn't give me any help. Its experience is all fabulous; its sign-posts point to castles in Spain. Whatever happens between me and Emilio I could never find my way back to it. Respectability must lose its criterion.

'It pleased me to know that Emilio had been honest after his fashion. I can't pretend I admire him or even that I very much like him. The only creditable feeling I have is a sort of glow of the heart when he behaves less badly than I expect. These are the credentials of my passion; credential really, but the word is plural. Passion, I call it, but a shorter word describes it better. It does seem a little hard that now I have gone through so much, given up so much, I have no sense of exaltation, no impulse left. I suppose the effort of clearing the jungle of past associations has taken all my strength. I have made a desert and called it peace.'

Next morning a letter accompanied Lavinia's breakfast. She opened it listlessly; she had hardly slept, and all her sensations seemed second-hand.

'No, my dear Lavinia,' she read, 'you do not deceive me, though you do surprise me. I hope this letter will find you in America, but if it doesn't, if you have flouted my commands and are still eating your heart out in Venice, it may still serve a useful purpose. How simple you were to imagine I should be taken in by the apocryphal Miss Perkins! If you hadn't been in your weak way so catty about her, I might have thought twice about believing in her; but your letters, you know, are always crammed with things like this: "Dear Caroline, what a saint she is, she sent me a thimble at Christmas".

'I will now give you some rules for your guidance and I earnestly counsel you to follow them. As to your design of shipping the adored to Boston, I don't like to say what I feel about it; but this I will say: it alarmed me for you. Lavinia, you are not at all cut out for what I might call the guerrilla warfare of love. Your irregularities would be much too irregular.

'Now listen to me, Simonetta Perkins, you who were once recommended to Mrs. Johnstone, then rejected by her, and have now devolved upon yourself. The great thing to do is to have a programme. At ten, say, go and have a straight talk with your mother; tell her to get up, there's nothing the matter with her, and she's only wasting her time in bed. At 10.30 go to your bedroom or some inaccessible place, the roof if possible, ring the bell and tell the waiter to bring you a cocktail. Nothing is so successful in restoring one's self-respect as giving servants a great deal of trouble. At eleven, sit down and write some letters, preferably a testimonial to me saying you are following my instructions and deriving benefit. At twelve you might visit one of the larger churches. I suggest SS. Giovanni e Paolo: don't look at the church, look at the tourists, and despise them. Order your luncheon with care and see that you get what you like and like what you get. In the afternoon go to the Lido, or else buy yourself some trifle at a curiosity shop (I recommend one in the Piazzetta dei Leoncini, kept by a man with a name like a Spanish golfer, —— della Torre). At five you should call on a Venetian hostess, submit to universal introduction (they will hate you if you don't and think you *mal élevée*), praise the present administration and listen politely to the descendants of the doges. If the flutter in your heart is still unsubdued go to Zampironi's on the way to your hotel and get some bromide: they have it on tap there. In the evening, if you haven't been asked to a party, go to Florian's and drink liqueurs—strega, I suggest. Or, if you want a shorter way to oblivion, their horrible benedictine punch. Repeat the time-table on Thursday, and on Friday, by the time your train reaches Verona, certainly when it reaches Brescia, you will have forgotten your gondolier, his name, his face, everything about him.

'But whatever you do, Lavinia, don't make your plight fifty times worse by dragging morality into it. I suspect you of examining your conscience, chalking up black marks against yourself, wearing a Scarlet Letter and generally working yourself into a state. Put all such notions from you. The whole thing is a question of convenience. It arises constantly, it is not at all serious. Obviously you can't marry the man; he is probably married already, and has a large family nearly as old as himself: they marry very young. If you were anyone else you might have him as a lover. I shouldn't advise it, but with reasonable precautions it could be successfully carried through. But really, Lavinia, for you to have a *cavalier servente* of that kind would be the greatest folly; you would reproach yourself and feel you had done wrong. And it's not a question of right and wrong, as I said: only a child of the 'fifties would think it was. So good-bye Lavinia, and if you can bring me a snapshot of him we will laugh over it together.

With love,

Elizabeth Templeman.'

Lavinia read the letter with relief, with irritation, finally, without emotion of any kind. It was soothing to have her situation made light of; it was irritating to have it made fun of. But in proposing a solution based on reason Miss Templeman had missed the mark altogether, while her appeal to convention added another to Lavinia's store of terrors. She could face the reproaches of her friends, the intimate disapproval of her conscience; they were part of her ordinary life. But the enmity of convention was outside her experience, for she had always been its ally, marched in its van. She could not placate it because it was implacable; its function was to disapprove.

The Evanses had gone, Stephen had gone, the Kolynopulos had gone, the de Wintons had gone; Elizabeth had failed to come, and Mrs. Johnstone would not rise till noon. Lavinia was alone.

Emilio did not desert her; he came in all his finery, he was delighted to see her. Stepping into the gondola Lavinia felt almost satisfied. It was a prize she had fought for against odds during a fortnight, and at last it was hers. 'Comandi, Signorina?' Emilio said, slowly moving his oar backwards and forwards. 'Am I his Anthea?' thought Lavinia. 'Can I command him anything?' But she only suggested they should go to San Salvatore. '*Chiesa molto bella*,' she hazarded. '*Si, si*,' returned Emilio, '*e molto antica.*' That was the sort of conversation she liked, so easy, like fitting together two halves of a proverb. She felt deliciously weary. Suddenly she heard a shout. Emilio answered it, more loquaciously than was his wont. She looked up: it was only a passing gondolier, saying good-morning. Another shout. This time a whole sentence followed, in those clipped syllables which Lavinia could never catch. Emilio ceased rowing and answered at length, speaking in short bursts and with great conviction. A minute later a similar, even longer, interchange took place. The whole army of gondoliers seemed to take an interest in Emilio, to know his business and to be congratulating him on some success. Suddenly it seemed to Lavinia that from every pavement, traghetto, doorstep, and window a fire of enquiries was being directed upon her gondolier; and the enquirers all looked at her.

'It's my imagination,' she thought; but in the afternoon the same thing happened again; it was like a nightmare. Convention, even Venetian convention, was showing its teeth, growling through the walls of its glass house. Lavinia was seized with a contempt for all these people, mopping and mowing and poking their noses into other people's business. 'What are they,' she thought, 'this population of Lascars and Dagoes?' For a moment she felt Emilio to belong to them, a rift opened between her and him: she saw him as it were through the wrong end of a telescope, minute, insignificant, menial, not worth a thought. In his place appeared all the generations of the Johnstones, sincere, simple, grave from the performance of municipal and even higher functions, servants of their own time, benefactors of the time to come.

They were the people upon whom America had depended; America owed everything to them. From the sixteen-thirties when they arrived until the beginnings of vulgarization in the eighteen-eighties, for two hundred and fifty years they had persisted, an aristocracy unconscious of its own aristocratic principle, homely, solid, and affluent. If they remembered their descent — and Lavinia could recollect every generation of hers — they remembered it historically, not personally: the matter of genealogy was common knowledge: it was a bond to hold them together, not a standard for others to fall short of. It was domestic, this society to which they belonged, it was respectable, it was as democratic as an aristocracy could well be. And still, though threatened on all sides by an undifferentiated plutocracy, it kept its character, it preserved its primness, its scrupulosity, its air of something home-made and old-fashioned, without gloss or glitter. The lives of rich people now-a-days tended to follow the line of least resistance. They could go where they wanted, see what they wanted, do what they wanted; but the range of their desires was miserably contracted; with them personality was a mere drop in the bucket of prosperity. If they possessed a Gainsborough, they only possessed a name. 'But if we have a Gainsborough,' Lavinia mused, 'we are not thereby debarred cherishing the lines of the family tea-pot; and it would hurt me more to lose my grandmother's brooch than my pearl necklace.' 'That is it,' she continued, elated, feeling herself necessary to civilization: 'we have not lost touch with small things although we have had experience of great affairs; we can still discriminate, we still have an intimacy that does not need to wear its heart upon its sleeve or barter its secrets in the open market.' Higher and higher mounted the tide of her self-complacency. For days the mood had been a stranger to her; now she encouraged it, indulged it, exulted in it, thinking, in her buoyancy, it would never leave her.

'We didn't take things lightly,' she boasted, 'we made life hard for ourselves. We thought that prosperity followed a good conscience, not, as they think now, that a good conscience follows prosperity. We did not find an excuse for wickedness in high places.' Unaccountably the rhythm of her thought faltered; it had felt itself free of the heavens, but it was singed, and drooped earthward with damaged wing. 'If Hester Prynne had lived in Venice,' she thought, 'she needn't have stood in the pillory.' For a moment she wished that Hawthorne's heroine could have found a country more congenial to her temperament. 'It was my ancestors who punished her,' she thought. 'They had to: they had to stick at something. One must mind something, or else the savour goes out of life, and it stinks.' She glanced uneasily round the room. It had taken back its friendship and had an air of lying in wait for her to disgrace herself. 'Take that,' she muttered, slamming the wardrobe door. But it swung back at her, as though something inside wanted to have a look. 'All right,' she threatened, 'gim-crack stuff in a paste-board palazzo. At home, if I shut a door, it shuts.' But the brave words didn't convince her, and when she tried to visualize her home, she couldn't. The breakdown in her imaginative faculty alarmed her. Suppose that, for the remainder of her life, when she wanted to evoke an image, it wouldn't come? Tentatively, not committing herself to too great an effort, she trained her mind's eye upon the portrait of her great-aunt, Sophia. There was a blur, then a blank: and in turn, as she called upon them, each of the portraits evaded her summons. 'It is unkind of you,' she murmured, almost in tears, 'after I have given you all such a good character.' Then suddenly, as her mind relaxed, the images she had striven for flooded uncontrollably into it, bending their disapproving stare upon her, proclaiming their hostility.

Who was she to commend them? Small thanks would they have given her for her praise: they could only relish a compliment if it came from a virtuous person. They wouldn't want her even to agree with them: they would distrust their very thoughts if she said she shared them. In whom, then, could she confide and to whom could she go for help? Not to the dead and gone Johnstones, for by no act of renunciation could she ingratiate herself with them. She could plume herself with their prestige if she liked; they could not stop her making a snob of herself. But any closer identification, any claim on their long-preserved integrity, any assumption that she, for what she should now give up, was entitled to take her place beside them—this, their grave displeased faces, still circling about her, positively forbade. She might trade on their name, but their goodwill, the vitality of their tradition, could never be hers. They disowned her.

'Well, let them go,' thought Lavinia. 'In the face of life, what use is a recipe from the past? I have fed myself too long upon illusions to want to add another to them.' She was aware of the grapes going sour; in her mouth was a bitter, salty taste; in her eyes the vision of her fate, limitless, agoraphobic, its last barricade thrown down; in her ears, perhaps, defunctive music, the leave-taking of the gods she loved.

The glory of the Johnstones seemed to crumble; root, branch, and stem they were stricken and the virtue passed out of them. She walked up and down the room, conscious of an amazing exhilaration. The rivers of her being, long forced uphill, turned back upon themselves, joined and flowed away unhindered in one dark current. At last she had reached a state of mind that did not need working for, that could be maintained without effort, that absorbed her and left nothing over. The sense of being at odds with herself disappeared; the general awareness of friction and unease that had subtly cramped her movements as well as her thought slid from her; her very skin lay more lightly on her.

'I am lost!' Lavinia cried. It was a moment of ecstasy, but it passed and she burst into tears.

'Well, I don't want you to go, but you must be back by eleven. Re-member we've got to get up early.' Lavinia heard her mother's voice, the firm voice of the recovered Mrs. Johnstone, but it sounded a long way off. She closed her bedroom door and locked it.

' "Amo" is all right,' she muttered, fluttering the leaves of a diction-ary, 'though it has a smack of the Latin Grammar, but should I say "*io*" too? "*Io*" is emphatic, it might be taken to mean that I love him but other people don't; "*io ti amo*": "I love you to the exclusion of" – and that would offend him and be silly besides: everyone must love him. "*Ti amo, ti amo*", I must remember that.' Lavinia breathed quickly and lay down for a moment on her bed. She rose, restless, and looked at the place where she had lain. There was a small depression, scarcely noticeable, and the pillow had filled out again. 'I make very little mark,' she said to herself, and the thought, absurdly enough, filled her with self-pity. She went to the looking-glass and stared at her face as though she would never see it again. 'I ought to have had a photograph taken,' she thought inconsequently. 'I could have done: I had time.' Still standing in front of the mirror she opened her purse; it was empty. Quickly she went to a box, fidgeted with the key and walked slowly back, a bunch of notes in her hand. One by one she stuffed them in her purse. 'Another?' she muttered and looking up, met her questioning eyes in the glass. She shuddered and walked unsteadily into a corner of the room behind the wardrobe, as though it were not enough to keep out of her own sight. To the intruder she unconsciously feared, she would have presented the appearance of a naughty child, taking its punishment. 'One more?' she muttered, in her new, stifled voice. 'How can I tell?'

17

'*Comandi, Signorina?*' Emilio asked. Lavinia started. '*Alla musica,*' she said, '*e poi, al Canal grande della Giudecca.*'

They drifted slowly towards the swaying lanterns, and drew up alongside another gondola. The Toreador's song blared across the water; a man was singing it also, at the second barge, the serenata of St. Mark, only a few hundred feet away. The unfortunate coincidence gave Lavinia a feeling of insanity. The song became a kind of canon;

each singer paused to hear where the other had got; the little orchestra hesitated, scraped, decided to go on. Lavinia could not endure it. *'Alla Giudecca,'* she said.

'Va bene, Signorina.'

The canal opened out, very black and very still. They passed under the shadow of a trawler.

'Ferma qui,' said Lavinia suddenly.

The gondola stopped.

'Emilio,' Lavinia said, *'Ti amo.'*

'Comandi, Signorina?' murmured the gondolier, absently.

'I shall have to say it again,' thought Lavinia.

This time he heard, and understood.

At what time would she like to be home?

At eleven.

'Impossibile.'

At half-past eleven?

'Si, Signorina.'

Rapidly the gondola pressed its way alongside the Fondamenta delle Zattere. With each stroke it shivered and thrilled. They turned into a little canal, turned again into a smaller one, almost a ditch. The V-shaped ripple of the gondola clucked and sucked at the walls of crumbling tenements. Ever and again the prow slapped the water with a clopping sound that, each time she heard it, stung Lavinia's nerves like a box on the ear. She was afraid to look back, but in her mind's eye she could see, repeated again and again, the arrested rocking movement of the gondolier. The alternation of stroke and recovery became dreadful to her, suggesting no more what was useful or romantic, but proclaiming a crude physical sufficiency, at once relentless and unwilling. It came to her overwhelmingly that physical energy was dangerous and cruel, just in so far as it was free; there flashed across her mind the straining bodies in Tiepolo and Tintoretto, one wielding an axe, another tugging at a rope, a third heaving the Cross aloft, a fourth turning his sword upon the Innocents. And Emilio with his hands clasping the oar was such another; a minister at her martyrdom.

She strove to rid her mind of symbols. 'The oar is just a lever,' she thought. ' "We have the long arm of the lever over here. The long arm of the lever – the long arm of the lever".' The silly words stuck in her head like a refrain. Still, with unabated pace, the gondola pushed on. Which side would it stop? 'It'll be this one,' she thought, catching sight of some steps dully outlined against the darkness. 'No, not that, this.'

A dozen times apprehension was succeeded by relief. 'I'm having a run of luck,' she told herself, her mind confusedly adverting to the gaming tables: 'perhaps I shall get off after all.' But let the red turn up as often as it liked, one day the black would win. The odds were against her. But there were no odds; the die was cast. The solace of independent thought, that stuffs out with its bright colours whatever crevices of the mind the tide of misery has forgotten to fill, was taken from her. A wall of darkness, thought-proof and rigid like a fire-curtain, rattled down upon her consciousness. She was cut off from herself; a kind of fizzing, a ghastly mental effervescence, started in her head.

It suddenly seemed to Lavinia that she was going down a tunnel that grew smaller and smaller; something was after her. She ran, she crawled; she flung herself on her face, she wriggled . . . . .

'*Gondoliere!*' she cried, '*Torniamo al hotel.*'

'*Subito Signorina?*'

'*Subito, subito.*'

The next morning Lavinia was sitting by her mother's side in the Orient express. They had been travelling some hours. The train pulled up at a station.

'Brescia?' she thought. 'Why do I remember Brescia? But Elizabeth was wrong. I shall never forget him.'

THE TRAVELLING GRAVE

The Travelling Grave *was first published
in Great Britain in 1951*

A VISITOR FROM DOWN UNDER

'And who will you send to fetch him away?'

AFTER a promising start, the March day had ended in a wet evening. It was hard to tell whether rain or fog predominated. The loquacious bus conductor said, 'A foggy evening,' to those who rode inside, and 'A wet evening,' to such as were obliged to ride outside. But in or on the buses, cheerfulness held the field, for their patrons, inured to discomfort, made light of climatic inclemency. All the same, the weather was worth remarking on: the most scrupulous conversationalist could refer to it without feeling self convicted of banality. How much more the conductor who, in common with most of his kind, had a considerable conversational gift.

The bus was making its last journey through the heart of London before turning in for the night. Inside it was only half full. Outside, as the conductor was aware by virtue of his sixth sense, there still remained a passenger too hardy or too lazy to seek shelter. And now, as the bus rattled rapidly down the Strand, the footsteps of this person could be heard shuffling and creaking upon the metal-shod steps.

'Anyone on top?' asked the conductor, addressing an errant umbrella-point and the hem of a mackintosh.

'I didn't notice anyone,' the man replied.

'It's not that I don't trust you,' remarked the conductor pleasantly, giving a hand to his alighting fare, 'but I think I'll go up and make sure.'

Moments like these, moments of mistrust in the infallibility of his observation, occasionally visited the conductor. They came at the end of a tiring day, and if he could he withstood them. They were signs of weakness, he thought; and to give way to them matter for self-reproach. 'Going barmy, that's what you are,' he told himself, and he casually took a fare inside to prevent his mind dwelling on the unvisited outside. But his unreasoning disquietude survived this distraction, and murmuring against himself he started to climb the steps.

To his surprise, almost stupefaction, he found that his misgivings were justified. Breasting the ascent, he saw a passenger sitting on the right-hand front seat; and the passenger, in spite of his hat turned down, his collar turned up, and the creased white muffler that showed between the two, must have heard him coming; for though the man was looking straight ahead, in his outstretched left hand, wedged between the first and second fingers, he held a coin.

'Jolly evening, don't you think?' asked the conductor, who wanted to say something. The passenger made no reply, but the penny, for such it was, slipped the fraction of an inch lower in the groove between the pale freckled fingers.

'I said it was a damn wet night,' the conductor persisted irritably, annoyed by the man's reserve.

Still no reply.

'Where you for?' asked the conductor, in a tone suggesting that wherever it was, it must be a discreditable destination.

'Carrick Street.'

'Where?' the conductor demanded. He had heard all right, but a slight peculiarity in the passenger's pronunciation made it appear reasonable to him, and possibly humiliating to the passenger, that he should not have heard.

'Carrick Street.'

'Then why don't you say Carrick Street?' the conductor grumbled as he punched the ticket.

There was a moment's pause, then:

'Carrick Street,' the passenger repeated.

'Yes, I know, I know, you needn't go on telling me,' fumed the conductor, fumbling with the passenger's penny. He couldn't get hold of it from above; it had slipped too far, so he passed his hand underneath the other's and drew the coin from between his fingers.

It was cold, even where it had been held. 'Know?' said the stranger suddenly. 'What do you know?'

The conductor was trying to draw his fare's attention to the ticket, but could not make him look round.

'I suppose I know you are a clever chap,' he remarked. 'Look here, now. Where do you want this ticket? In your button-hole?'

'Put it here,' said the passenger.

'Where?' asked the conductor. 'You aren't a blooming letter-rack.'

'Where the penny was,' replied the passenger. 'Between my fingers.'

The conductor felt reluctant, he did not know why, to oblige the passenger in this. The rigidity of the hand disconcerted him: it was stiff, he supposed, or perhaps paralysed. And since he had been standing on the top his own hands were none too warm. The ticket doubled up and grew limp under his repeated efforts to push it in. He bent lower, for he was a good-hearted fellow, and using both hands, one above and one below, he slid the ticket into its bony slot.

'Right you are, Kaiser Bill.'

Perhaps the passenger resented this jocular allusion to his physical infirmity; perhaps he merely wanted to be quiet. All he said was:

'Don't speak to me again.'

'Speak to you!' shouted the conductor, losing all self-control. 'Catch me speaking to a stuffed dummy!'

Muttering to himself he withdrew into the bowels of the bus.

At the corner of Carrick Street quite a number of people got on board. All wanted to be first, but pride of place was shared by three women who all tried to enter simultaneously. The conductor's voice made itself audible over the din: 'Now then, now then, look where you're shoving! This isn't a bargain sale. Gently, *please*, lady; he's only a pore old man.' In a moment or two the confusion abated, and the conductor, his hand on the cord of the bell, bethought himself of the passenger on top whose destination Carrick Street was. He had forgotten to get down. Yielding to his good nature, for the conductor was averse from further conversation with his uncommunicative fare, he mounted the steps, put his head over the top and shouted 'Carrick Street! Carrick Street!' That was the utmost he could bring himself to do. But his admonition was without effect; his summons remained unanswered; nobody came. 'Well, if he wants to stay up there he can,' muttered the conductor, still aggrieved. 'I won't fetch him down, cripple or no cripple.' The bus moved on. He slipped by me, thought the conductor, while all that Cup-tie crowd was getting in.

The same evening, some five hours earlier, a taxi turned into Carrick Street and pulled up at the door of a small hotel. The street was empty. It looked like a cul-de-sac, but in reality it was pierced at the far end by an alley, like a thin sleeve, which wound its way into Soho.

'That the last, sir?' inquired the driver, after several transits between the cab and the hotel.

'How many does that make?'

'Nine packages in all, sir.'

'Could you get all your worldly goods into nine packages, driver?'

'That I could; into two.'

'Well, have a look inside and see if I have left anything.' The cabman felt about among the cushions. 'Can't find nothing, sir.'

'What do you do with anything you find?' asked the stranger.

'Take it to New Scotland Yard, sir,' the driver promptly answered.

'Scotland Yard?' said the stranger. 'Strike a match, will you, and let me have a look.'

But he, too, found nothing, and reassured, followed his luggage into the hotel.

A chorus of welcome and congratulation greeted him. The manager, the manager's wife, the Ministers without portfolio of whom all hotels are full, the porters, the lift-man, all clustered around him.

'Well, Mr. Rumbold, after all these years! We thought you'd forgotten us! And wasn't it odd, the very night your telegram came from Australia we'd been talking about you! And my husband said, "Don't you worry about Mr. Rumbold. He'll fall on his feet all right. Some fine day he'll walk in here a rich man." Not that you weren't always well off, but my husband meant a millionaire.'

'He was quite right,' said Mr. Rumbold slowly, savouring his words. 'I am.'

'There, what did I tell you?' the manager exclaimed, as though one recital of his prophecy was not enough. 'But I wonder you're not too grand to come to Rossall's Hotel.'

'I've nowhere else to go,' said the millionaire shortly. 'And if I had, I wouldn't. This place is like home to me.'

His eyes softened as they scanned the familiar surroundings. They were light grey eyes, very pale, and seeming paler from their setting in his tanned face. His cheeks were slightly sunken and very deeply lined; his blunt-ended nose was straight. He had a thin, straggling moustache, straw-coloured, which made his age difficult to guess. Perhaps he was nearly fifty, so wasted was the skin on his neck, but his movements, unexpectedly agile and decided, were those of a younger man.

'I won't go up to my room now,' he said, in response to the manageress's question. 'Ask Clutsam—he's still with you?—good—to unpack my things. He'll find all I want for the night in the green suitcase. I'll take my despatch-box with me. And tell them to bring me a sherry and bitters in the lounge.'

As the crow flies it was not far to the lounge. But by the way of the tortuous, ill-lit passages, doubling on themselves, yawning with dark entries, plunging into kitchen stairs—the catacombs so dear to *habitués* of Rossall's Hotel—it was a considerable distance. Anyone posted in the shadow of these alcoves, or arriving at the head of the basement staircase, could not have failed to notice the air of utter content which marked Mr. Rumbold's leisurely progress: the droop of his shoulders, acquiescing in weariness; the hands turned inwards and swaying slightly, but quite forgotten by their owner; the chin, always prominent, now pushed forward so far that it looked relaxed and helpless, not at all defiant. The unseen witness would have envied Mr. Rumbold, perhaps even grudged him his holiday air, his untroubled acceptance of the present and the future.

A waiter whose face he did not remember brought him the *apéritif*, which he drank slowly, his feet propped unconventionally upon a ledge of the chimneypiece; a pardonable relaxation, for the room was empty. Judge therefore of his surprise when, out of a fire-engendered drowsiness, he heard a voice which seemed to come from the wall above his head. A cultivated voice, perhaps too cultivated, slightly husky, yet careful and precise in its enunciation. Even while his eyes searched the room to make sure that no one had come in, he could not help hearing everything the voice said. It seemed to be talking to him, and yet the rather oracular utterance implied a less restricted audience. It was the utterance of a man who was aware that, though it was a duty for him to speak, for Mr. Rumbold to listen would be both a pleasure and a profit.

' . . . A Children's Party,' the voice announced in an even, neutral tone, nicely balanced between approval and distaste, between enthusiasm and boredom; 'six little girls and six little' (a faint lift in the voice, expressive of tolerant surprise) 'boys. The Broadcasting Company has invited them to tea, and they are anxious that you should share some of their fun.' (At the last word the voice became completely colourless.) 'I must tell you that they have had tea, and enjoyed it, didn't you, children?' (A cry of 'Yes,' muffled and timid, greeted this leading question.) 'We should have liked you to hear our table-talk, but there wasn't much of it, we were so busy eating.' For a moment the voice identified itself with the children. 'But we can tell you what we ate. Now, Percy, tell us what you had.'

A piping little voice recited a long list of comestibles; like the children in the treacle-well, thought Rumbold, Percy must have been, or soon would be, very ill. A few others volunteered the items of their repast. 'So you see,' said the voice, 'we have not done so badly. And now we are going to have crackers, and afterwards' (the voice hesitated and seemed to dissociate itself from the words) 'Children's Games.' There was an impressive pause, broken by the muttered exhortation of a little girl. 'Don't cry, Philip, it won't hurt you.' Fugitive sparks and snaps of sound followed; more like a fire being kindled, thought Rumbold, than crackers. A murmur of voices pierced the fusillade. 'What have you got, Alec, what have you *got*?' 'I've got a cannon.' 'Give it to me.' 'No.' 'Well, lend it to me.' 'What do you want it for?' 'I want to shoot Jimmy.'

Mr. Rumbold started. Something had disturbed him. Was it imagination, or did he hear, above the confused medley of sound, a tiny click? The voice was speaking again. 'And now we're going to begin the Games.' As though to make amends for past lukewarmness a faint flush of anticipation gave colour to the decorous voice. 'We will commence with that old favourite, Ring-a-Ring of Roses.'

The children were clearly shy, and left each other to do the singing. Their courage lasted for a line or two and then gave out. But fortified by the speaker's baritone, powerful though subdued, they took heart, and soon were singing without assistance or direction. Their light wavering voices had a charming effect. Tears stood in Mr. Rumbold's eyes. 'Oranges and Lemons' came next. A more difficult game, it yielded several unrehearsed effects before it finally got under way. One could almost see the children being marshalled into their places, as though for a figure in the Lancers. Some of them no doubt had wanted to play another game; children are contrary; and the dramatic side of 'Oranges and Lemons,' though it appeals to many, always affrights a few. The disinclination of these last would account for the pauses and hesitations which irritated Mr. Rumbold, who, as a child, had always had a strong fancy for this particular game. When, to the tramping and stamping of many small feet, the droning chant began, he leaned back and closed his eyes in ecstasy. He listened intently for the final accelerando which leads up to the catastrophe. Still the prologue maundered on, as though the children were anxious to extend the period of security, the joyous carefree promenade which the great Bell of Bow, by his inconsiderate profession of ignorance, was so rudely to curtail. The Bells of Old Bailey pressed their usurer's question; the Bells of Shoreditch answered with becoming flippancy; the Bells of Stepney posed their ironical query, when suddenly, before the great Bell of Bow had time to get his word in, Mr. Rumbold's feelings underwent a strange revolution. Why couldn't the game continue, all sweetness and sunshine? Why drag in the fatal issue? Let payment be deferred; let the bells go on chiming and never strike the hour. But heedless of Mr. Rumbold's squeamishness, the game went its way.

After the eating comes the reckoning.

> Here is a candle to light you to bed,
> And here comes a chopper to chop off your head!
> Chop—chop—chop.

A child screamed, and there was silence.

Mr. Rumbold felt quite upset, and great was his relief when, after a few more half-hearted rounds of 'Oranges and Lemons,' the Voice announced, 'Here We Come Gathering Nuts and May.' At least there was nothing sinister in that. Delicious sylvan scene, comprising in one splendid botanical inexactitude all the charms of winter, spring, and autumn. What superiority to circumstances was implied in the conjunction of nuts and May! What defiance of cause and effect! What a testimony to coincidence! For cause and effect is against us, as witness the fate of Old Bailey's debtor; but coincidence is always on our side, teaching us how to eat our cake and have it! The long arm of coincidence! Mr. Rumbold would have liked to clasp it by the hand.

Meanwhile his own hand conducted the music of the revels and his foot kept time. Their pulses quickened by enjoyment, the children put more heart into their singing; the game went with a swing; the ardour and rhythm of it invaded the little room where Mr. Rumbold sat. Like heavy fumes the waves of sound poured in, so penetrating, they ravished the sense; so sweet, they intoxicated it; so light, they fanned it into a flame. Mr. Rumbold was transported. His hearing, sharpened by the subjugation and quiescence of his other faculties, began to take in new sounds; the names, for instance, of the players who were 'wanted' to make up each side, and of the champions who were to pull them over. For the listeners-in, the issues of the struggles remained in doubt. Did Nancy Price succeed in detaching Percy Kingham from his allegiance? Probably. Did Alec Wharton prevail against Maisie Drew? It was certainly an easy win for someone: the contest lasted only a second, and a ripple of laughter greeted it. Did Violet Kingham make good against Horace Gold? This was a dire encounter, punctuated by deep irregular panting. Mr. Rumbold could see, in his mind's eye, the two champions straining backwards and forwards across the white, motionless handkerchief, their faces red and puckered with exertion. Violet or Horace, one of them had to go: Violet might be bigger than Horace, but then Horace was a boy: they were evenly matched: they had their pride to maintain. The moment when the will was broken and the body went limp in surrender would be like a moment of dissolution. Yes, even this game had its stark, uncomfortable side. Violet or Horace, one of them was smarting now: crying perhaps under the humiliation of being fetched away.

The game began afresh. This time there was an eager ring in the children's voices: two tried antagonists were going to meet: it would be a battle of giants. The chant throbbed into a war-cry.

> Who will you have for your Nuts and May,
> Nuts and May, Nuts and May;
> Who will you have for your Nuts and May
> On a cold and frosty morning?

They would have Victor Rumbold for Nuts and May, Victor Rumbold, Victor Rumbold: and from the vindictiveness in their voices they might have meant to have had his blood, too.

> And who will you send to fetch him away,
> Fetch him away, fetch him away;
> Who will you send to fetch him away
> On a cold and frosty morning?

Like a clarion call, a shout of defiance, came the reply:

> We'll send Jimmy Hagberd to fetch him away,
> Fetch him away, fetch him away;
> We'll send Jimmy Hagberd to fetch him away
> On a wet and foggy evening.

This variation, it might be supposed, was intended to promote the contest from the realms of pretence into the world of reality. But Mr. Rumbold probably did not hear that his abduction had been antedated. He had turned quite green, and his head was lolling against the back of the chair.

'Any wine, sir?'
'Yes, Clutsam, a bottle of champagne.'
'Very good, sir.'
Mr. Rumbold drained the first glass at one go.
'Anyone coming in to dinner besides me, Clutsam?' he presently inquired. 'Not now, sir, it's nine o'clock,' replied the waiter, his voice edged with reproach.
'Sorry, Clutsam, I didn't feel up to the mark before dinner, so I went and lay down.'

The waiter was mollified.

'Thought you weren't looking quite yourself, sir. No bad news, I hope.'

'No, nothing. Just a bit tired after the journey.'

'And how did you leave Australia, sir?' inquired the waiter, to accommodate Mr. Rumbold, who seemed anxious to talk.

'In better weather than you have here,' Mr. Rumbold replied, finishing his second glass, and measuring with his eye the depleted contents of the bottle.

The rain kept up a steady patter on the glass roof of the coffee-room.

'Still, a good climate isn't everything. It isn't like home, for instance,' the waiter remarked.

'No, indeed.'

'There's many parts of the world as would be glad of a good day's rain,' affirmed the waiter.

'There certainly are,' said Mr. Rumbold, who found the conversation sedative.

'Did you do much fishing when you were abroad, sir?' the waiter pursued.

'A little.'

'Well, you want rain for that,' declared the waiter, as one who scores a point. 'The fishing isn't preserved in Australia, like what it is here?'

'No.'

'Then there ain't no poaching,' concluded the waiter philosophically. 'It's every man for himself.'

'Yes, that's the rule in Australia.'

'Not much of a rule, is it?' the waiter took him up. 'Not much like law, I mean.'

'It depends what you mean by law.'

'Oh, Mr. Rumbold, sir, you know very well what I mean. I mean the police. Now if you was to have done a man in out in Australia— murdered him, I mean—they'd hang you for it if they caught you, wouldn't they?'

Mr. Rumbold teased the champagne with the butt-end of his fork and drank again.

'Probably they would, unless there were special circumstances.'

'In which case you might get off?'

'I might.'

'That's what I mean by law,' pronounced the waiter. 'You know what the law is: you go against it, and you're punished. Of course I don't mean you, sir; I only say "you" as—as an illustration to make my meaning clear.'

'Quite, quite.'

'Whereas if there was only what you call a rule,' the waiter pursued, deftly removing the remains of Mr. Rumbold's chicken, 'it might fall to the lot of any man to round you up. Might be anybody; might be me.'

'Why should you or they,' asked Mr. Rumbold, 'want to round me up? I haven't done you any harm, or them.'

'Oh, but we should have to, sir.'

'Why?'

'We couldn't rest in our beds, sir, knowing you was at large. You might do it again. Somebody'd have to see to it.'

'But supposing there was nobody?'

'Sir?'

'Supposing the murdered man hadn't any relatives or friends: supposing he just disappeared, and no one ever knew that he was dead?'

'Well, sir,' said the waiter, winking portentously, 'in that case he'd have to get on your track himself. He wouldn't rest in his grave, sir, no, not he, and knowing what he did.'

'Clutsam,' said Mr. Rumbold suddenly, 'bring me another bottle of wine, and don't trouble to ice it.'

The waiter took the bottle from the table and held it to the light.

'Yes, it's dead, sir.'

'Dead?'

'Yes, sir; finished; empty; dead.'

'You're right,' Mr. Rumbold agreed. 'It's quite dead.'

It was nearly eleven o'clock. Mr. Rumbold again had the lounge to himself. Clutsam would be bringing his coffee presently. Too bad of Fate to have him haunted by these casual reminders; too bad, his first day at home. 'Too bad, too bad,' he muttered, while the fire warmed the soles of his slippers. But it was excellent champagne; he would take no harm from it: the brandy Clutsam was bringing him would do the rest. Clutsam was a good sort, nice old-fashioned servant . . . nice old-fashioned house. . . . Warmed by the wine, his thoughts began to pass out of his control.

'Your coffee, sir,' said a voice at his elbow.

'Thank you, Clutsam, I'm very much obliged to you,' said Mr. Rumbold, with the exaggerated civility of slight intoxication. 'You're an excellent fellow. I wish there were more like you.'

'I hope so, too, I'm sure,' said Clutsam, trying in his muddle-headed way to deal with both observations at once.

'Don't seem many people about,' Mr. Rumbold remarked. 'Hotel pretty full?'

'Oh, yes, sir, all the suites are let, and the other rooms, too. We're turning people away every day. Why, only to-night a gentleman rang up. Said he would come round late, on the off-chance. But, bless me, he'll find the birds have flown.'

'Birds?' echoed Mr. Rumbold.

'I mean there ain't any more rooms, not for love nor money.'

'Well, I'm sorry for him,' said Mr. Rumbold, with ponderous sincerity. 'I'm sorry for any man, friend or foe, who has to go tramping about London on a night like this. If I had an extra bed in my room, I'd put it at his disposal.'

'You have, sir,' the waiter said.

'Why, of course I have. How stupid. Well, well. I'm sorry for the poor chap. I'm sorry for all homeless ones, Clutsam, wandering on the face of the earth.'

'Amen to that,' said the waiter devoutly.

'And doctors and such, pulled out of their beds at midnight. It's a hard life. Ever thought about a doctor's life, Clutsam?'

'Can't say I have, sir.'

'Well, well, but it's hard; you can take that from me.'

'What time shall I call you in the morning, sir?' the waiter asked, seeing no reason why the conversation should ever stop.

'You needn't call me Clutsam,' replied Mr. Rumbold, in a sing-song voice, and rushing the words together as though he were excusing the waiter from addressing him by the waiter's own name. 'I'll get up when I'm ready. And that may be pretty late, pretty late.' He smacked his lips over the words.

'Nothing like a good lie, eh, Clutsam?'

'That's right, sir, you have your sleep out,' the waiter encouraged him. 'You won't be disturbed.'

'Good-night, Clutsam. You're an excellent fellow, and I don't care who hears me say so.'

'Good-night, sir.'

Mr. Rumbold returned to his chair. It lapped him round, it ministered to his comfort: he felt at one with it. At one with the fire, the clock, the tables, all the furniture. Their usefulness, their goodness, went out to meet his usefulness, his goodness, met, and were friends.

Who could bind their sweet influences or restrain them in the exercise of their kind offices? No one: certainly not a shadow from the past. The room was perfectly quiet. Street sounds reached it only as a low continuous hum, infinitely reassuring. Mr. Rumbold fell asleep.

He dreamed that he was a boy again, living in his old home in the country. He was possessed, in the dream, by a master-passion; he must collect firewood, whenever and wherever he saw it. He found himself one autumn afternoon in the wood-house; that was how the dream began. The door was partly open, admitting a little light, but he could not recall how he got in. The floor of the shed was littered with bits of bark and thin twigs; but, with the exception of the chopping-block which he knew could not be used, there was nowhere a log of sufficient size to make a fire. Though he did not like being in the wood-house alone he stayed long enough to make a thorough search. But he could find nothing. The compulsion he knew so well descended on him, and he left the wood-house and went into the garden. His steps took him to the foot of a high tree, standing by itself in a tangle of long grass at some distance from the house. The tree had been lopped; for half its height it had no branches, only leafy tufts, sticking out at irregular intervals. He knew what he would see when he looked up into the dark foliage. And there, sure enough, it was: a long dead bough, bare in patches where the bark had peeled off, and crooked in the middle like an elbow.

He began to climb the tree. The ascent proved easier than he expected, his body seemed no weight at all. But he was visited by a terrible oppression, which increased as he mounted. The bough did not want him; it was projecting its hostility down the trunk of the tree. And every second brought him nearer to an object which he had always dreaded; a growth, people called it. It stuck out from the trunk of the tree, a huge circular swelling thickly matted with twigs. Victor would have rather died than hit his head against it.

By the time he reached the bough twilight had deepened into night. He knew what he had to do: sit astride the bough, since there was none near by from which he could reach it, and press with his hands until it broke. Using his legs to get what purchase he could, he set his back against the tree and pushed with all his might downwards. To do this he was obliged to look beneath him, and he saw, far below him on the ground, a white sheet spread out as though to catch him; and he knew at once that it was a shroud.

Frantically he pulled and pushed at the stiff, brittle bough; a lust to break it took hold of him; leaning forward his whole length he seized the bough at the elbow joint and strained it away from him. As it cracked he toppled over and the shroud came rushing upwards. . . .

Mr. Rumbold waked in a cold sweat to find himself clutching the curved arm of the chair on which the waiter had set his brandy. The glass had fallen over and the spirit lay in a little pool on the leather seat. 'I can't let it go like that,' he thought. 'I must get some more.' A man he did not know answered the bell. 'Waiter,' he said, 'bring me a brandy and soda in my room in a quarter of an hour's time. Rumbold, the name is.' He followed the waiter out of the room. The passage was completely dark except for a small blue gas-jet, beneath which was huddled a cluster of candlesticks. The hotel, he remembered, maintained an old-time habit of deference towards darkness. As he held the wick to the gas-jet, he heard himself mutter, 'Here is a candle to light you to bed.' But he recollected the ominous conclusion of the distich, and fuddled though he was he left it unspoken.

Shortly after Mr. Rumbold's retirement the door-bell of the hotel rang. Three sharp peals, and no pause between them. 'Someone in a hurry to get in,' the night porter grumbled to himself. 'Expect he's forgotten his key.' He made no haste to answer the summons; it would do the forgetful fellow good to wait: teach him a lesson. So dilatory was he that by the time he reached the hall door the bell was tinkling again. Irritated by such importunity, he deliberately went back to set straight a pile of newspapers before letting this impatient devil in. To mark his indifference he even kept behind the door while he opened it, so that his first sight of the visitor only took in his back; but this limited inspection sufficed to show that the man was a stranger and not a visitor at the hotel.

In the long black cape which fell almost sheer on one side, and on the other stuck out as though he had a basket under his arm, he looked like a crow with a broken wing. A bald-headed crow, thought the porter, for there's a patch of bare skin between that white linen thing and his hat.

'Good evening, sir,' he said. 'What can I do for you?'

The stranger made no answer, but glided to a side-table and began turning over some letters with his right hand.

'Are you expecting a message?' asked the porter.

'No,' the stranger replied. 'I want a room for the night.'

'Was you the gentleman who telephoned for a room this evening?'

'Yes.'

'In that case, I was to tell you we're afraid you can't have one; the hotel's booked right up.'

'Are you quite sure?' asked the stranger. 'Think again.'

'Them's my orders, sir. It don't do me no good to think.'

At this moment the porter had a curious sensation as though some important part of him, his life maybe, had gone adrift inside him and was spinning round and round. The sensation ceased when he began to speak.

'I'll call the waiter, sir,' he said.

But before he called the waiter appeared, intent on an errand of his own.

'I say, Bill,' he began, 'what's the number of Mr. Rumbold's room? He wants a drink taken up, and I forgot to ask him.'

'It's thirty-three,' said the porter unsteadily. 'The double room.'

'Why, Bill, what's up?' the waiter exclaimed. 'You look as if you'd seen a ghost.'

Both men stared round the hall, and then back at each other. The room was empty.

'God!' said the porter. 'I must have had the horrors. But he was here a moment ago. Look at this.'

On the stone flags lay an icicle, an inch or two long, around which a little pool was fast collecting.

'Why, Bill,' cried the waiter, 'how did that get here? It's not freezing.'

'*He* must have brought it,' the porter said.

They looked at each other in consternation, which changed into terror as the sound of a bell made itself heard, coming from the depths of the hotel.

'Clutsam's there,' whispered the porter. 'He'll have to answer it, whoever it is.'

Clutsam had taken off his tie and was getting ready for bed. He slept in the basement. What on earth could anyone want in the smoking-room at this hour? He pulled on his coat and went upstairs.

Standing by the fire he saw the same figure whose appearance and disappearance had so disturbed the porter.

'Yes, sir?' he said.

'I want you to go to Mr. Rumbold,' said the stranger, 'and ask him if he is prepared to put the other bed in his room at the disposal of a friend.'

In a few moments Clutsam returned.

'Mr. Rumbold's compliments, sir, and he wants to know who it is.'

The stranger went to the table in the centre of the room. An Australian newspaper was lying there which Clutsam had not noticed before.

The aspirant to Mr. Rumbold's hospitality turned over the pages. Then with his finger, which appeared even to Clutsam standing by the door unusually pointed, he cut out a rectangular slip, about the size of a visiting card, and, moving away, motioned the waiter to take it.

By the light of the gas-jet in the passage Clutsam read the clipping. It seemed to be a kind of obituary notice; but of what possible interest could it be to Mr. Rumbold to know that the body of Mr. James Hagberd had been discovered in circumstances which suggested that he had met his death by violence?

After a longer interval Clutsam returned, looking puzzled and a little frightened.

'Mr. Rumbold's compliments, sir, but he knows no one of that name.'

'Then take this message to Mr. Rumbold,' said the stranger. 'Say, "Would he rather that I went up to him, or that he came down to me?" '

For the third time Clutsam went to do the stranger's bidding. He did not, however, upon his return open the door of the smoking-room, but shouted through it:

'Mr. Rumbold wishes you to Hell, sir, where you belong, and says, "Come up if you dare!" '

Then he bolted.

A minute later, from his retreat in an underground coal-cellar, he heard a shot fired. Some old instinct, danger-loving or danger-disregarding, stirred in him, and he ran up the stairs quicker than he had ever run up them in his life. In the passage he stumbled over Mr. Rumbold's boots. The bedroom door was ajar. Putting his head down he rushed in. The brightly lit room was empty. But almost all the movables in it were overturned and the bed was in a frightful mess. The pillow with its five-fold perforation was the first object on which Clutsam noticed bloodstains. Thenceforward he seemed to see them everywhere. But what sickened him and kept him so long from going down to rouse the others was the sight of an icicle on the window-sill, a thin claw of ice curved like a Chinaman's nail, with a bit of flesh sticking to it.

That was the last he saw of Mr. Rumbold. But a policeman patrolling Carrick Street noticed a man in a long black cape, who seemed, by the position of his arm, to be carrying something heavy. He called out to the man and ran after him; but though he did not seem to be moving very fast, the policeman could not overtake him.

PODOLO

THE evening before we made the expedition to Podolo we talked it over, and I agreed there was nothing against it really.

'But why did you say you'd feel safer if Walter was going too?' Angela asked me. And Walter said, 'What good should I be? I can't help to row the gondola, you know.'

Then I felt rather silly, for everything I had said about Podolo was merely conversational exaggeration, meant to whet their curiosity, like a newspaper headline: and I knew that when Angela actually saw the dull little island, its stony and inhospitable shore littered with broken bottles and empty tins, she would think what a fool I was, with my romancing. So I took back everything I said, called my own bluff, as it were, and explained that I avoided Podolo only because of its exposed position: it was four miles from Venice, and if a boisterous bora got up (as it sometimes did, without warning) we should find getting back hard work, and might be late home. 'And what will Walter say,' I wound up, 'if he comes back from Trieste' (he was going there for the day on business) 'and finds no wife to welcome him?' Walter said, on the contrary, he had often wished such a thing might happen. And so, after some playful recriminations between this lately married, charming, devoted couple we agreed that Podolo should be the goal for tomorrow's picnic. 'You must curb my wife's generous impulses,' Walter warned me; 'she always wants to do something for somebody. It's an expensive habit.' I assured him that at Podolo she would find no calls on her heart or her purse. Except perhaps for a rat or two it was quite uninhabited. Next morning in brilliant sunshine Walter gulped down his breakfast and started for the station. It seemed hard that he should have to spend six hours of this divine day in a stuffy train. I stood on the balcony watching his departure.

The sunlight sparkled on the water; the gondola, in its best array, glowed and glittered. 'Say good-bye to Angela for me,' cried Walter as the gondolier braced himself for the first stroke. 'And what is your postal address at Podolo?' 'Full fathom five,' I called out, but I don't think my reply reached him.

Until you get right up to Podolo you can form no estimate of its size. There is nothing near by to compare it with. On the horizon it looks like a foot-rule. Even now, though I have been there many times, I cannot say whether it is a hundred yards long or two hundred. But I have no wish to go back and make certain.

We cast anchor a few feet from the stony shore. Podolo, I must say, was looking its best, green, flowery, almost welcoming. One side is rounded to form the shallow arc of a circle: the other is straight. Seen from above, it must look like the moon in its first quarter. Seen as we saw it from the water-line with the grassy rampart behind, it forms a kind of natural amphitheatre. The slim withy-like acacia trees give a certain charm to the foreground, and to the background where they grow in clumps, and cast darker shadows, an air of mystery. As we sat in the gondola we were like theatre-goers in the stalls, staring at an empty stage.

It was nearly two o'clock when we began lunch. I was very hungry, and, charmed by my companion and occupied by my food, I did not let my eyes stray out of the boat. To Angela belonged the honour of discovering the first denizen of Podolo.

'Why,' she exclaimed, 'there's a cat.' Sure enough there was: a little cat, hardly more than a kitten, very thin and scraggy, and mewing with automatic regularity every two or three seconds. Standing on the weedy stones at the water's edge it was a pitiful sight. 'It's smelt the food,' said Angela. 'It's hungry. Probably it's starving.'

Mario, the gondolier, had also made the discovery, but he received it in a different spirit. '*Povera bestia*,' he cried in sympathetic accents, but his eyes brightened. 'Its owners did not want it. It has been put here on purpose, one sees.' The idea that the cat had been left to starve caused him no great concern, but it shocked Angela profoundly.

'How abominable!' she exclaimed. 'We must take it something to eat at once.'

The suggestion did not recommend itself to Mario, who had to haul up the anchor and see the prospect of his own lunch growing more remote: I too thought we might wait till the meal was over. The cat would not die before our eyes. But Angela could brook no delay. So to the accompaniment of a good deal of stamping and heavy breathing the prow of the gondola was turned to land.

Meanwhile the cat continued to miaow, though it had retreated a little and was almost invisible, a thin wisp of tabby fur, against the parched stems of the outermost grasses.

Angela filled her hand with chicken bones.

'I shall try to win its confidence with these,' she said, 'and then if I can I shall catch it and put it in the boat and we'll take it to Venice. If it's left here it'll certainly starve.'

She climbed along the knife-like gunwale of the gondola and stepped delicately on to the slippery boulders.

Continuing to eat my chicken in comfort, I watched her approach the cat. It ran away, but only a few yards: its hunger was obviously keeping its fear at bay. She threw a bit of food and it came nearer: another, and it came nearer still. Its demeanour grew less suspicious; its tail rose into the air; it came right up to Angela's feet. She pounced. But the cat was too quick for her; it slipped through her hands like water. Again hunger overpowered mistrust. Back it came. Once more Angela made a grab at it; once more it eluded her. But the third time she was successful. She got hold of its leg.

I shall never forget seeing it dangle from Angela's (fortunately) gloved hand. It wriggled and squirmed and fought, and in spite of its tiny size the violence of its struggles made Angela quiver like a twig in a gale. And all the while it made the most extraordinary noise, the angriest, wickedest sound I ever heard. Instead of growing louder as its fury mounted, the sound actually decreased in volume, as though the creature was being choked by its own rage. The spitting died away into the thin ghost of a snarl, infinitely malevolent, but hardly more audible from where I was than the hiss of air from a punctured tyre.

Mario was distressed by what he felt to be Angela's brutality. 'Poor beast!' he exclaimed with pitying looks. 'She ought not to treat it like that.' And his face gleamed with satisfaction when, intimidated by the whirling claws, she let the cat drop. It streaked away into the grass, its belly to the ground.

Angela climbed back into the boat. 'I nearly had it,' she said, her voice still unsteady from the encounter. 'I think I shall get it next time. I shall throw a coat over it.' She ate her asparagus in silence, throwing the stalks over the side. I saw that she was preoccupied and couldn't get the cat out of her mind. Any form of suffering in others affected her almost like an illness. I began to wish we hadn't come to Podolo; it was not the first time a picnic there had gone badly.

'I tell you what,' Angela said suddenly, 'if I can't catch it I'll kill it. It's only a question of dropping one of these boulders on it. I could do it quite easily.' She disclosed her plan to Mario, who was horror-struck. His code was different from hers. He did not mind the animal dying of slow starvation; that was in the course of nature. But deliberately to kill it! '*Poveretto!* It has done no one any harm,' he exclaimed with indignation. But there was another reason, I suspected, for his attitude. Venice is overrun with cats, chiefly because it is considered unlucky to kill them. If they fall into the water and are drowned, so much the better, but woe betide whoever pushes them in.

I expounded the gondolier's point of view to Angela, but she was not impressed. 'Of course I don't expect him to do it,' she said, 'nor you either, if you'd rather not. It may be a messy business but it will soon be over. Poor little brute, it's in a horrible state. Its life can't be any pleasure to it.'

'But we don't know that,' I urged, still cravenly averse from the deed of blood. 'If it could speak, it might say it preferred to live at all costs.' But I couldn't move Angela from her purpose.

'Let's go and explore the island,' she said, 'until it's time to bathe. The cat will have got over its fright and be hungry again by then, and I'm sure I shall be able to catch it. I promise I won't murder it except as a last resource.'

The word 'murder' lingered unpleasantly in my mind as we made our survey of the island. You couldn't imagine a better place for one. During the war a battery had been mounted there. The concrete emplacement, about as long as a tennis court, remained: but nature and the weather had conspired to break it up, leaving black holes large enough to admit a man. These holes were like crevasses in a glacier, but masked by vegetation instead of snow. Even in the brilliant afternoon sunlight one had to tread cautiously. 'Perhaps the cat has its lair down there,' I said, indicating a gloomy cavern with a jagged edge. 'I suppose its eyes would shine in the dark.' Angela lay down on the pavement and peered in. 'I thought I heard something move,' she said, 'but it might be anywhere in this rabbit-warren.'

Our bathe was a great success. The water was so warm one hardly felt the shock of going in. The only drawback was the mud, which clung to Angela's white bathing shoes, nasty sticky stuff. A little wind

had got up. But the grassy rampart sheltered us; we leaned against it
and smoked. Suddenly I noticed it was past five.

'We ought to go soon,' I said. 'We promised, do you remember, to
send the gondola to meet Walter's train.'

'All right,' said Angela, 'just let me have a go at the cat first. Let's
put the food' (we had brought some remnants of lunch with us) 'here
where we last saw it, and watch.'

There was no need to watch, for the cat appeared at once and made
for the food. Angela and I stole up behind it, but I inadvertently kicked
a stone and the cat was off like a flash. Angela looked at me reproachfully. 'Perhaps you could manage better alone,' I said. Angela seemed
to think she could. I retreated a few yards, but the cat, no doubt scent-
ing a trap, refused to come out.

Angela threw herself on the pavement. 'I can see it,' she muttered.
'I must win its confidence again. Give me three minutes and I'll catch
it.'

Three minutes passed. I felt concerned for Angela, her lovely hair
floating over the dark hole, her face as much as one could see of it, a
little red. The air was getting chilly.

'Look here,' I said, 'I'll wait for you in the gondola. When you've
caught it, give a shout and I'll have the boat brought to land.' Angela
nodded; she dare not speak for fear of scaring her prey.

So I returned to the gondola. I could just see the line of Angela's
shoulders; her face, of course, was hidden. Mario stood up, eagerly
watching the chase. 'She loves it so much,' he said, 'that she wants to
kill it.' I remembered Oscar Wilde's epigram, rather uncomfortably;
still, nothing could be more disinterested than Angela's attitude to the
cat. 'We ought to start,' the gondolier warned me. 'The signore will
be waiting at the station and wonder what has happened.'

'What about Walter?' I called across the water. 'He won't know
what to do.'

Her mind was clearly on something else as she said: 'Oh, he'll find
his own way home.'

More minutes passed. The gondolier smiled. 'One must have patience
with ladies,' he said; 'always patience.'

I tried a last appeal. 'If we started at once we could just do it.'

She didn't answer. Presently I called out again. 'What luck, Angela?
Any hope of catching him?'

There was a pause: then I heard her say, in a curiously tense voice.
'I'm not trying to *catch* him now.'

The need for immediate hurry had passed, since we were irrevocably late for Walter. A sense of relaxation stole over me; I wrapped the rug round me to keep off the treacherous cold sirocco and I fell asleep. Almost at once, it seemed, I began to dream. In my dream it was night; we were hurrying across the lagoon trying to be in time for Walter's train. It was so dark I could see nothing but the dim blur of Venice ahead, and the little splash of whitish water where the oar dipped. Suddenly I stopped rowing and looked round. The seat behind me seemed to be empty. 'Angela!' I cried; but there was no answer. I grew frightened. 'Mario!' I shouted. 'Where's the signora? We have left her behind! We must go back at once!' The gondolier, too, stopped rowing and came towards me; I could just distinguish his face; it had a wild look. 'She's there, signore,' he said. 'But where? She's not on the seat.' 'She wouldn't stay on it,' said the gondolier. And then, as is the way in dreams, I knew what his next words would be. 'We loved her and so we had to kill her.'

An uprush of panic woke me. The feeling of relief at getting back to actuality was piercingly sweet. I was restored to the sunshine. At least I thought so, in the ecstasy of returning consciousness. The next moment I began to doubt, and an uneasiness, not unlike the beginning of nightmare, stirred in me again. I opened my eyes to the daylight but they didn't receive it. I looked out on to darkness. At first I couldn't believe my eyes: I wondered if I was fainting. But a glance at my watch explained everything. It was past seven o'clock. I had slept the brief twilight through and now it was night, though a few gleams lingered in the sky over Fusina.

Mario was not to be seen. I stood up and looked round. There he was on the poop, his knees drawn up, asleep. Before I had time to speak he opened his eyes, like a dog.

'Signore,' he said, 'you went to sleep, so I did too.' To sleep out of hours is considered a joke all the world over; we both laughed. 'But the signora,' he said. 'Is *she* asleep? Or is she still trying to catch the cat?'

We strained our eyes towards the island which was much darker than the surrounding sky.

'That's where she was,' said Mario, pointing, 'but I can't see her now.'

'Angela!' I called.

There was no answer, indeed no sound at all but the noise of the waves slapping against the gondola.

We stared at each other.

'Let us hope she has taken no harm,' said Mario, a note of anxiety in his voice. 'The cat was very fierce, but it wasn't big enough to hurt her, was it?'

'No, no,' I said. 'It might have scratched her when she was putting her face—you know—into one of those holes.'

'She was trying to kill it, wasn't she?' asked Mario.

I nodded.

'*Ha fatto male*,' said Mario. 'In this country we are not accustomed to kill cats.'

'*You* call, Mario,' I said impatiently. 'Your voice is stronger than mine.'

Mario obeyed with a shout that might have raised the dead. But no answer came.

'Well,' I said briskly, trying to conceal my agitation, 'we must go and look for her or else we shall be late for dinner, and the signore will be getting worried. She must be a—a heavy sleeper.'

Mario didn't answer.

'*Avanti!*' I said. '*Andiamo! Coraggio!*' I could not understand why Mario, usually so quick to execute an order, did not move. He was staring straight in front of him.

'There *is* someone on the island,' he said at last, 'but it's not the signora.'

I must say, to do us justice, that within a couple of minutes we had beached the boat and landed. To my surprise Mario kept the oar in his hand. 'I have a pocket-knife,' he remarked, 'but the blade is only so long,' indicating the third joint of a stalwart little finger.

'It was a man, then?' said I.

'It looked like a man's head.'

'But you're not sure?'

'No, because it didn't walk like a man.'

'How then?'

Mario bent forward and touched the ground with his free hand. I couldn't imagine why a man should go on all fours, unless he didn't want to be seen.

'He must have come while we were asleep,' I said. 'There'll be a boat round the other side. But let's look here first.'

We were standing by the place where we had last seen Angela. The grass was broken and bent; she had left a handkerchief as though to mark the spot. Otherwise there was no trace of her.

'Now let's find his boat,' I said.

We climbed the grassy rampart and began to walk round the shallow curve, stumbling over concealed brambles.

'Not here, not here,' muttered Mario.

From our little eminence we could see clusters of lights twinkling across the lagoon; Fusina three or four miles away on the left, Malamocco the same distance on the right. And straight ahead Venice, floating on the water like a swarm of fire-flies. But no boat. We stared at each other bewildered.

'So he didn't come by water,' said Mario at last. 'He must have been here all the time.'

'But are you quite certain it wasn't the signora you saw?' I asked. 'How could you tell in the darkness?'

'Because the signora was wearing a white dress,' said Mario. 'And this one is all in black—unless he is a negro.'

'That's why it's so difficult to see him.'

'Yes, we can't see him, but he can see us all right.'

I felt a curious sensation in my spine.

'Mario,' I said, 'he must have seen her, you know. Do you think he's got anything to do with her not being here?'

Mario didn't answer.

'I don't understand why he doesn't speak to us.'

'Perhaps he can't speak.'

'But you thought he was a man. . . . Anyhow, we are two against one. Come on. You take the right. I'll go to the left.'

We soon lost sight of each other in the darkness, but once or twice I heard Mario swearing as he scratched himself on the thorny acacias. My search was more successful than I expected. Right at the corner of the island, close to the water's edge, I found one of Angela's bathing shoes: she must have taken it off in a hurry for the button was torn away. A little later I made a rather grisly discovery. It was the cat, dead, with its head crushed. The pathetic little heap of fur would never suffer the pangs of hunger again. Angela had been as good as her word.

I was just going to call Mario when the bushes parted and something hurled itself upon me. I was swept off my feet. Alternately dragging and carrying me my captor continued his headlong course. The next thing I knew I was pitched pell-mell into the gondola and felt the boat move under me.

'Mario!' I gasped. And then—absurd question—'What have you done with the oar?'

The gondolier's white face stared down at me.

'The oar? I left it— it wasn't any use, signore. I tried. . . . What it wants is a machine gun.'

He was rowing frantically with my oar: the island began to recede. 'But we can't go away!' I cried.

The gondolier said nothing, but rowed with all his strength. Then he began to talk under his breath. 'It was a good oar, too,' I heard him mutter. Suddenly he left the poop, climbed over the cushions and sat down beside me.

'When I found her,' he whispered, 'she wasn't quite dead.'

I began to speak but he held up his hand.

'She asked me to kill her.'

'But, Mario!'

' "Before it comes back," she said. And then she said, "*It's* starving, too, and it won't wait. . . ." ' Mario bent his head nearer but his voice was almost inaudible.

'Speak up,' I cried. The next moment I implored him to stop.

Mario clambered on to the poop.

'You don't want to go to the island now, signore?'

'No, no. Straight home.'

I looked back. Transparent darkness covered the lagoon save for one shadow that stained the horizon black. Podolo. . . .

THREE, OR FOUR, FOR DINNER

IT was late July in Venice, suffocatingly hot. The windows of the bar in the Hotel San Giorgio stood open to the Canal. But no air came through. At six o'clock a little breeze had sprung up, a feebler repetition of the mid-day sirocco, but in an hour it had blown itself out.

One of the men got off his high stool and walked somewhat unsteadily to the window.

'It's going to be calm all right,' he said. 'I think we'll go in the gondola. I see it's there, tied up at the usual post.'

'As you please, Dickie,' said his friend from the other stool.

Their voices proclaimed them Englishmen; proclaimed also the fact that they were good clients of the barman.

'Giuseppe!' called the man at the window, turning his eyes from the Salute with its broad steps, its mighty portal and its soaring dome back to the counter with the multi-coloured bottles behind it. 'How long does it take to row to the Lido?'

'Sir?'

'Didn't you say you'd lived in England, Giuseppe?'

'Yes, sir, eight years at the Hôtel Métropole.'

'Then why——?'

His friend intervened, pacifically, in Italian.

'He wants to know how long it takes to row to the Lido.'

Relief in his voice, the barman answered, 'That depends if you've got one oar or two.'

'Two.'

'If you ask me,' said Dickie, returning to his stool, 'I don't think Angelino, or whatever his damned name is, counts for much. It's the chap in front who does the work.'

'Yes, sir,' said the barman, solicitously. 'But the man at the back he guide the boat, he give the direction.'

'Well,' said Dickie, 'as long as he manages to hit the Lido. . . . We want to be at the Splendide by eight. Can we do it?'

'Easily, sir, you have got an hour.'

'Barring accidents.'

'We never have accidents in Venice,' said the barman, with true Italian optimism.

'Time for another, Phil?'

'Three's my limit, Dickie.'

'Oh, come on, be a man.'

They drank.

'You seem to know a lot,' said Dickie more amiably to the barman. 'Can you tell us anything about this chap who's dining with us—Joe O'Kelly, or whatever his name is?'

The barman pondered. He did not want to be called over the coals a second time. 'That would be an English name, sir?'

'English! Good Lord!' exploded Dickie. 'Does it sound like English?'

'Well, now, as you say it, it does,' remonstrated his companion. 'Or rather Irish. But wait—here's his card. Does that convey anything to you, Giuseppe?'

The barman turned the card over in his fingers. 'Oh, now I see, sir—Giacomelli—il Conte Giacomelli.'

'Well, do you know him?'

'Oh yes, sir. I know him very well.'

'What's he like?'

'He's a nice gentleman, sir, very rich . . .'

'Then he must be different from the rest of your aristocracy,' said Dickie, rather rudely. 'I hear they haven't two penny pieces to rub together.'

'Perhaps he's not so rich now,' the barman admitted, mournfully. 'None of us are. Business is bad. He is *grand azionista*—how do you say?' he stopped, distressed.

'Shareholder?' suggested Philip.

'Good Lord!' exclaimed Dickie, 'I didn't know you were so well up in this infernal language. You're a regular Wop!'

The barman did not notice the interruption.

'Yes, shareholder, that's it,' he was saying delightedly. 'He is a great shareholder in a *fabbrica di zucchero*——'

'Sugar-factory,' explained Philip, not without complacence.

The barman lowered his voice. 'But I hear they are . . .' He made a curious rocking movement with his hand.

'Not very flourishing?' said Philip.

The barman shrugged his shoulders. 'That's what they say.'

'So we mustn't mention sugar,' said Dickie, with a yawn. 'Come on, Phil, you're always so damned abstemious. Have another.'

'No, no, really not.'

'Then I will.'

Philip and even the barman watched him drink with awe on their faces.

'But,' said Philip as Dickie set down his glass, 'Count Giacomelli lives in Venice, doesn't he?'

'Oh yes, sir. Usually he comes in here every night. But it's four— five days now I do not see him.'

'Pity,' said Philip, 'we might have given him a lift. But perhaps he has a launch?'

'I don't think he's using his launch now, sir.'

'Oh well, he'll find some way of getting there, you may be sure,' said Dickie. 'How shall we know him, Giuseppe?'

'I expect you'll see him double, my poor Dickie,' remarked his friend.

The barman, with his usual courtesy, began replying to Dickie's question.

'Oh, he's a common-looking gentleman like yourself, sir. . . .'

'I, common?'

'No,' said the barman, confused. 'I mean *grande come lei*—as tall as you.'

'That's nothing to go by. Has he a beard and whiskers and a moustache?'

'No, he's clean-shaven.'

'Come on, come on,' said Philip. 'We shall be late, and perhaps he won't wait for us.'

But his friend was in combative mood. 'Damn it! how are we to dine with the chap if we don't recognize him? Now, Giuseppe, hurry up; think of the Duce and set your great Italian mind working. Isn't there anything odd about him? Is he cross-eyed?'

'No, sir.'

'Does he wear spectacles?'

'Oh no, sir.'

'Is he minus an arm?'

'*Nossignore,*' cried the barman, more and more agitated.

'Can't you tell us anything about him, except that he's common-looking, like me?'

The barman glanced helplessly round the room. Suddenly his face brightened. 'Ah, *ecco*! He limps a little.'

'That's better,' said Dickie. 'Come on, Philip, you lazy hound, you always keep me waiting.' He got down from the stool. 'See you later,' he said over his shoulder to the barman. 'Mind you have the whisky pronto. I shall need it after this trip.'

The barman, gradually recovering his composure, gazed after Dickie's receding, slightly lurching figure with intense respect.

The gondola glided smoothly over the water towards the island of San Giorgio Maggiore, the slender campanile of which was orange with the light of the setting sun. On the left lay the Piazzetta, the two columns, the rich intricate stonework of St. Mark's, the immense façade of the Ducal Palace, still perfectly distinct for all the pearly pallor in the air about them. But, as San Giorgio began to slide past them on the right, it was the view at the back of the gondola which engrossed Philip's attention. There, in the entrance of the Grand Canal, the atmosphere was deepening into violet while the sky around the dome of the Salute was of that clear deep blue which, one knows instinctively, may at any moment be pierced by the first star. Philip, who was sitting on his companion's left, kept twisting round to see the view, and the gondolier, whose figure blocked it to some extent, smiled each time he did so, saying '*Bello, non è vero?*' almost as though from habit. Dickie, however, was less tolerant of his friend's æsthetic preoccupations.

'I wish to goodness you wouldn't keep wriggling about,' he muttered, sprawling laxly in the depths of the more comfortable seat. 'You make me feel seasick.'

'All right, old chap,' said Philip, soothingly. 'You go to sleep.'

Dickie hauled himself up by the silk rope which was supported by the brass silhouette of a horse at one end and by a small but solid brass lion at the other.

He said combatively: 'I don't want to go to sleep. I want to know what we're to say to this sugar-refining friend of yours. Supposing he doesn't talk English? Shall we sit silent through the meal?'

'Oh, I think all foreigners do.' Philip spoke lightly; his reply was directed to the first of Dickie's questions; it would have been obviously untrue as an answer to the second. 'Jackson didn't tell me; he only gave me that letter and said he was a nice fellow and could get us into palaces and so on that ordinary people don't see.'

'There are too many that ordinary people do see, as it is, if you ask me,' groaned Dickie. 'For God's sake don't let him show us any more sights.'

'He seems to be a well-known character,' said Philip. 'He'll count as a sight himself.'

'If you call a limping dago a sight, I'm inclined to agree with you,' Dickie took him up crossly.

But Philip was unruffled.

'I'm sorry, Dickie, but I had to do it — couldn't ignore the letter, you know. We shall get through the evening somehow. Now, sit up and look at the lovely scenery. *Cosa è questa isola?*' he asked the gondolier, indicating an island to the right that looked if it might be a monastery.

'*Il manicomio,*' said the gondolier, with a grin. Then, as Philip looked uncomprehending, he tapped his forehead and smiled still more broadly.

'Oh,' said Philip, 'it's the lunatic asylum.'

'I do wish,' said Dickie, plaintively, 'if you must show me things, you'd direct my attention to something more cheerful.'

'Well, then,' said Philip, 'look at these jolly old boats. They're more in your line.'

A couple of tramp-steamers, moored stern to stern, and, even in the fading twilight, visibly out of repair — great gangrenous patches of rust extending over their flanks — hove up on the left. Under the shadow of their steep sides the water looked oily and almost black.

Dickie suddenly became animated. 'This reminds me of Hull,' he exclaimed. 'Good old Hull! Civilization at last! Nothing picturesque and old-world. Two ugly useful old ships, nice oily water and lots of foreign bodies floating about in it. At least,' he said, rising unsteadily to his feet, 'I take that to be a foreign body.'

'*Signore, signore!*' cried the first gondolier, warningly.

A slight swell, caused perhaps by some distant motor-boat, made the gondola rock alarmingly. Dickie subsided — fortunately, into his seat; but his hand was still stretched out, pointing, and as the water was suddenly scooped into a hollow, they all saw what he meant: a dark object showed up for an instant in the trough of the wave.

'Looks like an old boot,' said Philip, straining his eyes. '*Cosa è, Angelino?*'

The gondolier shrugged his shoulders.

'*Io non so. Forsè qualche gatto,*' he said, with the light-heartedness with which Italians are wont to treat the death of animals.

'Good God, does the fellow think I don't know a cat when I see one?' cried Dickie, who had tumbled to the gondolier's meaning. 'Unless it's a cat that has been in the water a damned long time. No, it's— it's . . .'

The gondoliers exchanged glances and, as though by mutual consent, straightened themselves to row. '*E meglio andare, signori,*' said Angelino firmly.

'What does he say?'

'He says we'd better be going.'

'I'm not going till I've found out what that is,' said Dickie obstinately. 'Tell him to row up to it, Phil.'

Philip gave the order, but Angelino seemed not to understand.

'*Non è niente interesssante, niente interessante,*' he kept repeating stubbornly.

'But it is interesting to me,' said Dickie, who like many people could understand a foreign language directly his own wishes were involved. 'Go to it! There!' he commanded.

Reluctantly the men set themselves to row. As the boat drew up alongside, the black patch slid under the water and there appeared in its place a gleam of whiteness, then features—a forehead, a nose, a mouth. . . . They constituted a face, but not a recognizable one.

'Ah, *povero annegato,*' murmured Angelino, and crossed himself.

The two friends looked at each other blankly.

'Well, this has torn it,' said Dickie, at last. 'What are we going to do now?'

The gondoliers had already decided. They were moving on.

'Stop! Stop!' cried Philip. 'We can't leave him like this.' He appealed to the men. '*Non si può lasciarlo così.*'

Angelino spread his hands in protest. The drowned man would be found by those whose business it was to patrol the waters. Who knew what he had died of? Perhaps some dreadful disease which the signori would catch. There would be difficulties with the police; official visits. Finally, as the Englishmen still seemed unconvinced, he added, '*Anche fa sporca la gondola. Questo tappeto, signori, m'ha costato più che mille duecento lire.*'

Somewhat grimly Philip explained to Dickie this last, unanswerable reason for not taking the drowned man on board. 'He will dirty the gondola and spoil the carpet, which cost twelve hundred lire.'

'Carpet be damned!' exclaimed Dickie. 'I always told you dagoes were no good. Here, catch hold of him.'

Together they pulled the dead man into the boat, though not before Angelino had rolled back his precious carpet. And when the dead man was lying in the bottom of the boat, decently covered with a piece of brown water-proof sheeting, he went round with sponge and wash-leather and carefully wiped away every drop of water from the gun-wale and its brass fittings.

Ten minutes sufficed to take them to the Lido. The little *passeggiata* that had started so pleasantly had become a funeral cortege. The friends hardly spoke. Then, when they were nearing the landing-stage and the ugly white hotel, an eyesore all the way across the lagoon, impended over them with its blazing lights and its distressing symmetry, Dickie said:

'By Jove, we shall be late for that fellow.'

'He'll understand,' said Philip. 'It'll be something to talk to him about.'

He regretted the words the moment they were out of his mouth: they sounded so heartless.

The landing-stage was almost deserted when the gondola drew up at the steps, but the aged, tottering and dirty *rampino* who hooked it in and held out his skinny hand for *soldi*, soon spread the news. While Philip was conferring with the gondoliers upon the proper course to be taken, a small crowd collected and gazed, expressionlessly but persistently, at the shapeless mound in the gondola. The *rampino* professed himself capable of keeping watch; the gondoliers declared they could not find a *vigile* unless they went together; they hinted that it might take some time. At last Dickie and Philip were free. They walked along the avenue under acacia trees stridently lighted by arc-lamps, towards the sea and the Hotel Splendide. As they looked back they saw that the little knot of spectators was already dispersing.

No, they were told: Count Giacomelli had not yet arrived. But that is nothing, smiled the *maître d'hôtel*; the Signore Conte is often late. Would the gentlemen take a cocktail while they waited?

Dickie agreed with enthusiasm. 'I think we've earned it,' he said. 'Think of it, but for us that poor chap would be floating about the lagoons till Doomsday and none of his dusky offspring know what had happened to him.'

'Do you think they will now?' asked Philip.

'You mean . . .? Oh, I think anyone who really knew him could tell.'

They were sitting at a table under the trees. The air was fresh and pleasant; the absence of mosquitoes almost miraculous. Dickie's spirits began to rise.

'I say,' he said. 'It's damned dull waiting. He's twenty minutes late. Where's that boy?'

When a second round had been served, Dickie motioned the page to stay. Philip looked at him in surprise.

'Listen,' said Dickie, in a thick, excited undertone. 'Wouldn't it be a lark if we sent this lad down to the gondola and told him to ask the chap that's resting inside to come and dine with us?'

'A charming idea, Dickie, but I doubt whether they understand practical jokes in this country.'

'Nonsense, Phil, that's a joke that anyone could understand. Now, put on your thinking-cap and find the appropriate words. I'm no good; you must do it.'

Philip smiled.

'We don't want to be four at dinner, do we? I'm sure the Count wouldn't like having to sit down with a—a drowned rat.'

'That's absurd; he may be a man of excellent family; it's generally the rich who commit suicide.'

'We don't know that he did.'

'No, but all that's beside the point. Now just tell this boy to run down to the jetty, or whatever it is called, give our message and bring us back the answer. It won't take him ten minutes. I'll give him five lire to soothe his shattered nerves.'

Philip appeared to be considering it. 'Dick, I really don't think—a foreign country and all, you know. . . .'

The boy looked interrogatively from one to the other.

'It's a good idea,' repeated Philip, 'and I don't want to be a spoil-sport. But really, Dickie, I should give it up. The boy would be very scared, perhaps tell his parents, and then we might be mobbed and thrown into the Canal. It's the kind of thing that gives us a bad name abroad,' he concluded, somewhat pompously.

Dickie rose unsteadily to his feet.

'Bad name be hanged!' he said. 'What does it matter what we do in this tuppeny ha'penny hole? If you won't tell the boy I'll arrange it with the concierge. He understands English.'

'All right,' agreed Philip, for Dickie was already lurching away, the light of battle in his eye. 'I don't expect it'd do any harm, really. *Senta piccolo!*' He began to explain the errand.

'Don't forget,' admonished Dickie, 'we expect the gentleman *subito*. He needn't bother to dress or wash or brush up or anything.'

Philip smiled in spite of himself.

'*Dica al signore,*' he said, '*di non vestirsi nero.*'

'Not "smoking"?' said the boy, pertly, delighted to display his English.

'No, not "smoking".'

The boy was off like a streak.

It must be boring waiting for a bomb to go off; it is almost equally tedious waiting for a practical joke to take effect. Dickie and Philip found the minutes drag interminably and they could think of nothing to say.

'He must be there now,' said Dickie, at last, taking out his watch.

'What's the time?'

'Half-past eight. He's been gone seven minutes.'

'How dark it is,' said Philip. 'Partly the trees, I suppose. But it wouldn't be dark in England now.'

'I've told you, much better stick to the Old Country. More daylight, fewer corpses, guests turn up to dinner at the proper time. . . .'

'Giacomelli's certainly very late. Over half an hour.'

'I wonder if he ever got your message.'

'Oh yes, he answered it.'

'You never told me. How long ago was that?'

'Last Wednesday. I wanted to give him plenty of time.'

'Did he write?'

'No, he telephoned. I couldn't understand very well. The servant said the Count was away but he would be delighted to dine with us. He was sorry he couldn't write, but he had been called away on business.'

'The sugar factory, perhaps?'

'Very likely.'

'It's bloody quiet, as the navvy said,' remarked Dickie.

'Yes, they are all dining in that glass place. You can see it through the leaves.'

'I suppose they'll know to bring him here.'

'Oh, yes.'

Silence fell, broken a moment later by Philip's exclamation, 'Ah, here's the boy!'

With no little excitement they watched his small figure approaching over the wilderness of small grey pebbles which serve the Venetians in lieu of gravel. They noticed at once that his bearing was erect and important; if he had had a shock he bore no traces of it. He stopped by them, smiling and breathing hard.

'*Ho fatto un corso,*' he said, swelling with pride.

'What's that?'

'He says he ran.'

'I expect he did.'

The friends exchanged amused glances.

'I must say he's got a good pluck,' remarked Dickie, ruefully admiring. Their joke had fallen flat. 'But I expect these Italian kids see corpses every day. Anyhow, ask him what the gentleman said.'

'*Che cosa ha detto il signore?*' asked Philip.

Still panting, the boy replied:

'*Accetta con molto piacere. Fra pochi minuti sarà qui.*'

Philip stared at the page in amazement.

'*Sì, sì, signore,*' repeated the boy. '*Così ha detto, "vengo con molto piacere".*'

'What does he say?' asked Dickie irritably.

'He says that the gentleman accepts our invitation with great pleasure and will be here in a few minutes.'

'Of course,' said Dickie, when the boy had gone off with his *mancia*, whistling, 'he's having us on. But he's a tough youngster. Can't be more than twelve years old.'

Philip was looking all round him, clenching and unclenching his fingers.

'I don't believe he invented that.'

'But if he didn't?'

Philip did not answer.

'How like a cemetery the place looks,' he said, suddenly, 'with all the cypresses and this horrible monumental mason's road-repairing stuff all round.'

'The scene would look better for a few fairy-lights,' rejoined Dickie. 'But your morbid fancies don't help us to solve the problem of our friend in the boat. Are we being made fools of by this whippersnapper, or are we not?'

'Time will show,' said Philip. 'He said a few minutes.'

They both sat listening.

'This waiting gives me the jim-jams,' said Dickie at last. 'Let's call the little rascal back and make him tell us what really did happen.'

'No, no, Dickie, that would be too mortifying. Let's try to think it out; let's proceed from the known to the unknown, as they do in detective stories. The boy goes off. He arrives at the landing stage. He finds some ghoulish loafers hanging about. . . .'

'He might not,' said Dickie. 'There were only two or three corpse-gazers when we left.'

'Anyhow, he finds the *rampino* who swore to mount guard.'

'He might have slipped in for a drink,' said Dickie. 'You gave him the wherewithal, and he has to live like others.'

'Well, in that case, the boy would see — what?'

'Just that bit of tarpaulin stuff, humped up in the middle.'

'What would he do, then? Put yourself in his place, Dickie.'

Dickie grimaced slightly.

'I suppose he'd think the man was resting under the water-proof and he'd say, "Hullo, there!" in that ear-splitting voice Italians have, fit to wake. . . .'

'Yes, yes. And then?'

'Then perhaps, as he seems an enterprising child, he'd descend into the hold and give the tarpaulin a tweak and — well, I suppose he'd stop shouting,' concluded Dickie lamely. 'He'd see it was no good. You must own,' he added, 'it's simpler to assume that half way down the street he met a pal who told him he was being ragged: then he hung about and smoked a cigarette and returned puffing with this cock-and-bull story — simply to get his own back on us.'

'That is the most rational explanation,' said Philip. 'But just for fun, let's suppose that when he called, the tarpaulin began to move and rear itself up and a hand came round the edge, and——'

There was a sound of feet scrunching on the stones, and the friends heard a respectful voice saying, '*Per qui, signor Conte.*'

At first they could only see the robust, white-waistcoated figure of the concierge advancing with a large air and steam-roller tread; behind him they presently descried another figure, a tall man dressed in dark clothes, who walked with a limp. After the concierge's glorious effulgence, he seemed almost invisible.

'Il Conte Giacomelli,' announced the concierge, impressively.

The two Englishmen advanced with outstretched hands, but their guest fell back half a pace and raised his arm in the Roman salute.

'How do you do?' he said. His English accent was excellent. 'I'm afraid I am a little late, no?'

'Just a minute or two, perhaps,' said Philip. 'Nothing to speak of.' Furtively, he stared at the Count. A branch of the overhanging ilex tree nearly touched his hat; he stood so straight and still in the darkness that one could fancy he was suspended from the tree.

'To tell you the truth,' said Dickie bluntly, 'we had almost given you up.'

'Given me up?' The Count seemed mystified. 'How do you mean, given me up?'

'Don't be alarmed,' Philip laughingly reassured him. 'He didn't mean give you up to the police. To give up, you know, can mean so many things. That's the worst of our language.'

'You can give up hope, isn't it?' inquired the Count.

'Yes,' replied Philip cheerfully. 'You can certainly give up hope. That's what my friend meant: we'd almost given up hope of seeing you. We couldn't give *you* up—that's only an idiom—because, you see, we hadn't got you.'

'I see,' said the Count. 'You hadn't got me.' He pondered.

The silence was broken by Dickie.

'You may be a good grammarian, Phil,' he said, 'but you're a damned bad host. The Count must be famished. Let's have some cock-tails here and then go in to dinner.'

'All right, you order them. I hope you don't mind,' he went on when Dickie had gone, 'but we may be four at dinner.'

'Four?' echoed the Count.

'I mean,' said Philip, finding it absurdly difficult to explain, 'we asked someone else as well. I—I think he's coming.'

'But that will be delightful,' the Count said, raising his eyebrows slightly. 'Why should I mind? Perhaps he is a friend of mine, too—your—your other guest?'

'I don't think he would be,' said Philip, feeling more than ever at a loss. 'He—he . . .'

'He is not *de notre monde*, perhaps?' the Count suggested, indulgently.

Philip knew that foreigners refer to distinctions of class more openly than we do, but all the same, he found it very difficult to reply.

'I don't know whether he belongs to our world or not,' he began, and realizing the ludicrous appropriateness of the words, stopped suddenly. 'Look here,' he said, 'I can't imagine why my friend is staying so long. Shall we sit down? Take care!' he cried as the Count was moving towards a chair. 'It's got a game leg—it won't hold you.'

He spoke too late; the Count had already seated himself. Smiling, he said: 'You see, she carries me all right.'

Philip marvelled.

'You must be a magician.'

The Count shook his head. 'No, not a magician, a—a ...,' he searched for the word. 'I cannot explain myself in English. Your friend who is coming—does he speak Italian?'

Inwardly Philip groaned.

'I—I really don't know.'

The Count tilted his chair back.

'I don't want to be curious, but is he an Englishman, your friend?'

Oh God, thought Philip. Why on earth did I start this subject? Aloud he said: 'To tell you the truth I don't know much about him. That's what I wanted to explain to you. We only saw him once and we invited him through a third person.'

'As you did me?' said the Count, smiling.

'Yes, yes, but the circumstances were different. We came on him by accident and gave him a lift.'

'A lift?' queried the Count. 'You were in a hotel, perhaps?'

'No,' said Philip, laughing awkwardly. 'We gave him a lift—a ride —in the gondola. How did you come?' he added, thankful at last to have changed the subject.

'I was given a lift, too,' said the Count.

'In a gondola?'

'Yes, in a gondola.'

'What an odd coincidence,' said Philip.

'So, you see,' said the Count, 'your friend and I will have a good deal in common.'

There was a pause. Philip felt a growing uneasiness which he couldn't define or account for. He wished Dickie would come back: he would be able to divert the conversation into pleasanter channels. He heard the Count's voice saying:

'I'm glad you told me about your friend. I always like to know something about a person before I make his acquaintance.'

Philip felt he must make an end of all this. 'Oh, but I don't think you will make his acquaintance,' he cried. 'You see, I don't think he exists. It's all a silly joke.'

'A joke?' asked the Count.

'Yes, a practical joke. Don't you in Italy have a game on the first of

April making people believe or do silly things? April Fools, we call them.'

'Yes, we have that custom,' said the Count, gravely, 'only we call them *pesci d'Aprile* – April Fish.'

'Ah,' said Philip, 'that's because you are a nation of fishermen. An April fish is a kind of fish you don't expect – something you pull out of the water and——'

'What's that?' said the Count. 'I heard a voice.'

Philip listened.

'Perhaps it's your other guest.'

'It can't be him. It can't be!'

The sound was repeated: it was only just audible, but it was Philip's name. But why did Dickie call so softly?

'Will you excuse me?' said Philip. 'I think I'm wanted.'

The Count inclined his head.

'But it's the most amazing thing,' Dickie was saying, 'I think I must have got it all wrong. But here they are and perhaps you will be able to convince them. I think they're mad myself – I told them so.'

He led Philip into the hall of the hotel. The concierge was there and two *vigili*. They were talking in whispers.

'*Ma è scritto sul fazzoletto*,' one of them was saying.

'What's that?' asked Dickie.

'He says it's written on his handkerchief,' said Philip.

'Besides, we both know him,' chimed in the other policeman.

'What *is* this all about?' cried Philip. 'Know whom?'

'Il Conte Giacomelli,' chanted the *vigili* in chorus.

'Well, do you want him?' asked Philip.

'We *did* want him three days ago,' said one of the men. 'But now it's too late.'

'Too late? But he's . . .' Philip stopped suddenly and looked across at Dickie.

'I tell them so,' shouted the concierge, who seemed in no way disposed to save Count Giacomelli from the hands of justice. 'Many times, many times, I say: "The Count is in the garden with the English gentlemen." But they do not believe me.'

'But it's true!' cried Philip. 'I've only just left him. What do the *vigili* say?'

'They say that he is dead,' said the concierge. 'They say he is dead and his body is in your boat.'

There was a moment of silence. The *vigili*, like men exhausted by argument, stood apart, moody and indifferent. At last one of them spoke.

'It is true, *signori. Si è suicidato*. His affairs went badly. He was a great swindler—and knew he would be arrested and condemned. *Cosi si è salvato.*'

'He may be a swindler,' said Philip, 'but I'm certain he's alive. Come into the garden and see.'

Shaking their heads and shrugging their shoulders, the *vigili* followed him out of the hotel. In a small group they trooped across the stony waste towards the tree. There was no one there.

'You see, *signori*,' said one of the *vigili*, with an air of subdued triumph, 'it's as we said.'

'Well, he must have gone away,' said Philip, obstinately. 'He was sitting on this chair—so. . . .' But his effort to give point to his contention failed. The chair gave way under him and he sprawled rather ludicrously and painfully on the stony floor. When he had picked himself up one of the policemen took the chair, ran his hand over it, and remarked:

'It's damp.'

'Is it?' said Philip expressionlessly.

'I don't think anyone could have sat on this chair,' pursued the policeman.

He is telling me I am a liar, thought Philip, and blushed. But the other *vigile*, anxious to spare his feelings, said:

'Perhaps it was an impostor whom you saw—a confidence man. There are many such, even in Italy. He hoped to get money out of the *signori*.' He looked round for confirmation; the concierge nodded.

'Yes,' said Philip, wearily. 'No doubt that explains it. Will you want us again?' he asked the *vigili*. 'Have you a card, Dickie?'

The *vigili*, having collected the information they required, saluted and walked off.

Dickie turned to the concierge.

'Where's that young whippersnapper who took a message for us?'

'Whippersnapper?' repeated the concierge.

'Well, page-boy?'

'Oh, the *piccolo*? He's gone off duty, sir, for the night.'

'Good thing for him,' said Dickie. 'Hullo, who's this? My poor nerves won't stand any more of this Maskelyne and Devant business.'

It was the *maître d'hôtel*, bowing obsequiously.

'Will there be three gentlemen, or four, for dinner?' he asked.

Philip and Dickie exchanged glances and Dickie lit a cigarette.

'Only two gentlemen,' he said.

THE TRAVELLING GRAVE

HUGH CURTIS was in two minds about accepting Dick Munt's invitation to spend Sunday at Lowlands. He knew little of Munt, who was supposed to be rich and eccentric and, like many people of that kind, a collector. Hugh dimly remembered having asked his friend Valentine Ostrop what it was that Munt collected, but he could not recall Valentine's answer. Hugh Curtis was a vague man with an unretentive mind, and the mere thought of a collection, with its many separate challenges to the memory, fatigued him. What he required of a week-end party was to be left alone as much as possible, and to spend the remainder of his time in the society of agreeable women. Searching his mind, though with distaste, for he hated to disturb it, he remembered Ostrop telling him that parties at Lowlands were generally composed entirely of men, and rarely exceeded four in number. Valentine didn't know who the fourth was to be, but he begged Hugh to come.

'You will enjoy Munt,' he said. 'He really doesn't pose at all. It's his nature to be like that.'

'Like what?' his friend had inquired.

'Oh, original and—and strange, if you like,' answered Valentine. 'He's one of the exceptions—he's much odder than he seems, whereas most people are more ordinary than they seem.'

Hugh Curtis agreed. 'But I like ordinary people,' he added. 'So how shall I get on with Munt?'

'Oh,' said his friend, 'but you're just the type he likes. He prefers ordinary—it's a stupid word—I mean normal, people, because their reactions are more valuable.'

'Shall I be expected to react?' asked Hugh, with nervous facetiousness.

98

'Ha! Ha!' laughed Valentine, poking him gently—'we never quite know what he'll be up to. But you will come, won't you?'

Hugh Curtis had said he would.

All the same, when Saturday morning came he began to regret his decision and to wonder whether it might not honourably be reversed. He was a man in early middle life, rather set in his ideas, and, though not specially a snob, unable to help testing a new acquaintance by the standards of the circle to which he belonged. This circle had never warmly welcomed Valentine Ostrop; he was the most unconventional of Hugh's friends. Hugh liked him when they were alone together, but directly Valentine fell in with kindred spirits he developed a kind of foppishness of manner that Hugh instinctively disliked. He had no curiosity about his friends, and thought it out of place in personal relationships, so he had never troubled to ask himself what this altered demeanour of Valentine's, when surrounded by his cronies, might denote. But he had a shrewd idea that Munt would bring out Valentine's less sympathetic side. Could he send a telegram saying he had been unexpectedly detained? Hugh turned the idea over; but partly from principle, partly from laziness (he hated the mental effort of inventing false circumstances to justify change of plans), he decided he couldn't. His letter of acceptance had been so unconditional. He also had the fleeting notion (a totally unreasonable one) that Munt would somehow find out and be nasty about it.

So he did the best he could for himself; looked out the latest train that would get him to Lowlands in decent time for dinner, and telegraphed that he would come by that. He would arrive at the house, he calculated, soon after seven. 'Even if dinner is as late as half-past eight,' he thought to himself 'they won't be able to do me much harm in an hour and a quarter.' This habit of mentally assuring to himself periods of comparative immunity from unknown perils had begun at school. 'Whatever I've done,' he used to say to himself, 'they can't kill me.' With the war, this saving reservation had to be dropped: they could kill him, that was what they were there for. But now that peace was here the little mental amulet once more diffused its healing properties; Hugh had recourse to it more often than he would have admitted. Absurdly enough he invoked it now. But it annoyed him that he would arrive in the dusk of the September evening. He liked to get his first impression of a new place by daylight.

Hugh Curtis's anxiety to come late had not been shared by the other two guests. They arrived at Lowlands in time for tea. Though they had not travelled together, Ostrop motoring down, they met practically on the doorstep, and each privately suspected the other of wanting to have his host for a few moments to himself.

But it seemed unlikely that their wish would have been gratified even if they had not both been struck by the same idea. Tea came in, the water bubbled in the urn, but still Munt did not present himself, and at last Ostrop asked his fellow-guest to make the tea.

'You must be deputy-host,' he said; 'you know Dick so well, better than I do.'

This was true. Ostrop had long wanted to meet Tony Bettisher who, after the death of someone vaguely known to Valentine as Squarchy, ranked as Munt's oldest and closest friend. He was a short, dark, thick-set man, whose appearance gave no clue to his character or pursuits. He had, Valentine knew, a job at the British Museum, but, to look at, he might easily have been a stockbroker.

'I suppose you know this place at every season of the year,' Valentine said. 'This is the first time I've been here in the autumn. How lovely everything looks.'

He gazed out at the wooded valley and the horizon fringed with trees. The scent of burning garden-refuse drifted in through the windows.

'Yes, I'm a pretty frequent visitor,' answered Bettisher, busy with the teapot.

'I gather from his letter that Dick has just returned from abroad,' said Valentine. 'Why does he leave England on the rare occasions when it's tolerable? Does he do it for fun, or does he have to?' He put his head on one side and contemplated Bettisher with a look of mock despair.

Bettisher handed him a cup of tea.

'I think he goes when the spirit moves him.'

'Yes, but *what* spirit?' cried Valentine with an affected petulance of manner. 'Of course, our Richard is a law unto himself: we all know that. But he must have some motive. I don't suppose he's *fond* of travelling. It's *so* uncomfortable. Now Dick cares for his comforts. That's why he travels with so much luggage.'

'Oh does he?' inquired Bettisher. 'Have you been with him?'

'No, but the Sherlock Holmes in me discovered that,' declared Valentine triumphantly. 'The trusty Franklin hadn't time to put it away. Two large crates. Now would you call that *personal* luggage?'

His voice was for ever underlining: it pounced upon 'personal' like a hawk on a dove.

'Perambulators, perhaps,' suggested Bettisher laconically.

'Oh, do you think so? Do you think he collects perambulators? That would explain everything!'

'What would it explain?' asked Bettisher, stirring in his chair.

'Why, his collection, of course!' exclaimed Valentine, jumping up and bending on Bettisher an intensely serious gaze. 'It would explain why he doesn't invite us to see it, and why he's so shy of talking about it. Don't you see? An unmarried man, a bachelor, *sine prole* as far as we know, with whole *attics-full* of perambulators! It would be *too* fantastic. The world would laugh, and Richard, much as we love him, is terribly serious. Do you imagine it's a kind of vice?'

'All collecting is a form of vice.'

'Oh no, Bettisher, don't be hard, don't be cynical—a *substitute* for vice. But tell me before he comes—he *must* come soon, the laws of hospitality demand it—am I right in my surmise?'

'Which? You have made so many.'

'I mean that what he goes abroad for, what he fills his house with, what he thinks about when we're not with him—in a word, what he collects, is perambulators?'

Valentine paused dramatically.

Bettisher did not speak. His eyelids flickered and the skin about his eyes made a sharp movement inwards. He was beginning to open his mouth when Valentine broke in:

'Oh no, of course, you're in his confidence, your lips are sealed. Don't tell me, you mustn't, I forbid you to!'

'What's that he's not to tell you?' said a voice from the other end of the room.

'Oh, Dick!' cried Valentine, 'what a start you gave me! You must learn to move a little less like a dome of silence, mustn't he, Bettisher?'

Their host came forward to meet them, on silent feet and laughing soundlessly. He was a small, thin, slightly built man, very well turned out and with a conscious elegance of carriage.

'But I thought you didn't know Bettisher?' he said, when their greetings had been accomplished. 'Yet when I come in I find you with difficulty stemming the flood of confidences pouring from his lips.'

His voice was slightly ironical, it seemed at the same moment to ask a question and to make a statement.

'Oh, we've been together for *hours*,' said Valentine airily, 'and had the most enchanting conversation. Guess what we talked about.'

'Not about me, I hope?'

'Well, about something very dear to you.'

'About you, then?'

'Don't make fun of me. The objects I speak of are both solid and useful.'

'That does rather rule you out,' said Munt meditatively. 'What are they useful for?'

'Carrying bodies.'

Munt glanced across at Bettisher, who was staring into the grate.

'And what are they made of?'

Valentine tittered, pulled a face, answered, 'I've had little experience of them, but I should think chiefly of wood.'

Munt got up and looked hard at Bettisher, who raised his eyebrows and said nothing.

'They perform at one time or another,' said Valentine, enjoying himself enormously, 'an essential service for us all.'

There was a pause. Then Munt asked—

'Where do you generally come across them?'

'Personally I always try to avoid them,' said Valentine. 'But one meets them every day in the street and—and here, of course.'

'Why do you try to avoid them?' Munt asked rather grimly.

'Since you think about them, and dote upon them, and collect them from all the corners of the earth, it pains me to have to say it,' said Valentine with relish, 'but I do not care to contemplate lumps of human flesh lacking the spirit that makes flesh tolerable.'

He struck an oratorical attitude and breathed audibly through his nose. There was a prolonged silence. The dusk began to make itself felt in the room.

'Well,' said Munt, at last, in a hard voice, 'you are the first person to guess my little secret, if I can give it so grandiose a name. I congratulate you.'

Valentine bowed.

'May I ask how you discovered it? While I was detained upstairs, I suppose you—you—poked about?' His voice had a disagreeable ring; but Valentine, unaware of this, said loftily:

'It was unnecessary. They were in the hall, plain to be seen by any-one. My Sherlock Holmes sense (I have eight or nine) recognized them immediately.'

Munt shrugged his shoulders, then said in a less constrained tone:
'At this stage of our acquaintance I did not really intend to enlighten
you. But since you know already, tell me, as a matter of curiosity,
were you horrified?'

'Horrified?' cried Valentine. 'I think it a charming taste, *so* original,
so—so human. It ravishes my æsthetic sense; it slightly offends my
moral principles.'

'I was afraid it might,' said Munt.

'I am a believer in Birth Control,' Valentine prattled on. 'Every
night I burn a candle to Stopes.'

Munt looked puzzled. 'But then, how can you object?' he began.

Valentine went on without heeding him.

'But of course by making a corner in the things, you *do* discourage
the whole business. Being exhibits they have to stand idle, don't they?
you keep them empty?'

Bettisher started up in his chair, but Munt held out a pallid hand and
murmured in a stifled voice:

'Yes, that is, most of them are.'

Valentine clapped his hands in ecstasy.

'But some are not? Oh, but that's too ingenious of you. To think of
the darlings lying there quite still, not able to lift a finger, much less
scream! A sort of mannequin parade!'

'They certainly seem more complete with an occupant,' Munt
observed.

'But who's to push them? They can't go of themselves.'

'Listen,' said Munt slowly. 'I've just come back from abroad, and
I've brought with me a specimen that does go by itself, or nearly. It's
outside there where you saw, waiting to be unpacked.'

Valentine Ostrop had been the life and soul of many a party. No one
knew better than he how to breathe new life into a flagging joke.
Privately he felt that this one was played out; but he had a social conscience; he realized his responsibility towards conversation, and sum-
moning all the galvanic enthusiasm at his command he cried out:

'Do you mean to say that it looks after itself, it doesn't need a helping
hand, and that a fond mother can entrust her precious charge to it without a nursemaid and without a tremor?'

'She can,' said Munt, 'and without an undertaker and without a
sexton.'

'Undertaker . . . ? Sexton . . . ?' echoed Valentine. 'What have they
to do with perambulators?'

There was a pause, during which the three figures, struck in their respective attitudes, seemed to have lost relationship with each other.

'So you didn't know,' said Munt at length, 'that it was coffins I collected.'

An hour later the three men were standing in an upper room, looking down at a large oblong object that lay in the middle of a heap of shavings and seemed, to Valentine's sick fancy, to be burying its head among them. Munt had been giving a demonstration.

'Doesn't it look funny now it's still?' he remarked. 'Almost as though it had been killed.' He touched it pensively with his foot and it slid towards Valentine, who edged away. You couldn't quite tell where it was coming; it seemed to have no settled direction, and to move all ways at once, like a crab. 'Of course the chances are really against it,' sighed Munt. 'But it's very quick, and it has that funny gift of anticipation. If it got a fellow up against a wall, I don't think he'd stand much chance. I didn't show you here, because I value my floors, but it can bury itself in wood in three minutes and in newly turned earth, say a flower-bed, in one. It has to be this squarish shape, or it couldn't dig. It just doubles the man up, you see, directly it catches him—backwards, so as to break the spine. The top of the head fits in just below the heels. The soles of the feet come uppermost. The spring sticks a bit.' He bent down to adjust something. 'Isn't it a charming toy?'

'Looking at it from the criminal's standpoint, not the engineer's,' said Bettisher, 'I can't see that it would be much use in a house. Have you tried it on a stone floor?'

'Yes, it screams in agony and blunts the blades.'

'Exactly. Like a mole on paving-stones. And even on an ordinary carpeted floor it could cut its way in, but there would be a nice hole left in the carpet to show where it had gone.'

Munt conceded this point, also. 'But it's an odd thing,' he added, 'that in several of the rooms in this house it would really work, and baffle anyone but an expert detective. Below, of course, are the knives, but the top is inlaid with real parquet. The grave is so sensitive—you saw just now how it seemed to grope—that it can feel the ridges, and adjust itself perfectly to the pattern of the parquet. But of course I agree with you. It's not an indoor game, really: it's a field sport. You go on, will you, and leave me to clear up this mess. I'll join you in a moment.'

Valentine followed Bettisher down into the library. He was very much subdued.

'Well, that was the funniest scene,' remarked Bettisher, chuckling.

'Do you mean just now? I confess it gave me the creeps.'

'Oh no, not that: when you and Dick were talking at cross-purposes.'

'I'm afraid I made a fool of myself,' said Valentine dejectedly. 'I can't quite remember what we said. I know there was something I wanted to ask you.'

'Ask away, but I can't promise to answer.'

Valentine pondered a moment.

'Now I remember what it was.'

'Spit it out.'

'To tell you the truth, I hardly like to. It was something Dick said. I hardly noticed at the time. I expect he was just playing up to me.'

'Well?'

'About these coffins. Are they real?'

'How do you mean "real"?'

'I mean, could they be used as—'

'My dear chap, they have been.'

Valentine smiled, rather mirthlessly.

'Are they full-size—life-size, as it were?'

'The two things aren't quite the same,' said Bettisher with a grin. 'But there's no harm in telling you this: Dick's like all collectors. He prefers rarities, odd shapes, dwarfs, and that sort of thing. Of course any anatomical peculiarity has to have allowance made for it in the coffin. On the whole his specimens tend to be smaller than the general run—shorter, anyhow. Is that what you wanted to know?'

'You've told me a lot,' said Valentine. 'But there was another thing.'

'Out with it.'

'When I imagined we were talking about perambulators—'

'Yes, yes.'

'I said something about their being empty. Do you remember?'

'I think so.'

'Then I said something about them having mannequins inside, and he seemed to agree.'

'Oh, yes.'

'Well, he couldn't have meant that. It would be too—too realistic.'

'Well, then, any sort of dummy.'

'There are dummies and dummies. A skeleton isn't very talkative.'
Valentine stared.

'He's been away,' Bettisher said hastily. 'I don't know what his latest idea is. But here's the man himself.'

Munt came into the room.

'Children,' he called out, 'have you observed the time? It's nearly seven o'clock. And do you remember that we have another guest coming? He must be almost due.'

'Who is he?' asked Bettisher.

'A friend of Valentine's. Valentine, you must be responsible for him. I asked him partly to please you. I scarcely know him. What shall we do to entertain him?'

'What sort of man is he?' Bettisher inquired.

'Describe him, Valentine. Is he tall or short? I don't remember.'

'Medium.'

'Dark or fair?'

'Mouse-coloured.'

'Old or young?'

'About thirty-five.'

'Married or single?'

'Single.'

'What, has he no ties? No one to take an interest in him or bother what becomes of him?'

'He has no near relations.'

'Do you mean to say that very likely nobody knows he is coming to spend Sunday here?'

'Probably not. He has rooms in London, and he wouldn't trouble to leave his address.'

'Extraordinary the casual way some people live. Is he brave or timid?'

'Oh, come, what a question! About as brave as I am.'

'Is he clever or stupid?'

'All my friends are clever,' said Valentine, with a flicker of his old spirit. 'He's not intellectual: he'd be afraid of difficult parlour games or brilliant conversation.'

'He ought not to have come here. Does he play bridge?'

'I don't think he has much head for cards.'

'Could Tony induce him to play chess?'

'Oh, no, chess needs too much concentration.'

'Is he given to wool-gathering, then?' Munt asked. 'Does he forget to look where he's going?'

'He's the sort of man,' said Valentine, 'who expects to find everything just so. He likes to be led by the hand. He is perfectly tame and confiding, like a nicely brought up child.'

'In that case,' said Munt, 'we must find some childish pastime that won't tax him too much. Would he like Musical Chairs?'

'I think that would embarrass him,' said Valentine. He began to feel a tenderness for his absent friend, and a wish to stick up for him. 'I should leave him to look after himself. He's rather shy. If you try to make him come out of his shell, you'll scare him. He'd rather take the initiative himself. He doesn't like being pursued, but in a mild way he likes to pursue.'

'A child with hunting instincts,' said Munt pensively. 'How can we accommodate him? I have it! Let's play "Hide-and-Seek." We shall hide and he shall seek. Then he can't feel that we are forcing ourselves upon him. It will be the height of tact. He will be here in a few minutes. Let's go and hide now.'

'But he doesn't know his way about the house.'

'That will be all the more fun for him, since he likes to make discoveries on his own account.'

'He might fall and hurt himself.'

'Children never do. Now you run away and hide while I talk to Franklin,' Munt continued quietly, 'and mind you play fair, Valentine — don't let your natural affections lead you astray. Don't give yourself up because you're hungry for your dinner.'

The motor that met Hugh Curtis was shiny and smart and glittered in the rays of the setting sun. The chauffeur was like an extension of it, and so quick in his movements that in the matter of stowing Hugh's luggage, putting him in and tucking the rug round him, he seemed to steal a march on time. Hugh regretted this precipitancy, this interference with the rhythm of his thoughts. It was a foretaste of the effort of adaptability he would soon have to make; the violent mental readjustment that every visit, and specially every visit among strangers, entails: a surrender of the personality, the fanciful might call it a little death.

The car slowed down, left the main road, passed through white gateposts and followed for two or three minutes a gravel drive shadowed by trees. In the dusk Hugh could not see how far to right and left these extended. But the house, when it appeared, was plain enough: a large, regular, early nineteenth-century building, encased in cream-coloured stucco and pierced at generous intervals by large windows, some round-headed, some rectangular. It looked dignified and quiet, and in the twilight seemed to shine with a soft radiance of its own. Hugh's spirits began to rise. In his mind's ear he already heard the welcoming buzz of voices from a distant part of the house. He smiled at the man who opened the door. But the man didn't return his smile, and no sound came through the gloom that spread out behind him.

'Mr. Munt and his friends are playing "Hide-and-Seek" in the house, sir,' the man said, with a gravity that checked Hugh's impulse to laugh. 'I was to tell you that the library is home, and you were to be "He", or I think he said, "It", sir. Mr. Munt did not want the lights turned on till the game was over.'

'Am I to start now?' asked Hugh, stumbling a little as he followed his guide, — 'or can I go to my room first?'

The butler stopped and opened a door. 'This is the library,' he said. 'I think it was Mr. Munt's wish that the game should begin immediately upon your arrival, sir.'

A faint coo-ee sounded through the house.

'Mr. Munt said you could go anywhere you liked,' the man added as he went away.

Valentine's emotions were complex. The harmless frivolity of his mind had been thrown out of gear by its encounter with the harsher frivolity of his friend. Munt, he felt sure, had a heart of gold which he chose to hide beneath a slightly sinister exterior. With his travelling graves and charnel-talk he had hoped to get a rise out of his guest, and he had succeeded. Valentine still felt slightly unwell. But his nature was remarkably resilient, and the charming innocence of the pastime on which they were now engaged soothed and restored his spirits, gradually reaffirming his first impression of Munt as a man of fine mind and keen perceptions, a dilettante with the personal force of a man of action, a character with a vein of implacability, to be respected but not to be feared. He was conscious also of a growing desire to see Curtis; he wanted to see Curtis and Munt together, confident that two people he liked could not fail to like each other. He pictured the pleasant encounter after the mimic warfare of Hide-and-Seek — the captor and the caught laughing a little breathlessly over the diverting circumstances of their reintroduction. With every passing moment his mood grew more sanguine.

Only one misgiving remained to trouble it. He felt he wanted to confide in Curtis, tell him something of what had happened during the day; and this he could not do without being disloyal to his host. Try as he would to make light of Munt's behaviour about his collection, it was clear he wouldn't have given away the secret if it had not been surprised out of him. And Hugh would find his friend's bald statement of the facts difficult to swallow.

But what was he up to, letting his thoughts run on like this? He must hide, and quickly too. His acquaintance with the lie of the house, the fruits of two visits, was scanty, and the darkness did not help him. The house was long and symmetrical; its principal bedrooms lay on the first floor. Above were servants' rooms, attics, boxrooms, probably — plenty of natural hiding-places. The second storey was the obvious refuge.

He had been there only once, with Munt that afternoon, and he did not specially want to revisit it; but he must enter into the spirit of the game. He found the staircase and went up, then paused: there was really no light at all.

'This is absurd,' thought Valentine. 'I must cheat.' He entered the first room to the left, and turned down the switch. Nothing happened: the current had been cut off at the main. But by the light of a match he made out that he was in a combined bed-and-bathroom. In one corner was a bed, and in the other a large rectangular object with a lid over it, obviously a bath. The bath was close to the door.

As he stood debating he heard footsteps coming along the corridor. It would never do to be caught like this, without a run for his money. Quick as thought he raised the lid of the bath, which was not heavy, and slipped inside, cautiously lowering the lid.

It was narrower than the outside suggested, and it did not feel like a bath, but Valentine's inquiries into the nature of his hiding-place were suddenly cut short. He heard voices in the room, so muffled that he did not at first know whose they were. But they were evidently in disagreement.

Valentine lifted the lid. There was no light, so he lifted it farther. Now he could hear clearly enough.

'But I don't know what you really want, Dick,' Bettisher was saying. 'With the safety-catch it would be pointless, and without it would be damned dangerous. Why not wait a bit?'

'I shall never have a better opportunity than this,' said Munt, but in a voice so unfamiliar that Valentine scarcely recognized it.

'Opportunity for what?' said Bettisher.

'To prove whether the Travelling Grave can do what Madrali claimed for it.'

'You mean whether it can disappear? We know it can.'

'I mean whether it can effect somebody else's disappearance.'

There was a pause. Then Bettisher said: 'Give it up. That's my advice.'

'But he wouldn't leave a trace,' said Munt, half petulant, half pleading, like a thwarted child. 'He has no relations. Nobody knows he's here. Perhaps he isn't here. We can tell Valentine he never turned up.'

'We discussed all that,' said Bettisher decisively, 'and it won't wash.'

There was another silence, disturbed by the distant hum of a motor-car.

'We must go,' said Bettisher.

But Munt appeared to detain him. Half imploring, half whining, he said:

'Anyhow, you don't mind me having put it there with the safety-catch down.'

'Where?'

"By the china-cabinet. He's certain to run into it.'

Bettisher's voice sounded impatiently from the passage:

'Well, if it pleases you. But it's quite pointless.'

Munt lingered a moment, chanting to himself in a high voice, greedy with anticipation: 'I wonder which is up and which is down.'

When he had repeated this three times he scampered away, calling out peevishly: 'You might have helped me, Tony. It's so heavy for me to manage.'

It was heavy indeed. Valentine, when he had fought down the hysteria that came upon him, had only one thought: to take the deadly object and put it somewhere out of Hugh Curtis's way. If he could drop it from a window, so much the better. In the darkness the vague outline of its bulk, placed just where one had to turn to avoid the china-cabinet, was dreadfully familiar. He tried to recollect the way it worked. Only one thing stuck in his mind. 'The ends are dangerous, the sides are safe.' Or should it be, 'The sides are dangerous, the ends are safe?' While the two sentences were getting mixed up in his mind he heard the sound of 'coo-ee,' coming first from one part of the house, then from another. He could also hear footsteps in the hall below him.

Then he made up his mind, and with a confidence that surprised him put his arms round the wooden cube and lifted it into the air. He hardly noticed its weight as he ran with it down the corridor. Suddenly he realized that he must have passed through an open door. A ray of moonlight showed him that he was in a bedroom, standing directly in front of an old-fashioned wardrobe, a towering, majestic piece of furniture with three doors, the middle one holding a mirror. Dimly he saw himself reflected there, his burden in his arms. He deposited it on the parquet without making a sound; but on the way out he tripped over a footstool and nearly fell. He was relieved at making so much clatter, and the grating of the key, as he turned it in the lock, was music to his ears.

Automatically he put it in his pocket. But he paid the penalty for his clumsiness. He had not gone a step when a hand caught him by the elbow.

'Why, it's Valentine!' Hugh Curtis cried. 'Now come quietly, and take me to my host. I must have a drink.'

'I should like one, too,' said Valentine, who was trembling all over. 'Why can't we have some light?'

'Turn it on, idiot,' commanded his friend.

'I can't—it's cut off at the main. We must wait till Richard gives the word.'

'Where is he?'

'I expect he's tucked away somewhere. Richard!' Valentine called out, 'Dick!' He was too self-conscious to be able to give a good shout. 'Bettisher! I'm caught! The game's over!'

There was silence a moment, then steps could be heard descending the stairs.

'Is that you, Dick?' asked Valentine of the darkness.

'No, Bettisher.' The gaiety of the voice did not ring quite true.

'I've been caught,' said Valentine again, almost as Atalanta might have done, and as though it was a wonderful achievement reflecting great credit upon everybody. 'Allow me to present you to my captor. No, this is me. We've been introduced already.'

It was a moment or two before the mistake was corrected, the two hands groping vainly for each other in the darkness.

'I expect it will be a disappointment when you see me,' said Hugh Curtis in the pleasant voice that made many people like him.

'I want to see you,' declared Bettisher. 'I will, too. Let's have some light.'

'I suppose it's no good asking you if you've seen Dick?' inquired Valentine facetiously. 'He said we weren't to have any light till the game was finished. He's so strict with his servants; they have to obey him to the letter. I daren't even ask for a candle. But *you* know the faithful Franklin well enough.'

'Dick will be here in a moment surely,' Bettisher said, for the first time that day appearing undecided.

They all stood listening.

'Perhaps he's gone to dress,' Curtis suggested. 'It's past eight o'clock.'

'How can he dress in the dark?' asked Bettisher.

Another pause.

'Oh, I'm tired of this,' said Bettisher. 'Franklin! Franklin!' His voice boomed through the house and a reply came almost at once from the hall, directly below them. 'We think Mr. Munt must have gone to dress,' said Bettisher. 'Will you please turn on the light?'

'Certainly, sir, but I don't think Mr. Munt is in his room.'

'Well, anyhow—'

'Very good, sir.'

At once the corridor was flooded with light, and to all of them, in greater or less degree according to their familiarity with their surroundings, it seemed amazing that they should have had so much difficulty, half an hour before, in finding their way about. Even Valentine's harassed emotions experienced a moment's relaxation. They chaffed Hugh Curtis a little about the false impression his darkling voice had given them. Valentine, as always the more loquacious, swore it seemed to proceed from a large gaunt man with a hare-lip. They were beginning to move towards their rooms, Valentine had almost reached his, when Hugh Curtis called after them:

"I say, may I be taken to my room?'

'Of course,' said Bettisher, turning back. 'Franklin! Franklin! Franklin, show Mr. Curtis where his room is. I don't know myself.' He disappeared and the butler came slowly up the stairs.

'It's quite near, sir, at the end of the corridor,' he said. 'I'm sorry, with having no light we haven't got your things put out. But it'll only take a moment.'

The door did not open when he turned the handle.

'Odd! It's stuck,' he remarked: but it did not yield to the pressure of his knee and shoulder. 'I've never known it to be locked before,' he muttered, thinking aloud, obviously put out by this flaw in the harmony of the domestic arrangements. 'If you'll excuse me, sir, I'll go and fetch my key.'

In a minute or two he was back with it. So gingerly did he turn the key in the lock he evidently expected another rebuff; but it gave a satisfactory click and the door swung open with the best will in the world.

'Now I'll go and fetch your suitcase,' he said as Hugh Curtis entered.

'No, it's absurd to stay,' soliloquized Valentine, fumbling feverishly with his front stud, 'after all these warnings, it would be insane. It's what they do in a "shocker", linger on and on, disregarding revolvers and other palpable hints, while one by one the villain picks them off, all except the hero, who is generally the stupidest of all, but the luckiest. No doubt by staying I should qualify to be the hero: I should survive; but what about Hugh, and Bettisher, that close-mouthed rat-trap?' He studied his face in the glass: it looked flushed. 'I've had an alarming increase in blood-pressure: I am seriously unwell: I must go away at once to a nursing home, and Hugh must accompany me.' He gazed round wretchedly at the charmingly appointed room, with its chintz and polished furniture, so comfortable, safe, and unsensational. And for the hundredth time his thoughts veered round and blew from the opposite quarter. It would equally be madness to run away at a moment's notice, scared by what was no doubt only an elaborate practical joke. Munt, though not exactly a jovial man, would have his joke, as witness the game of Hide-and-Seek. No doubt the Travelling Grave itself was just a take-in, a test of his and Bettisher's credulity. Munt was not popular, he had few friends, but that did not make him a potential murderer. Valentine had always liked him, and no one, to his knowledge, had ever spoken a word against him. What sort of figure would he, Valentine, cut, after this nocturnal flitting? He would lose at least two friends, Munt and Bettisher, and cover Hugh Curtis and himself with ridicule.

Poor Valentine! So perplexed was he that he changed his mind five times on the way down to the library. He kept repeating to himself the sentence, 'I'm so sorry, Dick, I find my blood-pressure rather high, and I think I ought to go into a nursing home to-night — Hugh will see me safely there' — until it became meaningless, even its absurdity disappeared.

Hugh was in the library alone. It was now or never; but Valentine's opening words were swept aside by his friend, who came running across the room to him.

'Oh, Valentine, the funniest thing has happened.'

'Funny? Where? What?' Valentine asked.

'No, no, not funny in the sinister sense, it's not in the least serious. Only it's so *odd*. This is a house of surprises. I'm glad I came.'

'Tell me quickly.'

'Don't look so alarmed. It's only very amusing. But I must show it you, or you'll miss the funny side of it. Come on up to my room; we've got five minutes.'

But before they crossed the threshold Valentine pulled up with a start.

'Is *this* your room?'

'Oh, yes. Don't look as if you had seen a ghost. It's a perfectly ordinary room, I tell you, except for one thing. No, stop a moment; wait here while I arrange the scene.'

He darted in, and after a moment summoned Valentine to follow.

'Now, do you notice anything strange?'

'I see the usual evidences of untidiness.'

A coat was lying on the floor and various articles of clothing were scattered about.

'You do? Well then—no deceit, gentlemen.' With a gesture he snatched the coat up from the floor. 'Now what do you see?'

'I see a further proof of slovenly habits—a pair of shoes where the coat was.'

'Look well at those shoes. There's nothing about them that strikes you as peculiar?'

Valentine studied them. They were ordinary brown shoes, lying side by side, the soles uppermost, a short pace from the wardrobe. They looked as though someone had taken them off and forgotten to put them away, or taken them out, and forgotten to put them on.

'Well,' pronounced Valentine at last, 'I don't usually leave my shoes upside-down like that, but you might.'

'Ah,' said Hugh triumphantly, 'your surmise is incorrect. They're *not* my shoes.'

'Not yours? Then they were left here by mistake. Franklin should have taken them away.'

'Yes, but that's where the coat comes in. I'm reconstructing the scene, you see, hoping to impress you. While he was downstairs fetching my bag, to save time I began to undress; I took my coat off and hurled it down there. After he had gone I picked it up. So he never saw the shoes.'

'Well, why make such a fuss? They won't be wanted till morning. Or would you rather ring for Franklin and tell him to take them away?'

'Ah!' cried Hugh, delighted by this. 'At last you've come to the heart of the matter. He *couldn't* take them away.'

'Why couldn't he?'

'Because they're fixed to the floor!'

'Oh, rubbish!' said Valentine. 'You must be dreaming.'

He bent down, took hold of the shoes by the welts, and gave a little tug. They did not move.

'There you are!' cried Hugh. 'Apologize. Own that it is unusual to find in one's room a strange pair of shoes adhering to the floor.'

Valentine's reply was to give another heave. Still the shoes did not budge.

'No good,' commented his friend. 'They're nailed down, or gummed down, or something. The dinner-bell hasn't rung; we'll get Franklin to clear up the mystery.'

The butler when he came looked uneasy, and surprised them by speaking first.

'Was it Mr. Munt you were wanting, sir?' he said to Valentine. 'I don't know where he is. I've looked everywhere and can't find him.'

'Are these his shoes by any chance?' asked Valentine.

They couldn't deny themselves the mild entertainment of watching Franklin stoop down to pick up the shoes, and recoil in perplexity when he found them fast in the floor.

'These should be Mr. Munt's, sir,' he said doubtfully — 'these should. But what's happened to them that they won't leave the floor?'

The two friends laughed gaily.

'That's what *we* want to know,' Hugh Curtis chuckled. 'That's why we called you: we thought you could help us.'

'They're Mr. Munt's right enough,' muttered the butler. 'They must have got something heavy inside.'

'Damned heavy,' said Valentine, playfully grim.

Fascinated, the three men stared at the upturned soles, so close together that there was no room between for two thumbs set side by side.

Rather gingerly the butler stooped again, and tried to feel the uppers. This was not as easy as it seemed, for the shoes were flattened against the floor, as if a weight had pressed them down.

His face was white as he stood up.

'There *is* something in them,' he said in a frightened voice.

'And his shoes were full of feet,' carolled Valentine flippantly. 'Trees, perhaps.'

'It was not as hard as wood,' said the butler. 'You can squeeze it a bit if you try.'

They looked at each other, and a tension made itself felt in the room.

'There's only one way to find out,' declared Hugh Curtis suddenly, in a determined tone one could never have expected from him.

'How?'

'Take them off.'

'Take what off?'

'His shoes off, you idiot.'

'Off what?'

'That's what I don't know yet, you bloody fool!' Curtis almost screamed; and kneeling down, he tore apart the laces and began tugging and wrenching at one of the shoes.

'It's coming, it's coming,' he cried. 'Valentine, put your arms around me and pull, that's a good fellow. It's the heel that's giving the trouble.'

Suddenly the shoe slipped off.

'Why, it's only a sock,' whispered Valentine; 'it's so thin.'

'Yes, but the foot's inside it all right,' cried Curtis in a loud strange voice, speaking very rapidly. 'And here's the ankle, see, and here's where it begins to go down into the floor, see; he must have been a very small man; you see I never saw him, but it's all so crushed—'

The sound of a heavy fall made them turn.

Franklin had fainted.

FEET FOREMOST

THE house-warming at Low Threshold Hall was not an event that affected many people. The local newspaper, however, had half a column about it, and one or two daily papers supplemented the usual August dearth of topics with pictures of the house. They were all taken from the same angle, and showed a long, low building in the Queen Anne style flowing away from a square tower on the left which was castellated and obviously of much earlier date, the whole structure giving somewhat the impression to a casual glance of a domesticated church, or even of a small railway train that had stopped dead on finding itself in a park. Beneath the photograph was written something like 'Suffolk Manor House re-occupied after a hundred and fifty years,' and, in one instance, 'Inset, (L.) Mr. Charles Ampleforth, owner of Low Threshold Hall; (R.) Sir George Willings, the architect responsible for the restoration of this interesting mediæval relic.' Mr. Ampleforth's handsome, slightly Disraelian head, nearly spiked on his own flagpole, smiled congratulations at the grey hair and rounded features of Sir George Willings who, suspended like a bubble above the Queen Anne wing, discreetly smiled back.

To judge from the photograph, time had dealt gently with Low Threshold Hall. Only a trained observer could have told how much of the original fabric had been renewed. The tower looked particularly convincing. While as for the gardens sloping down to the stream which bounded the foreground of the picture—they had that old-world air which gardens so quickly acquire. To see those lush lawns and borders as a meadow, that mellow brickwork under scaffolding, needed a strong effort of the imagination.

But the guests assembled in Mr. Ampleforth's drawing-room after dinner and listening to their host as, not for the first time, he enlarged upon the obstacles faced and overcome in the work of restoration, found it just as hard to believe that the house was old. Most of them had been taken to see it, at one time or another, in process of reconstruction; yet even within a few days of its completion, how unfinished a house looks! Its habitability seems determined in the last few hours. Magdalen Winthrop, whose beautiful, expressive face still (to her hostess' sentimental eye) bore traces of the slight disappointment she had suffered earlier in the evening, felt as if she were in an Aladdin's palace. Her glance wandered appreciatively from the Samarcand rugs to the pale green walls, and dwelt with pleasure on the high shallow arch, flanked by slender columns, the delicate lines of which were emphasized by the darkness of the hall behind them. It all seemed so perfect and so new; not only every sign of decay but the very sense of age had been banished. How absurd not to be able to find a single grey hair, so to speak, in a house that had stood empty for a hundred and fifty years! Her eyes, still puzzled, came to rest on the company, ranged in an irregular circle round the open fireplace.

'What's the matter, Maggie?' said a man at her side, obviously glad to turn the conversation away from bricks and mortar. 'Looking for something?'

Mrs. Ampleforth, whose still lovely skin under the abundant white hair made her face look like a rose in snow, bent forward over the cream-coloured satin bedspread she was embroidering and smiled. 'I was only thinking,' said Maggie, turning to her host whose recital had paused but not died upon his lips, 'how surprised the owls and bats would be if they could come in and see the change in their old home.'

'Oh, I do hope they won't,' cried a high female voice from the depths of a chair whose generous proportions obscured the speaker.

'Don't be such a baby, Eileen,' said Maggie's neighbour in tones that only a husband could have used. 'Wait till you see the family ghost.'

'Ronald, please! Have pity on my poor nerves!' The upper half of a tiny, childish, imploring face peered like a crescent moon over the rim of the chair.

'If there is a ghost,' said Maggie, afraid that her original remark might be construed as a criticism, 'I envy him his beautiful surroundings. I would willingly take his place.'

'Hear, hear,' agreed Ronald. 'A very happy haunting-ground. Is there a ghost, Charles?'

There was a pause. They all looked at their host.

'Well,' said Mr. Ampleforth, who rarely spoke except after a pause and never without a slight impressiveness of manner, 'there is and there isn't.'

The silence grew even more respectful.

'The ghost of Low Threshold Hall,' Mr. Ampleforth continued, 'is no ordinary ghost.'

'It wouldn't be,' muttered Ronald in an aside Maggie feared might be audible.

'It is, for one thing,' Mr. Ampleforth pursued, 'exceedingly considerate.'

'Oh, how?' exclaimed two or three voices.

'It only comes by invitation.'

'Can anyone invite it?'

'Yes, anyone.'

There was nothing Mr. Ampleforth liked better than answering questions; he was evidently enjoying himself now.

'How is the invitation delivered?' Ronald asked. 'Does one telephone, or does one send a card: "Mrs. Ampleforth requests the pleasure of Mr. Ghost's company on — well — what is to-morrow? — the eighteenth August, Moaning and Groaning and Chain Rattling. R.S.V.P."?'

'That would be a sad solecism,' said Mr. Ampleforth. 'The ghost of Low Threshold Hall is a lady.'

'Oh,' cried Eileen's affected little voice. 'I'm so thankful. I should be less frightened of a female phantom.'

'She hasn't attained years of discretion,' Mr. Ampleforth said. 'She was only sixteen when—'

'Then she's not "out"?'

'Not in the sense you mean. I hope she's not "out" in any sense,' said Mr. Ampleforth, with grim facetiousness.

There was a general shudder.

'Well, I'm glad we can't ask her to an evening party,' observed Ronald. 'A ghost at tea-time is much less alarming. Is she what is called a "popular girl"?'

'I'm afraid not.'

'Then why do people invite her?'

'They don't realize what they're doing.'

'A kind of pig in a poke business, what? But you haven't told us yet how we're to get hold of the little lady.'

'That's quite simple,' said Mr. Ampleforth readily. 'She comes to the door.'

The drawing-room clock began to strike eleven, and no one spoke till it had finished.

'She comes to the door,' said Ronald with an air of deliberation, 'and then—don't interrupt, Eileen, I'm in charge of the cross-examination—she—she hangs about—'

'She waits to be asked inside.'

'I suppose there is a time-honoured formula of invitation: "Sweet Ermyntrude, in the name of the master of the house I bid thee welcome to Low Threshold Hall. There's no step, so you can walk straight in." Charles, much as I admire your house, I do think it's incomplete without a doorstep. A ghost could just sail in.'

'There you make a mistake,' said Mr. Ampleforth impressively. 'Our ghost cannot enter the house unless she is lifted across the threshold.'

'Like a bride,' exclaimed Magdalen.

'Yes,' said Mr. Ampleforth. 'Because she came as a bride.' He looked round at his guests with an enigmatic smile.

They did not disappoint him. 'Now, Charlie, don't be so mysterious! Do tell us! Tell us the whole story.'

Mr. Ampleforth settled himself into his chair. 'There's very little to tell,' he said, with the reassuring manner of someone who intends to tell a great deal, 'but this is the tale. In the time of the Wars of the Roses the owner of Low Threshold Hall (I need not tell you his name was not Ampleforth) married *en troisièmes noces* the daughter of a neighbouring baron much less powerful than he. Lady Elinor Stortford was sixteen when she came and she did not live to see her seventeenth birthday. Her husband was a bad hat (I'm sorry to have to say so of a predecessor of mine), a very bad hat. He ill-treated her, drove her mad with terror, and finally killed her.'

The narrator paused dramatically but the guests felt slightly disappointed. They had heard so many stories of that kind.

'Poor thing,' said Magdalen, feeling that some comment was necessary, however flat. 'So now she haunts the place. I suppose it's the nature of ghosts to linger where they've suffered, but it seems illogical to me. I should want to go somewhere else.'

'The Lady Elinor would agree with you. The first thing she does when she gets into the house is make plans for getting out. Her visits, as far as I can gather, have generally been brief.'

'Then why does she come?' asked Eileen.

'She comes for vengeance,' Mr. Ampleforth's voice dropped at the word. 'And apparently she gets it. Within a short time of her appearance, someone in the house always dies.'

'Nasty spiteful little girl,' said Ronald, concealing a yawn. 'Then how long is she in residence?'

'Until her object is accomplished.'

'Does she make a dramatic departure—in a thunderstorm or something?'

'No, she is just carried out.'

'Who carries her this time?'

'The undertaker's men. She goes out with the corpse. Though some say—'

'Oh, Charlie, do stop!' Mrs. Ampleforth interrupted, bending down to gather up the corners of her bedspread. 'Eileen will never sleep. Let's go to bed.'

'No! No!' shouted Ronald. 'He can't leave off like that. I must hear the rest. My flesh was just beginning to creep.'

Mr. Ampleforth looked at his wife.

'I've had my orders.'

'Well, well,' said Ronald, resigned. 'Anyhow, remember what I said. A decent fall of rain, and you'll have a foot of water under the tower there, unless you put in a doorstep.'

Mr. Ampleforth looked grave. 'Oh no, I couldn't do that. That would be to invite er—er—trouble. The absence of a step was a precaution. That's how the house got its name.'

'A precaution against what?'

'Against Lady Elinor.'

'But how? I should have thought a draw-bridge would have been more effective.'

'Lord Deadham's immediate heirs thought the same. According to the story they put every material obstacle they could to bar the lady's path. You can still see in the tower the grooves which contained the portcullis. And there was a flight of stairs so steep and dangerous they couldn't be used without risk to life and limb. But that only made it easier for Lady Elinor.'

'How did it?'

'Why, don't you see, everyone who came to the house, friends and strangers alike, had to be helped over the threshold! There was no way of distinguishing between them. At last when so many members of the family had been killed off that it was threatened with extinction, some-one conceived a brilliant idea. Can you guess what it was, Maggie?'

'They removed all the barriers and levelled the threshold, so that any stranger who came to the door and asked to be helped into the house was refused admittance.'

'Exactly. And the plan seems to have worked remarkably well.'

'But the family did die out in the end,' observed Maggie.

'Yes,' said Mr. Ampleforth, 'soon after the middle of the eighteenth century. The best human plans are fallible, and Lady Elinor was very persistent.'

He held the company with his glittering raconteur's eye.

But Mrs. Ampleforth was standing up. 'Now, now,' she said, 'I gave you twenty minutes' grace. It will soon be midnight. Come along, Maggie, you must be tired after your journey. Let me light you a candle.' She took the girl's arm and piloted her into the comparative darkness of the hall. 'I think they must be on this table,' she said, her fingers groping; 'I don't know the house myself yet. We ought to have had a light put here. But it's one of Charlie's little economies to have as few lights as possible. I'll tell him about it. But it takes so long to get anything done in this out-of-the-way spot. My dear, nearly three miles to the nearest clergyman, four to the nearest doctor! Ah, here we are, I'll light some for the others. Charlie is still holding forth about Lady Elinor. You didn't mind that long recital?' she added, as, accompanied by their shadows, they walked up the stairs. 'Charlie does so love an audience. And you don't feel uncomfortable or anything? I am always so sorry for Lady Elinor, poor soul, if she ever existed. Oh, and I wanted to say we were so disappointed about Antony. I feel we got you down to-day on false pretences. Something at the office kept him. But he's coming to-morrow. When is the wedding to be, dearest?'

'In the middle of September.'

'Quite soon now. I can't tell you how excited I am about it. I think he's such a dear. You both are. Now which is your way, left, right, or middle? I'm ashamed to say I've forgotten.'

Maggie considered. 'I remember; it's to the left.'

'In that black abyss? Oh, darling, I forgot; do you feel equal to going on the picnic to-morrow? We shan't get back till five. It'll be a long day: I'll stay at home with you if you like—I'm tired of ruins.'

'I'd love to go.'

'Good-night, then.'

'Good-night.'

In the space of ten minutes the two men, left to themselves, had succeeded in transforming the elegant Queen Anne drawing-room into something that looked and smelt like a bar-parlour.

'Well,' observed Ronald who, more than his host, had been responsible for the room's deterioration, 'time to turn in. I have a rendezvous with Lady Elinor. By the way, Charles,' he went on, 'have you given the servants instructions in anti-Elinor technique—told them only to admit visitors who can enter the house under their own steam, so to speak?'

'Mildred thought it wisest, and I agree with her,' said Mr. Ampleforth, 'to tell the servants nothing at all. It might unsettle them, and we shall have hard work to keep them as it is.'

'Perhaps you're right,' said Ronald. 'Anyhow it's no part of their duty to show the poor lady out. Charles, what were you going to say that wasn't fit for ears polite when Mildred stopped you?'

Mr. Ampleforth reflected. 'I wasn't aware—'

'Oh, yes, she nipped your smoking-room story in the bud. I asked "Who carries Lady Elinor out?" and you said "The undertaker's men; she goes out with the corpse," and you were going to say something else when you were called to order.'

'Oh, I remember,' said Mr. Ampleforth. 'It was such a small point, I couldn't imagine why Mildred objected. According to one story, she doesn't go out *with* the corpse, she goes out in it.'

Ronald pondered. 'Don't see much difference, do you?'

'I can't honestly say I do.'

'Women are odd creatures,' Ronald said. 'So long.'

The cat stood by the library door, miaowing. Its intention was perfectly plain. First it had wanted to go out; then it strolled up and down outside the window, demanding to come in; now it wanted to go out again. For the third time in half an hour Antony Fairfield rose from his comfortable chair to do its bidding. He opened the door gently—all his movements were gentle; but the cat scuttled ignominiously out, as though he had kicked it. Antony looked round. How could he defend himself from disturbance without curtailing the cat's liberty of movement? He might leave the window and the door open, to give the animal freedom of exit and entrance; though he hated sitting in a room with the door open, he was prepared to make the sacrifice. But he couldn't leave the window open because the rain would come in and spoil Mrs. Ampleforth's beautiful silk cushions. Heavens, how it rained! Too bad for the farmers, thought Antony, whose mind was always busying itself with other people's misfortunes. The crops had been looking so well as he drove in the sunshine from the station, and now this sudden storm would beat everything down. He arranged his chair so that he could see the window and not keep the cat waiting if she felt like paying him another visit. The pattering of the rain soothed him. Half an hour and they would be back — Maggie would be back. He tried to visualize their faces, all so well known to him: but the experiment was not successful. Maggie's image kept ousting the others; it even appeared, somewhat grotesquely, on the top of Ronald's well-tailored shoulders. They mustn't find me asleep, thought Antony; I should look too middle-aged. So he picked up the newspaper from the floor and turned to the cross-word puzzle. 'Nine points of the law' in nine — ten letters. That was a very easy one: 'Possession.' Possession, thought Antony; I must put that down. But as he had no pencil and was too sleepy to get one, he repeated the word over and over again: Possession, Possession. It worked like a charm. He fell asleep and dreamed.

In his dream he was still in the library, but it was night and somehow his chair had got turned around so that he no longer faced the window, but he knew that the cat was there, asking to come in; only someone — Maggie — was trying to persuade him not to let it in. 'It's not a cat at all,' she kept saying; 'it's a Possession. I can see its nine points, and they're very sharp.' But he knew that she was mistaken, and really meant nine lives, which all cats have: so he thrust her aside and ran to the window and opened it. It was too dark to see so he put out his hand where he thought the cat's body would be, expecting to feel the warm fur; but what met his hand was not warm, nor was it fur. . . . He woke with a start to see the butler standing in front of him. The room was flooded with sunshine.

'Oh, Rundle,' he cried, 'I was asleep. Are they back?'

The butler smiled.

'No, sir, but I expect them every minute now.'

'But you wanted me?'

'Well, sir, there's a young lady called, and I said the master was out, but she said could she speak to the gentleman in the library? She must have seen you, sir, as she passed the window.'

'How very odd. Does she know me?'

'That was what she said, sir. She talks rather funny.'

'All right, I'll come.'

Antony followed the butler down the long corridor. When they reached the tower their footsteps rang on the paved floor. A considerable pool of water, the result of the recent heavy shower, had formed on the flagstones near the doorway. The door stood open, letting in a flood of light; but of the caller there was no sign.

'She was here a moment ago,' the butler said.

'Ah, I see her,' cried Antony. 'At least, isn't that her reflected in the water? She must be leaning against the door-post.'

'That's right,' said Rundle. 'Mind the puddle, sir. Let me give you a hand. I'll have this all cleared up before they come back.'

Five minutes later two cars, closely following each other, pulled up at the door, and the picnic party tumbled out.

'Dear me, how wet!' cried Mrs. Ampleforth, standing in the doorway. 'What has happened, Rundle? Has there been a flood?'

'It was much worse before you arrived, madam,' said the butler, disappointed that his exertions with mop, floor-cloth, scrubbing-brush, and pail were being so scantily recognized. 'You could have sailed a boat on it. Mr. Antony, he —'

'Oh, has he arrived? Antony's here, isn't that splendid?'

'Antony!' they all shouted. 'Come out! Come down! Where are you?'

'I bet he's asleep, the lazy devil,' remarked Ronald.

'No, sir,' said the butler, at last able to make himself heard. 'Mr. Antony's in the drawing-room with a lady.'

Mrs. Ampleforth's voice broke the silence that succeeded this announcement.

'With a lady, Rundle? Are you sure?'

'Well, madam, she's hardly more than a girl.'

'I always thought Antony was that sort of man,' observed Ronald. 'Maggie, you'd better —'

'It's too odd,' interposed Mrs. Ampleforth hastily, 'Who in the world can she be?'

'I don't see there's anything odd in someone calling on us,' said Mr. Ampleforth. 'What's her name, Rundle?'

'She didn't give a name, sir.'

'That is rather extraordinary. Antony is so impulsive and kind-hearted. I hope — ah, here he is.'

Antony came towards them along the passage, smiling and

waving his hands. When the welcoming and hand-shaking were over:

'We were told you had a visitor,' said Mrs. Ampleforth.

'Yes,' said Ronald. 'I'm afraid we arrived at the wrong moment.'

Antony laughed and then looked puzzled. 'Believe me, you didn't,' he said. 'You almost saved my life. She speaks such a queer dialect when she speaks at all, and I had reached the end of my small talk. But she's rather interesting. Do come along and see her: I left her in the library.'

They followed Antony down the passage. When they reached the door he said to Mrs. Ampleforth:

'Shall I go in first? She may be shy at meeting so many people.'

He went in. A moment later they heard his voice raised in excitement.

'Mildred! I can't find her! She's gone!'

Tea had been cleared away, but Antony's strange visitor was still the topic of conversation. 'I can't understand it,' he was saying, not for the first time. 'The windows were shut, and if she'd gone by the door we must have seen her.'

'Now, Antony,' said Ronald severely, 'let's hear the whole story again. Remember, you are accused of smuggling into the house a female of doubtful reputation. Furthermore the prosecution alleges that when you heard us call (we were shouting ourselves hoarse, but he didn't come at once, you remember) you popped her out of that window and came out to meet us, smiling sheepishly, and feebly gesticulating. What do you say?'

'I've told you everything,' said Antony. 'I went to the door and found her leaning against the stonework. Her eyes were shut. She didn't move and I thought she must be ill. So I said, "Is anything the matter?" and she looked up and said, "My leg hurts." Then I saw by the way she was standing that her hip must have been broken once and never properly set. I asked her where she lived, and she didn't seem to understand me; so I changed the form of the question, as one does on the telephone, and asked where she came from, and she said, "A little further down," meaning down the hill, I suppose.'

'Probably from one of the men's cottages,' said Mr. Ampleforth.

'I asked if it was far, and she said "No," which was obvious, otherwise her clothes would have been wet and they weren't, only a little muddy. She even had some mud on her mediæval bridesmaid's head-dress (I can't describe her clothes again, Mildred; you know how bad

I am at that). So I asked if she'd had a fall, and she said, "No, she got dirty coming up," or so I understood her. It wasn't easy to understand her; I suppose she talked the dialect of these parts. I concluded (you all say you would have known long before) that she was a little mad, but I didn't like to leave her looking so rotten, so I said, "Won't you come in and rest a minute?" Then I wished I hadn't.'

'Because she looked so pleased?'

'Oh, much more than pleased. And she said, "I hope you won't live to regret it," rather as though she hoped I should. And then I only meant just to take her hand, because of the water, you know, and she was lame—'

'And instead she flung herself into the poor fellow's arms—'

'Well, it amounted to that. I had no option! So I carried her across and put her down and she followed me here, walking better than I expected. A minute later you arrived. I asked her to wait and she didn't. That's all.'

'I should like to have seen Antony doing the St. Christopher act!' said Ronald. 'Was she heavy, old boy?'

Antony shifted in his chair. 'Oh no,' he said, 'not at all. Not at all heavy.' Unconsciously he stretched his arms out in front of him, as though testing an imaginary weight. 'I see my hands are grubby,' he said with an expression of distaste. 'I must go and wash them. I won't be a moment, Maggie.'

That night, after dinner, there was some animated conversation in the servants' hall.

'Did you hear any more, Mr. Rundle?' asked a house-maid of the butler, who had returned from performing his final office at the dinner-table.

'I did,' said Rundle, 'but I don't know that I ought to tell you.'

'It won't make any difference, Mr. Rundle, whether you do or don't. I'm going to give in my notice to-morrow. I won't stay in a haunted house. We've been lured here. We ought to have been warned.'

'They certainly meant to keep it from us,' said Rundle. 'I myself had put two and two together after seeing Lady Elinor; what Wilkins said when he came in for his tea only confirmed my suspicions. No gardener can ever keep a still tongue in his head. It's a pity.'

'Wouldn't you have told us yourself, Mr. Rundle?' asked the cook.

'I should have used my discretion,' the butler replied. 'When I informed Mr. Ampleforth that I was no longer in ignorance, he said, "I rely on you, Rundle, not to say anything which might alarm the staff." '

'Mean, I call it,' exclaimed the kitchen-maid indignantly. 'They want to have all the fun and leave us to die like rats in a trap.'

Rundle ignored the interruption.

'I told Mr. Ampleforth that Wilkins had been tale-bearing and would he excuse it in an outdoor servant, but unfortunately we were now in possession of the facts.'

'That's why they talked about it at dinner,' said the maid who helped Rundle to wait.

'They didn't really throw the mask off till after you'd gone, Lizzie,' said the butler. 'Then I began to take part in the conversation.'

He paused for a moment.

'Mr. Ampleforth asked me whether anything was missing from the house, and I was able to reply, "No, everything was in order." '

'What else did you say?' inquired the cook.

'I made the remark that the library window wasn't fastened, as they thought, but only closed, and Mrs. Turnbull laughed and said, "Perhaps it's only a thief, after all," but the others didn't think she could have got through the window anyhow, unless her lameness was all put on. And then I told them what the police had said about looking out for a suspicious character."

'Did they seem frightened?' asked the cook.

'Not noticeably,' replied the butler. 'Mrs. Turnbull said she hoped the gentlemen wouldn't stay long over their port. Mr. Ampleforth said, "No, they had had a full day, and would be glad to go to bed." Mrs. Ampleforth asked Miss Winthrop if she wanted to change her bedroom, but she said she didn't. Then Mr. Fairfield asked if he could have some iodine for his hand, and Miss Winthrop said she would fetch him some. She wanted to bring it after dinner, but he said, "Oh, to-morrow morning will do, darling." He seemed rather quiet.'

'What's he done to his hand?'

'I saw the mark when he took his coffee. It was like a burn.'

'They didn't say they were going to shut the house up, or anything?'

'Oh, Lord, no. There's going to be a party next week. They'll all have to stay for that.'

'I never knew such people,' said the kitchen-maid. 'They'd rather die, and us too, than miss their pleasures. I wouldn't stay another day if I wasn't forced. When you think she may be here in this very room, listening to us!' She shuddered.

'Don't you worry, my girl,' said Rundle, rising from his chair with a gesture of dismissal. 'She won't waste her time listening to you.'

'We really might be described as a set of crocks,' said Mr. Ampleforth to Maggie after luncheon the following day. 'You, poor dear, with your headache; Eileen with her nerves; I with – well – a touch of rheumatism; Antony with his bad arm.'

Maggie looked troubled.

'My headache is nothing, but I'm afraid Antony isn't very well.'

'He's gone to lie down, hasn't he?'

'Yes.'

'The best thing. I telephoned for the doctor to come this evening. He can have a look at all of us, ha! ha! Meanwhile, where will you spend the afternoon? I think the library's the coolest place on a stuffy day like this; and I want you to see my collection of books about Low Threshold – my Thresholdiana, I call them.'

Maggie followed him into the library.

'Here they are. Most of them are nineteenth-century books, publications of the Society of Antiquaries, and so on; but some are older. I got a little man in Charing Cross Road to hunt them out for me; I haven't had time to read them all myself.'

Maggie took a book at random from the shelves.

'Now I'll leave you,' said her host. 'And later in the afternoon I know that Eileen would appreciate a little visit. Ronald says it's nothing, just a little nervous upset, stomach trouble. Between ourselves, I fear Lady Elinor is to blame.'

Maggie opened the book. It was called *An Enquiry into the Recent Tragicall Happenings at Low Threshold Hall in the County of Suffolk, with some Animadversions on the Barbarous Customs of our Ancestors.* It opened with a rather tedious account of the semi-mythical origins of the Deadham family. Maggie longed to skip this, but she might have to discuss the book with Mr. Ampleforth, so she ploughed on. Her persistence was rewarded by a highly coloured picture of Lady Elinor's husband and an account of the cruelties he practised on her. The story would have been too painful to read had not the author (Maggie felt) so obviously drawn upon a very vivid imagination. But suddenly her eyes narrowed. What was this? 'Once in a Drunken Fitt he so mishandled her that her thigh was broken near the hip, and her screames were so loud they were heard by the servants through three closed doores; and yet he would not summon a Chirurgeon, for (quoth he)' — Lord Deadham's reason was coarse in the extreme; Maggie hastened on.

'And in consequence of these Barbarities her nature which was soft and yielding at the first was greatly changed, and those who sawe her now (but Pitie seal'd their lips) would have said she had a Bad Hearte.'

No wonder, thought Maggie, reading with a new and painful interest how the murdered woman avenged herself on various descendants, direct and collateral, of her persecutor. 'And it hath been generally supposed by the vulgar that her vengeance was directed only against members of that family from which she had taken so many Causeless Hurtes; and the depraved, defective, counterfeit records of those times have lent colour to this Opinion. Whereas the truth is as I now state it, having had access to those death-bed and testamentary depositions which, preserved in ink however faint, do greater service to verity than the relations of Pot-House Historians, enlarged by Memory and confused by Ale. Yet it is on such Testimonies that rash and sceptical Heads rely when they assert that the Lady Elinor had no hand in the late Horrid Occurrence at Low Threshold Hall, which I shall presently describe, thinking that a meer visitor and no blood relation could not be the object of her vengeance, notwithstanding the evidence of two serving-maids, one at the door and one craning her neck from an upper casement, who saw him beare her in: The truth being that she maketh no distinction between persons, but whoso admits her, on him doth her vengeance fall. Seven times she hath brought death to Low Threshold Hall; Three, it is true, being members of the family, but the remaining four indifferent Persons and not connected with them, having in common only this piece of folie, that they, likewise, let her in. And in each case she hath used the same manner of attack, as those who have beheld her first a room's length, then no further than a Lovers Embrace, from her victim have *in articulo mortis* delivered. And the moment when she is no longer seen, which to the watchers seems the Clarion and Reveille of their hopes, is in reality the knell; for she hath not withdrawn further, but approached nearer, she hath not gone out but entered in: and from her dreadful Citadel within the body rejoyces, doubtless, to see the tears and hear the groanes, of those who with Comfortable Faces (albeit with sinking Hearts), would soothe the passage of the parting Soul. Their lacrimatory Effusions are balm to her wicked Minde; the sad gale and ventilation of their sighs a pleasing Zephyre to her vindictive spirit.'

Maggie put down the book for a moment and stared in front of her. Then she began again to read.

'Once only hath she been cheated of her Prey, and it happened thus. His Bodie was already swollen with the malignant Humours she had stirred up in him and his life despaired of when a kitchen-wench was taken with an Imposthume that bled inwardly. She being of small account and but lately arrived they did only lay her in the Strawe, charging the Physician (and he nothing loth, expecting no Glory or Profit from attendance on such a Wretched creature) not to Divide his Efforts but use all his skill to save their Cousin (afterwards the twelfth Lord). Notwithstanding which precaution he did hourly get worse until sodainely a change came and he began to amend. Whereat was such rejoicing (including an Ox roasted whole) that the night was spent before they heard that the serving-maid was dead. In their Revels they gave small heed to this Event, not realizing that they owed His life to Hers; for a fellow-servant who tended the maid (out of charity) declared that her death and the cousin's recovery followed as quickly as a clock striking Two. And the Physician said it was well, for she would have died in any case.

'Whereby we must conclude that the Lady Elinor, like other Apparitions, is subject to certain Lawes. One, to abandon her Victim and seeking another tenement to transfer her vengeance, should its path be crossed by a Body yet nearer Dissolution: and another is, she cannot possess or haunt the corpse after it has received Christian Buriall. As witness the fact that the day after the Interment of the tenth Lord she again appeared at the Doore and being recognized by her inability to make the Transit was turned away and pelted. And another thing I myself believe but have no proof of is: That her power is circumscribed by the walls of the House; those victims of her Malignitie could have been saved but for the dreadful swiftnesse of the disease and the doctors unwillingness to move a Sicke man; otherwise how could the Termes of her Curse that she pronounced be fulfilled: "They shall be carried out Feet Foremost"?'

Maggie read no more. She walked out of the library with the book under her arm. Before going to see how Antony was she would put it in her bedroom where no one could find it. Troubled and oppressed she paused at the head of the stairs. Her way lay straight ahead, but her glance automatically travelled to the right where, at the far end of the passage, Antony's bedroom lay. She looked again; the door, which she could only just see, was shut now. But she could swear it had closed upon a woman. There was nothing odd in that; Mildred might have gone in, or Muriel, or a servant. But all the same she could not rest. Hurriedly she changed her dress and went to Antony's room. Pausing at the door she listened and distinctly heard his voice, speaking rapidly and in a low tone; but no one seemed to reply. She got no answer to her knock, so, mustering her courage, she walked in.

The blind was down and the room half dark, and the talking continued, which increased her uneasiness. Then, as her eyes got used to the darkness, she realized, with a sense of relief, that he was talking in his sleep. She pulled up the blind a little, so that she might see his hand. The brown mark had spread, she thought, and looked rather puffy as though coffee had been injected under the skin. She felt concerned for him. He would never have gone properly to bed like that, in his pyjamas, if he hadn't felt ill, and he tossed about restlessly. Maggie bent over him. Perhaps he had been eating a biscuit: there was some gritty stuff on the pillow. She tried to scoop it up but it eluded her. She could make no sense of his mutterings, but the word 'light' came in a good deal. Perhaps he was only half asleep and wanted the blind down. At last her ears caught the sentence that was running on his lips: 'She was so light.' Light? A light woman? Browning. The words conveyed nothing to her, and not wishing to wake him she tiptoed from the room.

'The doctor doesn't seem to think seriously of any of us, Maggie, you'll be glad to hear," said Mr. Ampleforth, coming into the drawing-room about six o'clock. 'Eileen's coming down to dinner. I am to drink less port—I didn't need a doctor, alas! to tell me that. Antony's the only casualty: he's got a slight temperature, and had better stay where he is until to-morrow. The doctor thinks it is one of those damnable horse-flies: his arm is a bit swollen, that's all.'

'Has he gone?' asked Maggie quickly.

'Who, Antony?'

'No, no, the doctor.'

'Oh, I'd forgotten your poor head. No, you'll just catch him. His car's on the terrace.'

The doctor, a kindly, harassed middle-aged man, listened patiently to Maggie's questions.

'The brown mark? Oh, that's partly the inflammation, partly the iodine—he's been applying it pretty liberally, you know; amateur physicians are all alike; feel they can't have too much of a good thing.'

'You don't think the water here's responsible? I wondered if he ought to go away.'

'The water? Oh no. No, it's a bite all right, though I confess I can't see the place where the devil got his beak in. I'll come to-morrow, if you like, but there's really no need.'

The next morning, returning from his bath, Ronald marched into Antony's room. The blind went up with a whizz and a smack, and Antony opened his eyes.

'Good morning, old man,' said Ronald cheerfully. 'Thought I'd look in and see you. How goes the blood-poisoning? Better?'

Antony drew up his sleeve and hastily replaced it. The arm beneath was chocolate-coloured to the elbow.

'I feel pretty rotten,' he said.

'I say, that's bad luck. What this?' added Ronald, coming nearer. 'Have you been sleeping in both beds?'

'Not to my knowledge,' murmured Antony.

'You have, though,' said Ronald. 'If this bed hasn't been slept in, it's been slept on, or lain on. That I can swear. Only a head, my boy, could have put that dent in the pillow, and only a pair of muddy — hullo! The pillow's got it, too.'

'Got what?' asked Antony drowsily.

'Well, if you ask me, it's common garden mould.'

'I'm not surprised. I feel pretty mouldy, too.'

'Well, Antony; to save your good name with the servants, I'll remove the traces.'

With characteristic vigour Ronald swept and smoothed the bed.

'Now you'll be able to look Rundle in the face.'

There was a knock on the door.

'If this is Maggie,' said Ronald, 'I'm going.'

It was, and he suited the action to the word.

'You needn't trouble to tell me, dearest,' she said, 'that you are feeling much better, because I can see that you aren't.'

Antony moved his head uneasily on the pillow.

'I don't feel very flourishing, to tell you the honest truth.'

'Listen' — Maggie tried to make her voice sound casual — 'I don't believe this is a very healthy place. Don't laugh, Antony; we're all of us more or less under the weather. I think you ought to go away.'

'My dear, don't be hysterical. One often feels rotten when one wakes up. I shall be all right in a day or two.'

'Of course you will. But all the same if you were in Sussex Square you could call in Fosbrook – and, well, I should be more comfortable.'

'But you'd be here!'

'I could stay at Pamela's.'

'But, darling, that would break up the party. I couldn't do it; and it wouldn't be fair to Mildred.'

'My angel, you're no good to the party, lying here in bed. And as long as you're here, let me warn you they won't see much of me.'

A look of irritation Maggie had never noticed before came into his face as he said, almost spitefully:

'Supposing the doctor won't allow you to come in? It may be catching, you know.'

Maggie concealed the hurt she felt.

'All the more reason for you to be out of the house.'

He pulled up the bedclothes with a gesture of annoyance and turned away.

'Oh, Maggie, don't keep nagging at me. You ought to be called Naggie, not Maggie.'

This was an allusion to an incident in Maggie's childhood. Her too great solicitude for a younger brother's safety had provoked the gibe. It had always wounded her, but never so much as coming from Antony's lips. She rose to go.

'Do put the bed straight,' said Antony, still with face averted. 'Otherwise they'll think you've been sleeping here.'

'What?'

'Well, Ronald said something about it.'

Maggie closed the door softly behind her. Antony was ill, of course, she must remember that. But he had been ill before, and was always an angelic patient. She went down to breakfast feeling miserable.

After breakfast, at which everyone else had been unusually cheerful, she thought of a plan. It did not prove so easy of execution as she hoped.

'But, dearest Maggie,' said Mildred, 'the village is nearly three miles away. And there's nothing to see there.'

'I love country post-offices,' said Maggie; 'they always have such amusing things.'

'There is a post-office,' admitted Mildred. 'But are you sure it isn't something we could do from here? Telephone, telegraph?'

'Perhaps there'd be a picture-postcard of the house,' said Maggie feebly.

'Oh, but Charlie has such nice ones,' Mildred protested. 'He's so house-proud, you could trust him for that. Don't leave us for two hours just to get postcards. We shall miss you so much, and think of poor Antony left alone all the morning.'

Maggie had been thinking of him.

'He'll get on all right without me,' she said lightly.

'Well, wait till the afternoon when the chauffeur or Ronald can run you over in a car. He and Charlie have gone into Norwich and won't be back till lunch.'

'I think I'll walk,' said Maggie. 'It'll do me good.'

'I managed that very clumsily,' she thought, 'so how shall I persuade Antony to tell me the address of his firm?'

To her surprise his room was empty. He must have gone away in the middle of writing a letter, for there were sheets lying about on the writing-table and, what luck! an envelope addressed to Higgins & Stukeley, 312 Paternoster Row. A glance was all she really needed to memorize the address; but her eyes wandered to the litter on the table. What a mess! There were several pages of notepaper covered with figures. Antony had been making calculations and, as his habit was, decorating them with marginal illustrations. He was good at drawing faces, and he had a gift for catching a likeness. Maggie had often seen, and been gratified to see, slips of paper embellished with portraits of herself—full-face, side-face, three-quarter-face. But this face that looked out from among the figures and seemed to avoid her glance, was not hers. It was the face of a woman she had never seen before but whom she felt she would recognize anywhere, so consistent and vivid were the likenesses. Scattered among the loose leaves were the contents of Antony's pocket-book. She knew he always carried her photograph. Where was it? Seized by an impulse, she began to rummage among the papers. Ah, here it was. But it was no longer hers! With a few strokes Antony had transformed her oval face, unlined and soft of feature, into a totally different one, a pinched face with high cheekbones, hollow cheeks, and bright hard eyes, from whose corners a sheaf of fine wrinkles spread like a fan: a face with which she was already too familiar.

Unable to look at it she turned away and saw Antony standing behind her. He seemed to have come from the bath for he carried a towel and was wearing his dressing-gown.

'Well,' he said. 'Do you think it's an improvement?'

She could not answer him, but walked over to the washstand and took up the thermometer that was lying on it.

'Ought you to be walking about like that,' she said at last, 'with a temperature of a hundred?'

'Perhaps not,' he replied, making two or three goat-like skips towards the bed. 'But I feel rather full of beans this morning.'

Maggie edged away from his smile towards the door.

'There isn't anything I can do for you?'

'Not to-day, my darling.'

The term of endearment struck her like a blow.

Maggie sent off her telegram and turned into the village street. The fact of being able to do something had relieved her mind: already in imagination she saw Antony being packed into the Ampleforths' Daimler with rugs and hot-water bottles, and herself, perhaps, seated by the driver. They were endlessly kind, and would make no bones about motoring him to London. But though her spirits were rising her body felt tired; the day was sultry, and she had hurried. Another bad night like last night, she thought, and I shall be a wreck. There was a chemist's shop over the way, and she walked in.

'Can I have some sal volatile?'

'Certainly, madam.'

She drank it and felt better.

'Oh, and have you anything in the way of a sleeping draught?'

'We have some allodanol tablets, madam.'

'I'll take them.'

'Have you a doctor's prescription?'

'No.'

'Then I'm afraid you'll have to sign the poison book. Just a matter of form.'

Maggie recorded her name, idly wondering what J. Bates, her predecessor on the list, meant to do with his cyanide of potassium.

'We must try not to worry,' said Mrs. Ampleforth, handing Maggie her tea, 'but I must say I'm glad the doctor has come. It relieves one of responsibility, doesn't it? Not that I feel disturbed about Antony—he was quite bright when I went to see him just before lunch. And he's been sleeping since. But I quite see what Maggie means. He doesn't seem himself. Perhaps it would be a good plan, as she suggests, to send him to London. He would have better advice there.'

Rundle came in.

'A telegram for Mr. Fairfield, madam.'

'It's been telephoned: "Your presence urgently required Tuesday morning—Higgins & Stukeley." Tuesday, that's to-morrow. Everything seem to point to his going, doesn't it, Charles?'

Maggie was delighted, but a little surprised, that Mrs. Ampleforth had fallen in so quickly with the plan of sending Antony home.

'Could he go to-day?' she asked.

'To-morrow would be too late, wouldn't it?' said Mr. Ampleforth drily. 'The car's at his disposal: he can go whenever he likes.'

Through her relief Maggie felt a little stab of pain that they were both so ready to see the last of Antony. He was generally such a popular guest.

'I could go with him,' she said.

Instantly they were up in arms. Ronald the most vehement of all. 'I'm sure Antony wouldn't want you to. You know what I mean, Maggie, it's such a long drive, in a closed car on a stuffy evening. Charlie says he'll send a man, if necessary.'

Mr. Ampleforth nodded.

'But if he were ill!' cried Maggie.

The entrance of the doctor cut her short. He looked rather grave.

'I wish I could say I was satisfied with Mr. Fairfield's progress,' he said, 'but I can't. The inflammation has spread up the arm as far as the shoulder, and there's some fever. His manner is odd, too, excitable and apathetic by turns.' He paused. 'I should like a second opinion.'

Mr. Ampleforth glanced at his wife.

'In that case wouldn't it be better to send him to London? As a matter of fact, his firm has telegraphed for him. He could go quite comfortably in the car.'

The doctor answered immediately:

'I wouldn't advise such a course. I think it would be most unwise to move him. His firm—you must excuse me—will have to do without him for a day or two.'

'Perhaps,' suggested Maggie trembling, 'it's a matter that could be arranged at his house. They could send over someone from the office. I know they make a fuss about having him on the spot,' she concluded lamely.

'Or, doctor,' said Mr. Ampleforth, 'could you do us a very great kindness and go with him? We could telephone to his doctor to meet you, and the car would get you home by midnight.'

The doctor squared his shoulders: he was clearly one of those men whose resolution stiffens under opposition.

'I consider it would be the height of folly,' he said, 'to move him out of the house. I dare not do it on my responsibility. I will get a colleague over from Ipswich to-morrow morning. In the meantime, with your permission, I will arrange for a trained nurse to be sent to-night.'

Amid a subdued murmur of final instructions, the doctor left.

As Maggie, rather late, was walking upstairs to dress for dinner she met Rundle. He looked anxious.

'Excuse me, miss,' he said, 'but have you seen Mr. Fairfield? I've asked everyone else, and they haven't. I took him up his supper half an hour ago, and he wasn't in his room. He'd got his dress clothes out, but they were all on the bed except the stiff shirt.'

'Have you been to look since?' asked Maggie.

'No, miss.'

'I'll go and see.'

She tiptoed along the passage to Antony's door. A medley of sounds, footsteps, drawers being opened and shut, met her ears.

She walked back to Rundle. 'He's in there all right,' she said. 'Now I must make haste and dress.'

A few minutes later a bell rang in the kitchen.

'Who's that?'

'Miss Winthrop's room,' said the cook. 'Hurry up, Lettice, or you'll have Rundle on your track—he'll be back in a minute.'

'I don't want to go,' said Lettice. 'I tell you I feel that nervous——'

'Nonsense, child,' said the cook. 'Run along with you.'

No sooner had the maid gone than Rundle appeared.

'I've had a bit of trouble with Master Antony,' he said. 'He's got it into his head that he wants to come down to dinner. "Rundle," he said to me, confidentially, "do you think it would matter us being seven? I want them to meet my new friend." "What friend, Mr. Fairfield?" I said. "Oh," he said, "haven't you seen her? She's always about with me now." Poor chap, he used to be the pick of the bunch, and now I'm afraid he's going potty.'

'Do you think he'll really come down to dinner?' asked the cook, but before Rundle could answer Lettice rushed into the room.

'Oh,' she cried, 'I knew it would be something horrid! I knew it would be! And now she wants a floor cloth and a pail! She says they mustn't know anything about it! But I won't go again—I won't bring it down, I won't even touch it!'

'What won't you touch?'

'That waste-paper basket.'

'Why, what's the matter with it?'

'It's . . . it's all bloody!'

When the word was out she grew calmer, and even seemed anxious to relate her experience.

'I went upstairs directly she rang' ('That's an untruth to start with,' said the cook) 'and she opened the door a little way and said, "Oh, Lettice, I've been so scared!" And I said, "What's the matter, miss?" And she said, "There's a cat in here." Well, I didn't think that was much to be frightened of, so I said, "Shall I come in and catch him, miss?" and she said (deceitful-like, as it turned out), "I should be so grateful." Then I went in but I couldn't see the cat anywhere, so I said, "Where is he?" At which she pointed to the waste-paper basket away by the dressing-table, and said, "In that waste-paper basket." I said, "Why, that makes it easier, miss, if he'll stay there." She said, "Oh, he'll stay there all right." Of course I took her meaning in a moment, because I know cats do choose queer, out-of-the-way places to die in, so I said, "You mean the poor creature's dead, miss?" and I was just going across to get him because ordinarily I don't mind the body of an animal when she said (I will do her that justice), "Stop a minute, Lettice, he isn't dead; he's been murdered." I saw she was all trembling, and that made me tremble, too. And when I looked in the basket—well——'

She paused, partly perhaps to enjoy the dramatic effect of her announcement. 'Well, if it wasn't our Thomas! Only you couldn't have recognized him, poor beast, his head was bashed in that cruel.'

'Thomas!' said the cook. 'Why he was here only an hour ago.'

'That's what I said to Miss Winthrop. "Why, he was in the kitchen only an hour ago," and then I came over funny, and when she asked me to help her clean the mess up I couldn't, not if my life depended on it. But I don't feel like that now,' she ended inconsequently. 'I'll go back and do it!' She collected her traps and departed.

'Thomas!' muttered Rundle. 'Who could have wished the poor beast any harm? Now I remember, Mr. Fairfield did ask me to get him out a clean shirt. . . . I'd better go up and ask him.'

He found Antony in evening dress seated at the writing-table. He had stripped it of writing materials and the light from two candles gleamed on its polished surface. Opposite to him on the other side of the table was an empty chair. He was sitting with his back to the room; his face, when he turned it at Rundle's entrance, was blotchy and looked terribly tired.

'I decided to dine here after all, Rundle,' he said. Rundle saw that the Bovril was still untouched in his cup.

'Why, your supper'll get cold, Mr. Fairfield,' he said.

'Mind your own business,' said Antony. 'I'm waiting.'

The Empire clock on the drawing-room chimney-piece began to strike, breaking into a conversation which neither at dinner nor afterwards had been more than desultory.

'Eleven,' said Mr. Ampleforth. 'The nurse will be here any time now. She ought to be grateful to you, Ronald, for getting him into bed.'

'I didn't enjoy treating Antony like that,' said Ronald.

There was a silence.

'What was that?' asked Maggie suddenly.

'It sounded like the motor.'

'Might have been,' said Mr. Ampleforth. 'You can't tell from here.'

They strained their ears, but the rushing sound had already died away. 'Eileen's gone to bed, Maggie,' said Mrs. Ampleforth. 'Why don't you? We'll wait up for the nurse, and tell you when she comes.'

Rather reluctantly Maggie agreed to go.

She had been in her bedroom about ten minutes, and was feeling too tired to take her clothes off, when there came a knock at the door. It was Eileen.

'Maggie,' she said, 'the nurse has arrived. I thought you'd like to know.'

'Oh, how kind of you,' said Maggie. 'They were going to tell me, but I expect they forgot. Where is she?'

'In Antony's room. I was coming from the bath and his door was open.'

'Did she look nice?'

'I only saw her back.'

'I think I'll go along and speak to her,' said Maggie.

'Yes, do. I don't think I'll go with you.'

As she walked along the passage Maggie wondered what she would say to the nurse. She didn't mean to offer her professional advice. But even nurses are human, and Maggie didn't want this stranger to imagine that Antony was, well, always like that—the spoilt, tiresome, unreasonable creature of the last few hours. She could find no harsher epithets for him, even after all his deliberate unkindness. The woman would probably have heard that Maggie was his fiancée; Maggie would try to show her that she was proud of the relationship and felt it an honour.

The door was still open so she knocked and walked in. But the figure that uncoiled itself from Antony's pillow and darted at her a look of malevolent triumph was not a nurse, nor was her face strange to Maggie; Maggie could see, so intense was her vision at that moment, just what strokes Antony had used to transform her own portrait into Lady Elinor's. She was terrified, but she could not bear to see Antony's rather long hair nearly touching the floor nor the creature's thin hand on his labouring throat. She advanced, resolved at whatever cost to break up this dreadful tableau. She approached near enough to realize that what seemed a strangle-hold was probably a caress, when Antony's eyes rolled up at her and words, frothy and toneless like a chain of bursting bubbles, came popping from the corner of his swollen mouth: 'Get out, damn you!' At the same moment she heard the stir of presences behind her and a voice saying, 'Here is the patient, nurse; I'm afraid he's half out of bed, and here's Maggie, too. What *have* you been doing to him, Maggie?' Dazed, she turned about. 'Can't you see?' she cried; but she might have asked the question of herself, for when she looked back she could only see the tumbled bed, the vacant pillow, and Antony's hair trailing the floor.

The nurse was a sensible woman. Fortified by tea, she soon bundled everybody out of the room. A deeper quiet than night ordinarily brings invaded the house. The reign of illness had begun.

A special embargo was laid on Maggie's visits. The nurse said she had noticed that Miss Winthrop's presence agitated the patient. But Maggie extracted a promise that she should be called if Antony got worse. She was too tired and worried to sleep, even if she had tried to, so she sat up fully dressed in a chair, every now and then trying to allay her anxiety by furtive visits to Antony's bedroom door.

The hours passed on leaden feet. She tried to distract herself by reading the light literature with which her hostess had provided her. Though she could not keep her attention on the books, she continued to turn their pages, for only so could she keep at bay the conviction that had long been forming at the back of her mind and that now threatened to engulf her whole consciousness: the conviction that the legend about Low Threshold was true. She was neither hysterical nor superstitious, and for a moment she had managed to persuade herself that what she had seen in Antony's room was an hallucination. The passing hours robbed her of that solace. Antony was the victim of Lady

Elinor's vengeance. Everything pointed to it: the circumstances of her appearance, the nature of Antony's illness, the horrible deterioration in his character—to say nothing of the drawings, and the cat.

There were only two ways of saving him. One was to get him out of the house; she had tried that and failed; if she tried again she would fail more signally than before. But there remained the other way.

The old book about *The Tragicall Happenings at Low Threshold Hall* still reposed in a drawer; for the sake of her peace of mind Maggie had vowed not to take it out, and till now she had kept her vow. But as the sky began to pale with the promise of dawn and her conviction of Antony's mortal danger grew apace, her resolution broke down.

'Whereby we must conclude,' she read, 'that the Lady Elinor, like other Apparitions, is subject to certain Lawes. One, to abandon her Victim and seeking another tenement enter into it and transfer her vengeance, should its path be crossed by a Body yet nearer Dissolution. . . .'

A knock, that had been twice repeated, startled her out of her reverie.

'Come in!'

'Miss Winthrop,' said the nurse, 'I'm sorry to tell you the patient is weaker. I think the doctor had better be telephoned for.'

'I'll go and get someone,' said Maggie. 'Is he much worse?'

'Very much, I'm afraid.'

Maggie had no difficulty in finding Rundle; he was already up.

'What time is it, Rundle?' she asked. 'I've lost count.'

'Half-past four, miss.' He looked very sorry for her.

'When will the doctor be here?'

'In about an hour, miss, not more.'

Suddenly she had an idea. 'I'm so tired, Rundle, I think I shall try to get some sleep. Tell them not to call me unless . . . unless . . .'

'Yes, miss,' said Rundle. 'You look altogether done up.'

About an hour! So she had plenty of time. She took up the book again. 'Transfer her vengeance . . . seeking another tenement . . . a Body nearer Dissolution.' Her idle thoughts turned with compassion to the poor servant girl whose death had spelt recovery to Lord Deadham's cousin but been so little regarded: 'the night was spent' before they heard that she was dead. Well, this night was spent already. Maggie shivered. 'I shall die in my sleep,' she thought. 'But shall I feel her come?' Her tired body sickened with nausea at the idea of such a loathsome violation. But the thought still nagged at her. 'Shall I realize even for a moment that I'm changing into . . . into?' Her mind refused to frame the possibility. 'Should I have time to do anyone an injury?' she wondered. 'I could tie my feet together with a handkerchief; that would prevent me from walking.' Walking . . . walking. . . . The word let loose on her mind a new flood of terrors. She could not do it! She could not lay herself open for ever to this horrible occupation! Her tormented imagination began to busy itself with the details of her funeral; she saw mourners following her coffin into the church. But Antony was not amongst them; he was better but too ill to be there. He could not understand why she had killed herself, for the note she had left gave no hint of the real reason, referred only to continual sleeplessness and nervous depression. So she would not have his company when her body was committed to the ground. But that was a mistake; it would not be her body, it would belong to that other woman and be hers to return to by the right of possession.

All at once the screen which had recorded such vivid images to her mind's eye went blank; and her physical eye, released, roamed wildly about the room. It rested on the book she was still holding. 'She cannot possess or haunt the corpse,' she read, 'after it has received Christian Buriall.' Here was a ray of comfort. But (her fears warned her) being a suicide she might not be allowed Christian burial. How then? Instead of the churchyard she saw a cross-roads, with a slanting signpost on which the words could no longer be read; only two or three people were there; they kept looking furtively about them and the gravedigger had thrown his spade aside and was holding a stake. . . .

She pulled herself together with a jerk. 'These are all fancies,' she thought. 'It wasn't fancy when I signed the poison book.' She took up the little glass cylinder; there were eighteen tablets and the dose was one or two. Daylight was broadening apace; she must hurry. She took some notepaper and wrote for five minutes. She had reached the words 'No one is to blame' when suddenly her ears were assailed by a tremendous tearing, whirring sound: it grew louder and louder until the whole room vibrated. In the midst of the deafening din something flashed past the window, for a fraction of a second blotting out the daylight. Then there was a crash such as she had never heard in her life.

All else forgotten, Maggie ran to the window. An indescribable scene of wreckage met her eyes. The aeroplane had been travelling at a terrific pace: it was smashed to atoms. To right and left the lawn was littered with fragments, some of which had made great gashes in the grass, exposing the earth. The pilot had been flung clear; she could just see his legs sticking out from a flower-bed under the wall of the house. They did not move and she thought he must be dead.

While she was wondering what to do she heard voices underneath the window.

'We don't seem to be very lucky here just now, Rundle,' said Mr. Ampleforth.

'No, sir.'

There was a pause. Then Mr. Ampleforth spoke again.

'He's still breathing, I think.'

'Yes, sir, he is, just.'

'You take his head and I'll take his feet, and we'll get him into the house.'

Something began to stir in Maggie's mind. Rundle replied:

'If you'll pardon my saying so, sir, I don't think we ought to move him. I was told once by a doctor that if a man's had a fall or anything it's best to leave him lying.'

'I don't think it'll matter if we're careful.'

'Really, sir, if you'll take my advice——'

There was a note of obstinacy in Rundle's voice. Maggie, almost beside herself with agitation, longed to fling open the window and cry 'Bring him in! Bring him in!' But her hand seemed paralysed and her throat could not form the words.

Presently Mr. Ampleforth said:

'You know we can't let him stay here. It's beginning to rain.'

(Bring him in! Bring him in!)

'Well, sir, it's your responsibility . . .'

Maggie's heart almost stopped beating.

'Naturally I don't want to do anything to hurt the poor chap.'

(Oh, bring him in! Bring him in!)

The rain began to patter on the pane.

'Look here, Rundle, we must get him under cover.'

'I'll fetch that bit of wing, sir, and put over him.'

(Bring him in! Bring him in!)

Maggie heard Rundle pulling something that grated on the gravel path. The sound ceased and Mr. Ampleforth said:

'The very thing for a stretcher, Rundle! The earth's so soft, we can slide it under him. Careful, careful!' Both men were breathing hard. 'Have you got your end? Right.' Their heavy, measured footfalls grew fainter and fainter.

The next thing Maggie heard was the motor-car returning with the doctor. Not daring to go out, and unable to sit down, she stood, how long she did not know, holding her bedroom door ajar. At last she saw the nurse coming towards her.

'The patient's a little better, Miss Winthrop. The doctor thinks he'll pull through now.'

'Which patient?'

'Oh, there was never any hope for the other poor fellow.'

Maggie closed her eyes.

'Can I see Antony?' she said at last.

'Well, you may just peep at him.'

Antony smiled at her feebly from the bed.

THE COTILLON

'B UT,' protested Marion Lane, 'you don't mean that we've all got to dance the cotillon in masks? Won't that be terribly hot?'

'My dear,' Jane Manning, her friend and hostess, reminded her, 'this is December, not July. Look!' She pointed to the window, their only protection against a soft bombardment of snowflakes.

Marion moved across from the fireplace where they were sitting and looked out. The seasonable snow had just begun to fall, as though in confirmation of Mrs. Manning's words. Here and there the gravel still showed black under its powdery coating, and on the wing of the house which faced east the shiny foliage of the magnolia, pitted with pockets of snow, seemed nearly black too. The trees of the park which yesterday, when Marion arrived, were so distinct against the afternoon sky that you could see their twigs, were almost invisible now, agitated shapes dim in the slanting snow. She turned back to the room.

'I think the cotillon's a good idea, and I don't want to make difficulties,' she said. 'I'm not an obstructionist by nature, am I? Tell me if I am.'

'My dear, of course you're not.'

'Well, I was thinking, wouldn't half the fun of the cotillon be gone if you didn't know who was who? I mean, in those figures when the women powder the men's faces, and rub their reflections off the looking-glass, and so on. There doesn't seem much point in powdering a mask.'

'My darling Marion, the mask's only a bit of black silk that covers the top part of one's face; you don't imagine we shan't recognize each other?'

'You may,' said Marion, 'find it difficult to recognize the largest, barest face. I often cut my best friends in the street. They needn't put on a disguise for me not to know them.'

'But you can tell them by their voices.'

'Supposing they won't speak?'

'Then you must ask questions.'

'But I shan't know half the people here.'

'You'll know all of us in the house,' her friend said; 'that's sixteen to start with. And you know the Grays and the Fosters and the Boltons. We shall only be about eighty, if as many.'

'Counting gate-crashers?'

'There won't be any.'

'But how will you be able to tell, if they wear masks?'

'I shall know the exact numbers, for one thing, and for another, at midnight, when the cotillon stops, everyone can take their masks off— must, in fact.'

'I see.'

The room was suddenly filled with light. A servant had come in to draw the curtains. They sat in silence until he had finished the last of the windows; there were five of them in a row.

'I had forgotten how long this room was,' Marion said. 'You'll have the cotillon here, I suppose?'

'It's the only possible place. I wish it were a little longer, then we could have a cushion race. But I'm afraid we shall have to forgo that. It would be over as soon as it began.'

The servant arranged the tea-table in front of them and went away.

'Darling,' said Jane suddenly, 'before Jack comes in from shooting with his tired but noisy friends, I want to say what a joy it is to have you here. I'm glad the others aren't coming till Christmas Eve. You'll have time to tell me all about yourself.'

'Myself?' repeated Marion. She stirred in her chair. 'There's nothing to tell.'

'Dearest, I can't believe it! There must be, after all these months. My life is dull, you know—no, not dull, quiet. And yours is always so *mouvementée*.'

'It used to be,' admitted Marion. 'It used to be; but now I——'

There was a sound of footsteps and laughter at the door, and a voice cried 'Jenny, Jenny, have you some tea for us?'

'You shall have it in a moment,' Mrs. Manning called back. Sighing, she turned to her friend.

'We must postpone our little séance.'

Five days had gone by — it was the evening of the twenty-seventh, the night of the ball. Marion went up to her room to rest. Dinner was at half-past eight, so she had nearly two hours' respite. She lay down on the bed and turned out all the lights except the one near her head. She felt very tired. She had talked so much during the past few days that even her thoughts had become articulate; they would not stay in her mind; they rose automatically to her lips, or it seemed to her that they did. 'I am glad I did not tell Jenny,' she soliloquised; 'it would only have made her think worse of me, and done no good. What a wretched business.' She extinguished the light, but the gramophone within her went on more persistently than ever. It was a familiar record; she knew every word of it: it might have been called *The Witness for the Defence.* 'He had no reason to take me so seriously,' announced the machine in self-excusatory accents. 'I only wanted to amuse him. It was Hugh Travers who introduced us: he knows what I am like; he must have told Harry; men always talk these things over among themselves. Hugh had a grievance against me, too, once; but he got over it; I have never known a man who didn't.' For a moment Marion's thoughts broke free from their bondage to the turning wheel and hovered over her past life. Yes, more or less, they had all got over it. 'I never made him any promise.' pursued the record, inexorably taking up its tale: 'what right had he to think he could coerce me? Hugh ought not to have let us meet, knowing the kind of man he was — and — and the kind of woman I was. I was very fond of him, of course; but he would have been so exacting, he *was* so exacting. All the same,' continued the record — sliding a moment into the major key only to relapse into the minor — 'left to myself I could have managed it all right, as I always have. It was pure bad luck that he found me that night with the other Harry. That was a dreadful affair.' At this point the record, as always, wobbled and scratched: Marion had to improvise something less painful to bridge over the gap. Her thoughts flew to the other Harry and dwelt on him tenderly; he would never have made a scene if he could have helped it; he had been so sweet to her afterwards. 'It was just bad luck,' the record resumed; 'I didn't want to blast his happiness and wreck his life, or whatever he says I did.'

What had he actually said? There was an ominous movement in Marion's mind. The mechanism was being wound up, was going through the whole dreary performance again. Anything rather than that! She turned on the light, jumped off the bed, and searched among her letters. The moment she had it in her hand, she realized that she knew it by heart.

DEAR MARION,

After what has happened I don't suppose you will want to see me again, and though I want to see you, I think it better for us both that I shouldn't. I know it sounds melodramatic to say it, but you have spoilt my life, you have killed something inside me. I never much valued Truth for its own sake, and I am grateful to Chance for affording me that peep behind the scenes last night. I am more grateful to you for keeping up the disguise as long as you did. But though you have taken away so much, you have left me one flicker of curiosity: before I die (or after, it doesn't much matter!) I should like to see you (forgive the expression) unmasked, so that for a moment I can compare the reality with the illusion I used to cherish. Perhaps I shall. Meanwhile good-bye.

Yours once, and in a sense still yours,

HENRY CHICHESTER.

Marion's eyes slid from the letter to the chair beside her where lay mask and domino, ready to put on. She did not feel the irony of their presence; she did not think about them; she was experiencing an immense relief—a relief that always came after reading Harry's letter. When she thought about it it appalled her; when she read it it seemed much less hostile, flattering almost; a testimonial from a wounded and disappointed but still adoring man. She lay down again, and in a moment was asleep.

Soon after ten o'clock the gentlemen followed the ladies into the long drawing-room; it looked unfamiliar even to Jack Manning, stripped of furniture except for a thin lining of gilt chairs. So far everything had gone off splendidly; dinner, augmented by the presence of half a dozen neighbours, had been a great success; but now everyone, including the host and hostess, was a little uncertain what to do next. The zero hour was approaching; the cotillon was supposed to start at eleven and go on till twelve, when the serious dancing would begin; but guests motoring from a distance might arrive at any time. It would spoil the fun of the thing to let the masked and the unmasked meet before the cotillon started; but how could they be kept apart? To preserve the illusion of secrecy Mrs. Manning had asked them to announce themselves at the head of the staircase, in tones sufficiently discreet to be heard by her alone. Knowing how fallible are human plans, she had left in the cloakroom a small supply of masks for those men who, she knew, would forget to bring them. She thought her arrangements were proof against mischance, but she was by no means sure; and as she looked about the room and saw the members of the dinner-party stealing furtive glances at the clock, or plunging into frantic and short-lived conversations, she began to share their uneasiness.

'I think,' she said, after one or two unsuccessful efforts to gain the ear of the company, 'I think you had all better go and disguise yourselves, before anyone comes and finds you in your natural state.' The guests tittered nervously at this pleasantry, then with signs of relief upon their faces they began to file out, some by one door, some by the other, according as the direction of their own rooms took them. The long gallery (as it was sometimes magniloquently described) stood empty and expectant.

'There,' breathed Mrs. Manning, 'would you have recognized that parlour bandit as Sir Joseph Dickinson?'

'No,' said her husband, 'I wouldn't have believed a mask and a domino could make such a difference. Except for a few of the men, I hardly recognized anyone.'

'You're like Marion; she told me she often cuts her best friends in the street.'

'I dare say that's a gift she's grateful for.'

'Jack! You really mustn't. Didn't she look lovely to-night! What a pity she has to wear a mask, even for an hour!'

Her husband grunted.

'I told Colin Chillingworth she was to be here: you know he's always wanted to see her. He is such a nice old man, so considerate — the manners of the older generation.'

'Why, because he wants to see Marion?'

'No, idiot! But he had asked me if he might bring a guest——'

'Who?'

'I don't remember the man's name, but he has a bilious attack or something, and can't come, and Colin apologized profusely for not letting us know: his telephone is out of order, he said.'

'Very civil of him. How many are we then, all told?'

'Seventy-eight; we should have been seventy-nine.'

'Anyone else to come?'

'I'll just ask Jackson.'

The butler was standing half-way down the stairs. He confirmed Mrs. Manning's estimate. 'That's right, Madam; there were twenty-two at dinner and fifty-six have come in since.'

'Good staff-work,' said her husband. 'Now we must dash off and put on our little masks.'

They were hurrying away when Mrs. Manning called over her shoulder: 'You'll see that the fires are kept up, Jackson?'
'Oh, yes, Madam,' he replied. 'It's very warm in there.'

It was. Marion, coming into the ballroom about eleven o'clock was met by a wave of heat, comforting and sustaining. She moved about among the throng, slightly dazed, it is true, but self-confident and elated. As she expected, she could not put a name to many of the people who kept crossing her restricted line of vision, but she was intensely aware of their eyes — dark, watchful but otherwise expressionless eyes, framed in black. She welcomed their direct regard. On all sides she heard conversation and laughter, especially laughter; little trills and screams of delight at identities disclosed; voices expressing bewilderment and polite despair — 'I'm very stupid, I really cannot imagine who you are,' gruff rumbling voices, and high falsetto squeaks, obviously disguised. Marion found herself a little impatient of this childishness. When people recognized her, as they often did (her mask was as much a decoration as a concealment) she smiled with her lips but did not try to identify them in return. She felt faintly scornful of the women who were only interesting provided you did not know who they were. She looked forward to the moment when the real business of the evening would begin.

But now the band in the alcove between the two doors had struck up, and a touch on her arm warned her that she was wanted for a figure. Her partner was a raw youth, nice enough in his way, eager, good-natured and jaunty, like a terrier dog. He was not a type she cared for, and she longed to give him the slip.

The opportunity came. Standing on a chair, rather like the Statue of Liberty in New York Harbour, she held aloft a lighted candle. Below her seethed a small group of masked males, leaping like salmon, for the first to blow the candle out would have the privilege of dancing with the torch-bearer. Among them was her partner; he jumped higher than the rest, as she feared he would; but each time she saw his Triton-like mouth soaring up she forestalled his agility and moved the candle out of his reach. Her arm began to tire; and the pack, foiled so often, began to relax their efforts. She must do something quickly. Espying her host among the competitors, she shamelessly brought the candle down to the level of his mouth.

'Nice of you,' he said, when, having danced a few turns, they were sitting side by side. 'I was glad of that bit of exercise.'

'Why, do you feel cold?'

'A little. Don't you?'

Marion considered. 'Perhaps I do.'

'Funny thing,' said her host, 'fires seem to be blazing away all right, and it was too hot ten minutes ago.'

Their eyes travelled inquiringly round the room. 'Why,' exclaimed Manning, 'no wonder we're cold; there's a window open.'

As he spoke, a gust of wind blew the heavy curtains inwards, and a drift of snow came after them.

'Excuse me a moment,' he said. 'I'll soon stop that.'

She heard the sash slam, and in a few moments he was back at her side.

'Now who on earth can have done it?' he demanded, still gasping from contact with the cold air. 'The window was wide open!'

'Wide enough to let anyone in?'

'Quite.'

'How many of us ought there to be?' asked Marion. 'I'm sure you don't know.'

'I do — there are——'

'Don't tell me, let's count. I'll race you.'

They were both so absorbed in their calculations that the leaders of the cotillon, coming round armed with favours for the next figure, dropped into their laps a fan and a pocket book and passed on unnoticed.

'Well, what do you make it?' they cried almost in unison.

'Seventy-nine,' said Marion. 'And you?'

'Seventy-nine, too.'

'And how many ought there to be?'

'Seventy-eight.'

'That's a rum go,' said Manning. 'We can't both be mistaken. I suppose someone came in afterwards. When I get a chance I'll talk to Jackson.'

'It can't be a burglar,' said Marion, 'a burglar wouldn't have chosen that way of getting in.'

'Besides, we should have seen him. No, a hundred to one it was just somebody who was feeling the heat and needed air. I don't blame them, but they needn't have blown us away. Anyhow, if there is a stranger among us he'll soon have to show up, for in half an hour's time we can take off these confounded masks. I wouldn't say it of everyone, but I like you better without yours.'

'Do you?' smiled Marion.

'Meanwhile, we must do something about these favours. The next figure's beginning. I say, a fur rug would be more suitable, but may I give this fan to you?'

'And will you accept this useful pocket book?'

They smiled and began to dance.

Ten minutes passed; the fires were heaped up, but the rubbing of hands and hunching of shoulders which had followed the inrush of cold air did not cease. Marion, awaiting her turn to hold the looking-glass, shivered slightly. She watched her predecessor on the chair. Armed with a handkerchief, she was gazing intently into the mirror while each in his turn the men stole up behind her, filling the glass with their successive reflections; one after another she rubbed the images out. Marion was wondering idly whether she would wait too long and find the candidates exhausted when she jumped up from her chair, handed the looking-glass to the leader of the cotillon, and danced away with the man of her choice. Marion took the mirror and sat down. A feeling of unreality oppressed her. How was she to choose between these grotesque faces? One after another they loomed up, dream-like, in the glass, their intense, almost hypnotic eyes searching hers. She could not tell whether they were smiling, they gave so little indication of expression. She remembered how the other women had paused, peered into the glass, and seemed to consider; rubbing away this one at sight, with affected horror, lingering over that one as though sorely tempted, only erasing him after a show of reluctance. She had fancied that some of the men looked piqued when they were rejected; they walked off with a toss of the head; others had seemed frankly pleased to be chosen. She was not indifferent to the mimic drama of the figure, but she couldn't contribute to it. The chill she still felt numbed her mind, and made it drowsy; her gestures seemed automatic, outside the control of her will. Mechanically she rubbed away the reflection of the first candidate, of the second, of the third. But when the fourth presented himself, and hung over her chair till his mask was within a few inches of her hair, the onlookers saw her pause; the hand with the handkerchief lay motionless in her lap, her eyes were fixed upon the mirror. So she sat for a full minute, while the man at the back, never shifting his position, drooped over her like an earring.

'She's taking a good look this time,' said a bystander at last, and the remark seemed to pierce her reverie — she turned round slowly and then gave a tremendous start; she was on her feet in a moment. 'I'm so sorry,' someone heard her say as she gave the man her hand, 'I never saw you. I had no idea that anyone was there.'

A few minutes later Jane Manning, who had taken as much share in the proceedings as a hostess can, felt a touch upon her arm. It was Marion.

'Well, my dear,' she said. 'Are you enjoying yourself?'

Marion's voice shook a little. 'Marvellously!' She added in an amused tone:

'Queer fellow I got hold of just now.'

'Queer-looking, do you mean?'

'Really I don't know; he was wearing a sort of death-mask that covered him almost completely, and he was made up as well, I thought, with French chalk.'

'What else was queer about him?'

'He didn't talk. I couldn't get a word out of him.'

'Perhaps he was deaf.'

'That occurred to me. But he heard the music all right; he danced beautifully.'

'Show him to me.'

Marion's eyes hovered round the room without catching sight of her late partner.

'He doesn't seem to be here.'

'Perhaps he's our uninvited guest,' said Jane, laughing. 'Jack told me there was an extra person who couldn't be accounted for. Now, darling, you mustn't miss this figure: it's the most amusing of them all. After that, there are some favours to be given, and then supper. I long for it.'

'But don't we take off our masks first?'

'Yes, of course, I'd forgotten that.'

The figure described by Mrs. Manning as being the most amusing of all would have been much more amusing, Marion thought, if they had played it without masks. If the dancers did not recognize each other, it lost a great deal of its point. Its success depended on surprise. A space had been cleared in the middle of the room, an oblong space like a badminton court, divided into two, not by a net but by a large white sheet supported at either end by the leaders of the cotillon, and held nearly at arm's length above their heads. On one side were grouped the men, on the other the women, theoretically invisible to each other; but Marion noticed that they moved about and took furtive peeps at each other round the sides, a form of cheating which, in the interludes, the leaders tried to forestall by rushing the sheet across to intercept the view. But most of the time these stolen glimpses went on unchecked, to the accompaniment of a good deal of laughter; for while the figure was in progress the leaders were perforce stationary. One by one the men came up from behind and clasped the top edge of the sheet, so that their gloved fingers, and nothing else, were visible the farther side. With becoming hesitation a woman would advance and take these anonymous fingers in her own; then the sheet was suddenly lowered and the dancers stood face to face, or rather mask to mask. Sometimes there were cries of recognition, sometimes silence, the masks were as impenetrable as the sheet had been.

It was Marion's turn. As she walked forward she saw that the gloved hands were not resting on the sheet like the rest; they were clutching it so tightly that the linen was caught up in creases between the fingers and crumpled round their tips. For a moment they did not respond to her touch, then they gripped with surprising force. Down went the leader's arms, down went the corners of the sheet. But Marion's unknown partner did not take his cue. He forgot to release the sheet, and she remained with her arms held immovably aloft, the sheet falling in folds about her and almost covering her head. 'An unrehearsed effect, jolly good, I call it,' said somebody. At last, in response to playful tugs and twitches from the leaders, the man let the sheet go and discovered himself to the humiliated Marion. It was her partner of the previous figure, that uncommunicative man. His hands, that still held hers, felt cold through their kid covering.

'Oh,' she cried, 'I can't understand it—I feel so cold. Let's dance.'

They danced for a little and then sat down. Marion felt chillier than ever, and she heard her neighbours on either side complaining of the temperature. Suddenly she made a decision and rose to her feet.

'Do take me somewhere where it's warmer,' she said. 'I'm perished here.'

The man led the way out of the ballroom, through the ante-room at the end where one or two couples were sitting, across the corridor into a little room where a good fire was burning, throwing every now and then a ruddy gleam on china ornaments and silver photograph frames. It was Mrs. Manning's sitting-room.

'We don't need a light, do we?' said her companion. 'Let's sit as we are.'

It was the first time he had volunteered a remark. His voice was somehow familiar to Marion, yet she couldn't place it; it had an alien quality that made it unrecognizable, like one's own dress worn by someone else.

'With pleasure,' she said. 'But we mustn't stay long, must we? It's only a few minutes to twelve. Can we hear the music from here?'

They sat in silence, listening. There was no sound.

'Don't think me fussy,' Marion said. 'I'm enjoying this tremendously, but Jenny would be disappointed if we missed the last figure. If you don't mind opening the door, we should hear the music begin.'

As he did not offer to move, she got up to open it herself, but before she reached the door she heard her name called.

'Marion!'

'Who said that, you?' she cried, suddenly very nervous.

'Don't you know who I am?'

'Harry!'

Her voice shook and she sank back into her chair, trembling violently.

'How was it I didn't recognize you? I'm—I'm so glad to see you.'

'You haven't seen me yet,' said he. It was like him to say that, playfully grim. His words reassured her, but his tone left her still in doubt. She did not know how to start the conversation, what effect to aim at, what note to strike; so much depended on divining his mood and playing up to it. If she could have seen his face, if she could even have caught a glimpse of the poise of his head, it would have given her a cue; in the dark like this, hardly certain of his whereabouts in the room, she felt hopelessly at a disadvantage.

'It was nice of you to come and see me—if you did come to see me,' she ventured at last.

'I heard you were to be here.' Again that non-committal tone! Trying to probe him she said:

'Would you have come otherwise? It's rather a childish entertainment, isn't it?'

'I should have come,' he answered, 'but it would have been in—in a different spirit.'

She could make nothing of this.

'I didn't know the Mannings were friends of yours,' she told him. 'He's rather a dear, married to a dull woman, if I must be really truthful.'

'I don't know them,' said he.

'Then you gate-crashed?'

'I suppose I did.'

'I take that as a compliment,' said Marion after a pause. 'But—forgive me—I must be very slow—I don't understand. You said you were coming in any case.'

'Some friends of mine called Chillingworth offered to bring me.'

'How lucky I was! So you came with them?'

'Not with them, after them.'

'How odd. Wasn't there room for you in their car? How did you get here so quickly?'

'The dead travel fast.'

His irony baffled her. But her thoughts flew to his letter, in which he accused her of having killed something in him; he must be referring to that.

'Darling Hal,' she said. 'Believe me, I'm sorry to have hurt you. What can I do to—to——'

There was a sound of voices calling, and her attention thus awakened caught the strains of music, muffled and remote.

'They want us for the next figure. We must go,' she cried, thankful that the difficult interview was nearly over. She was colder than ever, and could hardly keep her teeth from chattering audibly.

'What is the next figure?' he asked, without appearing to move.

'Oh, you know—we've had it before—we give each other favours, then we unmask ourselves. Hal, we really ought to go! Listen! Isn't that midnight beginning to strike?'

Unable to control her agitation, aggravated by the strain of the encounter, the deadly sensation of cold within her, and a presentiment of disaster for which she could not account, she rushed towards the door and her outstretched left hand, finding the switch, flooded the room with light. Mechanically she turned her head to the room; it was empty. Bewildered she looked back over her left shoulder, and there, within a foot of her, stood Harry Chichester, his arms stretched across the door.

'Harry,' she cried, 'don't be silly! Come out or let me out!'

'You must give me a favour first,' he said sombrely.

'Of course I will, but I haven't got one here.'

'I thought you always had favours to give away.'

'Harry, what do you mean?'

'You came unprovided?'

She was silent.

'*I* did not. I have something here to give you—a small token. Only I must have a *quid pro quo.*'

He's mad, thought Marion. I must humour him as far as I can.

'Very well,' she said, looking around the room. Jenny would forgive her—it was an emergency. 'May I give you this silver pencil?'

He shook his head.

'Or this little vase?'

Still he refused.

'Or this calendar?'

'The flight of time doesn't interest me.'

'Then what can I tempt you with?'

'Something that is really your own—a kiss.'

'My dear,' said Marion, trembling, 'you needn't have asked for it.'

'Thank you,' he said. 'And to prove I don't want something for nothing, here is your favour.'

He felt in his pocket. Marion saw a dark silvery gleam; she held her hand out for the gift.

It was a revolver.

'What am I to do with this?' she asked.

'You are the best judge of that,' he replied. 'Only one cartridge has been used.'

Without taking her eyes from his face she laid down the revolver among the bric-à-brac on the table by her side.

'And now your gift to me.'

'But what about our masks?' said Marion.

'Take yours off,' he commanded.

'Mine doesn't matter,' said Marion, removing as she spoke the silken visor. 'But you are wearing an entirely false face.'

'Do you know why?' he asked, gazing at her fixedly through the slits in the mask.

She didn't answer.

'I was always an empty-headed fellow,' he went on, tapping the waxed covering with his gloved forefinger, so that it gave out a wooden hollow sound—'there's nothing much behind this. No brains to speak of, I mean. Less than I used to have, in fact.'

Marion stared at him in horror.

'Would you like to see? Would you like to look right into my mind?'

'No! No!' she cried wildly.

'But I think you ought to,' he said, coming a step nearer and raising his hands to his head.

'Have you seen Marion?' said Jane Manning to her husband. 'I've a notion she hasn't been enjoying herself. This was in a sense her party, you know. We made a mistake to give her Tommy Cardew as a partner; he doesn't carry heavy enough guns for her.'

'Why, does she want shooting?' inquired her husband.

'Idiot! But I could see they didn't get on. I wonder where she's got to—I'm afraid she may be bored.'

'Perhaps she's having a quiet talk with a howitzer,' her husband suggested.

Jane ignored him. 'Darling, it's nearly twelve. Run into the ante-room and fetch her; I don't want her to miss the final figure.'

In a few seconds he returned. 'Not there,' he said. 'Not there, my child. Sunk by a twelve-inch shell, probably.'

'She may be sitting out in the corridor.'

'Hardly, after a direct hit.'

'Well, look.'

They went away and returned with blank faces. The guests were standing about talking; the members of the band, their hands ready on their instruments, looked up inquiringly.

'We shall have to begin without her,' Mrs. Manning reluctantly decided. 'We shan't have time to finish as it is.'

The hands of the clock showed five minutes to twelve.

The band played as though inspired, and many said afterwards that the cotillon never got really going, properly warmed up, till those last five minutes. All the fun of the evening seemed to come to a head, as though the spirit of the dance, mistrustful of its latter-day devotees, had withheld its benison till the final moments. Everyone was too excited to notice, as they whirled past that the butler was standing in one of the doorways with a white and anxious face. Even Mrs. Manning, when at last she saw him, called out cheerfully, almost without pausing for an answer:

'Well, Jackson, everything all right, I hope?'

'Can I speak to you a moment, Madam?' he said. 'Or perhaps Mr. Manning would be better.'

Mrs. Manning's heart sank. Did he want to leave?

'Oh, I expect I shall do, shan't I? I hope it's nothing serious.'

'I'm afraid it is, Madam, very serious.'

'All right, I'll come.' She followed him on to the landing.

A minute later her husband saw her threading her way towards him.
'Jack! Just a moment.'
He was dancing and affected not to hear. His partner's eyes looked surprised and almost resentful, Mrs. Manning thought; but she persisted none the less.
'I know I'm a bore and I'm sorry, but I really can't help myself.'
This brought them to a stand.
'Why, Jane, has the boiler burst?'
'No, it's more serious than that, Jack,' she said, as he disengaged himself from his partner with an apology. 'There's been a dreadful accident or something at the Chillingworths'. That guest of theirs, do you remember, whom they were to have brought and didn't——'
'Yes, he stayed behind with a headache—rotten excuse—'
'Well, he's shot himself.'
'Good God! When?'
'They found him half an hour ago, apparently, but they couldn't telephone because the machine was out of order, and had to send.'
'Is he dead?'
'Yes, he blew his brains out.'
'Do you remember his name?'
'The man told me. He was called Chichester.'
They were standing at the side of the room, partly to avoid the dancers, partly to be out of earshot. The latter consideration need not have troubled them, however. The band, which for some time past had been playing nineteenth-century waltzes, now burst into the strains of *John Peel*. There was a tremendous sense of excitement and climax. The dancers galloped by at break-neck speed; the band played fortissimo; the volume of sound was terrific. But above the din—the music, the laughter and the thud of feet—they could just hear the clock striking twelve.
Jack Manning looked doubtfully at his wife.'Should I go and tell Chillingworth now? What do you think?'
'Perhaps you'd better—it seems so heartless not to. Break it to him as gently as you can, and don't let the others know if you can help it.'
Jack Manning's task was neither easy nor agreeable, and he was a born bungler. Despairing of making himself heard, he raised his hand and cried out, 'Wait a moment!' Some of the company stood still and, imagining it was a signal to take off their masks, began to do so; others

went on dancing; others stopped and stared. He was the centre of attention; and before he had got his message fairly delivered, it had reached other ears than those for which it was intended. An excited whispering went round the room: 'What is it? What is it?' Men and women stood about with their masks in their hands, and faces blanker than before they were uncovered. Others looked terrified and incredulous. A woman came up to Jane Manning and said:

'What a dreadful thing for Marion Lane.'

'Why?' Jane asked.

'Didn't you know? She and Harry Chichester were the greatest friends. At one time it was thought—'

'I live out of the world, I had no idea,' said Jane quickly. Even in the presence of calamity, she felt a pang that her friend had not confided in her.

Her interlocutor persisted: 'It was talked about a great deal. Some people said—you know how they chatter—that she didn't treat him quite fairly. I hate to make myself a busybody, Mrs. Manning, but I do think you ought to tell her; she ought to be prepared.'

'But I don't know where she is!' cried Jane, from whose mind all thought of her friend had been banished. 'Have you seen her?'

'Not since the sheet incident.'

'Nor have I.'

Nor, it seemed, had anyone. Disturbed by this new misadventure far more than its trivial nature seemed to warrant, Jane hastened in turn to such of her guests as might be able to enlighten her as to Marion's whereabouts. Some of them greeted her inquiry with a lift of the eyebrows but none of them could help her in her quest. Nor could she persuade them to take much interest in it. They seemed to have forgotten that they were at a party, and owed a duty of responsiveness to their hostess. Their eyes did not light up when she came near. One and all they were discussing the suicide, and suggesting its possible motive. The room rustled with their whispering, with the soft hissing sound of 'Chichester' and the succeeding 'Hush!' which was meant to stifle but only multiplied and prolonged it. Jane felt that she must scream.

All at once there was silence. Had she screamed? No, for the noise they had all heard came from somewhere inside the house. The room seemed to hold its breath. There it was again, and coming closer; a cry, a shriek, the shrill tones of terror alternating in a dreadful rhythm with a throaty, choking sound like whooping-cough. No one could have recognized it as Marion Lane's voice, and few could have told for

Marion Lane the dishevelled figure, mask in hand, that lurched through the ballroom doorway and with quick stumbling steps, before which the onlookers fell back, zigzagged into the middle of the room.

'Stop him!' she gasped. 'Don't let him do it!' Jane Manning ran to her.

'Dearest, what is it?'

'It's Harry Chichester,' sobbed Marion, her head rolling about on her shoulders as if it had come loose. 'He's in there. He wants to take his mask off, but I can't bear it! It would be awful! Oh, do take him away!'

'Where is he?' someone asked.

'Oh, I don't know! In Jane's sitting-room. I think, He wouldn't let me go. He's so cold, so dreadfully cold.'

'Look after her, Jane,' said Jack Manning. 'Get her out of here. Anyone coming with me?' he asked, looking round. 'I'm going to investigate.'

Marion caught the last words. 'Don't go,' she implored. 'He'll hurt you.' But her voice was drowned in the scurry and stampede of feet. The whole company was following their host. In a few moments the ballroom was empty.

Five minutes later there were voices in the ante-room. It was Manning leading back his troops. 'Barring, of course, the revolver,' he was saying, 'and the few things that had been knocked over, and those scratches on the door, there wasn't a trace. Hullo!' he added, crossing the threshold, 'what's this?'

The ballroom window was open again; the curtains fluttered wildly inwards; on the boards lay a patch of nearly melted snow.

Jack Manning walked up to it. Just within the further edge, near the window, was a kind of smear, darker than the toffee-coloured mess around it, and roughly oval in shape.

'Do you think that's a footmark?' he asked of the company in general.

No one could say.

A CHANGE OF OWNERSHIP

THE motor-car felt its way cautiously up the little street that opened upon a field on one side, and somehow looked less suburban by night than it did by day.

'Here?' asked the driver, peering into the semi-rural darkness.

'Just a little farther, if you don't mind,' said his friend. 'Where you can see that black patch in the wall: that's the gate.'

The car crept on.

'Cold?' demanded the man at the wheel. 'These October nights *are* cold. Stuffy place, the theatre.'

'Did I sound cold?' asked his companion, the faint quiver renewing itself in his voice. 'Oh, I can't be, it's such a little way. Feel that,' he added, holding out his hand.

The driver applied his cheek to it and the car wobbled, bumping against the kerb.

'Feels warm enough to me,' he said, 'hot, in fact. Whoa! Whoa! good horse. This it?' he added, turning the car's head round.

'Yes, but don't bother to come in, Hubert. The road is so twisty and there may be a branch down. I'm always expecting them to fall, and I've had a lot of them wired. You never know with these elm-trees.'

'Jumpy kind of devil, aren't you?' muttered Hubert, extricating himself from the car and standing on the pavement. In the feeble moon-light he looked enormous; Ernest, fiddling with the door on his side, wondered where his friend went to when he tucked himself under the wheel. It must dig into him, he thought.

'It's a bit stiff, but you're turning it the wrong way,' said Hubert, coming round to Ernest's side. 'Easy does it. There you are.' He held the door open; Ernest stumbled out, missed his footing and was for a moment lost to sight between the more important shadows of his friend and his friend's car.

'Hold up, hold up,' Hubert enjoined him. 'The road doesn't need rolling.' He set Ernest on his feet and the two figures, so unequal in size, gazed mutely into the black square framed by the gateway. Through the trees, which seemed still to bear their complement of boughs, they could just see the outlines of the house, which repeated by their rectangularity the lines of the gateway. It looked like a large black hat-box, crowned at one corner by a smaller hat-box that was, in fact, a tower. There was a tiny light in the tower, otherwise the house was dark, the windows being visible as patches of intense black, like eyeless sockets in a negro's face.

'You said you were alone in the house,' remarked Hubert, breaking the silence.

'Yes,' his friend replied. 'In a sense I am.' He went on standing where he was, with the motor between him and the gateway.

'In what sense?' persisted his friend. 'Queer devil you are, Ernest; you must either be alone or not alone. Do I scent a romance? In that room with the light in it, for instance——'

'Oh, no,' Ernest protested, fidgeting with his feet. 'That's only the gas in the box-room. I don't know how it comes to be alight. It ought not to be. The least thing blows it out. Sometimes I get up in the night and go and see to it. Once I went four times, because it's so difficult with gas to make sure it's properly turned off. If you turn it off with your thumb you may easily turn it on again with your little finger, and never notice.'

'Well, a little puff of gas wouldn't hurt you,' observed Hubert, walking to the front of the car and looking at it as though in a moment he would make it do something it didn't like. 'Make you sleep better. How's the insomnia?'

'Oh, so-so.'

'Don't want anyone to hold your hand?'

'My dear Hubert, of course not.'

Ernest dashingly kicked a pebble which gyrated noisily on the metal surface. When it stopped all sound seemed to cease with it.

'Tell me about this shadowy companion, Ernest,' said Hubert, giving one of the tyres such a pinch that Ernest thought the car would scream out.

'Companion?' echoed Ernest, puzzled. 'I—I have no companion.'

'What did you mean, then, by saying you were only alone "in a

sense"?' demanded Hubert. 'In what sense? Think that out, my boy,'
He took a spanner, adjusted it, and gave a savage heave. The car shuddered through its whole length and subsided with a sigh.

'I only meant——' began Ernest.

'Please teacher, I only meant,' mocked Hubert grimly.

'I only meant,' said Ernest, 'that there is a charwoman coming tomorrow at half-past six.'

'And what time is it now?'

'A quarter to twelve.'

As Ernest spoke a distant clock chimed the three-quarters—a curious unsatisfied chime that ended on a note of interrogation.

'How the devil did you know that?' asked Hubert, his voice rising in protest as if such knowledge were not quite nice.

'During the night,' replied Ernest, a hint of self-assertion making itself heard for the first time in his voice, 'I am very sensitive to the passage of time.'

'You ought to loan yourself to our dining-room clock,' observed Hubert. 'It hasn't gone these fifteen months. But where are your servants, Ernest? Where's the pretty parlourmaid? Tell me she's there and I'd come and stop the night with you.'

'She isn't,' said Ernest. 'They're away, all three of them. I came home earlier than I meant. But would you really stay, Hubert? You've got a long way to go—eighteen miles, isn't it?'

'Afraid I can't, old man. Got some business to do early to-morrow.'

'What a pity,' said Ernest. 'If I'd asked you sooner perhaps you could have stayed.'

His voice expressed dejection and Hubert, who was making ready to get into the motor, turned round, holding the door half open.

'Look here, Ernest, I'll stay if it's any consolation to you.'

Ernest seemed to be revolving something in his mind.

'You really think you could?'

'You've only to say the word.'

Again Ernest hesitated.

'I don't think there's a bed aired.'

'Give me a shake-down in that room with the leaky light.'

Ernest turned aside so that his friend might not see the struggle in his face.

'Thank you a thousand times, Hubert. But really there's no need. Truly there isn't. Though it was most kind of you to suggest it.' He spoke as though he was trying to soothe an apprehensive child. 'I couldn't ask you to.'

'Well,' said Hubert, setting his foot on the self-starter, 'on your own head be it. On your tombstone they'll write "Here lieth one who turned a friend into the street at midnight".'

'Oh, no,' said Ernest, like a child.

'Won't they? Damn this self-starter.'

'Isn't it going to work?' asked Ernest hopefully.

'Just you wait a moment and I'll give it hell,' declared Hubert. He got out and wrung the starting-handle furiously. Still the car refused.

'It doesn't seem to want to go,' said Ernest. 'You'd much better stay here.'

'What, *now*?' Hubert exclaimed, as if the car must be taught a lesson, at whatever cost to himself. And then, as though it knew it had met its match, the engine began to throb.

'Good-night, Ernest. Pleasant dreams!'

'Good-night, Hubert, and thank you so much. And, oh . . . Hubert!'

The motor began to slow down as Hubert heard Ernest's cry, and his footsteps pattering down the street.

'I only wanted to ask what your telephone number was.'

'Don't I wish I knew! Number double o double o infinity. The thing's been coming every day for six weeks.'

'It's not likely to have been put in to-day while you were away?'

'No, old boy: more likely when I'm there. Good-night, and don't let yourself get blown up.'

In a few seconds all sound of the motor died away. The god had departed in his car.

'Shall I shut the gates?' thought Ernest. 'No, someone might want to come in. People don't usually drive up to a house in the dead of night, but you can't be sure: there are always accidents, petrol runs out; or it might be an old friend, turned up from abroad. Stranded after leaving the boat-train. "London was so full I couldn't get in anywhere, so I came on here, Ernest, to throw myself on your mercy." "You were quite right, Reggie; wait a moment, and I'll have you fixed up." How easy it would have been to say that to Hubert. But I was quite right, really, to let him go: I mustn't give way to myself, I must learn to live alone, like other people. How nice to be some poor person, a street-arab, for instance, just left school, who had come into some money and naturally bought this house. He's spent a jolly evening with a friend,

been to a theatre and comes home quite late, well, almost at midnight.'
And no sooner had the word crossed Ernest's mind than he heard, almost with a sense of private complicity, almost as though he had uttered them himself, the first notes of the midnight chime. He could not think against them; and looking round a little dazed he saw he had come only a very few steps into the garden. But already the house seemed larger; he could make out the front door, plumb in the middle of the building, sunk in its neo-Gothic ogee arch. He was standing on a closely clipped lawn; but to his right, across the carriageway, he knew there was that odd flat tract in the long grass. It always looked as if something large had trampled upon it, lain upon it, really: it was like the form of an enormous hare, and each blade of grass was broken-backed and sallow, as though the juice had been squeezed out of it.

But the new householder doesn't mind that, not he. His mind is full of the play. He only thinks, 'Polkin will have some trouble when he comes to mow *that* bit.' And of course he likes the trees; he doesn't notice that the branches are black and dead at the tips, as though the life of the tree were ebbing, dropping back into its trunk, like a failing fountain. He hasn't taken a ladder to peer into that moist channel where the branches fork; it oozes a kind of bright sticky froth, and if you could bring yourself to do it, you could shove your arm in up to the elbow, the wood is so rotten. 'Well, Polkin, if the tree's as far gone as you say, by all means cut it down: I don't myself consider it dangerous, but have it your own way. Get in a couple of Curtis's men, and fell it to-morrow.' So the new owner of Stithies hadn't really liked the tree? Oh, it's not that; he's a practical man; he yields to circumstances. 'Well, the old chap will keep us warm in the winter evenings, Polkin.' 'Yes, sir, and I do hope you'll have some company. You must be that lonely all by yourself, if I may say so, sir.' 'Company, my good Polkin, I should think so! I'm going to give a couple of dances, to start off with.' How reassuring, how reanimating, this glimpse into the life of the New Proprietor!

More insistently than ever, as the house drew near, did Ernest crave the loan of this imaginary person's sturdy thoughts. He had lived always in cramped, uncomfortable rooms; perhaps shared a bedroom with three or four others, perhaps even a bed! What fun for him, after these constricted years, to come home to a big house of his own, where he has three or four sitting-rooms to choose from, each of which he may occupy by himself! What a pleasure it is for him, in the long evenings, to sit perfectly still in the dining-room, with time hanging on his hands, hearing the clock tick. How he laughs when suddenly, from under the table or anyhow from some part of the floor, one doesn't quite know where, there comes that strange loud thump, as though someone, lying on his back, had grown restive and given the boards a terrific kick! In an old house like this, of course, the floor-boards do contract and expand; they have seen a great deal; they have something to say, and they want to get it off their chests.

Ernest paused. His reverie had brought him to the edge of the lawn, only a few yards from his front door. On either side the house stretched away, reaching out with its flanks into the night. Well, so would the new proprietor pause, to take a last look at the domain he so dearly loved — the symbol of his escape from an existence which had been one long round of irritating chores, always at somebody's beck and call, always having to think about something outside himself, never alone with his own thoughts! How he had longed for the kind of self-knowledge that only comes with solitude. And now, just before tasting this ecstasy of loneliness at its purest, he pauses. In a moment he will stride to the door which he hasn't troubled to lock, turn the handle and walk in. The hall is dark, but he finds a chair and mounting it lights the gas. Then he goes his nightly round. With what sense of possession, what luxury of ownership, does he feel the catches of the windows. Just a flick to make sure it's fast. As he picks his way through the furniture to the glimmering panes he congratulates himself that now he can look out on a view — as far as the sulky moonlight admits a view — of trees, shrubs, shadows; no vociferous callboys, no youthful blades returning singing after a wet night. Nothing but darkness and silence, within and without. What balm to the spirit! What a vivid sensation of security and repose! Down he goes into the cellar where the gas meter ticks. The window-sash is a flimsy thing — wouldn't keep out a determined man, perhaps; the new proprietor just settles it in its socket, and passes on into the wine-cellar. But no, the sort of man we are considering wouldn't bother to lock up the wine-cellar: such a small window could only let in cats and hedgehogs. It had let in both, and they were discovered afterwards, starved and dead: but that was before the occupancy of the new proprietor. Then upstairs, and the same ceremonial, so rapid and efficient, a formality, really, hardly taking a quarter of an hour: just the eight bedrooms, and the maids' rooms, since they were away. These might take longer. Last of all the box-room, with its unsatisfactory by-pass. It would be dealt with firmly and definitely and never revisited, like a sick person, during the watches of the night. And then, pleasantly tired and ready for bed, the new proprietor would turn to his friend Hubert, whom he had brought back from the play, and bid him good-night.

So absorbed was Ernest in the evocation of this pleasant bed-time scene that, with the gesture of someone retiring to rest, he half held out his hand. But no one took it; and he realized, with a sinking of the heart, that the new proprietor had let him down, was a craven like himself. He walked unsteadily to the door and turned the handle. Nothing happened. He turned it the other way. Still the door resisted him. Suddenly he remembered how once, returning home late at night from taking some letters to the post, the door of the stable, where he kept his bicycle, had been similarly recalcitrant. But when he pushed harder the door yielded a little, as though someone stronger than he was holding it against him and meant to let him in slowly before doing him an injury. He had exerted all his strength. Suddenly the door gave. It was only a tennis-ball that had got wedged between the door and the cobblestone: but he never forgot the episode. For a moment he sat down on the stone step before renewing his attack. He must have managed it clumsily. The door needed drawing towards him or else pushing away from him. He recalled his failure to negotiate the catch of Hubert's car. But his second attempt was as vain as the first. The door wouldn't open, couldn't: it must have been locked on the inside.

Ernest knew, as well as he knew anything, that he had left it unfastened. The lock was of an old-fashioned pattern; it had no tricks of its own. You could be quite certain it was locked, the key turned so stiffly: it had never given Ernest a moment's uneasiness nor demanded nocturnal forfeits from his nervous apprehension. It was locked all right; but who had locked it?

Supposing there was a man who disliked his house, thought Ernest, hated it, dreaded it, with what emotions of relief would he discover, when he returned from a dull play at the witching hour, that the house was locked against him? Supposing this man, from a child, had been so ill at ease in his own home that the most familiar objects, a linen-press or a waste-paper basket, had been full of menace for him: wouldn't he rejoice to be relieved, by Fate, of the horrible necessity of spending the night alone in such a house? And wouldn't he rather welcome than otherwise the burglar or whoever it might be who had so providentially taken possession—the New Proprietor? The man was an abject funk; could scarcely bear to sit in a room alone; spent the greater part of the night prowling about the house torn between two fears — the fear of staying in bed and brooding over neglected windows and gas jets, and the fear of getting up and meeting those windows and gas jets in the dark. Lucky chap to lose, through no fault of his own, all his fears and all his responsibilities. What a weight off his mind! The streets were open to him, the nice noisy streets, even at night-time half full of policemen and strayed revellers, in whose company he could gaily pass what few hours remained till dawn.

But somehow the Old Expropriated had less success, as an imaginative lure, than the New Proprietor. 'I must get in,' thought Ernest. 'It's perfectly simple. There are one, two, three windows I can get in by if I try: four counting the window of the box-room. But first I'll ring the bell.' He rang and a wild peal followed which might have come from the hall instead of the kitchen, it seemed so near. He waited, while at ever-increasing intervals of time the clangour renewed itself, like an expiring hiccough. 'I'll give him another minute,' thought Ernest, taking out his watch. The minute passed but no one came.

When a policeman has tried the handle of the door and found it shut, he often, if he is a true guardian of the law, proceeds to examine the windows. 'Hullo, there, hullo! hullo!' And a handful of gravel, maybe, rattles against the window-panes. Leaping or creeping out of bed, according to his temperament, the startled householder goes to the window. 'What's the matter?' 'Nothing's the matter, only your window's unfastened. There are queer people about tonight — gypsies. You had better come down and fasten it unless you want your silver stolen.' 'Thank you very much, officer; good-night.' And down patters paterfamilias in his warm slippers and his dressing-gown, while the constable patrols the garden with comfortable tread. No one dare molest him, not even if he is ever so wicked. And whoever heard of a wicked policeman? thought Ernest, reconnoitring, at some distance, the dining-room window. He tramps through the shrubberies, cats fly before him, his bull's-eye lantern turns night into day, he could walk through the spinney where the mound is and never turn a hair. And this is how he would open the dining-room window.

It was a sash-window, hanging loose in its grooves. Ernest inserted his pocket-knife in the crevice and started to prize it open. To his delight and dismay the sash began to move. Half an inch higher and he would be able to get his fingers under it. He was using the haft of the knife now, not the blade. The sash began to move more easily. He curled his fingers under and round it. His face, twisted with exertion, stared blankly upon the cream-coloured blind inside. The blind stirred. He must have let in a current of air. He redoubled his exertions. The sash slid up six inches, and then stuck fast. And he could see why. A hand, pressed flat along the bottom of the sash, was holding it down.

Ernest let go with a cry, and the window was slowly and smoothly closed. He had an impulse to run but he resisted it, and forced himself to walk back to the window. The hand was gone.

Imagine you were a window-cleaner and wanted to open a window and some playful member of the family — a great over-grown lout of a boy, for instance — took it into his head to play a prank like that on you. You know what boys are; they have no mercy; there is a bully embedded in all of them, and pretty near the surface in most. That being so, what would you make of the young gentleman's interference? What line would you take? Clearly he won't hurt you, and he can't, besides, be everywhere at once. Perhaps somebody calls him, or he finds the cat and pulls its tail or blows tobacco-smoke into the spaniel's eyes. For such a lad as that there are a hundred distractions; and while you are quietly going on with your job at the drawing-room window he will be making an apple-pie bed for his small sister in the nursery: too engrossed, my dear Ernest, to remember your existence, certainly too much occupied to follow you about.

And it did seem that Ernest the window cleaner was likely to be more successful than Ernest the policeman. Crouching like an animal, his hands hanging down in front of him, keeping close to the wall, brushing himself against creepers, scratched by thorns and blackened by soot, at last he reached the drawing-room window and flung himself on his face beneath the sill. The sill was a low one. Half kneeling, half supporting himself on his elbows, he raised himself till his eyes were level with the glass. The fitful moonlight played on this side of the house; a treacherous light, but it served to show him that the Puck of Stithies was occupied elsewhere. With extreme caution, holding his breath, he negotiated the difficult preliminaries; then he stood up straight, and heaved with all his might. The window rushed up a foot and then stuck. Involuntarily he glanced down: yes, there was the hand, flattened on the frame: there was another hand, holding back the blind, and there was a face, not very distinct, but certainly a face.

It was the hand that Ernest, cowering under the thick umbrage of. the drooping-ash, remembered best. The face was anybody's face, not really unlike Hubert's: a ruddy, capable face: not exactly angry, but stern, official-looking. But the odd thing about the hand was that it didn't seem like the hand of another person. It was larger than Ernest's, yet he had felt, for the moment that it was presented before his eyes, that it would respond to his volition, move as he wanted it to move. He had been too frightened, at the moment, to act upon this fantastic notion; but couldn't he act upon it next time? Next time. But why not? Imagine a man of average capabilities, physically none too robust, but with a good headpiece on him. He can afford to spare himself; even when he takes on a job that is strange to him he will find out the easiest way, will know just the right moment to bring to bear what little strength he has. Many a slenderly built chap, at the bidding of necessity, has transformed himself into a passable coal-heaver. But to carry a sack of coal or a sack of anything one needs a knack: it's no good taking the load into your arms, you must hoist it on to your back. And when you've carried a sack or two like that, who knows that your luck mayn't change? Many a man who carried a sack in his time, in later life has supped with princes.

Ernest scrambled up the slates, slithered down a gully and grasped the balustrade of the battlement. He had found his way instinctively, or did he remember it? If he hadn't been familiar with the lie of the roofs, even to the point of knowing what slates were loose and would crack or, worse, creak when you trod, how could he have avoided a sprained ankle or a serious fall? Yes, certainly he knew his way about the leads and slates; who wouldn't, if they had lived in a house from childhood, and loved it, though it frightened them, and wanted to have it, and meant to have it, and what went with it, though by a slip of the pen it belonged to someone else?

The window of the Blue Room was just round the corner. Imagine yourself a steeplejack. How delicious to know, while you went about your work with a crowbar or a hammer or whatever heavy, unwieldy instrument it might be, that there was a railing of stone and mortar, two feet high and six inches thick, between you and the ground! The steeplejack would feel he wasn't earning his pay when his life was safe-guarded like that. Well, here's a foolproof job! Like putting a grown man in a child's cot, with a high brass *chevaux-de-frise* round it. But nevertheless, rounding the bend, Ernest was overtaken by nausea and lay for some moments stretched out upon the leaden gully, twitching.

But supposing a man was kept out by force from his possessions, or what should have been his? Who would blame him, who would not applaud him, if he went to any reasonable length to recover his property? Should he consult his own safety, or anyone's safety, when he was engaged upon such an undertaking?

Ernest dragged himself to the window. His head was level with the upper sash which was fast in the wall, and looked as if it was fixed there. But the lower sash was about six inches open, with the fold of a blue blind projecting from it.

Up went the sash a long, long way as it seemed, much farther than the others. But as he lifted it there was a whirring sound; the tegument of the blind vanished. The new proprietor was standing there. Ernest stared at him. Was it the face of the poor man who had come into money and acquired Stithies? Or of the coward who owned it? Or of the policeman who protected it, or of the man who cleaned its windows? Or of the coal-heaver or of the steeplejack or of the man who wouldn't let anything stand in his way? It seemed in turn to be all these, yet its essential character never changed. Dazed as he was, Ernest remembered to drop his hands. The apparition dropped his; the window was unguarded. Slowly Ernest lowered and advanced his head. But he had not reckoned on his enemy's faculty for imitation. The simulacrum bowed, leant forward, pressed its face to within three inches of Ernest's. And as it hung there the last expression faded out of it, and was replaced by a featureless oval, dimly phosphorescent. Yet something began to take shape in that mobile, almost fluid tract. Ernest did not wait for it to declare itself, this new visage whose lines he could almost see graven in the air before they settled and bit deep into the flesh.

He was on the dripstone of the tower now, clinging with his fingers to the sham machicolations. Suppose a man meant to commit a murder, did he shrink from risking his own life? Wasn't anything easy to him, in the presence of such a determination? Hadn't it been easy to him, Ernest, when he stood, some ten years ago, on this same dizzy ledge and found, after three failures, the one vulnerable point of Stithies, the box-room window?

Sweating and gasping he reached the window and clung to the stanchion, his back, weak with exhaustion, bending outwards like a bow. But his prescient tormentor had outstripped him. This time the face did not alter. It was Ernest's own face, a hateful face, and the face of a murderer.

Punctually at half-past six, in the gathering light, Mrs. Playward passed through the open gateway into the garden of Stithies Court. 'Bless me,' she thought. 'What with the maids away and the young gentleman in bed I shan't be able to get in.' The suspicion that she had made the journey for nothing weighed heavily on Mrs. Playward. 'It's not as if I am as young as I was,' she told herself. But, having come so far, it was worth while to make sure that none of the doors was unlocked. The front door seemed to open of itself, such was her amazement at finding it unfastened. 'Well, I never,' she declared. 'And he always said to be so fidgety about robbers.' She heaved a sigh. 'Best to get it over,' she muttered. 'If there's one step there's eighty.' Having collected the machinery of her profession she mounted the spiral staircase that led to the box-room. Her eyesight was defective, a fact to which, when reproached for apparent negligence, she often drew the attention of her clients. The staircase was lighted by a couple of slit windows, set deep in the wall. At the second of them she paused, partly to recover her breath, partly to relieve her eyes from the strain of peering into the gloom. By leaning forward she could just see the road below. 'Well, I declare,' she muttered, 'if Polkin hasn't been and left his overcoat out on the path all night. That good black one he told me he was promised by Mr. Ernest. Some men don't know when they're well off.' Breathing heavily she resumed her journey. The condition of this box-room was heart-breaking, trunks, cardboard boxes, gas-rings, fenders, disused furniture all covered with a layer of dust. But she hardly noticed that because a stranger sight claimed her attention. The casement window was wide open.

She walked towards it. A huge black trunk with a flat top stood directly under the window, and in the dust which thickly coated it there were four curious marks. Two pairs of each. The farther ones, the marks nearest the window, she made out at once. They were the prints of hands. The fingers, pointing into the room, were splayed out and unnaturally elongated; where the hand joined the wrist there was a long shapeless smear. Opposite them, and within an arm's length, were the other marks. At first they meant nothing to her: two symmetrical black smudges with rounded tops and a thin track of dust between them. The imprint of a man's knees perhaps? Panic descended on Mrs. Playward. She fled, screaming 'Mr. Ernest, Mr. Ernest, something has happened in the box-room!' No one answered her; when she hammered on Mr. Ernest's door no one replied, and when she went in, the room was empty.

THE THOUGHT

HENRY GREENSTREAM had always looked forward to his afternoon walk. It divided the day for him. In ideal circumstances a siesta preceded it and he awoke to a new morning, a false dawn, it is true, but as pregnant with unexpressed promise as the real one. For some weeks now, however, sleep had deserted his after-luncheon cushion; he could get to the brink of unconsciousness, when thoughts and pictures drifted into his mind independently of his will, but not over.

Still, the walk was the main thing even if he started on it a little tired. It calmed, it satisfied, it released. For an hour and twenty-five minutes he enjoyed the freedom of the birds of the air. Impressions and sensations offered themselves to him in an unending flow, never outstaying their welcome, never demanding more from his attention than a moment's recognition. Lovely and pleasant voices that tonelessly proclaimed the harmony between him, Henry Greenstream, and the spirit of all created things.

Or they had proclaimed it till lately. Lately the rhythm of his thoughts had been disturbed by an interloper, yes, an interloper, but an interloper from within. Like a cuckoo that soon ceased to be a visitor, the stranger had entered his mind and now dwelt there, snatching at the nourishment meant for its legitimate neighbours. They pined, they grew sickly while Henry Greenstream suckled the parasite.

He knew what it was and whence it came. It was an infection from his conscience which had taken offence at an act so trivial that surely no other conscience would have noticed it. Indeed, he had himself almost forgotten what it originated in — something about a breach of confidence that (reason assured him a thousand times) could have harmed nobody. And when it stirred inside him it was not to remind him of his fault and recall the circumstances of his lapse, but simply to hurt him; to prick the tender tegument which, unpierced, assures comfort to the mind.

If it did not spoil his life it fretted him, reducing his capacity for enjoyment; and most of all did it make its presence felt when he took his afternoon exercise. The aery shapes that then haunted his imagination could not suppress it, nor was the scenery through which he passed such as to distract him from himself. Town gave way to suburb; suburb to ribbon development; only when it was time to turn back did he emerge into the unspoilt countryside. Motors rushed by; an occasional tramp asked for a match; dogs idled on the pavement. All this was uninspiring but at the same time it fostered his mood; even the ugly little houses, with their curtains drawn aside to reveal a plant or a pretentious piece of china, invited pleasing speculations. Confidently he looked forward to his reunion with these humble landmarks. But they had lost their power to draw him out, and lately he had invented a new and less satisfying form of mental pastime. Much less satisfying; for it consisted in counting the minutes that elapsed between one visitation of the Thought and the next. Even so might a Chinese malefactor seek to beguile himself while under the water-torture by calculating the incidence of the drops.

Where the signpost pointed to Aston Highchurch Mr. Greenstream paused. He had been walking half an hour and the Thought had recurred twenty-two times; that was an average of nearly once a minute, a higher average than yesterday, when he had got off with fourteen repetitions. It was in fact a record: a bad record. What could he do to banish this tedious symptom? Stop counting, perhaps? Make his mind a blank? He wandered on with uncertain footsteps unlike his ordinary purposeful stride. Ahead of him the October sun was turning down the sky, behind, the grass (for the fields now began to outnumber the houses) took on a golden hue; above, the clouds seemed too lazy to obey what little wind there was. It was a lovely moment that gathered to itself all the harmony of which the restless earth was capable. Mr. Greenstream opened his heart to the solace of the hour and was already feeling refreshed when ping! the Thought stung him again.

'I must do something about this,' thought Mr. Greenstream, 'or I shall go mad.'

He looked round. To his left, in the hedge beyond the grass verge, was a wicket-gate, and from it a path ran diagonally over the shoulder of a little hill, a shabby asphalt path that gleamed in the sunlight and disappeared, tantalizingly, into the horizon. Mr. Greenstream knew where it led, to Aston Highchurch; but so conservative was he that in all these years of tramping down the main road he had never taken it. He did so now. In a few minutes he was on the high land in what seemed a different world, incredibly nearer the sky. Turning left along a country lane bordered by trees and less agreeably by chicken runs, he kept catching sight of a church; and at length he came to a path that led straight to it across a stubble field. It lay with its back to him, long and low, with a square tower at the further end that gave it the look of a cat resting on tucked-in legs, perhaps beginning to purr.

Mr. Greenstream stopped at the churchyard gate and stared up at the tower to make out what the objects were which, hanging rather crazily at the corners below the parapet, had looked in the distance like whiskers, and completed the feline impression made by the church. A whiskered church! The idea amused Mr. Greenstream until his watchful tormentor, ever jealous of his carefree moments, prodded him again. With a sigh he entered the porch and listened. No sound. The door opened stiffly to confront him with a pair of doors, green baize this time. He went back and shut the outer door, then the inner ones, and felt he had shut out the world. The church was empty; he had it to himself.

It was years since Mr. Greenstream had been inside a church except on ceremonial occasions or as a sightseer, and he did not quite know what to do. This was a Perpendicular church, light, airy and spacious, under rather than over furnished. The seats were chairs made of wood so pale as to be almost white: they were lashed together with spars, and the whole group, with its criss-cross of vertical and horizontal lines, made an effect that was gay and pretty and in so far as it suggested rigging, faintly nautical.

Mr. Greenstream wandered up the nave but felt a reluctance, for which he could not quite account, to mount the chancel steps: in any case there was little of note there and the east window was evidently modern. Straying back along the north aisle wall he read the monumental inscriptions, black lettering on white marble or white lettering on black marble. Then he came face to face with the stove, an impressive cylinder from which issued a faint crackling. His tour seemed to be over; but he was aware of a feeling of expectancy, as if the church were waiting for him to do something.

'After all, why not?' he thought, sinking to his knees. But he could not pray at once — he had lost the habit, he did not know how to begin. Moreover he felt ashamed of coming to claim the benefits of religion when for many years he had ignored its obligations. Such a prayer would be worse than useless; it was an insult; it would put God against him. Then the Thought came with its needle-jab and he waited no longer but prayed vehemently and incoherently for deliverance. But a morbid fear assailed him that it was not enough to think the words, for some of them, perhaps the most operative, might be left out, telescoped or elided by the uncontrollable hurry of his mind, so he repeated his petition out loud. Until he had ceased to speak he did not notice how strange his voice sounded in the empty church, almost as if it did not belong to him. Rising shakily to his feet he blinked, dazzled by the daylight, and stumbled out of the church without a backward look.

Not once on the homeward journey to his narrow house in Midgate was Mr. Greenstream troubled by the Thought. His relief and gratitude were inexpressible; but it was not till the next day that he realized that the visit to Aston Highchurch had been a turning point in his life. Doctors had told him that his great enemy was his morbid sense of guilt. Now, so long as St. Cuthbert's, Aston Highchurch, stood, he need not fear it.

Fearful yet eager he began to peer down a future in which, thanks to the efficacy of prayer, the desires of his heart would meet with no lasting opposition from the voice of his conscience. He could indulge them to the full. Whatever they were, however bad they were, he need not be afraid that they would haunt him afterwards. The Power whose presence he had felt in church would see to that.

It was a summer evening and the youth of Aston Highchurch would normally have been playing cricket on the village green, but the game fell through because a handful of the regulars had failed to turn up. There was murmuring among the disappointed remnant, and inquiry as to what superior attraction had lured away the defaulters.

'I know,' said a snub-nosed urchin, 'because I heard them talking about it.'

'Well, tell us, Tom Wignall.'

'They said I wasn't to.'

'Come on, you tell us or . . .'

According to their code a small but appreciable amount of physical torture released the sufferer from further loyalty to his plighted word. After a brief but strident martyrdom the lad, nothing loth, yielded to the importunity of his fellows.

'It's about that praying chap.'

'What, old Greenpants?'

'Yes. They've gone to watch him at it.'

'Where?'

'In the tower gallery. Fred Buckland pinched the key when the old man wasn't looking.'

'Coo, they'll cop it if they're caught.'

'Why, they aren't doing no harm. You can't trespass in a church.'

'That's all you know. They haven't gone there just to watch, neither.'

'Why, what are they going to do?'

'Well,' said Tom Wignall importantly, 'they're going to give him a fright. Do you know what he does?'

'He prays, doesn't he?'

'Yes, but he don't pray to himself. He prays out loud, and he shouts sometimes, and rocks himself about. And he doesn't pray for his father and mother——'

'He hasn't got any, so I've heard,' said an older boy, who, to judge from his caustic tone, seemed to be listening with some impatience to Tom Wignall's revelations. 'He's an orphan.'

'Anyhow,' the speaker resumed unabashed, 'he doesn't pray for his king or his country, or to be made good or anything like that. He confesses his sins.'

'Do you mean he's done a murder?'

'Fred Buckland couldn't hear what it was, but it must have been something bad or he wouldn't have come all this way to confess it.'

This reasoning impressed the audience.

'Must have been murder,' they assured each other, 'or forgery anyhow.'

'But that isn't all,' continued the speaker, intoxicated by the attention he was receiving. 'He prays for what he didn't ought.'

'Why, you can pray for anything you like,' opined one of the listeners.

'That you can't. There's heaps of things you mustn't pray for. You mustn't pray to get rich, for one thing, and (he lowered his voice) you mustn't pray for anyone to die.'

'Did he do that?'

'Fred Buckland said that's what it sounded like.'

There was a pause.

'I think the poor chap's balmy if you ask me,' said the older boy. 'I bet his prayers don't do no one any harm nor him any good either.'

'That's where you make a mistake,' said the spokesman of the party.

'That's where you're wrong. Fred Buckland says he's got much, much richer these last six months. Why, he's got a car and a chauffeur and all. Fred Buckland says he wouldn't be surprised if he's a millionaire.'

'You bet he is,' scoffed the older boy. 'You bet that when he prayed somebody dropped down dead and left him a million. Sounds likely, doesn't it?'

The circle of listeners stirred. All the faces broadened with scepticism and one boy took up his bat and played an imaginary forward stroke. Tom Wignall felt that he was losing ground. He was like a bridge-player who has held up his ace too long.

'Anyhow,' he said defiantly, 'Fred Buckland says that church is no place for the likes of him who've got rich by praying in a way they ought to be ashamed of. And I tell you, he's going to give old Green-pants a fright. He's going to holler down at him from the tower in a terrible deep voice, and Greenpants'll think it's God answering him from Heaven, or perhaps the Devil, and he'll get such a fright he'll never set foot in Aston again. And good riddance, I say.'

Tom's own voice rose as he forced into it all the dramatic intensity he could muster. But he had missed his moment. One or two of his companions looked serious and nodded, but the rest, with the unerring instinct of boys for a change of leadership, a shifting of moral ascendancy, threw doubtful glances towards their senior. They were wavering. They would take their cue from him.

'Lousy young bastards,' he said, 'leaving us all standing about like fools on a fine evening like this. I should like to tan their hides.'

There was a murmur of sympathetic indignation, and he added, 'What makes them think the chap's coming to-day to pray, anyhow?'

Tom Wignall answered sullenly: 'He comes most days now. . . . And if you want to know, Jim Chantry passed him on his motor-bike the other side of Friar's Bridge. He didn't half jump when Jim honked in his ear,' Tom concluded with unrepentant relish. 'He'll be here any time now.'

'Well,' said the older boy stretching himself luxuriously, 'you chaps can go and blank yourselves. There's nothing else for you to do. I'm off.' He sauntered away, grandly, alone, towards the main road. Those silly mutts need a lesson. I'll spoil their little game for them, he thought.

The tower gallery at St. Cuthbert's, Aston Highchurch, was a feature most unusual in parish churches. But the tower was rather unusual too. Its lower storey, which rose fifty or more feet to the belfry floor, was open to the main body of the building; only an arch divided it from the nave. The gallery, a stone passage running along the tower wall just above the west window, was considerably higher than the apex of the arch. It was only visible from the western end of the church, and itself commanded a correspondingly restricted view—a view that was further impeded by the lightly swaying bell-ropes. But Fred Buckland and his four conspirators could see, through the flattened arc of the arch, a portion of the last six rows of chairs. The sunlight coming through the window below them fell on the chairs, picking them out in gold and making a bright patch like the stage of a theatre.

'He ought to be here by now, didn't he?' one urchin whispered.

'Shut up!' hissed the ringleader. 'It'll spoil everything if he hears us.'

They waited, three of them with their backs pressed against the wall, their faces turned this way and that as in a frieze, looking very innocent and naughty. Fred, who had more than once sung carols from this lofty perch, embraced a baluster and let his feet dangle over the edge.

Five minutes passed, ten, a quarter of an hour. The sinking sun no longer lay so brightly on the foreground; shadows began to creep in from the sides. The boys even began to see each other less plainly.

'I'm frightened,' whispered a voice. 'I wish we hadn't come. I want to go home.'

'Shut up, can't you?'

More minutes passed and the church grew darker.

'I say, Fred,' a second voice whispered, 'what time does your old man come to shut the church up?'

'Seven o'clock these evenings. It still wants a quarter to.'

They waited; then one whispered in a tense voice, 'I believe that's him.'

'Who?'

'Old Greenpants, of course.'

'Did you hear anything?'

'No, but I thought I saw something move.'

'You're balmy. That's the shadow of the bell-rope.'

They strained their eyes.

'I don't think it was, Fred. It moves when the bell-rope doesn't.'

'Funny if somebody else should be spying on old Greenpants.'

'Maybe it's him who's spying on us.'

'What, old Greenpants?'

'Of course. Who else could it be?'

'I wish I could see what that was moving,' the boy said again. 'There, close by the stove.'

'I suppose it couldn't get up to us?'

'Not unless it came by the bell-rope,' said Fred decisively. 'I've locked the door of the stairs and the only other key my dad has. You're in a funk, that's your trouble. Only the Devil could shin up one of them ropes.'

'They wouldn't let him come into church, would they?'

'He might slip in if the north door was open.'

Almost as he spoke a puff of wind blew up in their faces and the six bell-ropes swayed in all directions lashing each other and casting fantastic shadows.

'That's him,' Fred hissed. 'Don't you hear his footsteps? I bet that's him. Just wait till he gets settled down. Now, all together: "God is going to punish thee, Henry Greenstream, thou wicked man".'

In creditable unison, their voices quavered through the church. What result they expected they hardly knew themselves, nor did they have time to find out; for the sacristan, appearing with a clatter of boots at the gallery door, had them all like rats in a trap. Fear of committing sacrilege by blasphemy for a moment took away his powers of speech; then he burst out, 'Come on, you little blackguards! Get down out of here! Oh, you'll be sore before I've finished with you!'

A spectator, had there been one, would have noticed that the sounds of snivelling and scuffling were momentarily stilled as the staircase swallowed them up. A minute later they broke out again, with louder clamour; for though Fred got most of the blows the others quickly lost their morale, seeing how completely their leader had lost his.

'I'll take a strap to you when I get you home,' thundered the sacristan, 'trying to disturb a poor gentleman at his devotions.'

'But, Dad, he wasn't in the church!' protested Fred between his sobs.

'It wasn't your fault if he wasn't,' returned his father grimly.

For some months after being warned Henry Greenstream came no more to St. Cuthbert's, Aston Highchurch. Perhaps he found another sanctuary, for certainly there was no lack of them in the district. Perhaps, since he had a motor, he found it more convenient to drive out into the country where (supposing he needed them) were churches in sparsely populated areas, untenanted by rude little boys. He had never been a man to advertise his movements, and latterly his face had worn a closed look, as if he had been concealing them from himself. But he had to tell the chauffeur where to go, and the man was immensely surprised when, one December afternoon, he received an order to drive to Aston Highchurch. 'We hadn't taken that road for an age,' he afterwards explained.

'Stop when I tap the window,' Mr. Greenstream said, 'and then I shall want you to do something for me.'

At the point where the footpath leads across the fields Mr. Greenstream tapped and got out of the car.

'I'm going on to the church now,' he said, 'but I want you to call at the Rectory, and ask the Reverend Mr. Ripley if he would step across to the church and . . . and hear my confession. Say it's rather urgent. I don't know how long I shall be gone.'

The chauffeur, for various reasons, had not found Mr. Greenstream's service congenial; he had in fact handed his notice in that morning. But something in his employer's tremulous manner touched him, and surprising himself, he said:

'You wouldn't like me to go with you as far as the church, sir?'

'Oh, no, thank you, Williams, I think I can get that far.'

'I only thought you didn't look very fit, sir.'

'Is that why you decided to leave me?' asked Mr. Greenstream, and the man bit his lip and was silent.

Mr. Greenstream walked slowly towards the church, absently and unsuccessfully trying to avoid the many puddles left by last night's storm. It had been a violent storm, and now though the wind was gone, the sky, still burning streakily as with the embers of its own ill-temper, had a wild, sullen look.

Mr. Greenstream reached the porch but didn't go in. Instead he walked round the church, stumbling among the graves, for some were unmarked by headstones; and on the north side, where no one ever went, the ground was untended and uneven.

It took him some minutes to make the circuit, but when he had completed it he started again. It was on his second tour that he discovered— literally stumbled against—the gargoyle, which, of course, has been replaced now. The storm had split it but the odd thing was that the two halves, instead of being splintered and separated by their fall, lay intact on the sodden grass within a few inches of each other. Mr. Greenstream could not have believed the grinning mask was so big. It had split where the spout passed through it: one half retained the chin, the other was mostly eye and cheek and ear. Mr. Greenstream could see the naked spout hanging out far above him, long and bent and shining like a black snake. The comfortless sight may have added to the burden of his thoughts, for he walked on more slowly. This time, however, he did not turn aside at the porch, but went straight in, carefully shutting the inner and outer doors behind him.

It was past four o'clock and the church was nearly dark, the windows being only visible as patches of semi-opaque brightness. But there *was* a light which shone with a dull red glow, a burning circle hanging in the air a foot or two from the ground. It looked like a drum that had caught fire within, but it was not truly luminous; it seemed to attract the darkness rather than repel it. For a moment Mr. Greenstream could not make out what the strange light was. But when he took a step or two towards it and felt the heat on his face and hands he knew at once. It was the stove. The zealous sacristan, mindful of the chilly day, had stoked it up until it was red hot.

Mr. Greenstream was grateful for the warmth, for his hands were cold and his teeth chattering. He would have liked to approach the stove and bend over it. But the heat was too fierce for that, it beat him back. So he withdrew to the outer radius of its influence. Soon he was kneeling, and soon—the effect of the warmth on a tired mind and a tired body, asleep.

It must have been the cold that woke him, cold, piercing cold, that seemed solid, like a slab of ice pressing against his back. The stove still glared red in front of him, but it had no more power to warm him physically than has a friendly look or a smiling face. Whence did it come, this deadly chill? Ah! He looked over his left shoulder and saw that the doors, which he remembered shutting, were now open to the sky and the north wind. To shut them again was the work of a moment. But why were they open? he wondered, turning back into the church. Why, of course, of course, the clergyman had opened them, the Rector of Aston Highchurch, who was coming at his request to hear his confession. But where was he, and why did he not speak? And what was the reddish outline that moved towards him in the darkness? For a moment his fancy confused it with the stove, or it might be the stove's reflection, thrown on one of the pillars. But on it came, bearing before it that icy breath he now knew had nothing to do with the north wind.

'Mr. Ripley, Mr. Ripley,' he murmured, falling back into the warmth of the stove, feeling upon his neck its fierce assault. Then he heard a voice like no voice he had ever heard, as if the darkness spoke with the volume of a thousand tongues.

'I am your confessor. What have you to say?'

'My death must be my answer,' he replied, the consciousness of annihilation on him.

When Mr. Greenstream's chauffeur learned that the Rector was not at home he left a message and then returned to the car, for he knew from experience that his master's unaccountable church-going often kept him a long time. But when an hour had gone by he felt vaguely anxious and decided to see if anything was the matter. To his surprise he found the church door open, and noticed a smell coming from it which he had never associated with a church. Moving gingerly in the dark, he advanced towards where a sound of hissing made itself heard. Then he struck a match, and what he saw caused him to turn and run in terror for the door. On the threshold he almost collided with Mr. Ripley, hastening from the Rectory on his errand of mercy. Together they overcame the repugnance which either of them would have felt singly, lifted Mr. Greenstream's body from the stove across which it hung and laid it reverently on the pavement.

The newspapers at first gave out that Mr. Greenstream had been burned to death, but the medical authorities took a different view.

'In my opinion,' one doctor said, 'he was dead before he even touched the stove, and paradoxical as it may seem, the physical signs indicate that he was frozen, not burned to death.

'He was perhaps trying to warm himself—why, we shall never know.'

CONRAD AND THE DRAGON

ONCE upon a time there was a boy who lived with his mother and father in a country five day's journey beyond the boundaries of Europe. As he was only twelve years old when this story begins, he did not have to work for his living, but played about in the woods in which his house was, generally by himself. But sometimes he would stand and watch his two brothers felling trees and sawing them up, for, like his father, they were foresters, and every now and then they would let him ride home astride a tree-trunk, jogging up and down above the horses. This he enjoyed, when once he got over the fear of falling off, and he would have joined them oftener, but he was afraid lest Leo might say, 'Now, Conrad, it's your turn to do something; just mind those horses for ten minutes,' or 'Conrad, come here and lean your heavy weight against this sapling, so that I can get the axe to it.' Then Conrad would have to go; unless Rudolph chimed in with, 'Oh, let the boy alone, Leo, he's more hindrance than help.' Conrad would be half glad and half sorry at Rudolph's intervention; he wanted to lend a hand, but he was afraid the horse might tread on his toes, or the sapling spring up and hit him. He was very fond of his brothers, especially the younger, Rudolph, and he admired them, they were so strong and capable; he did not believe he would ever be able to do what they did, even when he grew up. 'I am not meant to be a forester,' he told himself.

It so happened that one afternoon Leo put the axe in his hands, and tried more persistently than ever to teach him how to use it. Conrad had been only half attending; he swung the axe clumsily, and it glanced off the tree on to his foot, making a deep gash in his boot. Leo spoke sharply to him for his awkwardness, and Conrad, without waiting to hear what Rudolph might say in his defence, dropped the axe and ran away, crying, nor did he pause for breath until the sounds that came from the clearing had ceased altogether.

Here the forest was very thick and silent, and though there seemed to be plenty of little paths going hither and thither, a stranger to the wood would have found that they led nowhere in particular, to an abandoned clearing, perhaps, or just into the undergrowth. But Conrad, who knew this part of the wood by heart, was not at all alarmed. He was feeling too hurt and angry with his brothers to be sorry that he had damaged his boot, though it would mean his father buying another pair; what he dreaded was that the axe might have cut his foot, in which case he would have to swallow his pride and go back to his brothers to beg a ride, for he was a long way from home.

He examined the gash as well as the dim light permitted, but there was no sign of blood; and when he took off his boot to look closer he found that the stocking was lightly cut, but the skin below it was unharmed. What a lucky escape! It must be magic, Conrad thought, white magic, much rarer than the black kind which he had been warned against, and which was all too common in this part of the world. How nice if he could meet, in some dell or coppice, the good fairy who, at the critical moment, had turned the axe's edge! He peered about; he kissed the air, hoping to attract her; but if she was there she remained invisible. But Conrad, encouraged by the discovery that he was unhurt, felt twice the boy he was; so far from running back to his brothers, he would prove to them that he did not need their protection; he would press on through the forest further than he had ever gone before, and would not be home till nightfall. He had some food in his satchel and, as it was early autumn, there were plenty of berries on the trees. He started off.

Soon the wood changed its character. Instead of being flat, it turned into a succession of narrow valleys which Conrad always seemed to have to cross at their deepest point, scrambling up and down as best he could, for path there was none. He began to feel tired, and the sharp, hard leather of his damaged boot stuck into him and hurt him. He kept on meaning to turn back, but whenever he reached the crest of a ridge, it looked such a little way to the next that he always decided to cross just one more valley. They were long and empty, lit up their whole length by the sun which, away on Conrad's right, was now so low that he could see it without lifting his eyes. It would soon be night. Suddenly he lost heart and made up his mind to stop at the next hilltop. It was only a few yards' climb.

But once there, what a sight met his eyes — worth the whole journey, worth far, far more than all the efforts he had made. An immense valley, like the others, only larger, and flooded with orange light, stretched away to the left; and blocking the end a huge square rock, almost a mountain, with a castle built into its summit, so cunningly you could not tell where rock ended and stone began. Conrad strained his eyes. In the clear air of that country, of course, it was possible to see an immense distance; the castle might be five miles away, might be ten, might be twenty. But there was a picture of it in the kitchen at home, and he recognized it at once. It was the royal castle, the palace of the King.

Clearly there was a ceremony in progress, for the castle was gaily decorated with large and little flags; bright-coloured rugs and tapestries hung from the windows, and scarlet streamers attached to the pinnacles flapped and floated in the breeze. Where the valley narrowed to a gorge in front of the castle was a huge black mass, divided by a white road; this mass Conrad presently made out to be a great crowd of people ranged on either side of the highway; soldiers on horseback posted at the corners and at regular intervals along the track were keeping the road clear, while along it in fours marched heralds blowing trumpets, and moving so slowly they scarcely seemed to move at all.

All at once the trumpeters halted, turned, stepped back and lined the road, their trumpets still extended. There was a pause in which nothing seemed to move; the breeze held its breath, the flags, hanging straight down, looked little thicker than their poles. Then, in the mouth of the long white channel appeared four men on horseback, followed at some distance by a single horseman, whose uniform glittered as though with jewels and on whose helmet was a great white plume. His head was slightly bent, whether in pride or humility, Conrad could not tell; perhaps he was acknowledging the cheers of the spectators, who had broken into frenzied movement, waving their arms and flinging their hats into the air.

So, in the heart of a welcome he could never have known before, he proceeded, until the whole crowd, and Conrad with it, had stared their fill at him, and the first flight of steps seemed only a few yards away. Exactly what happened then Conrad never remembered. There was a movement in the face of the living rock, a wrinkling and crumbling, and a drift of powdery smoke flung up into the air. A hole appeared in the hillside, and out of it came a head — a snake-like head, blacker than the hole it issued from, solid as ebony, large as the shadow of a cloud.

It writhed this way and that on its thick round neck, then suddenly darted forward. The crowd gave way on either hand, leaving in the centre a bulging space like an egg. Conrad saw the plumed horseman look back over his shoulder. That way lay safety; but he preferred not to save himself. Conrad did not wait to see him ride to his death; his last impression of the scene, before he took to his heels, was of a sudden hurricane that caught the face of the castle and stripped it bare of every flag, carpet and tapestry that emblazoned it.

Ill news travels fast, and thus it was that when night fell, Conrad's absence from home was scarcely noticed. 'What can have happened to the boy?' his mother asked more than once, but nobody took the matter up; they were too busy, the brothers and their friends, discussing the awful fate that had overtaken Princess Hermione's suitor. As they all talked at once, I had better give the substance of what they said. The Princess was to have been betrothed that day to the heir of a neighbouring monarch. He was a handsome young man, gallant and brave, an excellent match in every way.

'Had the Princess ever seen him?' asked Conrad's mother.

'How does that affect the matter?' exclaimed her husband. 'The alliance would have made us the strongest nation upon earth. Who will want to marry her now?'

'There will be plenty,' said Leo promptly. 'The Princess is but seventeen, and the most beautiful woman in the world.'

Nobody denied this, for it was known to be true. The Princess's beauty was so great it had already become a proverb. The men of other countries, when they wanted to describe a beautiful woman, said she was as lovely as a rose, or as the day, or as a star; but the people of this country, if they wanted to praise something, said it was as beautiful as Princess Hermione. She was so beautiful that anything she did, even speaking, made her less lovely, ruffled her beauty, as it were; so she did little and spoke seldom. Also she rarely went about in public, it was unfair to people, they could not help falling in love with her. So retiring was her nature that ordinary folk like Conrad and his brothers knew little about her except that she was lovely.

'Of course,' said Leo, 'someone will have to go properly armed to fight this dragon. That poor fellow didn't have a chance in his fine clothes. The king may call out the militia; or perhaps they'll just stop its hole up and starve it out.'

'I'm afraid it will be a great shock to the Princess,' their mother said. Thereupon they fell to arguing as to where the Princess could have been when the Dragon burst out from the cliff and devoured her luck-less suitor. One said she had been seen at a window; another that she was praying in the chapel. Of course it was all hearsay, but they defended their versions with great vigour. At last their father, tired of the fruitless argument, observed:

'I don't suppose she was anywhere in particular.'

'Why, she must have been somewhere,' they protested.

'Well, I've told you what I think,' said he; and at that moment Conrad came in.

He expected a beating for being so late, and at any other time he might have got it. But to-night, so great was the excitement, his tardy arrival was treated as something of a joke. To turn their attention away from his lateness he meant to tell them, at once, the story of what he had seen in the wood—he had got it by heart. But no sooner had he begun than, partly from exhaustion but more from sickness as the details came up before his mind, he turned faint and had to stop. His brothers laughed at him, and returned to their own pet theories of what happened at the castle. Conrad felt disappointed. Though coming home had taken him twice as long as going, it had all been a marvellous adventure, which he thought his parents and brothers would clamour to hear about! Whereas Leo hardly took any interest in his story, and even Rudolph said that from such a position he couldn't have seen anything with certainty. Just because they were grown up they did not believe his experiences could matter to anyone. They went on discuss-ing how many people besides the Prince the Dragon had eaten, and what had happened to the torrent of black blood it was supposed to have emitted—things they knew nothing about. What a tame ending to an exciting day!

Of course, the court went into mourning, and a general fast was proclaimed, for it was rightly decided to neglect nothing that might lead to the Dragon's destruction. But from the first the Prince's would-be avengers were faced by an almost insuperable obstacle. The Dragon had utterly disappeared, leaving no trace; even the hole by which it came out had closed up; and professional mountaineers tied to ropes searched the face of the rock with pickaxes and even micro-scopes, to find an opening, without success. The very wall-flowers that the Princess was reported to be so fond of, bloomed there just as before; and popular opinion became irritated against the experts who, it said, were looking in the wrong place and deliberately prolonging their job. Short of blasting the rock, which would have endangered the castle, every means was tried to make the Dragon come out. A herald was sent, quaking with fright, to ask it to state its terms; because those learned in dragonology declared that in the past dragons had been appeased by an annual sacrifice of men and maidens. When the Dragon made no reply the herald was instructed to play upon its vanity, and issue a formal challenge on behalf of one or other of the most redoubtable champions in the country: let it name a day and settle the matter by single combat. Still the Dragon made no sign, and the herald, emboldened by this display of cowardice, said that since it was such a poor spirited thing he was ready to fight it himself, or get his little brother to do so. But the Dragon took no notice at all.

As the weeks lengthened into months without any demonstration by the Dragon, public confidence grew apace. One circumstance especially fostered this. It was feared that the neighbouring monarch who had so unluckily lost his eldest son would demand compensation, possibly with threats. But his attitude proved unexpectedly conciliatory. He absolved them of all negligence, he said; no one could be forearmed against a Dragon; and his son had met a gallant death on behalf (as it were) of the most beautiful lady in the world. After this handsome declaration it was hoped that he himself might come forward as a candidate for Princess Hermione's hand, for he was a widower. But he did not.

Suitors were not lacking, however; indeed, since the appearance of the Dragon they had multiplied enormously. The fame of that event went aboard, carrying the Princess's name into remote countries where even the rumour of her beauty had failed to penetrate. Now she was not only beautiful, she was unfortunate: the Dragon, some said, was the price she had paid for her beauty. All this, combined with the secrecy which made her way of life a matter of speculation, invested the Princess with an extraordinary glamour. Everyone in the land, even the humblest, wanted to do something for her, they knew not what. Daily she received sackfuls of letters, all telling the same tale: that she was the most wonderful of women, that the writer adored her and wished that he, not the Prince, had had the honour of dying for her. A few even expressed the hope that the Dragon would reappear, so that they might put their devotion to the test.

But of course no one believed that it really would. Some who had not been eyewitnesses declared that the Dragon was an hallucination; that the Prince had just died of joy upon finding himself at last so near the Princess, and that the spectators, drunk with excitement, had imagined the rest. The majority felt confident for a different reason. Dragons, like comets and earthquakes, were things of rare occurrence. We know little about them, they argued, but at any rate we can be sure of this: if we have seen *one* dragon in our lives, we are not likely to see another. Many carried this argument a step further, and maintained that the kingdom had never been so safe from visitation by dragons as it was now; it had got the Dragon over, so to speak.

Before eighteen months were up the Dragon had passed into a joke. In effigy it was dragged round at fairs and processions, and made to perform laughable antics. Writers in the newspapers, when they wanted to describe a groundless fear, or a blessing in disguise, referred to it as 'Princess Hermione's Dragon'. Such as gave the monster serious thought congratulated themselves that it had come and gone without doing them any personal harm. Factories sprang up and business flourished, and in the tide of national prosperity, a decent period having elasped, another suitor presented himself for the honour of winning Princess Hermione's hand.

He came of a royal house scarcely less distinguished (the newspapers said more distinguished) than his predecessor's. Preparations for his reception were made on a grander scale than before, to illustrate the growing resources of the country, and they were made on a completely different plan, so that there might be no question of comparison with the former ceremony. One alteration was this: at the instance of the Minister of War, who said it would stimulate recruiting, a detachment of machine-gunners, armed with a new type of gun and carrying many rounds of blank ammunition, was posted on a convenient ledge commanding the spot where the Dragon had broken out. And there was to be one further change. The Princess's first suitor, when he realized his danger and turned to face the Dragon, had cried out 'Dearest Hermione!' or something to that effect, some protestation of loyalty and love; he had not time to say much, but nobody could recollect his exact words. The new pretendant proposed, and his idea was universally applauded, that he should kneel at the foot of the steps and make a little speech, half a prayer, amplifying the sentiments of adoration and devotion that imminent death had wrung from the lips of his predecessor.

And so, when the day came, the people assembled to enjoy the spectacle in greater numbers than before. They were in the highest spirits, for the ceremony had a double appeal: it was to celebrate the betrothal of their beloved Princess, and her deliverance from the

Dragon. Salvoes from the machine-gun emplacements above their heads, mingling with the strains of martial music and the caterwauling of private instruments, raised their excitement to frenzy. The silence in which the Prince kneeled down to do homage to his bride-to-be was painful in its intensity. But no sooner had the last words passed his lips than there came a rumbling roar, a convulsion in the cliff, and the poor wretch was whirled aloft between the Dragon's jaws, to disappear in the mysterious recesses of the hillside.

The scene that followed was indescribable, and for a week, throughout the length and breadth of the kingdom, panic reigned. Frantic efforts were made to explain the causes of the calamity in the wickedness of individuals or in the mismanagement of the country. Impostors appeared and won a short hour of notoriety and influence by declaring that so-and-so was the culprit; and many innocent persons whose only fault was that they were uglier or richer or somehow different from the rest, perished at the hands of the mob. The government, more composed, arranged a few judicial executions, among the sufferers being the officers who had served the machine-gunners with blank ammunition. Even the King was covertly censured, and not allowed to contribute to the enormous indemnity which the Prime Minister, in the name of the country, handed over to the dead Prince's father: a sum so large that it had to be raised by a wholesale increase of taxation.

Only the Princess escaped blame. As before, she was alone, no one knew exactly where, at the precise moment of the catastrophe; but when she was found, a few minutes later, half-swooning in her room, her courage impressed everyone. She was soon able to write with her own hand a letter of condolence to the man who had so nearly been her father-in-law; when published in the newspapers, its eloquent phrases touched all hearts. Most miserable of women, she said, she had been the means of bringing death to two brave men—the second perhaps even more promising than the first. But what raised such a fury of protest was her concluding sentence—that she thought she must retire from the world. From all quarters of the country came letters begging her not to, so numerous that special mail-trains had to be run.

There was no difficulty in finding fresh champions for the Princess; her fame had increased with her misfortunes. She had never been so popular. Public confidence was reinvigorated by the verdict of military experts, who asserted that the disaster could not have happened if the machine-gunners had been properly armed. 'Give it a few rounds rapid,' they said, 'and we shan't be troubled by it any more.' The populace believed them. There had been too much muddling along; preparations for the Princess's coming betrothal must be put in the hands of the military. The commander-in-chief announced that no member of the general public would be admitted to the ceremony, for the Dragon, though its days were now numbered, was still not to be trifled with. The Prince's escort (he had already been chosen) was to be formed exclusively of picked troops, drilled to perfection and armed with the latest weapons. As they marched along the valley to take up their positions, the sun shone down on thousands of steel helmets: they looked invincible.

Alas, alas. The Prince had no sooner voiced his passionate plea than the hillside quaked and the Dragon darted out. It was warmly welcomed. Ten thousand soft-nosed rifle bullets must have struck it, and volleys of machine-gun fire, but in vain. The cruel eyes never even blinked. One satisfaction it missed, however. The firing continued long after the Prince was in mid-air. He must have been riddled with bullets, stone-dead, before the Dragon got him into its lair. He had been killed by his own defenders, a possibility that had never entered into the calculations of the military authorities.

To chronicle the events of the next two years is a grievous task, and one that the historian would gladly skip. The country went through a miserable time. The supply of eligible Princes would not last for ever, so it was decided to accept the offers of champions who, though of good birth, were more remarkable for valour than for rank. Supposing it did not fall to the spear of the first, seven different warriors were to engage the Dragon on seven successive days. If it survived these encounters, it would at any rate be tired, and in no fit state to engage the Prince of royal blood, though of no great personal prowess, who was to attempt it on the eighth day. But the Dragon was not exhausted at all; it seemed to have profited from practice, and found the Royal Prince as easy a prey as his seven predecessors.

So ended the first phase. The country's nobility shed its blood in gallons and still volunteers pressed forward, drawn from its thinning ranks. But then began an agitation, founded partly on democratic feeling, partly on the devotion which every man in the country worthy of the name, aye, and many outside it, cherished for the Princess Hermione: why should the glory of her rescue be confined to a privileged class? The King gave his consent; the Chamberlain's office was nearly stampeded; and at last a blacksmith, a redoubtable fellow, was selected as the People's Champion against the Dragon.

Of course there was no thought of his marrying her, nor did he presume to such an honour. As he stood at the foot of the steps accompanied only by a handful of friends who came at their own risk (the public had long since been excluded) he would gladly have allayed his nervousness by saying a few words, if not of love to the Princess at least of defiance to the Dragon. But he was not allowed to speak; and this, much as he resented it at the time, undoubtedly saved his life; for the Dragon did not condescend to appear.

No, its hate, rage, and lust of blood were clearly reserved for those who really loved the Princess and were in a position to marry her. The Dragon was not the enemy of the people, but the enemy of the Princess.

As soon as this was realized, there was obviously only one thing to do, and the King gave his consent to it, though sorely against his will. Anyone, of whatever station in life, who could kill the Dragon, should marry the Princess and have half the kingdom as well.

As always when a last desperate step is taken, hope surged up to greet the new proposal. It was obviously the right solution; why had no one thought of it before, and saved all this bloodshed? Enthusiasm ran high; combats were of almost daily occurrence; and in each one, though the upshot was always the same, the newspapers (seeing that they ran no risk, the public was again admitted to the scene) found some encouraging circumstance: the Dragon had lost a tooth, or its inky crest was streaked with grey, or it was a second late in appearing, or it was fat and slow with good living, or it had grinned and looked almost benevolent. The unfortunate heroes had displayed this one a neat piece of foot-work, that, a shrewd thrust which might have pierced the side of a ship: while they were all commended for some original phrase, some prettily-turned compliment in the address to the Princess.

Not the least part of the whole ordeal was the framing of this preliminary speech; it was the only way by which the competitors could measure their skill against each other, since their performances against the Dragon hardly differed at all. There was no doubt the Dragon disliked hearing the Princess praised; the more ardent and graceful the language in which she was wooed, the more vigorous was its onslaught.

Leo, Conrad's brother, was one of the first to volunteer, but his actual encounter with the Dragon tarried because he lacked scholarship to put into words the love that burned in him. But his production, to judge from the zest with which the monster gobbled him up, must have had some literary merit. Conrad missed his fiery, impatient brother. Little had his parents realized that the Dragon, which had seemed an affair for Kings and Queens and Governments, would take its toll from them. But their pride in their son's sacrifice upheld them, and lessened their grief.

Conrad, however, grew more despondent daily. He dreaded lest Rudolph, his favourite brother, should take it into his head to challenge the Dragon. Rudolph was less hot-headed than Leo and—surely a great safeguard—he was engaged to be married. Married men were prohibited (or, as Conrad put it to himself, exempted) from Dragon-baiting—though more than one, concealing his true condition, had gone out to meet a bachelor's death.

Conrad lost no opportunity of urging the charms of Charlotte, his brother's sweetheart; in and out of season he proclaimed them and begged Rudolph to marry her. In his anxiety for his brother's safety he more than once let drop a disparaging remark about the Princess, comparing her unfavourably to Charlotte. Rudolph told him to shut up or he would get himself into trouble: a madman who had spoken disrespectfully of the Princess had been torn to pieces by the mob.

'Of course the Princess is beautiful,' Conrad admitted, 'but she is fair: you told me you only admired dark women. Promise me you will marry Charlotte before the month is out.'

'How can I?' asked Rudolph, 'when I've no money and no home to take her to?'

Conrad knew that this was not strictly true; his brother was a gay young man, but he had some money laid by. Conrad, though he earned little, spent nothing at all.

'If you marry her a fortnight from to-day,' he begged, 'you shall have all my savings, and I will be a forester instead of going to the University.'

It cost him something to say this, but Rudolph answered with his light laugh:

'Keep your money, my dear Conrad, you will want it when your turn comes to fight the Dragon.'

This was not very encouraging, and Conrad began to ask himself was there no other way of keeping Rudolph out of harm's reach. The King had offered an enormous prize to anyone who could suggest a solution to the Dragon problem, and many women, cripples, elderly men and confirmed husbands had sent in suggestions. One was that the intending suitor should visit the castle in disguise. This was turned down because, even if the man got safely in, the Dragon would still be at large. Another proposed that the Royal Magician should give place to one more competent. To this the Home Secretary replied that it was a bad plan to change horses in mid-stream; the Magician had a world-wide reputation; he had performed many noteworthy feats in the past, he knew the lay-out of the castle as no one else did, and he was a close friend of Princess Hermione: it would be cruel to deprive her of his presence.

Most of the proposals, though meant helpfully, only put the authorities' backs up, implying as they did some dissatisfaction with the way things were being handled. One malcontent even dared to remark that at this rate the Princess would never get married. The newspapers made fun of him and he lost his job.

'If only I could get *inside* the castle,' thought Conrad, 'I might be able to do something. But I shall have to be very tactful.'

He began to write, but the pen would not answer to his thoughts. It seemed to have a will of its own, which was struggling against his. Instead of the valuable suggestion he wanted to make, a message of very different import kept appearing on the paper, in broken phrases like, 'my life to your service,' 'no better death than this.' Tired of trying to control it, he let the pen run on; when it stopped, he found he had written a little love-address to the Princess, very like those printed between heavy black lines (almost every day now) in the memorial columns of the newspapers. Puzzled, he threw the thing aside and applied himself to his task. Now it went better; he signed it, wrote 'The Princess Hermione' on the envelope and took it to the post. It would be some days before it reached her, if it ever did; she must have so many letters to deal with.

When he got home he found Rudolph in the room. He was standing by the table holding something in his hand.

'Ha, ha!' said he, 'I've found you out.'

Conrad could not imagine what he meant.

'Yes,' went on Rudolph, putting his hands behind his back . 'You've been deceiving me. You're in love with the Princess. You've been trying to persuade me not to fight the Dragon because you want the glory of killing it yourself.'

Rudolph was laughing, but Conrad cried out in agitation, 'No, no, you don't understand.'

'Well, listen then,' said Rudolph, and he began to read Conrad's declaration of love to the Princess; mockingly at first, then more seriously, and finally with a break in his voice and tears standing in his eyes.

They were silent for a moment, then Conrad held out his hand for the paper. But Rudolph would not part with it.

'Don't be silly,' Conrad pleaded. 'Give it to me.'

'What do you want it for?' asked Rudolph.

'I want to burn it!' cried Conrad recklessly.

'No, no!' said Rudolph, half laughing and gently pushing his brother away. 'I must have it—it may come in useful—who knows.'

He went out, taking the paper with him. Conrad felt uncomforable; somehow he guessed he had done a silly thing.

He had. Two days later Rudolph casually announced that he had sent in his name as a candidate for the privilege of freeing Princess Hermione from her tormentor and that his application had been accepted.

'It's fixed for Thursday,' he remarked gaily. 'Poor old Dragon.'

His mother burst into tears, his father left the room and did not come back for an hour; but Conrad sat in his chair, without noticing what was going on round him. At last he said:

'What about Charlotte?'

'Oh,' said Rudolph airily, 'she's anxious for me to go. She's not like you pretend to be. She's sorry for the Princess. "I expected you'd want to go," she said to me. "I shall be waiting for you when you come back."'

'Was that all?' asked Conrad.

'Oh, she gave me her blessing.'

Conrad pondered. 'Did you tell her you were in love with the Princess?' he asked at length.

Rudolph hesitated. 'I couldn't very well tell her that, could I? It wouldn't have been kind. Besides, I'm not really in love with the Princess, of course: that's the difficulty. It was that speech you wrote — you know' (Conrad nodded) 'made me feel I was. I shall just try to be in love with her as long as the combat lasts. If I wasn't, you know, the Dragon wouldn't come out and I should miss my chance. But,' he added more cheerfully, 'I shall recite your address, and that will deceive it.'

'And then?'

'Oh, then I shall just come back and marry Charlotte. She understands that. You can give us some of your money if you like. I won't take it all. I'm not greedy.'

He went off whistling. Conrad's heart sank. He knew his brother's moods: this careless manner betokened that his mind was made up.

Who the first founder of the royal castle was, and when he built it, no one precisely knew. The common people ascribed its origin to the whim of some god or hero; and professional historians, though they scoffed at this idea, had no definite theory to put in its place—at least none that they all agreed upon. But the castle had been many times rebuilt, at the bidding of changing fashions, and of the present edifice it was doubtful whether any part was more than a thousand years old. Its position on the solitary rock, defended by precipices on all sides save one, gave it so much natural strength that it was generally considered impregnable. According to common report, there were more rooms hollowed out of the rock than built of stones and mortar. Later architects, taking advantage of this, had concentrated their efforts on giving a grace and elegance to the exterior that no other fortress could boast, adorning it with turrets and balconies of an aery delicacy and windows embellished with the richest tracery their imaginations could devise. Windows that generously admitted the sun into wide, spacious rooms, the damasks and brocades of which, thus exposed to the noonday glare, had need of constant renewal.

But the Princess Hermione had chosen for her favourite sitting-room a chamber in another part of the castle, so deeply embedded in the rock that the light of day reached it only by an ingenious system of reflectors. Nor could you tell what the season was, for a fire burned there all the year round. The room was not easy of access, nor did the Princess mean it to be. There was one known way into it, by a narrow, winding stair; but if report could be believed, there were several ways out—dark passages leading probably to bolt-holes in the rock. For years no one had troubled to explore them, but they had a fascination for the Princess, who knew them by heart and sometimes surprised her parents by appearing suddenly before them, apparently from nowhere.

She was sitting by the fireside, deep in a chair, and looking at some papers, which neither the firelight nor the twilight reflected down from above quite allowed her to read. Suddenly a shadow fell across the page and she could see nothing. The Princess looked up: a man was standing in front of her, shutting out the firelight; she knew no more than you or I how he had got there, but she was not surprised to see him.

'Well,' said the magician, for it was he. 'Are you still unsatisfied?'

The Princess turned her head, hidden by the chair-back, invisible to us; but the shadow of her features started up on the wall, a shadow so beautiful that (report said) it would not disappear when the Princess turned again, but clung on with a life of its own, until dissolved by the magician.

'Yesterday, at any rate, was a success,' the Princess murmured.

'Will you read me what he said?' asked the magician.

'Give me some light,' she commanded, and the room began to fill with radiance.

The Princess turned over the papers in her lap.

'Rudolph, Rudolph,' she muttered. 'Here he is – Do you really want to hear what the poor oaf says?'

'Is it like the others?'

'Exactly the same, only a particularly fine specimen.'

Though she tried to make her voice sound unconcerned, the Princess spoke with a certain relish; and her silhouette, stretched upon the wall, trembled and changed and became less pleasing. She turned and noticed it.

'Oh, there's that thing at its tricks again,' she sighed irritably. 'Take it away.'

The shadow faded.

'Well,' she said, settling herself again in the depths of her chair. 'Here it is.'

Her voice, slightly mimicking the peasants' burr, was delicious to hear.

' "Most Gracious Princess: Men have been known to pity the past and dread the future, never, it seems to me, with much reason until now. But now I say, in the past there was no Princess Hermione; in the future, in the far future, dearest angel (may you live for ever), there will be none; none to live for, none to die for. Therefore I say, Wretched Past! Miserable Future! And I bless this present hour in which Life and Death are one, one act in your service, one poem in your honour!'

The Princess paused: then spoke in her own voice.

'Didn't he deserve eating?'

'Your Highness, he did.'

'But now,' she continued in a brisker tone, 'I've got something different to read to you. Altogether different. In fact I've never received anything like it before.'

The shadow, which, like a dog that dreads reproof but cannot bear its banishment, had stolen back to the wall, registered a tiny frown on the Princess's forehead.

For the letter was certainly an odd one. The writer admitted frankly that he was not brave, nor strong, nor skilled in arms. He was afraid of a mouse, so what could he do against a dragon? The Princess was a lady of high intelligence, she would be the first to see the futility of such a sacrifice. She was always in his thoughts, and he longed to do some tiny service for her. He could not bear to think of her awaiting alone the issue of the combat between her champion and the Dragon. The strain must be terrible. He would count himself ever honoured if she would allow him to bear her company, even behind a screen, even outside the door, during those agonising moments.

'What a pity I can't grant his request!' said the Princess, when she had finished. 'I like him. I like him for not wanting to offer up his life for me. I like him for thinking that women have other interests than watching men gratify their vanity by running into danger. I like him because he credits me with intelligence. I like him because he considers my feelings, and longs to be near me when there is no glory to be gained by it. I like him because he would study my moods and find out what I needed, and care for me for all the day long, even when I was in no particular danger. I like him because he would love me without a whole population of terrified half-wits egging him on! I like him for a thousand things—I think I love him.'

'Your Highness! Your Highness!' said the magician, stirring uneasily. 'Remember the terms of the spell.'

'Repeat them: I have forgotten.'

> 'If he loves you
> And you love not,
> Your suitor's life's
> Not worth a jot,'

sang the magician cheerfully.

'That's all we need to know,' sighed the Princess, who really recollected the spell perfectly. 'It always happens that way, and always will. But go on.'

> 'If he loves you
> And you love him,
> I cannot tell
> What Chance may bring,'

chanted the magician in a lower tone.

'But if the "he" were Conrad,' said the Princess teasingly, 'surely you could make a guess? And now for the last condition.'

The magician's voice sank to a whisper:

'If you love him
And he reject you,
A thousand spells
Will not protect you.'

'Ha! Ha!' cried the Princess, rocking with laughter so that the shadow on the wall flickered like a butterfly over a flower, 'all the same I love this Conrad!'

'He's but a lad, your Highness, barely turned seventeen.'

'The best age—I love him.'

'He's a slothful sort, his letter shows; a dreamer, not a man.'

'I love him.'

'While you were reading, I summoned his likeness here—he is ill-favoured—has lost a front tooth.'

'Regular features are my abhorrence—I love him.'

'He is sandy-haired and freckled and untidy in his dress.'

'Never mind, I love him.'

'He is self-willed and obstinate; his parents can do nothing with him.'

'I could: I love him.'

'He likes insects and crawling things: his pockets are full of spiders and centipedes.'

'I shall love them for his sake.'

'He cares for waterfalls and flowers and distant views.'

'I love him more than ever!'

'But,' said the magician, suddenly grave, 'I'm not sure that he loves you.'

'Ah!' cried the Princess, jubilation in her voice. 'I love him most of all for that!'

There was a pause. The shadow on the wall swooned from the oppression of its beauty, and slid to the floor.

'But of course he loves me,' the Princess murmured to herself. 'Everyone does, and so must he.'

She looked up at the magician for confirmation; but he had gone. Then she saw that something was missing.

'Magician! Magician!' she cried. 'You've taken my Conrad's letter. I want it back!'

But the magician, if he heard her, did not answer.

Conrad's suggestion, when published in the papers, produced a disagreeable impression. It was called mawkish and unmanly and insulting to the dignity of the Princess. *Forester's Son Wants To Be Male*

Nurse, ran the headline. However, the letter was so inept, it could not be taken seriously. Conrad was evidently a little weak in the head. The Princess had all the virtues, but especially two: courage and unselfishness. Naturally she would have liked company in the hour of trial—and many were ready to offer it, from the King downwards: she had no need of the services of a woodman's unlicked cub. But she preferred to spare her friends the sight of her mental and physical anguish. It was the best she could do, she said in her gracious, winning way, to soften the burden a miserable fate had cast, through her, upon her countrymen. So she retired and encountered her dark destiny alone, with the aid of such courage as she could summon. Conrad, the article concluded charitably, was no doubt too thick in the head to understand such delicacy of feeling; but surely his parents might have stopped him from making a fool of himself in public: the noble example of his brothers might have stopped him.

Conrad was too miserable after Rudolph's death to mind cutting a sorry figure in the public eye. Fortunately for him he had few acquaintances and spent much time in the woods alone; so at first he was scarcely aware of his unpopularity. But the neighbours were quick to point out to his parents what a dishonour their son had brought on the district; it has set the whole province by the ears, they said, and started a government inquiry as to why our part of the world has been so backward in sending volunteers to fight the Dragon. This touched to the quick many people who had never heard of Conrad, and who now realized they might be called on to display their heroism in front of the castle, whether they would or no; for it was whispered that there might be an official round-up of likely young men.

His father and mother did their best to keep all this from Conrad. They were hurt and puzzled by his action, but they knew what a blow his brother's death had been, and did not want to distress him needlessly. But as he walked about the woods, especially at night-time, he would hear a stone go whizzing by him, or see a stick break at his feet; and demanding the cause of these attentions from one of the culprits, a lad rather smaller than himself, he was told very fully and in words that hurt. His foolish letter had got the place a bad name and he himself was this, that, and the other.

Conrad tried to take no notice and go his own way. But after five years in increasing calamity, the temper of the people had changed. True, the Princess found champions enthusiastic as ever; but they were men of a different kidney, always discovering good reasons why others should go out to battle and they themselves remain at home. These busybodies could not let Conrad alone, and Conrad, who was enjoying life far less than five years ago had seemed possible, saw there was only one thing to do. He must challenge the Dragon himself.

He did not go into training, as his brothers had done, with walks before breakfast and nourishing, unappetising food; he did not, if he chanced to spy a fantastic-looking bush, set spurs to his horse and with a wild cry aim at it with his axe. Had he made the experiment he would have fallen off, for his horsemanship had not improved. Nor did he spend his savings on the purchase of costly weapons, and a military equipment of plume, breastplate, and golden epaulette, to charm the spectator's eye. His preparations were quite simple and only one of them cost him thought. This was the speech he would have to make at the foot of the steps.

He knew that it must be a declaration of love, or the Dragon would ignore it. But since Rudolph's death, his indifference to the Princess had deepened into positive dislike, almost hatred. He could not bring himself to say he loved her, even without meaning it. So he set himself to devise a form of words which would sound to the greedy, stupid Dragon sufficiently like praise, but to him, the speaker, would mean something quite different. When this was done, there still remained one thing: to leave his savings to Charlotte, his brother's fiancée. These last few weeks, when no one had a kind word for him, and even his parents seemed neutral, she had gone out of her way to be nice to him.

A letter came written on parchment under a great red seal, calling him by flattering and endearing terms, and fixing three o'clock as the hour for the contest. Conrad started early, before the November morning was well astir. He was riding the horse his father had lent him: the Dragon did not fancy horsemeat. Conrad would have felt safer on foot, but besides his luncheon he had an axe to carry, and the castle was seventeen miles away. He was wearing his old suit, as it seemed a pity to spoil his best one. As he went along, mostly walking, but occasionally trotting if the horse stumbled, people stopped work or came out of their houses to look at him. They knew why he was there and though they did not cheer or clap, they did not insult or ridicule him, which was some comfort.

But when six hours later the portals of the ravine opened before him, the castle burst into view, and the whole scene branded so long on his memory renewed itself, and at such dreadfully close quarters, his heart sank. He had not been able to eat his luncheon and still carried it (having been taught not to throw food away) in a satchel hung round his neck. This embarrassed him, for he thought the onlookers would laugh. But at present there were very few onlookers; the spectacle had become so common, it hardly awakened any interest.

Soon he was near enough to the flight of stairs to be able to distinguish the separate steps, and the crowd began to thicken somewhat. A little boy blew a sudden blast on a tin trumpet in the very ear of Conrad's horse. It pranced about in alarm, and Conrad, clutching wildly at its mane and neck, was ignominiously thrown. He was rather shaken, but not too much shaken to hear the crowd laugh and ask each other what sort of champion was this, who couldn't sit on his horse properly.

Conrad dared not remount his horse for fear of falling off; and a good-natured man offered to lead it for him, a few paces in the rear, so that he could get on if he liked. He was glad to be rid of it on such easy terms. But he was aware of cutting an awkward figure on foot, in dusty clothes, trailing an axe which he tried to use as a walking-stick. The crowd, who liked its champions gay, reckless, and handsome, received him coldly. He felt they grudged their admiration and withheld their good-will. Once at school, through hard work and industry, he had won a prize. To receive it he had to pass through a long lane of his schoolfellows. They applauded for a moment—it was the rule—and then fell to staring at him critically and resentfully. He remembered the scene.

But in the castle the Princess Hermione, her face pressed against the window-pane, watched every inch of his progress. 'It's he, it's Conrad. I knew it was!' she cried. 'You must let me wait another moment, Magician. Just one more moment!'

Conrad was trying to distract his mind by repeating over and over the address he meant to deliver to the Princess. When he was nervous his memory always betrayed him. He had a copy of the speech in his cap, to read if his mind became a blank. He wished he could do something to propitiate the spectators, besides smiling nervously at them; he knew that his tactics with the Dragon would shock them, for he carried in his pocket a phial of chloroform, wrapped in a handkerchief; he meant to break and wave this in the Dragon's face before using the steel. Suddenly he was aware that the horse was no longer following. The man had drawn it to one side and was standing in front of it, his hands over its eyes. The crowd had fallen back. Conrad had reached the steps. The castle clock struck three.

He knelt down, took off his cap, and said:

'Most Wonderful Princess,

'This is a moment I have long looked forward to, with what feelings you best may guess. The many who have knelt before me have been eloquent in your praise; who am I to add a syllable to their tributes? But I know it is not the words you value, most discerning Princess, but the heart that inspires them.'

At this moment the rock heaved, the Dragon came forth and hung over Conrad with lolling tongue. He could feel its hot breath on his cheek. The words died on his lips, he stared wildly round, then remembered the cue in his cap, and went on without looking up.

'All have loved you well, but some (dare I say it?) have voiced their love less happily than others. They said: "This my love, though great, is but an acorn that will grow with years into an oak." But when I remember what you have done for me: rescued me from the dull round of woodland life; raised me from obscurity into fame; transformed me from a dreamer into a warrior, an idler into a hunter of Dragons; deigned to make yourself the limit of my hopes and the end of my endeavours — I have no words to thank you, and I cannot love you more than I do now!'

The more sensitive in the crowd had already turned away. The hardier spirits, with eyes glued to the scene, saw an unfamiliar thing. The Dragon swayed, dipped, hesitated. Its tongue licked the dust at Conrad's feet. He, who had hitherto done nothing to defend himself, drew out the handkerchief and threw it awkwardly but with lucky aim, right into the Dragon's scarlet mouth. The beast roared, snorted, coughed, whimpered, and in a moment looked less terrible. Conrad, taking heart, lifted the axe and struck at the scaly neck towering above him. It was a clumsy blow, unworthy of a woodman, but it found its mark. A torrent of green blood gushed out, evaporating before it reached the ground. The Dragon's claws lost their hold on the rock, and it sprawled outwards, exposing a long, black tubular body no one had seen till now. The neck dropped to within easy reach of Conrad's axe, and encouraged by the frenzied cheering behind him, he hacked at it again and again. Its balance lost, the Dragon seemed bewildered and helpless; a child could have tackled it, it was as passive under the axe as a felled tree. Conrad seemed to be having matters all his own way, when suddenly the Dragon made a convulsive movement and wriggled backwards into the rock, which closed over it. Conrad was left in possession of the field.

The crowd stopped cheering; no one quite knew what to do, least of all Conrad, who was still standing by the steps, half-dazed. That the Dragon had retired wounded and discomfited was plain to all; but perhaps it was only biding its time, gathering its strength for a fresh attack. It had so long seemed invincible; they could not believe it was dead.

But when seconds passed and nothing happened, they began to surge round Conrad, weeping and laughing and trying to take his hand. From the castle, too, came signs of rejoicing, a faint cheering and fluttering of handkerchiefs, then a full-throated roar and flags waved from every window. A little throng began to form at the top of the steps, the King in the centre, his sceptre in his hand and his crown on his head. They were all laughing and talking together; it was clear they had never expected Conrad to win, they had made no plans for his reception, and were all rather enjoying the informal meeting. They called and beckoned to Conrad to come up; but he did not understand, so the crowd came behind and pushed him. As he moved up, the King came down, alone; they met in midstair, the King kissed Conrad and embraced him, and they walked up to the castle arm-in-arm.

'And now I must present you to my daughter,' the King was saying as they reached the top, and the members of the Court were pressing forward with shining eyes to congratulate the victor of the Dragon. 'Where is she? She's away somewhere, she'll come in a minute. Silly child, she's missed all the fun.'

'Hermione! Your Royal Highness!' called the ladies of the Court, in their light, eager voices, peering into the hall, staring up at the windows. And the crowd, nearly ninety feet below, took up the cry, 'Hermione! We want Princess Hermione!' It was an immense crowd now, for all the town was running to the spot, and the volume of sound was terrific. Everyone was delighted with the noise that he or she was making; even the group by the castle door winked and nudged and poked each other in the ribs, while they cried 'Hermione!' at the top of their voices. Only Conrad did not join in the cry.

But still she delayed. The crowd shouted itself hoarse; the ladies of the Court coughed and wrinkled up their faces and looked appealingly at each other; the King frowned slightly, for he felt she ought to be here now; but still the Princess did not come.

Then they all burst out excitedly, 'Where can she be? Let's go and look for her,' while others said, 'No, no, the shock would harm her, we must break it to her gradually.' There was quite a little confusion and uproar of voices arguing this way and that, stirring the general

gaiety to an even higher pitch. They flocked into the castle dividing
hither and thither, their silvery laughter lost among the corridors and
colonnades.

Conrad had been torn from the King's side and hurried into the
building before he knew what he was doing. Several people promised
to show him the way, but when they had gone a little distance, they
forgot about him, and flew off, with shouts of laughter, to join their
own friends. Conrad seemed to be alone in the long dark corridor, but
when he looked round, there was a man standing at the far end of it.
Conrad walked towards him, calling out to him to wait; but the fellow
hurried on, though how he could go like that, his face looking backwards all the time, Conrad did not understand.

Through doors, along passages, down steps they went, always with
the same distance between them, always getting lower and lower;
Conrad felt the cold on his cheeks and hands. At last a door, indistin-
guishable from the surrounding masonry, opened, showing a room.
Conrad followed his guide in, then lost sight of him.

On a couch by the wall lay the Princess, her head turned away, and
in the whiteness of her neck a gash dreadful to behold. On the wall
above her hung the shadow to which her indescribable beauty had
lent a kind of life: it could not long survive her, and just as Conrad
took in the perfection of its loveliness, it faded.

He fell on his knees by the couch. How long he knelt, he could not
tell, but when he looked up, the room was full of people.

'You have killed her,' someone said.

Conrad rose and faced them.

'I did not kill her: I killed the Dragon!'

'Look,' said another voice. 'She has the same wound in her neck.'

'That wound I gave the Dragon.'

'And what is this?' asked a third, pointing to a ball of linen, tightly
grasped in Princess Hermione's outstretched hand. He took it and shook
it out: the smell of chloroform filled the air. A cluster of eyes read the
name in the corner of the handkerchief: it was Conrad's.

'And you poisoned her as well!' they gasped.

'That poison,' said Conrad, 'I gave to the Dragon.'

One or two nodded their heads; but the rest shouted:

'But you *must* have killed her! How else did she die?'

Conrad passed his hand across his face.

'Why should I kill her? I love her,' he said in a broken voice. 'It was
the Dragon I killed.'

Then, as they all gazed at him fascinated, he added:

'But the Dragon was the Princess!'

Immediately there was a terrible hubbub, and to shouts of 'Liar,' 'Murderer,' 'Traitor,' Conrad was hustled from the room and lodged in a neighbouring dungeon. He was released almost immediately and never brought up for trial, though a section of the Press demanded it.

A story was put about that the Princess had somehow met her death defending Conrad from the Dragon; and Conrad, when asked if this was so, would not altogether deny it. His hour of popularity as slayer of the Dragon soon passed, and in its place he incurred the lasting odium of having been somehow concerned in the Princess's death. 'He ought never to have used that chloroform,' was a criticism repeated with growing indignation from mouth to mouth. 'No sportsman would have.' It was a mark of patriotism to make light of the Dragon's misdeeds, for their long continuance redounded little to the country's credit and capacity. They were speedily forgotten, while the fame of Princess Hermione, a national treasure, went mounting ever higher in the hearts of her countrymen. Before the year was out, Conrad heard a man in the street say to his friend:

'What does it matter if the Princess did change herself into a dragon? She only did it for a lark.'

Conrad went back to his home, but he soon received an official intimation that in his own and the common interest, he ought to leave the country. The government would find him a passport and pay his fare. This was all the reward he got for killing the Dragon, but he went gladly enough—the more gladly that Charlotte consented to go with him. She stipulated, however, that they should make their home in a Republic. There they were married and lived happily ever after.

THE ISLAND

H o w well I remembered the summer aspect of Mrs. Santander's island, and the gratefully deciduous trees among the pines of that countryside coming down to the water's edge and over it! How their foliage, sloping to a shallow dome, sucked in the sunlight, giving it back all grey and green! The sea, tossing and glancing, refracted the light from a million spumy points; the tawny sand glared, a monochrome unmitigated by shades; and the cliffs, always bare, seemed to have achieved an unparalleled nudity, every speck on their brown flanks clamouring for recognition.

Now every detail was blurred or lost. In the insufficient, ill-distributed November twilight the island itself was invisible. Forms and outlines survive but indistinctly in the memory; it was hard to believe that the spit of shingle on which I stood was the last bulwark of that huge discursive land-locked harbour, within whose meagre mouth Mrs. Santander's sea-borne territory seemed to ride at anchor. In the summer I pictured it as some crustacean, swallowed by an ill-turned starfish, but unassimilated. How easy it had been to reach it in Mrs. Santander's gay plunging motor-boat! And how inaccessible it seemed now, with the motor-boat fallen, as she had written to tell me, into war-time disuse, with a sea running high and so dark that, save for the transparent but scarcely luminous wave-tips, it looked like an agitated solid. The howling of the wind, and the oilskins in which he was encased, made it hard to attract the ferryman's attention. I shouted to him: 'Can you take me over to the island?'

'No, I can't,' said the ferryman, and pointed to the tumultuous waves in the harbour.

'What are you here for?' I bawled. 'I tell you I must get across; I have to go back to France to-morrow.'

In such circumstances it was impossible to argue without heat. The ferryman turned, relenting a little. He asked querulously in the tone of one who must raise a difficulty at any cost: 'What if we both get drowned?'

What a fantastic objection! 'Nonsense,' I said. 'There's no sea to speak of; anyhow, I'll make it worth your while.'

The ferryman grunted at my unintentional pleasantry. Then, as the landing stage was submerged by the exceptionally high tide, he carried me on his back to the boat, my feet trailing in the water. The man lurched at every step, for I was considerably heavier than he; but at last, waist-deep in water, he reached the boat and turned sideways for me to embark. How uncomfortable the whole business was. Why couldn't Mrs. Santander spend November in London like other people? Why was I so infatuated as to follow her here on the last night of my leave when I might have been lolling in the stalls of a theatre? The craft was behaving oddly, rolling so much that at every other stroke one of the boatman's attenuated seafaring oars would be left high and dry. Once, when we happened to be level with each other, I asked him the reason of Mrs. Santander's seclusion. At the top of his voice he replied: 'Why, they do say she be lovesick. Look out!' he added, for we had reached the end of our short passage and were "standing by" in the succession of breakers. But the ferryman misjudged it. Just as the keel touched the steep shingle bank, a wave caught the boat, twisted it round and half over, and I lost my seat and rolled about in the bottom of the boat, getting very wet.

How dark it was among the trees. Acute physical discomfort had almost made me forget Mrs. Santander. But as I stumbled up the grassy slope I longed to see her.

She was not in the hall to welcome me. The butler, discreetly noticing my condition, said: 'We will see about your things, sir.' I was thankful to take them off, and I flung them about the floor of my bedroom—that huge apartment that would have been square but for the bow-window built on to the end. The wind tore at this window, threatening to drive it in; but not a curtain moved. Soundlessness, I remembered, was characteristic of the house. Indeed, I believe you might have screamed yourself hoarse in that room and not have been heard in the adjoining bathroom. Thither I hastened and wallowed long and luxuriously in the marble bath; deliberately I splashed the water over the side, simply to see it collected and marshalled away down the little grooves that unerringly received it. When I emerged, swathed in hot towels, I found my clothes already dried and pressed. Wonderful household. A feeling of unspeakable well-being descended upon me as, five minutes before dinner-time, I entered the drawing-room. It was empty. What pains Mrs. Santander must be bestowing on her toilette! Was it becoming her chief asset? I wondered. Perish the thought! She had a hundred charms of movement, voice and expression, and yet she defied analysis. She was simply irresistible! How Santander, her impossible husband, could have retired to South America to nurse an injured pride, or as he doubtless called it, an injured honour, passed my comprehension. She had an art to make the most commonplace subject engaging. I remembered having once admired the lighting of the house. I had an odd fancy that it had a quality not found elsewhere, a kind of whiteness, a power of suggesting silence. It helped to give her house its peculiar hush. 'Yes,' she had said, 'and it's all so simple; the sea makes it, just by going in and out!' A silly phrase, but her intonation made it linger in the memory like a charm.

I sat at the piano and played. There were some songs on the music-rest—Wolf, full of strange chords and accidentals so that I couldn't be sure I was right. But they interested me; and I felt so happy that I failed to notice how the time was drawing on—eight o'clock, and dinner should have been at a quarter to. Growing a little restless, I rose and walked up and down the room. One corner of it was in shadow, so I turned on all the lights. I had found it irritating to watch the regular expansion and shrinkage of my shadow. Now I could see everything; but I still felt constrained, sealed up in that admirable room. It was always a shortcoming of mine not to be able to wait patiently. So I wandered into the dining-room and almost thought—such is the power of overstrung anticipation—that I saw Mrs. Santander sitting at the head of the oval table. But it was only an effect of the candlelight. The two places were laid, hers and mine; the glasses with twisty stems were there, such a number of glasses for the two of us! Suddenly I remembered I was smoking and, taking an almond, I left the room to its four candles. I peeped inside the library; it was in darkness, and I realized, as I fumbled for the switch without being able to find it, that I was growing nervous. How ridiculous! Of course, Mrs. Santander wouldn't be in the library and in the dark. Abandoning the search for the switch, I returned to the drawing-room.

I vaguely expected to find it altered, and yet I had ceased to expect to see Mrs. Santander appear at any moment. That always happens when one waits for a person who doesn't come. But there *was* an alteration—in me. I couldn't find any satisfaction in struggling with Wolf; the music had lost its hold. So I drew a chair up to the china-cabinet; it had always charmed me with its figures of Chinamen, those white figures, conventional and stiff, but so smooth and luminous and significant. I found myself wondering, as often before, whether the ferocious pleasure in their expressions was really the Oriental artist's conception of unqualified good humour, or whether they were not, after all, rather cruel people. And this disquieting topic aroused others that I had tried successfully to repress: the exact connotation of my staying in the house as Mrs. Santander's guest, an unsporting little mouse playing when the cat was so undeniably, so effectually away. To ease myself of these obstinate questionings, I leant forward to open the door of the cabinet, intending to distract myself by taking one of the figures into my hands. Suddenly I heard a sound and looked up. A man was standing in the middle of the room.

'I'm afraid the cabinet's locked,' he said.

In spite of my bewilderment, something in his appearance struck me as odd: he was wearing a hat. It was a grey felt hat, and he had an over-coat that was grey too.

'I hope you don't take me for a burglar,' I said, trying to laugh.

'Oh no,' he replied, 'not that.' I thought his eyes were smiling, but his mouth was shadowed by a dark moustache. He was a handsome man. Something in his face struck me as familiar; but it was not an unusual type and I might easily have been mistaken.

In the hurry of getting up I knocked over a set of fire-irons—the cabinet flanked the fireplace—and there was a tremendous clatter. It alarmed and then revived me. But I had a curious feeling of defenceless-ness as I stooped down to pick the fire-irons up, and it was difficult to fix them into their absurd sockets. The man in grey watched my opera-tions without moving. I began to resent his presence. Presently he moved and stood with his back to the fire, stretching out his fingers to the warmth.

'We haven't been introduced,' I said.

'No,' he replied, 'we haven't.'

Then, while I was growing troubled and exasperated by his behavi-our, he offered an explanation. 'I'm the engineer Mrs. Santander calls in now and then to superintend her electric plant. That's how I know my way about. She's so inventive, and she doesn't like to take risks.' He volunteered this. 'And I came in here in case any of the fittings needed adjustment. I see they don't.'

'No,' I said, secretly reassured by the stranger's account of himself; 'but I wish – of course, I speak without Mrs. Santander's authority – I wish you'd have a look at the switches in the library. They're damned inconvenient.' I was so pleased with myself for having compassed the expletive that I scarcely noticed how the engineer's fingers, still avid of warmth, suddenly became rigid.

'Oh, you've been in the library, have you?' he said.

I replied that I had got no further than the door. 'But if you can wait,' I added politely to this superior mechanic who liked to style himself an engineer, 'Mrs. Santander will be here in a moment.'

'You're expecting her?' asked the mechanic.

'I'm staying in the house,' I replied stiffly. The man was silent for several moments. I noticed the refinement in his face, the good cut of his clothes. I pondered upon the physical disability that made it impossible for him to join the army.

'She makes you comfortable here?' he asked; and a physical disturbance, sneezing or coughing, I supposed, seized him, for he took out his handkerchief and turned from me with all the instinct of good breeding. But I felt that the question was one his station scarcely entitled him to make, and ignored it. He recovered himself.

'I'm afraid I can't wait,' he said. 'I must be going home. The wind is dropping. By the way,' he added, 'we have a connection in London. I think I may say it's a good firm. If ever you want an electric plant installed! – I left a card somewhere.' He searched for it vainly. 'Never mind,' he said, with his hand on the door, 'Mrs. Santander will give you all particulars.' Indulgently I waved my hand, and he was gone.

A moment later it seemed to me that he wouldn't be able to cross to the mainland without notifying the ferryman. I rang the bell. The butler appeared. 'Mrs. Santander is very late, sir,' he said.

'Yes,' I replied, momentarily dismissing the question. 'But there's a man, a mechanic or something – you probably know.' The butler looked blank. 'Anyhow,' I said, 'a man has been here attending to the lighting; he wants to go home; would you telephone the boatman to come and fetch him away?'

When the butler had gone to execute my order, my former discomfort and unease returned. The adventure with the engineer had diverted my thoughts from Mrs. Santander. Why didn't she come? Perhaps she had fallen asleep, dressing. It happened to women when they were having their hair brushed. Gertrude was imperious and difficult; her maid might be afraid to wake her. Then I remembered her saying in her letter, 'I shall be an awful fright because I've had to give my maid the sack.' It was funny how the colloquialisms jarred when you saw them in black and white; it was different when she was speaking. Ah, just to hear her voice! Of course, the loss of her maid would hinder her, and account for some delay. Lucky maid, I mused confusedly, to have her hair in your hands! Her image was all before me as I walked aimlessly about the room. Half tranced with the delight of that evocation, I stopped in front of a great bowl, ornamented with dragons, that stood on the piano. Half an hour ago I had studied its interior that depicted terra-cotta fish with magenta fins swimming among conventional weeds. My glance idly sought the pattern again. It was partially covered by a little slip of paper. Ah! the engineer's card! His London connection! Amusedly I turned it over to read the fellow's name.

'*Mr. Maurice Santander.*'

I started violently, the more that at the same moment there came a knock at the door. It was only the butler; but I was so bewildered I scarcely recognized him. Too well-trained, perhaps, to appear to notice my distress, he delivered himself almost in a speech. 'We can't find any trace of the person you spoke of, sir. The ferryman's come across and he says there's no one at the landing-stage.'

'The gentleman,' I said, 'has left this,' and I thrust the card into the butler's hand.

'Why, that must be Mr. Santander!' the servant of Mr. Santander's wife at last brought out.

'Yes,' I replied, 'and I think perhaps as it's getting late, we ought to try and find Mrs. Santander. The dinner will be quite spoiled.'

Telling the butler to wait and not to alarm the servants, I went alone to Gertrude's room. From the end of a long passage I saw the door standing partly open; I saw, too, that the room was in darkness. There was nothing strange in that, I told myself; but it would be methodical, it would save time, to examine the intervening rooms first. Examine! What a misleading word. I banished it, and 'search' came into my mind. I rejected that too. As I explored the shuttered silences I tried to find a formula that would amuse Gertrude, some facetious understatement of my agitated quest. 'A little tour of inspection' — she would like that. I could almost hear her say: 'So you expected to find me under a sofa!' I wouldn't tell her that I had looked under the sofas, unless to make a joke of it: something about dust left by the housemaid. I rose to my knees, spreading my hands out in the white glow. Not a speck.

But wasn't conversation — conversation with Gertrude — made up of little half-truths, small forays into fiction? With my hand on the door — it was of the last room and led on to the landing — I rehearsed the pleasantry aloud: 'During the course of a little tour of inspection, Gertrude, I went from one dust-heap to another, from dust unto dust I might almost say. . . .' This time I must overcome my unaccountable reluctance to enter her room. Screwing up my courage, I stepped into the passage, but for all my resolution I got no further.

The door still stood as I had first seen it — half open; but there was a light in the room — a rather subdued light, possibly from the standard lamp by the bed. I knocked and called 'Gertrude!' and when there was no reply I pushed open the door. It moved from right to left so as not to expose the bulk of the room, which lay on the left side. It seemed a long time before I was fairly in.

I saw the embers of the fire, the pale troubled lights of the mirror, and, vivid in the pool of light by the bed, a note. It said: 'Forgive me dearest, I have had to go. I can't explain why, but we shall meet some time. All my love, G.' There was no envelope, no direction, but the handwriting was hers and the informality characteristic of her. It was odd that the characters, shaky as they were, did not seem to have been written in haste. I was trying to account for this, trying to stem, by an act of concentration, the tide of disappointment that was sweeping over me, when a sudden metallic whirr sounded in my ear. It was the telephone — the small subsidiary telephone that communicated with the servants' quarters. 'It will save their steps,' she had said, when I urged her to have it put in; and I remembered my pleasure in this evidence of consideration, for my own motives had been founded in convenience and even in prudence. Now I loathed the black shiny thing that buzzed so raucously and never moved. And what could the servants have to say to me except that Mr. Santander had — well, gone. What else was there for him to do? The instrument rang again and I took up the receiver.

'Yes?'

'Please, sir, dinner is served.'

'Dinner!' I echoed. It was nearly ten, but I had forgotten about that much-postponed meal.

'Yes, sir. Didn't you give orders to have it ready immediately? For two, I think you said, sir.' The voice sounded matter-of-fact enough, but in my bewilderment I nearly lost all sense of what I was doing. At last I managed to murmur in a voice that might have been anybody's: 'Yes, of course, for two.'

On second thoughts, I left the telephone disconnected. I felt just then that I couldn't bear another summons. And, though my course was clear, I did not know what to do next; my will had nothing but confusion to work with. In the dark, perhaps, I might collect myself. But it didn't occur to me to turn out the light; instead, I parted the heavy curtains that shut off the huge bow-window and drew them behind me. The rain was driving furiously against the double casements, but not a sound vouched for its energy. A moon shone at intervals, and by the light of one gleam, brighter than the rest, I saw a scrap of paper, crushed up, lying in a corner. I smoothed it out, glad to have employment for my fingers, but darkness descended on the alcove again and I had to return to the room. In spite of its crumpled condition I made out the note—easily, indeed, for it was a copy of the one I had just read. Or perhaps the original; but why should the same words have been written twice and even three times, not more plainly, for Gertrude never tried to write plainly, but with a deliberate illegibility?

There was only one other person besides Gertrude, I thought, while I stuffed the cartridges into my revolver, who could have written that note, and he was waiting for me downstairs. How would he look, how would he explain himself? This question occupied me to the exclusion of a more natural curiosity as to *my* appearance, *my* explanation. They would have to be of the abruptest. Perhaps, indeed, they wouldn't be needed. There were a dozen corners, a dozen points of vantage all well known to Mr. Santander between me and the dining-room door. It came to me inconsequently that the crack of a shot in that house would make no more noise than the splintering of a tooth-glass on my washing-stand. And Mr. Santander, well versed no doubt in South American revolutions, affrays, and shootings-up, would be an adept in the guerilla warfare to which military service hadn't accustomed me. Wouldn't it be wiser, I thought, irresolutely contemplating the absurd bulge in my dinner jacket, to leave him to his undisputed mastery of the situation, and not put it to the proof? It was not like cutting an ordinary engagement. A knock on the door interrupted my confused consideration of social solecisms.

'Mr. Santander told me to tell you he is quite ready,' the butler said. Through his manifest uneasiness I detected a hint of disapproval. He looked at me askance; he had gone over. But couldn't he be put to some use? I had an idea.

'Perhaps you would announce me,' I said. He couldn't very well refuse, and piloted by him I should have a better chance in the passages and an entry valuably disconcerting. 'I'm not personally known to Mr. Santander,' I explained. 'It would save some little awkwardness.'

Close upon the heels of my human shield I threaded the passages. Their bright emptiness reassured me; it was inconceivable, I felt, after several safely negotiated turns, that anything sinister could lurk behind those politely rounded corners — Gertrude had had their angularities smoothed into curves; it would be so terrible, she said, if going to bed one stumbled (one easily might) and fell against an *edge*! But innocuous as they were, I preferred to avoid them. The short cut through the library would thus serve a double purpose, for it would let us in from an unexpected quarter, from that end of the library, in fact, where the large window, so perilous-looking — really so solid on its struts and stays — perched over the roaring sea.

'This is the quickest way,' I said to the butler, pointing to the library door. He turned the handle. 'It's locked, sir.'

'Oh, well.'

We had reached the dining-room at last. The butler paused with his hand on the knob as though by the mere sense of touch he could tell whether he were to be again denied admittance. Or perhaps he was listening or just thinking. The next thing I knew was that he had called out my name and I was standing in the room. Then I heard Mr. Santander's voice. 'You can go, Collins.' The door shut.

My host didn't turn round at once. All I could make out, in the big room lighted only by its four candles and the discreet footlights of dusky pictures, was his back, and — reflected in the mirror over the mantelpiece — his eyes and forehead. The same mirror showed my face too, low down on the right-hand side, curiously unrelated. His arms were stretched along the mantelpiece and he was stirring the fire with his foot. Suddenly he turned and faced me.

'Oh, you're there,' he said. 'I'm so sorry.'

We moved to the table and sat down. There was nothing to eat.

I fell to studying his appearance. Every line of his dinner-jacket, every fold in his soft shirt, I knew by heart; I seemed always to have known them.

'What are you waiting for?' he suddenly demanded rather loudly. 'Collins!' he called. 'Collins!' His voice reverberated through the room, but no one came. 'How stupid of me,' he muttered; 'of course, I must ring.' Oddly enough he seemed to look to me for confirmation. I nodded. Collins appeared, and the meal began.

Its regular sequence soothed him, for presently he said: 'You must forgive my being so distrait. I've had rather a tiring journey—come from a distance, as they say. South America, in fact.' He drank some wine reflectively. 'I had one or two things to settle before . . . before joining the Army. Now I don't think it will be necessary.'

'Necessary to settle them?' I said.

'No,' he replied. 'I have settled them.'

'You mean that you will claim exemption as an American citizen?'

Again Mr. Santander shook his head. 'It would be a reason, wouldn't it? But I hadn't thought of that.'

Instinct urged me to let so delicate a topic drop; but my nerves were fearful of a return to silence. There seemed so little, of all that we had in common, to draw upon for conversation.

'You suffer from bad health, perhaps?' I suggested. But he demurred again.

'Even Gertrude didn't complain of my health,' he said, adding quickly, as though to smother the sound of her name: 'But you're not drinking.'

'I don't think I will,' I stammered. I had meant to say I was a tee-totaller.

My host seemed surprised. 'And yet Gertrude had a long bill at her wine merchant's,' he commented, half to himself.

I echoed it involuntarily: 'Had?'

'Oh,' he said, 'it's been paid. That's partly,' he explained, 'why I came home—to pay.'

I felt I couldn't let this pass.

'Mr. Santander,' I said, 'there's a great deal in your behaviour that I don't begin (is that good American?) to understand.'

'No?' he murmured, looking straight in front of him.

'But,' I proceeded, as truculently as I could, 'I want you to rea-lize——'

He cut me short. 'Don't suppose,' he said, 'that I attribute all my wife's expenditure to you.'

I found myself trying to defend her. 'Of course,' I said, 'she has the house to keep up; it's not run for a mere song, a house like this.' And with my arm I tried to indicate to Mr. Santander the costly immensity of his domain. 'You wouldn't like her to live in a pigsty, would you? And there's the sea to keep out—why, a night like this must do pounds' worth of damage!'

'You are right,' he said, with a strange look; 'you even under-estimate the damage it has done.'

Of course, I couldn't fail to catch his meaning. He meant the havoc wrought in his affections. They had been strong, report said—strong enough for her neglect of them to make him leave the country. They weren't expressed in half-measures, I thought, looking at him with a new sensation. He must have behaved with a high hand, when he arrived. How he must have steeled himself to drive her out of the house, that stormy night, ignoring her piteous protestations, her turns and twists which I had never been able to ignore! She was never so alluring, never so fertile in emotional appeals, as when she knew she was in for a scolding. I could hear her say, 'But, Maurice, however much you hate me, you couldn't really want me to get *wet*!' and his reply: 'Get out of this house, and don't come back till I send for you. As for your lover, leave me to look after him.' He was looking after me, and soon, no doubt, he would send for her. And for her sake, since he had really returned to take part in her life, I couldn't desire this estrangement. Couldn't I even bridge it over, bring it to a close? *Beati pacifici*. Well, I would be a peace-maker too.

Confident that my noble impulses must have communicated themselves to my host, I looked up from my plate and searched his face for signs of abating rigour. I was disappointed. But should I forego or even postpone my atonement because he was stiff-necked? Only it was difficult to begin. At last I ventured.

'Gertrude is really very fond of you, you know.'

Dessert had been reached, and I, in token of amity and good-will, had helped myself to a glass of port wine.

For answer he fairly glared at me. 'Fond of me!' he shouted.

I was determined not to be browbeaten out of my kind offices.

'That's what I said; she has a great heart.'

'If you mean,' he replied, returning to his former tone, 'that it has ample accommodation!—but your recommendations come too late; I have delegated her affections.'

'To me?' I asked, involuntarily.

He shook his head. 'And in any case, why to you?'

'Because I——'

'Oh, no,' he exclaimed passionately. 'Did she deceive you—has she deceived you into believing *that*—that *you* are the alternative to *me*? You aren't unique—you have your reduplications, scores of them!'

My head swam, but he went on, enjoying his triumph. 'Why, no one ever told me about you! She herself only mentioned you once.

You are the least—the least of all her lovers!' His voice dropped. 'Otherwise you wouldn't be here.'

'Where should I be?' I fatuously asked. But he went on without regarding me.

'But I remember this house when its silence, its comfort, its isolation, its uniqueness were for us, Gertrude and me and . . . and for the people we invited. But we didn't ask many—we preferred to be alone. And I thought at first she was alone,' he wound up, 'when I found her this evening.'

'Then why,' I asked, 'did you send her away and not me?'

'Ah,' he replied with an accent of finality, 'I wanted you.'

While he spoke he was cracking a nut with his fingers and it must have had sharp edges, for he stopped, wincing, and held the finger to his mouth.

'I've hurt my nail,' he said. 'See?'

He pushed his hand towards me over the polished table. I watched it, fascinated, thinking it would stop; but still it came on, his body following, until if I hadn't drawn back, it would have touched me, while his chin dropped to within an inch of the table, and one side of his face was pillowed against his upper arm.

'It's a handicap, isn't it?' he said, watching me from under his brows.

'Indeed it is,' I replied; for the fine acorn-shaped nail was terribly torn, a jagged rent revealing the quick, moist and gelatinous. 'How did you manage to do that?' I went on, trying not to look at the mutilation which he still held before my eyes.

'Do you really want to know how I did it?' he asked. He hadn't moved, and his question, in its awkward irregular delivery, seemed to reflect the sprawled unnatural position of his body.

'Do tell me,' I said, and added, nervously jocular, 'but first let me guess. Perhaps you met with an accident in the course of your professional activities, when you were mending the lights, I mean, in the library.'

At that he jumped to his feet. 'You're very warm,' he said, 'you almost burn. But come into the library with me, and I'll tell you.'

I prepared to follow him.

But unaccountably he lingered, walked up and down a little, went to the fireplace and again (it was evidently a favourite relaxation) gently kicked the coals. Then he went to the library door, meaning apparently to open it, but he changed his mind and instead turned on the big lights of the dining-room. 'Let's see what it's really like,' he said. 'I hate this half-light.' The sudden illumination laid bare that great rich still room, so secure, so assured, so content. My host stood looking at it. He was fidgeting with his dinner-jacket and had so little self-control that, at every brush of the material with his damaged finger, he whimpered like a child. His face, now that I saw it fairly again, was twisted and disfigured with misery. There wasn't one imaginable quality that he shared with his sumptuous possessions.

In the library darkness was absolute. My host preceded me, and in a moment I had lost all sense of even our relative positions. I backed against the wall, and by luck my groping fingers felt the switch. But its futile click only emphasized the darkness. I began to feel frightened, with an acute immediate alarm very different from my earlier apprehensions and forebodings. To add to my uneasiness my ears began to detect a sound, a small irregular sound; it might have been water dripping, yet it seemed too definitely consonantal for that; it was more like an inhuman whisper. 'Speak up,' I cried, 'if you're talking to me!' But it had no more effect, my petulant outcry, than if it had fallen on the ears of the dead. The disquieting noise persisted, but another note had crept into it—a soft labial sound, like the licking of lips. It wasn't intelligible, it wasn't even articulate, yet I felt that if I listened longer it would become both. I couldn't bear the secret colloquy; and though it seemed to be taking place all round me, I made a rush into what I took to be the middle of the room. I didn't get very far, however. A chair sent me sprawling, and when I picked myself up it was to the accompaniment of a more familiar sound. The curtains were being drawn apart and the moonlight, struggling in, showed me shapes of furniture and my own position, a few feet from the door. It showed me something else, too.

How could my host be drawing the curtains when I could see him lounging, relaxed and careless, in an armchair that, from its position by the wall, missed the moon's directer ray? I strained my eyes. Very relaxed, very careless he must be, after what had passed between us, to stare at me so composedly over his shoulder, no, more than that, over his very back! He faced me, though his shoulder, oddly enough, was turned away. Perhaps he had practised it—a contortionist's trick to bewilder his friends. Suddenly I heard his voice, not from the armchair at all but from the window.

'Do you know now?'

'What?' I said.

'How I hurt my finger?'

'No,' I cried untruthfully, for that very moment all my fears told me. 'I did it strangling my wife!'

I rushed towards the window, only to be driven back by what seemed a solid body of mingled sleet and wind. I heard the creak of the great casement before it whirled outwards, crashing against the mullion and shattering the glass. But though I fought my way to the opening I wasn't quick enough. Sixty feet below the eroding sea sucked, spouted and roared. Out of it jags of rock seemed to rise, float for a moment and then be dragged under the foam. Time after time great arcs of spray sprang hissing from the sea, lifted themselves to the window as though impelled by an insatiable curiosity, condensed and fell away. The drops were bitter on my lips. Soaked to the skin and stiff with cold, I turned to the room. The heavy brocade curtains flapped madly or rose and streamed level with the ceiling, and through the general uproar I could distinguish separate sounds, the clattering fall of small objects and the banging and scraping of pictures against the walls. The whole weather-proof, soundproof house seemed to be ruining in, to be given up to darkness and furies . . . and to me. But not wholly, not unreservedly, to me. Mrs. Santander was still at her place in the easy chair.

NIGHT FEARS

THE coke-brazier was elegant enough but the night-watchman was not, consciously at any rate, sensitive to beauty of form. No; he valued the brazier primarily for its warmth. He could not make up his mind whether he liked its light. Two days ago, when he first took on the job, he was inclined to suspect the light; it dazzled him, made a target of him, increased his helplessness; it emphasized the darkness. But to-night he was feeling reconciled to it; and aided by its dark, clear rays, he explored his domain—a long narrow rectangle, fenced off from the road by poles round and thick as flag-posts and lashed loosely at the ends. By day they seemed simply an obstacle to be straddled over; but at night they were boundaries, defences almost. At their junctions, where the warning red lanterns dully gleamed, they bristled like a barricade. The night-watchman felt himself in charge of a fortress.

He took a turn up and down, musing. Now that the strangeness of the position had worn off he could think with less effort. The first night he had vaguely wished that the 'No Thoroughfare' board had faced him instead of staring uselessly up the street: it would have given his thoughts a rallying-point. Now he scarcely noticed its blankness. His thoughts were few but pleasant to dwell on, and in the solitude they had the intensity of sensations. He arranged them in cycles, the rotation coming at the end of ten paces or so when he turned to go back over his tracks. He enjoyed the thought that held his mind for the moment, but always with some agreeable impatience for the next. If he surmised there would be a fresh development in it, he would deliberately refrain from calling it up, leave it fermenting and ripening, as it were, in a luxury of expectation.

The night-watchman was a domesticated man with a wife and two children, both babies. One was beginning to talk. Since he took on his job wages had risen, and everything at home seemed gilt-edged. It made a difference to his wife. When he got home she would say, as she had done on the preceding mornings, 'Well, you do look a wreck. This night work doesn't suit you, I'm sure.' The night-watchman liked being addressed in that way and hearing his job described as night work; it showed an easy competent familiarity with a man's occupation. He would tell her, with the air of one who had seen much, about the incidents of his vigil, and what he hadn't seen he would invent, just for the pleasure of hearing her say: 'Well, I never! You do have some experiences, and no mistake.' He was very fond of his wife. Why, hadn't she promised to patch up the old blue-paper blinds, used once for the air-raids, but somewhat out of repair as a consequence of their being employed as a quarry for paper to wrap up parcels? He hadn't slept well, couldn't get accustomed to sleeping by day, the room was so light; but these blinds would be just the thing, and it would be nice to see them and feel that the war was over and there was no need for them, really.

The night-watchman yawned as for the twentieth time perhaps he came up sharp against the boundary of his walk. Loss of sleep, no doubt. He would sit in his shelter and rest a bit. As he turned and saw the narrowing gleams that transformed the separating poles into thin lines of fire, he noticed that nearly at the end, just opposite the brazier in fact and only a foot or two from the door of his hut, the left line was broken. Someone was sitting on the barrier, his back turned on the night-watchman's little compound. 'Strange I never heard him come,' thought the man, brought back with a jerk from his world of thoughts to the real world of darkness and the deserted street—well, no, not exactly deserted, for here was someone who might be inclined to talk for half an hour or so. The stranger paid no attention to the watchman's slowly advancing tread. A little disconcerting. He stopped. Drunk, I expect, he thought. This would be a real adventure to tell his wife. 'I told him I wasn't going to stand any rot from him. "Now, my fine fellow, you go home to bed; that's the best place for you," I said.' He had heard drunk men addressed in that way, and wondered doubtfully whether he would be able to catch the tone; it was more important than the words, he reflected. At last, pulling himself together, he walked up to the brazier and coughed loudly, and feeling ill-at-ease, set about warming his hands with such energy he nearly burned them.

As the stranger took no notice, but continued to sit wrapped in thought, the night-watchman hazarded a remark to his bent back. 'A fine night,' he said rather loudly, though it was ridiculous to raise one's voice in an empty street. The stranger did not turn round.

'Yes,' he replied, 'but cold; it will be colder before morning.' The night-watchman looked at his brazier, and it struck him that the coke was not lasting so well as on the previous nights. I'll put some more on, he thought, picking up a shovel; but instead of the little heap he had expected to see, there was nothing but dust and a few bits of grit — his night's supply had been somehow overlooked. 'Won't you turn round and warm your hands?' he said to the person sitting on the barrier. 'The fire isn't very good, but I can't make it up, for they forgot to give me any extra, unless somebody pinched it when my back was turned.' The night-watchman was talking for effect; he did not really believe that anyone had taken the coke. The stranger might have made a movement somewhere about the shoulders.

'Thank you,' he said, 'but I prefer to warm my back.'

Funny idea that, thought the watchman.

'Have you noticed,' proceeded the stranger, 'how easily men forget? This coke of yours, I mean; it looks as if they didn't care about you very much, leaving you in the cold like this.' It had certainly grown colder, but the man replied cheerfully: 'Oh, it wasn't that. They forgot it. Hurrying to get home, you know.' Still, they might have remembered, he thought. It was Bill Jackson's turn to fetch it — Old Bill, as the fellows call him. He doesn't like me very much. The chaps are a bit stand-offish. They'll be all right when I know them better.

His visitor had not stirred. How I would like to push him off, the night-watchman thought, irritated and somehow troubled. The stranger's voice broke in upon his reflections.

'Do you like this job?'

'Oh, not so bad,' said the man carelessly; 'good money, you know.'

'Good money,' repeated the stranger scornfully. 'How much do you get?'

The night-watchman named the sum.

'Are you married, and have you got any children?' the stranger persisted.

The night-watchman said 'Yes,' without enthusiasm.

'Well, that won't go very far when the children are a bit older,' declared the stranger. 'Have you any prospect of a rise?' The man said no, he had just had one.

'Prices going up, too,' the stranger commented.

A change came over the night-watchman's outlook. The feeling of hostility and unrest increased. He couldn't deny all this. He longed to say, 'What do you think you're getting at?' and rehearsed the phrase under his breath, but couldn't get himself to utter it aloud; his visitor had created his present state of mind and was lord of it. Another picture floated before him, less rosy than the first: an existence drab-coloured with the dust of conflict, but relieved by the faithful support of his wife and children at home. After all, that's the life for a man, he thought; but he did not cherish the idea, did not walk up and down hugging it, as he cherished and hugged the other.

'Do you find it easy to sleep in the daytime?' asked the stranger presently.

'Not very,' the night-watchman admitted.

'Ah,' said the stranger, 'dreadful thing, insomnia.'

'When you can't go to sleep, you mean,' interpreted the night-watchman, not without a secret pride.

'Yes,' came the answer. 'Makes a man ill, mad sometimes. People have done themselves in sooner than stand the torture.'

It was on the tip of the night-watchman's tongue to mention that panacea, the blue blinds. But he thought it would sound foolish, and wondered whether they would prove such a sovereign remedy after all.

'What about your children? You won't see much of them,' remarked the stranger, 'while you are on this job. Why, they'll grow up without knowing you! Up when their papa's in bed, and in bed when he's up! Not that you miss them much, I dare say. Still, if children don't get fond of their father while they're young, they never will.'

Why didn't the night-watchman take him up warmly, assuring him they were splendid kids; the eldest called him daddy, and the younger, his wife declared, already recognized him. She knew by its smile, she said. He couldn't have forgotten all that; half an hour ago it had been one of his chief thoughts. He was silent.

'I should try and find another job if I were you,' observed the stranger. 'Otherwise you won't be able to make both ends meet. What will your wife say then?'

The man considered; at least he thought he was facing the question, but his mind was somehow too deeply disturbed, and circled wearily and blindly in its misery. 'I was never brought up to a trade,' he said hesitatingly; 'father's fault.' It struck him that he had never confessed that before; had sworn not to give his father away. What am I coming to? he thought. Then he made an effort. 'My wife's all right, she'll stick to me.' He waited, positively dreading the stranger's next attack. Though the fire was burning low, almost obscured under the coke ashes that always seem more lifeless than any others, he felt drops of perspiration on his forehead, and his clothes, he knew, were soaked. I shall get a chill, that'll be the next thing, he thought; but it was involuntary: such an idea hadn't occurred to him since he was a child, supposedly delicate.

'Yes, your wife,' said the stranger at last, in tones so cold and clear that they seemed to fill the universe; to admit of no contradiction; to be graven with a fine unerring instrument out of the hard rock of truth itself. 'You won't see much of her either. You leave her pretty much to herself, don't you? Now with these women, you know, that's a *risk*.' The last word rang like a challenge; but the night-watchman had taken the offensive, shot his one little bolt, and the effort had left him more helpless than ever.

'When the eye doth not see,' continued the stranger, 'the heart doth not grieve; on the contrary, it makes merry.' He laughed, as the night-watchman could see from the movement of his shoulders. 'I've known cases very similar to yours. When the cat's away, you know! It's a pity you're under contract to finish this job' (the night-watchman had not mentioned a contract), 'but as you are, take my advice and get a friend to keep an eye on your house. Of course, he won't be able to stay the night—of course not; but tell him to keep his eyes open.'

The stranger seemed to have said his say, his head drooped a little more; he might even be dropping off to sleep. Apparently he did not feel the cold. But the night-watchman was breathing hard and could scarcely stand. He tottered a little way down his territory, wondering absurdly why the place looked so tidy; but what a travesty of his former progress. And what a confusion in his thoughts, and what a thumping in his temples. Slowly from the writhing, tearing mass in his mind a resolve shaped itself; like a cuckoo it displaced all others. He loosened the red handkerchief that was knotted round his neck, without remembering whose fingers had tied it a few hours before, or that it had been promoted (not without washing) to the status of a garment from the menial function of carrying his lunch. It had been an extravagance, that tin carrier, much debated over, and justified finally by the rise in the night-watchman's wages. He let the handkerchief drop as he fumbled for the knife in his pocket, but the blade, which was stiff, he got out with little difficulty. Wondering vaguely if he would be able to do it, whether the right movement would come to him, why he hadn't practised it, he took a step towards the brazier. It was the one friendly object in the street. . . .

Later in the night the stranger, without putting his hands on the pole to steady himself, turned round for the first time and regarded the body of the night-watchman. He even stepped over into the little compound and, remembering perhaps the dead man's invitation, stretched out his hands over the still warm ashes in the brazier. Then he climbed back and, crossing the street, entered a blind alley opposite, leaving a track of dark, irregular footprints; and since he did not return it is probable that he lived there.

THE KILLING BOTTLE

UNLIKE the majority of men, Jimmy Rintoul enjoyed the hour or so's interval between being called and having breakfast; for it was the only part of the day upon which he imposed an order. From nine-fifteen onwards the day imposed its order upon him. The 'bus, the office, the hasty city luncheon; then the office, the 'bus, and the unsatisfactory interval before dinner: such a promising time and yet, do what he would with it, it always seemed to be wasted. If he was going to dine alone at his club, he felt disappointed and neglected; if, as seldom happened, in company, he felt vaguely apprehensive. He expected a good deal from his life, and he never went to bed without the sense of having missed it. Truth to tell, he needed a stimulus, the stimulus of outside interest and appreciation, to get the best out of himself. In a competitive society, with rewards dangled before his eyes, his nature fulfilled itself and throve. How well he had done at school, and even afterwards, while his parents lived to applaud his efforts. Now he was thirty-three; his parents were dead; there was no one close enough to him to care whether he made a success of his life or not. Nor did life hand out to grown-up men incontestable signs of merit and excellence, volumes bound in vellum or silver cups standing proudly on ebony pedestals. No, its awards were far less tangible, and Jimmy, from the shelter of his solicitors' office, sometimes felt glad that its more sensational prizes were passing out of his reach—that he need no longer feel obliged, as he had once felt, to climb the Matterhorn, play the *Moonlight Sonata*, master the Spanish language, and read the *Critique of Pure Reason* before he died. His ambition was sensibly on the ebb.

But not in the mornings. The early mornings were still untouched by the torpors of middle-age. Dressing was for Jimmy a ritual, and like all rituals it looked forward to a culmination. Act followed act in a recognized sequence, each stage contributing its peculiar thrill, opening his mind to a train of stimulating and agreeable thoughts, releasing it, encouraging it. And the culmination: what was it? Only his morning's letters and the newspaper! Not very exciting. But the newspaper might contain one of those helpful, sympathetic articles about marriage, articles that warned the reader not to rush into matrimony, but to await the wisdom that came with the early and still more with the late thirties; articles which, with a few tricks of emphasis, of skipping here and reading between the lines there, demonstrated that Jimmy Rintoul's career, without any effort of his own, was shaping itself on sound, safe lines. The newspaper, then, for reassurance; the letters for surprise! And this morning an interesting letter would be particularly welcome. It would distract his mind from a vexing topic that even the routine of dressing had not quite banished—the question of his holiday, due in a fortnight's time.

Must it be Swannick Fen again? Partly for lack of finding others to take their place, he had cherished the interests of his boyhood, of which butterfly-collecting was the chief. He was solitary and competitive, and the hobby ministered to both these traits. But alas! he had not the patience of the true collector; his interest fell short of the lesser breeds, the irritating varieties of Wainscots and Footmen and whatnots. It embraced only the more sensational insects—the large, the beautiful, and the rare. His desire had fastened itself on the Swallow-tail butterfly as representing all these qualities. So he went to Swannick, found the butterfly, bred it, and presently had a whole hutch-full of splendid green caterpillars. Their mere number, the question of what to do with them when they came out, whether to keep them all in their satiating similarity, to give them away, or to sell them; to let them go free so that the species might multiply, to the benefit of all collectors; to kill all but a few, thus enhancing the value of his own—these problems vexed his youthful, ambitious, conscientious mind. Finally he killed them all. But the sight of four setting-boards plastered with forty identical insects destroyed by a surfeit his passion for the Swallow-tail butterfly. He had coaxed it with other baits: the Pine Hawk moth, the Clifden Nonpareil; but it would not respond, would accept no substitute, being, like many passions, monogamous and constant. Every year, in piety, in conservatism, in hope, he still went to Swannick Fen; but with each visit the emotional satisfaction diminished. Soon it would be gone..

However, there on his dressing-table (for some reason) stood the killing bottle—mutely demanding prey. Almost without thinking he released the stopper and snuffed up the almond-breathing fumes. A safe, pleasant smell; he could never understand how anything died of it, or why cyanide of potassium should figure in the chemists' book of poisons. But it did; he had had to put his name against it. Now, since the stuff was reputed to be so deadly, he must add a frail attic to the edifice of dressing and once more wash his hands. In a fortnight's time, he thought, I shall be doing this a dozen times a day.

On the breakfast-table lay a large, shiny blue envelope. He did not recognize the handwriting, nor, when he examined the post-mark, did it convey anything to him. The flap, gummed to the top and very strong, resisted his fingers. He opened it with a knife and read:

VERDEW CASTLE.

MY DEAR RINTOUL,

How did you feel after our little dinner on Saturday? None the worse, I hope. However, I'm not writing to inquire about your health, which seems pretty good, but about your happiness, or what I should like to think would be your happiness. Didn't I hear you mutter (the second time we met, I think it was, at Smallhouse's) something about going for a holiday in the near future? Well, then, couldn't you spend it here with us, at Verdew? Us being my brother Randolph, my wife, and your humble servant. I'm afraid there won't be a party for you; but we could get through the day somehow, and play bridge in the evenings. Randolph and you would make perfect partners, you would be so kind to each other. And didn't you say you collected bugs? Then by all means bring your butterfly-net and your killing bottle and your other engines of destruction and park them here; there are myriads of green-flies, bluebottle-flies, may-flies, dragon-flies, and kindred pests which would be all the better for your attentions. Now don't say no. It would be a pleasure to us, and I'm sure it would amuse you to see ye olde castle and us living in our mediæval seclusion. I await the favour of a favourable reply, and will then tell you the best way of reaching the Schloss, as we sometimes call it in our German fashion.

Yours,

ROLLO VERDEW.

Jimmy stared at this facetious epistle until its purport faded from his mind, leaving only a blurred impression of redundant loops and twirls. Verdew's handwriting was like himself, bold and dashing and unruly. At least, this was the estimate Jimmy had formed of him, on the strength of three meetings. He had been rather taken by the man's bluff, hearty manner, but he did not expect Verdew to like him: they were birds of a different feather. He hadn't felt very well after the

dinner, having drunk more than was good for him in the effort to fall
in with his host's mood; but apparently he had succeeded better than
he thought. Perhaps swashbucklers like Verdew welcomed mildness in
others. If not, why the invitation? He considered it. The district might
be entomologically rich. Where exactly was Verdew Castle? He had,
of course, a general idea of its locality, correct to three counties; he
knew it was somewhere near the coast. Further than that, nothing; and
directly he began to sift his knowledge he found it to be even less helpful than he imagined. The notepaper gave a choice of stations: wayside
stations they must be, they were both unknown to him. The postal,
telegraphic, and telephonic addresses all confidently cited different
towns—Kirton Tracy, Shrivecross, and Pawlingham—names which
seemed to stir memories but never fully awakened recollection. Still,
what did it matter? Verdew had promised to tell him the best route,
and it was only a question of getting there, after all. He could find his
own way back.

Soon his thoughts, exploring the future, encountered an obstacle and
stopped short. He was looking ahead as though he had made up his
mind to go. Well, hadn't he? The invitation solved his immediate
difficulty: the uncertainty as to where he should take his holiday. The
charm of Swannick had failed to hold him. And yet, perversely enough,
his old hunting-ground chose this very moment to trouble him with
its lures: its willows, its alders, the silent clumps of grey rushes with the
black water in between. The conservatism of his nature, an almost
superstitious loyalty to the preferences of his early life, protested against
the abandonment of Swannick—Swannick, where he had always done
exactly as he liked, where bridge never intruded, and the politenesses
of society were unknown. For Jimmy's mind had run forward again,
and envisaged existence at Verdew Castle as divided between holding
open the door for Mrs. Rollo Verdew and exchanging compliments
and forbearances and commiseration with Rollo's elder (or perhaps
younger, he hadn't said) brother Randolph across the bridge-table,
with a lot of spare time that wasn't really spare and a lot of being left
to himself that really meant being left to everybody.

Jimmy looked at the clock: it was time to go. If it amused his imagination to fashion a mythical Verdew Castle, he neither authorized nor
forbade it. He still thought himself free to choose. But when he reached
his office his first act was to write his friend a letter of acceptance.

Four days later a second blue envelope appeared on his breakfast-
table. It was evidently a two-days' post to Verdew Castle, for Rollo

explained that he had that moment received Jimmy's welcome communication. There followed a few references, necessarily brief, to matters of interest to them both. The letter closed with the promised itinerary:

> So we shall hope to see you in ten days' time, complete with lethal chamber and big-game apparatus. I forget whether you have a car; but if you have, I strongly advise you to leave it at home. The road bridge across the estuary has been dicky for a long time. They may close it any day now, since it was felt to wobble the last time the Lord-Lieutenant crossed by it. You would be in a mess if you found it shut and had to go trailing thirty miles to Amplesford (a hellish road, since it's no one's interest to keep it up). If the bridge carried the Lord-Lieutenant it would probably bear you, but I shouldn't like to have your blood on my head! Come, then, by train to Verdew Grove. I recommend the four o'clock; it doesn't get here till after dark, but you can dine on it, and it's almost express part of the way. The morning train is too bloody for anything: you would die of boredom before you arrived, and I should hate that to happen to any of my guests. I'm sorry to present you with such ghastly alternatives, but the Castle was built here to be out of everyone's reach, and by Heaven, it is! Come prepared for a long stay. You must. I'm sure the old office can get on very well without you. You're lucky to be able to go away as a matter of course, like a gentleman. Let us have a line and we'll send to meet you, not my little tin kettle but Randolph's majestic Daimler. Good-bye.
>
> Yours,
> ROLLO.

It was indeed a troublesome, tedious journey, involving changes of train and even of station. More than once the train, having entered a terminus head first, steamed out tail first, with the result that Rintoul lost his sense of direction and had a slight sensation of vertigo whenever, in thought, he tried to recapture it. It was half-past nine and the sun was setting when they crossed the estuary. As always in such places the tide was low, and the sun's level beams illuminated the too rotund and luscious curves of a series of mud-flats. The railway-line approached the estuary from its marshy side, by a steep embankment. Near by, and considerably below, ran the road bridge — an antiquated affair of many arches, but apparently still in use, though there seemed to be no traffic on it. The line curved inwards, and by straining his neck Rintoul could see the train bent like a bow, and the engine approaching a hole, from which a few wisps of smoke still issued, in the ledge of rock that crowned the farther shore. The hole rushed upon him; Rintoul pulled

in his head and was at once in darkness. The world never seemed to get
light again. After the long tunnel they were among hills that shut out
the light that would have come in, and stifled the little that was left
behind. It was by the help of the station lantern that he read the name,
Verdew Grove, and when they were putting his luggage on the motor
he could scarcely distinguish between the porter and the chauffeur
One of them said:

'Did you say it was a rabbit?'

And the other: 'Well, there was a bit of fur stuck to the wheel.'

'You'd better not let the boss see it,' said the first speaker.

'Not likely.' And so saying, the chauffeur, who seemed to be referring to an accident, climbed into the car. As Rollo had said, it was a
very comfortable one. Jimmy gave up counting the turns and trying to
catch glimpses of the sky over the high hedges, and abandoned himself to drowsiness. He must have dozed, for he did not know whether
it was five minutes or fifty before the opening door let in a gust of cool
air and warned him that he had arrived.

For a moment he had the hall to himself. It did not seem very large,
but to gauge its true extent was difficult, because of the arches and the
shadows. Shaded lamps on the tables gave a diffused but very subdued
glow; while a few unshaded lights, stuck about in the groining of the
vault, consuming their energy in small patches of great brilliancy,
dazzled rather than assisted the eye. The fact that the spaces between
the vaulting-ribs were white-washed seemed to increase the glare. It
was curious and not altogether happy, the contrast between the brilliance above and the murk below. No trophies of the chase adorned the
walls; no stags' heads or antlers, no rifles, javelins, tomahawks, assegais,
or krisses. Clearly the Verdews were not a family of sportsmen. In
what did Randolph Verdew's interests lie? Rintoul wondered, and he
was walking across to the open grate, in whose large recess a log-fire
flickered, when the sound of a footfall startled him. It came close, then
died away completely, then still in the same rhythm began again. It
was Rollo.

Rollo with his black moustaches, his swaggering gait, his large expansive air, his noisy benevolence. He grasped Jimmy's hand.

But before he could say more than 'Damned glad,' a footman appeared. He came so close to Jimmy and Rollo that the flow of the
latter's eloquence was checked.

'Mr. Rintoul is in the Pink Room,' announced the footman.

Rollo put his little finger in his mouth and gently bit it.

'Oh, but I thought I said——'

'Yes, sir,' interrupted the footman. 'But Mr. Verdew thought he might disturb Mr. Rintoul in the Onyx Room, because sometimes when he lies awake at night he has to move about, as you know, sir. And he thought the Pink Room had a better view. So he gave orders for him to be put there, sir.'

The footman finished on a tranquil note and turned to go. But Rollo flushed faintly and seemed put out.

'I thought it would have been company for you having my brother next door,' he said. 'But he's arranged otherwise, so it can't be helped. Shall I take you to the room now, or will you have a drink first? That is, if I can find it,' he muttered. 'They have a monstrous habit of sometimes taking the drinks away when Randolph has gone to bed. And by the way, he asked me to make his excuses to you. He was feeling rather tired. My wife's gone, too. She always turns in early here; she says there's nothing to do at Verdew. But, my God, there's a lot that wants doing, as I often tell her. This way.'

Though they found the whisky and soda in the drawing-room, Rollo still seemed a little crestfallen and depressed; but Jimmy's spirits, which sometimes suffered from the excessive buoyancy of his neighbour's, began to rise. The chair was comfortable; the room, though glimpses of stone showed alongside the tapestries, was more habitable and less ecclesiastical than the hall. In front of him was an uncurtained window through which he could see, swaying their heads as though bent on some ghostly conference, a cluster of white roses. I'm going to enjoy myself here, he thought.

Whatever the charms of the Onyx Room, whatever virtue resided in the proximity of Mr. Randolph Verdew, one thing was certain: the Pink Room had a splendid view. Leaning out of his window the next morning Jimmy feasted his eyes on it. Directly below him was the moat, clear and apparently deep. Below that again was the steep conical hill on which the castle stood, its side intersected by corkscrew paths and level terraces. Below and beyond, undulating ground led the eye onwards and upwards to where, almost on the horizon, glittered and shone the silver of the estuary. Of the castle were visible only the round wall of Jimmy's tower, and a wing of the Tudor period, the gables of which rose to the level of his bedroom window. It was half-past eight and he dressed quickly, meaning to make a little tour of the castle precincts before his hosts appeared.

His intention, however, was only partially fulfilled, for on arriving in the hall he found the great door still shut, and fastened with a variety of locks and bolts, of antique design and as hard to open, it seemed, from within as from without. He had better fortune with a smaller door, and found himself on a level oblong stretch of grass, an island of green, bounded by the moat on the east and on the other side by the castle walls. There was a fountain in the middle. The sun shone down through the open end of the quadrangle, making the whole place a cave of light, flushing the warm stone of the Elizabethan wing to orange, and gilding the cold, pale, mediaeval stonework of the rest. Jimmy walked to the moat and tried to find, to right or left, a path leading to other parts of the building. But there was none. He turned round and saw Rollo standing in the doorway.

'Good-morning,' called his host. 'Already thinking out a plan of escape?'

Jimmy coloured slightly. The thought had been present in his mind, though not in the sense that Rollo seemed to mean it.

'You wouldn't find it very easy from here,' remarked Rollo, whose cheerful humour the night seemed to have restored. 'Because even if you swam the moat you couldn't get up the bank: it's too steep and too high.'

Jimmy examined the farther strand and realized that this was true.

'It would be prettier,' Rollo continued, 'and less canal-like, if the water came up to the top; but Randolph prefers it as it used to be. He likes to imagine we're living in a state of siege.'

'He doesn't seem to keep any weapons for our defence,' commented Jimmy. 'No arquebuses or bows and arrows; no vats of molten lead.'

'Oh, he wouldn't hurt anyone for the world,' said Rollo. 'That's one of his little fads. But it amuses him to look across to the river like one of the first Verdews and feel that no one can get in without his leave.'

'Or out either, I suppose,' suggested Jimmy.

'Well,' remarked Rollo, 'some day I'll show you a way of getting out. But now come along and look at the view from the other side; we have to go through the house to see it.'

They walked across the hall, where the servants were laying the breakfast-table, to a door at the end of a long narrow passage. But it was locked. 'Hodgson!' shouted Rollo.

A footman came up.

'Will you open this door, please?' said Rollo. Jimmy expected him to be angry, but there was only a muffled irritation in his voice. At his leisure the footman produced the key and let them through.

'That's what comes of living in someone else's house,' fumed Rollo, once they were out of earshot. 'These lazy devils want waking up. Randolph's a damned sight too easy-going.'

'Shall I see him at breakfast?' Jimmy inquired.

'I doubt it.' Rollo picked up a stone, looked round, for some reason, at the castle, and threw the pebble at a thrush, narrowly missing it. 'He doesn't usually appear till lunchtime. He's interested in all sorts of philanthropical societies. He's always helping them to prevent something. He hasn't prevented you, though, you naughty fellow,' he went on, stooping down and picking up from a stone several fragments of snails' shells. 'This seems to be the thrushes' Tower Hill.'

'He's fond of animals, then?' asked Jimmy.

'Fond, my boy?' repeated Rollo. 'Fond is not the word. But we aren't vegetarians. Some day I'll explain all that. Come and have some bacon and eggs.'

That evening, in his bath, a large wooden structure like a giant's coffin, Jimmy reviewed the day, a delightful day. In the morning he had been taken round the castle; it was not so large as it seemed from outside—it had to be smaller, the walls were so thick. And there were, of course, a great many rooms he wasn't shown, attics, cellars, and dungeons. One dungeon he had seen: but he felt sure that in a fortress of such pretensions there must be more than one. He couldn't quite get the "lie" of the place at present; he had his own way of finding his room, but he knew it wasn't the shortest way. The hall, which was like a Clapham Junction to the castle's topographical system, still confused him. He knew the way out, because there was only one way, across a modernized drawbridge, and that made it simpler. He had crossed it to get at the woods below the castle, where he had spent the afternoon, hunting for caterpillars. 'They' had really left him alone— even severely alone! Neither of Rollo's wife nor of his brother was there yet any sign. But I shall see them at dinner, he thought, wrapping himself in an immense bath-towel.

The moment he saw Randolph Verdew, standing pensive in the drawing-room, he knew he would like him. He was an etherealized version of Rollo, taller and slighter. His hair was sprinkled with grey and he stooped a little. His cloudy blue eyes met Jimmy's with extraordinary frankness as he held out his hand and apologized for his previous non-appearance.

'It is delightful to have you here,' he added. 'You are a naturalist, I believe?'

His manner was formal but charming, infinitely reassuring.

'I am an entomologist,' said Jimmy, smiling.

'Ah, I love to watch the butterflies fluttering about the flowers — and the moths, too, those big heavy fellows that come in of an evening and knock themselves about against the lights. I have often had to put as many as ten out of the windows, and back they come — the deluded creatures. What a pity that their larvae are harmful and in some cases have to be destroyed! But I expect you prefer to observe the rarer insects?'

'If I can find them,' said Jimmy.

'I'm sure I hope you will,' said Randolph, with much feeling. 'You must get Rollo to help you.'

'Oh,' said Jimmy, 'Rollo——'

'I hope you don't think Rollo indifferent to nature?' asked his brother, with distress in his voice and an engaging simplicity of manner. 'He has had rather a difficult life, as I expect you know. His affairs have kept him a great deal in towns, and he has had little leisure — very little leisure.'

'He must find it restful here,' remarked Jimmy, again with the sense of being more tactful than truthful.

'I'm sure I hope he does. Rollo is a dear fellow; I wish he came here oftener. Unfortunately his wife does not care for the country, and Rollo himself is very much tied by his new employment — the motor business.'

'Hasn't he been with Scorcher and Speedwell long?'

'Oh no: poor Rollo, he is always trying his hand at something new. He ought to have been born a rich man instead of me.' Randolph spread his hands out with a gesture of helplessness. 'He could have done so much, whereas I — ah, here he comes. We were talking about you, Rollo.'

'No scandal, I hope; no hitting a man when he's down?'

'Indeed no. We were saying we hoped you would soon come into a fortune.'

'Where do you think it's coming from?' demanded Rollo, screwing up his eyes as though the smoke from his cigarette had made them smart.

'Perhaps Vera could tell us,' rejoined Randolph mildly, making his way to the table, though his brother's cigarette was still unfinished. 'How is she, Rollo? I hoped she would feel sufficiently restored to make a fourth with us this evening.'

'Still moping,' said her husband. 'Don't waste your pity on her. She'll be all right to-morrow.'

They sat down to dinner.

The next day, or it might have been the day after, Jimmy was coming home to tea from the woods below the castle. On either side of the path was a hayfield. They were mowing the hay. The mower was a new one, painted bright blue; the horse tossed its head up and down; the placid afternoon air was alive with country sounds, whirring, shouts, and clumping footfalls. The scene was full of an energy and gentleness that refreshed the heart. Jimmy reached the white iron fence that divided the plain from the castle mound, and, with a sigh, set his feet upon the zigzag path. For though the hill was only a couple of hundred feet high at most, the climb called for an effort he was never quite prepared to make. He was tramping with lowered head, conscious of each step, when a voice hailed him.

'Mr. Rintoul!'

It was a foreign voice, the i's pronounced like e's. He looked up and saw a woman, rather short and dark, watching him from the path above.

'You see I have come down to meet you,' she said, advancing with short, brisk, but careful and unpractised steps. And she added, as he still continued to stare at her: 'Don't you know? I am Mrs. Verdew.'

By this time she was at his side.

'How could I know?' he asked, laughing and shaking the hand she was already holding out to him. All her gestures seemed to be quick and unpremeditated.

'Let us sit here,' she said, and almost before she had spoken she was sitting, and had made him sit, on the wooden bench beside them. 'I am tired from walking downhill; you will be tired by walking uphill; therefore we both need a rest.'

She decided it all so quickly that Jimmy, whose nature had a streak of obstinacy, wondered if he was really so tired after all.

'And who should I have been, who could I have been, but Mrs. Verdew?' she demanded challengingly.

Jimmy saw that an answer was expected, but couldn't think of anyone who Mrs. Verdew might have been.

'I don't know,' he said feebly.

'Of course you don't, silly,' said Mrs. Verdew. 'How long have you been here?'

'I can't remember. Two or three days, I think,' said Jimmy, who disliked being nailed down to a definite fact.

'Two or three days? Listen to the man, how vague he is!' commented Mrs. Verdew, with a gesture of impatience apostrophizing the horizon. 'Well, whether it's three days or only two, you must have learnt one thing—that no one enters these premises without leave.'

'Premises?' murmured Jimmy.

'Hillside, garden, grounds, premises,' repeated Mrs. Verdew. 'How slow you are! But so are all Englishmen.'

'I don't think Rollo is slow,' remarked Jimmy, hoping to carry the war into her country.

'Sometimes too slow, sometimes too fast, never the right pace,' pronounced his wife. 'Rollo misdirects his life.'

'He married you,' said Jimmy gently.

Mrs. Verdew gave him a quick look. 'That was partly because I wanted him to. But only just now, for instance, he has been foolish.'

'Do you mean he was foolish to come here?'

'I didn't mean that. Though I hate the place, and he does no good here.'

'What good could he do?' asked Jimmy, who was staring vacantly at the sky. 'Except, perhaps, help his brother to look after—to look after——'

'That's just it,' said Mrs. Verdew. 'Randolph doesn't need any help, and if he did he wouldn't let Rollo help him. He wouldn't even have him made a director of the coal-mine!'

'What coal-mine?' Jimmy asked.

'Randolph's. You don't mean to say you didn't know he had a coal-mine? One has to tell you everything!'

'I like you to tell me things!' protested Jimmy.

'As you don't seem to find out anything for yourself, I suppose I must. Well, then: Randolph has a coal-mine, he is very rich, and he spends his money on nothing but charitable societies for contradicting the laws of nature. And he won't give Rollo a penny—not a penny though he is his only brother, his one near relation in the world! He won't even help him to get a job!'

'I thought he had a job,' said Jimmy, in perplexity.

'You thought that! You'd think anything' exclaimed Mrs. Verdew, her voice rising in exasperation.

'No, but he told me he came here for a holiday,' said Jimmy pacifically.

'Holiday, indeed! A long holiday. I can't think why Rollo told you that. Nor can I think why I bore you with all our private troubles. A man can talk to a woman about anything; but a woman can only talk to a man about what interests him.'

'But who is to decide that?'

'The woman, of course; and I see you're getting restless.'

'No, no. I was so interested. Please go on.'

'Certainly not. I am a Russian, and I often know when a man is bored sooner than he knows himself. Come along,' pulling him from the bench much as a gardener uproots a weed; 'and I will tell you something very interesting. Ah, how fast you walk! Don't you know it's less fatiguing to walk uphill slowly—and you with all those fishing-nets and pill-boxes. And what on earth is that great bottle for?'

'I try to catch butterflies in these,' Jimmy explained. 'And this is my killing bottle.'

'What a horrible name. What is it for?'

'I'm afraid I kill the butterflies with it.'

'Ah, what a barbarian! Give it to me a moment. Yes, there are their corpses, poor darlings. Is that Randolph coming towards us? No, don't take it away. I can carry it quite easily under my shawl. What was I going to tell you when you interrupted me? I remember—it was about the terrace. When I first came here I used to feel frightfully depressed— it was winter and the sun set so early, sometimes before lunch! In the afternoons I used to go down the mound, where I met you, and wait for the sun to dip below that bare hill on the left. And I would begin to walk quite slowly towards the castle, and all the while the sun was balanced on the hilltop like a ball! And the shadow covered the valley and kept lapping my feet, like the oncoming tide! And I would wait till it reached my ankles, and then run up into the light, and be safe for a moment. It was such fun, but I don't expect you'd enjoy it, you're too sophisticated. Ah, here's Randolph. Randolph, I've been showing Mr. Rintoul the way home; he didn't know it—he doesn't know anything! Do you know what he does with this amusing net? He uses it to catch tiny little moths, like the ones that get into your furs. He puts it over them and looks at them, and they're so frightened, they think they can't get out; then they notice the little holes, and out they creep and fly away! Isn't it charming?'

'Charming,' said Randolph, glancing away from the net and towards the ground.

'Now we must go on. We want our tea terribly!' And Mrs. Verdew swept Jimmy up the hill.

With good fortune the morning newspaper arrived at Verdew Castle in time for tea, already a little out of date. Jimmy accorded it, as a rule, the tepid interest with which, when abroad, one contemplates the English journals of two days ago. They seem to emphasize one's remoteness, not lessen it. Never did Jimmy seem farther from London, indeed, farther from civilization, than when he picked up the familiar sheet of *The Times*. It was like a faint rumour of the world that had somehow found its way down hundreds of miles of railway, changed trains and stations, rumbled across the estuary, and threaded the labyrinth of lanes and turnings between Verdew Grove and the castle. Each day its news seemed to grow less important, or at any rate less important to Jimmy. He began to turn over the leaves. Mrs. Verdew had gone to her room, absent-mindedly taking the killing bottle with her. He was alone; there was no sound save the crackle of the sheets. Unusually insipid the news seemed. He turned more rapidly. What was this? In the middle of page fourteen, a hole? No, not a mere hole: a deliberate excision, the result of an operation performed with scissors. What item of news could anyone have found worth reading, much less worth cutting out? To Jimmy's idle mind, the centre of page fourteen assumed a tremendous importance, it became the sun of his curiosity's universe. He rose; with quick cautious fingers he searched about, shifting papers, delving under blotters, even fumbling in the more public-looking pigeon-holes.

Suddenly he heard the click of a door opening, and with a bound he was in the middle of the room. It was only Rollo, whom business of some kind had kept all day away from home.

'Enter the tired bread-winner,' he remarked. 'Like to see the paper? I haven't had time to read it.' He threw something at Jimmy and walked off.

It was *The Times*. With feverish haste Jimmy turned to page fourteen and seemed to have read the paragraph even before he set eyes on it. It was headed: *Mysterious Outbreak at Verdew.*

'The sequestered, little-known village of Verdew-le-Dale has again been the scene of a mysterious outrage, recalling the murders of John Didwell and Thomas Presland in 1910 and 1912, and the occasional killing of animals which has occurred since. In this instance, as in the others, the perpetrator of the crime seems to have been actuated by some vague motive of retributive justice. The victim was a shepherd dog, the property of Mr. J. R. Cross. The dog, which was known to worry cats, had lately killed two belonging to an old woman of the parish. The Bench, of which Mr. Randolph Verdew is chairman, fined Cross and told him to keep the dog under proper control, but did not order its destruction. Two days ago the animal was found dead in a ditch, with its throat cut. The police have no doubt that the wound was made by the same weapon that killed Didwell and Presland, who, it will be remembered, had both been prosecuted by the R.S.P.C.A. for cruelty and negligence resulting in the deaths of domestic animals. At present no evidence has come to light that might lead to the detection of the criminal, though the police are still making investigations.'

'And I don't imagine it will ever come to light,' Jimmy muttered.

'What do you suppose won't come to light?' inquired a voice at his elbow. He looked up. Randolph Verdew was standing by his chair and looking over his shoulder at the newspaper.

Jimmy pointed to the paragraph.

'Any clue to the identity of the man who did this?'

'No,' said Randolph after a perceptible pause. I don't suppose there will be.' He hesitated a moment and then added:

'But it would interest me much to know how that paragraph found its way back into the paper.'

Jimmy explained.

'You see,' observed Randolph, 'I always cut out, and paste into a book, any item of news that concerns the neighbourhood, and especially Verdew. In this way I have made an interesting collection.'

'There seem to have been similar occurrences here before,' remarked Jimmy.

'There have, there have,' Randolph Verdew said.

'It's very strange that no one has even been suspected.'

Randolph Verdew answered obliquely:

'Blood calls for blood. The workings of justice are secret and incalculable.'

'Then you sympathize a little with the murderer?' Jimmy inquired.

'I?' muttered Randolph. 'I think I hate cruelty more than anything in the world.'

'But wasn't the murderer cruel?' persisted Jimmy.

'No,' said Randolph Verdew with great decision. 'At least,' he added in a different tone, 'the victims appear to have died with the minimum of suffering. But here comes Vera. We must find a more cheerful topic of conversation. Vera, my dear, you won't disappoint us of our bridge to-night?'

Several days elapsed, days rendered slightly unsatisfactory for Jimmy from a trivial cause. He could not get back his killing bottle from Mrs. Verdew. She had promised it, she had even gone upstairs to fetch it; but she never brought it down. Meanwhile, several fine specimens (in particular a large female Emperor moth) languished in match-boxes and other narrow receptacles, damaging their wings and even having to be set at liberty. It was very trying. He began to feel that the retention of the killing bottle was deliberate. In questions of conduct he was often at sea. But in the domain of manners, though he sometimes went astray, he considered that he knew very well which road to take, and the knowledge was a matter of pride to him. The thought of asking Mrs. Verdew a third time to restore his property irked him exceedingly. At last he screwed up his courage. They were walking down the hill together after tea.

'Mrs. Verdew,' he began.

'Don't go on,' she exclaimed. 'I know exactly what you're going to say. Poor darling, he wants to have his killing bottle back. Well, you can't. I need it myself for those horrible hairy moths that come in at night.'

'But Mrs. Verdew——!' he protested.

'And please don't call me Mrs. Verdew. How long have we known each other? Ten days! And soon you've got to go! Surely you could call me Vera!'

Jimmy flushed. He knew that he must go soon, but didn't realize that a term had been set to his stay.

'Listen,' she continued, beginning to lead him down the hill. 'When you're in London I hope you'll often come to see us.'

'I certainly will,' said he.

'Well, then, let's make a date. Will you dine with us on the tenth? That's to-morrow week.'

'I'm not quite sure——' began Jimmy unhappily, looking down on to the rolling plain and feeling that he loved it.

'How long you're going to stay?' broke in Mrs Verdew, who seemed to be able to read his thoughts. 'Why do you want to stay? There's nothing to do here: think what fun we might have in London. You can't like this place and I don't believe it's good for you; you don't look half as well as you did when you came.'

'But you didn't see me when I came, and I feel very well,' said Jimmy.

'Feeling is nothing,' said Mrs. Verdew. 'Look at me. Do I look well?' She turned up to him her face: it was too large, he thought, and dull and pallid with powder; the features were too marked; but undeniably it had beauty. 'I suppose I do: I feel well. But in this place I believe my life might stop any moment of its own accord! Do you never feel that?'

'No,' said Jimmy, smiling.

'Sit down,' she said suddenly, taking him to a seat as she had done on the occasion of their first meeting, 'and let me have your hand—not because I love you, but because I'm happier holding something, and it's a pretty hand.' Jimmy did not resist: he was slightly stupefied, but somehow not surprised by her behaviour. She held up his drooping hand by the wrist, level with her eyes, and surveyed it with a smile, then she laid, it palm upward, in her lap. The smile vanished from her face: she knitted her brows.

'I don't like it,' she said, a sudden energy in her voice.

'I thought you said it was a pretty hand,' murmured Jimmy.

'I did; you know I don't mean that. It is pretty: but you don't deserve to have it, not your eyes, nor your hair; you are idle and complacent and unresponsive and ease-loving—you only think of your butterflies and your killing bottle!' She looked at him fondly; and Jimmy for some reason was rather pleased to hear all this. 'No, I meant that I see danger in your hand, in the lines.'

'Danger to me?'

'Ah, the conceit of men! Yes, to you.'

'What sort of danger—physical danger?' inquired Jimmy, only moderately interested.

'*Danger de mort*,' pronounced Mrs. Verdew.

'Come, come,' said Jimmy, bending forward and looking into Mrs. Verdew's face to see if she was pretending to be serious. 'When does the danger threaten?'

'Now,' said Mrs. Verdew.

Oh, thought Jimmy, what a tiresome woman! So you think I'm in danger, do you, Mrs. Verdew, of losing my head at this moment? God, the conceit of women! He stole a glance at her; she was looking straight ahead, her lips pursed up and trembling a little, as though she wanted him to kiss her. Shall I? he thought, for compliance was in his blood and he always wanted to do what was expected of him. But at that very moment a wave of irritability flooded his mind and changed it: she had taken his killing bottle, spoilt and stultified several precious days, and all to gratify her caprice. He turned away.

'Oh, I'm tougher than you think,' he said.

'Tougher?' she said. 'Do you mean your skin? All Englishmen have thick skins.' She spoke resentfully; then her voice softened. 'I was going to tell you——' She uttered the words with difficulty, and as though against her will. But Jimmy, not noticing her changed tone and still ridden by his irritation, interrupted her.

'That you'd restore my killing bottle?'

'No, no,' she cried in exasperation, leaping to her feet. 'How you do harp on that wretched old poison bottle! I wish I'd broken it!' She caught her breath, and Jimmy rose too, facing her with distress and contrition in his eyes. But she was too angry to heed his change of mood. 'It was something I wanted you to know—but you make things so difficult for me! I'll fetch you your bottle,' she continued wildly, 'since you're such a child as to want it! No, don't follow me; I'll have it sent to your room.'

He looked up; she was gone, but a faint sound of sobbing disturbed the air behind her.

It was evening, several days later, and they were sitting at dinner. How Jimmy would miss these meals when he got back to London! For a night or two, after the scene with Mrs. Verdew, he had been uneasy under the enforced proximity which the dining-table brought; she looked at him reproachfully, spoke little, and when he sought occasions to apologize to her, she eluded them. She had never been alone with him since. She had, he knew, little control over her emotions, and perhaps her pride suffered. But her pique, or whatever it was, now seemed to have passed away. She looked lovely to-night, and he realized he would miss her. Rollo's voice, when he began to speak, was like a commentary on his thoughts.

'Jimmy says he's got to leave us Randolph,' he said. 'Back to the jolly old office.'

'That is a great pity,' said Randolph in his soft voice. 'We shall miss him, shan't we, Vera?'

Mrs. Verdew said they would.

'All the same, these unpleasant facts have to be faced,' remarked Rollo. 'That's why we were born. I'm afraid you've had a dull time, Jimmy, though you must have made the local flora and fauna sit up. Have you annexed any prize specimens from your raids upon the countryside?'

'I have got one or two good ones,' said Jimmy with a reluctance that he attributed partially to modesty.

'By the way,' said Rollo, pouring himself out a glass of port, for the servants had left the room, 'I would like you to show Randolph that infernal machine of yours, Jimmy. Anything on the lines of a humane killer bucks the old chap up no end.' He looked across at his brother, the ferocious cast of his features softened into an expression of fraternal solicitude.

After a moment's pause Randolph said: 'I should be much interested to be shown Mr. Rintoul's invention.'

'Oh, it's not my invention,' said Jimmy a little awkwardly.

'You'll forgive me disagreeing with you, Rollo,' Mrs. Verdew, who had not spoken for some minutes, suddenly remarked. 'I don't think it's worth Randolph's while looking at it. I don't think it would interest him a bit.'

'How often have I told you, my darling,' said Rollo, leaning across the corner of the table towards his wife, 'not to contradict me? I keep a record of the times you agree with me: December, 1919, was the last.'

'Sometimes I think that was a mistake,' said Mrs. Verdew, rising in evident agitation, 'for it was then I promised to marry you.' She reached the door before Jimmy could open it for her.

'Ah, these ladies!' moralized Rollo, leaning back and closing his eyes. 'What a dance the dear things lead us, with their temperaments.' And he proceeded to enumerate examples of feminine caprice, until his brother proposed that they should adjourn to the bridge table.

The next morning Jimmy was surprised to find a note accompany his early morning tea.

Dear Mr. Rintoul (it began), since I mustn't say 'Dear Jimmy.' ('I never said she mustn't' Jimmy thought.) I know it isn't easy for any man, most of all an Englishman, to understand moods, but I do beg you to forgive my foolish outburst of a few days ago. I think it must have been the air or the lime in the water that made me *un po' nervosa*, as the Italians say. I know you prefer a life utterly flat and dull and even—it would kill me, but there! I am sorry. You can't expect me to change, *à mon âge*! But anyhow try to forgive me.

Yours,

VERA VERDEW.

P.S.—I wouldn't trouble to show that bottle to Randolph. He has quite enough silly ideas in his head as it is.

What a nice letter, thought Jimmy drowsily. He had forgotten the killing bottle. I won't show it to Randolph, Jimmy thought, unless he asks me.

But soon after breakfast a footman brought him a message: Mr. Verdew was in his room and would be glad to see the invention (the man's voice seemed to put the word into inverted commas) at Mr. Rintoul's convenience. 'Well,' reflected Jimmy, 'if he's to see it working it must have something to work on.' Aimlessly he strolled over the drawbridge and made his way, past blocks of crumbling wall, past grassy hummocks and hollows, to the terraces. They were gay with flowers; and looked at from above, the lateral stripes and bunches of colour, succeeding each other to the bottom of the hill, had a peculiarly brilliant effect. What should he catch? A dozen white butterflies presented themselves for the honour of exhibiting their death-agony to Mr. Randolph Verdew, but Jimmy passed them by. His collector's pride demanded a nobler sacrifice. After twenty minutes' search he was rewarded; his net fell over a slightly battered but still recognizable specimen of the Large Tortoiseshell butterfly. He put it in a pill-box and bore it away to the house. But as he went he was visited by a reluctance, never experienced by him before, to take the butterfly's life in such a public and coldblooded fashion; it was not a good specimen, one that he could add to his collection; it was just cannon-fodder. The heat of the day, flickering visibly upwards from the turf and flowers, bemused his mind; all around was a buzzing and humming that seemed to liberate his thoughts from contact with the world and give them the intensity of sensations. So vivid was his vision, so flawless the inner quiet from which it sprang, that he came up with a start against his own bedroom door. The substance of his day-dream had been forgotten; but it had left its ambassador behind it — something that whether apprehended by the mind as a colour, a taste, or a local inflammation, spoke with an insistent voice and always to the same purpose: 'Don't show Randolph Verdew the butterfly; let it go, here, out of the window, and send him an apology.'

For a few minutes, such was the force of this inward monitor, Jimmy did contemplate setting the butterfly at liberty. He was prone to sudden irrational scruples and impulses, and if there was nothing definite urging him the other way he often gave in to them. But in this case there was. Manners demanded that he should accede to his host's request; the rules of manners, of all rules in life, were the easiest to recognize and the most satisfactory to act upon. Not to go would be a breach of manners.

'How kind of you,' said Randolph, coming forward and shaking Jimmy's hand, a greeting that, between two members of the same household, struck him as odd. 'You have brought your invention with you?' Jimmy saw that it was useless to disclaim the honour of its discovery. He unwrapped the bottle and handed it to Randolph.

Randolph carried it straight away to a high window, the sill of which was level with his eyes and above the top of Jimmy's head. He held the bottle up to the light. Oblong in shape and about the size of an ordinary jam jar, it had a deep whitish pavement of plaster, pitted with brown furry holes like an overripe cheese. Resting on the plaster, billowing and coiling up to the glass stopper, stood a fat column of cotton-wool. The most striking thing about the bottle was the word *poison* printed in large, loving characters on a label stuck to the outside.

'May I release the stopper?' asked Randolph at length.

'You may,' said Jimmy, 'but a whiff of the stuff is all you want.'

Randolph stared meditatively into the depths of the bottle. 'A rather agreeable odour,' he said. 'But how small the bottle is. I had figured it to myself as something very much larger.'

'Larger?' echoed Jimmy. 'Oh, no, this is quite big enough for me. I don't need a mausoleum.'

'But I was under the impression,' Randolph Verdew remarked, still fingering the bottle, 'that you used it to destroy pests.'

'If you call butterflies pests,' said Jimmy, smiling.

'I am afraid that some of them must undeniably be included in that category,' pronounced Mr. Verdew, his voice edged with a melancholy decisiveness. 'The cabbage butterfly, for instance. And it is, of course, only the admittedly noxious insects that need to be destroyed.'

'All insects are more or less harmful,' Jimmy said.

Randolph Verdew passed his hand over his brow. The shadow of a painful thought crossed his face, and he murmured uncertainly:

'I think that's a quibble. There are categories . . . I have been at some pains to draw them up. . . . The list of destructive lepidoptera is large, too large. . . . That is why I imagined your lethal chamber would be a vessel of considerable extent, possibly large enough to admit a man, and its use attended by some danger to an unpractised exponent.'

'Well,' said Jimmy, 'there's enough poison here to account for half a town. But let me show you how it works.' And he took the pill-box from his pocket. Shabby, battered and cowed, the butterfly stood motionless, its wings closed and upright.

'Now,' said Jimmy, 'you'll see.'

The butterfly was already between the fingers and half-way to the bottle, when he heard, faint but clear, the sound of a cry. It was two-syllabled, like the interval of the cuckoo's call inverted, and might have been his own name.

'Listen!' he exclaimed. 'What was that? It sounded like Mrs. Verdew's voice.' His swiftly turning head almost collided with his host's chin, so near had the latter drawn to watch the operation, and chased the tail-end of a curious look from Randolph Verdew's face.

'It's nothing,' he said. 'Go on.'

Alas, alas, for the experiment in humane slaughter! The butterfly must have been stronger than it looked; the power of the killing bottle had no doubt declined with frequent usage. Up and down, round and round flew the butterfly; its frantic flutterings could be heard through the thick walls of its glass prison. It clung to the cotton-wool, pressed itself into corners, its straining, delicate tongue coiling and uncoiling in the effort to suck in a breath of living air. Now it was weakening. It fell from the cotton-wool and lay with its back on the plaster slab. It jolted itself up and down and, when strength for this movement failed, it clawed the air with its thin legs as though pedalling an imaginary bicycle. Suddenly, with a violent spasm, it gave birth to a thick cluster of yellowish eggs. Its body twitched once or twice and at last lay still.

Jimmy shrugged his shoulders in annoyance and turned to his host. The look of horrified excitement whose vanishing vestige he had seen a moment before, lay full and undisguised upon Randolph Verdew's face. He only said:

'Of what flower or vegetable is that dead butterfly the parasite?'

'Oh, poor thing,' said Jimmy carelessly, 'it's rather a rarity. Its caterpillar may have eaten an elm-leaf or two—nothing more. It's too scarce to be a pest. It's fond of gardens and frequented places, the book says—rather sociable, like a robin.'

'It could not be described as injurious to human life?'

'Oh, no. It's a collector's specimen really. Only this is too damaged to be any good.'

'Thank you for letting me see the invention in operation,' said Randolph Verdew, going to his desk and sitting down. Jimmy found his silence a little embarrassing. He packed up the bottle and made a rather awkward, self-conscious exit.

The four bedroom candles always stood, their silver flashing agreeably, cheek by jowl with the whisky decanter and the hot-water kettle and the soda. Now, the others having retired, there were only two, one of which (somewhat wastefully, for he still had a half-empty glass in his hand) Rollo was lighting.

'My dear fellow,' he was saying to Jimmy, 'I'm sorry you think the new model insecticide fell a bit flat. But Randolph's like that, you know: damned undemonstrative cove, I must say, though he's my own brother.'

'He wasn't exactly undemonstrative,' answered Jimmy, perplexity written on his face.

'No, rather like an iceberg hitting you amidships,' said his friend. 'Doesn't make a fuss, but you feel it all the same. But don't you worry, Jimmy; I happen to know that he enjoyed your show. Fact is, he told me so.' He gulped down some whisky.

'I'm relieved,' said Jimmy, and he obviously spoke the truth. 'I've only one more whole day here, and I should be sorry if I'd hurt his feelings.'

'Yes, and I'm afraid you'll have to spend it with him alone,' said Rollo, compunction colouring his voice. 'I was coming to that. Fact is, Vera and I have unexpectedly got to go away to-morrow for the day.' He paused; a footman entered and began walking uncertainly about the room. 'Now, Jimmy,' he went on, 'be a good chap and stay on a couple of days more. You do keep us from the blues so. That's all right, William, we don't want anything,' he remarked parenthetically to the footman's retreating figure. 'I haven't mentioned it to Randolph, but he'd be absolutely charmed if you'd grace our humble dwelling a little longer. You needn't tell anyone anything: just stay, and we shall be back the day after to-morrow. It's hellish that we've got to go, but you know this bread-winning business: it's the early bird that catches the worm. And talking of that, we have to depart at cock-crow. I may not see you again—that is, unless you stay, as I hope you will. Just send a wire to the old blighter who works with you and tell him to go to blazes.'

'Well,' said Jimmy, delighted by the prospect, 'you certainly do tempt me.'

'Then fall, my lad,' said Rollo, catching him a heavy blow between the shoulder-blades. 'I shan't say good-bye, but "au revoir." Don't go to bed sober; have another drink.'

But Jimmy declined. The flickering candles lighted them across the hall and up the stone stairs.

And it's lucky I have a candle, Jimmy thought, trying in vain the third and last switch, the one on the reading-lamp by the bed. The familiar room seemed to have changed, to be closing hungrily, with a vast black embrace, upon the nimbus of thin clear dusk that shone about the candle. He walked uneasily up and down, drew a curtain and let in a ray of moonlight. But the silver gleam crippled the candlelight without adding any radiance of its own, so he shut it out. This window must be closed, thought Jimmy, that opens on to the parapet, for I really couldn't deal with a stray cat in this localized twilight. He opened instead a window that gave on to the sheer wall. Even after the ritual of tooth-cleaning he was still restless and dissatisfied, so after a turn or two he knelt by the bed and said his prayers— whether from devotion or superstition he couldn't tell: he only knew that he wanted to say them.

'Come in!' he called next morning, in answer to the footman's knock.

'I can't come in, sir,' said a muffled voice. 'The door's locked.'

How on earth had that happened? Then Jimmy remembered. As a child he always locked the door because he didn't like to be surprised saying his prayers. He must have done so last night, unconsciously. How queer! He felt full of self-congratulation—he didn't know why. 'And—oh, William!' he called after the departing footman.

'Yes, sir?'

'The light's fused, or something. It wouldn't go on last night.'

'Very good, sir.'

Jimmy addressed himself to the tea. But what was this? Another note from Mrs. Verdew!

DEAR JIMMY (he read),

You will forgive this impertinence, for I've got a piece of good news for you. In future, you won't be able to say that women never help a man in his career! (Jimmy was unaware of having said so.) As you know, Rollo and I have to leave to-morrow morning. I don't suppose he told you why, because it's rather private. But he's embarking on a big undertaking that will mean an enormous amount of litigation and lawyer's fees! Think of that! (Though I don't suppose you think of anything else.) I know he wants you to act for him: but to do so you positively *must* leave Verdew to-morrow. Make any excuse to Randolph; send yourself a telegram if you want to be specially polite: but you must catch the night train to London. It's the chance of a life. You can get through to Rollo on the telephone next morning. Perhaps we could lunch together—or dine? *A bientôt*, therefore.   VERA VERDEW.

P.S.—I shall be furious if you don't come.

Jimmy pondered Mrs. Verdew's note, trying to read between its lines. One thing was clear: she had fallen in love with him. Jimmy smiled at the ceiling. She wanted to see him again, so soon, so soon! Jimmy smiled once more. She couldn't bear to wait an unnecessary day. How urgent women were! He smiled more indulgently. And, also, how exacting. Here was this cock-and-bull story, all about Rollo's 'undertaking' which would give him, Jimmy, the chance of a lifetime! And because she was so impatient she expected him to believe it! Luncheon, indeed! Dinner! How could they meet for dinner, when Rollo was to be back at Verdew that same evening? In her haste she had not even troubled to make her date credible. And then: 'I shall be furious if you don't come.' What an argument! What confidence in her own powers did not that sentence imply! Let her be furious, then, as furious as she liked.

Her voice, just outside his door, interrupted his meditation.

'Only a moment, Rollo, it will only take me a moment!'

And Rollo's reply, spoken in a tone as urgent as hers, but louder:

'I tell you there isn't time: we shall miss the train.'

He seemed to hustle her away downstairs, poor Vera. She had really been kind to Jimmy, in spite of her preposterous claims on his affection. He was glad he would see her again to-morrow. . . . Verdew was so much nicer than London. . . . He began to doze.

On the way back from the woods there was a small low church with a square tower and two bells – the lower one both cracked and flat. You could see up into the belfry through the slats in the windows. Close by the church ran a stream, choked with green scum except where the cattle went down to drink, and crossed by a simple bridge of logs set side by side. Jimmy liked to stand on the bridge and listen to the unmelodious chime. No one heeded it, no one came to church, and it had gone sour and out of tune. It gave Jimmy an exquisite, slightly morbid sense of dereliction and decay, which he liked to savour in solitude; but this afternoon a rustic had got there first.

'Good-day,' he said.

'Good-day,' said Jimmy.

'You're from the castle, I'm thinking?' the countryman surmised.

'Yes.'

'And how do you find Mr. Verdew?'

'Which Mr. Verdew?'

'Why, the squire, of course.'

'I think he's pretty well,' said Jimmy.

'Ah, he may appear to be so,' the labourer observed; 'but them as has eyes to see and ears to hear, knows different.'

'Isn't he a good landlord?' asked Jimmy.

'Yes,' said the old man. 'He's a tolerably good landlord. It isn't that.' He seemed to relish his mysteriousness.

'You like Mr. Rollo Verdew better?' suggested Jimmy.

'I wouldn't care to say that, sir. He's a wild one, Mr. Rollo.'

'Well, anyhow, Mr. Randolph Verdew isn't wild.'

'Don't you be too sure, sir.'

'I've never seen him so.'

'There's not many that have. And those that have—some won't tell what they saw and some can't.'

'Why won't they?'

'Because it's not their interest to.'

'And why can't the others?'

'Because they're dead.'

There was a pause.

'How did they die?' asked Jimmy.

'That's not for me to say,' the old man answered, closing his mouth like a trap. But this gesture, as Jimmy had already learned, was only part of his conversational technique. In a moment he began again:

'Did you ever hear of the Verdew murders?'

'Something.'

'Well, 'twasn't only dogs that was killed.'

'I know.'

'But they were all killed the same way.'

'How?'

'With a knife,' said the old man. 'Like pigs. From ear to ear,' he added, making an explanatory gesture; 'from ear to ear.' His voice became reminiscent. 'Tom Presland was a friend o' mine. I seed him in the evening and he said, he says, "That blamed donkey weren't worth a ten-pound fine." And I said, "You're lucky not to be in prison," for in case you don't know, sir, the Bench here don't mind fellows being a bit hasty with their animals, although Mr. Verdew is the chairman. I felt nigh killing the beast myself sometimes, it was that obstinate. "But, Bill," he says, "I don't feel altogether comfortable when I remember what happened to Jack Didwell." And sure enough he was found next morning in the ditch with his throat gapin' all white at the edges, just like poor old Jack. And the donkey was a contrary beast, that had stood many a knock before, harder than the one what killed him.'

'And why is Mr. Verdew suspected?'

'Why, sir, the servants said he was in the castle all night and must have been, because the bridge was drawed. But how do they know he had to use the bridge? Anyhow, George Wiscombe swears he saw him going through Nape's Spinney the night poor old Tom was done in. And Mr. Verdew has always been cruel fond of animals, that's another reason.'

How easy it is, thought Jimmy, to lose one's reputation in the country!

'Tell me,' he said, 'how does Mr. Verdew satisfy his conscience when he eats animals and chickens, and when he has slugs and snails killed in the garden?'

'Ah, there you've hit it,' said the old man, not at all nonplussed. 'But they say Mr. Rollo Verdew has helped him to make a mighty great list of what may be killed and what mayn't, according as it's useful-like to human beings. And anybody kills anything, they persuade him it's harmful and down it goes on the black list. And if he don't see the thing done with his own eyes, or the chap isn't hauled up before the Bench, he doesn't take on about it. And in a week or less it's all gone from his mind. Jack and Tom were both killed within a few days of what they'd done becoming known; so was the collie dog what was found here a fortnight back.'

'Here?' asked Jimmy.

'Close by where you're standing. Poor beast, it won't chase those b——y cats no more. It was a mess. But, as I said, if what you've done's a week old, you're safe, in a manner of speaking.'

'But why, if he's really dangerous,' said Jimmy, impressed in spite of himself by the old man's tacit assumption of Randolph's guilt, 'doesn't Mr. Rollo Verdew get him shut up?' This simple question evoked the longest and most pregnant of his interlocutor's pauses. Surely, thought Jimmy, it will produce a monstrous birth, something to make suspicion itself turn pale.

'Now don't you tell nothing of what I'm saying to you,' said the old man at length. 'But it's my belief that Mr. Rollo don't want his brother shut up; no, nor thought to be mad. And why? Because if people know he's mad, and he goes and does another murder, they'll just pop him in the lunatic asylum and all his money will go to government and charity. But if he does a murder like you or me might, and the circumstances are circumstantial, he'll be hanged for it, and all the money and the castle and the coal-mine will go into the pockets of Mr. Rollo.'

'I see,' said Jimmy. 'It sounds very simple.'

'I'm not swearing there's anything of the sort in Mr. Rollo's mind,' said the old man. 'But that's the way I should look at it if I was him. Now I must be getting along. Good-night, sir.'

'Good-night.'

Of course it wasn't really night, only tea-time, five o'clock; but he and his acquaintance would meet no more that day, so perhaps the man was right to say good-night. Jimmy's thoughts, as he worked his way up the castle mound, were unclear and rather painful. He didn't believe a tithe of what the old man said. It was not even a distortion of the truth; it was ignorant and vulgar slander, and had no relation to the truth except by a kind of contiguity. But it infected his mood and gave a disagreeable direction to his thoughts. He was lonely; Randolph had not appeared at lunch, and he missed Rollo, and even more he missed (though this surprised him) Rollo's wife. He hadn't seen much of them, but suddenly he felt the need of their company. But goodness knows where they are, thought Jimmy; I can't even telephone to them. In the midst of these uneasy reflections he reached his bedroom door. Walking in, he could not for a moment understand why the place looked so strange. Then he realized; it was empty. All his things had been cleared out of it.

'Evidently,' thought Jimmy, 'they've mistaken the day I was going away, and packed me!' An extraordinary sensation of relief surged up into his heart. Since his luggage was nowhere to be seen, it must have been stacked in the hall, ready for his departure by the evening train. Picturing himself at the booking-office of Verdew Grove station buying a ticket for London, Jimmy started for the hall.

William cut short his search.

'Were you looking for your things, sir?' he asked, with a slight smile. 'Because they're in the Onyx Room. We've moved you, sir.'

'Oh,' said Jimmy, following in the footman's wake. 'Why?'

'It was Mr. Verdew's orders, sir. I told him the light was faulty in your bedroom, so he said to move you into the Onyx Room.'

'The room next his?'

'That's right, sir.'

'Couldn't the fuse be mended?'

'I don't think it was the fuse, sir.'

'Oh, I thought you said it was.'

So this was the Onyx Room—the room, Jimmy suddenly remembered, that Rollo had meant him to have in the beginning. Certainly its colours were dark and lustrous and laid on in layers, but Jimmy didn't care for them. Even the ceiling was parti-coloured. Someone must have been given a free hand here; perhaps Vera had done the decoration. The most beautiful thing in the room was the Chinese screen masking the door that communicated, he supposed, with Randolph's bedroom. What a clatter it would make if it fell, thought Jimmy, studying the heavy, dark, dully-shining panels of the screen. The door opening would knock it over. He heard the footman's voice.

'Is it for one night or more, sir? I've packed up some of your things.'

'I'm not sure yet,' said Jimmy. 'William, will this screen move?'

The footman took hold of the screen with both hands and telescoped it against his chest. There was revealed an ordinary-looking door covered with green baize. Jimmy could see the point of a key-head, so the door was probably not very thick.

'This used to be the dressing-room,' William volunteered, as though making a contribution to Jimmy's unspoken thoughts.

'Thank you,' said Jimmy, 'and would you mind putting the screen back? . . . And, William!'

The footman stopped.

'There's still time to send a telegram?'

'Oh yes, sir. There's a form here.'

All through his solitary tea Jimmy debated with himself as to whether he should send the telegram—a telegram of recall, of course, it would be. The message presented no difficulty. 'Wire if Croxford case opens Tuesday.' He knew that it did, but his attendance was not at all necessary. He was undoubtedly suffering from a slight attack of nerves; and nowadays one didn't defy nerves, one yielded to them gracefully. 'I know that if I stay I shall have a bad night,' he thought; 'I might as well spend it in the train.' But of course he hadn't meant to go at all; he had even promised Rollo to stay. He had wanted to stay. To leave abruptly to-night would be doubly rude: rude to Randolph, rude to Rollo. Only Vera would be pleased. Vera, whose clumsy attempt to lure him to London he had so easily seen through. Vera, whose 'I shall be furious if you don't come' rankled whenever he thought of it. Every moment added its quota to the incubus of indecision that paralysed his mind. Manners, duty, wishes, fears, all were contradictory, all pulled in different directions. A gust of apprehension sent him hot-foot to the writing-table. The telegram was ready written when, equally strong, an access of self-respect came and made him tear it up. At last he had an idea. At six o'clock he would send the telegram; the office might still be open. There might still be time to get a reply. If, in spite of his twofold obstacle he had an answer, he would take it as the voice of fate, and leave that night. . . .

At half-past seven William came in to draw the curtains; he also brought a message. Mr. Verdew begged Mr. Rintoul to excuse him, but he felt a little unwell, and was dining in his own room. He hoped to see Mr. Rintoul to-morrow to say good-bye. 'You are going, then, sir?' added the footman.

Jimmy blindfolded his will, and took an answer at random from among the tablets of his mind.

'Yes. And — William!' he called out.

'Sir?'

'I suppose it's too late now for me to get an answer to my telegram?'

'I'm afraid so, sir.'

For a second Jimmy sunned himself in a warm flow of recovered self-esteem. Luck had saved him from a humiliating flight. Now his one regret was that his nerves had cheated him of those few extra days at Verdew. 'If there had been a bolt on my side of the green door,' he said to himself, 'I should never have sent that telegram.'

How like in some ways, was the last evening to the first. As bedtime approached, he became acutely conscious of his surroundings — of the stone floors, the vaulted passages, the moat, the drawbridge — all those concrete signs which seemed to recall the past and substitute it for the present. He was completely isolated and immured; he could scarcely believe he would be back in the real, living world to-morrow. Another glass of whisky would bring the centuries better into line. It did; and, emboldened by its heady fumes, he inspected, with the aid of his candle (for the ground-floor lights had been turned out) the defences of door and window, and marvelled anew at their parade of clumsy strength. Why all these precautions when the moat remained, a flawless girdle of protection?

But was it flawless? Lying in bed, staring at the painted ceiling, with its squares and triangles and riot of geometrical designs, Jimmy smiled to remember how Rollo had once told him of a secret entrance, known only to him. He had promised to show it to Jimmy, but he had forgotten. A nice fellow Rollo, but he didn't believe they would ever know each other much better. When dissimilar natures come together, the friendship blossoms quickly, and as quickly fades. Rollo and Jimmy just tolerated each other—they didn't share their lives, their secrets, their secret passages. . . .

Jimmy was lying on his back, his head sunk on the brightly lit pillow, his mind drowsier than his digestion. To his departing consciousness the ceiling looked like a great five of diamonds spread over his head; the scarlet lozenges moved on hinges, he knew that quite well, and as they moved they gave a glimpse of black and let in a draught. Soon there would be a head poking through them all, instead of through this near corner one, and that would be more symmetrical. But if I stand on the bed I can shut them; they will close with a click. If only this one wasn't such a weight and didn't stick so. . . .

Jimmy awoke in a sweat, still staring at the ceiling. It heaved and writhed like a half-dead moth on the setting-board. But the walls stood still, so that there was something more than whisky at the back of it. And yet, when he looked again, the ceiling did not budge.

The dream was right; he could touch the ceiling by standing on the bed. But only with the tips of his fingers. What he needed was a bar of some kind with which to prise it open. He looked round the room, and could see nothing suitable but a towel-horse. But there were plenty of walking-sticks downstairs. To light his candle and put on his dressing-gown and slippers was the work of a moment. He reached the door in less time than it takes to tell. But he got no further, because the door was locked.

Jimmy's heart began to beat violently. Panic bubbled up in him like water in a syphon. He took a wild look around the room, ran to the bed-head, and pressed the bell-button as though he meant to flatten it in its socket. Relief stole in his heart. Already he heard in imagination the quick patter of feet in the corridor, the hurried, whispered explanations, the man's reassuring voice: 'I'll be with you in a moment, sir.' Already he felt slightly ashamed of his precipitate summons, and began to wonder how he should explain it away. The minutes passed, and nothing happened. He need not worry yet; it would take William some time to dress, and no doubt he had a long way to come. But Jimmy's returning anxiety cried out for some distraction, so he left the edge of the bed where he had been sitting, fetched the towel-horse, and, balancing unsteadily on the mattress, began to prod the ceiling. Down came little flakes and pellets of painted plaster; they littered the sheets, and would be very uncomfortable to sleep on. . . . Jimmy stooped to flick them away, and saw from the tail of his eye that since he rang five minutes had gone by. He resumed the muffled tattoo on the ceiling.

Suddenly it gave; the red diamond shot upwards and fell back, revealing a patch of black and letting in a rush of cool air.

As, stupefied, Jimmy lowered his eyes, they fell upon the screen. It was moving stealthily outwards, toppling into the room. Already he could see a thin strip of the green door. The screen swayed, paused, seemed to hang by a hair. Then, its leaves collapsing inwards upon each other, it fell with a great crash upon the floor. In the opening stood Randolph, fully dressed; he had a revolver in his right hand, and there was a knife between his teeth. It was curved and shining, and he looked as though he were taking a bite out of the new moon.

The shot missed Jimmy's swaying legs, the knife only grazed his ankle, and he was safe in the darkness of the attic, with the bolt of the trap-door securely shut. He ran trembling in the direction the draught came from, and was rewarded first by a sense of decreasing darkness, and then by a glimpse, through a framed opening in the roof, of the stars and the night sky.

The opening was low down, and to climb out was easy. He found himself in a leaden gully, bounded on one side by a shallow parapet two feet high, and on the other, as it seemed, by the slope of the roof. Finding his way along the gully, he was brought up sharp against an octagonal turret, that clearly marked the end of the building. The moat was directly below him. Turning to the left, he encountered another similar turret, and turning to the left again he found himself up against a wall surmounted by tall chimneys. This wall appeared to be scored with projections and indentations — soot-doors he guessed them to be; he hoped to be able to use them to climb the wall, but they were awkwardly spaced, close to the parapet, and if he missed his footing he ran the risk of falling over its edge.

He now felt a curious lightheartedness, as though he had shuffled off every responsibility: responsibility towards his pyjamas, which were torn and dirty, towards his foot, which was bleeding, towards trains, letters, engagements — all the petty and important demands of life. Cold, but not unhappy, he sat down to await daybreak.

The clock had just chimed three-quarters, which three-quarters he did not know, when he heard a scraping sound that seemed to come from the corresponding parapet across the roof. He listened, crouching in the angle between the chimney wall and the battlement. His fears told him that the sound was following the track by which he had come; the shuffling grew indistinct, and then, the first turret passed, began to draw nearer. It could only be Randolph, who clearly had some means of access to the roof other than the trap-door in Jimmy's bedroom. He must have, or he could not have reached it to spy on his victim while he was asleep. Now he was turning the last corner. Jimmy acted quickly and with the courage of desperation. At the corner where he crouched there projected above the battlement three sides of an octagonal turret, repeating the design of the true turrets at the end. Grasping the stone as well as he could, he lowered himself into space. It was a terrible moment, but the cautious shuffle of Randolph's approach deadened his fear. His arms almost at their full stretch, he felt the dripstone underneath his feet. It seemed about six inches wide, with a downward curve, but it sufficed. He changed his grip from the plain stone band of the parapet to the pierced masonry beneath it, which afforded a better purchase, and held his breath. Randolph could not find him unless he leant right over the balustrade. This he did not do. He muttered to himself; he climbed up to the apex of the roof; he examined the flue-doors, or whatever they were. All this Jimmy could clearly see through the quatrefoil to which he was clinging. Randolph muttered, 'I shall find him when the light comes,' and then he disappeared. The clock struck four, four-fifteen, four-thirty, and then a diffused pallor began to show itself in the eastern sky.

The numbness that had taken hold of Jimmy's body began to invade his mind, which grew dull and sleepy under the effort of compelling his tired hands to retain their hold. His back curved outwards, his head sank upon his breast; the changes of which his cramped position admitted were too slight to afford his body relief. So that he could not at once look round when he heard close above his head the sound of an opening door and the sharp rattle of falling mortar. He recognized the figure as it passed him—Rollo's.

Jimmy restrained his impulse to call out. Why had Rollo come back? Why was he swaggering over the roofs of Verdew Castle at daybreak looking as though he owned it? It was not his yet. Rollo turned, and in the same leisurely fashion walked back towards Jimmy's corner. His face was set and pale, but there was triumph in his eyes, and cruelty, and the marks of many passions which his everyday exterior had concealed. Then his eyebrows went up, his chin quivered, and his underlip shot out and seemed to stretch across his face. 'Just five minutes more, five minutes more; I'll give him another five minutes,' he kept muttering to himself. He leaned back against the wall. Jimmy could have touched the laces of his shoes, which were untied and dirty. 'Poor old Jimmy, poor old James!' Rollo suddenly chanted, in a voice that was very distinct, but quite unlike his own. To Jimmy's confused mind he seemed to be speaking of two different people, neither of whom was connected with himself. 'Never mind, Jimmy,' Rollo added in the conciliatory tone of one who, overcome by his better nature, at last gives up teasing. 'Anyhow, it's ten to one against.' He stumbled down the gully and round the bend.

Jimmy never knew how he summoned strength to climb over the parapet. He found himself sprawling in the gully, panting and faint. But he had caught sight of a gaping hole like a buttery hatch amid the tangle of soot-doors, and he began to crawl towards it. He was trying to bring his stiff knee up to his good one when from close by his left ear he heard a terrible scream. It went shooting up, and seemed to make a glittering arc of sound in the half-lit sky. He also thought he heard the words, 'Oh, God, Randolph, it's me!' but of this he was never certain. But through all the windings of Rollo's bolt-hole, until it discharged itself at the base of a ruined newel-staircase among the outbuildings, he still heard the agonized gasping, spasmodic, yet with a horrible rhythm of its own, that followed Rollo's scream. He locked the cracked, paintless door with the key that Rollo had left, and found himself among the lanes.

Late in the evening of the same day a policeman asked to see Mrs. Verdew, who was sitting in a bedroom in the King's Head inn at Fremby, a market town ten miles from Verdew Castle. She had been sitting there all day, getting up from time to time to glance at a slip of paper pinned to one of the pillows. It was dated, '7.30 a.m., July 10th,' and said, 'Back in a couple of hours. Have to see a man about a car. Sorry—Rollo.' She wouldn't believe the constable when he said that her husband had met with an accident some time early that morning, probably about five o'clock. 'But look! But look!' she cried. 'See for yourself! It is his own handwriting! He says he went away at half-past seven. Why are all Englishmen so difficult to convince?'

'We have a statement from Mr. Randolph Verdew,' said the policeman gently. 'He said that he . . . he . . . he met Mr. Rollo at the castle in the early hours of the morning.'

'But how can you be so stupid!' cried Mrs. Verdew. 'It wasn't Rollo —it was Mr. Rintoul who . . .'

'What name is that?' asked the policeman, taking out his notebook.

THE WHITE WAND

THE WHITE WAND

C.F. TOLD me this story and I shall re-tell it, as nearly as I can, in his own words. He would certainly have wished to be anonymous, and I shall respect his wish.

'Last summer,' he said, 'after an absence of many years, I revisited Venice. I used to stay there for long stretches at a time before the war, and had many friends in the Anglo-American colony. My reasons for going to Venice were partly curiosity, to see if the old spell still held, and partly in order to write—I've always been able to write in Venice. The apartment I used to take had been let, and I had found a new one, though of course I hadn't seen it. Nor had I notified my friends of my arrival; I'll tell you why Arthur, presently.

'But I didn't expect to be altogether alone, nor did I want to be. I had one stand-by. My gondolier, Antonio, who had served me all the times I was in Venice, was at the station to meet me. Italians are very good at welcoming one. He greeted me rapturously; he could hardly stand still: excitement wriggled from the top of his greying head to the soles of his feet. It was as if a fund of affection had been accumulating in him during the war years and now he was pouring it all out.

'Alone of my Venetian friends I had kept in touch with him during the War. Somehow or other, by way of Portugal, or the Vatican, or the Red Cross, we had managed to communicate, and the very difficulty entailed by those manœuvres seemed to have made our friendship more precious. Though I had never succeeded in hating him as an enemy, the reaction was just as strong as if I had, and I think the same was true of him. He was much more articulate about his feelings than I was. All the way from the station to my flat, which was somewhere behind the Zattere—I'll try to tell you where later, it's so hard to describe where anything is in Venice – I kept screwing my head round on the cushion and looking up at him, while he leaned over his oar, his words tripping over each other he talked so fast.

'I got more feeling from that conversation that hostilities had come to an end than I did from V.E. day or V.J. day, or indeed from anything before or since. The cold war with Russia had not yet got under way, and talking to Antonio I felt that human solidarity was once more a fact.

'So enveloping was his personality and so infectious his goodwill that I was hardly aware of the strangeness of my new abode, he was like a strong dose of familiarity that transformed the unknown into the known. I only noticed that it was up a great many steps.

'There was only one subject I didn't discuss with him, and that was my friends in Venice. Partly because I thought that he wouldn't know about them (though he was by nature a know-all), partly, and illogically, because I thought he might tell me something I didn't want to hear, but chiefly because – well, you know how I have felt about people since the war. The whole thing was such a ghastly disappointment to me that even my closest friends were somehow involved in it – even you, Arthur. I saw even the people I liked best as somehow at each other's throats. My personal relationships were a tender area, as the doctors say. I had dreaded my meeting with Antonio, in case it turned sour on me, like food on an acid stomach. I had jumped that hurdle, but I thought the others could be taken later. It's one thing talking to a servant who more or less has to agree with you (at least, Italian servants feel they must), and another to broach highly controversial topics with people whose minds and feelings have to be approached as warily as if they were a Foreign Power. And I was in no mood for circumspection. If I couldn't see eye to eye with someone, I didn't want to see him; I couldn't bear to be disagreed with, and I wasn't over eager to be agreed with, either. So I didn't ask Antonio for news of my friends, and he didn't for the moment volunteer any.

'I might have noticed that he and Giuseppina, the maid of all work who "went" with my new flat, were not hitting it off; but if I did notice, it didn't register. In the confusion of arriving I forgot to introduce them to each other formally. This was a breach of etiquette, but I don't think it would have made any difference if I had. There is never any love lost between gondoliers and indoor servants, and I think they were jealous of each other from the start. Giuseppina had not been warned that I should have this attendant, and Antonio did not trouble to disguise from her the fact that he regarded me as his possession. She looked about fifty; he was ten years older. She never let him out of her sight if she could help it, and she didn't want him to unpack for me. At about seven o'clock, before going out, as was his custom, to celebrate with his friends, he asked me if there was anything I wanted — tobacco, cigarettes, cognac? I said I should like some cognac and he brought it back with him when he returned to wait on me at dinner. Afterwards, when he was standing in the dimly-lit sala, saying goodnight, which took him a long time for he had by no means rubbed off the patina of absence, Giuseppina circled round him like a cat round a retriever, and when he had gone she shot the big bolt — the catenaccio — across the door with a sigh of satisfaction.

'I dined well and slept well, and the next morning what was my surprise and pleasure when Antonio appeared at eight o'clock bringing my early morning tea and beaming at me like the sun. In his other hand he was carrying something else — a bottle. He did everything with a flourish.

' "What have you got there?" I asked, when he had gone through our morning salutations and inquiries which, so strong is habit, took the same form they had taken in pre-war years. "It isn't time to begin drinking yet."

'His expression changed and became serious, even severe.

' "O signore," he said accusingly, "what a lot of cognac you drank last night!"

'He held the bottle up to the light; it was about three-quarters full. I was surprised that I had drunk so much and said so. "I was drinking a toast to my return to Venice," I added, apologizing for excess.

'He accepted my explanation graciously but still with a touch of disapproval in his manner; and then suddenly his face relaxed and became sunny again.

' "Good news," he said. "Signor Gretton is in Venice, he is staying at the Grand Hotel."

'I was dumbfounded. It was anything but good news to me. Gretton was an old friend of mine of pre-war days, not a member of the colony but a constant visitor to Venice, as I was. I liked him but I didn't want to see him, and he would bring the whole colony buzzing round my ears.

' "Yes, signore," Antonio went on, "he was leaving to-morrow, but when he heard that you were here he put his departure off a day."

' "How did he know that I was here?" I asked — a silly question from someone who knew the workings of the Venetian bush-telegraph as well as I did; but I was so relieved that Gretton was so to speak on the wing that I hardly knew what I was saying.

'Antonio shrugged his shoulders. "His gondolier must have told him," he said—forbearing to add, "And I told his gondolier." "And he wants to know if he may dine with you to-night. He thought you would prefer that to going to his hotel—I expect he is short of money like all the English, alas." This was a reasonable inference, but quite groundless, for Gretton is the soul of hospitality.

'So Gretton came to dinner and it wasn't at all the flop I thought it would be. The moment I saw his tall, thin figure Venice seemed to become itself and I could scarcely believe that so many years had rolled by. Gretton is a man of generous impulses, quick enthusiasms and equally quick resentments. But I didn't feel uneasy with him, still less quarrel with him, for the things that upset him were always personal matters—someone had treated him badly or had treated badly someone in whom he was interested. If he simmered with small resentments or flared up in sudden indignation these outbursts were like safety-valves, and no pressure of basic disagreement could form while they were spurting; he didn't reawaken the slumbering feud I had with almost everyone. There was just one thing: his eyes didn't light up when he saw me, and he didn't smile; he looked surprised, and I know why. It wasn't only that I looked much older; it was the sour expression I have now—you needn't tell me I haven't, I catch a glimpse of it in the glass sometimes.

'Well, it was very hot and we sat on the terrace with the night above us and below us, sipping iced water—it was much too hot to drink anything else. I went back in Gretton's gondola to his hotel, and walked home, revelling in the Venetian night which was like gold thread on black velvet: and it was nearly one o'clock when I reached the flat.

'Next morning Antonio again appeared with my early tea and I remember not feeling surprised—for I was in the befuddled state between sleeping and waking, when one is disposed to accept everything as a matter of course—to see the brandy bottle in his other hand. Having greeted me he assumed a stern, even a shocked expression, and said:

' "O signore, what a lot of cognac you and Mr. Gretton drank last night! Ma quanto! Quanto! What a lot, what a lot!" And he held the bottle up for my inspection: it was more than half empty.

' "But, Antonio," I said, now thoroughly mystified, "we didn't drink any cognac. It was much too hot."

'He turned away, but not before I had seen his expression change, and went to the window and looked out.

' "Forsè mi sbaglio," he said. "Perhaps I am mistaken."

' "But you can't be mistaken," I said. "Someone has drunk it."

'At that he turned away from the window and observed, significantly:

' "Signore, you were better off in your old flat."

'It was plain what he meant. He meant that if I hadn't drunk the brandy, Giuseppina had. I didn't answer, but I suddenly remembered how, all those years ago in my old flat, my stock of brandy sometimes used to dwindle, not in this sensational and dramatic fashion, but little by little. After breakfast I was still pondering upon this, and wondering who was the culprit, when in came Giuseppina. She said nothing but beckoned to me, and I saw that she was carrying in her hand a key. She led me from the room where I was sitting to the dining-room, where she fitted the key into the lock of the cellarette. Then she pursed her lips, raised her eyebrows, and withdrew.

'Later in the morning Gretton called to say good-bye to me. I was so pleased to see him and thought it so good of him to come, on the morning of his departure, that I forgot the problem of the missing brandy. But when I was asking him if he would have a drink I remembered it and told him.

'He was up in arms at once.

' "How monstrous! Let me see the bottle."

'I brought it and before I could protest, indeed before I knew what he was up to, he had taken out his fountain pen and scored a thick black line across the label to mark the level of the brandy.

' "That'll teach him," he said.

'After Gretton was gone I wondered if I should lock the cellarette and take away the key. I couldn't bring myself to do that; it was too flagrantly hostile an act, and against someone to whom I was very much attached. But all the same, my resentment mounted. I shouldn't have minded so much if Antonio had just sipped the brandy on the sly; it was this ridiculous act he had put on this "commedia" as the Italians call it, imagining he could so easily throw dust in my eyes. You can't throw dust in people's eyes without getting some of it in your own; and that's what had happened to him. And then, when he saw the first cock wouldn't fight, to try to put the blame on Giuseppina! Was there every such a misguided piece of cleverness? What a fool he must think me! That is the Italians all over, I thought; they are not content with theft, they must give it a panache, an extra twist to make them feel how smart they are, what artists. No doubt Antonio was telling the story to his fellow-gondoliers at the traghetto, and it would lose nothing in the telling. In Italy, I thought, there is no public opinion against dishonesty; as long as a man is ingenious about it, and successful (for Italians adore success), they think the better of him.

'I would willingly have given Antonio a bottle of brandy if he had asked me, but he would rather steal it than take it as a gift, because any nit-wit can have something given to him, but only the clever can steal it. I suppose you would say it's one of the things that make Italians so human.'

It was time to break in.

'I shouldn't say so,' I protested.

'Well, I thought you might. But I couldn't see it in that light. All through the war, in England, stopping at strange hotels and places up and down the country, and not only at hotels, I had been the victim of innumerable acts of pilfering — don't tell me, Arthur, please don't tell me, that the war has done our morals any good. All the little trinkets I possessed — yes, and necessities, too — were pinched from me — watches, watch-chains, cuff-links, travelling clocks — even the shirt off my back, when it was new enough. The war turned us into a nation of thieves — oh yes, it did, Arthur, whatever you may say. And to have this happening all over again in Venice it was *too* maddening.' My friend looked away from me and the sour look came into his face.

'All the rest of that day, until dinner-time, Antonio was charming — so attentive, he couldn't do enough for me. It seemed as though he could hardly get used to the idea that I was back and had a fresh shock of pleasure every time he saw me. I have never been able to find the same thing more than once, but he seemed able to rediscover me many times. That is all very well, I thought; but how do I know that this mood is more genuine than the other? How do I know that it isn't the brandy he is rediscovering, not me? So I turned a rather glum face to his smiles. But I didn't take any further steps and didn't mean to take any, so that when the storm burst it took me completely by surprise.

'It happened while he was laying the table for dinner. In my old flat he always laid the table. He had his own way of doing it, which was not quite orthodox by English or indeed by Italian standards; and Giuseppina, in pointing this out to me, also observed that she was accustomed to doing it herself. I said that perhaps later on I would tell him not to bother with the table. But I didn't mean to, knowing it would hurt his feelings.

'Yet when he burst into my sitting-room with a face twisted and black with rage, my first thought was that it must have something to do with this dispute, this "questione" about the table-laying. Then I saw the brandy-bottle; he was not carrying it delicately in the palm of his large hand, he was grasping it by the neck and looked as if he meant to hit me with it: perhaps I was lucky that he didn't. I jumped up and said:

' "What's the matter, Antonio?"

'He came towards me and thrust the bottle under my eyes.

' "Who did this?" he demanded in (I don't exaggerate) a strangled voice.

'I saw the accusing black line across the label.

' "I did," I said. It was the easiest thing to say, the truth would have involved too many explanations which would, in any case, have been lost upon his fury. Besides, I was to blame for the line being there.

' "Does it mean that you have wished to suspect me——?" he began in the same choking voice.

'Suddenly I saw red. I wasn't sure that his anger was genuine. I thought he might be putting it on, using his bad temper as a weapon to terrorize me and bounce me into believing he was innocent; and this made me still more angry. I took a long breath.

' "I don't know whom to suspect," I said. "Tutti gli Italiani sono ladri, specialmente i gondolieri" – "all Italians are thieves, especially gondoliers."

'I shouldn't have said it, of course, but at the moment I was glad to have said it, I wanted to do him the greatest injury I could. I might have stuck a dagger into his heart if I had had one, and felt the same satisfaction.

'Antonio went as white as a sheet – the only time I have seen him without colour. His normal complexion was a shade darker than brick-red. I remember his once saying to me, alluding to his complexion, "I am red, I have always been red, and when I am dead I shall still be red."

'A moment later he was red again, redder than I have ever seen him. He looked away from me, dashed the bottle down on the mosaic terrazzo, squared his shoulders, turned round, and walked out of the room stiffly, like a soldier.

'I sat down and laughed weakly. In doing so I too was putting on an act, but to impress myself, not someone else. How long I sat there I don't know, but suddenly I noticed a strong smell and, looking down, I saw a long rivulet of brandy curling round my feet. Dark fragments of broken glass littered the terrazzo, which I now saw was slightly splintered where the bottle had struck it. What would Giuseppina say to all this? I went to look for her and found her in the kitchen, placidly beating up a zabaione.

'"Where is Antonio?" I asked.

'Her face became expressionless, as it always did when I mentioned his name.

'"Isn't he in the dining-room?" she said, as if the dining-room would be contaminated by his presence.

'But he wasn't. The oval dining-table was half laid, the door of the cellarette, from which Antonio had been getting out the drinks, stood open. The room had a provisional, expectant air like a child abandoned in the middle of being dressed.

'I knew Antonio's tantrums well. He had always had these moods of being what he called "nero" — "black" — and was rather proud of them. They were manifestations of his proper pride, the "amor proprio" so dear to the Italian heart; they showed that he knew his own value and was not going to be put upon. They lasted sometimes for a day or even two days, after which, and without apology or explanation, he would come out of them and be his sanguine, sunny self again. They must have cost him something, for during these times he ate but little and spoke hardly at all; they were a kind of possession. I used to wonder how his wife, who was devoted to him, stood them; they had a very upsetting effect on me. But perhaps like most Italian women she liked a man to be a man and respected his displays of temperament.

'To Giuseppina's unconcealed displeasure — she said she would have much preferred to do it herself — he had decided to wait on me at meals. After the first explosion, when he generally absented himself for a time, he never let his tempers interfere with the performance of what he considered his duties, and I fully expected he would come back to help me through dinner.

'But he didn't. Giuseppina served me; she made no comment on Antonio's absence but stood watching me. Any emotional upset affects my digestion, that is why I avoid them whenever I can, and have got the reputation, no doubt, of being an icicle. If I had given way to all the annoyance I have felt during the last twelve years I should long ago have been riddled with gastric ulcers. Oh yes, I should have, Arthur; you needn't look sceptical. I should have been well advised that evening to have eaten nothing; but how could I, I ask you, with Giuseppina watching my every mouthful? She was determined I should do her cooking justice, and she never took her eyes off me, or stopped talking, except between the courses. At last I could not help speaking of the subject uppermost in my mind, and asked her where she thought Antonio had gone.

'"Oh, him," she said, and made no other comment.

'By bedtime the nerves of my stomach were thoroughly demoralized and I knew I was in for a bad night. By half-past five in the morning, with the first summons of the Ave Mary bell, I knew that I was in for fever, too. I kept going over in my mind phrases of forgiveness which should also make it clear that there was nothing to forgive, for I did not doubt that Antonio would come in the morning. But instead it was Giuseppina who called me, bringing my tea-tray but no bottle of brandy. She looked more cheerful than I had ever seen her, and I, misinterpreting the signs, asked her if she had seen Antonio.

'"Yes," she said, "he came at seven o'clock and took the gondola away."

'"Took the gondola away?" I echoed.

'"Yes, signore, he said he was not going to serve you any more."

'"Did he say why?" I asked.

'She hesitated a moment and then said, "He said it was because you would not pay him enough."

'My illness was sharp and what was more it was recurrent. It was one of those gastric disorders that visitors to Venice sometimes get, and I expect I should have had it anyway: the row with Antonio only aggravated it. But I had never had it before and didn't quite know what was going to happen. I didn't call in a doctor because every day Giuseppina assured me I was better, and in the end she proved to be right. But it did for me what an illness so often does, it changed the orientation of my thoughts. The needle of anxiety pointed to myself, not to Antonio. I could think of him without agitation and without working myself into a state.

'I thought of him a good deal and remembered his many virtues. What patience he had! He never minded how long he was kept waiting. One of the grand ladies who used to employ him before he came to me, once forgot about him, went home another way, and left him out all night: but he didn't hold it against her—he thought it reflected credit on her, and was the way a great lady should behave.

'And what courage he had. Many gondoliers are afraid of the water; a puff of wind or a drop of rain will send them scurrying for shelter. Storms get up very suddenly on the lagoon: we had many picnics there in exposed places miles from Venice; often we had to fight our way home against a head wind (for I rowed, too), and it took hours and was really a little dangerous, for a gondola is a most unseaworthy boat. But Antonio never minded that, or getting wet to the skin. He never reproached me with disregarding his warnings about the weather; he contented himself with saying that no other gondolier would do what he did; he was nothing if not boastful, but this at least was true. He had a great regard for appearances and perhaps he saw himself as Ajax defying the lightning. But in a humbler, less exhibitionistic way, he could be very devoted. Like a policeman, he hated having to run; it upset his dignity. Though amphibious, he was primarily a sea-creature, and though by no means awkward on dry land, he had a stiff-legged way of running—throwing his weight from one foot to the other as if he were reaching out to crush a beetle. He must have known it was inelegant, and it was particularly unsuitable to Venice, where an unguarded movement may easily knock someone over. But he would dash off to the station with my late letters and come back breathless but triumphant, saying "Ho fatto un corso!"—"I ran like the wind!"—and without making any complaint.

'His dignity! It all came back to that. "Far figura"—how do you translate it? "Keeping up appearances"? Face-saving is at the root of the Italian character. He didn't mind being a thief, but he didn't like being called one. Among the popolo in Italy an insult is a thing in itself: un' offesa, and whether it be well founded or not makes little difference to the gravity of the offence, perhaps none. By taking umbrage he was only acting according to his principles; a less dramatic course would have lowered him in his own esteem. How easy it would have been to treat the whole thing as a joke! And perhaps I could have, if he hadn't wounded my own self-esteem by believing he could bamboozle me about the bottle—and all to satisfy his artistic sense! I had only to think of his stern accusing face—"What a lot of cognac you and Mr. Gretton drank last night, signore—what a lot, what a lot!" to feel myself getting hot under the collar. Of course I shouldn't have minded so much if I hadn't had all those things stolen from me in the war—all my trinkets, my cuff-links, my watch-chains, my travelling-clock—don't laugh, Arthur!'

'I wasn't laughing,' I said, though in fact I was on the verge of a nervous titter, such was his vehemence.

'You looked as if you might be going to. Of course materially, it wasn't serious, and yet in a way it was; before the war one bottle of brandy more or less didn't matter, you could replace it; but how can you replace three thousand lire now, I ask you? And it was the principle of the thing. Somehow I should have minded less if he had had one redeeming virtue instead of one damning vice. His whole being seemed to be organized for deceit. But most Italians are that way, I fancy.'

'I shouldn't choose a gondolier as a touchstone of moral behaviour, either in Italy or elsewhere,' I said, tired of his coat-trailing.

'Oh, you wouldn't, wouldn't you?' my friend said nastily. 'Why not? Because he is a poor man, I suppose?'

'No,' I said, not wishing to be hoisted on the petard of social snobbery. 'Because for centuries gondoliers have been dependent on the whims of well-to-do people like yourself, and have had to shape their conduct accordingly. With them it's a matter of economics, not of morals.'

'You would defend the Devil,' he said violently. Then with a sudden change of mood he went on:

'It was so ironical that during all the war years when we ought to have been wishing each other dead and so on, we hadn't had an unkind thought about each other, and now, when our Governments had graciously announced we could be friends, we weren't on speaking terms.

'As soon as I could I wrote him a letter, in effect apologizing to him for having let him rob me and asking him to come back. I couldn't bring myself to say that I had drunk the brandy myself or that Giuseppina had. I gave the letter to Giuseppina to post and never doubted it would do the trick. I've sometimes wondered whether she did post it, she hated him so much. Certainly he didn't answer, or come back. Did I afterwards find out he wasn't the real culprit? Unfortunately, no.

'Lacking Antonio, Venice seemed an utterly strange place to me. For one thing I had never been ill in Venice before. I had always been particularly well—and, for me, active. The question was how to find time for all the things I wanted to do. And you know how, in that state, one doesn't look about one very much. I won't say I never looked at Venice, but I looked at it with the eye of health and hurry—any eye that doesn't see much. Now I was a prisoner. My sphere of action was limited to one room and, as I got better, to two. I felt utterly cut off. In my old flat I had a telephone and Antonio to run errands for me: here I had no telephone, no Antonio, only Giuseppina as a link with the outside world: she had all the housework to do, as well as marketing and catering for me and, when I was ill, acting as my nurse: and I did not like to inflict any further duties on her, unless it was to ask her to post a letter.

'And I didn't want to write any letters. No! After Antonio's defection my unwillingness to make myself known to my friends in Venice increased, until it amounted to a nervous inhibition. When I thought I was getting over it, I was really getting used to it. A feeling of snugness enfolded me; I was enclosed in my anonymity as in a cocoon, and I had no wish at all to break my bonds; indeed, every day I spun new ones, I didn't want my convalescence to end and invented new symptoms which would keep me indoors. Giuseppina, with native shrewdness, was quick to discover this. "Si è impressionato," she said, "you are frightening yourself" — and so I was, though not quite in the way she meant.

'At the back of my mind was always the thought that Antonio, though absent as a friend was present as an enemy, and my dread of meeting him, if I went out, began to extend to all the inhabitants of Venice. So I was doubly a prisoner, a prisoner of myself and a prisoner of the flat; and when I got tired of the view of my own mind, I had the windows of my two rooms to look out of.

'From my bedroom windows I enjoyed a roofscape. Domes and towers gave it grandeur and formal beauty, but what chiefly fascinated me was the roofs themselves. I came to know them as intimately as did the sparrows that hopped about on them: a sparrow on the house-tops, that's what I was myself.

'Low-pitched, almost flat, the roofs reminded me of shallow pyramids or squat pagodas — Venice has many forms and contours that suggest the East. Red-brown and weather-stained, the tiles lay along them like strings of broken flower-pots, on which, when the sun came out, the lizards basked and darted. (It didn't come out very much: June had set in wet.) Instead of pots or cowls, the chimney-stacks had roofs on them like tables. Crowning some of the roofs, and higher than the chimney pots, were the altanas, platforms where the washing was hung out; flimsy-looking structures whose posts and palings made a pattern on the sky like Chinese Chippendale. Some of them had small hut-like attachments, bonnets or hoods to keep the weather out. There was something new every time one looked, some new arrangement of lines and surfaces; all, or nearly all, brown-pink and grey, with here and there the vivid green of a creeper, or the top of a cypress nodding against a wall.

'This view had the slightly hypnotic effect on me that an abstract or a cubist picture might have. It took me out of myself, but not, as you will easily believe, towards anyone else. Except for a woman shaking a duster from a window or hanging washing out on an altana, it was a roofscape without figures—a geometrical world.

'Below the two windows of my sitting-room was a canal with a pavement—a fondamenta—bordering it. You could only see the pavement by leaning out of the window, it was so far below; but what a rewarding sight it was! Together the canal and the fondamenta made a stage on which the scenery didn't vary much but the action was always changing. Though nothing sensational ever happened, something was always going to happen; and that something was heralded by shouts of warning or encouragement, advice or reproof: nothing that took place, or looked like taking place, escaped somebody's comment.

'It was a way of living by proxy, and it exactly suited me, in my limp convalescent state, to be a spectator of the spectators. I didn't try to write, I just sat looking. Very often I didn't even take the trouble to go to the windows: I could see from my chair a great deal—the houses opposite, the big acacia with its tufted top, sensitive to every air that blew, the terrace beside it, sometimes the scene of impassioned carpet-beating, sometimes of alfresco parties, the petunias in boxes along its balustrade, the luxuriant bignonia that dripped from it, and the scarcely less luxuriant wistaria that climbed in and out of the bignonia. It was mid-June; the bignonia was beginning to put out its scarlet tongues—an insult which I took in good part; the wistaria was blooming for the second time; their blossoms did not accord, yet there was something touching about their friendship: it was so intimate yet on so grand a scale.

'Next came the great palazzo to which the terrace was a foot-stool—the Palazzo Trevisan. It differed in plan from most Venetian palaces in having two wings with a courtyard in between. The courtyard was also a garden in the Italian sense— that is to say it possessed trees, shrubs, creepers and a fountain; but no flowers to speak of. It looked dreary in the rain but on bright days when the sunshine lay heavy on the house-tops it made a great patch of shade for which the eye was thankful; and I could imagine how cool it was beneath the trees. The garden had a water-gate let into the wall and a flight of stone steps, stained and seaweedy, that were submerged at high tide. But I never saw it opened. No gondola ever drew up at the steps; the gondolier's anxious cry, warning his fare against the slippery surface — "Piano — si scivola!" — was never heard. Not that the steps were unused. Barche and sandole — nondescript boats of all work — were moored to them, and moored, too, to the tall blue posts with their gilded and coroneted summits that stood, slanting this way and that, like a forest in the water.

'No one said them nay, no one told them to tie up elsewhere, for the noble family who owned the palace, and from whom it took its name, had long since left and now it was inhabited, so Giuseppina told me, by many families, some of whom were well to do, while some occupied tenements of no more than two rooms each. The palace had come down in the world. It was encased in pale grey stucco, and had the tall, round-headed windows of the late sixteenth century, each bordered by a thin band of Istrian stone; the balconies, the dripstones, the sham machicolations which held up the roof, were of the same material. The shutters were painted brown outside, but inside they were grey, a darker grey than the stucco, so that when they were open the palace was a symphony of shades from white to dark grey, and might, if it had looked smarter, have been compared to a fashionable elderly lady dressed for a garden-party; but it didn't look smart — no building in Venice does.

'Some of the occupants of the palace opened their shutters in the daytime, some left them ajar, some kept them closed; few kept them completely closed, for the front that faced me was the north front, and the sun only reached it in the evening. Venetians — perhaps all Italians — are very shutter-conscious. Facing south, my sitting-room got the full force of the sunshine, if there was any; whether there was or not, Giuseppina would come about midday and try to close my shutters, leaving me in darkness; otherwise, she said, the sun would fade the covers — she was very jealous of her mistress's possessions. But I insisted on having them left a little open, for me to see out by; when this had been done, my flat and the palace opposite were like two people looking at each other through half-closed eyes.

'When the sun had gone round I threw the shutters back and resumed my watch at the window. I must have sat for many hours of every day in this way, like a passenger in a railway train, not taking in any special feature of what I saw but passively enjoying the sense of sight.

'Several days passed and then, one morning, Giuseppina brought me a letter.

'I thought at once that it was a letter from Antonio, for there was no stamp on it, it had come by hand. But the handwriting told me it was not.

'Giuseppina watched me open it. It was written in Italian in a very sloping hand, with spidery letters not easy to read. I have it here,' my friend went on, and pulled out his pocket-book; but like a speaker who does not have to rely on his notes he read, or rather translated, without consulting it:

' "Egregio Signore, — It is many days now that I have seen you looking from your window and it seems to me that always your eyes have been fixed on me." '

My friend looked up, and almost as though he were illustrating the letter, he raised his eyes to mine. Then he dropped them and went on:

' "Perhaps I am mistaken, but I think you do not look at me without interest. It would not be possible to gaze so long at one object unless the object had aroused one's interest. And I, signore, am also interested in you. I know your face — ah, very well. I know — do not ask me how — that you are a foreigner. Ah! You would be surprised if you knew how much I know about you. Do not think it is because I am inquisitive. I cannot help knowing about you, any more than I can help knowing whether we have the sun or not. I ask only one thing, signore, do not leave Venice, do not leave me, without making a sign." '

My friend's voice grew a little unsteady at this point, and he broke off.

'How did she finish it?' I asked. 'Foreigners have such odd ways of ending letters.'

'She didn't finish it,' he answered.

'She didn't even give her name?'

He shook his head.

'But how could she expect you to make a sign when you didn't know her name or her address?'

He suddenly became too agitated to answer.

'But you know her name now?' I persisted.

'Yes, I know it now.'

After a moment or two my friend took up his tale.

'I was furious at the letter and my first reflection was: Now I shall never be able to sit at the window again. You don't know how essential it is for a writer, at least it is for me, to be able to be absolutely passive, well, not quite passive, but as unconscious of absorbing as the body when it breathes. You can't do that with someone watching you, watching you in a particular way, I mean; speculating about you, wondering what you're up to, trying to make contact through their eyes. I had enough of that from Giuseppina. She was always peeping

at me. I would look up to see the door ajar, and half a face showing —
to be followed at once by the entrance of its owner, looking disarmingly frank and innocent. It was bad enough to have this espionage
indoors, but to have it from outside as well, a cross-fire, was really too
much. I was seriously put out. You know how it is when one is nervous;
the full force of one's irritation concentrates on a single grievance. Then
I realized that by shifting my chair to the other window I could still
command a view — the view of the creeper-hung terrace — and be out
of sight of the harpy in the palace.

'She had asked me for a sign — well, now she had it.

'I meant to tear the letter up, but, as you see, I didn't. I kept it as one
does sometimes keep things, to sharpen the edge of my annoyance.
One's nature demands a sensitive place — a soft spot, a sore spot — that
will yield a thrill or a pang: at least mine does. As I had no soft spot at
the moment, the sore spot did just as well. It reminded me of all the
idle, inquisitive women who had from time to time plagued me un-
mercifully about my work, wasting my time as freely as if it was their
own; and whenever I sat down at my new gazebo I felt I was giving
them all a retrospective snub.

'But habit is sometimes stronger than spite and one morning, without being aware of it, I found myself sitting in my old place. I jumped
up, as if an enemy had caught me napping; but at the same moment a
nerve of curiosity twitched and I became all eyes. Like eyes, the windows of the palace stared back at me, and I thought I detected in the
depths of one which had its shutters ajar a sort of commotion, a confusion, a flurry, and then a movement of withdrawl, as if something
long and slender and white — I thought of it as a white wand — had been
pulled inwards. I've never been quite clear what did happen, but suddenly I felt ashamed of having scared a fellow-creature, and as if I was
a sort of ogre, and my confidence in the justice of my feelings was
shaken.'

'Did you then lean out and wave?' I asked.

'Oh no, I bolted back to the other window, but I didn't like the view
from there so well. The yellow campanile of Santa Eufemia on the
Giudecca looked like a water-tower, just as functional as the chimney-
stack beside it. And I saw a lot of other things that I didn't like, but they
didn't vanish just because I didn't like them. They weren't so accommodating as she was. All day long, through the narrow strait of blue
sky between the acacia and the palace wall, the swifts came, dive-
bombing and screaming. They had twice the lung-power of our

English swifts and made a target of me. Involuntarily I ducked.—
But I expect you are fond of birds?'

'Not extravagantly,' I said.

He gave me a sour smile.

'Most English people are. Well, after a time and as I began to feel
better and have fewer set-backs, my feelings about the unknown signorina—*la signorina sconosciuta* (for so I thought of her) underwent a
change. It seemed quite natural and excusable that she should want to
look at me—after all, a cat can look at a king. Convalescence creates
an appetite for life: I began to lose my morbid dread of being stared at.
And as for wanting me to make a sign, that was excusable in a woman,
too. I hadn't the smallest intention of making one, of course; but I
liked to think of her thinking that I might. So I moved back to my old
window and sat there rather self-consciously, with I dare say a complacent smile on my face, as if I was sitting for my portrait. And I used to
scan the window in which I thought I had seen the white wand, or
whatever it was, but I never saw it.

'After that my routine existence began to irk me. Venice called me.
I could no longer pretend I was an invalid; I wanted to join the chattering, clattering throng that drifts through the streets of Venice as slug-
gishly as the tide flows through its canals. Supposing I did run into
Antonio, what matter? And I wanted to see my friends, my friends
from whom I had been separated by years of war and my own bad
habit of not writing.

'I owed each of them a letter, some more than one; their letters, like
Antonio's had come by devious routes; they had arrived months,
sometimes years, after they were written, they were blacked out and
smudged, they told me as little of the sender's present state as if they
had been messages from the grave. And I hadn't answered, partly from
inertia, partly from lack of opportunity, but chiefly from a deeper feeling that with the war friendship had come to an end. In those days I
was internationally-minded, and it seemed to me that the breakdown
of international relationships meant the breakdown of individual relationships too. Peace is indivisible, as somebody said. I had friends in
many countries, some of them countries, like Italy, with which we
were at war. I could not hate them because the State ordered me to;
but neither could I like them as I had liked them. For me the war dried
up the springs of liking; the intercourse between souls seemed an activity
as meaningless and out-of-date as the other activities I had enjoyed.

'I don't believe I was alone in this, Arthur, I believe that for many people the steady warmth of personal relationships perished in the burning heat of September 1939. Certainly with me it did; I felt I had nothing to give out or to take in and this arid state continued, more or less, until the accident of my Venetian convalescence altered it. I won't say it has never come back.'

'So that is the explanation,' I broke in. 'We all thought——'

'No, that was it,' he said, firmly pushing aside what we had all thought. 'I felt as though the currency restrictions had—well—made all forms of communication impossible. The blight of political hatred was on everything. I'm not sure that it's gone yet. I believe people still say to themselves, 'I will really start to *feel*—for you, or you, or you—and my feeling will be worth something to us both—as soon as, as soon as—the hydrogen bomb is perfected, or this business in Korea is settled. Then I shall feel for you, and perhaps you will feel for me; but until then our feelings are provisional—we are trying them out—they don't involve us or commit us—they are on appro. We might make a deal in them on the hire-purchase system, but the day of settlement is infinitely remote. Meanwhile, nothing really counts." '

'I don't think I feel like that,' I said.

'Don't be too sure. Anyhow, one dismal afternoon,—I'd had a nap—under a blanket and an eiderdown, the day was so abominably cold—I started out to see my friends.

'I had no telephone and couldn't forewarn them: I had no one to send, and as for writing letters, I had suddenly become too impatient to wait for the answers. The need for friendship had come on me like a hunger.

'I decided I would call on three—the three who had meant the most to me. They lived a long way apart, one at San Severo, one—oh, but it doesn't matter where, it's impossible to describe where any place is in Venice. They were each under the protection of a local saint, though they were not exactly saints themselves. If you think of Venice as a flat fish swimming towards the mainland, one of my friends lived on its tail, another half-way up the north side of its body, and the third somewhere near its eye. They lived, as I said, a long way apart, and though they saw each other fairly often, they didn't like each other very much. In those days when I went in for personal relationships—when in fact they were almost my religion—I didn't like to see any two of these friends, still less the three of them, on one day, because they were so critical of each other. I suppose all that sounds rather priggish to you?'

'No,' I said primly. 'I think it does you credit.'

He shot me a suspicious glance. 'Oh well,' he said, 'I don't mind now, of course. But in those days I didn't like to hear one of my friends run down another, beyond a certain point, I mean, and despised myself for not taking the part of the absent one, or only taking it half-heartedly. Then, when I was with someone I was fond of, he or she was like a mirror to me: I don't only mean that they reflected me myself, which was agreeable, but the other reflections seemed to me true, unflawed and perfect also: I saw the world in a frame—their frame—and I could live in it and accept it. My vision of them and theirs of me were one— or could become one, I believed, and that was what I aimed at: the merging into one focus of our reciprocal reflections—a sort of fusion. Well, each of my friends was quite willing to play this game with me and we had plenty of conversational material, unconnected with the others, to make our meetings fun. They were all cultivated people, who had spent most of their lives abroad; their outlook was at once cosmopolitan and parochial, and they had several languages at their command. They all had taste, too, in their houses. Though Lady Porteous's house was by far the most beautiful, each of the three interiors had something that intimately satisfied and pleased me.

'I did sometimes ask myself what I had to give them, that they should make me welcome, and supposed it was that, coming from London, I could feed them with gossip they might not have got otherwise. Like most expatriates, they were keenly interested in what went on at home. Lady Porteous and Denys Constantine were both great gossips; Miranda Collier wasn't, she preferred to talk about a subject, but she too liked hearing the latest news. I had written a book or two, which gave me a certain status; and I have since thought that I took too much for granted the appreciation they showered on these callow works. I myself was so astonished at having produced them that I assumed too readily that others would share my wonderment—after all, writers are two a penny. Perhaps, being all people who might have written, but had not, they attached too much importance to the accident of literary creativeness. Come to that, their lives were a creation, for they made an art of living.

'But it occurs to me now—I can see you're going to laugh—that what I really had to offer was youth. Compared to them I was young. I was—but no matter how old I was. Their ages were carefully concealed, though always a matter for conjecture. (I rarely saw Denys Constantine without his telling me that Lady Porteous was nearer seventy than sixty.) Most of the colony were on the shady side of middle age, and they were glad to see someone who had the sun before him instead of at his back.

'So it was as a young man that I started out on my sentimental journey that cold, wet, blustery day in June, and as a young man that I faced the prospect of the five-mile walk which I should have to accomplish if I was to carry out my programme. No gondola for me. Few gondoliers would have turned out on such a day. Antonio would have, but he wasn't available.

'I got to the Piazza in good order but then I stopped, for it was like a lake, a lake with islands and peninsulas made by the dips and rises in the pavement, which were imperceptible at normal times. On these a few daring pedestrians stood stranded. The arcade by Florian's was above the flood-line, but so packed with people that one could hardly stir. In the distance, stretching across the façade of St. Mark's, a flimsy wooden bridge had been put up, and across it two lines of people were moving in contrary directions – if moving be the word: no traffic jam was ever more complete. I looked round and as I did so a stranger smiled at me. After a moment's hesitation I smiled back: he must, I thought, be some acquaintance from my Venetian past. Confusion spread over the man's face and he began to explain:

' "You are like somebody I know – the Engineer Tremontin – I was to meet him here."

'I bowed and we both tried to cover up the awkwardness – he his disappointment, I my pique at being taken for someone else. All at once he smiled:

' "Ah ecco! Here he is!" and following his eye I saw a man whose resemblance to me I at once recognized. And yet, I thought, he can't be really like me – he's an old man – that white hair, that whitening moustache! – while I'm a young one – and I remembered my age, which, like my friends in Venice, I had taken to concealing, even from myself.

'It has often happened to me to be mistaken for other men, but never before had my *alter ego* been almost simultaneously presented to my gaze, giving my vanity no chance to put a flattering interpretation on the likeness. Offence deepened into outrage; I looked with hatred at that Ancient of Days, my double. And the worst of it was we were jammed together in the crowd; and for several minutes, while we shoved or were being shoved towards the end of the arcade, I was forced to look at the greying stubble and the criss-cross wrinkles on the nape of his neck and wonder if mine had them too. Italians deserve their reputation for good manners, and from time to time the couple would turn their heads and made some civil remark, deprecating the crush; but I received these olive-branches so badly that they soon desisted. I was aware of a process of disacquaintance going on in me, which, to judge from their stiffened shoulders and reddening necks was also going on in them, and when we at last debouched it was, I'm sure, with a common hope that we should never, never, never meet again.'

'You don't look old,' I said. 'No one would ever take you for whatever age it is you are concealing.' He looked sixty, or thereabouts.

He smiled and answered, 'I'm not really vain, so it was specially annoying, at that moment, to have to admit I was.

'My way lay to the left of St. Mark's, through the Canonica; but to get there I should have to cross the trestle bridge, where progress was visibly slower than it had been even in the arcade. I couldn't face the sardine tin again, so I picked my way along the high ground of the Piazzetta towards the two columns and the Bacino. It was rather fun, I remember, like walking on a sandbank with the sea coming in both sides. The sea was dark green and white, the gondolas rode madly up and down between their posts, there was, distinct from all the other storm sounds, that unnerving creaking that wood makes scraping against wood; and all along the Molo, almost up to the arches of the Ducal Palace, there was a jagged line of seaweed and orange peel and other vegetable and marine matter, the detritus of the storm. The seashore in Venice! And in contrast to all this untidiness and uproar was a strange Claude-like feature which enchanted me; for where the sea was actually invading the stone floor of Venice, it came not in angry foam-flecked swirls but in tiny level ripples, which advanced with the utmost gentleness at intervals so regular that in the distance they looked like the steps of a staircase—a shallow staircase leading to the sea.

'Bludgeoned by the blast, I fought my way along the riva, meaning to strike inland when an opening offered—one of them, I knew, would lead to San Severo. The insult to my appearance was losing its smart, and I was wondering how I could make a story of it; it would make a good story to celebrate a reunion with an old friend. Not Denys perhaps; his hair was white and his moustache whitening when I last saw him. Nor Miranda; she would not miss the point, but she would not quite see how it affected me, she would generalize and philosophize about it, and perhaps start some theory of doppelgängers. But Lady Porteous—how she would enjoy the malign little episode! How perfectly its malice would accord with hers! She would equally enjoy laughing with me and laughing at me; and from among her inexhaustible annals she would find a much better anecdote to cap it with.

'I almost wished I had put her first on my itinerary instead of leaving her, like a bonne bouche, till last.

'Well, I reached my first destination and I reached my second, and was told at each that the person I had come to see had left Italy before the war broke out and never come back. I could have seen them any day in England during the last ten years, but I could not see them in Venice.'

My friend sighed and I sighed with him. Being a happily married man I did not subscribe to his gospel of multiple personal relationships: it seemed to me a *pis aller* — I was content with one. But I knew how much it meant, or had meant, to him, and perhaps I should have felt still sorrier for him if I also had not been one of his rejects, and had been banished for twelve years, not ten.

'One has a different self for every friend,' he was saying. 'That is their most precious gift to one — a new self. The boredom of being always the same person! I had condemned myself to it all those years — and yet it was not I, it was the war which somehow upset the balance of my feelings, offering them food they would not accept — rationed food, too — and then making what they would once have accepted, unacceptable. A's name, B's name, your name, meant as little to me as a column of strange names in the telephone book. I can't tell you how blighting it was: it's not much better now.

'Where was I? Oh, yes, under the statue of Bartolomeo Colleoni, one of the two great equestrian statues of the world. Was there friendship in it? There was not. There was pride, and insolence, and success, and glory; the glory of war and conquest: every quality the statue had, except the quality of art, repudiated every quality I valued. I nearly turned back; but then I remembered Lady Porteous and the extraordinary power that she had, and that her house had, of imposing their standards on one. They were not standards I would be altogether prepared to defend; they were worldly, they were snobbish, they were based on exclusiveness.

'Do you want me to go on?' he asked, suddenly and resentfully. 'I suppose you know what's coming?'

'I've not the faintest idea,' I said.

'Well, what Lady Porteous had — what even her husband Sir Hilary, the light-weight satellite who circled round her, had — was the gift of imparting her own sense of superiority. She made one a present of it — her wealth, her cleverness, her taste, her ability to see everyone as stuck at various levels lower than her own, struggling to reach hers, and failing. Humour was her weapon; she knew something about everyone that made them slightly absurd; the most august figures of our acquaintance, the most feared and revered figures in the world outside — Mussolini, Hitler, Stalin — seemed figures of fun when Caroline Porteous had done with them. There was a story, which I did not believe, that Mussolini had once called on her and had not been received. She obviously liked the story, would not altogether deny it, but she was too clever to authenticate it. Her version was that it was a muddle on the part of the servants, who were so overcome by the visitor's identity that when they announced him to her they got his name wrong. She would have admitted him, I'm sure. But "No Admittance" was her watchword. How ignoble, you will say, but it wasn't altogether, for along with much which hadn't the polish or the glitter to get in, she kept out a lot of things that were better kept out. She had a sort of moral shrewdness, though she was apt to relax her standards in favour of those whom she ironically termed "the great". Anyhow she had never kept me out, or only once or twice, and suddenly I felt an intense longing for her immense blue drawing-room. You could say it looked out on to the garden and the lagoon; but it would be truer to say that the garden and the lagoon looked into it — they had too much personality, they had sat too often for their portraits, by Guardi and others, to be merely landscapes. She was a little jealous of them, these illustrious outsiders (she would have thought it bourgeois not to be jealous) and didn't like one looking at them too much.

' "What am I here for?" she would ask, plaintively, if one stared out of the window. But she was also proud of them, and if one didn't look, and kept one's eyes in the boat, so to speak, she would grow restive and say: "You've not looked at the garden. But then you're not interested in gardens." One never quite knew where one was with her.

'How invulnerable she was, or seemed to be! And as one sat, listening to her unpredictable malice, which always had the note of collusion in it, one was almost aware of the subject's accessories strewn about the floor, as in a picture by Velasquez: the shield, the breastplate, the gauntlets — all the apparatus of defence. And as one by one the idols were thrown down, by hints at this or that little weakness, laughable and belittling, so, piece by piece, one put on the whole armour — not of righteousness, for Lady Porteous was too mundane to clothe herself in that — but of ridicule, which in some circumstances is a defence hardly less strong. I always left her feeling twice the man I was, for she had established the fallibility of mankind on such a firm foundation that with her one could laugh at anything, even at death itself. Indeed, I remember once writing an imaginary dialogue in which Death called at Lady Porteous's palazzo and was told he could not be received as he lacked the necessary social qualifications – he was in fact too *common*. So, snubbed, he turned away, leaving her immortal. I used to wonder whether I could show her this, for in certain moods she enjoyed a joke against herself, though she preferred that she should tell it.

'But I found that in my absence he had called, and had not been turned away; indeed, he had called twice and of the two it was the frail Sir Hilary who had put up the stiffer fight. The joke had been turned against Lady Porteous at last.

'And it had been turned against me, for I had boasted, not quite truthfully, that she was always at home to me. Perhaps her spirit enjoyed the joke, for she never liked one to call without having rung up first. "I might be out if you didn't ring up," she threatened. But Death hadn't been civil enough to make an appointment with her: she died of a stroke, I was told.

'I left the palace to its alien occupants,' my friend said, 'and got home somehow, feeling half the man I was. I hadn't counted on the weakening effect of my illness, and the long walk, punctuated by disappointments, was too much for me. I seemed to see "No Admittance" written on every door I passed. Closed doors, closed shutters, iron grilles, cats grimacing at me from behind the grilles: Venice on a wet day is barred like a fortress. I took to my bed again and was too much discouraged to write to my other friends who, in any case, didn't conjure up the real meaning of the word. But the expedition had created in me a hunger which I couldn't assuage. The idea of death haunted me as it sometimes does in Venice: the churches, the bells, the beauty, the overwhelming vitality of the people: all this insistence on what the senses can give one, on life: if one cannot accept it, what remains but its opposite, death? In Northern countries there are so many degrees of living: one can turn life down, like a gas-fire, and live by its dull glow: but Italy is a land of contrasts, not of half-tones. I felt that time was pressing and I had a legacy to give someone: myself.

'For my second convalescence I returned to my first window and when I looked out it wasn't in the spirit of a railway passenger, finding something in everything, pleased with just seeing: I had a particular object in view. Only the object was not in view. The palace had twenty-seven windows visible from my flat: it was not exactly opposite, it stood at a slight angle and the windows on the nearer side of the deep courtyard were hidden from me. Those I could see, and from which I could be seen, were of many shapes and sizes, some as tall as a modest-sized house, some squat and longitudinal. I scanned them all, and from time to time I would get up and lean out of my window and wave; and then, dazzled by the glare outside, turn back blinking into what seemed the darkness of my own room. But there was never an answering gesture.

'My month in Venice was running out and I had nothing to show for it. I had scarcely written a word. I had been ill and got better, I had been ill and got better, and I had made one expedition into Venice; otherwise my existence had been as pointless and unfruitful as the Lady of Shalott's, and far less decorative: you could not have made a poem out of it, you could not have made anything. All I had to show was the money I had ear-marked for Antonio's wages. On this I could live beyond the time-limit I had prescribed for myself. It was the fruit—the very tangible fruit—of my quarrel with Antonio, and as such had a bitter taste. A sense of utter futility and failure possessed me. It was both personal and moral. Moral for the feeling of time wasted that haunts every unproductive artist: that I was used to. And personally I was a failure: I hadn't made any contacts. I was used to that, too. But I was not so used to the idea of having let myself down by letting someone else down. La signorina sconosciuta who had found my appearance so interesting and who was so sure that I was interested in her: yielding to a small, spiteful impulse, I had snubbed her, I had rebuffed her, I had taken the line that my privacy was sacrosanct, I had behaved as if a chorus of admirers was egging me on.

'I had treated her as a nuisance, not as a human being, with feelings to be wounded or consoled.

'How brutal I had been, in my self-sufficiency, brushing her aside! Just because, in my life, a certain good fortune had attended me, I felt I could afford to treat her letter as an un-welcome item in a fan-mail.

'How good it was of her, I now thought, to single me out for her attention, how good of her to stay in Venice and wait for me, instead of going away, as Denys and Miranda had, or dying, as Lady Porteous had! In all this great city of Venice, which I had once known so well, she was the only human being left who seemed to care for me, and she was a stranger! She possessed the precious, the sacred gift of sympathy! She had pretended to know something about me, but what could she know?

The truth was she had felt the impulse to communicate, and she had acted on it, at whatever cost to pride.

'My visits to the window grew so frequent that in the end I had to ration them to one per quarter of an hour; but I made up for this self-denying ordinance by waving so frantically when I did go that passers-by might well have thought me mad.

'Several days went by like this, and then the second letter came. Shall I read it to you?' my friend asked. 'No, you won't want to hear it, and in any case it's unpardonable, undressing myself like this in front of you, and undressing—— No, it isn't decent. You should have stopped me long ago. I can't think why you let me go on.'

He was quite ready to be angry with me.

'Yes, please read it,' I said.

He took out his pocket-book but didn't open it.

'I could just give you the gist of it,' he said, eyeing me doubtfully.

'No, let me hear it.'

He cleared his throat and read rather loudly, in a voice that was quite unlike his own:

' "Carissimo, — At first I thought that you were angry with me, for what I had written, and then I saw your signals, and knew that you were not. But now you will be really angry for I must say no, no, no. I should never have written to you—it was madness. What possessed me I cannot think: it was something plus fort que moi. I have regretted it ever since: I have shed the bitterest tears. Do not think about me, do not ask about me, above all do not try to find me. But no, think about me a little, as someone who wishes you well but must be forever unknown to you." '

Without looking at me my friend replaced the letter in his note-case and the note-case in his pocket; and for a moment hardly seemed to know where he was. He made one or two false starts and then said, 'I asked Giuseppina who had brought the letter. She said she did not know; she had found it in the letter-box. She managed to suggest I had reproached her, both with knowing and not knowing; she was a past-master of reproach.

' "But can't you think of anybody?" I said stupidly.

' "But signore, there are so many people in Venice!"

'I got into an odd state of mind,' my friend went on. 'I didn't lean out of the window any more: I didn't even look out: if an atom bomb had fallen into the canal I shouldn't have noticed. My sole occupation was trying to imagine who my correspondent could be, and why she had behaved as she had. That she was beautiful I took for granted: I never doubted it for a moment. Her beauty grew on me with every hour. She was blonde, sumptuous, voluptous, Venetian, a Veronese figure. And why had she said we must not meet? My mind gave me a dozen answers to that question. She was of too high degree, she was of too low degree, she was ashamed of having made her feelings known to a stranger. For a time—for a few hours—for a few minutes—some one solution would satisfy me; then its plausibility would evaporate, and I would discard it and adopt another.

'Need I say that I had fallen in love with her? Perhaps I must, for you know me well enough to know that I had never been in love with any-one before. How different friendship is—a matter of adjustments, of balancing this with that, of alternating self-assertion and self-sacrifice—but all conducted under the rules—the more or less reasonable rules—of affection. Friendship fits into one's conception of life; with me, be-fore the war, it *was* my conception of life—it was the pattern of my picture. It had no rivals: I did not care about money, or position, or even present or posthumous fame, so long as I could feel about me the fabric of friendship protecting me equally against the heat and cold of life, its dangers, boredoms, even its sorrows, protecting me, some people would say—I suppose *you* would say—against life itself.

'Whereas love! Do you think life can contain love, Arthur? Come to terms with it, I mean? I don't, I think the two are deadly enemies. But I needn't tell you, no doubt you know better than I do, what love does. I don't mean love that has declined into friendship,' he went on scornfully, 'but the love that is a virus, a fever, an *attack*. Love keeps out friendship; it is a parasite, and drains life of its juices. Love keeps out friendship, or if friendship is there first, it ousts it like a cuckoo; how often has one seen it happen! And friendship, with any luck, keeps out love. But I was friendless, I had renounced friendship; and then, when I would have taken it back, friendship had renounced me. My heart was swept and garnished, and destitute of defenders: that was how love got in.

'But I didn't feel that way at the time. I don't mean that I didn't feel tormented, for I did. But the torment was part of the growing together, the fusion of all my faculties which I had so carefully kept separate, to meet, as far as I could, the diverse demands of life. Only so, I thought, could old age be made tolerable—by cultivating one's responses to the variety of life. Since the war I had neglected this exercise; I had felt the arteries of my mind harden, and been glad of it. For what was the use of trying to keep oneself up to a certain level of—what shall I say? general civilization, when the very people who were most vociferous in defending it were the first to abandon it—had to be, for, if not actually fighting, on them fell all the most decivilizing jobs — of waiting with empty minds and hands for something to happen, or of giving themselves up to some routine employment which an office-boy could have done as well. And feeding their minds with news—news, a quick mental pick-me-up, but how much food is there in it, I ask you, how many vitamins?

'Well, I see you disagree with me but I don't mind, not as I should have minded then. Then it was the only thing I minded, being disagreed with: and the less there was of me, the further I could contract into myself, the less there was to feel the pains of disagreement. I didn't feel much, I thought I had ceased to feel at all.

'But I hadn't, and feeling being new to me I felt much more. My feelings were blissful, for I believed my love to be returned; I never doubted that, indeed my love sprang out of it. And never, even when I was most tormented by the thought that it was all no use, that nothing could come of it, that it was like a cheque for a fortune that lacked the drawer's signature, I never felt any bitterness, none. Remorse and regret in plenty: for I told myself a hundred times a day that if only I had responded to her overture in the first place—before this dreadful second thought had taken hold of her mind—then all would have been well. We should have been together, we should have been whatever she wanted us to be; and—and my life would have had a meaning and a value that I never dreamed of for it. The belief that this meaning and this value were within my grasp gave me an exultation even while the thought of losing them tormented me. It didn't make me resentful that, like other lovers before me, I was plagued by the question of ways and means. The difficulty was like a challenge to me. Now that I knew my signals from the window would not be answered, I tried to think of other methods of getting in touch with her. It didn't occur to me, I'm afraid, to respect her prohibition: in fact the prohibition made me all the more eager: I assumed it was unreasonable, I regarded it simply as one more obstacle to be overcome.

'I could not expect any more help from the windows; they were blind eyes that did not see, or if they saw I could not read their expression. For my purposes the many-windowed façade of the palace, ranged around its deep, dividing chasm, might have been a blank wall, and as at a blank wall I looked at it, when I did look at it.

'I was up against a blank wall: how could I penetrate it? Suddenly it occurred to me, and I cursed myself for not thinking of it before, that the palace had a door as well as windows, a door through which, at one time or another, each of its occupants must go in and out. The door must be on the other side; it must open on the Zattere.

'I can never remember how well you know Venice, Arthur, but the Zattere is a mile-long promenade, with bridges and cafés and all the rest of it, that stretches from the Dogana to the south-west corner of Venice. It faces a great curved sheet of water as wide as the Thames at London Bridge. It gets all the sun there is, and all the moon there is, and all the air there is, and is thronged with people at all hours of the day and most hours of the night. Besides those who are going somewhere on business, there are always crowds of loungers, the licensed loiterers of all Italian towns: and these I joined. I took my stand opposite the great door, and when I was tired of standing there were stone benches to sit on, and round bollards, sturdy mushrooms of stone polished to a honey-coloured smoothness, which were not so comfortable, being convex, but had the advantage that on them one could swivel round in any direction. There I sat, sometimes literally for hours, watching the door as, at very irregular intervals, it opened and shut. Of those who came out I got a full front view; how unaware they seemed of being watched! Those who went in I could not see so well, because, having rung, they turned their backs on me and waited for the electric latch to buzz (I could sometimes hear it) and set the door ajar; then they pushed it and went in. But these I had longer to study, I could learn something of them by the way they waited, impatiently or patiently. And sometimes, as a change from sitting or standing, I would go up to the door myself, casually, as though struck by a sudden whim, and when someone opened it I would peep inside at the immense, murky entrata, with its cross-beams, its marbled stucco flaking from the walls, its solemn doorways crowned by architraves, and, far in the distance, the glimmer of light through the iron grille that opened on the garden and the fountain. To the right was the archway of the great staircase, the main artery of the palace; people went up it and came down it, and I marvelled at their unconcern.

'Sometimes the portinaia – the door-keeper – from her eyrie on the left, or her husband, or one of her children, would challenge the entrant, who would then answer something I could not catch: these, I supposed, were strangers to her. Those who went in without having their business asked were the habitués, the tenants, and these I gradually got to know.

'And also I got to know that none of them was she; for her I should have recognized instantly, I had as little doubt of that as I had that she would recognize me. And when she recognizes me she will not be able to help betraying it, I thought.

'Hope was so buoyant in me that for several days my failure to find the object of my search only made me more hopeful; I felt, illogically, that the odds against me were being exhausted, and it was a mathematical certainty that I should be successful. Only patience was needed, and I was unconscious of the need, for hope has no need of patience. But gradually it was borne in on me that the sands were running out, my days in Venice were numbered, and I might have to leave without accomplishing what I had come to think of as the aim and object not only of my visit but of my life.

'I tried to consider my predicament impartially, and relate it to the canons and requirements of ordinary, rational living; and then I began to suffer in earnest, for fantasy in the grip of facts is like a fly caught in the toils of a spider. I could not bring myself to go back on the promise I had made myself; it seemed like blasphemy against myself, as if I was requiring myself to deny my own existence. In vain, as a discipline, I tried to concentrate on what I was doing at the moment, to do things deliberately, and at set times, to make a ceremony of lighting a cigarette, to be critically conscious of the taste of food and wine, to remind myself, when walking, that I was putting one foot in front of another. Many such exercises in realism I went through, yet they had no reality for me—my only reality was in some room in the Palazzo Trevisan which I had begun to think I should never see.

'You know the Zattere and how it faces the long crescent of the Giudecca, with the canal in between as wide as the Thames at London Bridge and much deeper—but I told you all that. I'm getting old, I repeat myself—no, you needn't deny it, Arthur, it's the truth and I hope I'm not too old to recognize the truth. It's a wonderful view but I always turned my back on it, the palace interested me so much more.

'Well, one evening when I had gone out to keep my vigil, about six o'clock I think it was (I usually spent the two hours to dinner-time thus occupied) I was sitting on my stone seat staring at the palace when Antonio came by. My eyes recognized him but for a moment my mind didn't—he had become an absolute stranger to my thoughts. Then, my whole being welcomed him, I scarcely remembered what had come between us, and for a moment, so potent was his presence in bringing back the past, I could hardly associate myself with the ghost I had turned into — it seemed a dream.

'He was striding along between the brightly-coloured nurse-maids and their charges, and I jumped up with hand outstretched, meaning to cross his path. But he looked right through me, and if I hadn't swerved I believe he would have walked right through me, as if I had been indeed a ghost.

'Shaken, I sat down again, and for several moments I couldn't even think, I could only feel contrary tides of emotion sweeping over me. Then I saw that I was facing outwards, looking at the Giudecca, not at the palace, and I knew that whatever my mind might tell me, something more instinctive than my mind had given up hope.

'It was a heavy day threatening thunder, like so many June days in Venice; and in the thick, white sirocco sunlight the colours of the houses on the Giudecca — grey, yellow, terracotta, pink — seemed to merge and lose their proper qualities in a uniform lack of tone; and what stood out was the fenestration, the whitish oblongs and truncated ovals of the windows, monotonously repeated. Except for a dreadful travesty of Gothic, three enormous eyelets beyond the Redentore, scarcely a single pointed arch could I see.

'I suddenly felt a respect for the five factory chimneys, and I looked with indulgence, almost with affection, on the great bulk of Stucky's flour mill, battlemented, pinnacled, turreted, machicolated, a monument to the taste of 1870, that might have been built out of a child's box of bricks. A romantic intention had reared it, and left behind something that was solid and substantial and a benefit to mankind.

'I am short-sighted, and as my eye travelled backward from the mill, I saw something which I had taken to be a line of fishing boats moored in front of the houses opposite. But now I saw that it was not masts, and spars and rigging that was veiling the houses from me, it was scaffolding; I couldn't see the houses, but behind the scaffolding they were there all right, waiting to be repaired, to be cured of whatever sickness they were suffering from; it was just a cloud of invisibility, a temporary eclipse, and it would pass. Only let the workmen get on with their job — don't take them off for one of your European wars, Arthur — and the houses would be as good as ever. I don't know why, but this discovery put fresh heart in me; and the uprush of confidence brought an idea with it, as it so often does.

'I jumped off the seat and crossed over to the palace with as much determination as if it had been a fortress I was going to take by storm, and rang the bell as if I had every right to ring it. With the angry buzz of a trapped hornet the door opened, and I was inside. A sigh of fulfilment escaped me, as if something I had long been waiting for at last had come to pass. But where now? Which way? Which of the four staircases should I take? While I was debating a voice slanted down at me, like a shaft of sunlight piercing the shadow in a picture: "Chi xè?" it rasped. Who was I, what did I want? I could not answer either of those questions, I could not even consider them as questions, only as obstacles to my progress. I waved and shouted something, but it did not satisfy the caretaker: she came waddling down her private staircase, almost touching each side, so fat was she. She advanced across the damp flagstones of the entrata and barred my way. "Chi xè?" she asked again and this time I found a kind of answer.

' "Cerco una signorina!" I exclaimed. "I am looking for a young lady!"

'It wasn't really an answer, and it wouldn't have gone down in England: but in Italy it did.

' "Va bene!" she said, and my mind rather than my eye took note of her disappearance, as if she hadn't been a woman but a difficulty to be disposed of. Something seemed to guide my footsteps as I dashed up the main staircase: the steps were dirty under the grey and white stucco of the rounded ceiling, and sweating, as I was, from the sirocco. Almost before I was aware of it I had cannoned out into the great sala: I pulled up short on the slippery terrazzo like a schoolboy breaking off a slide. After the gloom of the entrata, the tall windows at either end made the gallery unexpectedly light. A row of doors faced me: I chose the middle one and rang the bell. A man appeared in his shirt sleeves, flanked by two small children who stared up at me with their fingers in their mouths.

' "What do you want?" he asked.

' "Cerco una signorina," I replied.

'He smiled, not altogether pleasantly. "But there are so many young ladies," he said. "What is her name?"

' "I don't know," I confessed. "She knows me, but I don't know her."

' "What does she look like?" he asked. "Is she dark or fair?"

'Again I had to say I didn't know, and a sense of the hopelessness of my quest began to steal over me: I felt how silly, and, above all, how unromantic I must look, at my age, looking for a young lady whom I didn't know.

' "But you would recognize her if you saw her?" the man asked.

'Again I had to say no; and then I had the presence of mind to add "But she would recognize me!"

'He nodded sagely, as if this was a situation that might easily arise and one which, as a man of the world, and a man of heart, he understood. Excusing himself, he turned away and called to someone inside the flat. A woman came out—his wife, I suppose; she was thin-faced and dark and wore long ear-rings. While he was explaining my quest to her I was again overwhelmed by a conviction of its hopelessness; yet she did not seem to share it; she kept looking at me with quick, measuring eyes as if she was trying to guess, from my appearance, the sort of person I should be interested in.

' "There are a score of signorinas living in the palace," she said to me; "would yours be young or old?"

'I stared; it had never occurred to me that a signorina could be old; but of course she could, the word only implied unmarried, and I was old; it was a natural question.

' "No, young, young," I cried, "I am sure she is young."

'The woman smiled and hesitated.

' "Proviamo!" she said. "Let us try!"

'Fascinated, I watched her ring the bell of the flat next to hers; the door opened, there were explanations, then a girl came out with her, a pretty girl of eighteen or so, who shyly looked me up and down, and then shook her head. Four or five times, at neighbouring doors, the process was repeated; once the couple drew a blank; once they came out with three signorinas all of whom politely looked as if they would have liked to recognize me if they could. Between each identity parade my hopes soared, only to be dashed again.

'All at once I realized it was over; no more signorinas were forthcoming; my well-wishers had exhausted their stock of suspects; now it was for me to prosecute my search, and they sincerely hoped I should be successful. I stood a moment encircled by their smiles, and then with Latin realism and acceptance of failure, the smiles were turned off and I found myself alone.

'Twilight was falling. It was thickest where I stood; I might have been in the middle of a tunnel, with a glimmer of violet light at either end. My excitement had evaporated and the shadow of defeat, which is also the shadow of reality, began to mingle with the other shadows.

Again, which way? At which end of the tunnel should I begin? Then I remembered, and was amazed at myself for having been so dense: it was the end that overlooked my flat that I must explore: the inspecting signorinas had come from the middle of the palace, which had no view of mine.

'With this realization my hopes revived. Looking through the four-arched window I could see my own: for once Giuseppina had not closed the shutters and I had the fancy that I could see myself, looking out, looking at something I didn't know was there, something I had created without knowing it, as the burning-glass knows nothing of the fire it starts.

'A puff of heat enveloped me, and all at once the sala, enormous as it was, seemed airless. How often, in Venice, the sirocco dies away at sunset just when it is most needed, making the nights seem hotter than the days. I did not remember this, but the sweat burst out on my forehead, and I felt my shirt sticking to my back. But it wasn't only my body trying to throw off something that oppressed it, it was my mind, trying to shake off the riding, driving impulse which possessed it, and which had begun to create, in the near distance of my mental landscape, a tract that wavered and trembled and did not, as painters say, explain itself —an agitation of moving shapes of light and dark, a tangle of branches in a high wind, with sometimes a flash of white among them, like a peeled stick tossed to and fro. You know Velasquez' picture of the Spinners?—well, it was as if the tapestry in the background of that picture had come to life and all its intricate design was wavering tremulously upwards. I was conscious of reality, like a pillar on each side of me, framing my view, but my thoughts were joined to that unstable centre where the vegetable flames were leaping, where nothing was clearly made out save the fact of flux.

Resist it as I would, I felt myself being sucked into this disturbance and soon my feet were moving in time with it rather than in answer to my own control—so that it was without really knowing what I was doing or even where I was that I rang first at one door and then at another, asking questions that I scarcely understood, though their urgency and intensity seemed to shake me, and receiving answers whose purport I gathered from the tone and gestures which accompanied them, not from the words themselves. Without knowing how, I found myself on other floors which might have been in another building, so different were they from the sala I had left: where the ceilings were low, the windows square or squat, where the whole plan of the palace had been be-devilled by party walls, divisions ply-wood thin, ingenious devices to wrest from the once noble simplicity of the great structure its last inch of living room.

'Up and down I went, by staircases broad and narrow, and I must have crossed the sala again, though I don't remember doing that, when I found another entry, another staircase and yet another range of doors.

'By this time I had lost all shyness or self-consciousness: I rang, I waited, I put my question with the impersonal authority of someone asking for help; only vaguely did I register the fact that these doors were better kept and that a different type of person answered them.

'The last door bell was answered by a maid: she stood in the doorway unsmiling and suspicious. She had a pinched face, hard eyes, and hair drawn tightly back.

' "C'è una signorina," I began. "There is a young lady——"

' "Si," she said, "yes"—and it was like the crack of a whip. "Ma la signorina non riceve nessuno" – "The young lady receives no one."

' "Receives no one?" I gasped, and something told me that I had come to the end of my quest. "She receives no one!" I repeated. "Are you sure?"

' "No one," the maid answered stubbornly, "proprio nessuno" – "no one at all."

'She was shutting the door on me when I cried:

' "But I have an appointment with her!"

' "How can you have an appointment with her?" the maid said scornfully. "I tell you she sees no one, only her family, and, and . . ." She stopped.

' "And who?" I demanded.

'But she had already changed her mind about telling me, and shook her head saying, "Non importa – it doesn't matter – it's not you."

'At that the pillars of reality seemed to dissolve, and framed in the doorway was not the maid keeping me out, or the wall of the passage behind her, but the green trees undulating upwards in golden light, a jungle in which forms had no time to harden into matter; and before the vision could be taken from me I pushed on into it, past the maid, through the door, down the passage whose terminal window faced my own, to where, on the left, another door stood open and the scent of flowers met me as I went through – met me and strengthened, and then I saw the flowers and the waving stems: they were banked up inside the open window, almost hiding it, keeping out the view, the view of me, keeping out what remained of the light, or I should have seen, much sooner than I did see, for the shadows of the leaves were playing on it and there was no other movement—the bed and the face on the pillow.'

My friend stopped and passed his hand across his face, whether to keep his mind's eye clear for its inner vision or to brush the vision aside I could not tell: and then, perhaps with the same intention, whichever it was, he closed and unclosed his eyes.

'Is that all?' I asked at length.

'No, it isn't all,' he said. 'How kind of you to have listened to me for so long, Arthur! It isn't all, but it's all that I feel I can tell—not because the rest's too private, though it is private, but because I can't—oh well—externalize it. What happened before, belonged to me; what happened afterwards, belonged to us: it was *shared*, that was the point of it. You can't say much about sharing, can you? Not to convey its meaning?'

I agreed.

'I suppose that's what I had been wanting all along,' he went on, 'to share something, and I did, we did—when I say I, I mean we. It all boiled down to that. I suppose I *could* tell you, but do you want to hear? Isn't there something rather putting off... unattractive... in the spectacle of somebody's meaning so much to someone else? Isn't it rather like watching a dog with a bone? You can tolerate it perhaps, but you can't like it. Besides . . .'

'Yes?' I prompted him.

'Well, I've never told anyone. I never meant to tell anyone. But when I've got as far as this, I might as well go on. But you will think badly of me. I'm sure you will. You think badly of me already.'

'Nonsense,' I said. 'Why do you keep imputing to me feelings I don't have?'

He frowned at my smile. 'Yes, but you will. Anyone would, and I couldn't bear that. Because at the time it seemed . . . well, perfect is a weak word for it. We haven't seen each other of late years, you and I, but you know enough of me and I've told you enough to know what small hopes I've ever had of obtaining perfection in my own experience. And it's the same with me now—a confirmed mental habit is so much stronger than the exception that breaks it. When I look back on that time, it's as if I was a plain-dweller—old and'—he looked at me and flushed—'and well, decrepit, looking up at a snow-capped mountain which he can hardly believe that he once climbed.'

'All the more credit to him for having climbed it once,' I said. 'He should be proud of that.'

My friend shook his head.

'I told you of my fancy of the archway, didn't I?' he said, 'and of the indeterminate springing greenness in between where there were no facts but just the raw material of facts, the inchoate substance of experience before it becomes one's own, well, in her room it was always there—the symbol and the thing itself, you see what I mean? Afterwards she used to have it dismantled so that we could see each other across the canal; but when I came back she would have it rearranged so that there was no need of blinds, but they don't go in for blinds in Venice—or shutters or anything to keep us to ourselves.'

'So you didn't leave Venice?' I said. 'You stayed on?'

'Yes, that was one of the facts,' he said, 'that at the time seemed so unimportant—I hardly remember how I arranged it. I had Antonio's money, you see. But in her room, there were no facts beside ourselves, everything was beginning, and it began afresh each time I saw her—for her as well as me, I know that, because we said to each other everything we'd been wanting to say all our lives. She was much younger than I was, but that didn't seem a fact, either. I don't speak Italian well, but do you know I was never once at a loss for a word—and I said things that I couldn't ever have said in English. I expect that was part of the enchantment: in another language I was another person.'

'But isn't all this rather lovely to look back on?' I said. 'It sounds as if it must be. So why——?'

'Yes,' he interrupted me, his brow clouding again, 'it is, in a way because in memory I can go back, but only sometimes, only as just, now, when I feel a sympathy outside myself that helps me—it's never come from a human being before—then I can remember what I want to remember, without the rest.

'In July the weather got much hotter—we were quite light-headed sometimes—yet I never felt the heat oppressive, never an enemy. I don't think I could have conceived the idea of an enemy in all that time.'

'Was there one?' I asked.

'Well, yes there was, Adele, the maid. Perhaps I ought not to call her an enemy: she only acted according to her lights. But she was jealous of me, or she wouldn't have done what she did, or not the way she did it. I couldn't have told: those Italian peasant women are so secret: she seemed only to want our happiness. How much that depended on her contriving, I never knew: I took it all for granted; my unobserved entrances and exits, and the untroubled hours between. I think I was quite a favourite with the portinaia of the palace: she always greeted me with a smile. She may have guessed why I came so often: perhaps any Italian would have guessed. But there were so many people going to and fro in the entrata and on the staircases, I seldom saw the same face twice. But I never looked much. The moment I was inside the building one thought possessed me. You know how wonderful that can be, Arthur, it's the only thing that matters, so long as it's the right thought. Everything else is a kind of stationariness that one shares with chairs and tables, the sense of being a fixture, imprisoned in oneself, never to alter, never to escape from the mould in which one has been cast. But then I had the freedom of a myriad existences, every day a change, a new growth, a new flower, like the plants in the window. And it wasn't egotism, for I have never felt less self-sufficient; indeed, I was so dependent on the thought of her that if it had been taken away I think I should have literally fallen over.'

'What was she like?' I asked. 'You haven't told me.'

My friend glanced at me and away again.

'I couldn't describe her, you know,' he said, 'feature by feature. She was Venice's reward to me, but she wasn't typically Venetian. Venetian women are golden and pink and brown and inclined to be plump when they are young: obvious beauties. They are out in the sun so much, they soak it up. Myself I never cared much for . . . for amplitude, or even for warm colours. I like the Alps, you know, with the snow coming down to the pine-forests. And a sailing ship, when you can see the spars and the rigging. Not all sail set, that's too oncoming and voluminous for my taste. There's a kind of opulence that's rather vulgar, I think: well, she didn't have it. Her colouring was Northern, though her hair was very dark, nearly black. She had a Gothic fragility and fineness, like a saint from Burgundy or Chartres that had somehow strayed into Venice, though of course there is Gothic in Venice. You remember what Vernon Lee said of Venice, that it was difficult to "isolate the *enough*", because of all the claims on one's attention. Well, it wasn't so with her. I never felt, with her, that round the corner there might be someone like her. A greeny light filtered into her room, a forest light—just enough to throw a shadow. Too much light hurt her eyes. And yet the room never seemed dark, there was so much white in it. I thought of it as a grove of silver birches. The walls were nearly white, the furniture was white, the muslin on the dressing-table was white, the bed-cover was white, and she . . .' he hesitated. 'She was a little pale.'

'And the white wand,' I asked, 'that you thought you saw tossed about among the green? Did you ever find out what that was? Was it an enchanter's wand?'

He took a long breath and said with difficulty:

'I think it may have been her arm. She was rather thin, you see.'

After a pause, I said:

'I understand the need for secrecy, and I can understand how it gave . . . at least how it didn't take away from the zest of the affair.'

An expression of distaste crossed my friend's face but I did not regret what I had said. Most of the lovers I have known have thought there was something sacrosanct about their relationship and the word 'affair' was too common to describe it.

'But,' I went on, 'didn't you get tired of meeting always in the same room? And wasn't it even a little risky? I mean, I don't know Venice well, but I should have thought it offered quite a number of retreats for clandestine couples—all those arches, and doorways, and dark entries.'

'You're right,' he said, 'it does. There are those places, and one seldom passes them, at night, without seeing a couple whispering in them. We often used to talk about Venice—of course she knew it much better than I did. And we went everywhere, you know, to—to the restaurants, and the churches and the islands. And we made expeditions to the mainland too, to Malcontenta and Maser and Asolo and Aquileia—all those places. We lingered a long time at the great gateway in the garden of Valsanzibio that looks towards Padua—the only place I know where the reality is equal to one's memory and expectations of it. Wherever we went, she was the *genius loci*; she knew just what to look for and how to feel and what to say. Oh, she was a wonderful guide and there was no fear, going with her, that the churches or the picture galleries would be shut, or that it would be raining; she knew the right day and the right time to choose. I have travelled a lot, as you know, but I've never travelled with anyone as far as I did with her never so far afield, never so far from my own base, so to speak.'

'But did you really go about like this?' I asked him. 'I somehow thought——' Suddenly I wondered if he had imagined the whole thing. He looked at me oddly and the light died from his face.

'No,' he said. 'We didn't. It wasn't real, that part. You see, she was a cripple. She'd had an illness, and she was a cripple.'

I cannot say how painfully, how disagreeably, this disclosure affected me. It was almost as if he had told me he had been in love with a skeleton. And I was angry with myself for not having foreseen it—for it, or something like it, was implicit in everything my friend had told me. I was angry because I had been taken in, angry because he had warned me I should be angry, angry with myself for being angry. I didn't know what to say, or where or how to look; I did not try to meet his eye.

To my intense relief he did not seem to notice my confusion, and went on:

'But the rest was real, the one real thing in my life. If only I had foreseen what was coming! If only I had given Adele, straight away, the tip that I meant to give her at the end! Only I didn't foresee an end. The time-factor had ceased to exist for me; I felt I should stay in Venice all my life. Perhaps Adele felt that too; perhaps she saw the prospect of her tip receding into the dateless future. Afterwards, she was full of excuses She said she never knew him come at that hour. She said he——'

'Who?' I asked.

My friend stared at me as though he couldn't believe I didn't know. 'The doctor. She said he found the flat door open and just walked in. But she contradicted herself, she gave herself away, for she also said she was alarmed for her mistress's state, thereby admitting she had told the doctor. It was all such nonsense! Every time she saw me——'

'Every time who saw you?' I interrupted. 'The maid, or . . . or . . . You haven't told me her name.'

'I couldn't,' he answered. 'At least, I'd rather not. Fate has some power over a name. But she . . . she said that never in her life had she felt so well. Life-giver was one of her names for me: she had so many!'

My friend bent his outraged, protesting gaze on mine, but I looked away, I could not meet his eye: he did not look at all life-giving then. 'And I could tell, too: I'm not a fool, am I?' he went on. 'Didn't I look at her with a doctor's eye, as well as with a lover's? I couldn't have been mistaken. I noticed every little change, and they were all changes towards health. How could it have been otherwise, when we were drawing all this glory down on us? How could all the other elements have united for her benefit, and one not? I said so to the doctor, once we were out of ear-shot. "You are a physician," I said, "don't you know that a patient's surest road to recovery is happiness? Do you deny," I said, "that she is happy, now, as she has never been happy before?"

'But he wouldn't listen to me; he kept on saying he would allow us one more meeting: "un solo incontro, un solo incontro". Then I got angry and asked him by what right he was depriving us of this blessing? We walked up and down the vestibule between the Victorian and Edwardian ladies and gentlemen whose coloured photographs hung on the walls. He became as agitated as I was, and poured out a flood of medical terms of which I understood very little. The shock alone, he said, might have killed her. I was still trembling from the shock myself, the irruption into our birch-grove of this alien figure, parting the branches, with the heat and dust and hurry of the streets still on him, holding his professional bag of tricks, wearing, until he saw us, his professional air of wary optimism. It might have been worse, it might have been much worse; but it was bad enough—the secret not only out, but you might say, exploding round us, and the sudden necessity we were under for the first time, to speak, almost to explain ourselves, to a third person.

' "I must go back to her," said the doctor, glancing impatiently at the closed door behind us; but he wouldn't hear of my going back, not then.

' "To-morrow if she is well enough, to-morrow, and for the last time." '

My friend paused. All this time with his face and his voice he had been dramatizing his interview with the doctor: first he was one, then the other.

'I can't pretend he underestimated what the separation would mean to us,' he said, 'he spoke with a gravity which made it seem more than ever final. "And supposing she doesn't consent?" I asked him. "Then you must make her," he said. "You must plead with her, for her sake, and yours too, to give up this suicidal folly. Do you want to kill her?"

' "Do *you* want to kill her?" I retorted.

'We had our last meeting. I won't say anything about it—it was in almost every way so unlike the others that it hardly counted. You see, they were all outside time, but, in this one, Time was so present he might have been standing over us with his scythe and hour-glass. The moment of real parting came much earlier, the doctor brought it in his bag, like a prescription. It took us unawares, like sudden death. Afterwards we were like ghosts, planning our reunion beyond the grave. I remember that even her voice sounded different. It had been ours, just as a song belongs to the listener as much as to the singer, but it became hers, a lovely voice expressing what she thought, but not what we thought, another person's voice. I believe we even argued a little about how soon she would be well enough, etc., and whether she shouldn't consult another doctor. I remember the long pauses, when we were thinking what to say, better than what we said. There had been no pauses before, only the sort of pauses that there are in music, leading up to the next theme. It seemed extraordinary that the world outside should be more real than the world contained in this room. We were only going to be as we had been before we met, it was no worse than that; and yet it seemed to both of us that such an existence, the existence we had known before, would be unbearable. Almost deliberately I tried to keep my thoughts away from hers, there was a refuge in egoism, for to think of her pain doubled mine. So I sat by her bedside as correct as a doctor, as unimplicated as a district visitor; and the love duet, without which no opera is complete, instead of swooning itself away in long, heart-broken phrases, grew more and more tense and staccato and inconsecutive with the things we had to say to keep silence at bay, but hated saying, until somehow I got myself out of the room, and out of the flat, and out of the palace, on to the Zattere where the heat blasted me, but it would have been the same if it had been freezing —I couldn't have recognized myself in any environment.'

My friend stopped as abruptly as if his memories had come up against a concrete obstacle. I was still uncomfortably aware of seeing the whole thing at an angle different from his, and of withholding some of the sympathy I should have liked to give; and all I could think of to say was:

'So she agreed to the parting?'

'Yes,' he answered listlessly, 'she agreed to it. In a way, she decreed it, for I should never have consented. But she was not herself that day.'

'No?' I said.

'No. It was the shock, of course, the mortal shock of the . . . discovery and then the strain of those last hours. She reproached herself a good deal . . . for having written to me. That was all nonsense. I could see she was not herself. But how could you expect her to be? I wasn't, either.' He added, with an effort: 'She had to take her tablets.'

'Had she never taken them before?' I asked.

'Never in my presence, I swear. They were for emergencies, you see. She kept them by her bed, in a tortoishell box. But the maid said she had taken them quite often, between times, and that was one reason why she was alarmed. I didn't and don't believe it.'

'You saw the maid again?'

'Oh yes, I saw her every day. I went—to ask, you know, and in case the . . . ban should be lifted. I couldn't keep away. And I wanted to make up to the maid for what I had left undone. But, do you know, I couldn't induce her to take it. She changed towards me completely, and was as grim as she had been on the first day. She wouldn't let me come any further than the door. She said she wished she'd never let me in.'

'Did you see the doctor again?' I asked.

My friend hesitated.

'Yes, but only once. He didn't want to see me, in fact he refused. I didn't know his name, so I couldn't go to his house, and the maid wouldn't tell me the hours when he made his visits. But I knew he came every day, so once more I kept watch outside the palace and caught him as he came in, about midday, it must have been.'

'What did he say?' I asked.

'Oh, the same technical stuff about her illness, and that she wasn't so well, and he was anxious about her, and would I kindly keep away, and so on. I waited till he came out again, a long time, but he wouldn't speak to me, he just shook his head and hurried off.'

'How unkind,' I commented.

'Yes, wasn't it? And I came to have a hatred for the place, for Venice, I mean, so in the end it wasn't so difficult to leave. I gave my address in England to the maid, and begged her to write to me as often as she could, since she said her mistress wasn't allowed to; but I only got one letter.'

'What did it say?'

'Oh, it was stuffed with lies.'

'What sort of lies?'

'Oh, ridiculous accusations against me, and against the English generally, and Sanctions, and the war, and how badly England had always treated Italy, and how we had won the war and were worse off than before, and she was thankful for that, and a lot more in the same vein.'

'But what did she accuse you of?' I asked.

'Oh, she said I had broken into the house like a burglar, and had been very wicked, and thought only of myself, and I wouldn't go away, and I ought to have been prosecuted, and the doctor had said this and that, and everyone agreed with him.'

'You could afford to disregard all that,' I remarked.

'Of course. And that the whole thing had been too much for her, and that she only went through with it because I forced her to, and that she would have sent me away only she was sorry for me, but it went on too long and that was why she died.'

'She died?'

'Yes, she died. That was the one fact in all that string of falsehoods.' He lowered his eyes and his voice. 'But I know one thing. It wasn't being with me that killed her—it was being without me. She died of a broken heart.'

He was silent for a time and then said:

'You agree with me, don't you?'

'Of course.'

'Because if I thought otherwise, I couldn't, I really couldn't——She died because I was taken away from her. You see that, don't you?'

'Of course,' I repeated.

'I don't value my life very much, and if I thought there was a word of truth in that letter, except the one fact of her death, well, I should want to kill myself. But there wasn't. You would agree there wasn't?'

'Of course,' I repeated.

'You are quite sure?'

'Quite sure.'

'Will you say it again?'

'I'm sure there wasn't a word of truth in it,' I pronounced firmly. He sighed.

'Thank you, thank you, Arthur. What a good friend you are!'

The tears were running down his face. I could not leave him like that, late as it was; I stayed with him and tried to comfort him, and it was not, until he had disagreed with me several times that I felt that I could, without unkindness, leave him to himself.

APPLES

'UNCLE TIM, Uncle Tim!' There was no escaping the voice. Uncle Tim hoisted himself out of his chair and limped towards the window. It still looked a long way off when the cry began again; close to, this time. 'Coming!' called Uncle Tim, but it made no difference; the mournful importunate anapaests followed each other without a break. 'Uncle Tim, Uncle Tim!' It was like a weary goods train climbing an incline. Uncle Tim threw open the window and leaned out.

'Yes, Rupert?'

'Oh, Uncle Tim,' said the child, and stopped, as though hypnotized by his own incantation.

'Well, Rupert?'

'I want an apple,' announced Rupert, with an air of detachment, and as though fetching his thoughts from afar. He proceeded with quick gasps. 'I want you to get me one. They're right up on the tree. Silly old tree!'

'Why is the tree silly?' asked Uncle Tim. He tried to speak indulgently, but a shadow of annoyance crossed his face.

'Because I can't get the apples,' answered Rupert, his voice growing shrill. 'Do come, Uncle Tim, please. I did say please.'

Uncle Tim was moving away when Rupert called him back.

'Uncle Tim! Come through the window, it's ever so much quicker. I must have the apples . . . I want them. I've wanted them ever since breakfast!'

'I'm afraid I'm not an acrobat,' said Uncle Tim.

'You're always thinking about your silly old leg,' argued Rupert. 'Mummy says so. It won't hurt you.'

'I'm not going to give it a chance,' said Uncle Tim, and he definitely withdrew.

Rupert was standing by the apple tree when his uncle arrived, leaning against it with one hand as though to introduce it to its despoiler. Around him on the grass lay instruments of assault, stones, sticks, toy bricks, even a doll that belonged to his little sister. There was a horrible gaping hole in its brilliant cheek, and its dress wanted smoothing down. Overhead the apples gleamed in the morning sunlight, each with a kind of halo, intolerably bright.

Uncle Tim steadied himself against the lichen-coated trunk and shook it. The rigid trunk gave a little and vibrated with a strong shudder, as though in pain; the apples tossed, noiselessly knocking each other in frantic mirth. But not one fell. Flushed with his effort, Uncle Tim turned and saw Rupert, his face parallel with the sky, staring into the branches with a bemused expression.

'Why, they're not ripe,' said Uncle Tim. 'They won't be ripe for a month.'

Rupert's jaw dropped and his face crinkled like a pond when a breeze crosses it.

'Don't cry, Rupert,' said Uncle Tim. 'In a month's time you'll have heaps; you won't know what to do with them, there'll be so many.'

'I shan't want them then,' said Rupert. 'I want them now.' He burst into tears.

The passing of thirty years had made a difference to the apple tree; even by the light of the candles Uncle Tim noticed that. There were five candles: four on the bridge-table and one on the improvised sideboard that held, rather precariously, the glasses and decanters. The tree seemed to have shrunk. Some of its lower boughs were dead; its plumpness was gone; its attitude was set and strained; its bark less adhesive. Even its leaves were sparse and small. But Rupert had bloomed. Not into a passion-flower, exactly, thought Uncle Tim, pausing just beyond the reach of the candle-light. The September night was dark, and very warm and still; the unwinking flames irradiated dully the great orb of Rupert's face. It glowed like tarnished copper and seemed of one colour with his lips, as his features shared their generous contours. His head lolled on the back of a basket-chair whose cushioned rim creaked beneath its weight; but his half-closed eyes, independent of those movements, never left his partner. She was playing the hand, but at times her jewelled fingers came abruptly across, twitching her fur with a gesture always provisional, always repeated. Suddenly she stopped.

'Four,' said Rupert. 'That's the rubber.'

Uncle Tim came out of the shadow.

'Isn't it very damp?' he said. 'And rather late? It's nearly three.'

Rupert was adding up the score and nobody spoke. At last Rupert said, 'I make it twelve hundred. Anybody got anything different?'

No one challenged the score.

'How do you feel about another?' Rupert asked, still ignoring Uncle Tim.

The man on Rupert's left found his voice.

'It depends what you mean by another. Another whisky, yes.'

'Help yourself,' said Rupert, 'and get me one too. It's Crême de Menthe for you, Birdie?'

'I don't mind,' said the lady so addressed.

During the pause that followed Rupert lit a cigar with great delibera-tion.

'Well, who's for going on?' he asked. Again there was a silence, broken finally by the other woman. She spoke in a tone that sounded extraordinarily cool and sweet.

'I think your uncle would like us to go in.'

'Oh, him,' said Rupert, rising heavily from his chair. 'He has such Vic — Victorian ideas. Haven't you, Uncle Tim?'

'I don't want to influence you,' said Uncle Tim. 'I only thought you mightn't have noticed how late it was.'

'Yes, it is late, deuced late,' Rupert drawled, refilling his glass. 'That's what I like about it. Whisky, Uncle Tim? Drown your sorrows.' He held the glass out with an unsteady hand. Meanwhile all the players had risen.

'I want to go to bye-bye,' said the other man.

'Put me in my little bed,' carolled Birdie, and they laughed.

Everyone blew out a candle except Rupert, who could not extin-guish his, and finally knocked it on to the ground where it continued to burn until smothered by his foot. The sudden darkness was confusing. Even Uncle Tim felt it; but Rupert lost his balance and fell heavily against the trunk of the apple tree. It seemed as though all the fruit had ripened simultaneously. It thudded softly on the turf, pattered sharply on the card-table, and crashed among the glasses. Uncle Tim struck a match to ascertain the damage. It was negligible. The fruit was lying all round in pre-Raphaelite profusion. Rupert recovered himself.

'Apples!' he cried. 'Look at those bloody apples!' He stooped to pick one up, but his stomach revolted from it and, clutching the tree, he tossed it, wounded by his teeth, away into the darkness.

The match went out.

'What about these things?' called Uncle Tim, who could not keep pace with the others. It was beginning to rain. 'Shall I leave them, Rupert?' There was no answer.

A SUMMONS

It could not have been long after midnight when I found myself awake, and so thoroughly awake, too. I did not feel the misty withdrawal or the drowsy approaches of sleep. I had apparently been reasoning, for some seconds, with admirable lucidity on the practical question: how had I come to wake up? The night was still. The ridiculous acorn-shaped appendage to the blind-cord no longer flapped in its eddying elliptical movement. And what of that odious bluebottle fly? Doubtless it had crept into some corner, a fold in the valance, perhaps. I could not believe it was asleep. It might be scratching itself with one foot, in the way flies have; a curious gesture that seems to imply a kind of equivocal familiarity with oneself—an insulting salute, a greeting one couldn't possibly acknowledge. Flies have a *flair* for putrefaction; what had brought this one to my bedside, what strange prescience had inspired its sharp, virulent rushes and brought that note of deadly exultation into its buzz? It had been all I could do to keep the creature off my face. Now it was biding its time, but my ears were apprehensive for the renewal of its message of mortality, its monotonous *memento mori*. That spray of virginia creeper, too, had apparently given up its desultory, stealthy, importunate attack upon the window. Perhaps it had annoyed the window-cleaner, and he, realizing the trouble it gave, had cut it off and dropped it to lie withering on the grass. I seemed to see its shrivelled, upturned leaves, its pathetic, strained curve of a creature that curls up to die. . . . Surely this was not particularly sensible. A thought came to me suddenly.

It must have been someone knocking. My small sister slept in the next room. I remembered her parting words, uttered in a voice that was half appeal, half command: 'Now, if I dream I'm being murdered I shall knock on the wall, and I shall expect you to come.' Of course, I reflected with uneasy amusement, my sister always had a lot to say at bedtime. It was a recognized device; it gained time; it gave an effect of stately deliberation to her departure. It was, in fact, the exercise of a natural right. One could not be packed off to bed in the middle of a sentence. One would linger over embraces, one would adopt attitudes and poses too rich and noble for irreverent interruption. One would drift into conversations and display a sudden interest. . . .

Tap — tap — tap — tap.

As I thought. Now what had put this silly idea into my sister's head? It was absurd that a child should dream of being murdered. It would not occur to her that there were such dreams. But perhaps someone had suggested it — a servant whose mind was brimful of horrors. I myself had mentioned a dream of my own. Well, it was nothing. Still it had something about a murder in it. Otherwise I suppose I shouldn't have thought it worth telling. Dreams seem so stupid to other people, so flat, so precisely the commonplace thing that wouldn't invade a first-rate imagination. Surely it is a privilege to be let into the secret of another person's dreams? And yet one recalls the despair, hurriedly transformed into a look of conventional interest, that greets confessions of this kind. But an elder brother's dreams are not to be dismissed lightly. Perhaps I had embroidered mine a little.

Tap — tap — tap.

If I went in, what, after all, could I do? Fears are intangible things, but they distort the features. It must be curious to see people looking very much frightened. Would their eyes bulge, their fingers twitch, their mouths be twisted into some unmeaning expression? As a general proposition it would be quite amusing. But to see one's sister in that deplorable condition! She would probably be in bed, clutching the sheet, peering over the edge like one of Bluebeard's wives; or perhaps chewing it, the first symptom of feeble-mindedness! Very likely, though, she would be huddled up under the bedclothes, a formless lump that I should be tempted to smack! But there are people who shrink from covering their heads, lest someone should come and hold down the bedclothes and stifle them. It is not very pleasant to think of such a person bending over you. . . . Perhaps the child wouldn't be in bed; she would have to get out to knock. At first I might not see her at all; she might be crouching behind some piece of furniture, or even hidden in the wardrobe with her head among the hooks. I should have to strike a match. How often they go out; you throw them on the carpet, and the smouldering head burns a little hole. How funny: if she were lying at my feet, I might drop several matches on her and never notice till she screamed.

Tap — tap.

It was much feebler that time. Better after all not to go in. It would create a sort of precedent, and one could not set up as a professional smoother of pillows. Besides, children grow out of this sort of thing much more quickly if left to themselves. Of course, I should not tell my sister I had heard her knocking; she might mistake my reason for not going to the rescue, and think I had somehow left her in the lurch. That would be absurd, for in spite of the cold I would get out this minute, slip on my dressing-gown, and say, 'There, there, everything's all right, it's only a dream!' Perhaps when my sister grew up I would tell her that I stayed away intentionally, feeling it was better for her to fight her battles alone; we had all gone through it. Everyone keeps a few such explanations up his sleeve; age mellows them, and there is a kind of pleasure in telling a story against oneself. For the present it was to remain my little secret. For my sister knew, or would know now at any rate, that I was a heavy sleeper; and if she referred to the matter at breakfast I would use a little pious dissimulation — children are so easily put off. Probably she would be ashamed to mention it. After all it wasn't my fault; I couldn't direct people's dreams; at her age, too, I slept like a top. Dreaming about murders . . . not very nice in a child. I would have to talk to her alone about it some time.

Minutes passed, and the knocking was not renewed. I turned over. The bed was comfortable enough, but I felt I should sleep sounder if my sister changed her room. This, after all, could easily be arranged.

A TONIC

'Is Sir Sigismund Keen at home?'

'I will just go and see, sir,' replied the man, opening a door on the left-hand side of the hall. 'What name shall I say?'

'Amber – Mr. Amber.'

Mr. Amber strayed into the waiting-room and sat down in the middle of an almost interminable sofa. On either hand it stretched away, a sombre crimson expanse figured with rather large fleurs-de-lys and flanked by two tight bolsters that matched the sofa, and each other. The room had heavy Oriental hangings, indian-red, and gilt French chairs, upholstered in pink. 'A mixture of incompatibles,' thought Mr. Amber, 'is contrary to the traditional usages of pharmacy, but in practice it may sometimes be not inadmissible.' His mind was sensitive to its environment. Framed in the table-top and table-legs was an anthracite stove, black and uninviting, this July Afternoon, as the gate of hell with the fire put out. Still the man did not come. Mr. Amber murmured against the formality of distinguished physicians. The appointment was a week old, it was Sir Sigismund's business to be at home; he had crossed the hall before Mr. Amber's eyes, and yet the servant must 'go and see'! Like a jealous landlord, fearful lest people should establish a common of pasture on his experience, the doctor kept up this figment of a kind of contingent existence. Mr. Amber was considering this problem when the footman appeared.

'Sir Sigismund is sorry, sir, but no appointment appears to have been made in your name. Sir Sigismund is to see a Mr. Coral at five o'clock.'

Mr. Amber changed colour.

'I made the appointment over the telephone, didn't I?'

'I don't know how it was made,' said the footman, who had moved to the front door and was holding it tightly as though it might escape.

318

Mr. Amber took a pace forward towards the street; then checked himself and said with a great effort: 'I think, I am sure, that I must be Mr. Coral.'

The footman stared. 'But you gave the name of Amber just now, sir.'

Suddenly the situation seemed easier to Mr. Amber. 'But they're both so much alike!' He was too much engrossed in his solution to see the slight change that came over the footman's manner.

'Oh yes, sir. Though coral is pink.'

'That's true,' replied Mr. Amber, restored to a quiet dignity. 'But if you think, they are both connected with the sea, they are both a substitute for jewels worn by people who would prefer to wear pearls — and, and the telephone is so confusing,' concluded Mr. Amber. 'I'm sure you find that if you have occasion to use it yourself.'

Satisfied to all appearances by this explanation, the footman disappeared, and Mr. Amber was presently ushered into Sir Sigismund's consulting-room.

'Take a chair, Mr. — er — Amber, is it?' said the doctor. 'It's not often I have the pleasure of meeting gentlemen with alternative names. But my friend the Superintendent of Police tells me they're not uncommon in the neighbourhood of Scotland Yard.'

Though Sir Sigismund's manner was reassuring, Mr. Amber declined the proffered chair and seated himself, as near the door as possible, on a towering sculptured edifice, the last in an ornamental series.

'I hope you don't think I'm a criminal, Sir Sigismund,' he began earnestly, 'or a lunatic. I should be sorry if I had given your servant that impression; he seemed such a nice man. It's the case with many people, isn't it, that the telephone confuses them and makes them say what they don't mean. I'm not unusual in that respect, am I?'

'Unusual, yes,' put in the doctor. 'Not, of course, unique!'

Mr. Amber looked troubled. 'Well, anyhow, not unique. But it wasn't about my aphasia — no, not aphasia, absent-mindedness' (he sought the doctor's eye for approval of this emendation, and the latter nodded) 'that I wanted to ask your advice, Sir Sigismund. It was about something else.'

Mr. Amber hesitated.

'Yes?' said Sir Sigismund Keen.

'I'm afraid you'll think me frivolous, seeming and looking as well as I do, to consult you on such a trifling matter. With your experience, I expect you only like attending cases that are almost desperate, cases of life and death?'

'Doctors are not undertakers,' replied Sir Sigismund. 'Let me assure you, Mr. Amber, that if only from a pecuniary point of view, I like to be in well before the death. My patients often recover. I'm sure I hope you will.'

'Oh,' said Mr. Amber, a little scared, 'it's not a question of recovery, not in *that* sense, so much as of establishing the health. I don't look ill, do I?'

'I can't see very well,' said the doctor. 'Won't you come a little nearer, Mr. Amber? This is a more comfortable chair, and it must tire you to talk from a distance.'

Mr. Amber, aware that his naturally confidential voice had to be raised rather ludicrously to make itself heard across the room, complied. He sat down nervously on the edge of the chair.

'Now,' said Sir Sigismund, 'tell me about yourself.'

'About myself?' echoed Mr. Amber, looking hopelessly round the room.

'Yes, yourself,' said Sir Sigismund energetically, 'and your symptoms.'

'Oh,' said Mr. Amber, on firm ground at last, 'I haven't any symptoms. I'm only a little run down. All I want is a tonic.'

'A tonic!' The idea seemed as unfamiliar to Sir Sigismund as the notion of his own personality had appeared strange to Mr. Amber.

'There,' said Mr. Amber in a melancholy tone, 'I was afraid you'd think me frivolous.'

Sir Sigismund recovered himself. 'No, not frivolous, Mr. Amber, anything but that. Your request is a very reasonable and sensible one. Only, you see, there are so many different tonics, suitable for different conditions in the patient. There is a type of man, I might say a figure of a man, for whom cod-liver oil would be less beneficial than, say, Parrish's Food.'

'Byno-Hypophosphites,' Mr. Amber corrected.

Sir Sigismund bowed.

'I've tried that,' said Mr. Amber. 'It didn't seem to do me any good; neither did Easton's Syrup, though there is said to be poison in it.'

There was a pause.

'I thought you would be able to recommend me something better,' said Mr. Amber at last, rather lamely.

'But you give me so little to go on!' cried Sir Sigismund, exasperated by his patient's marches and counter-marches. 'Better for what? On your own showing you are highly strung; if you want me to prescribe for your nerves, I shouldn't recommend a tonic but a sedative, bromide, perhaps.'

'Bromide!' repeated Mr. Amber, awestruck. 'Isn't that a drug?'

The doctor suppressed an exclamation.

'Yes, it is.'

'I haven't tried drugs,' said Mr. Amber reflectively. 'If I had a drug by me when an attack came on——'

'Tell me about your attacks,' said the doctor. 'You feel faint, perhaps?'

'Oh, no, not *faint*,' Mr. Amber protested. 'I feel giddy and ill, you know, and the room goes round; and then if I can, I lie down; or when I'm outside I sit on a doorstep; and if I have time I drink some brandy——'

'How do you mean,' said Sir Sigismund, 'if you have time?'

'Well,' said Mr. Amber reluctantly, 'sometimes there isn't time.'

'You mean, before you f——'

'Oh, no, I don't faint. Everything goes dim and dark, but it's all over in a minute. If I fainted, there might be something wrong with my heart, and that would be serious and—and interfere with my work perhaps.'

'But surely your attacks interfere with your work as it is?' the doctor asked.

'Only at odd times,' said Mr. Amber, 'If my heart was affected I should have to stay in bed like my Aunt Edith; she was my last relation left in the world, and she was bedridden for years.'

Sir Sigismund Keen fingered the stethoscope that lay on the table by his hand. But seeing a look of apprehension on his patient's face he let it drop and said tentatively, 'I could examine you quite easily without this.'

Alarm made Mr. Amber voluble.

'I've no doubt you could, Sir Sigismund. To a specialist of your standing the inventions of science must seem merely figureheads.' Anxiety to convey his sense of Sir Sigismund's superiority to ordinary practitioners almost choked Mr. Amber's utterance, and he went on more slowly. 'That's why I came to you. I knew you would be able to tell at a glance what . . . what kind of tonic would be best for me.'

Sir Sigismund did not raise his eyes from the blotting-paper on which he was scribbling.

'Yes, I can tell something.'

Mr. Amber's face showed a momentary discouragement; but he said with a forced cheerfulness: 'But it isn't anything serious, is it? Whereas if I had called in Dr. Wormwood, my own doctor, he would have insisted on examining me and then it would have been revealed' (Mr. Amber's voice dropped at the word) 'that I had angina pectoris and perhaps even pericarditis and hypertrophy as well.'

Sir Sigismund rose.

'I can assure you, Mr. Amber, that a medical examination doesn't necessarily reveal the presence of any of those disorders; and cases of the three being found together would be, to say the least, extremely rare.' He continued very kindly: 'You worry too much about yourself. You are——'

'A hypochondriac,' interposed Mr. Amber eagerly.

'Well, no, I wouldn't say that,' said the doctor. 'But it is evident from your unusual familiarity with medical terms and your—your apt use of them, that you have been uneasy about your health. Indeed, you told me so yourself.'

'I read about diseases for pleasure!' said Mr. Amber simply. 'But of course it is hard when you have so many of the symptoms, not to feel that you must have at any rate one or two of the diseases.'

Sir Sigismund Keen squared his shoulders against the chimney-piece.

'That is exactly my point. If I gave you my word of honour that you weren't such an exceptional victim of misfortune it would reassure you, wouldn't it?'

Mr. Amber admitted that it would.

'But before I can do that I'm afraid I must examine you.' It was Sir Sigismund's last word.

'No!' cried Mr. Amber, rising rather shakily to his feet. 'Why should I submit to such an indignity? I won't be examined, and take my clothes off in this icy room when I am so susceptible to chills!' His technical vocabulary hadn't deserted him, but, swaying slightly, he went on in a more conciliatory tone: 'You couldn't possibly want to examine me, Sir Sigismund! I am an uninteresting specimen; they told me so when I was passed for a sedentary occupation into the Army. They said I was a miserable specimen, too. They said I wasn't the sort of man you would want to look at twice.' Memories of Mr. Amber's dead life seemed to rush to the surface. 'And for all you say, I know you would tell me that I'm very ill, perhaps dying lingeringly! Though it would be worse to die suddenly.' Mr. Amber's voice dropped and he steadied himself by the arm of the chair. 'I only came to ask you for a tonic; surely that's a simple thing. A good strong tonic. I wouldn't have minded taking it, even if it had disagreed with me at first! But you doctors are all alike;

you will pry into the body of a perfectly uninteresting person, you will have your money's worth! You shan't be disappointed, Sir Sigismund. I'm not a rich man, but I can afford to pay your fee.' Mr. Amber fumbled desperately in his pockets, bringing up a strange medley of possessions and dropping them on the floor; but the effort had been too much for him and he had lost the support of the chair. Sir Sigismund caught him as he was falling and lifted him on to a sofa. Mr. Amber lay quite still. Sir Sigismund undid his collar which was fastened with a patent stud and, as he came round, conducted the examination which Mr. Amber, in his waking senses, had so passionately withstood.

Sir Sigismund Keen was writing at his desk when the dark dust thinned away from before Mr. Amber's eyes. He asked if he might have another cushion, and Sir Sigismund arranged it under his head.

'That's better,' said the patient. 'I must have had one of my attacks.'

As Sir Sigismund continued to write, Mr. Amber slid weakly off the sofa and tottered across the room to the doctor's side.

'Are you making out a prescription for me?' he asked in a subdued voice.

Sir Sigismund nodded.

'Is it a tonic?' he inquired timidly

'It will have a certain tonic effect,' Sir Sigismund answered guardedly.

'I'm sorry I made such a scene just now — you must have thought me very badly brought up,' Mr. Amber murmured, altogether crestfallen.

Sir Sigismund described a semi-circle with his head in order to lick an envelope. 'No, Mr. Amber; your reluctance to be examined was entirely understandable.'

'Then I am very ill?' asked Mr. Amber. The tenseness of his earlier manner had disappeared and he seemed happier.

'I have written to Dr. Wormwood about you,' replied the doctor. 'His address appears to be 19A, St. Mary's Buildings, Studdert Street, West.'

'West fourteen,' said Mr. Amber.

'West fourteen. I'm afraid your heart is affected, and you will have to take considerable care — great care. You must go to bed as soon as you get home. . . . Oh, never mind, Mr. Amber; you can send me a cheque.'

'A cheque?' said Mr. Amber doubtfully.

'It will be one guinea, then. Thank you.'

As the door closed on Mr. Amber, Sir Sigismund rang the bell. A nurse appeared.

'Nurse, I should be glad if you would see Mr. Amber to his home.'

'Yes, Sir Sigismund. Shall I inform the relatives?'

'You had better ask him,' Sir Sigismund Keen replied. 'But I forgot, he has no relatives.'

A CONDITION OF RELEASE

THERE are things one cannot get used to. A hot bath may, and perhaps ought to be, a habit; it rarely demands resolution; its frequency, within limits, is taken for granted, and, among ordinary people, scarcely commands respect. But a cold bath, however misrepresented by self-hypnotism or conscience, is usually a practice, seldom a habit, never an indulgence. Be the prospect of immersion never so attractive, the reality of it, the imminence even, sets one's inclinations in revolt. It is a chronic insurrection; the conscript forces of the will — that minion of manliness, respectability's redoubt — may scotch but cannot kill it.

But these are paltry encounters, bloodless Italian wars, compared with the campaign which opens with one's determination to bathe; and I, as with towel draped about my neck, I started on the 'good' twenty minutes' walk to the river, was complacently aware of this inward conflict. In the unwonted firmness — finality almost — of my farewells and in my avoidance of their tiresome sentimental frillings, resolution must, I thought, have been apparent; the snap of the gate was purposeful; my choice of the steep, adder-haunted path to the wood was unmistakable; I evidently meant business. On the reverse slope that dropped more gradually to the river this self-imposed tension gave way to a more legitimate excitement. Gleams of the river kindled anticipation. The brilliance of the sunlit grass glimpsed tantalizingly between twisted branches or framed in occasional openings, made my heart beat faster. I began to run.

But before reaching the little gate that led into the meadow I stopped. My thoughts took a gloomier turn. The danger of bathing when over-heated was only one of many perils; weeds, cramp, heart failure, the odious oozy circumstances of drowning. My loneliness increased, but I revelled in it; everything led up to it and emphasized it. Better to be drowned, I thought, than to be saved from drowning; fished out of a swimming-bath by an obese instructor, and 'brought round' by the relentless appliance of physical indignities in an atmosphere staled by the breath of obscenely curious urchins! Better be drowned than rescued to make a Brighton holiday by some officious tripper, who would wear the Royal Humane Society's medal and never weary of retelling his exploit.

In this intolerant mood, feeling that the very existence of the human race was an insult to my self-sufficiency, I approached the little green knoll whose further bank, I knew, sloped steeply to the water, but not so steeply as to forbid one to recline on it and bask in the sunshine. Essential solitude and privacy, protection militarily perfect awaited me in this declivity; a security almost tangible, an exquisite medium through which my thoughts could roam with something amounting to physical pleasure. Reaching the summit, I stopped; for my stronghold had been surprised.

A man was lying there in the most perfect, because the most unconscious, occupation. His formidable boots, his grey flannel shirt, his corduroy trousers were lying all about. Ordinarily, the thought that so much should be encased in so little gives a pathos to divested clothing; but his had an amplitude, an air of being successfully, if rudely worn, that forbade pity. The impression of size was repeated by their owner. His head, pivoted on a large arm, turned slowly; he said 'Good morning' indistinctly down two sides of a pipe, and resumed his reflections.

Hedged about by his ponderous garments, daunted and almost intimidated by his immobility, I undressed; it was a prosaic business, robbed of all romance. Subject as I was to scrutiny, observed, sized up, I had as little joy of the process as though I were stripping for a Medical Board. The man was intensely difficult to talk to; and his monosyllabic replies had, I was afterwards to remember, a sinister intonation as though he were secretly bargaining with Destiny for my downfall. Mechanically I stuffed my socks into my shoes, after them my spectacles and wristwatch, and sighed to think that this simple action should once have had all the thrill and significance of a final initiation. Instead of lingering on the bank until the forces of attraction and recoil had reached a delicate equilibrium — without giving the water a chance to get ready for me — I plunged in. The shock of the dive, usually as effective as a night's sleep in supplying a brand-new set of thoughts and sensations, left mine exactly as they were — small, thwarted and commonplace.

This was awful. I swam round a corner to be out of sight of the monster on the bank, uneasily conscious that his proximity gave me a pioneering impetus, a confidence in negotiating weeds that I lacked before. The sudden rising of fish, the startling croak of a moor-hen in the sparse discoloured reeds, had no terrors for me. With equanimity I clove my way through slow-moving groups of foamy, closely-massed bubbles, to which I was wont to give a wide berth—thinking them the expiring sighs of men long drowned. The climax of my courage came when I investigated and bestrode a great log. This in other days I would have shunned; its curious conformation in three coils suggested a serpent, and who knew how much it trailed, like an iceberg, below it in the water? I stood on a shelving bank of gravel and laughed to feel it suddenly wriggled under my feet; and I dived in deep water and brought up a huge, pale, fleshy weed. At last, trembling and feeling incredibly weak and heavy, I climbed out on to the bank and reached for my towel. My eyes were blurred, and it was some seconds before I noticed that the man on the bank was partially dressed; still longer before I realized that the trousers he was wearing were not his but my own. He had drawn my coat up to his side.

There might be all sorts of explanations; there were perhaps as many lines to take. One could not tell from his attitude whether he was a madman, a convict, or simply a practical joker. If he was a thief, why hadn't he decamped with the clothes? If he had meant it for a joke he wouldn't have left the job half done. There was nothing, moreover, in his appearance to suggest jocularity. Provisionally, I was forced to conclude that he was mad; and I thought perhaps the question might be thrashed out more amicably over a couple of cigarettes. I moved across to get them out of my coat pocket.

'Who asked you to touch that coat?' said he. 'It's mine.'

In spite of my surprise I managed to stammer, 'Oh, is it? Then I wonder if you would very much mind giving me a cigarette? I usually smoke one after bathing.' I heard my voice trailing away into uncertainty under the look of his eyes.

'Now look here,' he said, 'it ain't no —— good. I've taken a fancy to these clothes, and if you want any you can have mine.'

I was relieved to hear him swear, it made him more human. His madness, too, if such it were, had method in it; but I was not reassured. Sweet reasonableness, I felt, was the line to adopt.

'I'm afraid your clothes wouldn't be much use to me,' I remarked. 'Mind, I don't say there's anything wrong with them. They look very good wearing, and mine aren't that, as you'll find, I fear.' I stopped,

once more on a note of futility; his scornful, indifferent eyes held a mes-
age that I was beginning dimly to understand.

'You'd like them back, wouldn't you?' he said.

'Yes, I should,' I exclaimed in exasperation; but I could have bitten
my tongue off when I saw the look of grim satisfaction—the only expression he had yet worn to which you could give a name—cross his
face and die away. He said very quietly:

'That's how it is, is it? Then don't you think you'd better try and get
hold of them?'

At last, through his elementary sarcasm, the immitigable hostility of
his tone, the carefully maintained purposelessness of his outrageous behaviour, I saw his drift; I was up to his little game. He aimed at com-
passing my complete humiliation, my unconditional surrender to his
mastery of the situation. He expected me to go down on my knees, to
grovel, to display all the interesting symptoms of moral and physical
collapse. He was more subtle than I could have supposed.

I began to feel very cold—faint, too, and a little hysterical. Clouds
had darkened the sky and lowered it. My sense of the reality of the situation and of the circumstances that had led up to it was lost; and in its
place came a consciousness that I had reached an impasse, a cul-de-sac
against which thought continually hurled itself, only to fall away
bruised. Small practical movements lost their intention and faltered into
meaningless gestures. To convince myself that I retained the use of my
limbs I jumped to my feet. The man also rose; and his rising was a fine
affair, artistically considered; I was able to reflect that my trousers had
never assumed perpendicularity with so much dignity, or participated
in such a striking cumulative effect. Any hope I might have cherished of
forcibly recovering these garments fell from me. Their possessor's eyes
followed mine round the horizon.

'No, you don't,' he said.

I didn't, nor, as he might have seen, was I in any condition to; but the
formulation of this magnificent comprehensive negative riveted, so to
speak, my fetters. He came a step nearer.

'Look here,' he said, 'you can have this nice suit of yours back if——'
He lingered on the protasis like a schoolboy afraid of putting the verb
in the wrong tense. To give the consonant full play his lips curved back,
exposing his teeth, and his eyes, under the stress of unwonted mental
exertion, narrowed nearly to slits, preserving long after his lips had
abandoned it the sense, almost the sound, of that suppressed condition.
I was wondering what fantastic form his proposal would take when

suddenly he burst out laughing, slapped me a terrific blow on the shoulder and subsided on the ground convulsed with merriment. Somehow I fancied his heartiness was not wholly genuine. Presently he remarked:

'You can have them now; I've kept them aired for you.' An incredible peevishness, the result, I suppose, of reaction, seized me.

'I don't think I want to wear them after you,' I said; but instead of the outburst I expected he only remarked:

'Why the hell not? One man's legs are as good as another's.'

Without a word and as though for ocular proof of his assertion he thrust those limbs in front of me, half leaning on his back and half supporting himself with his hands. My trousers sagged round his ankles in an imperfect ellipse. Suddenly, as if impelled by an exterior force, I seized the garment and began to draw it off; but he held on to it with one hand from the other end, shouting 'pull' and roaring with laughter.

What have I done? I thought, as the trousers, released at last, gave a little spring into my hands. It struck me that they were none the worse for being a bit stretched. The man, who had relapsed into something more than his former gloom, was dressing with swift precision like a play-goer anxious to get away before the National Anthem.

Why had I undertaken to act as this creature's valet? My recovered garments were infinitely distasteful to me. Just because he would not be at the trouble to remove them himself I, I the injured party, the rightful owner, had stooped to that degrading office. It had been the culmination, the outward visible sign, of my abasement. He had not even asked me to do it. I had nothing to fear. He had withdrawn his foolish condition, he had 'shown friendly' after his uncouth manner, as my stinging shoulder still testified. He was just a high-spirited Briton, addicted, perhaps regrettably, to horseplay; and I, incredibly infatuated that I was, had made him a gratuitous offering of my self-respect. Why, I ought to have chucked him into the river and then argued with him from the bank. . . . His voice fell like a sword on the promising infant, my self-esteem.

'Why don't you get dressed instead of sitting there like the Light of Nature?'

I made no reply.

He took a step forward to adjust round his knee that traditional, much-affected encumbrance called, I believe, 'York to London.' The movement brought his face close to mine.

'So you did it after all,' said he.

'What?' I asked.

'Why, pulled them —— trousers of yours off my legs,' he explicitly replied, adding, with a preposterous straining after cultured pronunciation, ' 'Orace, I shall require my shaving water early to-morrow!'

That, then, was his suppressed condition — and I had complied with it.

WITHELING END

'For Witheling End?' asked my porter, his hand hovering over the glue-pot.

It is no longer to the people that one must go for traditional vulgarities of pronunciation. 'Willing End,' I commented. 'Yes, I suppose so.'

'This line is run for the convenience of intending passengers and bone-afied travellers,' remarked the porter, friendly but ironical. 'Think it over. You're not obliged. You needn't go if you don't want.'

Under the fierce assault of his brush the captive, peace-loving glue almost foamed in its agony.

'Ah,' I sighed, 'you don't know.'

Nor for that matter, I thought, as the train drew out of the dusky station, did I. Not yet. Logically, of course, it made no difference whether I stayed or went. It was the fact of the invitation that counted; the fact of its having, so menacingly, so—there was no burking it— disastrously come to hand. Just a week ago Oswald Clayton had been one of my most cherished friends. And now what was he? An enemy? Well, scarcely anything so personal as that. The others hadn't, as their turns came, regarded him as an enemy. On the contrary, they had no dealings with him, they hardly ever mentioned him. They acquiesced in, they almost connived at, their own ostracism. And one and all, when pressed to give an account of what had passed, they refused— betrayed uneasiness and turned the question off. Or they would hide their hurt behind a show of pride. 'Of course, a man with so many friends—he must grow tired of them.' And secure in Oswald's friendship one had considered, critically, the smarting cast-off, unattractive like all men with a grievance, and thought 'Oswald knows his own business best.'

It was odd that he should have chosen this particular method of conveying to his friends that their affection had become otiose. In other people's houses, in one's own house, he might be met without the slightest risk. Risk! With pleasure always, that rare pleasure that his off-handedness, his plain-speaking, his genius for being amused at one's expense, never failed to give. With his capacity for enjoyment (call it selfishness, now perhaps) he kindled the host in one as nobody else could. In fact the great privilege he conferred was the privilege of waiting on him hand and foot. He awoke in his friends a quite ravenous desire to please; not a repressive, conscientious self-effacement, but an active response to his needs, captious and exacting as they often were. His needs weren't material, he wasn't a common cadger, but he couldn't escape (I searched for a harsh term) the charge of being an emotional adventurer. Given leave, he would open up for one new fields of consciousness; he was the self-appointed prospector, he held the concession. But it was you who worked the field, did the digging and turned up the lumps of ore. His feeling for a relationship, his view of it to himself, happily stopped short of, didn't include the crucial fact that it was he who made the wheels go round. He thought or pretended to think, in any encounter, that he had stumbled across a little hive of happiness which had buzzed as gaily before he came as it would after he went away. In reality, both before and after, in as far as it buzzed at all, it buzzed to a very different tune. But while he was there, perching and flitting and settling in his agreeable way, his ingenuousness, his irresponsibility carried all before them. He affected to be amazed at the worldly wisdom of his friends; he declared that they were so many serpents, masquerading as doves, and threw himself on the mercy which they unstintingly provided. He only asked to be excused, permitted, taken care of.

Rather mournfully I made out for myself this inventory of his qualities, for, first-hand at any rate, I was to know them no more. It was to be for me his obituary notice, and I flattered myself that in this sad task I had shown both charity and discrimination; it would be the balsam of his memory, the entelecheia and soul of his subsistence. For I was certainly discarded. Of the half dozen or so who had spent those fatal week-ends at Witheling End, none had survived, none had told the tale. It had become a commonplace among us, the significance of an invitation to Oswald's home. It was a death warrant, and its probable incidence was the subject of jokes and even bets among the almost decimated battalion of his friends. And now the blow had fallen upon me.

What, after all, I asked myself while the train thundered remorselessly on, could Oswald do to enforce an estrangement? For it was to be an estrangement on both sides. Otherwise my predecessors in exile, granted that they were committed to keeping up appearances, must have made some slips. News would have leaked through of overtures, tentative essays in reconciliation that Oswald had sternly repelled. And they were not men to take a slight lying down. If they hadn't been proud before, the distinction of Oswald's friendship had lent them pride, and the inflation was theirs to keep. Oswald's tardy application of the pin would only have induced a new inflammation, flushed with anger against him and discharging venom. His creatures would have rounded upon him with all the weight of their derived, threatened importances. But—it came back to me again—they had done nothing of the kind. They had been content to watch their power, their glory pass without lifting a finger. They hadn't even permitted themselves the exquisite revenge, such was their pious resignation, of turning the other cheek. They seemed to have taken counsel of Desdemona's meekness; they approved of Oswald's scorn, they wouldn't hear of having him blamed.

Well, I was not so easily to be set aside. If Oswald meant to jettison me, he should have his work cut out. What, I wondered, would be his line of action? And when I considered the almost unlimited power to bore, embarrass and terrify which any host has at his command, I quailed. But, in justice to Oswald, I had to admit that his arsenal wouldn't be stocked with ordinary instruments of torture. He wouldn't spring upon me, my first evening, an obligatory charade which I should have to attend in some improvised costume—as a tinker perhaps, tricked out in domestic utensils, hung with saucepans, scoured, polished and sound beyond hope of dint or flaw. It was unlikely that I should be called upon to conceal my identity or exhibit a false one, with the implication that I was only tolerable in the likeness of somebody else. But there were other disguises, I pondered, less palpable and at first blush less disconcerting; but not less obligatory and far more exacting. False impressions, for instance. Oswald wouldn't launch me as a renowned arctic explorer, but he might convey, by a mere inflection of the voice, that I was something other than I really was, something I might love or loathe to be, it made no difference. I should be committed. Or he might put me to a severer test—the crucible of the haunted room. The reticence shown by his friends, indeed, argued some exposure of this kind. Coaxed, beguiled, flattered, browbeaten, perhaps bribed, they had undergone an experience which, for its very horror, they must for ever keep to themselves. And it needn't be a horror, I thought, that disclosed itself locally, that was charted, so to speak, and set and timed. That was the snare that was laid vainly in the sight of any bird. But supposing it was something strange in the character of my host, some baseness of fibre, some odious moral lapse or relaxation which he awaited in seclusion and the secret of which he imparted to his friends? Suppose my arrival were to chime with a (to him) calculable outbreak in some awful periodicity, whose convenient punctual eruptions he had cynically harnessed to his own ends—the incineration of spare acquaintances? Picking my way and holding my nose against the unsavoury conditions of my inquiry, I went a step farther. Lycanthropy lifted its head. Oswald might break the thread of conversation by becoming a wolf, furry on the outside, or, more horribly and incurably (for the malady had two forms) furry on the inside. Before such an object the most established affection might pardonably falter. By the time I reached the main-line station which boasted, as the least of its importances, that of being the junction for Witheling End, I had given up expecting to find in Oswald even the scarred outline of a human trait. He loomed before me the hero of some Near Eastern legend—marauding, predatory, fatal.

But the necessity to alight and pace the platform, to stand sentinel, unchallenged and ignored, by the luggage van, to stow away my things in the dirty branch-line carriage, to go through the routine, the mill, one might say, of 'changing', this prosaic occupation brought my thoughts to earth. Sadness succeeded terror. Of course, Oswald wouldn't need to call upon the resources of demonology for my eviction; he could dismiss me without that, as he had dismissed the others. If anyone practised black magic it would be I the following Monday, the day after to-morrow, the first day of my registered recognized exile. I might be excused if, to beguile my disconsolate homecoming, I stuck imaginary pins into his wasting receding image. However flattering the portent to my self-esteem, I needn't fear that merely out of sympathy with my eclipse the sun would turn into darkness, and the moon into blood. It wouldn't be necessary to mount me on a horse to reveal my poverty in deportment to the gaping 'county'. I could display unorthodoxy without being exposed by an archbishop; self-consciousness without the stimulus of a game of forfeits. What shortcoming was there, what social inadequacy or private self-sufficiency, I thought, with melancholy candour, that I couldn't show, and that without the least external help—without malicious arrangements of background, or predicaments contrived for my downfall? I had no aptitude for 'social surf-riding'.

Oswald's victory over me, if it consisted in a demonstration of my un-
fitness and unworthiness, needn't be costly, needn't be in the least Pyr-
rhic. I was shy-flowering, not all hardy or perennial; a hot-house plant,
I told myself, with a flamboyant impulse, that would thrive only in a
tepid air. It would be enough to turn off the heat and shut out the sun.
And that would be his line. A perfunctory welcome would be followed
by an evening's bridge—that game which, however listlessly played,
throws over everyone the chill of its formality or brings out the surly
side. Then, next morning, a dyspeptic and disorderly application to the
Sunday papers, the interchange of spare sheets over a strewn untidy
floor, the interchange too, of promiscuous tit-bits, scandalous items, in
lieu of conversation. Then the bleak three-quarters of an hour before
luncheon. . . . Why, that was the very entertainment I had given Oswald
himself at our last meeting. I had been too preoccupied to let his careless
good spirits have their way with me. Well, he would get his own back.
And what plea could I urge, what declaration could I make to compound
for my bad manners? There was nothing left me but my determination,
under however many affronts and provocations, never on my side to
let go, but be torn, protesting faithfulness, from the very horns of
Friendship's altar.

An hour later there came a tap on my bedroom door. It was Oswald
again. He peeped in furtively, as though fearful of committing a trespass
on my absolute occupation.

'You're sure you don't mind?'

'What?'

'Changing for dinner. I was afraid you might think it silly and pretentious when we're just to ourselves.'

'Of course not,' I said. 'I expected to. Look at all my finery. It would
have broken my heart not to wear it.'

Still as if on sufferance, he sidled appreciably farther into the warm,
light, admirably appointed room.

'Oh, so he has put them out for you. Then that's all right. And it
suits you, dining at eight?'

That had been the object of his first visit, to obtain my sanction for
the hour of dinner.

'Eight o'clock is quite my favourite time,' I assured him.

'Good,' he said, and discreetly withdrew.

Ever since he had greeted me on the steps of that solid red-brick house,
voluble explaining and regretting his failure to meet me at the station,

he had been—he had 'gone on', I felt inclined to say—like that. Apologetic, conciliatory, concerned, he had raised point after point, problem after problem, neglect of which, he seemed to think, would jeopardize my happiness. And though I had tried to meet his misgivings half-way with contra-assertions and confirmations, I couldn't convince him that I was satisfied, that I had made up my mind, as it were, to stay. He seemed to think that at the smallest domestic rub or breakdown, failure of the bell to ring or of the bath water to boil, I should stalk out of the house. The utmost he seemed to expect of me, his guest, was that I should consent to remain, that, like a captious newly-engaged servant, I should waive my prerogative of impermanence and 'settle'.

At first I was flattered. It hardly seemed necessary to congratulate myself on my success, it had come so easily. I even planned, in the interval before dinner, to write to my unluckier friends and tell them how deeply I had struck my roots. They, no doubt, had had to clean their own boots and wash at the pump in the stable-yard; whereas I was met at every turn by gratifying traces of the slaughter of the fatted calf. For them Oswald had been at his most casual—indifferent, irresponsible, careless of their creature comforts. For me, how different. In compliment to me he had put off his ordinary manner, the genial feckleness that sat on him so light, and assumed the air of an anxious housewife bristling (so far as his sobered attenuated demeanour allowed him to bristle) with *petits soins*. They were even embarrassing, these attentions, in their insistence, in their hydra-like quality of springing up double where one had been scotched. And so I went on, multiplying the instances, deepening the contrast, until the sound of a bell, hastily smothered like a rising indiscretion, invited me to dinner.

It was to be the keynote of my visit, I reflected, as I lay in bed—invitation. The bell had invited me to dinner; Oswald's man had invited me to take wine. Oswald himself in his first remarks, delivered ever so courteously across the oval table, had the air of inviting reply. He began:

'Perhaps you've never been in this part of the world before?'

I was encouraged to say 'No.'

After a moment's reflection in which, I supposed, he was passing the countryside in review, he said:

'There's Clum Abbey near by; would you care to see it?' I hesitated, not wholly from lukewarmness but because I was at a loss how to frame my answer, how to appear politely eager. He misinterpreted my silence. 'Don't feel obliged,' he said; 'only I generally take people there.'

Was this a threat? I longed to say, 'Take me anywhere else.' To my lively apprehensions the innocent ruin took on the hues and horrors of a Blue Chamber. But I complied; I succumbed to Clum.

Other invitations had followed: to smoke, to inspect the house, to play picquet, to take the younger hand first, to name the stakes.

'Give me some indication,' I said, wishing that he hadn't, after the insinuating fashion of the odd-job man, 'left it to me'.

'Do you think a shilling?'

'A point?'

'Just as you like,' he said.

I saw myself a financial cripple, perhaps a bankrupt; but it seemed impossible without vulgarizing the lofty accent of our intercourse, to suggest a humbler sum.

'The game generally ends all square, doesn't it?' I said, flying in the face of experience.

'I have known it not,' he admitted.

'You think, perhaps——?' Longingly I eyed the ignoble straw, not daring to clutch it. But he had seen it too.

'Well, I really meant a shilling a hundred.'

We were saved. But with what expense of spirit, with what reckless doles of hostages to misunderstanding! The appearance of whisky, with all its mitigating accessories, turned on a cascade of major and minor invitations. Fortunately for this contingency I was armed with ready desires; I directed, encouraged and restrained with a will; and, as a small return on my former prodigious outlay of reluctant adaptability, I did find the water hotter the whisky smoother, the sugar sweeter, the whole brew more grateful and harmonious, for the fact that it had been extracted, fought for, out of the inmost pattern and texture of polite behaviour. It was a stolen water, and if I had received it with some natural colloquialism such as 'Whisky, not half!' it would have tasted brackish and bitter. Instead, all the pleased propitiated forces of convention and propriety came to its aid, and poured their cautious sweetness into the cup. When, like a climacteric, the last invitation came, the invitation to bed, final and inevitable as I felt it to be, I detected stirrings of revolt, I almost jibbed. A defiant impulse came to me, as it might come to one on the summons of the Last Trump, to turn a deaf ear, to tender a qualified compliance, to suggest an alternative; almost to refuse.

But here I was in bed, and I had gone quietly enough. Refusal! that was the obverse of the golden coin that we had tossed each other, with rigid dexterity, throughout the evening. But only at the last had I managed to catch a glimpse of it; invitation's suave, deferential head was ever uppermost. I pondered over classical invitations: Weber's to the Valse; Shelley's less specifically to Jane. They didn't help because, from their buoyant confident tone one could see they didn't contemplate a refusal. But to all Oswald's invitations an engraved, an almost embossed R.S.V.P., was palpably subscribed. If he had just said 'Come away!' without troubling to call me 'best and brightest' or comparing the weather unfavourably with me, I would have gone with a light heart, ready for any enterprise, even excavations at Clum. Or if he had piped to me in Weber's florid strain I would have cried shame on my poor spirit, and plunged into the dance. And that was what he would have done before my visit, or the mysterious cause that determined my visit, had cast its blighting spell. I should have been given no time to decide; my hesitations and doubts would have been overridden or tossed aside, my self-consciousness anæsthetized. Instead of losing myself in this delirious experience I was condemned to sit eating unpalatable blackberries at a respectful distance from the still smouldering embers of the Burning Bush—for its blaze and crackle illuminated memory, unquenched by the berries' bitter juice. And for music I had the refrain of 'Will you, won't you, will you, won't you, join,' well what? The figured, frigid capering of conventional ghosts. I didn't want to, and I didn't want not to. Oswald flattered himself when he took such elaborate precautions against a possible refusal. It was a strain, too, negotiating his insipid proposals, threading my way through the tiresome labyrinth that promised no Minotaur.

'Will you, won't you?' Well, I wouldn't. I would refuse.

Daylight saw the ebb of my Dutch courage. It had receded infinitely far, leaving a barren strand. All day I waited for the tide to turn. On the horizon of my mind (never very distant, now stuffily close) I wrote the charmed word in letters of scarlet: refuse.

There seemed to be an opening at Clum. Among its treasures was a large squat perpendicular window, ribbed and tight-laced with massive angular tracery. Its forbidding aspect, presented successively to shrinking centuries, had kept injurious Time in awe. Oswald led me to a green knoll, which had a local reputation as a vantage-point from which this monster could be all too clearly seen. There it stood, or rather it didn't stand, it came 'at' you, secure in its harsh virginity, unmarried and unmarred, one of survival's most palpable mistakes. But Oswald invited my admiration; and I nearly withheld it. I hated to hear him speak with the voice if not with the accent (and that made it so much worse) of every tasteless tripper. And it wasn't *his* voice; it was the

voice that for the sake of safety, for the sake of maintaining the straddled flat-footed poise of the vulgar, he felt compelled to use to me. He
wouldn't be thrown off his balance; he would bring home to me, by
the persistence with which he applauded the second-rate and took refuge, for opinion, in the second-hand, the fact that I ceased to count.
How could I, with any feeling for my own dignity, challenge his im-
personality? I should only succeed in being rude. It was the triumph of
his policy to have brought our friendship to a pass where rudeness and
disagreement were synonymous.

But I didn't give up hope. I remembered my resolve; and though to
my inspection the altar of friendship appeared as cold, as foreign to
sacramental rites as Clum itself, I would still cling to it, though no one
should take enough interest to pull me off it. All swabbed and scraped
and slippery as it was, I couldn't help thinking that an acolyte had lately
been at work upon it, removing vestiges of former feasts. For though
swept it wasn't garnished, even with a vegetable marrow. It had an air
of dereliction, I noted maliciously, not of preparation. The manger
might be empty, but I was the only dog in the manger; it wasn't coldly
furnished forth with viands ear-marked for the next mongrel, denied to
me. Oswald didn't readily discuss our common friends, though after
dinner I tried to draw him, by dangling names, into this, often the most
rewarding of all forms of conversation. Perhaps it was snobbery; he
wouldn't rise to the minnows with which my poor line was forlornly
baited. I had resolved not to change the direction of my attack, but to
intensify it — to meet his most frigid propositions with passionate agreement, to glut his devouring sense of responsibility with continual tit-
bits. Zealous as I was, he easily outstripped me in the competition for
conferring favours. He looked all his own gift-horses in the mouth, before he presented them, whereas I was too apt to make mine show their
paces, too raw not to recommend them. I felt as the evening drew on
that something was sure to happen, some outburst, probably physical.
He would scream, or I should. We were playing picquet and I had won
the second partie.

'I'm terribly afraid you're rubiconed,' I said, adding up the score for
the third time.

'Well,' he replied, glancing sidelong at my figures, 'I shall hope to do
the same by you before the evening's out.'

Hope stirred in me. Was there to be a show-down? His words had an
ominous ring: last night we had been more jubilant under defeat.

'I shall not grudge you the last laugh,' I said, looking at him hard.

He laughed then, and rather bitterly, I thought.

'It will be a new experience for me.'

'Oh, surely,' I protested. In vision I saw a series of week-end cam-
paigns, lightning successes without a check; I saw too the casualties
privately wringing their hands.

'You held all the cards,' he said, still a little resentful.

'Oh, did I?' I replied, and added, 'But it was my misfortune. I'm so
sorry.'

He took up the cards.

'Should we cut?'

'I think we might.'

'After you, then.'

At length, all preliminary conditions satisfied, the game once more
got under way.

'And I've a quatorze of Kings, the whole phalanx,' I heard my host
say. It was the *coup-de-grâce*. I was 'repiqued'.

'Ninety-five,' he announced.

'Nothing.'

'Ninety-six.'

'Nothing.'

He played the cards almost vindictively, winning all the tricks and
'capotting' me. Again I noticed in his tone signs of excitement and satisfaction that were a betrayal of our code. We had taken our triumphs
sadly.

'With forty that makes you a hundred and forty-six,' I said, 'and
nothing for me, poor me.' I felt that, in view of his elation, I was entitled to a syllable of self-pity.

'You've forgotten the last trick,' he reminded me. 'I had to work for
it. That's a hundred and forty-seven, please. And why "poor you"?'

I was still smarting under the 'please', trying to explain it away as
ironical, when he repeated the question.

'Why "poor you"?'

I really had to think. It would have been much easier simply to be
annoyed.

'Because I got nothing, I suppose,' I said lamely. I thought it a sufficient explanation for a casual word, and even remarkably good-
tempered. But it had an unsettling effect on Oswald. He rose and went
to the fireplace.

'But you have everything!' he brought out at last. 'Everything!'

Like a bankrupt and with the unenviable sensations of a bankrupt, I

went over my meagre property, personal and real. The only considerable asset I had appeared to be my investment, my shares in the 'concern' that was Oswald—and then I was going to lose, had already lost.
He couldn't possibly—it was too heartless, be poking fun at my immi-
ment destitution. He couldn't seriously mean me to give him a financial
statement—an outline of my 'circumstances'. That they were straitened
was common property—the only sort of property, in fact, in which
they at all generously abounded. Judged by any standard the disparity
in our fortunes was tremendous and the advantages all his. It was my
luck with the cards, I decided, that had set growling the green-eyed
monster, which must have slumbered since its owner's childhood. And
this was a childish outburst, a childish solecism which I would overlook.

'I've been horribly lucky,' I said, looking up at him. 'I've won all
along the line. And I won last night too.'

I had, a paltry hundred.

He laughed and returned to his chair.

'Yes,' he said. 'You did. But I wasn't meaning that.' His face narrowed over the cards.

What, then, did he mean? I longed to ask; and last night, fortified by
toddy, perhaps I could have asked. But the interval had choked that
weakling, our intimacy, beneath a jungle of misunderstanding and constraint. I could no more ask the question than an actor could show
himself aware of a conventional aside spoken well within his hearing.
And if the saving mood failed me then, the next morning at breakfast, a
breakfast that looked so earnestly into the future that it seemed to have
outrun the present and be taking place at the station or even in the train
—this mood had faded into the shadow of a dream. I had ceased to take
pains, ceased even to cling. I suppose I cut an awkward figure, realizing
that if I didn't stand on my dignity I didn't stand at all. And it was from
this pedestal, and not from the horns of Friendship's altar, that I waved
Oswald Clayton good bye.

As far as London allowed of it, I passed the week that followed my visit
to Witheling End in seclusion. There was little to distract me. The cheerful or distinguished gatherings in which, as Oswald's familiar, I had
been welcome were closed to me; and I hadn't the heart to ogle the
other scarecrows of older standing, with which Oswald's waste ground
had been so thickly planted. Dully I realized that outlets were stopped
up; but even if I were robbed of motion, socially paralysed, I could still
hug my immobility and postpone the moment when I too must flap

and twirl for a warning to the rest. And so it was with sinking of the heart that I heard a bounding step on the stairs followed by a resounding voice. It was Ponting, the artist.

'Ha!' he said, drawing a fold of the window-curtain on to the table and sitting on it. 'What are you doing here, with a face as long as three wet days?' He had a vigorous vocabulary and his work was exuberantly morbid.

'I pass away the time,' I said.

'You should have been where I've come from,' he proclaimed. 'Then you wouldn't be looking like a candidate for confirmation.' I disliked his tone, and felt little interest in the place that had made him what he was; but he forestalled my inquiry.

'I've been at Witheling End.'

'Why,' I exclaimed in spite of myself, 'I was there a week ago!'

'And didn't you enjoy it?' he demanded.

'If you mean in the sense that one enjoys poor health,' I replied, 'I enjoyed it immensely. Frankly, I loathed every minute of it.'

He examined me curiously, as though I had some disease.

'Well!' he declared. 'You are a comical character.'

'I didn't amuse Oswald,' I said.

At that he laughed aloud, slipped off the table and danced up and down the room chanting:

'He's one of Oswald's misfits! He's one of Oswald's misfits!'

'Tell me the secret of your success,' I said, fascinated by his ungainly antics. 'I suppose you fitted like a glove.'

My friend struck an attitude.

'It was bone to his bone,' he assured me.

I tried to visualize this composite skeleton.

'When I arrived,' he went on, 'the place felt unhome-like. Oswald wanted to wrap me up in cotton-wool. But I soon put the lid on that.'

'How?' I asked.

'I waited till we were alone,' said Ponting. His face wore a puzzled expression, as though he were inwardly marvelling at his own astuteness, and he spoke slowly and emphatically, studying the exits and apertures of my room, anxious to bring home to me, by pantomime, the very scent and savour of his discretion.

'Yes?' I said.

He looked at me hard, to make sure I had taken it in.

'I waited till we were alone,' he repeated, 'and when we were alone I just touched him on the shoulder like that. Nothing more.'

He gave me a heavy pat. The 'more', from which he had refrained, would certainly have been a knock-down blow.

'Well,' I said, 'and then?'

'He seemed surprised,' Ponting said, 'so I drew him aside——'

'But you told me you were alone,' I objected.

'I drew him aside,' Ponting went on, 'and said, "Now that we're between ourselves, there's something I want to say to you," and Oswald said "Say on!" or something like that. I think it was "say on" he said.'

'And what *did* you say?' I asked.

'I didn't want to be heavy about it,' Ponting remarked carelessly. 'I said, "A truce to all this palaver. I shan't melt, Oswald, and I shan't break. There's no need to treat me like a Vestal Virgin." That was all; but it did the trick.'

'What trick?' I inquired.

'Why,' said Ponting, plunging into metaphor, 'the Gateless Barrier was surmounted; the walls of Jericho fell down. It was his soul to my soul, from that time forth. We talked — it was more than that — we conversed; for all the world like two love-birds on an identical twig. "Spit it out," I said, meaning his trouble, whatever it was. And he did, too. He told me everything.'

'Ah!' I breathed.

'I can't remember his exact words,' Ponting continued. 'I can remember better what *I* said. But he told me he never meant a week-end party to be a frost; his true intent, he said, was all for our delight. That was an eye-opener to me, I tell you, and it sounded like a quotation, that's how I came to recall it. He said he'd been afraid he'd offended me, and he mentioned you, and some others; so he asked us to Witheling End to make it up. He thought we had a down on him, while we thought he had a down on us,' Ponting lucidly explained. 'And then it struck me that I had been a bit snappy the last time he came to see me; I was feeling seedy, off colour, and got my tail thoroughly down. He stayed a long time and I got fed up, and said the studio wasn't a home for lost animals.'

'I didn't say anything like that,' I mused.

'No?' said Ponting. 'Well, everyone has his own way of being rude. I didn't mean any harm, but he must have taken it to heart. He said it made him nervous and shy, looking after people in his own house, especially when he felt he had got on their nerves. He did everything he could, he went out of his way to give them a jolly time; but it was killing work, he said, like trying to warm up an icicle; they just moped and drooped and dripped. What he really meant was, they were like warmed-up death. But he didn't blame them; he said it was all his fault. Then we laughed over the whole affair. Lord, how we laughed! My sides still ache!' He rocked with merriment and even I couldn't help laughing a little.

'Well,' Ponting said at last, 'I mustn't stop any longer, mooning about. Oswald's waiting for me.'

'Where?' I asked.

'Why, where I deposited him, I suppose,' said Ponting. 'To wit, at the foot of the stairs. He won't thank me for telling you, though. He didn't want you to know. Would you like to see him?'

I hesitated. 'I thought I would wait until he called on me.'

Ponting burst into another guffaw. 'But that's just what he said about you!'

I began to feel rather foolish. 'All right, then,' I said. 'Invite him to come up. But no, stop!' I cried, for Ponting was already on the landing. 'Tell him to come up!'

'I'll whistle him,' said Ponting, and I stopped my ears. Ponting was a genius; I should never have thought of that.

MR. BLANDFOOT'S PICTURE

How it became known in Settlemarsh that Mr. Blandfoot was the owner of an interesting picture it would be hard to say: the rumour of its existence seemed to come simultaneously from many quarters. But in the full tide of its popularity as a subject of discussion, when its authorship was being eagerly disputed at greater and lesser tea-parties, the question of its origin got somehow overlooked. No one with any reverence for the established order of Settlemarsh society could doubt that Mrs. Marling, of The Grove, would be the first to pronounce judgment on it, or that Mrs. Pepperthwaite, of The Pergola, would be among the first to make inquiry about it: their respective rôles were to ask questions and to answer them.

'So you haven't met him yet?' suggested Mrs. Pepperthwaite.

As always, Mrs. Marling paused before replying, and fixed upon her interlocutor that wintry look which had blighted so much budding conversation.

'Met him?' she said. 'No, why should I have met him?'

Mrs. Marling's questions were generally rhetorical.

'So you haven't heard about his picture?' Mrs. Pepperthwaite suggested.

'I don't see why you connect the two things,' rejoined Mrs. Marling. 'Have you heard about Raphael's pictures?'

'Yes.'

'Have you met Raphael?'

'No, but Raphael is dead, and Mr. Blandfoot is very much alive; I only just missed him yesterday at Mrs. Peets's. He had only that moment gone, she told me.'

'I can't think why you visit that woman,' Mrs. Marling observed. 'Tell me what you see in her.'

The conversation lapsed; but none the less a seed was sown, or rather it was watered. Of course, Mrs. Marling had heard about the picture; she heard about everything in Settlemarsh. But she never decided hastily. She collected evidence, she felt her way, and when the moment was ripe she acted. She invited or she did not invite, and on her action depended or was said to depend, the fate of the newcomer to Settlemarsh. It was chiefly due to her that though Settlemarsh was a large place its society remained a small one. Her verdicts seemed capricious, but they were not really the outcome of caprice; she took her duties as social censor much more seriously than those who murmured at but accepted her decrees would have believed. The reasons she gave for disliking people were generally frivolous, and painful to the parties concerned when they became known, as they nearly always did; but at the back of them, as often as not, was a valid objection which she had unearthed with difficulty and which, to do her justice, she did not always make public.

When her guests had gone she retired to her room, and sitting before the tarnished Venetian mirror which gave back a very subdued version of her dark, intelligent, aquiline, handsome face, she wrote a note: but first, as was her habit, she addressed the envelope:

> Mrs. Stornway,
> The Uplands,
> Little Settlemarsh.

Most of her friends lived in Little Settlemarsh; she herself still inhabited that part of the town which had been fashionable thirty years earlier.

DEAREST EVA (she wrote),

I cannot quite forgive you for not coming here to-day. You would have been *so* bored! but at any rate I should have had some amusement. Foremost among the bores was (dare I say it?) your foundling, Mrs. Pepperthwaite, or words to that effect—I forget the exact name and her card, if it ever reached me, has been mislaid. Among other subjects that she touched but did not adorn was Mr. Blandfoot and his picture, gossip she had heard at Mrs. Peets's. Now do tell me, what is all this about. And another time don't desert your poor distracted friend,

ALICE MARLING.

Next day brought an answer:

DEAREST ALICE,

A thousand apologies! I couldn't come yesterday because I was expecting
—who do you think? Mr. Blandfoot! He had proposed himself for that day,
but he never turned up. He sent me quite a civil note saying he had been
caught in a shower at the ninth hole, and had to take shelter, as he dare not
risk getting wet. I wonder why: he looks quite a strong man. He has taken
'Heather Patch' at the bottom of our garden and is putting in some orange-
and-blue curtains. More than that? and his golf, dearest, I simply do not
know! I expect we shall all see the picture when his house is straight—I don't
suppose he has even hung it yet. Horace thinks it may be of the Dutch School,
as Mr. Blandfoot is said to have been something in Java. I wish I could be
more helpful, dearest.

Yours,

E. S.

Such information as Mrs. Marling gleaned about the newcomer was
always fragmentary and unsatisfactory. The days passed, and still the
polite society of Settlemarsh awaited in vain a signal from its leader.

Meanwhile, there was no doubt of it, Mr. Blandfoot was making
headway; he joined clubs, was a fugitive visitor at tea-parties, he went
out in the evening and played bridge. In spite of Mrs. Marling's withheld permission, he seemed to be establishing himself. To those in whom
awe of Mrs. Marling was still as second nature, he seemed to go about
with a furtive air, like a foreigner without a passport. At any moment,
it was felt, some official, acting on her instructions, would come up and
ask for his credentials. It was observed that Mrs. Marling's immediate
circle still held aloof, and Mrs. Stornway never repeated the indiscretion of inviting him to tea. But people began to ask themselves, was his
case still *sub judice*? Had Mrs. Marling rejected him, or had she not? And
this uncertainty was new to Settlemarsh. For whatever else Mrs. Marling might be she was never indifferent, nor had she ever shirked the
responsibility of saying yes or no. In this matter of maintaining the
standard of Settlemarsh society her conscience and her honour were
involved. Her inactivity was inexplicable.

More than that, it was dangerous; dangerous to Mrs. Marling, dangerous to Settlemarsh. There had always been rebellious provinces on
the fringe of Mrs. Marling's dominion, and these, as the central authority seemed to weaken, began to hold up their heads. Mrs. Peets had to
order a new tea-service, so thronged was her table, and there were some
who preferred its vigorous blue and yellow stripes to Mrs. Marling's
gold and white, just as there were some who preferred her house with

its tiers of wooden balconies painted white to the Victorian exterior of The Grove. Everyone acknowledged that The Grove had been a good house in its day and for its time. But now even its habitués began to look at it with purged and critical eyes. They saw the brickwork, once yellow, now dingy with smoke, relieved by string-courses, also brick, of a hard, dark, metallic blue. They observed that the serviceable and decorative magnolias which swarmed the walls and were cut back (so Mrs. Peets said) to exhibit the blue-brick arabesque did not really conceal the scaffolding of drain-pipes with which Mrs. Marling's grandfather, at the coming of the bathroom age, had fortified the walls. At Mrs. Peets's you had air and light and virgin soil. But when you went to The Grove you were conscious that the trees from which it took its name, a respectable cluster, larger than a shrubbery but smaller than a spinney, were on their last legs, and that one was trying to do duty for two; that the soil was sour and impoverished and, like an old coat, looked the more threadbare for its careful raking and tending; that every shrub would be an elderberry if it could, every flower a lobelia, every fern an aspidistra.

'And how many of them have had their wish!' thought Mrs. Stornway, as she trod lightly over the earthy gravel of the drive, her eyes still dazzled by the remembrance of Mrs. Peets's carriage sweep, a veritable shingle-bank for depth and glitter. Poor Alice! Sooner or later she had to become a back number. How could she hope to keep pace, Mrs. Stornway ruminated, as a blue-slated turret of vaguely ogee outline burst into view, with the growth of the town, the newcomers who gave you cocktails at tea, and whose baths filled in a moment, so fierce and sudden was the rush of water? How could she make herself felt, exert her authority over a society whose members dropped in casually on each other, who might as easily as not precede the servant into the drawing-room, whose very clothes had a different aim from hers? How easily people of to-day moved! Just as the whim took them, they got up, they sat down, they sprawled, lounged, and smoked; their conversation was short, sharp, and informal, familiar and pert. Mrs. Marling's words, like her attitudes, were poured into a mould; they had no elasticity, no give-and-take! She had ruled, indeed, by getting people into her house and making them feel so strange, so tense, so awkward, so incapable of movement, that she could do anything she liked with them! She had no notion of how to make her guests feel relaxed and comfortable. 'Poor Alice!' thought Mrs. Stornway again. 'The sap of her mind is dried up. She can't absorb fresh subjects. Look how hide-bound she is about Mr. Blandfoot's picture! She affects not to take any interest in it. I really must speak to her seriously!'

But as she confronted Mrs. Marling's slightly ecclesiastical porch, smothered in soiled ivy and surmounted by crockets and finials, her brave thoughts began to change colour. And when, in response to her inquiry, the butler had gone to find out whether Mrs. Marling was in and Mrs. Stornway remembered that rarely as Mrs. Marling left her home, as rarely was she at it, those thoughts died completely. She waited; the sombre trophies from India and the Boxer Rebellion, scraps of armour without faces, scraps of faces without armour, pallid wooden hands projecting from hollow sleeves supporting flower pots, completed her discomfiture. She watched the butler returning from the far end of the long hall, his advancing figure silhouetted against a large window, enclosed in an oblong frame of stained glass. Till the man spoke, she could not tell, no one could have told, whether Mrs. Marling was at home or not. And as he conducted her towards the drawing-room, walking a little in front and a little to one side, he might have been taking one ghost to interview another.

At first Mrs. Marling did not seem to notice her visitor; she stretched her work out in front of her and peered over the edge in an abstracted fashion. Then suddenly she rose.

'My dear Eva, to think of you coming all this way, and in this heat, to talk to a poor imbecile like me! I can tell you how flattered I feel. Nobody ever comes to see me now.'

The slightly complacent tone in which she said this bewildered Mrs. Stornway.

'Of course they will always come, dearest Alice,' she ventured. 'You are our chief place of pilgrimage.'

But she had taken the wrong tack. Mrs. Marling seemed able to read what was in her mind.

'Oh, believe me I am quite *démodée*,' she said, more to the needlework than to her friend. 'And do you know, I like it? I hear of Mrs. Peets giving parties; Mrs. Pepperthwaite has At Homes; you, yourself, are organizing a garden fete, they tell me, and no doubt Mr. Blandfoot will soon be giving a ball. And here I sit, quite happy to be out of it all.'

'Everyone has missed you so much,' Mrs. Stornway murmured.

'How nice of you to say that! I have missed you, dear Eva, more than once: but the others——! No. I am really meant for solitude. Do you like my picture?' she went on, presenting to her friend's view a remarkable seascape. In a violet sea a man of war of the Nelson period, all square lines and portholes, had heeled over away from the spectator, and was sinking with all sail set. 'It's an emblem of my life, dearest Eva,' she continued. 'Do you think it would be considered more of a master-piece if I left it unfinished? Or better still, I might hide it away and just talk about it, and then I should make quite a name for myself, like your Mr. – Mr.——'

'Blandfoot,' put in Mrs. Stornway eagerly.

'Like him,' said Mrs. Marling, disdaining to repeat the name. 'Have you been seeing a lot of him, my dear?'

Mrs. Stornway would only admit to having seen him once or twice. Like most people, she could not tell a disagreeable truth to Mrs. Marling. 'But to-morrow I and one or two others thought of going in about tea-time to help him hang his pictures. Poor fellow, he is very helpless, like all men, and has no one in the house to lend a hand.'

'I suppose he invited you,' Mrs. Marling suddenly remarked.

'We sort of decided it between us,' said Mrs. Stornway hastily. 'And, of course,' she added, taking a run at it, and adopting the slightly self-conscious air that everyone who talked to Mrs. Marling sooner or later fell into—'we hope to be shown *the* picture.'

'What picture?' inquired Mrs. Marling.

'Why, the one everybody is talking about,' exclaimed Mrs. Storn-way. 'You mentioned it yourself a moment ago.'

'Oh, that,' said Mrs. Marling. 'I don't think that exists. Oh, no. It's just an idea that people have got into their heads. But I do pity you, my dear, heaving aloft those large photographic reproductions of the Blandfoot family portraits. I shall think of you, as I sit here listening to poor Mr. Hesketh. He does tire me.'

'Hesketh!' exclaimed Mrs. Stornway in awed tones. 'Not *the* Hesketh, the novelist? Is *he* coming to stay with you?'

'He is already here,' said Mrs. Marling, 'only as I wanted the pleasure of talking to you alone I sent him out for a walk. And now,' she went on briskly, relishing the visible pang of disappointment that crossed her visitor's face, let us have some tea. But don't forget to come and tell me what the picture is like, who painted it, and what it is worth.'

The conversation passed into other channels. Mrs. Stornway listened abstractedly, hoping that Mr. Hesketh would appear. But the minutes passed and he did not come.

Punctually at half-past four Mrs. Stornway was shown into the drawing-room of Heather Patch. She was, as she meant to be, the first to arrive;

Mrs. Peets and Mrs. Pepperthwaite were still unannounced, and her host himself lingered somewhere in the interior. Yes, there were the pictures, numbers of them, leaning against each other, their strings and wires sticking out untidily, their faces turned to the wall. Mrs. Stornway studied their brown backs with passionate interest. Which of them would be IT? A friend had once told her that she was psychic beyond ordinary women. Surely she could use this special power to pierce Mr. Blandfoot's secret? She stood still, emptied her mind of thought, and tried to let the brown shapes before her pass into it. At first she saw nothing but knowing-looking dogs with heads cocked sideways and pipes in their mouths. Then one picture began to oust the others: its subject remained obscure, but she recognized its material form and, tiptoeing across the room, took hold of the frame and began to draw it slowly backwards.

'Good afternoon, Mrs. Stornway.' The voice startled her so much that she let go the picture, which subsided with a thud. She rose awkwardly, her feet imprisoned by the picture-cords.

'Oh, Mr. Blandfoot, forgive me! I couldn't resist taking a look!'

'How charming of you to be so interested,' he said, coming forward, his large figure blocking up the light and casting a soft gloom before it. 'Tell me which one you were looking at.'

Mrs. Stornway's impulse was always to lie.

'This one,' she said, indicating one of the smaller pictures.

Mr. Blandfoot pulled it out.

'Ah, Jake,' he said, looking at it. 'Poor old Jake with a bandaged head.'

They went to the window. It was a dog—a dog with his head on one side and tied up in a handkerchief.

'Why, what's happened to him?' she said, looking from Mr. Blandfoot to the picture and back to Mr. Blandfoot again.

He was a tall man, put together so loosely that one or other of his limbs always seemed on the verge of dislocation. His hair, which was thin and pale, the same colour as his face, seemed to cling together, as though for protection, in half a dozen long lank wisps, showing pink tracts between. His face was bony, his features were irregular, and his eyes so light they seemed to have been bleached. He could never give an effect of neatness, thought Mrs. Stornway: even the skin on the hand which held the picture was unevenly tinted, it looked coarse and porous without being firm and hardly seemed to fit him.

'What's happened to the dog?' she repeated.

'Why,' he said slowly, 'dogs will be dogs. I had to teach him——'

But what the lesson was Mr. Blandfoot had sought to inculcate Mrs. Stornway never knew; Mrs. Peets and Mrs. Pepperthwaite arrived simultaneously, and they had tea in the bow-window, flanked by the orange-and-blue curtains. Outside could be seen the patches of heather which gave the house its name. It flowered with a commendable persistence, although in the forefront of villadom's advance — trenches, incipient walls, overturned wheelbarrows, splodges of whitewash, moist spots for mixing mortar. It looked as dry and wiry and tenacious as the owner of Heather Patch, only more beautiful, thought Mrs. Stornway unwillingly.

The work went on apace, and of the forty-odd pictures only a mere handful remained to be hung. Many of them had been photographs of the Far East, representing, as often as not, severe, thin men in shirt-sleeves, standing very erect outside their temporary dwellings, putting, as it seemed, the thought of tiffin behind them. Others showed native women holding their babies, or naked warriors in open formation holding spears. No one ever seemed to sit down. All the pictures suggested a sort of flimsy precarious verticality. For contrast there were views of English interiors, the dreams of nostalgia, where everyone was sitting or lying or reclining. The largest of these, a picture displaying a group of couchant rich people watching their children, dressed in costumes of a bygone age, resting from a game of Ring-a-ring of Roses, Mrs. Stornway hung over the piano. The picture and the instrument were exactly the same length.

'I believe,' she murmured, 'that Mrs. Marling has a copy of this, only not such a fine one, at The Grove. Do you remember it, Mrs. Peets?'

'You forget,' said Mrs. Peets, 'I've never seen the inside of the good lady's house.'

'Oh,' said Mrs. Stornway, with well-assumed confusion, 'I thought everyone—— You remember it, Muriel?'

'Yes,' said Mrs. Pepperthwaite, 'in the dining-room.'

'No, not in the dining-room,' Mrs. Stornway remarked complacently, 'it's upstairs, the second passage you come to, on the right, if my memory serves me. He really ought to see the house, oughtn't he, Mrs. Peets? Alice Marling has such interesting pictures.'

'You forget, I haven't had the privilege of going,' said Mrs. Peets again, busying herself with a picture. Only three remained unhung. The exaltation Mrs. Stornway had felt as one by one the pictures were disposed of in the various rooms deepened into ecstasy. She persuaded herself that the last of the three was the one she was examining when

Mr. Blandfoot interrupted her. They were back in the drawing-room; it was the largest room, and its walls still had empty spots, though they had thought it finished when they left it. In the intoxication that possessed her, as the moment of revelation drew near, Mrs. Stornway felt that there was no limit to her powers: she could say anything, do anything: she could bring Mahomet to the mountain, Mr. Blandfoot to Mrs. Marling, and everything she did would become her.

'I always think,' she said, 'that in all Settlemarsh there's no one so really worth while as Alice Marling.' To make this declaration she stopped working, came into the middle of the room and clasped her hands in front of her.

There was a pause. Then Mr. Blandfoot took another picture and, mounting the steps with the cord in his mouth, muttered, 'Why are you always talking about this Mrs. Marling?'

'Oh,' Mrs. Stornway exclaimed, her eyes aglow with the fire of evangelizing the heathen, 'she stands for all that is best in Settlemarsh — so it seems to me. There was a time when she used to keep open house.'

'She doesn't keep open house for me,' said Mrs. Peets.

'Nor for me,' Mr. Blandfoot echoed. Again his utterance was impeded, this time, as Mrs. Stornway saw when he turned his head, by a long nail that he held clamped between his teeth.

There they both stood, Mrs. Peets and Mr. Blandfoot, the rejected of Mrs. Marling, their faces to the wall and the silence deepening round them. Mrs. Pepperthwaite, who had taken the last picture but one, a study of Highland cattle in a mist, and was carrying it about while she gazed inquiringly but helplessly at the crowded picture-rail, flung herself into the breach.

'Why, there's only one more left!' she cried nervously. 'It must be the picture that everyone's been talking about! Now, let's all guess what it is.'

Her intervention was a complete success. The cloud cleared from the brow of Mrs. Peets; Mrs. Stornway's face lost its Sibylline look; and Mr. Blandfoot turned round and sat on the top of the steps, his knees projecting enormously, his chin supported by his hands while he looked down at them with an enigmatic smile.

'First of all, how did you get hold of it?' demanded Mrs. Peets.

'Yes,' echoed Mrs. Stornway a little wanly, 'how did it come into your possession?'

'Perhaps we ought not to ask him that,' said Mrs. Pepperthwaite coyly. Her success as a peacemaker had given a sense of power which she seldom enjoyed.

'Well, then, *where* did you get it? He can't mind telling us that,' said Mrs. Peets in her decided tone.

Fascinated, they stared at the medium-sized oblong of brown paper, Mrs. Stornway still convinced that it was the one her second sight had revealed to her.

'I got it in Java,' said Mr. Blandfoot from the steps.

They all three nodded at each other, as if a secret suspicion was at last openly confirmed.

'And how did you get it?' persisted Mrs. Peets. 'After everything we've done for you, three tired perspiring women, I think you might tell us.'

Mr. Blandfoot paused a moment. 'It was given me by a man I met,' he said at last. 'He painted it specially for me.'

'Ah, then, it's a portrait of you,' put in Mrs. Pepperthwaite quickly, as though to get her say in before the others could speak. 'Just the head, perhaps?' she suggested, scrutinizing the back of the picture which looked too small for a full length.

'No, it's not a portrait *of* me,' said Mr. Blandfoot, his voice dwelling on the preposition. 'It would be a pity to waste a good canvas on me, wouldn't it?' So yellow did his face look in the high shadowy place where he sat that for a moment nobody spoke. Mrs. Stornway's fluttering 'How can you say such a ridiculous thing?' came too late. Mr. Blandfoot seemed to have observed the pause, for there was a noticeable grimness in his voice as he added:

'In fact it's not a portrait at all — of any living person.'

'Oh, then he's dead,' concluded Mrs. Pepperthwaite quickly.

'There's more than one,' Mr. Blandfoot rejoined. 'Some would say they're dead; some would say they never lived at all; some would say they're still living. I'm a plain man: I can't pretend to judge.'

'You say you're plain,' said Mrs. Peets, a little impatiently. 'But you speak in riddles. I expect it's a mythological subject.'

'You're not far wrong,' said Mr. Blandfoot. 'Just a little blasphemous, that's all.'

'I don't care for them much myself,' observed Mrs. Peets. 'And how can it be a mythological subject, if it was painted specially for you? I thought they never did that sort of thing now.'

'By request,' said Mr. Blandfoot, who seemed to enjoy the conversation, 'they'll do almost anything.'

'Well, we've learned a certain amount,' said Mrs. Peets briskly, 'though I must say it's been like drawing blood out of a stone. It's a semi-mythological picture, painted in Java at Mr. Blandfoot's request. Who, may I ask, was the artist?'

'I'm afraid his name wouldn't mean anything to you, though in his time he was supreme,' said Mr. Blandfoot.

'Well, really, Mr. Blandfoot,' protested Mrs. Pepperthwaite bridling, 'you seem to think we don't know anything about Art. Settlemarsh isn't a big place, but we have a picture-gallery, as you should know by this time.'

'Yes, now that you've insulted us,' said Mrs. Peets, 'I think you ought to let us see the picture. We simply cannot wait another minute.'

'Well, there it is,' said Mr. Blandfoot. 'Look at it. Excuse me coming down, my foot's gone to sleep.' He began to wave it in the air.

Together they walked slowly towards the picture. Mrs. Peets took it and reverently but firmly turned it round towards the light. First came an impression of blue, stabbed by an arrow of white. Then the subject revealed itself to all their eyes.

'Why, it's the Matterhorn!' Mrs. Peets exclaimed.

'No, Mt. Cervin,' said Mrs. Pepperthwaite, examining it more closely.

'They're both the same,' said Mrs. Stornway, who had travelled.

'Then it's *not* the picture!' they cried in chorus, the inflexion of their voices making a very chord of disappointment.

'No,' said Mr. Blandfoot, 'it's not the picture. Why, did you think it was?'

'Now I call that too bad of you,' said Mrs. Peets.

'Isn't he a tease?' demanded Mrs. Pepperthwaite with ineffective playfulness.

'I don't believe they ever try to climb the Matterhorn from this side,' announced Mrs. Stornway. 'But the picture will go very nicely here.' As though fortified by the knowledge of Mrs. Marling's friendship she was the first to recover herself. There was a silence while she fitted the very blue print into a space between two photographic jungle-studies. When she had finished she looked round the crowded walls and said in a voice that sounded hurt but well-bred:

'But now there's no room for the real picture – the one Mr. Bland-foot wouldn't show us.'

'Oh,' said he, still from the top of the steps, 'that's hung already.'

'But we've been everywhere,' protested Mrs. Pepperthwaite, who couldn't forgo the appearance of curiosity as easily as could Mrs. Stornway.

'No,' said Mr. Blandfoot, his voice conveying reproach, 'not quite everywhere.'

Both of the other women suffered while Mrs. Pepperthwaite racked her memory for places they had not seen. Her mental processes were becoming clear even to herself when Mrs. Peets cut in:

'Not in the coal cellar, for instance.'

'No,' said Mr. Blandfoot. 'The picture has never been there.'

'So it walks about, does it?' said Mrs. Peets. 'How curious.' She was still ruffled, as they all were, by the practical joke that they felt had been played on them.

'I usually take it with me,' Mr. Blandfoot admitted.

'Then it must be a miniature,' declared Mrs. Pepperthwaite triumphantly. Her less sophisticated nature quickly threw off its mood of sulkiness, but her companions still stood on their dignity.

'No,' said Mr. Blandfoot, who always seemed pleased to disagree. 'It's a fair size — the ordinary size.'

'What is the ordinary size?' demanded Mrs. Peets.

'Oh,' Mr. Blandfoot replied, making a wide gesture on his airy perch, 'the size that fits the circumstances.'

'What are the circumstances?' Mrs. Peets persisted.

'Well, the flesh, for example, is the circumstances of the soul.'

The three women received this dictum in silence. Doubt and disappointment appeared in their faces. What a tame dull ending to an enterprise that had seemed so full of promise. Mrs. Pepperthwaite began looking behind the sofa for her bag; Mrs. Stornway picked up hers and started to put on her gloves. Only Mrs. Peets held her ground. She looked up thoughtfully at Mr. Blandfoot, who had the appearance of an umpire at a tennis match.

'I don't suppose you want to sell your picture?' she inquired. Her voice suggested that, little though it would fetch, the thought of selling it might easily have occurred to such a man as Mr. Blandfoot.

'Oh no,' said he, 'we are inseparable.'

'But if its value goes up, wouldn't you consider parting with it then?'

'I hope,' he answered rather gravely, 'I shan't have to part with it for many years,' He came down the steps, but so tall was he that Mrs. Pepperthwaite, whose grasp of facts was feeble and at the mercy of her imagination, could scarcely believe he was not still aloft. With various shades of ungraciousness they accepted his thanks for their kind offices, but something in his manner made them unwilling to show their disappointment openly. As they stood on the doorstep Mrs. Peets made a last appeal:

'So you won't show us the picture after all?'

For a moment he looked as though he might really oblige them, and all their curiosity flooded back.

'I'll tell you what I'll do,' he said suddenly. 'I'll show it to Mrs. Marling.'

He smiled down into their bewildered faces; and as he shut the door, they could still see, though his face was turned away, the smile lingering on his large, spare, yellowish cheek.

'I know the word to describe that man,' exclaimed Mrs. Stornway, who had just learned it and used it more often than the occasion warranted. 'He's sinister!'

Directly she reached home she telephoned to Mrs. Marling. Mrs. Marling, it was well known, resented the telephone as an intrusion upon private life: she was as inaccessible to it as to all other demands on her attention. But finally she came.

'Who's that?'

'Eva, Alice, Eva.'

'Eva Alice Eva: I don't know the name. Alice is my name: would you kindly spell yours?'

Mrs. Stornway spelt it.

'My darling Eva, how good of you to telephone, though of course you know I hardly ever use it, it makes me feel so deaf. Can't bear to feel deaf at my age. Had you anything to say, dearest?'

'Oh, Alice, I've got such heaps to tell you. May I come round to-morrow?'

'I'm afraid I'm engaged to-morrow.'

'Wednesday then?'

'Wednesday is no good.'

'What about Thursday?'

'Dearest Eva, you mustn't let me take up your whole week! Couldn't you tell me now?'

'It's about Mr. Blandfoot's picture.'

'His brick shirt?'

'No, his picture.'

'Oh,' in disappointed tones. 'Have you seen it?'

'No.'

'I thought not. Then what have you got to say about it?'

'He wants you to see it, he wants to show it to you.'

'To me? Oh no. That wouldn't do. Oh no. Not at my age. I'm too old to look at pictures: I make them myself now.'

'Well, that's what he said.'

'Darling, how frivolous you are. Come and see me on Friday. Yes, Mr. Hesketh will still be here. There's no sign of his going away.'

It was two days later. Dinner was over, and Mrs. Marling and Mr. Hesketh were sitting over their port: over his port, that is. It had ceased to circulate. As Mr. Hesketh raised his glass, his rich booming voice caused tiny tremors to appear on the surface of the wine.

'You ought to drink more port,' said Mrs. Marling. 'It's well known to be good for the throat.' Her pose was upright and her slender body never moved; but there was a hint of weariness in the lines round her eyes.

'Very kind of you, my dear Alice, I'm sure,' replied Mr. Hesketh, refilling his glass and staring into it. 'I shall take your advice to heart. How long has this very excellent port wine lain in your cellar?'

'You must ask Dodge,' said Mrs. Marling. 'He has the key. But I believe my husband put some down the same year that *The Logic of the Grape* came out – twenty-five years ago?'

'Thirty.'

'To look at you,' said Mrs. Marling, with one of her rare smiles, 'who would have thought it? Of the two vintages, if I may say so, I prefer your novel.' She sipped her wine.

'It has often occurred to me to wonder, Alice,' remarked Mr. Hesketh, pleased by the compliment – as everyone was pleased when Mrs. Marling said something nice to them, so clearly did she go out of her way to do it – 'why, when Richard died, you stayed on here, a triton among minnows?' He put his hands on the table-edge and looked hard at her, as though he really wanted an answer.

'But does that matter when whales like yourself, great, gambolling, famous, good-natured whales, come to stay with me?'

'Unfortunately, I can't be here all the time,' said Mr. Hesketh a trifle heavily.

'But you're here a good time – at least I mean when you're here I have a good time,' said Mrs. Marling.

'You are quite right,' the novelist agreed. Like many people slightly under the influence of alcohol, he was appealing to the Past to give up a decaying friendship, and he thought the best way of recovering it was by a series of intimate references to their common memories. 'With your talents, if you had lived in London, you might have done almost anything – you might have gone far, very far.'

'I'm afraid so,' replied Mrs. Marling. 'But don't you think it's better that I should be somebody in Settlemarsh than almost nobody in London?'

'Oh, my dear Alice,' Mr. Hesketh exclaimed, 'don't mistake my meaning. I was talking to Dick Gresham the other day, and Richard Gresham is not a man to use words lightly, and he said, "Of all the women I ever knew" (and he's known a great many) "the most brilliant by far was Alice Ingilby" (that's you, of course). "Most provincial towns are deadly," he said, "and Settlemarsh not least; but when you had met her, say just coming away from church, the very bricks and slates sparkled, and the streets were alive with joy!" Once, he said, when he had met you he counted all the palings between his house and Chittlegate, it was so impossible, after one had talked to you, not to find the world interesting! And now I come and I see you surrounded by wretched second-rate people swarming in jerry-built bungalows, with no feeling for the art of life, only an idle curiosity in what the day brings forth and a pitiful competitive snobbishness that has its goal, as it always had, in you.'

Mrs. Marling was silent for a moment after this tribute. To what emotion the slight movement of the muscles about her mouth testified, who could say? Then her eyes hardened, she leaned back as though taking control of the conversation and said:

'At least I haven't troubled you with these second-rate people. I kept them from you. It is true they can only take in one word at a time, and your longer speeches might be above their heads. I have always tried to do my best for everybody, Arthur! Even when that means not seeing them for months together! I have my duty to these unhappy creatures, you forget that. You're so mobile, you're such a gadabout and welcome in so many houses, you don't remember what it is to stay at home and hear about the gardener's baby. You have a large public which looks after you – I a small district which I look after – don't I seem,' she went on, her mood lightening. 'to have the cares of the community on my shoulders? And if you think I should like to live always among brilliant people like yourself you mistake me utterly, Arthur! You are a treat to me, a sugar-plum, a prize for a good, clever girl. But I'm not often good and hardly ever clever, and I couldn't have you here very much, I shouldn't dare. Oh no! Oh no!' she went on, wagging her finger at him. 'You and your standards would kill me. I must have my stupid friends, that you haven't been allowed to see, to come in and say one word at a time—one word at a time. "Does—Mrs.—Peets—dye—her hair?" That's the sort of thing I really enjoy. But now, tell me, where have you seen my second-rate friends, swarming in their bungalows? You can't have seen them. They live in fashionable Little Settlemarsh, far from this slum. You can't have heard their wireless sets, much less them.'

Mrs. Marling had put her question like an inquisitor, and the novelist, the wheels of whose conversational machinery had run down while she talked, did not answer immediately. Moreover, it was never easy to tell Mrs. Marling of an acquaintance of whom she might not approve.

'I ran into Catcomb yesterday,' he said as casually as he could.

'What, that man? I thought he was dead years ago!'

'No,' said Mr. Hesketh, his confidence returning now that the worst was over. 'He's very much alive and bubbling over with excitement.'

'He always was,' Mrs. Marling murmured with distaste.

'Excitement because a man has come to live in Settlemarsh who owns a picture of fabulous value. It's so valuable, it seems, that he won't let it out of his sight.'

'Or into anyone else's,' Mrs. Marling put in.

'I'm coming to that. In places like this people exaggerate. What they mean is he keeps it under lock and key. From the description, size, subject, etc., and the fact that it was found in Java, always a Dutch colony, I should judge it to be a Vermeer. In fact I'm practically sure it's a Vermeer: so few of them are known, there must be more somewhere.'

'Do you mean to say that this Mr. Blandfoot conceals about his person a picture by Vermeer?'

'No, no, but if he is a prudent man, and the picture is as yet unauthenticated, no doubt he keeps it in a safe place. But the point I was coming to is this.'

'Well?'

'You know how reluctant he has been—naturally, considering its value—to let anyone see the picture?'

'Yes, yes,' said Mrs. Marling. 'As you were saying, I live in Settlemarsh and unfortunately I can't be blind or deaf to all that goes on there.'

'Well,' said the novelist, 'Catcomb tells me that Blandfoot wants to show the picture to you.'

Mrs. Marling said nothing. Thoughts crowded into her mind: her youth when she had had Settlemarsh at her feet, the parties she had given, the people from the great world who had graced them, the larger ambitions she had entertained but which she had abandoned from cautiousness, from laziness, from conscience, for a dozen reasons. She thought of her empire which, like the Roman Empire under Hadrian, was now technically at its greatest extent. She had maintained it for many years against every kind of opposition and difficulty: assault, intrigue, her own diminished resources. The advent of Mr. Blandfoot troubled her, and taxed her powers as they had not been taxed for a long time. To the world of Settlemarsh it seemed that she was merely reserving her fire. But she knew too well that in her inactivity there lurked a grain of fatigue. She was not really weighing the reasons for and against Mr. Blandfoot's admission into her charmed circle; she was shirking her responsibilities as the mentor of Settlemarsh, she was letting things slide. And it troubled her the more to feel this lethargy, because she was aware that Mr. Blandfoot was already a centre of disaffection and revolt, and that he must be definitely assimilated into her system, or rejected from it. And her own indifference to whether he was admitted or not alarmed her: it was like the sound of the footsteps of old age gaining upon her. She must pull herself together and take the field. After all, what better occasion than the present, with a renowned novelist at her side to support her, supposing she needed support? She turned to Mr. Hesketh, who was meditatively eyeing the decanter.

'Dear Arthur, it must be very dull for you alone with such a fossil as me.'

'Alice, how can you say such a thing?' he protested.

'Oh no, oh no,' she said, 'in spite of your beautiful manners, I can see your eye wandering whenever I begin these long sentimental anecdotes about my early years. I see I am becoming a bore. Don't say "no" again. I can't bear to be contradicted. But I tell you what I'm going to do: I'm going to give a party for all those second-rate people you despise so much! For one evening at least their bungalows will know them no more. Then you will realize that I, like you, am a public benefactor. To make it amusing for them I shall say that you are here. And to make it amusing for you— do you know what I shall do?'

'Alice, you derange yourself too much!' murmured the novelist.

'I shall invite Mr. Blandfoot to come and show us his picture!'

'Ah!' cried Mr. Hesketh.

'And now,' said Mrs. Marling, rising briskly, 'I shall go and join the ladies. You must stay here and drink some port. You simply haven't

had any! What would my husband say, if he saw that poor little decanter still groaning with wine!'

Mr. Hesketh held the door open for her and she passed out of the
room, a slender, distinguished figure, seeming somehow to take up
even less space than her scanty envelope of flesh demanded. To say that
she fitted her rich heavy ugly surroundings did not do her justice; but
her presence completed a harmony whose innate grace and rarity the
amateur of life immediately recognized. Mr. Hesketh, watching her go,
suddenly felt grateful for her. A warm sentimental emotion welled up
in his heart — when she dies, he thought, she can never be replaced. He
tried to find words to describe that felicitous relationship between her
and her possessions in which her charm seemed to reside. He fancied
that the objects she passed made obeisance to her and that her graciousness flowed out, enveloping them in its gentle radiance. But the remembered asperity of her nature kept pricking his honeyed thoughts of her;
and returning to his port, he gave up trying to enclose her in a formula.

Alone in the drawing-room, Mrs. Marling sat down at her bureau.
She took out an envelope and wrote '—Blandfoot, Esq.' Then she hesitated. So written, the name had an unceremonious, unfriendly air. It
reminded her that she did not know Mr. Blandfoot: perhaps he would
resent being prefixed by a dash. She entertained the thought, however,
only to dismiss it. Who, among the servile population of Settlemarsh
would not be flattered to hear from her, by whatever style she addressed
them? For a moment she indulged her imagination with a prevision of
her party, and the room, as though aware of her thought, glowed softly
back at her, loosing for her all its influences of comfort and dignity and
order and security. The words flowed easily from her pen as she wrote
to the unknown art collector.

At nine o'clock the next morning the maid knocked at Mr. Blandfoot's
bedroom door — knocked several times, though with an air of misgiving. At last she heard a growl: 'Come in!' The room was so dark
she could see nothing and she paused on the threshold.

'How often have I told you,' said a voice, 'not to come until I ring.'

'Yes, sir,' said the maid, timidly.

'Well, come in, if you're coming,' said the voice, still implacable.

There was a vast heaving movement on the bed.

'Now the curtains, now the blinds, now the hot water, now the bath,'
the voice chanted rapidly and irritably, 'and you haven't told me why
you came at all yet.'

'Please, sir,' said the maid, stumbling towards the window, 'there's a letter marked "urgent", so I thought——'

'Why didn't you say so before?' snapped the voice. 'Well, hand it over.'

But in her flurry the maid had dropped the letter. She groped for it on the floor, obscurely feeling that she must not pull up the blind until she had given her master the letter. She did not know whereabouts in the room she was; she thought she must be near the bed, but she was afraid to touch it and every moment her movements grew more rigid.

'I had it only just now,' she murmured, almost crying.

'Clumsy, clumsy,' admonished the voice, in gentler accents. 'Here, I've got it.'

'Oh, that's all right then, sir,' said the maid, almost gasping with relief.

'No,' said the voice, drawing nearer.

'I want you to give it to me.'

Bewildered, the maid held out her hand in the darkness.

'No, just a little more this way,' persuaded the voice, still advancing to meet her.

Again she stumbled forward in the gloom, her hand stretched stiff like a fencer's. Mr. Blandfoot seemed to have reared himself up in the bed: she could see a vague outline towering above her.

'A shade to the left now,' said the voice.

The maid obeyed.

'And now straight into the letter-box.'

She made a half-hearted prodding movement. Something caught her finger: a sharp pain ran down her arm. She called out, and the whole room was suddenly flooded with light. Afterwards she realized it must have been electric light; but at the time she was aware only of the pain, of the sight of her finger wedged between Mr. Blandford's large irregular teeth, and of his face looking down at her with a smile that had no kindness in it. The blankets were tumbled together in the middle of the bed; the floor, as much of it as she could see, was lumpy with sorry-looking underclothes: the biscuit-coloured walls refracted the unsympathetic light, as did also Mr. Blandfoot's parchment-coloured face. The spiritless, yellow hues around her were infinitely uncomforting; she felt the world beginning to dissolve.

'There's the letter,' remarked Mr. Blandfoot, 'on the floor behind you.'

Her finger dropped from his mouth: obsequiously she picked up the letter and handed it to him. Her face was half averted; but she noticed that he pulled the jacket of his pyjamas more firmly across his chest, and this gesture, which seemed to recognize her right to be treated as a human being, restored her a little.

Mr. Blandfoot lay in the bath, the letter in his hand. Dabs of shaving soap had fallen on it, and steam had made the lines run. It was a pitiful object, fallen on evil days since it left Mrs. Marling's writing-table. We will read the letter over his shoulder. He has cleaned his razor on the envelope, but one has no difficulty in recognizing Mrs. Marling's elegant Italian hand.

DEAR MR. BLANDFOOT,

I hope you will forgive me for taking the liberty of writing to you without an introduction. I have long wanted to make your acquaintance but your friends are so jealous of you, they wouldn't let us meet: so I am defying convention and writing to you myself. I think I would not have dared had not my friend Arthur Hesketh given me courage—perhaps you know him, a most charming person, whatever one may feel about his later books. I want to discuss them with you. He leads me to hope that you will forgive my boldness on the score of my age, and spend next Thursday evening at my house—I have a few friends coming. He even whispered to me something about that picture we are all so longing to see—but this is mere naked presumption, and I feel I have tried your patience already too far. Let me have the pleasure of seeing you on Thursday evening at ten o'clock and I shall feel I am forgiven for my indiscretion. At your age (if I may say so) one can afford to postpone a pleasure. At mine, one can't; so you see I must indulge my impatience.

Hoping to see you.

Yours sincerely,

ALICE MARLING.

With astonishing dexterity Mr. Blandfoot converted the letter into a paper boat, and propelled it with his breath to the far end of the bath. Then he took aim with his sponge and an accurate shot sent the boat to the bottom. It did not reappear. Rising from the bath, Mr. Blandfoot arranged the towel round his waist like an apron. He walked slowly towards a pier glass. Except for a bright narrow margin round the edge, the mirror was misted over with steam; but so tall was Mr. Blandfoot that he could see his eyes reflected in the unclouded area at the top. Our observer, stationed discreetly by the door, could also see them and see the smile which, with ever-growing intensity, they gave back to Mr. Blandford's approaching figure.

'Do you think he's come yet?' asked Mrs. Pepperthwaite of Mrs. Stornway, glancing at the clock in the hall of Mrs. Marling's house. It showed a minute to ten.

'He told me at tea,' Mrs. Stornway whispered, 'that he might be a little late as he wanted to wash the picture. I said "Is that quite wise?" and he said "Yes, it makes the colours fresher." '

'You are the only person in Settlemarsh who is in his confidence!' exclaimed Mrs. Pepperthwaite simply.

'Oh no! But I do think that this time he really means to bring the picture. He practically told me so.'

They were led away. People who came to Mrs. Marling's house were taken into as many ante-chambers as possible before they were admitted to her presence. The turning of several corners confused them as to their physical and mental whereabouts, so that when they encountered their hostess such self-confidence as they possessed was considerably shaken. Like people who have been blindfolded in a children's game and whisked rapidly round, they were conscious of cutting an awkward figure.

'How good of you to come so soon,' said Mrs. Marling as she greeted them. 'I am always grateful when my oldest friends arrive early. This is Mr. Hesketh, Mrs. Stornway. An old friend of Settlemarsh. It was very different when you lived here, wasn't it, Arthur? You must tell him about the new building developments in your neighbourhood, Eva: he's fond of architecture: I wish he could have seen your new house before he went away: it would have interested him so much.'

The room began to fill. To Mrs. Pepperthwaite a party of any kind was like heaven. Her timidity, that distressed her in the company of two or three people, she felt to be an asset in the presence of forty or fifty: she knew instinctively that it pleased them to find someone less at ease than they were: she went the round of her acquaintance, making to each a small offering of her self-esteem, a sacrifice which, in the prevailing communal amiability, was always graciously accepted. Whereas most of her friends preferred to hide their ignorance, she was delighted to inquire who so-and-so was, whose photograph she had so often seen in the Settlemarsh *Clarion*, but whose name she could not remember. Never had she had so many opportunities of indulging her

craving for humility as to-night: all the chief personages of the neighbourhood were gathered together in Mrs. Marling's drawing-room.
Some of the citizens of Settlemarsh, headed by Mrs. Peets, were inclined
to cling together defensively, eyeing with hostility and apprehension
these visitants from a larger world. Mrs. Pepperthwaite was unconscious of their ignoble herd-feeling; she rejoiced in strange contacts and
she was justified in her confidence: everyone was nice to her. She wandered into the bridge-room and stood behind the chairs of the players.
When one of them took a trick she smiled as if she had taken it herself.
Once she leaned over the shoulder of a forbidding-looking man whose
name she scarcely knew and indicating a card said, 'I should play that.'
'Now would you?' he said, selecting a card from another part of his
hand, from a different suit indeed; but he smiled at her so charmingly
it was quite as if he had followed her suggestion. In a corner she found
a couple playing chess, their heads bent over the board.

'Can you play four games at once like Capablanca?' she asked at random of the two of them. One of the men looked up, the strain of concentration dying from his face like a cloud from the sky. 'Do you mean
me?' he said. 'I'm afraid I'm a very moderate player.' But Mrs. Pepperthwaite could see he was flattered that she had imagined him capable of
such a feat.

The sound of music recalled her to the drawing-room. It was Anton
Melzic at the piano: she recognized him the moment she saw him. He
had been plain Antony Mellish when he lived in Settlemarsh before he
had gone away and made a name for himself abroad. And now he had
come back to play for Mrs. Marling, though it was said she hadn't always been very kind to him when he practised scales and exercises in
the room above his father's bakehouse. But all that was forgotten: Time
had no revenges for Mrs. Marling; if he nourished any he relented at
the last moment, and transformed them into bouquets. How attentively
everyone was listening! Mrs. Pepperthwaite beat time with her forefinger, ecstatically aware of a harmony within herself more complete
than the imperfect copy of it rendered by the strains around her. When
the piece was over she would be the first to move across the room and
congratulate the pianist. The right words would rise to her lips: that
was the joy, the thrilling excitement and release, granted her by the
party. What a triumph for Alice Marling! Mrs. Pepperthwaite felt that
she and Mrs. Marling had been united for many years in a close bond
which had for object the perfect and appropriate entertainment of all
the choicer spirits in Settlemarsh. The executive power was Mrs.

Marling's, but surely the inspiration, the vital force, had been all hers! Mrs. Pepperthwaite gave Mrs. Marling, who was sitting at the far end of the room, a warm, confiding glance intended to convey this sense of partnership, and she fancied it was returned. The music was galloping ahead; a kind of recklessness had got into its rhythm, as though everything that went before had been provisional, looking forward to this. A loud brilliant passage was repeated twice as loudly and twice as brilliantly. The excitement which a perfect technique begets in the least musical of listeners was apparent on every face and in every pose. Mrs. Pepperthwaite scanned the guests, eagerly, even critically, as though about to visit with condign punishment the smallest sign of indifference or inattention. She was arranging her hands ready to clap when something jogged her elbow. The door against which she was standing was moving inwards. Someone was trying to come in. What a sacrilege at this moment of all moments. She peered round the door, fury written on her face, meaning to repel the intruder. Her outraged glance, travelling upwards, encountered the large yellowish face of Mr. Blandfoot, impending over her like a parchment lantern, in the dim light of the hall. She had completely forgotten his existence.

Shaken, she turned back to the room. The applause was tremendous, but her own contribution was half-hearted and pre-occupied. When the clapping died down the door opened and Mr. Blandfoot was announced. Mrs. Pepperthwaite noticed it was already eleven o'clock.

He stood in the middle of the room without seeming to face any one part of it, his figure so thin it was like a silhouette, his wide shoulders moving independently like the arms of a semaphore. He drew all eyes towards him and radiated a silence which threatened to stretch into the corners of the room. But Mrs. Marling was already on her feet.

'How nice to see you,' she said, 'and what a pity you missed the last piece.'

'I didn't,' said Mr. Blandfoot. 'I heard it from the passage, outside the door.'

'You would have been so much more comfortable in here,' returned Mrs. Marling, as though he had stayed outside on purpose. 'Now you must come and sit by me.' She piloted him to a chair by her side.

The pianist played again as brilliantly as ever and the guests listened entranced, but Mrs. Pepperthwaite knew that the party had changed its character. Before it was fulfilling itself as it went along: now it was leading up to something. Up or down? Mrs. Pepperthwaite had a sense of increasing velocity; her thoughts seemed to outstrip her and to leave her dissatisfied with the present. She felt that her remarks were now aimed at a moving target which they failed to hit. In the next interval she wandered uneasily into the buffet. Mr. Blandfoot was drinking a whisky and soda, even yellower than himself. Scraps of conversation kept coming to her ears. 'Oh — probably in the cloakroom with his hat.' 'But that's only a figure of speech, my dear, he can't sleep with it.' 'Really, I can't say, it might be a Vermeer: I know so little about the Dutch School,' 'They invented painting in oils.' 'But no one said it was an oil-painting.' 'But, my dear, the paint would run.' 'Not after all these years.' 'His waistcoat pocket? But it isn't a miniature.' 'Eva Stornway says it's not old at all: he had it made for himself.' 'Oh, he was kidding her; he looks just that sort of man. Hesketh must know better.'

Vaguely distressed she walked over to where Hesketh was standing, and heard him say to Mrs. Marling, with a smile:

'A bad fairy, I'm afraid.'

'Do you think he will cast a spell?'

'If he does, Alice, it is you who will be the Sleeping Beauty, not me.'

'Ah, but I invited him: he can't do me any harm: it's against the rules.

'When shall you ask him to——?'

'I don't quite know, Arthur. Yes, please, I will have some champagne. Perhaps after the next piece.'

The last piece was over. Some called for more, but the majority agreed, with a note of determination in their voices, that the pianist had been only too generous: they must not be greedy and presume upon his kindness. Mr. Melzic bowed to right and left, rising from his stool a little reluctantly: a monarch relinquishing his throne. The guests moved about studying pictures and *objets d'art*: it was midnight but they made no attempt to move, and they talked so little that everyone could hear the sound of his own voice.

'Where's Blandfoot?' asked someone, bolder than the rest.

'In the buffet, I think.'

'Shall I fetch him?'

'What for?'

'Oh, he'll know.'

At that moment Mr. Blandfoot entered. His cheek bones were flushed and his eyes bright. He walked on to the hearth-rug and stumbled over it, making a fold, which he unceremoniously kicked. The fold did not yield to his treatment, so he kicked it again, harder than before. Then he stared moodily at it while the others fell back into a rough semicircle.

There was literally a breach in the company. Mrs. Marling moved quietly into it.

'Don't trouble about the carpet, Mr. Blandfoot,' she said. 'It always behaves like that.'

'Bit dangerous, isn't it?'

'When you've been here a few more times,' said Mrs. Marling quietly, 'you'll get used to its ways.'

'I might have fallen over it.'

'How we should have laughed!' said Mrs. Marling, looking up at him with her bright eyes.

There was a pause.

'But do do something for us, Mr. Blandfoot,' she continued persuasively. 'Dance for us.'

'I can't dance,' he muttered.

'Then sing us a song?'

He was silent.

'Or tell us a story?'

He glowered down at her helplessly.

'He's a strong, silent man,' she said to the company at large. 'But there's something you can do for us, Mr. Blandfoot!'

'What?'

'Why, show us your picture!'

'Yes, do show it to us!' came in a confused murmur from the room. There was a general movement. The tension relaxed. Smiles broke out on puzzled faces: women made delicate gestures of eagerness; men settled themselves comfortably into their chairs. The optimistic party-spirit had reasserted itself, and once again Mrs. Marling's drawing-room breathed freely. Even Mr. Blandfoot smiled.

'Do you really want to see it?' he asked them.

'Yes, yes,' they cried, all looking towards him.

'But I must warn you,' he added, 'that it may be more than you bargain for.'

Mrs. Marling looked up from the chair in which, when Mr. Blandfoot showed signs of coming to heel, she had seated herself.

'Will it be like the head of Medusa? Will it turn us to stone?'

'I don't know what it will turn you into,' he said, looking round him reflectively.

They all smiled delightedly at each other.

'Nothing worse than donkeys?' suggested someone facetiously.

'I don't know,' said Mr. Blandfoot, 'how bad you can be.'

'And after to-night,' asked one of the guests, 'everyone will be able to see it—it will be hung up in your house?'

Mr. Blandfoot thought a moment. 'No,' he said. 'This is a private view, and I doubt if I shall show the picture again. You might not even want to see it a second time.'

There was a pause. Mrs. Marling stirred in her chair.

'Would you like me to send someone to fetch it?'

Everyone hung on Mr. Blandfoot's lips.

'No, thank you, I have it on me, here.'

'Dear me, how the man does tease us,' said a woman's voice.

'Come on, Blandfoot,' said a man from among the company. 'You can't get us more excited than we are now. You'll miss your market if you keep us on tenterhooks any longer.'

'He's forgotten it, and doesn't dare say so.'

'Blandfoot, we shall skin you alive if you disappoint us. Alice has all the engines of Oriental torture in the hall being heated ready for you, so hurry up!'

'I tell you what,' said Mr. Blandfoot, 'if you skin me alive you can have the picture to keep. There's an offer.'

Mrs. Marling rose from her chair. 'Mr. Blandfoot, I don't think you really want to show us the picture. Keep it for another time. It's late now, and we don't want to worry you,' She glanced at the clock.

Mr. Blandfoot pulled something slowly out of his pocket. Every eye was focused upon his wasitcoat, and when the object turned out to be in truth his watch, there was a general sigh, half of relief, half of disappointment.

'No, no,' he said, ignoring what was perhaps the most palpable hint Mrs. Marling had ever given in her life.

'Believe me, there's plenty of time. Only I should be much obliged if you would send and ask if my car is standing at the door.'

'I'm afraid all the servants have gone to bed,' said Mrs. Marling.

The silence that followed this pronouncement was broken by Mrs. Pepperthwaite's thin piping voice:

'There must be someone about to give us back our hats and coats.'

Mrs. Marling looked straight in front of her; and a man at the back of the room said in a good natured voice: 'All right, Blandfoot, I'll go and look.'

When he had gone the murmur of conversation began again, though Mr. Blandfoot and Mrs. Marling, at their posts on the hearth-rug, contributed nothing to it.

The man returned with a beaming smile, as though he had smoothed away every difficulty. 'The Rover? Yes, it's there all right. Now, Blandfoot. Out with the Murillo.'

Mrs. Marling and Mr. Blandfoot gave each other a long stare. Then Mrs. Marling spoke.

'I don't think we should find the picture very interesting. I hope, Mr. Blandfoot, you'll respect my wishes and not show it to us now.'

Instantly the room was alive with voices raised in protest. 'Really, Alice, you mustn't spoil the fun.' 'Oh, do let us see it, just for a moment! What harm can it do? It's only a picture.'

The various intonations of appeal and persuasion and protest united made quite a hubbub. Some rose to their feet and made oratorical gestures; some whispered fiercely into the ears of their neighbours, with heavy emphasis on single words; some studied the ceiling as though dissociating themselves from what was going on round them. Each, after speaking, looked as though no one on earth could challenge the reasonableness of his or her remarks. Mr. Blandfoot glanced from Mrs. Marling to the rebels, and back to Mrs. Marling again. His look spoke volumes. She turned to her unruly guests and said:

'In that case you must excuse me if I leave you.'

In the silence that followed she was preparing to depart when Mr. Blandfoot cried:

'Stop! You wanted to see it, and by God you shall!'

His hands flew to his collar; his pale face turned red, then purple and seemed to swell; he swayed, clutched at the mantelpiece and fell heavily on the carpet.

The man who had gone to find the car ran forward. 'Give him air!' he shouted. 'I'll unfasten his collar.' He wrenched at the starched linen, and at last it gave; the shirt front came open with it, disclosing a crimson stain. 'Ah, what's this?' he cried. 'Get back—it's more serious than we thought!' He bent over his patient, cutting him off from the view of those around. Another rending sound followed and further garments became apparent. 'What is it, what is it?' they cried. 'Is he dying?' 'Tell us what the matter is.' The man gave a laugh which sounded strangely on the ears of those who knew him well. 'It's nothing,' he said; 'it's his picture; it's his picture, that's all. I think he's coming round.' He began to laugh uncomfortably; but he did not move; his body still screened Mr. Blandfoot's chest from the eyes of the others. A man detached himself from the group of staring guests, walked across to the fallen man, paused, looked down and went on to the door, his expression scarcely

changing. 'Good night, good night, Alice,' he said. 'Thank you for a
most charming evening.' Another man left his chair, hesitated, walked
rather quickly to where Blandfoot lay, and peered down at him. Then
with a smile on his lips he gave the tips of his fingers to Mrs. Marling
and softly went away. Two other men did the same; the rest followed
the women who made a wide circuit to reach the door. 'Good night,
good night,' they said, in lower voices; but their hostess did not answer.
She looked neither at them nor at the figure on the carpet, but at the
ferns in the grate; she paid no heed to Hesketh who had taken her hand;
her lower lip twitched slightly and she seemed to have grown smaller.
'Never mind, never mind,' said the man at Mr. Blandfoot's side. 'Leave
him to us, Mrs. Marling. Don't you stay; he'll be all right in a moment.'
Then she too went. Mr. Blandfoot's face twitched. The man beside him
caught Hesketh's eye and the novelist reluctantly moved over to him.
'He's sweating,' said the man; 'better cover him up.' He folded Mr.
Blandfoot's garments over the tattoo-marks, his whole body quivering
with uncontrollable laughter, but his companion did not join in. 'I'm
glad you see something to laugh at,' he said.

THE PRICE OF THE ABSOLUTE

How stealthily, like the imperceptible approaches of a painless but fatal illness, does a passion for the antique grow on one! Timothy Carswell had inherited some Oriental china, enough to dress a chimney piece and fill a corner cupboard. His friends congratulated him and he was full of the pride of possession; when that wore off he lost interest and was half inclined to agree with his maid, that ornaments so breakable ought not to be left about.

But one day an elderly relation told him that in the time of his great-grandmother a certain plate had been used for feeding the chickens. Yes, here it was—great excitement—and as Timothy doubtless knew, was *famille verte* and valuable.

When she had gone Timothy studied the plate. From a circular yellow medallion in the centre radiated branches bearing blue flowers and mauve flowers, and terra-cotta roses with leaves of two shades of green. It was the leaves that especially fascinated Timothy. The point of transition between the two greens, where they leaned towards each other, affected him almost as deeply as a change of key in Schubert. He was horrified to think of the chickens pecking at the leaves and replaced the plate on the chimneypiece with exaggerated care.

Now the china was his chief delight, and though none of the other pieces gave him quite the same satisfaction as the plate, they all gave him something to read about, to discuss, and to contemplate in a dreamy mood between thought and feeling which he found extremely seductive.

And so it was with bitter disappointment that he learned from the porter of a London museum that the ceramics department was still closed for repairs. 'Come again in three years' time,' the man told him with a twinkle.

373

But to Timothy even three minutes seemed too long to wait. He had come up to London to see Chinese porcelain, and Chinese porcelain he would see. A bus hove in sight, going to a region north of the Park where antique shops abounded. Timothy got in.

The inside of the shop was much larger than one would have guessed from the street. A thick carpet muffled Timothy's tread. There was no one about, so he tip-toed up to the shelves which lined the walls and, looking at one piece after another, tried to measure in terms of feeling the attraction that each piece might have for him. Suddenly he stopped, for on a shelf above his head was a vase that arrested his attention as sharply as if it had spoken to him. Who can describe perfection? I shall not attempt to, nor even indicate the colour; for, like a pearl, the vase had its own colour, which floated on its surface more lightly than morning mist hangs on a river.

'You were looking at this vase,' said a voice at his elbow, a courteous voice but it made Timothy jump. 'You are right to admire it: it is a unique piece.'

The speaker was a clean-shaven man of middle height and middle age with an urbane manner and considerable presence.

'It is most beautiful,' said Timothy and was immediately abashed at having spoken to a stranger in such a heart-felt tone.

His interlocutor turned and called into the depth of the shop: 'Get the celadon vase down and show it to the gentleman.'

'Yes, Mr. Joshaghan.'

One of several men who had suddenly appeared from nowhere brought some steps and, with an expressionless face, took down the vase and set it on a table.

'Turn on the light!' commanded the proprietor. So illuminated, the vase shone as if brightness had been poured over it. It might have been floating in its own essence, so insubstantial did it look. Through layer on layer of soft transparency you seemed to see right into the heart of the vase.

'Clair-de-lune,' said Mr. Joshaghan. 'Ming?' he shrugged his shoulders. 'Perhaps. We do not guarantee. You like the vase, sir?'

'How much is it?' asked Timothy, absently.

He started when he was told the sum. And yet, he thought, it might have been much more. How can you put a price on perfection? He gave the proprietor a regretful smile to indicate that the vase was not for him.

'Too much, eh?' said Mr. Joshaghan in a business-like tone. 'Come here, Mr. Kirman, and tell this gentleman what you think about this vase.'

Mr. Kirman, detaching himself from the little pack, came forward and looked down thoughtfully at the vase.

'It is a wonderful piece, Mr. Joshaghan,' he said. 'In all our experience we have never had one like it. This gentleman would be well advised to buy it, if only as an investment.'

'You see?' said Mr. Joshaghan. 'Come here, Mr. Solstice, and tell this gentleman what you think about this vase.'

Dark-browed and aquiline like his predecessor, Mr. Solstice joined them and stared down at the vase.

'It is a bargain, indeed it is, sir,' he said earnestly. 'You would not find a vase like this wherever you looked. It is a piece of extraordinary good fortune that we are able to offer it to you.'

Mr. Joshaghan raised his eyebrows at Timothy and gave his hands a half-turn outwards. 'You hear? He agrees with the other. We will ask again. Come here, Mr. Doverman, and tell this gentleman——'

'No, no, please don't bother,' cried Timothy, forestalling almost rudely Mr. Doverman's testimony. 'I couldn't possibly——' He stopped and looked with distaste at the vase, its lustre dimmed by all the exudations of commerce that so thickly smeared it. How could he have dreamed? . . .

Into the moody silence round the vase came the sound of the shop door opening, and a shadow moved along the carpet.

'Ah!' exclaimed Mr. Joshaghan. 'What a good chance! Here is Mr. Smith of Manchester, in the nick of time. Mr. Smith, if you will be so kind, tell this gentleman what you think about this vase.'

Sharp-featured, sandy-haired and very English-looking, Mr. Smith seemed embarrassed. He stroked his chin, cleared his throat and said with an effort, 'Well, it speaks for itself, doesn't it?'

At once Timothy's mood changed. The others had all spoken for the vase. Mr. Smith, more perceptive, had said the vase spoke for itself. It did; it needed no recommendation from anyone. It had perfection; it was perfection; the Absolute in terms of a vase. If Timothy possessed it he would have the Absolute always at his command. Had his life been a quest, it would have ended here.

But the price was totally disproportionate to his capital, his income, his way of life and his prospects. To pay it would be a step towards madness. Worried by the pressure of the wills around him, he shook his head.

'Mr.——?' said Mr. Joshaghan softly. 'I do not have the pleasure of knowing your name.'

'Carswell,' said Timothy.

'Mr. Carswell,' said Mr. Joshaghan, as reverently as if the name was a benediction, 'do you know that Lord Mountbatten will soon be leaving India?'

Timothy stared at him. He had been so deeply absorbed in the vase that he could not get India into focus.

'I suppose so,' he said, doubtfully.

'Mr. Carswell,' repeated Mr. Joshaghan, 'India is a very *large* place.'

'Very large,' Timothy agreed, hoping he was not going to get drawn into a political argument.

'What would you say was the population of India?' Mr. Joshaghan eyed him closely.

Timothy was fond of statistics. 'Four hundred million,' he replied with unkind promptness. But to his surprise Mr. Joshaghan was not in the least put out.

'Four hundred and fifteen million, to be exact,' he said. 'And what fraction would that be of the total population of the world?'

'About a fifth.'

Again Mr. Joshaghan did not seem to mind having his aces trumped.

'You are quite right, Mr. Carswell,' he said, slowly and impressively. 'There are two thousand million people in the world, and not one of them could make this vase!'

The onlookers stood with downcast eyes, like donors in a picture. But to Timothy they had multiplied, multiplied into the two thousand million people of the world, for whom the making of this vase must for ever remain an unattainable ideal. The poetry of the idea swept over him, loosening his heart-strings.

'I'll have it,' he said.

'I congratulate you,' said Mr. Joshaghan.

Immediately the knot of tension broke; the cloud of witnesses, their faces indifferent now, melted away; even Mr. Joshaghan, still murmuring compliments, withdrew into his office. Timothy was left alone with his prize. How could he bear to be separated from it?

'But there is no need,' said Mr. Joshaghan, when consulted about payment. 'We will gladly accept your cheque and you can take the vase away with you.'

Joy surged up in Timothy again, and he could hardly refrain from embracing Mr. Joshaghan.

'I will arrange for it to be packed,' said Timothy's benefactor, pocketing his cheque and bowing himself away. 'Meanwhile, perhaps, you would like to have another look round. We may have other vases . . .'

Timothy smiled, for of course there were no other vases in the world. But there was plenty to look at, and plenty of reason, every time he looked, to congratulate himself that his vase was not as these.

His mind had travelled far before the assistant returned, bearing an immense square box which he respectfully tendered to Timothy. How solid beauty was! Clasping it, almost eclipsed by it, Timothy moved towards the door. Another customer had come in; another vase was being displayed; and as Timothy passed by he heard Mr. Joshaghan say, 'There are two thousand million people in the world, Mr. Gainfoot, and not one of them——'

But Timothy did not care, for before him, like a buckler against all those millions, he was carrying the Absolute.

A REWARDING EXPERIENCE

HENRY TARRANT had been asked to write a short story but he couldn't think of one.

He tried all sorts of devices. He studied the ornaments in his room (and they were many, for he was an inveterate collector); he recalled the circumstances in which he had inherited or acquired them. How many good stories had been written about objects! — *The Tinder Box, Le Peau de Chagrin, The Golden Bowl*. But his had nothing to tell him. They had risen above context, they were complete in themselves, they did not want to be questioned about their pasts.

Well, what about Nature? Many admirable stories had been written about Nature. Was not the sea the chief character in most of Conrad's novels? Did not the moors dominate *The Return of the Native*? Could *Green Mansions* have been written without trees?

Henry Tarrant knew about Nature, of course. Nature had made discreet appearances in his novels. He knew when flowers came out; he would never have committed Emily Brontë's blunder of making wallflowers blossom in September. But Nature had always come to him in his study. He did not have to go out in search of it, it was there when he took out his botany book. And if he wanted a more direct view he had only to go to his window, which commanded both the moors and the sea. What was Nature doing? He looked out. A September drizzle shrouded moors and sea, reducing the one to a pinkish, the other to a greyish monochrome. So much for Nature. He turned back with relief to his well-ordered room.

The date for the delivery of the story drew nearer, but Henry was no nearer to writing it. Art had failed him, Nature had failed him; they would not dramatize themselves in his mind.

There remained the human race. At the thought of the human race Henry's face, could he have seen it, lengthened. As a novelist he had written a lot about the human race, of course; he had even been complimented on his knowledge of it. And he did, he felt, know a lot about it, quite enough, too much. Sitting in his study he had paraded it before him. The human race had its apologists but Henry Tarrant was not among them. He was not going to say smooth things about it. It was a wonder that his public went on reading him, but from a sort of masochism, which was one of their less endearing traits, they did. They took their medicine and came back for more. Surely it should be easy to pour out another little dose?

Henry Tarrant was a bachelor and fiction-writing had confirmed him in the single state. The more he wrote about human beings the less he wanted to have anything to do with them. He had got them where he wanted them, and that was outside. Outside, they obeyed the rules – his rules. Critics had remarked on his aloofness, but it was perfectly in order for an artist to be aloof. A portrait-painter does not embrace his subject, at least he is under no obligation to; he stands away from it at whatever distance he finds convenient – in Henry's case, the range of a good pair of field glasses. But when he peered into the distance, once so thickly populated with unprepossessing figures, he could see nothing.

An idea came into his mind. 'I must provoke an incident,' he thought; 'I must provoke an incident.' He did not know where the words came from – perhaps they were an echo from some old newspaper. Dictators provoked incidents. But his whole life – nearly forty years of it now – had been designed to keep incidents at bay. He had kept illness at bay, the war at bay, marriage at bay: he had kept life itself at bay. Only art had he welcomed; and now art had gone back on him.

So how could he provoke an incident – ridiculous phrase? He looked round the snug little room. The only incidents that ever occurred in it were breakages. Sometimes he broke a thing himself and then his housekeeper would say: 'Well, sir, I'm glad it was you did it,' and this annoyed him, but it did not constitute an incident in the literary sense. One cannot provoke an incident with oneself.

In a panic he snatched up his hat, mackintosh and stick and hurried out. A sense of dislocated routine oppressed him, as if he was wearing someone else's clothes. The hour, six-thirty, was sacred to literary effort. The warm wet autumnal twilight wrapped him round. Which way? It didn't matter which way; he chose the road between occasional bungalows that led towards the golf house. Suddenly he saw a dog was following him. He didn't like dogs. 'Go away!' he said. But the animal wouldn't go away: it trotted beside him with a proprietary air as if it had adopted him.

Presently it halted. 'Good,' thought Henry, and walked on, thankful to be relieved of this encumbrance. Then he saw, some way ahead, a lady also with a dog: she must be giving it an airing. He heard a scamper; the yellow dog tore past him and bore down on the lady's dog. There was a moment's parley between the two; then a scuffle; then the indescribable ear-piercing uproar of a dog fight.

'Call off your dog, please, call off your dog!' the lady shouted.

'It isn't my dog!' Henry Tarrant replied.

'Well, please do something,' cried the lady, 'or my dog will get murdered.' She had no stick or whip, only a lead with which she was vainly thrashing the aggressor's back.

No pepper-pot, no bucket of water. Henry paused a moment, then plunged into the mêlée of gleaming eyes and snapping teeth.

The yellow dog had got the spaniel down and was literally wiping the floor with it; the blows of Henry's stick went off its back like water. Leaning down he seized it by the collar and lifted it into the air. It released the spaniel, wriggled round, and bit him to the bone. 'Ow!' he exclaimed and dropped the dog, which darted off into the gloom like the yellow streak it was.

Tall, dark and soft-featured, the lady bent over her pet. 'Poor Sherry! Poor Sherry!' she panted. The spaniel struggled to its feet and took some trial steps. She hadn't noticed Henry's hand. Better not tell her: let the incident be closed. But then she saw the blood flowing.

'Oh, your poor hand!'

'It's nothing,' said Henry, rather ungraciously.

'But it is! You must put something on it at once. Have you anyone to do it for you?'

'Well, no,' said Henry, which was not quite true.

'Then may I?'

'It's very kind of you,' said Henry in a distant voice.

'It's the least I can do,' the lady said. 'Do you live near here?'

Unwillingly Henry pointed to his house.

'Oh, then you're Henry Tarrant — how exciting!'

But Henry didn't ask the lady her name.

Later she said to him across the reassuring fumes of Dettol:

'But I thought you never saw anyone!'

'I don't,' said Henry, self-consciously.

'But,' she exclaimed inconsequently, 'it's such a pretty house!'

Henry Tarrant grunted. The basin was running with blood; the bathroom floor was splashed with blood; the towel was blood-stained. Blood everywhere: his blood. He felt absurdly proud of it. But the lady, following his eyes, suddenly realized the damage she had done, and was appalled. First she had wounded a writer and then wrecked his house. 'Oh,' she exclaimed, 'how you must wish you had never met us!'

'Not at all,' said Henry. 'It's been a most rewarding experience.'

He meant it, but she scented sarcasm and shook her head. And there was worse to follow when they went downstairs. The incident had been too much for Sherry's nerves, as a large, dark, sullen pool on Henry's best rug testified.

'At least let me——' she stammered.

'We'll do it together,' Henry said.

If only he could tell her how much better he liked the house this way, fouled and blood-stained! But he couldn't; he couldn't pierce the shell of her shame and remorse. He felt that they were turning her against him.

'Please stay and have a drink,' he begged. 'I have some sherry here— another kind of sherry,' he added, nervously facetious.

But she was firm. She could hardly bring herself to speak to him.

'Then I'll see you to the door.'

In silence they went down the flagged path to the gate. He held out his left hand.

'Good-bye,' he said, 'and thank you.'

Again she suspected sarcasm. 'Good-bye,' she said, and added with an effort, 'I think I should keep that arm in a sling.'

'How kind of you to think of it!'

She winced and did not answer. Henry opened the gate and there, waiting for them, its hackles rising, its teeth bared, its eyes ablaze as though it was a veritable hell-hound, stood the yellow dog. A deep growl came from its throat.

The lady screamed.

Henry hastily shut the gate. 'Now you simply *must* come back!' he said.

She heard the triumph in his voice and wonderingly followed him into the house.

W.S.

THE first postcard came from Forfar. 'I thought you might like a picture of Forfar,' it said. 'You have always been so interested in Scotland, and that is one reason why I am interested in you. I have enjoyed all your books, but do you really get to grips with people? I doubt it. Try to think of this as a handshake from your devoted admirer, W.S.'

Like other novelists, Walter Streeter was used to getting communications from strangers. Usually they were friendly but sometimes they were critical. In either case he always answered them, for he was conscientious. But answering them took up the time and energy he needed for his writing, so that he was rather relieved that W.S. had given no address. The photograph of Forfar was uninteresting and he tore it up. His anonymous correspondent's criticism, however, lingered in his mind. Did he really fail to come to grips with his characters? Perhaps he did. He was aware that in most cases they were either projections of his own personality or, in different forms, the antithesis of it. The Me and the Not Me. Perhaps W.S. had spotted this. Not for the first time Walter made a vow to be more objective.

About ten days later arrived another postcard, this time from Berwick-on-Tweed. 'What do you think of Berwick-on-Tweed?' it said. 'Like you, it's on the Border. I hope this doesn't sound rude. I don't mean that you are a border-line case! You know how much I admire your stories. Some people call them other-worldly. I think you should plump for one world or the other. Another firm handshake from W.S.'

Walter Streeter pondered over this and began to wonder about the sender. Was his correspondent a man or a woman? It looked like a man's handwriting — commercial, unself-conscious — and the criticism was like a man's. On the other hand, it was like a woman to probe — to want to make him feel at the same time flattered and unsure of himself. He felt the faint stirrings of curiosity but soon dismissed them; he was not a man to experiment with acquaintances. Still it was odd to think of this unknown person speculating about him, sizing him up. Other-worldly, indeed! He re-read the last two chapters he had written. Perhaps they didn't have their feet firm on the ground. Perhaps he was too ready to escape, as other novelists were nowadays, into an ambiguous world, a world where the conscious mind did not have things too much its own way. But did that matter? He threw the picture of Berwick-on-Tweed into his November fire and tried to write; but the words came haltingly, as though contending with an extra-strong barrier of self-criticism. And as the days passed he became uncomfortably aware of self-division, as though someone had taken hold of his personality and was pulling it apart. His work was no longer homogeneous, there were two strains in it, unreconciled and opposing, and it went much slower as he tried to resolve the discord. Never mind, he thought: perhaps I was getting into a groove. These difficulties may be growing pains, I may have tapped a new source of supply. If only I could correlate the two and make their conflict fruitful, as many artists have!

The third postcard showed a picture of York Minster. 'I know you are interested in cathedrals,' it said. 'I'm sure this isn't a sign of megalo-mania in your case, but smaller churches are sometimes more reward-ing. I'm seeing a good many churches on my way south. Are you busy writing or are you looking round for ideas? Another hearty handshake from your friend W.S.'

It was true that Walter Streeter was interested in cathedrals. Lincoln Cathedral had been the subject of one of his youthful fantasies and he had written about it in a travel book. And it was also true that he ad-mired mere size and was inclined to under-value parish churches. But how could W.S. have known that? And was it really a sign of megalo-mania? And who was W.S. anyhow?

For the first time it struck him that the initials were his own. No, not for the first time. He had noticed it before, but they were such common-place initials; they were Gilbert's, they were Maugham's, they were Shakespeare's—a common possession. Anyone might have them. Yet now it seemed to him an odd coincidence; and the idea came into his mind—suppose I have been writing postcards to myself? People did such things, especially people with split personalities. Not that he was one, of course. And yet there were these unexplained developments—the cleavage in his writing, which had now extended from his thought to his style, making one paragraph languorous with semi-colons and subordinate clauses, and another sharp and incisive with main verbs and full-stops.

He looked at the handwriting again. It had seemed the perfection of ordinariness — anybody's hand — so ordinary as perhaps to be disguised. Now he fancied he saw in it resemblances to his own. He was just going to pitch the postcard in the fire when suddenly he decided not to. I'll show it to somebody, he thought.

His friend said, 'My dear fellow, it's all quite plain. The woman's a lunatic. I'm sure it's a woman. She has probably fallen in love with you and wants to make you interested in her. I should pay no attention whatsoever. People whose names are mentioned in the papers are always getting letters from lunatics. If they worry you, destroy them without reading them. That sort of person is often a little psychic, and if she senses that she's getting a rise out of you she'll go on.'

For a moment Walter Streeter felt reassured. A woman, a little mouse-like creature, who had somehow taken a fancy to him! What was there to feel uneasy about in that? It was really rather sweet and touching, and he began to think of her and wonder what she looked like. What did it matter if she was a little mad? Then his subconscious mind, searching for something to torment him with, and assuming the authority of logic, said: Supposing those postcards are a lunatic's, and you are writing them to yourself, doesn't it follow that you must be a lunatic too?

He tried to put the thought away from him; he tried to destroy the postcard as he had the others. But something in him wanted to preserve it. It had become a piece of him, he felt. Yielding to an irresistible compulsion, which he dreaded, he found himself putting it behind the clock on the chimney-piece. He couldn't see it but he knew that it was there.

He now had to admit to himself that the postcard business had become a leading factor in his life. It had created a new area of thoughts and feelings and they were most unhelpful. His being was strung up in expectation of the next postcard.

Yet when it came it took him, as the others had, completely by surprise. He could not bring himself to look at the picture. 'I hope you are well and would like a postcard from Coventry,' he read. 'Have you ever been sent to Coventry? I have — in fact you sent me there. It isn't a pleasant experience, I can tell you. I am getting nearer. Perhaps we shall come to grips after all. I advised you to come to grips with your characters, didn't I? Have I given you any new ideas? If I have you ought to thank me, for they are what novelists want, I understand. I have been re-reading your novels, living in them, I might say. Another hard handshake. As always, W.S.'

A wave of panic surged up in Walter Streeter. How was it that he had never noticed, all this time, the most significant fact about the postcards — that each one came from a place geographically closer to him than the last? 'I am coming nearer.' Had his mind, unconsciously self-protective, worn blinkers? If it had, he wished he could put them back. He took an atlas and idly traced out W.S.'s itinerary. An interval of eighty miles or so seemed to separate the stopping-places. Walter lived in a large West Country town about ninety miles from Coventry.

Should he show the postcards to an alienist? But what could an alienist tell him? He would not know, what Walter wanted to know, whether he had anything to fear from W.S.

Better go to the police. The police were used to dealing with poison-pens. If they laughed at him, so much the better.

They did not laugh, however. They said they thought the postcards were a hoax and that W.S. would never show up in the flesh. Then they asked if there was anyone who had a grudge against him. 'No one that I know of,' Walter said. They, too, took the view that the writer was probably a woman. They told him not to worry but to let them know if further postcards came.

A little comforted, Walter went home. The talk with the police had done him good. He thought it over. It was quite true what he had told them — that he had no enemies. He was not a man of strong personal feelings such feelings as he had went into his books. In his books he had drawn some pretty nasty characters. Not of recent years, however. Of recent years he had felt a reluctance to draw a very bad man or woman: he thought it morally irresponsible and artistically unconvincing, too. There was good in everyone: Iagos were a myth. Latterly — but he had to admit that it was several weeks since he laid pen to paper, so much had this ridiculous business of the postcards weighed upon his mind — if he had to draw a really wicked person he represented him as a Communist or a Nazi — someone who had deliberately put off his human characteristics. But in the past, when he was younger and more inclined to see things as black or white, he had let himself go once or twice. He did not remember his old books very well but there was a character in one, 'The Outcast', into whom he had really got his knife. He had written about him with extreme vindictiveness, just as if he was a real person whom he was trying to show up. He had experienced a curious pleasure in attributing every kind of wickedness to this man. He never gave him the benefit of the doubt. He had never felt a twinge of pity for him, even when he paid the penalty for his misdeeds on the gallows. He had so worked himself up that the idea of this dark creature, creeping about brimful of malevolence, had almost frightened him.

Odd that he couldn't remember the man's name.

He took the book down from the shelf and turned the pages — even now they affected him uncomfortably. Yes, here it was, William . . . William . . . he would have to look back to find the surname. William Stainsforth.

His own initials.

Walter did not think the coincidence meant anything but it coloured his mind and weakened its resistance to his obsession. So uneasy was he that when the next postcard came it came as a relief.

'I am quite close now,' he read, and involuntarily he turned the postcard over. The glorious central tower of Gloucester Cathedral met his eye. He stared at it as if it could tell him something, then with an effort went on reading. 'My movements, as you may have guessed, are not quite under my control, but all being well I look forward to seeing you some time this week-end. Then we can really come to grips. I wonder if you'll recognize me! It won't be the first time you have given me hospitality. My hand feels a bit cold to-night, but my handshake will be just as hearty. As always, W.S.'

'P.S. Does Gloucester remind you of anything? Gloucester gaol?'

Walter took the postcard straight to the police station, and asked if he could have police protection over the week-end. The officer in charge smiled at him and said he was quite sure it was a hoax; but he would tell someone to keep an eye on the premises.

'You still have no idea who it could be?' he asked.

Walter shook his head.

It was Tuesday; Walter Streeter had plenty of time to think about the week-end. At first he felt he would not be able to live through the interval, but strange to say his confidence increased instead of waning. He set himself to work as though he *could* work, and presently he found he could — differently from before, and, he thought, better. It was as though the nervous strain he had been living under had, like an acid, dissolved a layer of non-conductive thought that came between him and his subject: he was nearer to it now, and his characters, instead of obeying woodenly his stage directions, responded wholeheartedly and with all their beings to the tests he put them to. So passed the days, and the dawn of Friday seemed like any other day until something jerked him out of his self-induced trance and suddenly he asked himself, 'When does a week-end begin?'

A long week-end begins on Friday. At that his panic returned. He went to the street door and looked out. It was a suburban, unfrequented street of detached Regency houses like his own. They had tall square gate-posts, some crowned with semi-circular iron brackets holding lanterns. Most of these were out of repair: only two or three were ever lit. A car went slowly down the street; some people crossed it: everything was normal.

Several times that day he went to look and saw nothing unusual, and when Saturday came, bringing no postcard, his panic had almost subsided. He nearly rang up the police station to tell them not to bother to send anyone after all.

They were as good as their word: they did send someone. Between tea and dinner, the time when week-end guests most commonly arrive, Walter went to the door and there, between two unlit gate-posts, he saw a policeman standing – the first policeman he had ever seen in Charlotte Street. At the sight, and at the relief it brought him, he realized how anxious he had been. Now he felt safer than he had ever felt in his life, and also a little ashamed at having given extra trouble to a hard-worked body of men. Should he go and speak to his unknown guardian, offer him a cup of tea or a drink? It would be nice to hear him laugh at Walter's fancies. But no – somehow he felt his security the greater when its source was impersonal and anonymous. 'P.C. Smith' was somehow less impressive than 'police protection'.

Several times from an upper window (he didn't like to open the door and stare) he made sure that his guardian was still there; and once, for added proof, he asked his housekeeper to verify the strange phenomenon. Disappointingly, she came back saying she had seen no policeman; but she was not very good at seeing things, and when Walter went a few minutes later he saw him plain enough. The man must walk about, of course, perhaps he had been taking a stroll when Mrs. Kendal looked.

It was contrary to his routine to work after dinner but to-night he did, he felt so much in the vein. Indeed, a sort of exaltation possessed him; the words ran off his pen; it would be foolish to check the creative impulse for the sake of a little extra sleep. On, on. They were right who said the small hours were the time to work. When his housekeeper came in to say good night he scarcely raised his eyes.

In the warm, snug little room the silence purred around him like a kettle. He did not even hear the door bell till it had been ringing for some time.

A visitor at this hour?

His knees trembling, he went to the door, scarcely knowing what he expected to find; so what was his relief on opening it, to see the doorway filled by the tall figure of a policeman. Without waiting for the man to speak —

'Come in, come in, my dear fellow,' he exclaimed. He held his hand out, but the policeman did not take it. 'You must have been very cold standing out there. I didn't know that it was snowing, though,' he added, seeing the snowflakes on the policeman's cape and helmet. 'Come in and warm yourself.'

'Thanks,' said the policeman. 'I don't mind if I do.'

Walter knew enough of the phrases used by men of the policeman's stamp not to take this for a grudging acceptance. 'This way,' he prattled on. 'I was writing in my study. By Jove, it *is* cold, I'll turn the gas on more. Now won't you take your traps off, and make yourself at home?'

'I can't stay long,' the policeman said, 'I've got a job to do, as *you* know.'

'Oh yes,' said Walter, 'such a silly job, a sinecure.' He stopped, wondering if the policeman would know what a sinecure was. 'I suppose you know what it's about — the postcards?'

The policeman nodded.

'But nothing can happen to me as long as you are here,' said Walter. 'I shall be as safe . . . as safe as houses. Stay as long as you can, and have a drink.'

'I never drink on duty,' said the policeman. Still in his cape and helmet, he looked round. 'So this is where you work,' he said.

'Yes, I was writing when you rang.'

'Some poor devil's for it, I expect,' the policeman said.

'Oh, why?' Walter was hurt by his unfriendly tone, and noticed how hard his gooseberry eyes were.

'I'll tell you in a minute,' said the policeman, and then the telephone bell rang. Walter excused himself and hurried from the room.

'This is the police station,' said a voice. 'Is that Mr. Streeter?'

Walter said it was.

'Well, Mr. Streeter, how is everything at your place? All right, I hope? I'll tell you why I ask. I'm sorry to say we quite forgot about that little job we were going to do for you. Bad co-ordination, I'm afraid.'

'But,' said Walter, 'you did send someone.'

'No, Mr. Streeter, I'm afraid we didn't.'

'But there's a policeman here, here in this very house.'

There was a pause, then his interlocutor said, in a less casual voice:

'He can't be one of our chaps. Did you see his number by any chance?'

'No.'

A longer pause and then the voice said:

'Would you like us to send somebody now?'

'Yes, p . . . please.'

'All right then, we'll be with you in a jiffy.'

Walter put back the receiver. What now? he asked himself. Should he barricade the door? Should he run out into the street? Should he try to rouse his housekeeper? A policeman of any sort was a formidable proposition, but a rogue policeman! How long would it take the real police to come? A jiffy, they had said. What was a jiffy in terms of minutes? While he was debating the door opened and his guest came in.

'No room's private when the street door's once passed,' he said. 'Had you forgotten I was a policeman?'

'Was?' said Walter, edging away from him. 'You *are* a policeman.'

'I have been other things as well,' the policeman said. 'Thief, pimp, blackmailer, not to mention murderer. *You* should know.'

The policeman, if such he was, seemed to be moving towards him and Walter suddenly became alive to the importance of small distances — the distance from the sideboard to the table, the distance from one chair to another.

'I don't know what you mean,' he said. 'Why do you speak like that? I've never done you any harm. I've never set eyes on you before.'

'Oh, haven't you?' the man said. 'But you've thought about me and' — his voice rose — 'and you've written about me. You got some fun out of me, didn't you? Now I'm going to get some fun out of you. You made me just as nasty as you could. Wasn't that doing me harm? You didn't think what it would feel like to be me, did you? You didn't put yourself in my place, did you? You hadn't any pity for me, had you? Well, I'm not going to have any pity for you.'

'But I tell you,' cried Walter, clutching the table's edge, 'I don't know you!'

'And now you say you don't know me! You did all that to me and then forgot me!' His voice became a whine, charged with self-pity. 'You forgot William Stainsforth.'

'William Stainsforth!'

'Yes. I was your scapegoat, wasn't I? You unloaded all your self-dislike on me. You felt pretty good while you were writing about me. You thought, what a noble, upright fellow you were, writing about this rotter. Now, as one W.S. to another, what shall I do, if I behave in character?'

'I . . . I don't know,' muttered Walter.

'You don't know?' Stainsforth sneered. 'You ought to know, you fathered me. What would William Stainsforth do if he met his old dad in a quiet place, his kind old dad who made him swing?'

Walter could only stare at him.

'You know what he'd do as well as I,' said Stainsforth. Then his face changed and he said abruptly, 'No, you don't, because you never really understood me. I'm not so black as you painted me.' He paused, and a flicker of hope started in Walter's breast. 'You never gave me a chance, did you? Well, I'm going to give you one. That shows you never understood me, doesn't it?'

Walter nodded.

'And there's another thing you have forgotten.'

'What is that?'

'I was a kid once,' the ex-policeman said.

Walter said nothing.

'You admit that?' said William Stainsforth grimly. 'Well, if you can tell me of one virtue you ever credited me with—just one kind thought —just one redeeming feature——'

'Yes?' said Walter, trembling.

'Well, then I'll let you off.'

'And if I can't?' whispered Walter.

'Well, then, that's just too bad. We'll have to come to grips and you know what that means. You took off one of my arms but I've still got the other. "Stainsforth of the iron hand" you called me.'

Walter began to pant.

'I'll give you two minutes to remember,' Stainsforth said. They both looked at the clock. At first the stealthy movement of the hand paralysed Walter's thought. He stared at William Stainsforth's face, his cruel, crafty face, which seemed to be always in shadow, as if it was something the light could not touch. Desperately he searched his memory for the one fact that would save him; but his memory, clenched like a fist, would give up nothing. 'I must invent something,' he thought, and suddenly his mind relaxed and he saw, printed on it like a photograph, the last page of the book. Then, with the speed and magic of a dream, each page appeared before him in perfect clarity until the first was reached, and he realized with overwhelming force that what he looked for was not there. In all that evil there was not one hint of good. And he felt, compulsively and with a kind of exaltation, that unless he testified to this the cause of goodness everywhere would be betrayed.

'There's nothing to be said for you!' he shouted. 'And you know it! Of all your dirty tricks this is the dirtiest! You want me to whitewash you, do you? The very snowflakes on you are turning black! How dare you ask me for a character? I've given you one already! God forbid that I should ever say a good word for you! I'd rather die!'

Stainsforth's one arm shot out. 'Then die!' he said.

The police found Walter Streeter slumped across the dining-table. His body was still warm, but he was dead. It was easy to tell how he died; for it was not his hand that his visitor had shaken, but his throat. Walter Streeter had been strangled. Of his assailant there was no trace. On the table and on his clothes were flakes of melting snow. But how it came there remained a mystery, for no snow was reported from any district on the day he died.

THE TWO VAYNES

THOSE garden-statues! My host was pardonably proud of them. They crowned the balustrade of the terrace; they flanked its steps; they dominated the squares and oblongs—high, roofless chambers of clipped yew —which, seen from above, had somewhat the appearance of a chessboard. In fact, they peopled the whole vast garden; and as we went from one to another in the twilight of a late September evening, I gave up counting them. Some stood on low plinths on the closely-shaven grass; others, water-deities, rose out of goldfish-haunted pools. Each was supreme in its own domain and enveloped in mystery, secrecy and silence.

'What do you call these?' I asked my host, indicating the enclosures. 'They have such an extraordinary shut-in feeling.'

'Temene,' he said, carefully stressing the three syllables. 'Temenos is Greek for the precincts of a god.'

'The Greeks had a word for it,' I said, but he was not amused.

Some of the statues were of grey stone, on which lichen grew in golden patches; others were of lead, the sooty hue of which seemed sun-proof. These were already gathering to themselves the coming darkness: perhaps they had never really let it go.

It was the leaden figures that my host most resembled; in his sober country clothes of almost clerical cut—breeches, tight at the knee, surmounting thin legs cased in black stockings, with something recalling a Norfolk jacket on top—he looked so like one of his own duskier exhibits that, as the sinking sun plunged the temene in shadow, and he stood with outstretched arm pointing at a statue that was also pointing, he might have been mistaken for one.

'I have another to show you,' he said, 'and then I'll let you go and dress.'

Rather to my surprise, he took my arm and steered me to the opening, which, I now saw, was in the further corner. (Each temenos had an inlet and an outlet, to connect it with its neighbours.) As we passed through, he let go of my arm and bent down as though to tie up his shoe-lace. I walked slowly on towards a figure which, even at this distance, seemed in some way to differ from the others.

They were all gods and goddesses, nymphs and satyrs, dryads and oreads, divinities of the ancient world: but this was not. I quickened my steps. It was the figure of a man in modern dress, and something about it was familiar. But was it a statue? Involuntarily I stood still and looked back. My host was not following me; he had disappeared. Yet here he was, facing me, with his arm stretched out, almost as if he were going to shake hands with me. But no; the bent forefinger showed that he was beckoning.

Again I looked behind me to the opening now shrouded in shadow, but there was no one. Stifling my repugnance, and to be frank, my fear, and putting into my step all the defiance I could muster, I approached the figure. It was smiling with the faint sweet smile of invitation that one sees in some of Leonardo's pictures. So life-like was the smile, such a close copy of the one I had seen on my host's face, that I stopped again, wondering which to believe: my common sense or my senses. While I was debating, a laugh rang out. I jumped – the figure might have uttered it; it sounded so near. But the smiling features never changed, and a second later I saw my host coming to me across the grass.

He laughed again, less histrionically, and rather uncertainly I joined in.

'Well,' he said, 'you must forgive my practical joke. But you'll understand how it amuses me to see what my guests will *do* when they see that figure. I've had a hole made through the hedge to watch. Some of them have been quite frightened. Some see through the trick at once and laugh before I get the chance to – the joke is then on me. But most of them do what you did – start and stop, and start and stop, wondering if they can trust their eyes. It's fun watching people when they don't know they are being watched. I can always tell which are the . . . the imaginative ones.'

I laughed a little wryly.

'Cheer up,' he said, though I would have rather he had not noticed my loss of poise. 'You came through the ordeal very well. Not an absolute materialist like the brazen ones, who know no difference between seeing and believing. And not – certainly not – well, a funk, like some of them. Mind you, I don't despise them for it. You stood your ground.

A well-balanced man, I should say, hard-headed but open-minded, cautious but resolute. You said you were a writer?'

'In my spare time,' I mumbled.

'Then you are used to looking behind appearances.'

While he was speaking, I compared him to the figure, and though the general resemblance was striking — the same bold nose, the same retreating forehead — I wondered how I could have been taken in by it. The statue's texture was so different! Lead, I supposed. Having lost my superstitious horror, I came nearer. I detected a thin crack in the black stocking, and thoughtlessly put my finger-nail into it.

'Don't do that,' he warned me. 'The plaster flakes off so easily.'

I apologized. 'I didn't mean to pull your leg. But is it plaster? It's so dark, as dark as, well — your suit.'

'It was painted that colour,' my host said, 'to make the likeness closer.'

I looked again. The statue's face and hands were paler than its clothes, but only a pale shade of the same tone. And this, I saw, was true to life. A leaden tint underlay my host's natural swarthiness.

'But the other statues are of stone, aren't they?' I asked.

'Yes,' he said, 'they are. This one was an experiment.'

'An experiment?'

'My experiment,' he said. 'I made it.' He did not try to conceal his satisfaction.

'How clever of you!' I exclaimed, stepping back to examine the cast more critically. 'It's you to the life. It almost seems to move.'

'Move?' he repeated, his voice distant and discouraging.

'Yes, move,' I said, excited by my fantasy. 'Don't you see how flat the grass is round it? Wouldn't a statue let the grass grow under its feet?'

He answered still more coldly: 'My gardeners have orders to clip the grass with shears.'

Snubbed and anxious to retrieve myself, I said, 'Oh, but it's the living image!' I remembered the motto on his crested writing-paper. '*Vayne sed non vanus*. I adore puns. "Vayne but not vain." You but not you. How do you translate it?'

'We usually say, "Vayne but not empty".' My host's voice sounded mollified.

'How apt!' I prattled on. 'It's Vayne all right, but is it empty? Is it just a suit of clothes?'

He looked hard at me and said:

'Doesn't the apparael oft proclaim the man?'

'Of course,' I said, delighted by the quickness of his answer. But isn't this Vayne a bigger man than you are—in the physical sense, I mean?'

'I like things to be over-life size,' he replied. 'I have a passion for the grand scale.'

'And here you are able to indulge it,' I said, glancing towards the great house which made a rectangle of intense dark in the night sky.

'But service isn't what it was before the war,' he rather platitudinously remarked. 'The trouble I've had, looking for a footman! Still, I think you'll find your bath has been turned on for you.'

I took the hint and was moving away when suddenly he called me back.

'Look!' he said, 'don't let's change for dinner. I've got an idea. Fairclough hasn't been before; it's his first visit, too. He hasn't seen the statues. After dinner we'll play a game of hide and seek. I'll hide, and you and he shall seek—here, among the statues. It may be a bit dull for you, because you'll be in the secret. But if you're bored, you can hunt for me, too—I don't think you'll find me. That's the advantage of knowing the terrain—perhaps rather an unfair one. We'll have a time-limit. If you haven't found me within twenty minutes, I'll make a bolt for home, whatever the circumstances.'

'Where will "home" be?'

'I'll tell you later. But don't say anything to Fairclough.'

I promised not to. 'But, forgive me,' I said, 'I don't quite see the point——'

'Don't you? What I want to happen is for Fairclough to mistake the statue for me. I want to see him . . . well . . . startled by it.'

'He might tackle it low and bring it crashing down.'

My host looked at me with narrowed eyes.

'If you think that, you don't know him. He's much too timid. He won't touch it—they never do until they know what it is.'

By 'they' I supposed him to mean his dupes, past, present and to come. We talked a little more and parted.

I found the footman laying out my dress-suit on the bed. I told him about not changing and asked if Mr. Fairclough had arrived yet.

'Yes, sir, he's in his room.'

'Could you take me to it?'

I followed along a passage inadequately lit by antique hanging lanterns, most of which were solid at the bottom.

Fairclough was changing. I told him we were to wear our ordinary clothes.

'What!' he exclaimed. 'But he always changes for dinner.'

'Not this evening.' I didn't altogether like my rôle of accomplice, but Fairclough had the weakness of being a know-all. Perhaps it would do him no harm to be surprised for once.

'I wonder if Postgate changed,' I said, broaching the topic which had been exercising my mind ever since I set foot in the house.

'He must have done,' said Fairclough. 'Didn't you know? His dress-clothes were never found.'

'I don't remember the story at all well,' I prompted him.

'There's very little to remember,' Fairclough said. 'He arrived, as we have; they separated to change for dinner, as we have; and he was never seen or heard of again.'

'There were other guests, weren't there?'

'Yes, the house was full of people.'

'When exactly did it happen?'

'Three years ago, two years after Vayne resigned the chairmanship.'

'Postgate had a hand in that, hadn't he?'

'Yes, don't you know?' said Fairclough. 'It was rather generous of Vayne to forgive him in the circumstances. It didn't make much differ-ence to Vayne; he'd probably have resigned in any case, when he inherited this place from his uncle. It was meant to be a sort of recon-ciliation party, burying the hatchet, and all that.'

I agreed that it was magnanimous of Vayne to make it up with some-one who had got him sacked. 'And he's still loyal to the old firm,' I added, 'or we shouldn't be here.'

'Yes, and we're such small fry,' Fairclough said. 'It's the company, not us, he's being kind to.'

I thought of the small ordeal ahead of Fairclough, but it hardly amounted to a breach of kindness.

'I suppose we mustn't mention Postgate to him?' I said.

'Why not? I believe he likes to talk about him. Much better for him than bottling it up.'

'Would you call him a vain man?' I asked.

'Certainly, Vayne by name and vain by nature.'

'He seemed rather pleased with himself as a sculptor,' I remarked.

'A sculptor?' echoed Fairclough.

I realized my indiscretion, but had gone too far to draw back. 'Yes, didn't you know?' I asked maliciously. 'He's done a statue. A sort of portrait. And he talks of doing some more. Portraits of his friends in plaster. He asked me if I'd be his model.'

'I wonder if he'd do one of me?' asked Fairclough, with instinctive egotism. 'I should make rather a good statue, I think.' Half-undressed, he surveyed himself in the mirror. Long and willowy, fair complexioned as his name, he had a bulging knobby forehead under a thin thatch of hair. 'Did you say yes?' he asked.

'I said I couldn't stand, but if he would make it a recumbent effigy, I would lie to him.'

We both laughed.

'Where's his studio?' asked Fairclough, almost humbly.

'Underground. He says he prefers to work by artificial light.'

We both thought about this, and some association of ideas made me ask:

'Is the house haunted?'

'Not that I ever heard of,' Fairclough said. 'But there's a legend about a bath.'

'A bath?'

'Yes, it's said to be on the site of an old lift-shaft, and to go up and down. Funny how such stories get about. And talking of baths,' Fairclough went on, 'I must be getting into mine. You may not know it, but he doesn't like one to be a minute late.'

'Just let me look at it,' I said. 'Mine's down a passage. You have one of your own, you lucky dog.'

We inspected the appointments, which were marble and luxurious, and very up to date, except for the bath itself, which was an immense, old-fashioned mahogany contraption with a lid.

'A lid!' I exclaimed. 'Don't you know the story of the Mistletoe Bough?' Fairclough clearly didn't, and with this parting shot I left him.

In spite of Fairclough's warning, I was a few minutes late for dinner. How that came about occupied my thoughts throughout the marvellous meal, though I could not bring myself to speak of it and would much rather not have thought about it. I'm afraid I was a dull guest, and Vayne himself was less animated than he had been before dinner. After dinner, however, he cheered up, and when he was giving us our orders for the evening, editing them somewhat for Fairclough's benefit, he had recovered all his old assurance. We were to divide, he said; I was to take the left-hand range of yew compartments, or temene, as he liked to call them, Fairclough the right. From the top of the terrace steps, a long steep flight, he indicated to us our spheres of action. 'And home will be here, where I'm standing,' he wound up. 'I'll call "coo-ee" when I'm ready.'

He strolled off in the direction of the house. Fairclough and I walked cautiously down the steps on to the great circle of grass from which the two blocks of temene diverged. Here we bowed ceremoniously and parted. Fairclough disappeared into the black wall of yew.

At last I was alone with my thoughts. Of course it was only another of Vayne's practical jokes; I realized that now. But at the moment when it happened, I was scared stiff. And I still couldn't help wondering what would have become of me if – well, if I had got into the bath. I just put my foot in, as I often do, to test the water. I didn't pull it out at once, for the water was rather cool. In fact I put my whole weight on it.

'Coo-ee!'

Now the hunt was up. Fairclough would be peering in the shadows. But mine was merely a spectator's rôle; I was Vayne's stooge. His stooge. . . .

Directly I felt something give, I pulled my foot out, and the lid came down and the bath sank through the floor like a coffin at a cremation service. Goodness, how frightened I was! I heard the click as the bath touched bottom; but I couldn't see it down the shaft. Then I heard rumbling again, and saw the bath-lid coming up. But I did not risk getting in, not I.

'Coo-ee!'

I jumped. It sounded close beside me. I moved into another temenos, trying to pretend that I was looking for Vayne. Really it would serve him right if I gave him away to Fairclough. He had no business to frighten people like that.

'Coo-ee!'

Right over on Fairclough's side, now. But it sounded somehow different; was it an owl? It might not be very easy to find Fairclough; there must be half a hundred of these blasted temene, and the moon was hidden by clouds. He might go out through one opening just as I was entering by another, and so we might go on all night. Thank goodness the night was warm. But what a silly farce it was.

I could just see to read my watch. Another quarter of an hour to go. Fairclough must be getting jumpy. I'll go and find him, I thought, and put him wise about the figure. Vayne would never know. Or would he? One couldn't tell where he was, he might be in the next temenos, watching me through a hole.

A light mist was descending, which obscured the heads of such statues as I could see projecting above the high walls of the temene. If it grew thicker, I might not see Fairclough even if he were close to me, and we might wander about till Doomsday—at least, for another ten minutes, which seemed just as long to wait.

I looked down, and saw that my feet had left tracks, dark patches in the wet grass. They seemed to lead in all directions. But were they all mine? Had I really walked about as much as that? I tried to identify the footprints and see if they tallied.

'Coo-ee!'

That almost certainly was an owl; the sound seemed to come from above. But perhaps Vayne added ventriloquism to his other accomplishments. He was capable of anything. Not a man one could trust. Postgate hadn't trusted him—not, at least, as the chairman of the company.

It was my duty, I now felt, to warn Fairclough. And I should be quite glad to see him myself, quite glad. But where was he?

I found myself running from one temenos to another and getting back to the one I started from. I could tell by the figure: at least that didn't move. I started off again. Steady, steady. Here was a temenos with no footprints on it—a virgin temenos. I crossed it and found myself in the central circle. I crossed that too.

Now I was in Fairclough's preserves. Poor Fairclough! To judge by the footprints, he had been running round even more than I had. But were they all his? Here was the figure of Pan—the god of panic. Very appropriate.

'Fairclough! Fairclough!' I began to call as loudly as I dared, having nearly but not quite lost my head.

'Fairclough! Fairclough!' I couldn't bring myself to hug the walls; the shadows were too thick; I stuck to the middle of each space.

I suppose I was expecting to find him, and yet when I heard him answer 'Here!' I nearly jumped out of my skin. He was crouching against a hedge. He evidently had the opposite idea from mine; he felt the hedge was a protection; and I had some difficulty in persuading him to come out into the open.

'Listen!' I whispered. 'What you've got to do is——'

'But I've seen him,' Fairclough said. 'There's his footmark.'

I looked: the footmark was long and slurred, quite unlike his or mine.

'If you were sure it was him,' I said, 'why didn't you speak to him?'

'I did,' said Fairclough, 'but he didn't answer. He didn't even turn round.'

'Someone may have got into the garden,' I said, 'some third person. But we'll find out. I'll take you to the statue.'

'The statue?'

'I'll explain afterwards.'

I had regained my confidence, but could not remember in which direction Vayne's statue lay.

Suddenly I had an idea.

'We'll follow the footprints.'

'Which?' asked Fairclough.

'Well, the other person's.'

Easy to say; easy to distinguish them from ours; but which way were they pointing? That was the question.

'He walks on his heels,' I said. 'It's this way.'

We followed and reached the temenos where the statue had stood. No possibility of mistake. We saw the patches of dead grass where its feet had been; we saw the footprints leading away from them. But the statue was not there.

'Vayne!' I shouted. 'Vayne!'

'Coo-ee!' came a distant call.

'To the steps,' I cried. 'To the steps! Let's go together!'

Vayne was standing on the terrace steps: I saw him plainly; and I also saw the figure that was stalking him: the other Vayne. Two Vaynes. Vayne our host, the shorter of the two, stood lordly, confident, triumphing over the night. 'Coo-ee!' he hooted to his moonlit acres. 'Coo-ee!' But the other Vayne had crept up the grass slope and was crouching at his back.

For a moment the two figures stood one behind the other, motionless as cats. Then a scream rang out; there was a whirl of limbs, like the Manxman's wheel revolving; a savage snarl, a headlong fall, a crash. Both fell, both Vaynes. When the thuds of their descent were over, silence reigned.

They were lying in a heap together, a tangled heap of men and plaster. A ceiling might have fallen on them, yet it was not a ceiling; it was almost a third man, for the plaster fragments still bore a human shape. Both Vaynes were dead but one of them, we learned afterwards, had been dead for a long time. And this Vayne was not Vayne at all, but Postgate.

MONKSHOOD MANOR

'HE's a strange man,' said Nesta.

'Strange in what way?' I asked.

'Oh, just neurotic. He has a fire-complex or something of the kind. He lies awake at night thinking that a spark may have jumped through the fireguard and set the carpet alight. Then he has to get up and go down to look. Sometimes he does this several times a night, even after the fire has gone out.'

'Does he keep an open fire in his own house?' I asked.

'Yes, he does, because it's healthier, and other people like it, and he doesn't want to give way to himself about it.'

'He sounds a man of principle,' I observed.

'He is,' my hostess said. 'I think that's half the trouble with Victor. If he would let himself go more he wouldn't have these fancies. They are his sub-conscious mind punishing him, he says, by making him do what he doesn't want to. But somebody has told him that if he could embrace his neurosis and really enjoy it——'

I laughed.

'I don't mean in that way,' said Nesta severely. 'What a mind you have, Hugo! And he conscientiously tries to. As if anyone could enjoy leaving a nice warm bed and creeping down cold passages to look after a fire that you pretty well know is out!'

'Are you sure that it *is* a fire he looks at?' I asked. 'I can think of another reason for creeping down a cold passage and embracing what lies at the end of it.'

Nesta ignored this.

'It's not only fires,' she said, 'it's gas taps, electric light switches, anything that he thinks might start a blaze.'

'But seriously, Nesta,' I said, 'there might be some method in his madness. It gives him an alibi for all sorts of things besides love-making: theft, for instance, or murder.'

'You say that because you don't know Victor,' Nesta said. 'He's almost a Buddhist—he wouldn't hurt a fly.'

'Does he want people to know about his peculiarity?' I asked. 'I know he's told you——'

'He does and he doesn't,' Nesta answered.

'It's obvious why he doesn't. It isn't so obvious why he does,' I observed.

'It's rather complicated,' Nesta said. 'I doubt if your terre-à-terre mind would understand it. The whole thing is mixed up in his mind with guilt——'

'There you are!' I exclaimed.

'Yes, but not real guilt. And he thinks that if someone caught him prowling about at night they might——'

'I should jolly well think they would!'

'And besides, he doesn't want to keep it a secret, festering. He would rather people laughed at him.'

'Laugh!' I repeated. 'I can't see that it's a laughing matter.'

'No, it isn't really. It all goes back to old Œdipus, I expect. Most men suffer from that, more or less. I expect you do, Hugo.'

'Me?' I protested. 'My father died before I was born. How could I have killed him?'

'You don't understand,' said Nesta, pityingly. 'But what I wanted to say was, if you should hear an unusual noise at night——'

'Yes?'

'Or happen to see somebody walking about——'

'Yes?'

'You'll know it's nothing to be alarmed at. It's just Victor, taking what he calls his safety precautions.'

'I'll count three before I fire,' I said.

Nesta and I had been taking a walk before the other week-end guests arrived.

The house came into sight, long and low with mullioned windows, crouching beyond the lawn. This was my first visit to Nesta's compara-tively new home. She was always changing houses. Leaving the subject of Victor we talked of the other guests, of their matrimonial intentions, prospects or entanglements. Our conversation had the pre-war air which Nesta could always command.

'Is Walter here?' I asked. Walter was her husband.

'No, he's away shooting. He doesn't come here very much, as you know. He never cared for Monkshood, I don't know why. Oh, by the way, Hugo,' she went on, 'I've an apology to make to you. I never put any books in your room. I know you're a great reader, but——'

'I'm not,' I said. 'I go to bed to sleep.'

She smiled. 'Then that's all right. Would you like to see the room?'

I said I would.

'It's called the Blue Bachelor's room, and it's on the ground floor.'

We joked a bit about the name.

'Bachelors are always in a slight funk,' I said, 'because of the designing females stalking them. But why didn't you give the room to Victor? It might have saved him several journeys up and down stairs.'

'It's rather isolated,' she said. 'I know you don't mind that, but he does.'

'Was that the real reason?' I asked, but she refused to answer.

I didn't meet Victor Chisholm until we assembled for drinks before dinner. He was a nondescript looking man, neither dark nor fair, tall nor short, fat nor thin, young nor old. I didn't have much conversation with him, but he seemed to slide off any subject one brought up—he didn't drop it like a hot coal, but after a little blowing on it, for politeness' sake, he quietly extinguished it. At least that was the impression I got. He smiled quite a lot, as though to prove he was not unsociable, and then retired into himself. He seemed to be saving himself up for something—a struggle with his neurosis, perhaps. After dinner we played bridge, and Victor followed us into the library, half meaning to play, I think; but when he found there was a four without him he went back into the drawing-room to join the three non-bridge playing members of the party. We sat up late trying to finish the last rubber, and I didn't see him again before we went to bed. The library had a large open fireplace in which a few logs were smouldering over a heap of wood-ash. The room had a shut-in feeling, largely because the door was lined with book-bindings to make it look like shelves, so that when it was closed you couldn't tell where it was. Towards midnight I asked Nesta if I should put another log on and she said carelessly, 'No. I shouldn't bother—we're bound to get finished sometime, if you'll promise not to overbid, Hugo,' which reminded me of Victor and his complex. So when at last we did retire I said meaningly, 'Would you like me to take a look at the drawing-room fire, Nesta?'

'Well, you might, but it'll be out by this time,' she said.

'And the dining-room?' I pursued, glancing at the others, to see if there was any reaction, which there was not. She frowned slightly and said, 'The dining-room's electric. We only run to two real fires,' and then we separated.

In spite of my boasting, for some reason I couldn't get to sleep. I tossed to and fro, every now and then turning the light on to see what time it was. My bedroom walls were painted dark blue, but by artificial light they looked almost black. They were so shiny and translucent that when I sat up in bed I could see my reflection in them, or at any rate my shadow. I grew tired of this and then it occurred to me that if I had a book I might read myself to sleep—it was one of the recognized remedies for insomnia. But I hadn't: there were two book-ends—soap-stone elephants, I remember, facing each other across an empty space. I gave myself till half-past two, then I got up, put on my dressing-gown and opened my bedroom door. All was in darkness. The library lay at the other end of the long house and to reach it I had to cross the hall. I had no torch and didn't know where the switches were, so my progress was slow. I tried to make as little noise as possible, then I remembered that if Nesta heard me she would think I was Victor Chisholm going his nightly rounds. After this I grew bolder and almost at once found the central switch panel at the foot of the staircase. This lit up the passage to the library. The library door was open and in I went, automatically fumbling for the switch. But no sooner had my hand touched the wall than it fell to my side, for I had a feeling that I was not alone in the room. I don't know what it was based on, but something was already implicit in my vision before it became physically clear to me: a figure at the far end of the room, in the deep alcove of the fireplace, bending, almost crouching over the fire. The figure had its back to me and was so near to the fire as to be almost in it. Whether it made a movement or not I couldn't tell, but a spurt of flame started up against which the figure showed darker than before. I knew it must be Victor Chisholm and I stifled an impulse to say 'Hullo!'—from a confused feeling that like a sleep-walker he ought not to be disturbed; it would startle and humiliate him. But I wanted a book, and my groping fingers found one. I withdrew it from the shelf, but not quite noiselessly, for with the tail of my eye I saw the figure move.

Back in my room I wondered if I ought to have left the hall lights on for Victor's return journey, but at once concluded that as he hadn't turned them on himself, he knew his way well enough not to need them. A sense of achievement possessed me: I had caught my fellow-guest out, and I had got my book. It turned out to be the fourth volume of John Evelyn's Diary; but I hadn't read more than a few sentences before I fell asleep.

When I met Victor Chisholm at breakfast I meant to ask him how he had slept. It was an innocent, conventional inquiry, but somehow I couldn't bring myself to put it. Instead, we congratulated each other on the bright, frosty, late October morning, almost as if we had been responsible for it. Presently the two other men joined us, but none of the ladies of the party, and lacking their conversational stimulus we relapsed into silence over our newspapers.

But I didn't want to keep my adventure to myself, and later in the morning, when I judged that Nesta would not be preoccupied with household management, I waylaid her.

'Your friend Victor Chisholm has been on the tiles again,' I began, and before she could get a word in I told her the story of last night's encounter. Half-way through I was afraid it might fall flat, for, after all, her guest's peculiarities were no news to her; but it didn't. She looked surprised and faintly worried.

'I oughtn't to have told you,' I said with assumed contrition, 'but I thought it would amuse you.'

She made an effort to smile.

'Oh well, it does,' she said, and then her serious look came back. 'But there's one thing that puzzles me.'

'What's that?'

'He told me he had had a very good night.'

'Oh well, he would say that. It's only civil if you're staying in someone's house. I should have said the same if you had asked me, only I thought you would want to hear about Victor.'

Nesta didn't take this up.

'But we know each other much too well,' she said, arguing with herself. 'Victor comes down here — well, he comes pretty often, and he *always* tells me if he's been taking his security measures. I can't understand it.'

Why does she seem so upset? I asked myself. Does she care more for Victor than she admits? Is she distressed by the thought that he should lie to her? Does she suspect him of infidelity?

'Oh, I expect he thought that for once he wouldn't bother you,' I said.

'You're quite sure it was Victor?' she asked, with an effort.

I opened my eyes.

'Who else could it have been?'

'Well, somebody else looking for a book.'

I said I thought this most unlikely. 'Besides, he wasn't looking for a book. He was looking at the fire—I think he stirred it with his foot.'

'Stirred it with his foot?'

'Well, something made a flame jump up.'

Nesta said nothing, but looked more anxious than before.

Hoping to make her say something that would enlighten me, I observed jokingly:

'But he's come to the right place. I saw a row of buckets in the hall and one of those patent fire-extinguishers——'

'Oh, Walter insisted on having them,' said Nesta, hurriedly. 'This is a very old house, you know, and we have to take reasonable precautions. Having a fire-complex doesn't mean there isn't such a thing as having a fire, any more than having persecution mania means there isn't such a thing as persecution.'

Then I remembered something.

'If he doesn't want to be taken for a burglar,' I said, 'why doesn't he turn on the lights?'

'But he does turn them on,' said Nesta, 'just for that reason.'

I shook my head.

'He didn't turn them on last night.'

The problem of Victor's nocturnal ramblings exercised me and made me unsociable. I never enjoy desultory conversation, and our pre-luncheon chit-chat seemed to me unusually insipid. So when the meal was over I excused myself from playing golf, though I had brought my clubs with me, and announced that I was going to have a siesta as I had slept badly. There was a murmur of sympathy, but Nesta made no comment and no one, least of all Victor, betrayed uneasiness.

In the middle of the afternoon I woke up and had an idea. I strode down to the village to search out the oldest inhabitant. To my surprise I found him, or his equivalent, digging in his front garden. Leaning over the wall I engaged him in conversation; and very soon he told me what I had somehow expected to hear, though, like so many pieces of knowledge that one picks up, it was difficult to act upon, and I rather wished I had never heard it. What chiefly intrigued me was the question: Did Victor know what I knew? It was clear, I thought, that Nesta did. But had she told him?

I did not think that I could ask her, it would seem too like prying; besides if she had wanted to tell me, she would have told me. What I had heard could be held to explain a good many things.

My secret gnawed at me and made the social contacts of the party seem unreal, as though I were a Communist in a Government office, my only accomplice being the head of the Department.

Suddenly, after tea I think it was, the conversation turned my way.

'Is the house haunted, Nesta?' asked one of the visitors, a woman, who like myself was a stranger to the house. 'It ought to be — it wouldn't be complete without a ghost!'

I watched Nesta as she answered carefully, 'No, I'm afraid I must disappoint you — it isn't.' And I watched Victor Chisholm, but he kept what might have been called his poker face — if it had been sinister, which it was not. The speaker wasn't to be satisfied; she returned to the charge more than once, suggesting various phantoms suitable to Monkshood Manor; but Nesta disowned them all, finally suppressing them with a yawn. One by one, on various pretexts, the company disbanded, and Victor Chisholm and I were left alone.

'I once stayed in a country house that was said to be haunted,' I remarked chattily.

'Oh, did you?' he said, with his air of being politely pleased to listen, while he was saving himself up for something in which one had no concern; 'was it fun?'

'Well, not exactly fun,' I said. 'I'll tell you about it if you can bear to hear. The house was an old one, like this, and the land on which it stood had belonged to the Church. Well, after the Dissolution of the Monasteries they pulled the Abbey, or whatever it was, down, and used some of the stones for building this house I'm telling you about. Nobody could stop them. But one of the old monks who had fallen into poverty, as a result of being dissolved, and who remembered the bygone days when they feasted and sang and wassailed and got fat and clapped each other on the back in the way you see in the pictures — he felt sore about it, and on his deathbed he laid a curse on the place and swore that four hundred years later he would come back from wherever he was and set fire to it.'

I watched Victor Chisholm for some sign of uneasiness but he showed none and all he said was:

'Do you think a ghost could do that? I've always understood that it wasn't very easy to set a house on fire. It isn't very easy to light a fire, is it, when it's been laid for the purpose, with paper and sticks and so on.'

This, I thought — and I congratulated myself upon my subtlety — is the voice of reassurance speaking: this is what well-meaning people tell him, and what he tells himself, hoping to calm his fears.

'I'm not up in the subject of ghosts,' I said, 'but they can clank chains and presumably some of them come from a hot place and wouldn't mind handling a burning brand or two. Or kicking one. That fire in the library, for instance——'

'Oh, but surely,' he said — and I saw that I had scared him — 'the library fire is absolutely safe? I — I'm sometimes nervous about fires myself, but I should never bother about that one. There's so much stone flagging around it. Do you really think——'

'I've no idea,' I said, feeling I had the answer to one of my questions. 'But my hostess at the time was certainly apprehensive. I had to worm the story out of her. It's a very usual one, of course, almost the regulation legend, very boring, really.'

'And was the house ever burnt down?' asked Victor.

'I never heard,' I said.

Of course Victor might have been dissembling. He might have known the legend of Monkshood Manor, he might have been afraid of the library fire: neurotic people are notoriously given to lying. But I didn't think so. Yet the alternative was too fantastic. I couldn't believe in it either, and gradually (for logic can sometimes be bluffed) I succeeded in disbelieving both alternatives at once.

Before nightfall I took the precaution of furnishing my blue room with books more interesting than Evelyn's Diary. But I didn't need them. I slept excellently, and so, to judge from discreet inquiries I made in the morning, did the rest of the party.

I couldn't get much out of Nesta. She rather avoided me, and for the first time in my life I felt like a policeman who must be treated with reserve in case he finds out too much. I still persuaded myself that Victor Chisholm had been and had not been in the library in the early hours of Saturday morning: if pressed, I should have said he had been. The third possibility, put forward by Nesta, that another guest had been searching for a book, I dismissed. My theory was that Nesta had a superstitious dread of a fire breaking out at Monkshood Manor and was keeping Victor in ignorance while she availed herself of his services as a night-watchman without warning him of the risk he ran.

Risk? There was no risk: yet I vaguely felt that I ought to do something about it, so I tried to make my social prevail over my private conscience and throw myself into the collective life of a week-end party. I thought about the form my coming Collins would take, and wondered if I ought to apologize for being a dull guest. In the meantime I could search Nesta out and make amends for something that I felt had been slightly critical in my attitude towards her.

My quest took me to the library. Nesta was not there but someone was — a housemaid on her hands and knees working vigorously at the carpet with a dust-pan and brush.

'Good heavens!' I exclaimed, surprised into speech by the sight of such antiquated cleaning methods; 'haven't you got a vacuum cleaner?'

The maid, who was pretty, looked up and said:

'Yes, but it won't bring these marks out.'

'Really?' I said. 'What sort of marks are they?'

'I don't know,' said the maid. 'But they look like footmarks.'

I bent down: they did look like footmarks, but they had another peculiarity which for some reason I refrained from commenting on. Instead I said, glancing at the fireplace:,

'It looks as though someone had been paddling in the ashes.'

'That's what I think,' she said, leaning back to study the marks on the carpet.

'Well, it's clean dirt,' I observed, 'and should come off all right.'

'Yes, it should,' she agreed. 'But it doesn't. It's my belief that it's been *burnt* in.'

'Oh no!' I assured her, but curiosity overcame me, and I, too, got down on my hands and knees, and buried my nose in the carpet.

'Hugo, what are you doing?' said Nesta's voice behind me.

I jumped up guiltily.

'What were you doing?' she repeated almost sternly.

I had an inspiration.

'To tell you the truth,' I said, 'I wanted to know whether this lovely Persian carpet had been dyed with an aniline dye. There's only one way to tell, you know — by licking it. Aniline tastes sour.'

'And does it?' asked Nesta.

'Not in the least.'

'I'm glad of that,' said Nesta, and leading me from the room she began to tell me the history of the carpet. This gave me an opportunity to praise the house and all its appointments.

'What treasures you have, Nesta,' I wound up. 'I hope they are fully insured.'

'Yes, they are,' she answered, rather dryly. 'But I didn't know you were an expert on carpets, Hugo.'

As soon as I could I returned to the library. The maid had done her work well: hardly a trace of the footmarks remained, and the smell of burning, which I thought I had detected, clinging to them, had quite worn off. You could still see the track they made, away from the fireplace towards the door: but they didn't reach the door or go in a direct line for it; they stopped at a point halfway between, against the inner wall, which was sheathed in books. There was nothing surprising in that: after a few steps the ashes would have been all rubbed off.

And there was another thing I couldn't see, and almost wondered if I had seen it—the mark of the big toe, which showed that the feet had been bare. Victor might have come down in his bare feet, to avoid making a noise; but it was odd, all the same, if not as odd as I had first thought it.

In the afternoon we went a long motor drive in two cars to have tea with a neighbour. As soon as Monkshood Manor was out of sight its problems began to fade, and in the confusion of the two parties joining forces round the tea-table they seemed quite unreal. And even when the house came into view again, stretched cat-like beyond the lawn, I only felt a twinge of my former uneasiness. By Sunday evening a week-end visit seems almost over; the threads with one's temporary residence are snapping; mentally one is already in next week. Before I got into bed I took out my diary and checked up my engagements. They were quite ordinary engagements for luncheon and dinner and so on, but suddenly they seemed extraordinarily desirable. I fixed my mind on them and went to sleep thinking about them.

I even dreamed about them, or one of them. It started as an ordinary dinner party but one of the guests was late and we had to wait for him. 'Who is he?' someone asked, and our host answered, 'I don't know, he will tell us when he comes.' Everyone seemed to accept this answer as reasonable and satisfactory, and we hung about talking and sipping cocktails until our host said, 'I don't think he can be coming after all. We won't wait any longer.' But just as we were sitting down to dinner there was a knock at the door and a voice said, 'May I come in?' And then I saw that we weren't at my friend's house in London, but back again at Monkshood, and the door that was opening was the library door, which was lined with bindings to make it look like bookshelves. For some reason it wasn't at the end of the wall but in the middle; and I said, 'Why is he coming in by that door?' 'Because it's the door he used to use,' somebody answered. The door was a long time opening, and it seemed to be opening by itself with nobody behind it; then came a hand and a sleeve—and a figure wearing a monk's cowl.

I woke with a start and was at once aware of a strong smell. For a moment I thought it was the smell of cooking, and wondered if it could be breakfast-time. If so, the cook had burnt something, for there was a smell of burning too. But it couldn't be breakfast time for not a glimmer of light showed round the window curtains. Actually, as I discovered when I turned on my bedside lamp, it was half-past two—the same hour that I had chosen for my sortie two nights before.

The smell seemed to be growing fainter, and I wondered if it could be an illusion, an effect of auto-suggestion. I opened the door and put my head into the passage and as quickly withdrew it. Not only because the smell was stronger there, but for another reason. The passage was not in darkness, as it had been the other night, for the hall lights had been turned on.

Well, let Victor see to it, I thought, whatever it is; no doubt he's on the prowl: let his be the glory. But curiosity overcame me and I changed my mind.

In the hall the smell was stronger. It seemed to come in waves, but where did it come from? My steps took me to the library. The door was open. A flickering light came through, and a smell strong enough to make my throat smart and my eyes water. I lingered, putting off the moment of going in: then I remembered the fire buckets in the hall and ran back for one. The water had a thick film of dust over it and I had an irrational feeling that it would be less effective so, and that I ought to change it. I did not do so, however, but hurried back and somehow forced myself to go into the room.

There were shadows, of course, and there was smoke, drifting about as smoke does. The two together make a shape that is almost opaque. And the shape was opaque that I saw before I saw anything else, a shape that seemed to rise from its knees beside the fireplace and glide slantwise across my vision towards the inner wall of the library. I might not have noticed it so particularly had it not recalled to me the shape of the late-comer in my dream. Before I could ask myself what it was, or meant, it had disappeared, chased perhaps from my attention by the obligation to act. I had the bucket: where should I begin? The dark mass of the big round library table was between me and the fireplace; beyond it should have been the card-table, but that I could not see. Except on the hearth no flames were visible.

Relief struggling with misgiving, I turned the light on and advanced towards the fireplace, but I stopped half-way, for lying in front of it, beside the overturned card-table, lay a body — Victor's. He was lying face downwards, curiously humped like a snail, under his brown Jaeger dressing-gown, which covered him and the floor around him. And it was from his dressing-gown, which was smouldering in patches, and stuck all over with playing cards, some of which were also alight, that the smell of burning came. Yes, and from Victor himself; for when I tried to lift him up I found beneath him a half-charred log, a couple of feet long, which the pressure of his body had almost extinguished, but not quite, and from which I could not at once release him, so deeply had it burnt into his flesh.

But the Persian carpet, being on the unburnt, underside of the log, was hardly scorched.

Afterwards, the explanation given was that the log had toppled off the fireplace and rolled on to the carpet; and Victor, coming down on a tour of inspection, had tripped over it and died of shock before being burnt. The evidence of shock was very strong, the doctor said. I don't know whether Nesta believed this: shortly afterwards she sold the house. I have since come to believe it, but I didn't at the time. At the time I believed that Victor had met his death defending the house against a fire-raising intruder, who, though defeated in his main object, had got the better of Victor in some peculiarly horrible way; for though one of Victor's felt slippers had caught fire, and was nearly burnt through, the other was intact, while the footprints leading to the wall — though they were fainter than they had been the other time — both showed the mark of a great toe. I pointed this out to the police who shrugged their shoulders. He might have taken his slippers off and put them on again, they said. One thing was certain: Victor had literally embraced his neurosis, and by doing so had rid himself of it for ever.

UP THE GARDEN PATH

I WAS surprised to get a letter from Christopher Fenton with a Rome postmark, for I did not know that he had gone abroad. I was surprised to get a letter from him at all, for we had not been on letter-writing terms for some time.

'My dear Ernest,' he began, and the opening, conventional as it was, gave me a slight twinge; 'How are you getting on? I've never had to ask you this before—I've always known! But it's my fault, I've let myself drop out of things, and it's a good deal thanks to all this gardening. Gardening was to have been the solace of my middle age, but it's become a tyrant, and holds me in a kind of spell while you have been forging ahead. Well, now I am punished because I've had to go abroad just as the rhododendrons and azaleas were coming out. They should have been nearly over, if they had obeyed the calendar, and I timed my departure accordingly, but, as you may have noticed, spring this year is three weeks late, and they have let me down. I promised R.M. I would pay him this visit and I can't possibly get out of it. All unwillingly I have made myself "the angel with the flaming sword".

'In a world bursting with sin and sorrow I oughtn't to make a grievance of such a small matter, but I can't bear to think of all my flowers (very good ones some of them) blooming without me. And this is where you come in, or where I hope you will. I know you're not much interested in gardens, you have more important fish to fry, but you used to quite enjoy them in the old days, so perhaps you would do me a kindness now. Will you spend a week-end—the week-end after next would be the best from the flowers' point of view—at Crossways? My couple are in charge. You were always one of their favourite visitors and I know they will do their best to make you comfortable. Please get what you like out of the cellar, I still have left a few bottles of the Mouton

Rothschild 1929 that you used to like. Make yourself thoroughly at home—but I know you will. I always think that a host's first duty is to absent himself as much as possible; I shall be with you in spirit, though not in the flesh. There's just one thing—I won't call it a condition or a stipulation, because in these days the burden of hospitality (if one can call it that) falls more heavily on the guest than on the host—what with tips, train-fares, the discomforts of travelling, etc., and, in your case, loss of valuable time. It is really for the host to write a Collins. So I will only say that if you consent to do this it will increase my sense of obligation. I know how tiresome other people's hobbies can be—lucky you, you never needed any, your career has always been your hobby. I don't suppose you will really want to look at the flowers very much—they toil not neither do they spin!—and a glance from the dining-room window may be all you will want to give my Eden. But all the same, I *do* want the flowers to be seen, even more urgently, perhaps, than I want *you* to see them. Somehow I feel that if no one sees them except the gardeners (who don't care much for flowers anyhow and just take them for granted) they might as well not exist. Perhaps, if Ronald Knox's limerick is true, they *don't* exist! All that glorious colour lost, as if it had never been, and the scent of the azaleas just fading into the sky! It is the only beauty I have ever created and I should like to think it was preserved in someone's mind. I really ought to have had the garden "thrown open" (ridiculous expression) to the public, but it needed more arranging than I now feel equal to. So would you, my dear Ernest, at four o'clock on the Sunday afternoon, stroll down what I magniloquently call the Long Walk, from the fountain at one end to what you once called the *temple d'amour* at the other? (The fountain is new, you haven't seen it.) And as you go, give the flowers a good look and don't hesitate to tread on the beds to read the names of anything that specially takes your fancy (but I don't suppose anything will). And try to keep me in mind at the time, as though you were looking through my eyes as well as yours.

'Will you do this for the sake of our old friendship? Will you even promise to do it?

'I know how busy you are, but perhaps you would send me a line to say yes or no.

'Yours ever, Christopher.'

Christopher was right. I was busy and though I didn't happen to have any engagement for the week-end he suggested, I didn't want to travel all the way down to the New Forest to spend a lonely Sunday. And I didn't want to get drawn again into what I felt to be the unreality of Christopher's life, of which this proposal was such an excellent example. He had never out-grown his adolescence or improved his adolescent gift for painting. He had allowed himself to become a back number. A private income had enabled him to indulge a certain contempt for the world where men strove, but he was jealous of it really; hence the digs and scratches in his letter. I had got on at the Bar, whereas he had not been even a successful dilettante. I imagine that he did now know the way that people talked about him, but perhaps he guessed. At Oxford he had been a leading figure in a group of which I was an inconspicuous member; we looked up to him then, and foretold a future for him, but I doubt if he would have achieved it, even without the handicap of his silver spoon. Except in what pertained to hospitality he was out of touch, *à côté de la vie*. He was good at pouring out drinks, and his friends, myself among them, appreciated this talent long after it was clear to most of us that his other talents would come to nothing. And though a drink is a drink, the satisfaction it gives one varies with whom one takes it with. At one time Christopher could afford drinks when we couldn't. Later, we would buy our own drinks and consume them in circumstances and in company which he couldn't attain to. There is a freemasonry of the successful which we shared and he did not. This he must have realized, for mine was not the only defection from his circle. I didn't dislike him — one couldn't dislike him — but equally one couldn't take him quite seriously as a human being.

So my first impulse was to say no, for I hate prolonging any relationship that the meaning has gone out of. But then I remembered Constantia and I thought again. I hadn't forgotten her but I had pushed her out of my mind while reading Christopher's letter.

Christopher hadn't mentioned Constantia in his letter but she was there all the same, in the wistful tone of it and the scarcely concealed bitterness. Yet he had no right to feel bitter; she told me that at one time she would have married him gladly if he had asked her. She was thirty-two and wanted to get married. But he didn't ask her. She hadn't told me, but I am sure that their relationship was never more than an *amitié amoureuse*. It was a sentimental attachment with the same unreality about it that there was in everything he did, and I felt no qualms about taking her from him. It is true that I met her through him — at Crossways, as a matter of fact, at a week-end party — and to that extent I owed her to him. But that is an unreal way of looking at things, and I did not think I was betraying his hospitality or anything of that sort, when I persuaded her that I could give her more than he could. He had no right to keep her indefinitely paddling in the shallows in which his own life was passing. But though we were lovers she hadn't said that she would marry me and I guessed it was some scruple about Christopher that stopped her.

I suppose some of her tenderness for him must have entered into me for when I read the letter again I felt that I ought to humour him, as much for her sake as for his. After all, she was the last, the only person who cared for him in the way he wanted to be cared for—whatever that was. I should get through the week-end somehow. I wrote to Christopher and I wrote to the Hancocks, Christopher's married couple, telling them the train that I should come by.

What surprised me, when I got there, was the familiarity of it all. I had forgotten what a frequent visitor I used to be.

'Why, Mr. Gretton,' Hancock said, 'you've deserted us, you're quite a stranger!' But I didn't feel one; I could have found my way about the house blindfolded.

'It's over a year since you came to us,' he reproached me. 'We often used to ask Mr. Fenton what had become of you.'

'And what did he say?' I asked.

'Oh, he said you were too busy, but as I said, you couldn't be too busy to get away at the week-end.'

'Oh, but I expect you have plenty of visitors without me,' I said.

'No, sir, we don't, not like we used to have. Of course it's a nuisance, food being what it is, but Mr. Fenton likes having them, and it's always a real treat to see you, sir. The new faces aren't the same by any means, not the same class of people either.' I took up the Visitors' Book and saw several names that were strange to me. Christopher had been trying out some new friends. But there weren't many names at all; to turn back a page was to turn back a year, and I soon found my own.

'It does seem too bad that you should be here when Mr. Fenton isn't,' Hancock prattled on. 'He always looks forward particularly to you coming, sir. Though now, of course, he's a good deal taken up with his garden. Often he works in it quite late. He's got to be terrible fond of flowers. Those rhododendrons he's so set on, sir, of course they looks after themselves, as you might say. But gardeners are all alike, sir, you can't get them to weed the flower-beds. Now this herbaceous border, sir, you can see it from the window——' His glance invited me to go to the window, but for some reason I didn't want to go. 'Often of an evening I go to the window and see him stooping and call out to him that dinner's ready. Would you like to see the garden, sir? He was ever so anxious you should see it.'

'Well, not just now,' I said. 'Of course I shall go and see it to-morrow. Now I think I shall have a bath. Dinner's at eight, I suppose?'

'Yes, sir, that's Mr. Fenton's hour, though there's many in these times has put it earlier. The wife she sometimes has a moan about it, but of course we have to respect Mr. Fenton's wishes.'

A question that had absurdly been nagging me all day now demanded utterance. 'I've brought my dinner-jacket, Hancock,' I said, 'because I know Mr. Fenton likes one to change for dinner. But as I'm going to be alone, do you suppose he would mind?'

'Well, sir, it's just as you like, of course, but you won't be alone because there's a lady coming.'

'A lady?'

'Yes, sir, didn't you know? But perhaps Mr. Fenton forgot to tell you. He's been very forgetful lately, we've both remarked on it. Yes, sir, Miss Constantia Corwen, you know her, don't you, you've stayed with her here several times. A tall lady.'

'Yes,' I said, 'I know her quite well. I wonder if Mr. Fenton told her I was going to be here.'

'Oh yes, sir, I expect so. He wouldn't forget the same thing twice.'

It was six o'clock. I went to my room, meaning to stay there till dinner-time, but when I heard the crunch of wheels curiosity overcame me and I tiptoed out on to the landing above the hall and listened.

'Yes, Miss,' I heard Hancock say, 'the master was dreadfully cut up about missing the flowers and all on account of spring being so late.'

I could understand Constantia making sympathetic noises, but there were tears in her voice as she said, 'Yes, it was terribly bad luck. I *am* so sorry. Is there time to go out and see the garden now?'

'Well, Miss, it's just as you like but dinner's at eight and there's a soufflé.'

'I shall only be a moment and I think I won't change for dinner as I shall be alone.'

There was quite a long pause and then Hancock said, in a puzzled, different voice, 'You won't be altogether alone, Miss, because you see Mr. Gretton's here.'

'Mr. Gretton?'

'Yes, Miss. Didn't Mr. Fenton tell you?'

'No, he must have forgotten. I think I'll go up to my room now.'

'Yes, Miss, it's the usual one. I'll bring your things.'

We were sitting together in the drawing-room after dinner, still a little in the shadow of our first embarrassed greeting. When we met in public we often didn't smile; but never until now had we not smiled when we met in private.

'Should we take a turn in the garden?' Constantia asked.

I demurred. 'It's too late, don't you think? Probably all the flowers are shut up for the night.'

'I don't think rhododendrons shut up,' Constantia said.

'Well, there isn't enough light to see them by.'

'Let's make sure,' said Constantia, and unwillingly I followed her to the bay window. It was a house of vaguely Regency date and the drawing-room was on the first floor. The Long Walk ran at right angles to it, nearly a hundred yards away. It made the southern boundary of the garden. We could see the tops of the rhododendrons, they were like a line of foam crowning a long dark billow; and in front of and below them the azaleas, a straggling line, hardly a line at all, gave an effect of sparseness and delicacy and fragility. But the colour hardly showed at all.

'You see,' I said. 'You can't see.'

She smiled. 'Perhaps you're right, but we'll go first thing in the morning.'

I laughed. 'First thing with you isn't very early.'

We went back into the room and sat one on each side of the fireplace, trying to look and feel at home; but the constraint had not left us and the house resisted us. It would not play the host. I felt an intruder, almost a trespasser, and caught myself listening for Christopher's footstep on the stairs.

'Christopher's absence is more potent than his presence,' I said as lightly as I could.

'Ah, poor Christopher,' Constantia said. 'I wish I could feel we were doing what he wanted us to do.'

'What did he want us to do,' I asked, 'besides look at the flowers?'

'I wish I knew,' Constantia answered.

I was glad to find myself growing annoyed. Christopher had somehow turned the tables on us; he had got us into his world of make-believe, his emotional climate of self-stultifying sentimentalism. He had becalmed us with his spell of inaction, which made the ordinary pursuits of life seem not worth-while. He had put us into an equivocal position; even in the conventional sense of the term it was equivocal. Well, I must get us out.

'Are you sure you wouldn't like me to go?' I said. 'The Tyrrel Arms is only a mile away.'

'No, no,' she answered. 'He wouldn't want you to, nor do I.'

'Listen,' I said. 'If it was a practical joke it was a damn bad one. You don't really think he forgot to warn us both that the other would be there?'

'Warn us?'

'Well, would you have come if you'd known I was to be here?'

'Would you?' she parried.

'Certainly,' I said, with more decision than I felt. 'I would go anywhere where you were, Constantia. It would be a plain issue to me. All the issues are plain where you are concerned. I don't have to dress them up in flowers.'

'Ah, the flowers,' she said, and turned again to the window.

'If he meant to make us doubt our feelings for each other,' I argued, 'he will be disappointed, as far as I'm concerned. He has thrown us together by a trick. He has arranged for us to be alone together in his house. He has put us into the position of an illicit couple. Why don't we accept the challenge?'

Constantia frowned. 'He wanted us to see the flowers,' she said, and she was still saying it, in effect if not in word, when the time came for week-end visitors to separate for the night.

I am usually a good sleeper but I could not sleep and was the more annoyed because I felt that Christopher's influence was gaining—it had spread from the emotional into the physical sphere. First he had surprised and kept me guessing; now he was keeping me awake. I had a shrewd idea that Constantia too was wakeful; and the irony and futility of our lying sleepless in separate rooms all because of some groundless scruple that Christopher had insinuated into our minds enraged me and made me more than ever wakeful, as anger will. About two o'clock I rose and, turning on the light, I stole along the passage towards Constantia's room. To reach it I had to pass the head of the staircase where it disappeared into the thick darkness of the hall below. Accentuated by the stillness of the night, the blackness seemed to come up at me, as though it was being brewed in a vat and given off like vapour; and though I wasn't frightened I felt that Christopher was trying to frighten me and this made me still more angry. I listened at Constantia's door and if I had heard a movement I should have gone in, but there was none, and I would not risk waking her; my love for her was intensified by my irritation against Christopher, and I could not bear to do her a disservice. So I turned away and deliberately bent my steps towards Christopher's room, for I knew that he left his letters lying about and I thought I might find something that would let me into the secret of his intentions — if intentions he had; but more and more I felt that the conception of the visit was an idle whim, with hardly enough purpose behind it to be mischievous.

I like a bedroom to be a bedroom, a place for sleeping in, not an extra sitting-room arranged for the display of modish and chi-chi-objects. Christopher's bedroom was even less austere than I remembered it; there were additions in the shape of fashionable Regency furniture, which I never care for. The bed looked as if it never had been and never could be slept in. And in contrast to this luxury were vases full of withered flowers, lilac and iris; the soup-green water they stood in smelt decidedly unpleasant. The Hancocks were not such perfect servants as Christopher liked to make out. Nothing looks so dead as a dead flower, and the bright light gave these a garish look as though they had been painted. But there was nothing to my purpose; no letters, sketches, no books even; only a tall pile of flower catalogues, topped by a Government pamphlet on pest control.

Pest control! It was the pamphlet, no less than the shrivelled flowers, which gave me the idea that burst into full bloom as soon as I was back in bed. The flowers, I felt, represented that part of Christopher with which I was least in sympathy; his instinct to substitute for life something that was apart from life — something that would prettify it, aromatize it, falsify it, enervate and finally destroy it. These flowers were pests and must, in modern parlance, be controlled and neutralized. Thinking how to do it I soon fell asleep.

I was sitting at Christopher's writing-table drafting an opinion when, at the hour at which well-to-do women usually make their first appearance, that is to say about half-past eleven, Constantia came in. She was dressed in grey country clothes the severity of which was relieved by a few frivolous touches here and there, and she was wearing a hat, or the rudiments of a hat. I kissed her and asked how she had slept.

'Not very well,' she said.

'Oh?' I said. 'Why not?'

'I was thinking about Christopher's flowers,' she said. 'I couldn't get them out of my head. I nearly went down to them in the watches of the night. But I'm going now. Will you come with me, Ernest, or are you too busy?'

'I am rather busy,' I said, 'and to tell you the truth, Constantia, I think this flower business is rather a bore.'

Constantia opened her grey eyes wide. 'Oh, why?' she said.

I pulled a chair towards the writing-table as if she was a client come to interview me, and sat down in Christopher's place.

'Because they distract you from me,' I replied. 'That's one thing. And another is, I have reasons for thinking they are not very good flowers.'

'Not?' queried Constantia, puzzled. 'But Christopher has spent so much time and money on them.'

'I know,' I said. 'But I also know that Christopher never gets anything quite right. You must have noticed that yourself.'

Constantia smiled. 'Poor Christopher, I suppose he doesn't quite, but still — Ernest, let's go out and look at them.'

'I hate the second-rate,' I said. 'My motto is, don't touch it.'

Constantia shifted in her chair and gave her dress a little pat. 'Oh well, if you don't want to, I'll——' she began.

'But I don't want you to, either,' I said, pointing my pen at her. 'You'll only regret it if you do.'

'Regret it?' she repeated. 'Ernest, darling, I quite understand if you don't want to go into the garden now, but please don't try to stop me.' She began to get up, but I motioned her to be seated.

'Yes, regret it,' I said, firmly. 'Do you know why Christopher played this trick on us?'

'But was it a trick?' Constantia asked doubtfully.

'Of course it was! He was leading us, if I may say so, up the garden path. I think he had two ideas in his mind, an upper and a lower one, and both were meant to separate us.'

She looked at me reproachfully and without speaking.

'The first was, frankly, to compromise us.'

'Oh, my dear Ernest!' Constantia protested.

'Yes, it was. He may not have put it to himself as crudely as that. He may not have meant to publish it abroad; that would have been the natural thing to do and he doesn't like the natural. No; the satisfaction he would get — will get — is from knowing that we know that he knows. It will enable him to practise a kind of gentle blackmail on us. We shall never be quite alone together any more; he will always be there, watching our thoughts. He will be like an agent — Cupid's agent — taking a ten per cent commission on our love. He will expect us to feel guilty and grateful at the same time and it will act like a poison — it will come between us.'

Constantia made a grimace of distaste. 'Really, Ernest, I don't think he meant anything of the sort.'

But I saw I had impressed her. 'He did, he did,' I said. 'You have no idea what fancies people get when they live alone and play at life.'

Constantia sighed but she did not meet my eye. 'What was the other idea?' she asked.

'I'll tell you,' I said. 'But first I must ask you a question which I think our relationship entitles me to ask. He was never your lover, was he?'

After a pause Constantia said, 'What do you want me to say?'

'No need for you to say anything,' I said. 'By shielding him you have answered my question. He was not. He kept you for years — where? In his enchanted garden, among the loves of the plants, despising this trivial act of union, infecting you with his unreality; and now he means us to meet in his Eden (he called it Eden in his letter) exposed to this same beauty of flowers, like Adam and Eve before the Fall, with this difference' — here I tapped the table with my pen and it gave out a sharp, dry sound — 'that *we* shall have been warned. We shan't dare to eat of the tree of knowledge; we shall be trapped for life in a labyrinth of false values, captives of a memory too gracious and delicate to be contaminated by such an ugly fact as man and wife. Yes,' I went on, for I saw that against herself she was being convinced, 'if you went out into that garden now you might well find a snake and what would it be? An incarnation of our old friend Chrisopher, luring us back to his eunuch's paradise!'

With frightened eyes Constantia looked about her; but I noticed that her glance avoided the window, through which I could see the rhododendrons stirring in the gentle summer breeze.

'Very well,' she said. 'I think you are more fanciful than poor Christopher ever was, but if you like I'll go and write some letters until lunch-time.'

'And you promise not to go into the garden?'

'Yes, since you're so childish.'

'And you won't even speak of going?'

'No, not till four o'clock.'

'All right,' I said. I knew that Constantia would be as good as her word.

After luncheon we decided that our morning's hard work entitled us to a siesta. Constantia had kept her promise, she had not even mentioned the garden; but she stipulated that Hancock should rouse us at a quarter to four, in case either of us overslept.

I did not sleep, however. The watch ticking on my wrist was not more careful of the minutes than I was. After half an hour of this I got up (it was just on three) and decided to take a walk. Where? I knew the walks round Crossways, of course, quite well. Two of them, the best two, were reached by the garden gate that opened on the lane. What of it? The flowers were dangerous to Constantia, but not to me. Anyhow, I needn't look. But as I started out my steps came slower; I stopped and glanced back at the house. 'Confound it!' I thought. 'Confound Christopher and all his works!' I found myself walking back to the house and my rage against him redoubled. Then I had an idea. I had brought a pair of dark glasses with me, sun-glasses, so strong they turned day into night. I put them on and started out with firmer tread. Such colours as I saw were wholly falsified by an admixture of dark sepia tints. I was not looking at Christopher's flowers. But indeed I kept my eyes fixed on the broad path, I did not have to look about me, and here was the gate, the door rather, that led into the lane; and according to Christopher's custom the key had been left in it, for the convenience of guests bent on exercise. The key out of Eden! I unlocked the door, locked it on the other side, put the key in my pocket, and drew a deep breath.

I had been walking for some time when my first plan occurred to me, and I wondered why I had not thought of it before, for it was such an obvious one. I would not go back; I would leave Constantia to keep her tryst with Christopher's spirit, for she would keep it: I had shaken her mind, but not her resolution. She would go through the silly ritual by herself and it would mean to her—well, whatever it did mean. It could not fail to be something of an anti-climax. She would wait, toeing the line like a runner, and looking round for me; she would give me a minute or two, and then she would start off. And as she went through that afternoon blaze of flowers, very slowly, drinking it in and thinking of Christopher, as no doubt he had enjoined her to—what would her reactions be? What would any woman's reactions be? Would she think less kindly of Christopher and more kindly of me? She would remember the many times she had walked there with him, wishing, no doubt, that he was other than he was, but indulgent to his faults, as women are, perhaps half liking him for them, not minding his ineffectualness. And the flowers would plead for him. She would not care if they were poor specimens (I had invented that), it would only make her feel sorry for him, and protective.

No, it would not do to let her go down the Long Walk alone. And nor would I escort her, for that would be the ultimate surrender to all that I was saving her from.

It was time to turn back and I still had formed no plan. I stopped and as I put my hands in my pockets the key of the garden door jingled and seemed to speak to me. At once the peace of decision, unknown to men of Christopher's type, descended on me. I felt that the problem of the garden was already solved. I had plenty of time to get back by a quarter to four, so I did not hurry, indeed I loitered. Suddenly I wondered why the familiar landscape looked so odd, and I remembered I was still wearing my dark glasses. I took them off and immediately felt interested in the wayside flowers, the dog-roses and honeysuckle of the hedgerows. In spite of what Christopher said I am really quite fond of flowers, and it gave me an intimate sense of power and freedom to examine these, which he had not asked me to examine. What plainer proof could I have that I was free of him and that my will was uncontaminated by his?

But when I reached the lane that bordered his garden wall I stopped botanizing and put on my sun-glasses again, for I still judged it better not to take risks. And I had thought out all my actions during the next twenty minutes so carefully that it came as a great surprise when I found that something had happened outside my calculations.

The garden door was open.

There could only be one explanation and it disturbed me: Constantia must have opened the door, and to do so must have passed through the garden. She must have asked Hancock for one of the several duplicate keys that Christopher had had made (the key of the garden door was always getting lost) and gone for a walk as I had. I did not want to disturb the rest of my plan so I left the door as it was and went towards the house. I did not return by the Long Walk; I went another way, invisible from the house, for I did not want to be seen by anyone just then.

But Constantia had not gone out; she was sitting by the drawing-room window. She jumped up. 'Oh,' she said, 'thank goodness, here you are. I was afraid you were going to be late. But I have a bone to pick with you. You stole a march on me.'

'How?' I challenged her.

'You've been to see the flowers already.'

'What makes you think so?'

'I saw you in the Long Walk, don't tell me it wasn't you!'

'When?'

'About ten minutes ago.'

'What was I doing?'

'Oh, Ernest, don't be so mysterious! You were looking at the flowers, of course.'

I joined her at the window.

'You couldn't see from here,' I said.

'Of course I could! And you were ashamed—you didn't want to be seen, you dodged in and out of the bushes, and pretended to be a rhododendron. But I knew you by your hat.'

Nothing she said made any sense to me; I hadn't gone out in a hat; but I said quickly, 'I think you're imagining things, but afterwards I'll explain.' It was like being back on the main road after a traffic diversion. 'Now what is our plan of campaign? At the stroke of four we are to walk from the fountain to the temple?'

Constantia hurriedly searched in her bag and brought out a letter. 'No, no, Ernest,' she said in agitation. 'He says from the temple to the fountain.'

'Are you sure?'

'Quite sure.'

'Did you promise him to do it?'

'Yes, did you?'

'Well, I suppose I did. But my instructions were the other way round. He means us to meet in the middle, then.'

'Yes. What time is it, Ernest? We mustn't be late.'

'Three minutes to four. Just let me get my stick.'

'Stick, you won't want a stick. What do you want a stick for?'

'To beat you with,' I said.

She smiled. 'Be quick, then.'

I hurried out, shutting the door behind me and turning the key in the lock. Suddenly feeling tired I sat down on a chair on the landing.

In the hall below me the grandfather clock struck four.

Oh, the ecstasy of that moment! It seemed to me that my whole life was being fulfilled in it. I heard Constantia's voice calling 'Ernest! Ernest!' But I could not move, I could not even think, for the waves of delight that were surging through me. I heard the rattle of the door-handle; I could see it stealthily turning, backwards and forwards, in a cramped semi-circle. Soon she began to beat upon the door. 'Her little fists will soon get tired of that,' I thought. 'And she can't get out through the window: there's a drop of twenty feet into the garden.'

As distinctly as if there had been no door between us I saw her face clenched in misery and fury. Ah, but this was real! This was no sentimental saunter down a garden-path! Presently the hammering ceased and another sound began. Constantia was crying: she did not do it prettily: she did not know she had a listener: she coughed her tears out. That, too, ministered to my ecstasy; I was the king of pain. I sat on, savouring it till all sounds ceased, except the ticking of the clock below.

How long my drowse lasted I cannot tell, but it was broken by the crack of a shot. It seemed to be inside me, it hurt me so much. I jumped up as if it was I who had been hit. I pressed the key against the lock too hard: it turned unwillingly, but at last I was in the room.

She was sitting bent forward with her face in her hands, blood was trickling from her broken knuckles, and for a moment I believed that she was dead. But she raised her face and looked at me unrecognizingly. 'Ernest?' she said, as if it was a question. 'Ernest?'

'I'm sorry, Constantia,' I said. 'Something delayed me. Shall we go into the garden now?'

She rose without a word and followed me downstairs, and we went out through the french windows in Christopher's room.

'Here we divide,' I said. 'You go to the temple and I'll go to the fountain, and we'll meet in the middle, Constantia.' She obeyed me like a child.

I looked at the flowers as Christopher wished me to. I did not look at anything else, though when I raised my eyes I could see Constantia, very small and far away, coming towards me. The afternoon sunshine lay thick on all these thousands of blooms. Not a single one seemed to be in shadow: all were displayed for us to look at, as Christopher had wished them to be. Constantia and I were representing the public, the great public, in fact the world, to whom Christopher had felt this strange obligation to make known the beauty he had helped to create. And now I was not only willing but eager to fall in with his plan. Methodically I zig-zagged from one side of the grass path to the other, from the rhododendrons to the azaleas, from the Boucher-like luxuriance of the one to the Chinese delicacy and tenuousness of the other. I went on the flower-beds; I lifted the brown labels, trying to decipher rain-smudged names; I stooped to the earth, yes, from time to time I knelt, to read the inscriptions on the leaden markers. Nothing that he would have wished me to see escaped me; the smallest effect was as clear to me as the largest; I found no faults — no dissonance, even, between the prevailing pink of the rhododendrons and the prevailing orange of the azaleas, which had hitherto always offended my eye when these flowers were juxtaposed. Yes, I thought, he has brought it off, he has established a harmony; the flowers all sing together an anthem to his glory.

I was approaching the middle of the Long Walk and my journey's end when I heard Constantia scream. Instantly the garden was in ruins, its spell broken.

I did not see her at first. Like me, she had been going to and fro among the flower-beds, and it was there, under the shadow of a towering rhododendron that I found her, bending over Christopher. Something or someone — perhaps Christopher, perhaps Constantia in the shock of her discovery, had shaken the bush, for the body was covered with rose-pink petals, and his forehead, his damaged forehead, was adrift with them. Even the revolver in his hand had petals on it, softening its steely gleam. But for that, and for something in his attitude that suggested he was defying Nature, not obeying her, one might have supposed that he had fallen asleep under his own flowers.

In his pocket we afterwards found a letter. It was addressed to both of us and dated Sunday 4.30. 'I had meant to join you at the garden-party,' it said, 'but now I feel it's best I shouldn't. Only half an hour, but long enough to be convinced that I have messed things up. And yet I can't quite understand it, for I felt so differently at four o'clock. Was it too much to ask, that you should keep your promise to me, or too little? All my life I have been asking myself this question, in one form or another, and perhaps this is the only answer. Bless you, my children, be happy. — Christopher.'

'But don't you *see*,' I said to Constantia, 'it all proves what I said? He couldn't come to terms with life, he didn't know how to live, and so he had to die?'

'You may be right,' she answered listlessly. 'But I shall never forgive myself for failing him — or you.'

I argued with her — I even got angry with her — but she would not see reason, and after the inquest we never met again.

HILDA'S LETTER

It may take time to get over an obsession, even after the roots have been pulled out. Eustace was satisfied that 'going away' did not mean that he was going to die; but at moments the fiery chariot still cast its glare across his mind, and he was thankful to shield himself behind the prosaic fact that going away meant nothing worse than going to school. In other circumstances the thought of going to school would have alarmed him; but as an alternative to death it was almost welcome.

Unconsciously he tried to inoculate himself against the future by aping the demeanour of the schoolboys he saw about the streets or playing on the beach at Anchorstone. He whistled, put his hands in his pockets, swayed as he walked, and assumed the serious but detached air of someone who owes fealty to a masculine corporation beyond the ken of his womenfolk: a secret society demanding tribal peculiarities of speech and manner. As to the thoughts and habits of mind which should inspire these outward gestures, he found them in school stories; and if they were sometimes rather lurid they were much less distressing than the fiery chariot.

His family was puzzled by his almost eager acceptance of the trials in store. His aunt explained it as yet another instance of Eustace's indifference to home-ties, and an inevitable consequence of the money he had inherited from Miss Fothergill. She had to remind herself to be fair to him whenever she thought of this undeserved success. But to his father the very fact that it was undeserved made Eustace something of a hero. His son was a dark horse who had romped home, and the sight of Eustace often gave him a pleasurable tingling, an impulse to laugh and make merry, such as may greet the evening paper when it brings news of a win. A lad of such mettle would naturally want to go to school.

To Minney her one time charge was now more than ever 'Master' Eustace; in other ways her feeling for him remained unchanged by anything that happened to him. He was just her little boy who was obeying the natural order of things by growing up. Barbara was too young to realize that the hair she sometimes pulled belonged to an embryo schoolboy. In any case, she was an egotist, and had she been older she would have regarded her brother's translation to another sphere from the angle of how it affected her. She would have set about finding other strings to pull now that she was denied his hair.

Thus, the grown-ups, though they did not want to lose him, viewed Eustace's metamorphosis without too much misgiving; and moreover they felt that he must be shown the forbearance and accorded the special privileges of one who has an ordeal before him. Even Aunt Sarah, who did not like the whistling or the hands in the pockets or the slang, only rebuked them half-heartedly.

But Hilda, beautiful, unapproachable Hilda, could not reconcile herself to the turn events had taken. Was she not and would she not always be nearly four years older than her brother Eustace? Was she not his spiritual adviser, pledged to make him a credit to her and to himself and to his family?

He was her care, her task in life. Indeed, he was much more than that; her strongest feelings centred in him and at the thought of losing him she felt as if her heart was being torn out of her body.

So while Eustace grew more perky, Hilda pined. She had never carried herself well, but now she slouched along, hurrying past people she knew as if she had important business to attend to, and her beauty, had she been aware of it, might have been a pursuer she was trying to shake off.

Eustace must not go to school, he must not. She knew he would not want to, when the time came; but then it would be too late. She had rescued him from Anchorstone Hall, the lair of the highwayman, Dick Staveley, his hero and her *bête noire*; and she would rescue him again. But she must act, and act at once.

It was easy to find arguments. School would be bad for him. It would bring out the qualities he shared with other little boys, qualities which could be kept in check if he remained at home.

'What are little boys made of?' she demanded, and looked round in triumph when Eustace ruefully but dutifully answered:

'Snips and snails and puppy-dogs' tails
And *that's* what *they* are made of.'

He would grow rude and unruly and start being cruel to animals. Schoolboys always were. And he would fall ill; he would have a return of his bronchitis. Anchorstone was a health-resort. Eustace (who loved statistics and had a passion for records) had told her that Anchorstone had the ninth lowest death-rate in England. (This thought had brought him some fleeting comfort in the darkest hours of his obsession.) If he went away from Anchorstone he might die. They did not want him to die, did they?

Her father and her aunt listened respectfully to Hilda. Since her mother's death they had treated her as if she was half grown up, and they often told each other that she had an old head on young shoulders.

Hilda saw that she had impressed them and went on to say how much better Eustace was looking, which was quite true, and how much better behaved he was, except when he was pretending to be a schoolboy (Eustace reddened at this). And, above all, what a lot he knew; far more than most boys of his age, she said. Why, besides knowing that Anchorstone had the ninth lowest death-rate in England, he knew that Cairo had the highest death-rate in the world, and would speedily have been wiped out had it not also had the highest birthrate. (This double pre-eminence made the record-breaking city one of Eustace's favourite subjects of contemplation.) And all this he owed to Aunt Sarah's teaching.

Aunt Sarah couldn't help being pleased; she was well-educated herself and knew that Eustace was quick at his lessons.

'I shouldn't be surprised if he gets into quite a high class,' his father said; 'you'll see, he'll be bringing home a prize or two, won't you, Eustace?'

'Oh, but boys don't always learn much at school,' objected Hilda.

'How do you know they don't?' said Mr. Cherrington teasingly. 'She never speaks to any other boys, does she, Eustace?'

But before Eustace had time to answer, Hilda surprised them all by saying: 'Well, I do, so there! I spoke to Gerald Steptoe!'

Everyone was thunderstruck to hear this, particularly Eustace, because Hilda had always had a special dislike for Gerald Steptoe, who was a sturdy, round-faced, knockabout boy with rather off-hand manners.

'I met him near the post office,' Hilda said, 'and he took off his cap, so I had to speak to him, hadn't I?'

Eustace said nothing. Half the boys in Anchorstone, which was only a small place, knew Hilda by sight and took their caps off when they passed her in the street, she was so pretty; and grown-up people used to stare at her, too, with a smile dawning on their faces. Eustace had often seen Gerald Steptoe take off his cap to Hilda, but she never spoke to him if she could help it, and would not let Eustace either.

Aunt Sarah knew this.

'You were quite right, Hilda. I don't care much for Gerald Steptoe, but we don't want to be rude to anyone, do we?'

Hilda looked doubtful.

'Well, you know he goes to a school near the one—St. Ninian's—that you want to send Eustace to.'

'Want to! That's good,' said Mr. Cherrington. 'He *is* going, poor chap, on the seventeenth of January—that's a month from to-day—aren't you, Eustace? Now don't you try to unsettle him, Hilda.'

Eustace looked nervously at Hilda and saw the tears standing in her eyes.

'Don't say that to her, Alfred,' said Miss Cherrington. 'You can see she minds much more than he does.'

Hilda didn't try to hide her tears, as some girls would have; she just brushed them away and gave a loud sniff.

'It isn't Eustace's feelings I'm thinking about. If he wants to leave us all, let him. I'm thinking of his—his education.' She paused, and noticed that at the word education their faces grew grave. 'Do you know what Gerald told me?'

'Well, what did he tell you?' asked Mr. Cherrington airily, but Hilda saw he wasn't quite at his ease.

'He told me they didn't teach the boys *anything* at St. Ninian's,' said Hilda. 'They just play games all the time. They're very good at games, he said, better than his school—I can't remember what it's called.'

'St. Cyprian's,' put in Eustace. Any reference to a school made him feel self-important.

'I knew it was another saint. But the boys at St. Ninian's aren't saints at all, Gerald said. They're all the sons of rich swanky people who go there to do nothing. Gerald said that what they don't know would fill books.'

There was a pause. No one spoke, and Mr. Cherrington and his sister exchanged uneasy glances.

'I expect he exaggerated, Hilda,' said Aunt Sarah. 'Boys do exaggerate sometimes. It's a way of showing off. I hope Eustace won't learn to. As you know, Hilda, we went into the whole thing very thoroughly. We looked through twenty-nine prospectuses before we decided, and your father thought Mr. Waghorn a very gentlemanly, understanding sort of man.'

'The boys call him "Old Foghorn",' said Hilda, and was rewarded by seeing Miss Cherrington stiffen in distaste. 'And they imitate him blowing his nose, and take bets about how many times he'll clear his throat during prayers. I don't like having to tell you this,' she added virtuously, 'but I thought I ought to.'

'What are bets, Daddy?' asked Eustace, hoping to lead the conversation into safer channels.

'Bets, my boy?' said Mr. Cherrington. 'Well, if you think something will happen, and another fellow doesn't, and you bet him sixpence that it will, then if it does he pays you sixpence, and if it doesn't you pay him sixpence.'

Eustace was thinking that this was a very fair arrangement when Miss Cherrington said, 'Please don't say "you", Alfred, or Eustace might imagine that you were in the habit of making bets yourself.'

'Well—' began Mr. Cherrington.

'Betting is a very bad habit,' said Miss Cherrington firmly, 'and I'm sorry to hear that the boys of St. Ninian's practise it—if they do: again, Gerald may have been exaggerating, and it is quite usual, I imagine, for the boys of one school to run down another. But there is no reason that Eustace should learn to. To be exposed to temptation is one thing, to give way is another, and resistance to temptation is a valuable form of self-discipline.'

'Oh, but they don't resist!' cried Hilda. 'And Eustace wouldn't either. You know how he likes to do the same as everyone else. And if any boy, especially any new boy, tries to be good and different from the rest they tease him and call him some horrid name (Gerald wouldn't tell me what it was), and sometimes punch him, too.'

Eustace, who had always been told he must try to be good in all circumstances, turned rather pale and looked down at the floor.

'Now, now, Hilda,' said her father, impatiently. 'You've said quite enough. You sound as if you didn't want Eustace to go to school.'

But Hilda was unabashed. She knew she had made an impression on the grown-ups.

'Oh, it's only that I want him to go to the right school, isn't it, Aunt Sarah?' she said. 'We shouldn't like him to go to a school where he learned bad habits and—and nothing else, should we? He would be much better off as he is now, with you teaching him and me helping. Gerald said they really knew *nothing*; he said he knew more than the oldest boys at St. Ninian's, and he's only twelve.'

'But he does boast, doesn't he?' put in Eustace timidly. 'You used to

say so yourself, Hilda.' Hilda had never had a good word for Gerald
Steptoe before to-day.

'Oh, yes, you all boast,' said Hilda sweepingly. 'But I don't think he
was boasting. I asked him how much he knew, and he said, The Kings
and Queens of England, so I told him to repeat them and he broke down
down at Richard II. Eustace can say them perfectly, and he's only ten,
so you see for the next four years he wouldn't be learning anything, he'd
just be forgetting everything, wouldn't he, Aunt Sarah? Don't let him
go, I'm sure it would be a mistake.'

Minney, Barbara's nurse, came bustling in. She was rather short and
had soft hair and gentle eyes. 'Excuse me, Miss Cherrington,' she said,
'but it's Master Eustace's bedtime.'

Eustace said good night. Hilda walked with him to the door and
when they were just outside she said in a whisper:

'I think I shall be able to persuade them.'

'But I think I want to go, Hilda!' muttered Eustace.

'It isn't what you want, it's what's good for you,' exclaimed Hilda,
looking at him with affectionate fierceness. As she turned the handle of
the drawing-room door she overheard her father saying to Miss Cherrington: 'I shouldn't pay too much attention to all that, Sarah. If the
boy didn't want to go it would be different. As the money's his, he
ought to be allowed to please himself. But he'll be all right, you'll see.'

The days passed and Hilda wept in secret. Sometimes she wept openly,
for she knew how it hurt Eustace to see her cry. When he asked her why
she was crying she wouldn't tell him at first, but just shook her head.
Later on she said, 'You know quite well: why do you ask me?' and, of
course, Eustace did know. It made him unhappy to know he was making her unhappy and besides, as the time to leave home drew nearer, he
became much less sure that he liked the prospect. Hilda saw that he was
weakening and she played upon his fears and gave him *Eric or Little by
Little* as a Christmas present, to warn him of what he might expect
when he went to school. Eustace read it and was extremely worried; he
didn't see how he could possibly succeed where a boy as clever, and
handsome, and good as Eric had been before he went to school, had
failed. But it did not make him want to turn back, for he now felt that
if school was going to be an unpleasant business, all the more must he go
through with it—especially as it was going to be unpleasant for him,
and not for anyone else; which would have been an excuse for backing
out. 'You see it won't really matter,' he explained to Hilda, 'they can't

kill me—Daddy said so—and he said they don't even roast boys at preparatory schools, only at public schools, and I shan't be going to a public school for a long time, if ever. I expect they will just do a few things to me like pulling my hair and twisting my arm and perhaps kicking me a little, but I shan't really mind that. It was much worse all that time after Miss Fothergill died, because then I didn't know what was going to happen and now I do know, so I shall be prepared.' Hilda was nonplussed by this argument, all the more so because it was she who had told Eustace that it was always good for you to do something you didn't like. 'You say so now,' she said, 'but you won't say so on the seventeenth of January.' And when Eustace said nothing but only looked rather sad and worried she burst into tears. 'You're so selfish,' she sobbed. 'You only think about being good—as if that mattered—you don't think about me at all. I shan't eat or drink anything while you are away, and I shall probably die.'

Eustace was growing older and he did not really believe that Hilda would do this, but the sight of her unhappiness and the tears (which sometimes started to her eyes unbidden the moment he came into the room where she was) distressed him very much. Already, he thought, she was growing thinner, there were hollows in her cheeks, she was silent, or spoke in snatches, very fast and with far more vehemence and emphasis than the occasion called for; she came in late for meals and never apologized, she had never been interested in clothes, but now she was positively untidy. The grown-ups, to his surprise, did not seem to notice.

He felt he must consult someone and thought at once of Minney, because she was the easiest to talk to. But he knew she would counsel patience; that was her idea, that people would come to themselves if they were left alone. Action was needed and she wouldn't take any action. Besides, Hilda had outgrown Minney's influence; Minney wasn't drastic enough to cut any ice with her. Aunt Sarah would be far more helpful because she understood Hilda. But she didn't understand Eustace and would make him feel that he was making a fuss about nothing, or if he did manage to persuade her that Hilda was unhappy she would somehow lay the blame on him. There remained his father. Eustace was nervous of consulting his father, because he never knew what mood he would find him in. Mr. Cherrington could be very jolly and treat Eustace almost as an equal; then something Eustace said would upset him and he would get angry and make Eustace wish he had never spoken. But since Miss Fothergill's death his attitude to Eustace had changed.

His outbursts of irritation were much less frequent and he often asked Eustace his opinion and drew him out and made him feel more self-confident. It all depended on finding him in a good mood.

Of late Mr. Cherrington had taken to drinking a whisky and soda and smoking a cigar when he came back from his office in Ousemouth; this was at about six o'clock, and he was always alone then, in the drawing-room, because Miss Cherrington did not approve of this new habit. When he had finished she would go in and throw open the windows, but she never went in while he was there.

Eustace found him with his feet up enveloped in the fumes of whisky and cigar smoke, which seemed to Eustace the very being and breath of manliness. Mr. Cherrington stirred. The fragrant cloud rolled away and his face grew more distinct.

'Hullo,' he said, 'here's the Wild Man.' The Wild Man from Borneo was in those days an object of affection with the general public. 'Sit down and make yourself comfortable. Now, what can I do for you?'

The armchair was too big for Eustace: his feet hardly touched the floor.

'It's about Hilda,' he said.

'Well, Hilda's a nice girl, what about her?' said Mr. Cherrington, his voice still jovial. Eustace hesitated and then said with a rush:

'You see, she doesn't want me to go to school.'

Mr. Cherrington frowned, and sipped at his glass.

'I know, we've heard her more than once on that subject. She thinks you'll get into all sorts of bad ways.' His voice sharpened; it was too bad that his quiet hour should be interrupted by these nursery politics. 'Have you been putting your heads together? Have you come to tell me you don't want to go either?'

Eustace's face showed the alarm he felt at his father's change of tone.

'Oh, no, Daddy. At least—well—I . . .'

'You don't want to go. That's clear,' his father snapped.

'Yes, I do. But you see . . .' Eustace searched for a form of words which wouldn't lay the blame too much on Hilda and at the same time excuse him for seeming to shelter behind her. 'You see, though she's older than me she's only a girl and she doesn't understand that men have to do certain things'—Mr. Cherrington smiled, and Eustace took heart—'well, like going to school.'

'Girls go to school, too,' Mr. Cherrington said. Eustace tried to meet this argument. 'Yes, but it's not the same for them. You see, girls are always nice to each other; why, they always call each other by their

Christian names even when they're at school. Fancy that! And they never bet or' (Eustace looked nervously at the whisky decanter) or drink, or use bad language, or kick each other, or roast each other in front of a slow fire.' Thinking of the things that girls did not do to each other, Eustace began to grow quite pale.

'All the better for them, then,' said Mr. Cherrington robustly. 'School seems to be the place for girls. But what's all this leading *you* to?'

'I don't mind about those things,' said Eustace eagerly. 'I . . . I should quite enjoy them. And I shouldn't even mind, well, you know, not being so good for a change, if it was only for a time. But Hilda thinks it might make me ill as well. Of course, she's quite mistaken, but she says she'll miss me so much and worry about me, that she'll never have a peaceful moment, and she'll lose her appetite and perhaps pine away and . . .' He paused, unable to complete the picture. 'She doesn't know I'm telling you all this, and she wouldn't like me to, and at school they would say it was telling tales, but I'm not at school yet, am I? Only I felt I must tell you because then perhaps you'd say I'd better not go to school, though I hope you won't.'

Exhausted by the effort of saying so many things that should (he felt) have remained locked in his bosom, and dreading an angry reply, Eustace closed his eyes. When he opened them his father was standing up with his back to the fireplace. He took the cigar from his mouth and puffed out an expanding cone of rich blue smoke.

'Thanks, old chap,' he said. 'I'm very glad you told me, and I'm not going to say you shan't go to school. Miss Fothergill left you the money for that purpose, so we chose the best school we could find; and why Hilda should want to put her oar in I can't imagine — at least, I can, but I call it confounded cheek. The very idea!' his father went on, working himself up and looking at Eustace as fiercely as if it was his fault, while Eustace trembled to hear Hilda criticized. 'What she needs is to go to school herself. Yes, that's what she needs.' He took a good swig at the whisky, his eyes brightened and his voice dropped. 'Now I'm going to tell you something, Eustace, only you must keep it under your hat.'

'Under my hat?' repeated Eustace, mystified. 'My hat's in the hall. Shall I go and get it?'

His father laughed. 'No, I mean you must keep it to yourself. You mustn't tell anyone, because nothing's decided yet.'

'Shall I cross my heart and swear?' asked Eustace anxiously. 'Of course, I'd rather not.'

'You can do anything you like with yourself as long as you don't tell Hilda,' his father remarked, 'but just see the door's shut.'

Eustace tiptoed to the door and cautiously turned the handle several times, after each turn giving the handle a strong but surreptitious tug. Coming back still more stealthily, he whispered, 'It's quite shut.'

'Very well, then,' said Mr. Cherrington. 'Now give me your best ear.'

'My best ear, Daddy?' said Eustace, turning his head from side to side. 'Oh, I see!' and he gave a loud laugh which he immediately stifled. 'You just want me to listen carefully.'

'You've hit it,' and between blue, fragrant puffs Mr. Cherrington began to outline his plan for Hilda.

While his father was speaking Eustace's face grew grave, and every now and then he nodded judicially. Though his feet still swung clear of the floor, to be taken into his father's confidence seemed to add inches to his stature.

'Well, old man, that's what I wanted to tell you,' said his father at length. 'Only you mustn't let on, see? Mum's the word.'

'Wild horses won't drag it out of me, Daddy,' said Eustace earnestly.

'Well, don't you let them try. By the way, I hear your friend Dick Staveley's back.'

Eustace started. The expression of an elder statesman faded from his face and he suddenly looked younger than his years.

'Oh, is he? I expect he's just home for the holidays.'

'No, he's home for some time, he's cramming for Oxford or something.'

'Cramming?' repeated Eustace. His mind suddenly received a most disagreeable impression of Dick, his hero, transformed into a turkey strutting and gobbling round a farmyard.

'Being coached for the 'Varsity. It may happen to you one day. Somebody told me they'd seen him, and I thought you might be interested. You liked him, didn't you?'

'Oh, *yes*,' said Eustace. Intoxicating visions began to rise, only to be expelled by the turn events had taken. 'But it doesn't make much difference now, does it? I mean, I shouldn't be able to go there, even if he asked me.'

Meanwhile, Hilda on her side had not been idle. She turned over in her mind every stratagem and device she could think of that might keep Eustace at home. Since the evening when she so successfully launched her bombshell about the unsatisfactory state of education and morals at

St. Ninian's, she felt she had been losing ground. Eustace did not respond, as he once used to, to the threat of terrors to come; he professed to be quite pleased at the thought of being torn limb from limb by older stronger boys. She didn't believe he was really unmoved by such a prospect, but he successfully pretended to be. When she said that it would make her ill he seemed to care a great deal more; for several days he looked as sad as she did, and he constantly, and rather tiresomely, begged her to eat more—requests which Hilda received with a droop of her long, heavy eyelids and a sad shake of her beautiful head. But lately Eustace hadn't seemed to care so much. When Christmas came he suddenly discovered the fun of pulling crackers. Before this year he wouldn't even stay in the room if crackers were going off; but now he revelled in them and made almost as much noise as they did, and his father even persuaded him to grasp the naked strip of cardboard with the explosive in the middle, which stung your fingers and made even grown-ups pull faces. Crackers bored Hilda; the loudest report did not make her change her expression, and she would have liked to tell Eustace how silly he looked as, with an air of trumph, he clasped the smoking fragment; but she hadn't the heart to. He might be at school already, his behaviour was so unbridled. And he had a new way of looking at her, not unkind or cross or disobedient, but as if he was a gardener tending a flower and watching to see how it was going to turn out. This was a reversal of their rôles; she felt as though a geranium had risen from its bed and was bending over her with a watering-can.

As usual, they were always together and if Hilda did not get the old satisfaction from the company of this polite but aloof little stranger (for so he seemed to her) the change in his attitude made her all the more determined to win him back, and the thought of losing him all the more desolating. She hated the places where they used to play together and wished that Eustace, who was sentimental about his old haunts, would not take her to them. 'I just want to see it once again,' he would plead, and she did not like to refuse him, though his new mantle of authority sat so precariously on him. Beneath her moods, which she expressed in so many ways, was a steadily increasing misery; the future stretched away featureless without landmarks; nothing beckoned, nothing drew her on.

Obscurely she realized that the change had been brought about by Miss Fothergill's money. It had made Eustace independent, not completely independent, not as independent as she was, but it had given a force to his wishes that they never possessed before. It was no good trying to make him not want to go to school; she must make him want to stay at home. In this new state of affairs she believed that if Eustace refused to go to school his father would not try to compel him. But how to go about it? How to make Anchorstone suddenly so attractive, so irresistibly magnetic, that Eustace would not be able to bring himself to leave?

When Eustace told her that Dick Staveley was coming to live at Anchorstone Hall he mentioned this (for him) momentous event as casually as possible. Hilda did not like Dick Staveley, she professed abhorrence of him; she would not go to Anchorstone Hall when Dick had invited her, promising he would teach her to ride. The whole idea of the place was distasteful to her; it chilled and shrivelled her thoughts, just as it warmed and expanded Eustace's. Even to hear it mentioned cast a shadow over her mind, and as to going there, she would rather die; and she had often told Eustace so.

It was a sign of emancipation that he let Dick's name cross his lips. He awaited the explosion, and it came.

'That man!'—she never spoke of him as a boy, though he was only a few years older than she was. 'Well, *you* won't see him, will you?' she added almost vindictively. 'You'll be at school.'

'Oh,' said Eustace, 'that won't make any difference. I shouldn't see him anyhow. You see, he never wanted to be friends with me. It was you he liked. If you had gone, I dare say he would have asked me to go too, just as your—well, you know, to hold the horse, and so on.'

'You and your horses!' said Hilda, scornfully. 'You don't know one end of a horse from the other.' He expected she would let the subject drop, but her eyes grew thoughtful and to his astonishment she said, 'Suppose I *had* gone?' 'Oh, *well*,' said Eustace, 'that would have changed everything. I shouldn't have had time to go to tea with Miss Fothergill —you see we should always have been having tea at Anchorstone Hall. Then she wouldn't have died and left me her money—I mean, she would have died; but she wouldn't have left me any money because she wouldn't have known me well enough. You have to know someone well to do that. And then I shouldn't be going to school now, because Daddy says it's her money that pays for me—and now' (he glanced up, the clock on the Town Hall, with its white face and black hands, said four o'clock) 'you would be coming in from riding with Dick, and I should be sitting on one of those grand sofas in the drawing-room at Anchorstone Hall, perhaps talking to Lady Staveley.'

Involuntarily Hilda closed her eyes against this picture—let it be confounded! Let it be blotted out! But aloud she said:

'Wouldn't you have liked that?'

'Oh, *yes*,' said Eustace fervently.

'Better than going to school?'

Eustace considered. The trussed boy was being carried towards a very large, but slow, fire; other boys, black demons with pitchforks, were scurrying about, piling on coals. His mood of heroism deserted him.

'Oh yes, much better.'

Hilda said nothing, and they continued to saunter down the hill, past the ruined cross, past the pierhead with its perpetual invitation, towards the glories of the Wolferton Hotel—winter-gardened, girt with iron fire-escapes—and the manifold exciting sounds, and heavy, sulphurous smells, of the railway station.

'Are we going to Mrs. Wrench's?' Eustace asked.

'No, why should we? We had fish for dinner; you never notice. Oh, I know, you want to see the crocodile.'

'Well, just this once. You see, I may not see it again for a long time.'

Hilda sniffed. 'I wish you wouldn't keep on saying that,' she said. 'It seems the only thing you can say. Oh, very well, then, we'll go in and look round and come out.'

'Oh, but we must buy something. She would be disappointed if we didn't. Let's get some shrimps. Aunt Sarah won't mind just for once, and I don't suppose I shall have any at St. Ninian's. I expect the Fourth Form gets them, though.'

'Why should they?'

'Oh, didn't you know, they have all sorts of privileges.'

'I expect they have shrimps every day at Anchorstone Hall,' said Hilda, meaningly.

'Oh, I expect they do. What a pity you didn't want to go. We have missed such a lot.'

Cautiously they crossed the road, for the wheeled traffic was thick here and might include a motor car. Fat Mrs. Wrench was standing at the door of the fish shop. She saw them coming, went in, and smiled expectantly from behind the counter.

'Well, Miss Hilda?'

'Eustace wants a fillet of the best end of the crocodile.'

'Oh Hilda, I don't!'

They all laughed uproariously, Hilda loudest of all; while the stuffed crocodile (a small one) sprawling on the wall with tufts of bright green

foliage glued round it, glared down on them malignantly. Eustace felt
the tremor of delighted terror that he had been waiting for.

'I've got some lovely fresh shrimps,' said Mrs. Wrench.

'Turn round, Eustace,' said Miss Cherrington.

'Oh must I again, Aunt Sarah?'

'Yes, you must. You don't want the other boys to laugh at you, do
you?'

Reluctantly, Eustace revolved. He hated having his clothes tried on.
He felt it was he who was being criticized, not they. It gave him a feeling of being trapped, as though each of the three pairs of eyes fixed on
him, impersonal, fault-finding, was attached to him by a silken cord
that bound him to the spot. He tried to restrain his wriggles within himself but they broke out and rippled on the surface.

'Do try to stand still, Eustace.'

Aunt Sarah was operating; she had some pins in her mouth with
which, here and there, she pinched grooves and ridges in his black jacket.
Alas, it was rather too wide at the shoulders and not wide enough
round the waist.

'Eustace is getting quite a corporation,' said his father.

'Corporation, Daddy?' Eustace was always interested in words.

'Well, I didn't like to say fat.'

'It's because you would make me feed up,' Eustace complained. 'I
was quite thin before. Nancy Steptoe said I was just the right size for a
boy.'

No one took this up; indeed, a slight chill fell on the company at the
mention of Nancy's name.

'Never mind,' Minney soothed him, 'there's some who would give a
lot to be so comfortable looking as Master Eustace is.'

'Would they, Minney?'

Eustace was encouraged.

'Yes, they would, nasty scraggy things. And I can make that quite all
right.' She inserted two soft fingers beneath the tight line round his
waist.

'Hilda hasn't said anything yet,' said Mr. Cherrington. 'What do you
think of your brother now, Hilda?'

Hilda had not left her place at the luncheon table, nor had she taken
her eyes off her plate. Without looking up she said:

'He'll soon get thin if he goes to school, if that's what you want.'

'*If* he goes,' said Mr. Cherrington. 'Of course he's going. Why do you suppose we took him to London to Faith Brothers if he wasn't? All the same, I'm not sure we ought to have got his clothes off the peg. . . . Now go and have a look at yourself, Eustace. Mind the glass doesn't break.'

Laughing, but half afraid of what he might see, Eustace tiptoed to the mirror. There stood his new personality, years older than a moment ago. The Eton collar, the black jacket cut like a man's, the dark grey trousers that he could feel through his stockings, caressing his calves, made a veritable mantle of manhood. A host of new sensations, adult, prideful, standing no nonsense, coursed through him. Involuntarily, he tilted his head back and frowned, as though he were considering a leg-break that might dismiss R. H. Spooner.

'What a pity he hasn't got the cap,' said Minney admiringly.

Eustace half turned his head. 'It's because of the crest, the White Horse of Kent. You see, if they let a common public tailor make that, anyone might wear it.'

'Don't call people common, please Eustace, even a tailor.'

'I didn't mean common in a nasty way, Aunt Sarah. Common just means anyone. It might mean me or even you.'

Hoping to change the subject, Minney dived into a cardboard box, noisily rustling the tissue paper.

'But we've got the straw hat. Put that on, Master Eustace. . . . There, Mr. Cherrington, doesn't he look nice?'

'Not so much on the back of your head, Eustace, or you'll look like Ally Sloper. That's better.'

'I wish it had a guard,' sighed Eustace, longingly.

'Oh well, one thing at a time.'

'And of course it hasn't got the school band yet. It's blue, you know, with a white horse.'

'What, another?'

'Oh, no, the same one, Daddy. You are silly.'

'Don't call your father silly, please, Eustace.'

'Oh, let him, this once. . . . Now take your hat off, Eustace, and bow.'

Eustace did so.

'Now say "Please sir, it wasn't my fault".'

Eustace did not quite catch what his father said.

'Please, sir, it was my fault.'

'No, no. *Wasn't* my fault.'

'Oh, I see, Daddy. Please, sir, it wasn't my fault. But I expect it would have been really. It nearly always is.'

'People will think it is, if you say so. Now say "That's all very well, old chap, but this time it's my turn".'

Eustace repeated the phrase, imitating his father's intonation and *dégagé* man-of-the-world air; then he said:

'What would it be my turn to do, Daddy?'

'Well, what do you think?' When Eustace couldn't think, his father said: 'Ask Minney.'

Minney was mystified but tried to carry it off.

'They do say one good turn deserves another,' she said, shaking her head wisely.

'That's the right answer as far as it goes. Your Aunt knows what I mean, Eustace, but she won't tell us.'

'I don't think you should teach the boy to say such things, Alfred, even in fun. It's an expression they use in a ... in a public house, Eustace.'

Eustace gave his father a look of mingled admiration and reproach which Mr. Cherrington answered with a shrug of his shoulders.

'Between you you'll make an old woman of the boy. Good Lord, at his age, I ...' he broke off, his tone implying that at ten years old he had little left to learn.' Now stand up, Eustace, and don't stick your tummy out.'

Eustace obeyed.

'Shoulders back.'

'Head up.'

'Don't bend those knees.'

'Don't arch your back.'

Each command set up in Eustace a brief spasm ending in rigidity, and soon his neck, back, and shoulders were a network of wrinkles. Miss Cherrington and Minney rushed forward.

'Give me a pin, please Minney, the left shoulder still droops.'

'There's too much fullness at the neck now, Miss Cherrington. Wait a moment, I'll pin it.'

'It's the back that's the worst, Minney. I can get my hand and arm up it — stand still, Eustace, one pin won't be enough — Oh, he hasn't buttoned his coat in front, that's the reason——'

Hands and fingers were everywhere, pinching, patting, and pushing; Eustace swayed like a sapling in a gale. Struggling to keep his balance on the chair, he saw intent eyes flashing round him, leaving gleaming streaks like shooting stars in August. He tried first to resist, then to abandon himself to all the pressures. At last the quickened breathing subsided, there were gasps and sighs, and the ring of electric tension round Eustace suddenly dispersed, like an expiring thunderstorm.

'*That's* better.'

'Really, Minney, you've made quite a remarkable improvement.'

'He looks quite a man now, doesn't he, Miss Cherrington? Oh, I *wish* he could be photographed, just to remind us. If only Hilda would fetch her camera——'

'Hilda!'

There was no answer. They all looked round.

The tableau broke up; and they found themselves staring at an empty room.

'Can I get down now, Daddy?' asked Eustace.

'Yes, run and see if you can find her.'

'She can't get used to the idea of his going away,' said Minney when Eustace had gone.

'No, I'm afraid she'll suffer much more than he will,' Miss Cherrington said.

Mr. Cherrington straightened his tie and shot his cuffs. 'You forget, Sarah, that she's going to school herself.'

'It's not likely I should forget losing my right hand, Alfred.'

After her single contribution to the problems of Eustace's school outfit, Hilda continued to sit at the table, steadily refusing to look in his direction, and trying to make her disapproval felt throughout the room. Unlike Eustace, she had long ago ceased to think that grown-up people were always right, or that if she was angry with them they possessed some special armour of experience, like an extra skin, that made them unable to feel it. She thought they were just as fallible as she was, more so, indeed; and that in this instance they were making a particularly big mistake. Her father's high-spirited raillery, as if the whole thing was a joke, exasperated her. Again, she projected her resentment through the æther, but they all had their backs to her, they were absorbed with Eustace. Presently his father made him stand on a chair. How silly he looked, she thought, like a dummy, totally without the dignity that every human being should possess. All this flattery and attention was making him conceited, and infecting him with the lax standards of the world, which she despised and dreaded. Now he was chattering about his school crest, as if that was anything to be proud of, a device woven on a cap, such as every little boy wore. He was pluming and preening himself, just as if she had never brought him up to know what was truly serious and worthwhile. A wave of bitter feeling broke against her. She could not let this mutilation of a personality go on; she must stop it, and there was only one way, though that way was the hardest she could take and the thought of it filled her with loathing.

Her aunt and Minney were milling round Eustace like dogs over a bone; sticking their noses into him. It was almost disgusting. To get away unnoticed was easy; if she had fired a pistol they would not have heard her. Taking her pencil box which she had left on the sideboard she slouched out of the room. A moment in the drawing-room to collect some writing paper and then she was in the bedroom which she still shared with Eustace. She locked the door and, clearing a space at the corner of the dressing-table, she sat down to write. It never crossed Hilda's mind that her plan could miscarry; she measured its success entirely by the distaste it aroused in her, and that was absolute — the strongest of her many strong feelings. She no more doubted its success than she doubted that, if she threw herself off the cliff, she would be dashed to pieces on the rocks below. In her mind, as she wrote, consoling her, was the image of Eustace, stripped of all his foolish finery, his figure restored to its proper outlines, his mouth cleansed of the puerilities of attempted schoolboy speech, his mind soft and tractable — forever hers.

But the letter did not come easily, partly because Hilda never wrote letters, but chiefly because her inclination battled with her will, and her sense of her destiny warned her against what she was doing. More than once she was on the point of abandoning the letter, but in the pauses of her thoughts she heard the excited murmur of voices in the room below. This letter, if she posted it, would still those voices and send those silly clothes back to Messrs. Faith Brothers. It could do anything, this letter, stop the clock, put it back even, restore to her the Eustace of pre-Miss Fothergill days. Then why did she hesitate? Was it an obscure presentiment that she would regain Eustace but lose herself?

DEAR MR. STAVELEY (she had written),
    Some time ago you asked me and Eustace to visit you, and we were not able to because . . . (Because why?)
    Because I didn't want to go, that was the real reason, and I don't want to now except that it's the only way of keeping Eustace at home.

Then he would see where he stood; she had sacrificed her pride by writing to him at all, she wouldn't throw away the rest by pretending she wanted to see him. Instinctively she knew that however rude and ungracious the letter, he would want to see her just the same.

So we can come any time you like, and would you be quick and ask us because Eustace will go to school, so there's no time to lose.

Yours sincerely,

HILDA CHERRINGTON.

Hilda was staring at the letter when there came a loud knock on the door, repeated twice with growing imperiousness before she had time to answer.

'Yes?' she shouted.

'Oh, Hilda, can I come in?'

'No, you can't.'

'Why not?'

'I'm busy, that's why.'

Eustace's tone gathered urgency and became almost menacing as he said:

'Well, you've got to come down because Daddy said so. He wants you to take my snapshot.'

'I can't. I couldn't anyhow because the film's used up.'

'Shall I go out and buy some? You see, it's very important, it's like a change of life. They want a record of me.'

'They can go on wanting, for all I care.'

'Oh, Hilda, I shan't be here for you to photograph this time next Thursday week.'

'Yes, you will, you see if you're not.'

'Don't you want to remember what I look like?'

'No, I don't. Go away, go away, you're driving me mad.'

She heard his footsteps retreating from the door. Wretchedly she turned to the letter. It looked blurred and misty, and a tear fell on it. Hilda had no blotting paper, and soon the tear-drop, absorbing the ink, began to turn blue at the edges.

'He mustn't see that,' she thought, and taking another sheet began to copy the letter out. 'Dear Mr. Staveley . . .' But she did not like what she had written; it was out of key with her present mood. She took another sheet and began again:

'Dear Mr. Staveley, My brother Eustace and I are now free . . .' That wouldn't do. Recklessly she snatched another sheet, and then another. 'Dear Mr. Staveley, Dear Mr. Staveley.' Strangely enough, with the repetition of the words he seemed to become almost dear; the warmth of dearness crept into her lonely, miserable heart and softly spread there — 'Dear Richard,' she wrote, and then, 'Dear Dick.' 'Dear' meant something to her now; it meant that Dick was someone of whom she could ask a favour without reserve.

DEAR DICK,

I do not know if you will remember me. I am the sister of Eustace Cherrington who was a little boy then and he was ill at your house and when you came to our house to ask after him you kindly invited us to go and see you. But we couldn't because Eustace was too delicate. And you saw us again last summer on the sands and told Eustace about the money Miss Fothergill had left him but it hasn't done him any good, I'm afraid, he still wants to go to school because other boys do but I would much rather he stayed at home and didn't get like them. If you haven't forgotten, you will remember you said I had been a good sister to him, much better than Nancy Steptoe is to Gerald. You said you would like to have me for a sister even when your own sister was there. You may not have heard but he is motherless and I have been a mother to him and it would be a great pity I'm sure you would agree if at this critical state of his development my influence was taken away. You may not remember but if you do you will recollect that you said you would pretend to be a cripple so that I could come and talk to you and play games with you like Eustace did with Miss Fothergill. There is no need for that because we can both walk over quite easily any day and the sooner the better otherwise Eustace will go to school. He is having his Sunday suit tried on at this moment so there is no time to lose. I shall be very pleased to come any time you want me and so will Eustace and we will do anything you want. I am quite brave Eustace says and do not mind strange experiences as long as they are for someone else's good. That is why I am writing to you now.

With my kind regards,
Yours sincerely,
HILDA CHERRINGTON.

She sat for a moment looking at the letter, then with an angry and despairing sigh she crossed out 'sincerely' and wrote 'affectionately'. But the word 'sincerely' was still legible, even to a casual glance; so she again tried to delete it, this time with so much vehemence that her pen almost went through the paper.

Sitting back, she fell into a mood of bitter musing. She saw the letter piling up behind her like a huge cliff, unscalable, taking away the sunlight, cutting off retreat. She dared not read it through but thrust it into an envelope, addressed and stamped it in a daze, and ran downstairs.

Eustace and his father were sitting together; the others had gone. Eustace kept looking at his new suit and fingering it as though to make sure it was real. They both jumped as they heard the door bang, and exchanged man-to-man glances.

'She seems in a great hurry,' said Mr. Cherrington.

'Oh yes, Hilda's always like that. She never gives things time to settle.'

'You'll miss her, won't you?'

'Oh, of *course*,' said Eustace. 'I shall be quite unconscionable.' It was the new suit that said the word; Eustace knew the word was wrong and hurried on.

'Of course, it wouldn't do for her to be with me there, even if she could be, in a boys' school, I mean, because she would see me being, well, you know, tortured, and that would upset her terribly. Besides, the other fellows would think she was bossing me, though I don't.'

'You don't?'

'Oh no, it's quite right at her time of life, but, of course, it couldn't go on always. They would laugh at me, for one thing.'

'If they did,' said Mr. Cherrington, 'it's because they don't know Hilda. Perhaps it's a good thing she's going to school herself.'

'Oh, she *is*?' Eustace had been so wrapped up in his own concerns that he had forgotten the threat which hung over Hilda. But was it a threat or a promise? Ought he to feel glad for her sake or sorry? He couldn't decide, and as it was natural for his mind to feel things as either nice or nasty, which meant right or wrong, of course, but one didn't always know that at the time, he couldn't easily entertain a mixed emotion, and the question of Hilda's future wasn't very real to him.

'Yes,' his father was saying, 'we only got the letter this morning, telling us we could get her in. The school is very full but they are making an exception for her, as a favour to Dr. Waghorn, your head-master.'

'Then it must be a good school,' exclaimed Eustace, 'if it's at all like mine.'

'Yes, St. Willibald's is a pretty good school,' said his father carelessly. 'It isn't so far from yours, either; just round the North Foreland. I shouldn't be surprised if you couldn't see each other with a telescope.'

Eustace's eyes sparkled, then he looked anxious. 'Do you think they'll have a white horse on their hats?' Mr. Cherrington laughed. 'I'm afraid I couldn't tell you that.' Eustace shook his head, and said earnestly:

'I hope they won't try to copy us too much. Boys and girls should be kept separate, shouldn't they?' He thought for a moment and his brow cleared. 'Of course, there was Lady Godiva.'

'I'm afraid I don't see the connection,' said his father.

'Well, she rode on a white horse.' Eustace didn't like being called on to explain what he meant. 'But only with nothing on.' He paused. 'Hilda will have to get some new clothes now, won't she? She'll have to have them tried on.' His eye brightened; he liked to see Hilda freshly adorned.

'Yes, and there's no time to lose. I've spoken to your aunt, Eustace, and she agrees with me that you're the right person to break the news to Hilda. We think it'll come better from you. Companions in adversity and all that, you know.'

Eustace's mouth fell open.

'Oh, Daddy, I couldn't. She'd—I don't know what she might not do. She's so funny with me now, anyway. She might almost go off her rocker.'

'Not if you approach her tactfully.'

'Well, I'll try,' said Eustace. 'Perhaps the day after to-morrow.'

'No, tell her this afternoon.'

'Fains I, Daddy. Couldn't *you*? It *is* your afternoon off.'

'Yes, and I want a little peace. Listen, isn't that Hilda coming in? Now run away and get your jumping-poles and go down on the beach.'

They heard the front door open and shut; it wasn't quite a slam but near enough to show that Hilda was in the state of mind in which things slipped easily from her fingers.

Each with grave news to tell the other, and neither knowing how, they started for the beach. Eustace's jumping-pole was a stout rod of bamboo, prettily ringed and patterned with spots like a leopard. By stretching his hand up he could nearly reach the top; he might have been a bear trying to climb up a ragged staff. As they walked across the green that sloped down to the cliff he planted the pole in front of him and took practice leaps over any obstacle that showed itself—a brick it might be, or a bit of fencing, or the cart-track which ran just below the square. Hilda's jumping-pole was made of wood, and much longer than Eustace's; near to the end it tapered slightly and then swelled out again, like a broom-handle. It was the kind of pole used by real pole-jumpers at athletic events, and she did not play about with it but saved her energy for when it should be needed. The January sun still spread a pearly radiance round them; it hung over the sea, quite low down, and was already beginning to cast fiery reflections on the water. The day was not cold for January, and Eustace was well wrapped up, but his bare knees felt the chill rising from the ground, and he said to Hilda:

'Of course, trousers would be much warmer.'

She made no answer but quickened her pace so that Eustace had to run between his jumps. He had never known her so preoccupied before.

In silence they reached the edge of the cliff and the spiked railing at the head of the concrete staircase. A glance showed them the sea was coming in. It had that purposeful look and the sands were dry in front of it. A line of foam, like a border of white braid, was curling round the outermost rocks.

Except for an occasional crunch their black beach shoes made no sound on the sand-strewn steps. Eustace let his pole slide from one to the other, pleased with the rhythmic tapping.

'Oh, don't do that, Eustace. You have no pity on my poor nerves.'

'I'm so sorry, Hilda.'

But a moment later, changing her mind as visibly as if she were passing an apple from one hand to the other, she said, 'You can, if you like. I don't really mind.'

Obediently Eustace resumed his tapping but it now gave him the feeling of something done under sufferance and was not so much fun. He was quite glad when they came to the bottom of the steps and the tapping stopped.

Here, under the cliff, the sand was pale and fine and powdery; it lay in craters inches deep and was useless for jumping, for the pole could get no purchase on such a treacherous foundation; it turned in mid air and the jumper came down heavily on one side or the other. So they hurried down to the beach proper, where the sand was brown and close and firm, and were soon among the smooth, seaweed-coated rocks which bestrewed the shore like a vast colony of sleeping seals.

Eustace was rapidly and insensibly turning into a chamois or an ibex when he checked himself and remembered that, for the task that lay before him, some other pretence might be more helpful. An ibex *could* break the news to a sister-ibex that she was to go to boarding school in a few days' time, but there would be nothing tactful, subtle, or imaginative in such a method of disclosure; he might almost as well tell her himself. They had reached their favourite jumping ground and he took his stand on a rock, wondering and perplexed.

'Let's begin with the Cliffs of Dover,' he said. The Cliffs of Dover, so called because a sprinkling of barnacles gave it a whitish look, was a somewhat craggy boulder about six feet away. Giving a good foothold it was their traditional first hole, and not only Hilda but Eustace could clear the distance easily. When he had alighted on it, feet together, with the soft springy pressure that was so intimately satisfying, he pulled his

pole out of the sand and stepped down to let Hilda do her jump. Hilda
landed on the Cliffs of Dover with the negligent grace of an alighting
eagle; and, as always, Eustace, who had a feeling for style, had to fight
back a twinge of envy.

'Now the Needles,' he said. 'You go first.' The Needles was both
more precipitous and further away, and there was only one spot on it
where you could safely make a landing. Eustace occasionally muffed it,
but Hilda never; what was his consternation therefore to see her swerve
in mid-leap, fumble for a foothold, and slide off on to the sand.

'Oh, hard luck, sir!' exclaimed Eustace. The remark fell flat. He
followed her in silence and made a rather heavy-footed but successful
landing.

'You're one up,' said Hilda. They scored as in golf over a course of
eighteen jumps, and when Hilda had won usually played the bye before
beginning another round on a different set of rocks. Thus, the miniature
but exciting landscape of mountain, plain and lake (for many of the
rocks stood in deep pools, starfish-haunted), was continually
changing.

Eustace won the first round at the nineteenth rock. He could hardly
believe it. Only once before had he beaten Hilda, and that occasion was
so long ago that all he could remember of it was the faint, sweet feeling
of triumph. In dreams, on the other hand, he was quite frequently victorious. The experience then was poignantly delightful, utterly beyond
anything obtainable in daily life. But he got a whiff of it now. Muffled
to a dull suggestion of itself, like some dainty eaten with a heavy cold,
it was still the divine elixir.

Hilda did not seem to realize how momentous her defeat was, nor,
happily, did she seem to mind. Could she have lost on purpose? Eustace
wondered. She was thoughtful and abstracted. Eustace simply had to
say something.

'Your sandshoes are very worn, Hilda,' he said. 'They slipped every
time. You *must* get another pair.'

She gave him a rather sad smile, and he added tentatively:

'I expect the ibex sheds its hoofs like its antlers. You're just going
through one of those times.'

'Oh, so *that's* what we're playing,' said Hilda, but there was a touch
of languor in her manner, as well as scorn.

'Yes, but we can play something else,' said Eustace. Trying to think
of a new pretence, he began to make scratches with his pole on the
smooth sand. The words 'St. Ninian's' started to take shape. Quickly he

obliterated them with his foot, but they had given him an idea. They had given Hilda an idea, too.

He remarked as they moved to their new course, 'I might be a boy going to school for the first time.'

'You might be,' replied Hilda, 'but you're not.'

Eustace was not unduly disconcerted.

'Well, let's pretend I am, and then we can change the names of the rocks, to suit.'

The incoming tide had reached their second centre, and its advancing ripples were curling round the bases of the rocks.

'Let's re-christen this one,' said Eustace, poised on the first tee. 'You kick off. It used to be "Aconcagua",' he reminded her.

'All right,' said Hilda, 'call it Cambo.'

Vaguely Eustace wondered why she had chosen the name of their house, but he was so intent on putting ideas into her head that he did not notice she was trying to put them into his.

'Bags I this one for St. Ninian's,' he ventured, naming a not too distant boulder. Hilda winced elaborately.

'Mind you don't fall off,' was all she said.

'Oh, no. It's my honour, isn't it?' asked Eustace diffidently. He jumped.

Perhaps it was the responsibility of having chosen a name unacceptable to Hilda, perhaps it was just the perversity of Fate; anyhow, he missed his aim. His feet skidded on the slippery seaweed and when he righted himself he was standing in water up to his ankles.

'Now we must go home,' said Hilda. In a flash Eustace saw his plan going to ruin. There would be no more rocks to name; he might have to tell her the news outright.

'Oh, please not, Hilda, please not. Let's have a few more jumps. They make my feet warm, they really do. Besides, there's something I want to say to you.'

To his astonishment Hilda agreed at once.

'I oughtn't to let you,' she said, 'but I'll put your feet into mustard and hot water, privately, in the bathroom.'

'Crikey! That would be fun.'

'And I have something to say to you, too.'

'Is it something nice?'

'You'll think so,' said Hilda darkly.

'Tell me now.'

'No, afterwards. Only you'll have to pretend to be a boy who isn't going to school. Now hurry up.'

They were both standing on Cambo with the water swirling round them.

'Say "Fains I" if you'd like me to christen the next one,' said Eustace hopefully. 'It used to be called the Inchcape Rock.'

'No,' said Hilda slowly, and in a voice so doom-laden that anyone less preoccupied than Eustace might have seen her drift. 'I'm going to call it "Anchorstone Hall".'

'Good egg!' said Eustace. 'Look, there's Dick standing on it. Mind you don't knock him off!'

Involuntarily Hilda closed her eyes against Dick's image. She missed her take-off and dropped a foot short of the rock, knee-deep in water.

'Oh, *poor* Hilda!' Eustace cried, aghast.

But wading back to the rock she turned to him an excited, radiant face.

'Now it will be mustard and water for us both.'

'How ripping!' Eustace wriggled with delight. 'That'll be something to tell them at St. Ninian's. I'm sure none of the other men have sisters who dare jump into the whole North Sea!'

'Quick, quick!' said Hilda. 'Your turn.'

Anchorstone Hall was by now awash, but Eustace landed easily. The fear of getting his feet wet being removed by the simple process of having got them wet, he felt gloriously free and ready to tell anyone anything.

'All square!' he announced. 'All square and one to play. Do you know what I am going to call this one?' He pointed to a forbiddingly bare, black rock, round which the water surged, and when Hilda quite graciously said she didn't, he added:

'But first you must pretend to be a girl who's going to school.'

'Anything to pacify you,' Hilda said.

'Now I'll tell you. It's St. Willibald's. Do you want to know why?'

'Not specially,' said Hilda. 'It sounds such a silly name. Why should Willie be bald?' When they had laughed their fill at this joke, Eustace said:

'It's got something to do with you. It's . . . well, you'll know all about it later on.'

'I hope I shan't,' said Hilda loftily. 'It isn't worth the trouble of a pretence. Was this all you were going to tell me?'

'Yes, you see it's the name of your school.'

Hilda stared at him. 'My school? What do you mean, my school? Me a school-mistress? You must be mad.'

Eustace had not foreseen this complication.

'Not a school-mistress, Hilda,' he gasped. 'You wouldn't be old enough yet. No, a schoolgirl, like I'm going to be a schoolboy.'

'A schoolgirl?' repeated Hilda. 'A schoolgirl?' she echoed in a still more tragic voice. 'Who said so?' she challenged him.

'Well, Daddy did. They all did, while you were upstairs. Daddy told me to tell you. It's quite settled.'

Thoughts chased each other across Hilda's face, thoughts that were incomprehensible to Eustace. They only told him that she was not as angry as he thought she would be, perhaps not angry at all. He couldn't imagine why she wasn't, but the relief was overwhelming.

'We shall go away almost on the same day,' he said. 'Won't that be fun? I mean it would be much worse if one of us didn't. And we shall be quite near to each other, in Kent. It's called the Garden of England. That's a nice name. You're glad, aren't you?'

Her eyes, swimming with happy tears, told him she was; but he could hardly believe it, and her trembling lips vouchsafed no word. He felt he must distract her.

'You were going to tell me something, Hilda. What was it?'

She looked at him enigmatically, and the smile playing on her lips restored them to speech.

'Oh, that? That was nothing.'

'But it must have been something,' Eustace persisted. 'You said it was something I should like. Please tell me.'

'It doesn't matter now,' she said, 'now that I am going to school.' Her voice deepened and took on its faraway tone. 'You will never know what I meant to do for you — how I nearly sacrificed *all* my happiness.'

'Will anyone know?' asked Eustace.

He saw he had made a false step. Hilda turned pale and a look of terror came into her eyes, all the more frightening because Hilda was never frightened. So absorbed had she been by the horrors that the letter would lead to, so thankful that the horrors were now removed, that she had forgotten the letter itself. Yes. Someone would know. . . .

Timidly Eustace repeated his question.

The pole bent beneath Hilda's weight and her knuckles went as white as her face.

'Oh, don't nag me, Eustace! Can't you see? . . . What's the time?' she asked sharply. 'I've forgotten my watch.'

'But you never forget it, Hilda.'

'Fool, I tell you I *have* forgotten it! What's the time?'

Eustace's head bent towards the pocket in his waistline where his watch was lodged, and he answered with maddening slowness, anxious to get the time exactly right:

'One minute to four.'

'And when does the post go?'

'A quarter past, But you know that better than I do, Hilda.'

'Idiot, they might have changed it.' She stiffened. The skies might fall but Eustace must be given his instructions.

'Listen, I've got something to do. You go straight home, slowly, mind, and tell them to get the bath water hot and ask Minney for the mustard.'

'How topping, Hilda! What fun we shall have.'

'Yes, it must be boiling. I shall hurry on in front of you, and you mustn't look to see which way I go.'

'Oh, no, Hilda.'

'Here's my pole. You can jump with it if you're careful. I shan't be long.'

'But, Hilda——'

There was no answer. She was gone, and he dared not turn round to call her.

A pole trailing from either hand, Eustace fixed his eyes on the waves and conscientiously walked backwards, so that he should not see her. Presently he stumbled against a stone and nearly fell. Righting himself he resumed his crab-like progress, but more slowly than before. Why had Hilda gone off like that? He could not guess, and it was a secret into which he must not pry. His sense of the inviolability of Hilda's feelings was a *sine qua non* of their relationship.

The tracks traced by the two poles, his and Hilda's, made a pattern that began to fascinate him. Parallel straight lines, he knew, were such that even if they were produced to infinity they could not meet. The idea of infinity pleased Eustace, and he dwelt on it for some time. But these lines were not straight; they followed a serpentine course, bulging at times and then narrowing, like a boa-constrictor that has swallowed a donkey. Perhaps with a little manipulation they could be made to meet.

He drew the lines closer. Yes, it looked as though they might converge. But would it be safe to try to make them when a law of Euclid said they couldn't?

A backward glance satisfied Hilda that Eustace was following her instructions. Her heart warmed to him. How obedient he was, in spite of everything. The tumult in her feelings came back, disappointment, relief, and dread struggling with each other. Disappointment that her plan had miscarried; relief that it had miscarried; dread that she would be too late to spare herself an unbearable humiliation.

She ran, taking a short cut across the sands, going by the promenade where the cliffs were lower. She flashed past the Bank with its polished granite pillars, so much admired by Eustace. Soon she was in the heart of the town.

The big hand of the post office clock was leaning on the quarter. Breathless, she went in. Behind the counter stood a girl she did not know.

'Please can you give me back the letter I posted this afternoon?'

'I'm afraid not, Miss. We're not allowed to.'

'Please do it this once. It's very important that the letter shouldn't go.'

The girl — she was not more than twenty herself — stared at the beautiful, agitated face, imperious, unused to pleading, the tall figure, the bosom that rose and fell, and it scarcely seemed to her that Hilda was a child.

'I could ask the postmaster.'

'No, please don't do that, I'd rather you didn't. It's a letter that I . . . regret having written.' A wild look came into Hilda's eye; she fumbled in her pocket.

'If I pay a fine may I have it back?'

How pretty she is, the girl thought. She seems thoroughly upset. Something stirred in her, and she moved towards the door of the letter box.

'I oughtn't to, you know. Who would the letter be to?'

'It's a gentleman.' Hilda spoke with an effort.

I thought so, the girl said to herself; and she unlocked the door of the letter box.

'What would the name be?'

The name was on Hilda's lips, but she checked it and stood speechless.

'Couldn't you let me look myself?' she said.

'Oh, I'm afraid that would be against regulations. They might give me the sack.'

'Oh, please, just this once. I . . . I shall never write to him again.'

The assistant's heart was touched. 'You made a mistake, then,' she said.

'Yes,' breathed Hilda. 'I don't know . . .' she left the sentence unfinished.

'You said something you didn't mean?'

'Yes,' said Hilda.

'And you think he might take it wrong?'

'Yes.'

The assistant dived into the box and brought out about twenty letters. She laid them on the counter in front of Hilda.

'Quick! quick!' she said. 'I'm not looking.'

Hilda knew the shape of the envelope. In a moment the letter was in her pocket. Looking at the assistant she panted; and the assistant panted slightly too. They didn't speak for a moment; then the assistant said:

'You're very young, dear, aren't you?'

Hilda drew herself up. 'Oh, no, I've turned fourteen.'

'You're sure you're doing the right thing? You're not acting impulsive-like? If you're really fond of him . . .'

'Oh, no,' said Hilda. 'I'm not . . . I'm not.' A tremor ran through her. 'I must go now.'

The assistant bundled the letters back into the box. There was a sound behind them: the postman had come in.

'Good evening, Miss,' he said.

'Good evening,' said the assistant languidly. 'I've been waiting about for you. You don't half keep people waiting, do you?'

'There's them that works, and them that waits,' said the postman.

The assistant tossed her head.

'There's some do neither,' she said tartly, and then, turning in a business-like way to Hilda:

'Is there anything else, Miss?'

'Nothing further to-day,' said Hilda, rather haughtily. 'Thank you very much,' she added.

Outside the post office, in the twilight, her dignity deserted her. She broke into a run, but her mind outstripped her, surging, exultant.

'I shall never see him now,' she thought, 'I shall never see him now,' and the ecstasy, the relief, the load off her mind, were such as she might have felt had she loved Dick Staveley and been going to meet him.

Softly she let herself into the house. The dining-room was no use: it had a gas fire. She listened at the drawing-room door. No sound. She tiptoed into the fire-stained darkness, crossed the hearthrug and dropped the letter into the reddest cleft among the coals. It did not catch at once so she took the poker to it, driving it into the heart of the heat. A flame sprang up, and at the same moment she heard a movement, and turning, saw the fire reflected in her father's eyes.

'Hullo, Hilda — you startled me. I was having a nap. Burning something?'

'Yes,' said Hilda, poised for flight.

'A love letter, I expect.'

'Oh, no, Daddy; people don't write love letters at my age.'

'At your age——' began Mr. Charrington. But he couldn't remember, and anyhow it wouldn't do to tell his daughter that at her age he had already written a love letter.

'Must be time for tea,' he said, yawning. 'Where's Eustace?'

As though in answer they heard a thud on the floor above, and the sound of water pouring into the bath.

'That's him,' cried Hilda. 'I promised him I would put his feet into mustard and water. He won't forgive me if I don't.'

She ran upstairs into the steam and blurred visibility, the warmth, the exciting sounds and comforting smells of the little bathroom. At first she couldn't see Eustace; the swirls of luminous vapour hid him; then they parted and disclosed him, sitting on the white curved edge of the bath with his back to the water and his legs bare to the knee, above which his combinations and his knickerbockers had been neatly folded back, no doubt by Minney's practised hand.

'Oh, there you are, Hilda!' he exclaimed. 'Isn't it absolutely spiffing! The water's quite boiling. I only turned it on when you came in. I wish it was as hot as boiling oil—boiling water isn't, you know.'

'How much mustard did you put in?' asked Hilda.

'Half a tin. Minney said she couldn't spare any more.'

'Well, turn round and put your feet in,' Hilda said.

'Yes. Do you think I ought to take off my knickers, too? You see I only got wet as far as my ankles. I should have to take off my combinations.'

Hilda considered. 'I don't think you need this time.'

Eustace swivelled round and tested the water with his toe.

'Ooo!'

'Come on, be brave.'

'Yes, but you must put your feet in too. It won't be half the fun if you don't. Besides, you said you would, Hilda.' In his anxiety to share the experience with her he turned round again. 'Please! You got much wetter than I did.'

'I got warm running. Besides, it's only salt water. Salt water doesn't give you a cold.'

'Oh, but my water was salt, too.'

'You're different,' said Hilda. Then, seeing the look of acute disappointment on his face, she added, 'Well, just to please you.'

Eustace wriggled delightedly, and, as far as he dared, bounced up and down on the bath edge.

'Take off your shoes and stockings, then,' It was delicious to give Hilda orders. Standing stork-like, first on one foot, then on the other, Hilda obeyed.

'Now come and sit by me. It isn't very safe, take care you don't lose your balance.'

Soon they were sitting side by side, looking down into the water. The clouds of steam rising round them seemed to shut off the outside world. Eustace looked admiringly at Hilda's long slim legs.

'I didn't fill the bath any fuller,' he said, in a low voice, 'because of the marks. It might be dangerous, you know.'

Hilda looked at the bluish chips in the enamel, which spattered the sides of the bath. Eustace's superstitions about them, and his fears of submerging them, were well known to her.

'They won't let you do that at school,' she said.

'Oh, there won't be any marks at school. A new system of plumbing and sanitarization was installed last year. The prospectus said so. That would mean new baths, of course. New baths don't have marks. Your school may be the same, only the prospectus didn't say so. I expect baths don't matter so much for girls.'

'Why not?'

'They're cleaner, anyway. Besides, they wash.' Eustace thought of washing and having a bath as two quite different, almost unconnected things. 'And I don't suppose they'll let us put our feet in mustard and water.'

'Why not?' repeated Hilda.

'Oh, to harden us, you know. Boys have to be hard. If they did, it would be for a punishment, not fun like this. . . . Just put your toe in, Hilda.'

Hilda flicked the water with her toe, far enough to start a ripple, and then withdrew it.

'It's still a bit hot. Let's wait a minute.'

'Yes,' said Eustace. 'It would spoil *everything* if we turned on the cold water.'

They sat for a moment in silence. Eustace examined Hilda's toes. They were really as pretty as fingers. His own were stunted and shapeless, meant to be decently covered.

'Now, both together!' he cried.

In went their feet. The concerted splash was magnificent, but the agony was almost unbearable.

'Put your arm round me, Hilda!'

'Then you put yours round me, Eustace!'

As they clung together their feet turned scarlet, and the red dye ran up far above the water-level almost to their knees. But they did not move, and slowly the pain began to turn into another feeling, a smart still, but wholly blissful.

'Isn't it wonderful?' cried Eustace. 'I could never have felt it without you!'

Hilda said nothing, and soon they were swishing their feet to and fro in the cooling water. The supreme moment of trial and triumph had gone by; other thoughts, not connected with their ordeal, began to slide into Eustace's mind.

'Were you in time to do it?' he asked.

'Do what?'

'Well, what you were going to do when you left me on the sands.'

'Oh, that,' said Hilda indifferently. 'Yes, I was just in time.' She thought a moment, and added: 'But don't ask me what it was, because I shan't ever tell you.'

TWO FOR THE RIVER

TWO FOR THE RIVER

MID-AUGUST was a dull time in my garden – the drought had seen to that. Flowers there were, but even the hardiest were only half their normal size; the Japanese anemones looked like shillings, not half-crowns. Because the garden lay beside the river, and sometimes, in wet seasons, under it, people thought the subsoil must be moist, but it was not; the rain ran off the steep slope without sinking in, the river drained the ground without irrigating it.

But the river-banks had just been in full glory, two interminable winding borders on which grew willow-weed and loosestrife, the lilac clusters of hemp agrimony, deep yellow ragwort, lemon-yellow chickweed, the peeping purple of the woody nightshade, the orange drops of the ranunculus, the youthful, tender teazle-cones of palest pink contrasting with their hard, brown, dried-up predecessors of the year before – and, a newcomer to the district but very much at home, the tall white balsam. Did the other flowers realize their danger from this rampant stranger with its innocent baby-face? Did they foresee the day when it, and only it, would occupy their standing room, making a close-set jungle through which a man could hardly force his way – while the plants, if it was their shooting season, popped off their pods at him? Nor would the invasion stop at the river-bank; it would follow up its conquest through the meadows. And how would the fishermen fare, who even now had to hack out from the massed vegetation steps and nests for themselves on competition days? Only the water-lilies would be safe, and the armies of reeds and rushes – the sword-shaped ones of yellow-green, the round pike-shafts of bluish-green, tufted with pennons – for they would have the water to protect them.

On the garden and river-bank alike autumn had already laid its spoiling finger, bringing languor and disarray to the luxuriance of summer, making it flop and sprawl. To this the river itself bore witness, for on its grey-green surface floated the earliest victims of the year's decline, yellow willow leaves tip-tilted like gondolas, that twirled and sported in the breeze, until the greedy water sucked them under.

But the flowers grew farther upstream. On my stretch of the river there were none; trees overhung it on both sides, on mine a copper beech, a mountain ash, a square-cut bay-tree, a silver birch, a box elder, and in the corner by the boathouse, threatening its foundations, a dome-capped sycamore. A low stone wall divided the river from the garden, which was narrow for its length and sloping steeply to the lawn; and from the outward-curving terrace in front of the house you could see the river, a mirror broken here and there by tree-trunks, and darkened by the reflections of the trees on the farther bank; or maybe by the image of a cow, suspended in mid-water upside-down, the shadowy feet seeming almost to touch the real feet. Sometimes these reflections were clearer than the things reflected, so little current was there in the summer, or breeze to ruffle them. But faithful likenesses though they were, they had no colour, except a darker shade of olive-green. The river imposed its own colour on everything it looked at, even the sky.

'Shall I bathe?' I thought. Flanking the boathouse was a flight of steps, ending in a large square flagstone, only a few inches above the water level. Ideal for a dive! And the water was deep almost at once, twenty feet deep, some said; I hadn't plumbed it. It did invite me. I laid aside my pen, for I was writing in the open air, a thing I seldom do — the open air has so many distractions, so many claims on one's attention: the river itself, for instance! But no, it was too late to bathe: the August sun hung over Follet Down, and my circulation wasn't what it used to be. Tomorrow at midday, perhaps . . .

As I was taking up my pen again, with the dull, cold sense of self-congratulation that an unwilling act of prudence sometimes brings, I saw a ripple spreading on the river, convex at first, then slightly concave. It was the swans, angry as usual. What trouble those odious birds had given me! He, the cob, was much the worse of the two; she was a nasty creature, with a supercilious, inquisitive expression, but she only aided and abetted him. He was a demon. An inveterate oarsman with a large experience of swans, I had often thought that this one was possessed: Jupiter in disguise perhaps, or not even in disguise. He seemed to think I had designs on her. A Leda-complex! I shouldn't have thought of bathing if I'd known he was about, for he had a bad record with bathers. And with boaters a worse one; but I was his favourite target.

He had only to see me in my skiff to go for me. It was a slender craft, hard to trim and easily upset: if I had had hair enough to matter I should have parted it in the middle. His methods of attack varied from in-fighting, when he would try to get his wing under the boat, to dive-bombing tactics. These were still more alarming. Spying me from afar he would come after me, skimming over the water and then, when I was bracing myself to take the impact of this living rocket, subside be-hind me in a smother of foam. The four-barred iron seat in the stern defended me: he dared not risk collision with it. But he had found a way round it, and now his system was to by-pass the stern and try to land on one of the sculls. So far he had missed his mark, but if he hit it . . .

What was he up to now? With snaky neck pressed down between outward-curving wings held taut for flight, he was forcing his way up-stream with powerful thrusts, using his feet for oars, as the Greek poet said. Behind him at a discreet distance came his mate, paddling fever-ishly, but with neck erect, not battened down as his was. Had they seen another swan perhaps, an interloper? For this was *their* reach of the river, as it had been mine, before they came, and they would not tolerate another swan on it.

They passed on, out of sight, but his baleful, malignant presence lingered with me; I have never seen, in any creature, such devilish in-tent as flashed from that wicked eye. Swollen with anger, he looked twice the size of other swans. Had it become a struggle for mastery be-tween us? Did he embody some spirit of opposition to me, that the place had? I loved it, but since I bought it, eleven years ago, so many vexatious and frustrating things had happened. . . .

Now all was peace. The river had regained its glassy surface and re-stored the sense of quietude which the contemplation of still water nearly always gives me. Just as the sudden cessation of a noise—a dog barking or someone hammering—induces sleep, so did the let-up in my swan-resentment prepare my mind for more congenial guests. Now for some real work.

Or so I promised myself, and rested my elbows on the iron table, painted green to match the garden. But my musings were once more interrupted before they became fertile. Another ripple spread across the river, and before I had time to wonder if it heralded another swan, I heard the sound of voices, a man's voice and a woman's. This didn't surprise me. Boats, other than mine, were infrequent on the river, be-cause of the weir, half a mile below, that protected it from the populous reach used by the townspeople. But hardier spirits sometimes lifted their boats round the weir and went on upstream into the unspoilt countryside.

Instead of carrying on past me, as I thought they would, the voices seemed to become stationary, and changed their tone. From being desultory they became animated; from being animated, argumentative. Which of the two prevailed I still don't know, but it was the man who called out to me.

'Sir!'

I was only a stone's throw from them, and not many feet above them, but as I am a little deaf I got up from my table, rather unwillingly, and went down the steps through the rockery and across the lawn in the direction the sounds came from. Leaning over the wall I saw them, in a smart, light new canoe, the man, who sat behind, holding on to the big flagstone that served as my diving-board.

I suppose they hadn't seen or heard me coming, for they looked up as if I was an apparition. They were both very fair, in their late twenties, I should guess, and both very good-looking—she especially. She had a longish face, deep blue eyes, and corn-gold hair piled high on her head. They were both wearing white.

He was the first to speak.

'Sir,' he said again (perhaps it was a tribute to my age), 'you must excuse us, but we wondered if you would let us use your landing-stage to change places in the boat? You see we are not skilled canoeists, and my wife is rather tired of paddling always on one side. We mustn't change places in mid-stream, I'm told. If you would allow us to land for a moment——'

His pleasant voice, her questioning, self-deprecatory smile, and their unassuming air (boating brings out rowdyism in so many people) made me take to them.

'Of course,' I said. 'But aren't you tired, having come all the way from Warmwell? Why not stop and have a drink, one for the river, before you go on?'

They exchanged a doubtful look. Does the prospect bore them? I thought, instantly suspicious. But the woman said:

'You're very kind. We'd like to.'

'Let me give you a hand,' I said. 'You mustn't rock the boat too much'—a timely warning, as it turned out, for they made a very awkward landing. 'I told you we were amateurs,' the man said. 'In fact we only bought this canoe yesterday. We're on our honeymoon; it's almost the first thing we've bought since we were married! We're staying in Warmwell to house-hunt,' he went on, 'and the river looked so inviting with the swans by Paulet Bridge, and all—we thought it would be fun to have our own boat, and go prospecting. That's what brought us here! But it's an awkward piece of luggage to travel with. Perhaps we shall give it away. But I hope——'

By this time we were half-way across the lawn. They fitted their long strides to mine; their graceful, white-clad figures were so tall I wondered how they tucked themselves into the boat.

We had drinks in my study, a darkish room in spite of its three windows. The creepers I once planted had rampaged. The jessamine looked in at one window, too intrusively, and the other two were darkened by the clematis which dripped from the veranda in untidy loops and streamers. But my visitors were enchanted.

'So this is where you work?' the woman asked.

'Yes, but how did you know?'

She looked towards my disorderly writing-desk, and smiling, shook her head.

'I recognize the signs . . . Besides——' she caught her husband's eye and stopped.

While I was pouring out the drinks a sort of telepathic communication stirred in me.

'Did you come out looking for a house?' I ventured.

Again they exchanged glances.

'In a way,' the man said. 'The agent told us——'

'Yes?'

'That there was a house on the river that might be for sale. We wondered if we could spot it.'

'Was that why you stopped and hailed me?'

They both coloured.

'No,' he said. 'We genuinely wanted to change places, for Sylvia was getting tired. My name is Harry,' he said hastily. 'Harry Marchmont. We're not the impostors that perhaps we look! But we did just think——'

'That this house was for sale?'

He nodded.

'Well, I'm the owner of it,' I said, 'and I can assure you that it isn't.'

I spoke more stiffly than I meant to, but one or two other people had been sent by agents to make the same inquiry. Why had it got about that I meant to sell the house? They blushed again, more deeply than before.

'Oh, we are so sorry,' Mrs. Marchmont said, while her husband made inarticulate noises of apology. 'Of course there are several other houses by the river——'

'But not owned by a writer,' said I, giving their embarrassment no time to wear off, 'and not quite on the river. They are cut off from it by a tow-path.'

'I'm sure they're not half so nice as this one,' Mrs. Marchmont said. She drained her glass. 'Now, Harry, we must be getting on our way, and not waste any more of Mr. . . . Mr. Minchin's time.'

So they knew my name, too.

We were all on our feet, the smiles of good-bye stiffening our faces, when to my great surprise I heard myself saying:

'But as you're here, won't you look over the house?'

In some confusion, protesting that they mustn't, that it was an imposition, that they had already trespassed too much on my kindness, they agreed.

We made a tour of the house, and they professed themselves delighted with everything they saw. At first their comments were strictly those of sightseers. 'Oh, what a lovely view! And that church tower between the trees on the hill! Has anybody painted it?' But soon their reactions grew more personal, and sharpened by the excitement of possible possession. 'This room would be perfect for a nursery, wouldn't it? Just put bars across the windows and a little gate outside to shut off the staircase . . . Are you married, Mr. Minchin?'

I was used to this question from women who were strangers to me. 'No.'

'Do you live in this big house all alone?'

'I'm overhoused, but several people live here; they help me in various ways, and I give them house-room. On the whole they seem contented.'

What uphill work it was, in these days, trying to run a private house! They were anachronisms, really. But the depression I sometimes felt about my domestic situation, which was so much easier than most people's, came of having no one at hand to grumble to, no confidant. Whereas this couple——

Mrs. Marchmont was saying: 'Of course we shouldn't want to alter anything. A bathroom here or there, perhaps . . .'

'My dear, you mustn't talk like that. It's Mr. Minchin's house, and he doesn't want to sell it.'

'Of course not, Mr. Minchin, I was just day-dreaming. But what would you do with all your beautiful things?'

'Supposing I sold it?'

'There I go again,' she said, all penitence. 'Of course you must keep it—it's such a perfect setting for them. We should only wreck it, shouldn't we, Harry?'

Embarrassed, he mumbled something.

My beautiful things! They had seemed so once, when one by one I had collected them: but how seldom had the glow of acquisition lasted from one side of the counter to the other! How soon one took them all for granted! Whereas the possessions of the mind!—It was the onset of old age, no doubt: once I hadn't felt that way. Nor would a young couple coming fresh to a place, with eyes and hearts alive to pretty things, feel that way, either.

We were back in my study.

'Well, it has been a great experience,' said Sylvia, the spokesman of the two, 'a great privilege, and one we didn't deserve. We ought to have been turned out on our ears. Instead, we've had a glimpse of Paradise.'

'It's odd you should say that,' I said, 'for "Paradise Paddock" is the name of the house.'

'What an unusual name, and how appropriate! Thank you so much, Mr. Minchin. Now Harry——'

She held her hand out, and I said:

'Just one more for the river?'

They laughed and Mr. Marchmont said: 'There's no law against being drunk in charge of a boat.'

We drank, and his wife said: 'Here's good luck, Mr. Minchin. You must never, never, never sell your house.'

The words struck my heart like a knell, and involuntarily I said:

'Supposing I wanted to sell it, would you buy it?'

'But you don't want to sell it.'

'But if I did?'

The tension in my feelings must have spread to the room: it seemed to listen for their answer.

'If you did, we should be buyers,' said Mr. Marchmont, quietly. 'Provided, of course . . .'

'That we could afford it,' put in his wife.

I felt they could; you didn't buy a canoe to give away if you were not well off.

'But where would you put all your lovely things?'

'They could go with the house.'

'Do you really mean that?' they asked me, almost in one breath.

'I think I do, I think I do, I must have time to think,' I babbled.

'Of course you must, of course you must.' They looked at me with extreme concern, as if I had been taken ill: but hope and joy sparkled in their eyes.

'Imagine it,' said Mrs. Marchmont, rapt, ecstatic, as if she saw a vision. 'Imagine living here!'

More to gain time than for any other reason I said:

'Another for the river!'

But this time they refused.

'Two must be our limit.'

'Telephone me from your hotel when you get back,' I said, 'and I'll let you know, one way or the other.'

Their faces fell at the uncertainty, and my heart missed a beat. Could I draw back? Had I committed myself?

'I'll see you safely off the premises,' I said.

At that they smiled, and I smiled with them. But whereas I smiled in relief, that I could put off, for the moment, my decision, they smiled because their minds were made up, and they thought mine was, too. Victory! Paradise Paddock was within their grasp. It was slipping out of mine; was that defeat?

Twilight was falling when I escorted them to the landing-stage.

'Let me go first, the steps are a bit tricky here.'

When we were safely on the lawn I said:

'You ring me up—or shall I ring you?'

'Oh, we'll ring you up,' Mr. Marchmont said. 'You see we don't know when we shall be back.'

We had reached the second flight of steps, that led from the garden wall to the landing-stage.

'Oh look, the boat is still here!' cried Mrs. Marchmont.

'Why,' said her husband, 'did you think it would have floated away?'

'I have no faith in your knots,' his wife replied.

We laughed at this, no doubt thinking of the marriage knot. I bent down to steady the canoe: its satin-smooth surface pleased my fingers: I had little or no experience of canoes. Mrs. Marchmont lowered herself into the back seat; he scrambled into the front one. The paddles dipped and gleamed.

'But you are going the wrong way!'

They back-watered clumsily towards me.

'We thought we'd see a little more of the river,' he said.

'You won't find another house on it,' I warned them.

'We don't want to! We don't want to!'

'When you come by again on your way back, give me a shout,' I said, 'and I'll tell you what I've decided—if I've decided anything.'

'Please let it be yes!'

They tried to wave; the frail craft lurched and teetered, and they were off. It was only as I saw them disappearing, their white-clad figures shining on the shadowed water, their busy paddles digging puddles in it, that I was reminded of the swans.

Back at my writing-table on the terrace a black mood settled on me. I had had many such, sometimes without cause; but this one had a cause: the house itself was accusing me. Every window was an eye that looked reproach, a speaking eye that said, 'Why are you deserting me? You have been happy here, as happy as your temperament would let you be! It was love at first sight, wasn't it? Didn't you make your mind up, then and there, to buy me? And think of your joy when you took possessions—vacant possession as they called it, but it wasn't vacant, for I was here and I am still here, the genius loci, your tutelary god! You wrote round to all your friends, "Paradise Paddock is its name, and a veritable paradise it is!" How have I failed you? Why have you changed?'

I couldn't answer, and the voice went on, 'I'll tell you why you have turned against me—it's for the same reason that you took to me. You fell in love with me and now you've fallen in love with them—that couple that were here a moment ago. You'd never set eyes on them before but they took your fancy, just as I did, and you thought: "I can identify myself with them! Their youth shall be my youth, their happiness my happiness, their children my children, their future mine!" Yes, grey-haired Mr. Minchin, you thought you could renew yourself in them, and lead vicariously the life you never led! But I'm not so fickle! I don't want them and their squalling children, who will deafen me with their clamour and never listen to my voice as you did, till they came. I don't want them, I tell you, and what's more, I won't have them!'

The voice of jealousy, no doubt, piercing what seemed a lifetime of sad, conflicting thoughts; but I had to heed it, for I could feel the house's enmity like a cold air at my back, feel too the threat of imminent and lasting rupture that a quarrel with an old friend brings. I tried to stop my ears but still the voice droned on, painting my future life away from Paradise Paddock in hues as dark as my own thoughts, as dark as the shadows gathering on the river, where a patch of light under the low branches might have been a swan. And not only my future, but the house's too. For the Marchmonts wouldn't keep it, the voice told me. Was it likely that a whim, born of being in love, fostered by a fine evening and stimulated by two dry martinis (dry, mind you) for the river, would *last*? With the servant difficulty, and all those flights of stairs? Oh, no, mark my words, within a year, Paradise Paddock will again be on the market, and what then? A road-house, will it be, with the river-bank a lido? Or an old people's home, an eventide home — fast falls the eventide! Or gutted and converted into flats — homes for the homeless, but not a home for you, you will have no home. That precious word will have no meaning for you. You have given your home up to the Marchmonts.

It was then I heard the beating of the swan's wings, a unique sound, there is nothing like it, an aspirated gasping, as if the atmosphere itself was labouring to keep that mighty body airborne, fourteen pounds of bone and flesh and fathers, the heaviest living thing that flies. It chilled my blood, for to me it was the prelude to attack, the throbbing drone of the bombers before they loosed their bombs. I could see nothing on the shrouded river, but in my mind's eye I could see it all — the long white wings skimming towards me, and between them the bottle-shaped fuselage of body tapering to the arrowy neck and head — and, the next moment, crisis! — the necessity to think and act only in self-defence, to lose myself in anger, in mindless hostility, just as it, the swan, had.

But of course it wasn't me the bird was after: I was on dry land, out of harm's way. Its quarry now would be another swan — had been, per-haps, for this swan was a killer. Two or three times I'd seen a drifting body, its neck once white gnawed bare by rats or fishes. And when I reported this to the Inspector of the R.S.P.C.A., hoping to enlist his aid against the river tyrant, he only said, 'Yes, swans are like that.'

All this went through my mind, was driven into it by those powerful wing-beats, as if by a hammer.

When, a few seconds later, the sound ceased, the air was unburdened of its urgency, and so was I; I got up as easily as if no panic spell had bound me, and took a turn along the terrace. I was my own master again and the house beside me as sightless and as speechless as any other house. A respite, but only for a moment, and then I must decide, say yes or no, and not on grounds of sentiment or fantasy. Could I afford to keep the house? Not as it should be kept. Could the Marchmonts? Ap-parently they could. Should I find a buyer with more feeling for it and its genius loci (how that creature had bullied me!) than they had? No,

I shouldn't. Then wasn't it more sensible to close with an offer which might not be repeated?

The answer must be yes.

I turned to my table on the terrace with my mind made up. Ignoring the foolscap that glimmered at me I let my elbows slide along the table and in a moment—I suppose it was the release from indecision—the darkness pressed down on my eyes and took me into it.

I dreamed and it was a dark dream, for the house was dark. I entered through the study door, but nowhere could I find the switch, and when at last I found it, it didn't work. This seemed to reinforce the darkness; I dared not move for fear of falling over something, and then I knew the house was hostile to me, something or someone didn't want me to come in. I was an outsider, but I couldn't get out any more than I could get in, for I couldn't tell where the door was. Where was I? If indoors, why did branches scrape against me? And what were these white flashes whirling round me, that clove the air like feathered scimitars? I tried to cry out but instead of my own voice I heard another, a jagged line of sound that struck against my ear and seemed to call my name. 'Mr. Minchin! Mr. Minchin!' The thin wail rose and fell. 'Remember to say yes,' I told myself. 'Yes is what you want and what they want. Yes, yes, yes, yes'—I was still saying it when I reached the river wall.

The sounds had stopped by then. Who knew how long the Marchmonts had been calling? Perhaps a long time; perhaps, getting no reply, they had given me up and were making tracks for Warmwell.

No, they were there, at least two people were who surely must be they—my visitors of who knew how long ago? My mind told me that they must be, though my eyes denied it, denied that this drenched couple in clothes no longer white but water-grey and so transparent that the skin showed through them, could be the Marchmonts. But their clothes were more recognizable than they were, for not a look I could remember, and hardly any awareness of themselves, each other, or of me, showed in their faces. The water in the canoe seemed to worry them, it was ankle-deep and they could not keep their feet still.

'You've had a spill,' I said. 'Come in and let me find you some dry clothes.'

Neither of them answered for a moment or two: Mrs. Marchmont was the first to find her tongue.

'No, thank you, we'll go on. We're not cold really. We shall be dry by the time we get to Warmwell. We stopped here because . . . Why did we stop, Harry?'

'Because we said we would,' he answered in a voice of which the inflexions were quite out of his control. 'Mr. . . . Mr. . . . was going to tell us something.'

'Look, you've had a shock,' I said, 'a nasty experience. Do come in and I'll give you something to warm you,'

'We did have a nasty experience,' he said in his lilting sing-song. 'That's why we . . . don't want to stay. That damned bird . . . it set about us——'

'Ah,' I said, 'I was afraid so.'

'It got us in the water where the banks were high. I didn't think we could climb out, with it thrashing around. It got on to her back, the great big bugger, and would have drowned her, but I was on the bank by that time and I bashed it . . . with the paddle, you know.'

'Did you kill it?' I asked.

'I think so. Do you see her dress, how torn it is, and her skin, all in ribbons. We'll have to see a doctor.'

I looked, and looked away.

'Yes,' I said, 'but do stay now. I'll call a doctor, if you like.'

He shook his head. 'We don't think the place is healthy for us, and we'd better be off, thanks all the same. And thanks for the drinks, too — what a big drink we nearly had! And thanks for everything. Now there was something we were going to tell you, or you were going to tell us, that's why we stopped. For the life of me, I can't think what it was.'

'It was about this house,' I said, 'Paradise Paddock. I was going to say that I would sell it if you wanted it.'

He laughed and laughed.

'Yes, that was it. What do you think, Sylvia, old girl?'

She shook her head and said, without looking up, and still twiddling her toes in the water, 'I'm afraid I don't want it now.'

'Don't think us rude, old chap,' her husband said, with sudden earnestness, 'but the fact is, we don't like your house any more. We think it's got a hoodoo on it. We don't want any more swan-songs.'

'I should feel the same,' I said, 'if I were you.' They shivered a little and I shivered in concert.

'No offence meant, if we say we think this place is a bit lousy.'

'Of course not.'

'You find that it suits you?'

'Well, yes and no,' I said. 'It may suit me better now.' I was wondering if the swan was really dead.

'Well, thanks for all the drinks you gave us, thanks a lot.'

'Don't speak of it,' I said.

'We shall often think of you,' said Mrs. Marchmont suddenly, 'sitting and writing, with all your treasures round you.'

My heart sank, then soared.

'So you won't be settling in Warmwell?'

'Not on your life, not on your life . . . Or ours,' he added. 'Excuse me—no offence intended.'

'I'm sorry about that,' I said. 'But you know best.' I saw that they were longing to be off, but didn't quite know how to take their leave.

'Let's tip the water out of the boat,' I suggested. 'You'll be more comfortable so.'

'Don't tip us out with it!'

'You'll have to debark first,' I said.

They laughed.

'We had forgotten that,' he said shakily.

When the operation was completed, and they were settled in again, he suddenly said: 'Would you accept this canoe as a memento, Mr. . . . Mr. . . . ?'

'Minchin,' put in his wife.

'Minchin, of course.'

'Most gratefully,' I said.

'I'll have it sent to Paradise Paddock, then . . .' He thought for a moment. 'Happy days,' he said. 'Have a good time,' said his wife, in an uncertain voice.

'And you!'

But they were already gone, and in a minute or two the darkness closed behind them.

I lingered by the river, trying to regain my faith in it, as one sometimes does with a friend after a quarrel. Mutely I apostrophized it. 'You have let me down, you have let me down! What have you to say?' But it was voiceless: the stealthy rustlings and stirring under the tree-laden banks were not meant for any ears, mine least of all. How vain to hope from nature a reciprocating mood, I thought—when suddenly, as though in answer to my thought, a V-shaped ripple stole along the river setting the water lapping at my feet, and after it a swan, a solitary swan. How changed she was! The anxious turning of the head from side to side, the questing, peering look, the jerky progress, that had lost its stately rhythm—they were quite unlike her; but most unlike was the little cry or call, louder than a moan, softer than a croak, that issued from her parted, yellow beak, which was so much less fearsome than his orange one.

She has never had to call for him before, I thought, and now he will not hear her.

There was nothing more to wait for; the air was turning cool; I had an irrational feeling that my clothes were wet. Stiffly I got up and climbed back to the house — my house, for it was mine after all: the swan had saved it for me. A moment's doubt remained: would the switch work? It did, and showed me what was still my own.

SOMEONE IN THE LIFT

'THERE's someone coming down in the lift, Mummy!'

'No, my darling, you're wrong, there isn't.'

'But I can see him through the bars—a tall gentleman.'

'You think you can, but it's only a shadow. Now, you'll see, the lift's empty.'

And it always was.

This piece of dialogue, or variations of it, had been repeated at intervals ever since Mr. and Mrs. Maldon and their son Peter had arrived at the Brompton Court Hotel, where, owing to a domestic crisis, they were going to spend Christmas. New to hotel life, the little boy had never seen a lift before and he was fascinated by it. When either of his parents pressed the button to summon it he would take up his stand some distance away to watch it coming down.

The ground floor had a high ceiling so the lift was visible for some seconds before it touched floor level: and it was then, at its first appearance, that Peter saw the figure. It was always in the same place, facing him in the left-hand corner. He couldn't see it plainly, of course, because of the double grille, the gate of the lift and the gate of the lift-shaft, both of which had to be firmly closed before the lift would work.

He had been told not to use the lift by himself—an unnecessary warning, because he connected the lift with the things that grown-up people did, and unlike most small boys he wasn't over-anxious to share the privileges of his elders: he was content to wonder and admire. The lift appealed to him more as magic than as mechanism. Acceptance of magic made it possible for him to believe that the lift had an occupant when he first saw it, in spite of the demonstrable fact that when it came to rest, giving its fascinating click of finality, the occupant had disappeared.

477

'If you don't believe me, ask Daddy,' his mother said.

Peter didn't want to do this, and for two reasons, one of which was easier to explain than the other.

'Daddy would say I was being silly,' he said.

'Oh no, he wouldn't, he never says you're silly.'

This was not quite true. Like all well-regulated modern fathers, Mr. Maldon was aware of the danger of offending a son of tender years: the psychological results might be regrettable. But Freud or no Freud, fathers are still fathers, and sometimes when Peter irritated him Mr. Maldon would let fly. Although he was fond of him, Peter's private vision of his father was of someone more authoritative and awe-inspiring than a stranger, seeing them together, would have guessed.

The other reason, which Peter didn't divulge, was more fantastic. He hadn't asked his father because, when his father was with him, he couldn't see the figure in the lift.

Mrs. Maldon remembered the conversation and told her husband of it. 'The lift's in a dark place,' she said, 'and I dare say he does see something, he's so much nearer to the ground than we are. The bars may cast a shadow and make a sort of pattern that we can't see. I don't know if it's frightening him, but you might have a word with him about it.'

At first Peter was more interested than frightened. Then he began to evolve a theory. If the figure only appeared in his father's absence, didn't it follow that the figure might be, could be, must be, his own father? In what region of his consciousness Peter believed this it would be hard to say; but for imaginative purposes he did believe it and the figure became for him 'Daddy in the lift'. The thought of Daddy in the lift did frighten him, and the neighbourhood of the lift-shaft, in which he felt compelled to hang about, became a place of dread.

Christmas Day was drawing near and the hotel began to deck itself with evergreens. Suspended at the foot of the staircase, in front of the lift, was a bunch of mistletoe, and it was this that gave Mr. Maldon his idea.

As they were standing under it, waiting for the lift, he said to Peter:

'Your mother tells me you've seen someone in the lift who isn't there.'

His voice sounded more accusing than he meant it to, and Peter shrank.

'Oh, not now,' he said, truthfully enough. 'Only sometimes.'

'Your mother told me that you always saw it,' his father said, again more sternly than he meant to. 'And do you know who I think it may be?'

Caught by a gust of terror Peter cried, 'Oh, please don't tell me!'

'Why, you silly boy,' said his father reasonably. 'Don't you want to know?'

Ashamed of his cowardice, Peter said he did.

'Why, it's Father Christmas, of course!'

Relief surged through Peter.

'But doesn't Father Christmas come down the chimney?' he asked.

'That was in the old days. He doesn't now. Now he takes the lift!'

Peter thought a moment.

'Will you dress up as Father Christmas this year,' he asked, 'even though it's an hotel?'

'I might.'

'And come down in the lift?'

'I shouldn't wonder.'

After this Peter felt happier about the shadowy passenger behind the bars. Father Christmas couldn't hurt anyone, even if he was (as Peter now believed him to be) his own father. Peter was only six but he could remember two Christmas Eves when his father had dressed up as Santa Claus and given him a delicious thrill. He could hardly wait for this one, when the apparition in the corner would at last become a reality.

Alas, two days before Christmas Day the lift broke down. On every floor it served, and there were five (six counting the basement), the forbidding notice 'Out of Order' dangled from the door-handle. Peter complained as loudly as anyone, though secretly, he couldn't have told why, he was glad that the lift no longer functioned; and he didn't mind climbing the four flights to his room, which opened out of his parents' room but had its own door too. By using the stairs he met the workmen (he never knew on which floor they would be) and from them gleaned the latest news about the lift-crisis. They were working overtime, they told him, and were just as anxious as he to see the last of the job. Sometimes they even told each other to put a jerk into it. Always Peter asked them when they would be finished, and they always answered, 'Christmas Eve at latest.'

Peter didn't doubt this. To him the workmen were infallible, possessed of magic powers capable of suspending the ordinary laws that governed lifts. Look how they left the gates open, and shouted to each other up and down the awesome lift-shaft, paying as little attention to the other hotel visitors as if they didn't exist! Only to Peter did they vouchsafe a word.

But Christmas Eve came, the morning passed, the afternoon passed, and still the lift didn't go. The men were working with set faces and a controlled hurry in their movements; they didn't even return Peter's 'Good night' when he passed them on his way to bed. Bed! He had begged to be allowed to stay up this once for dinner; he knew he wouldn't go to sleep, he said, till Father Christmas came. He lay awake, listening to the urgent voices of the men, wondering if each hammer-stroke would be the last; and then, just as the clamour was subsiding, he dropped off.

Dreaming, he felt adrift in time. Could it be midnight? No, because his parents had after all consented to his going down to dinner. Now was the time. Averting his eyes from the forbidden lift he stole down-stairs. There was a clock in the hall, but it had stopped. In the dining-room there was another clock; but dared he go into the dining-room alone, with no one to guide him and everybody looking at him?

He ventured in, and there, at their table, which he couldn't always pick out, he saw his mother. She saw him, too, and came towards him, threading her way between the tables as if they were just bits of furni-ture, not alien islands under hostile sway.

'Darling,' she said, 'I couldn't find you—nobody could, but here you are!' She led him back and they sat down. 'Daddy will be with us in a minute.' The minutes passed; suddenly there was a crash. It seemed to come from within, from the kitchen perhaps. Smiles lit up the faces of the diners. A man at a near-by table laughed and said, 'Something's on the floor! Somebody'll be for it!' 'What is it?' whispered Peter, too ex-cited to speak out loud. 'Is anyone hurt?' 'Oh, no, darling, somebody's dropped a tray, that's all.'

To Peter it seemed an anti-climax, this paltry accident that had stolen the thunder of his father's entry, for he didn't doubt that his father would come in as Father Christmas. The suspense was unbearable. 'Can I go into the hall and wait for him?' His mother hesitated and then said yes.

The hall was deserted, even the porter was off duty. Would it be fair, Peter wondered, or would it be cheating and doing himself out of a surprise, if he waited for Father Christmas by the lift? Magic has its rules which mustn't be disobeyed. But he was there now, at his old place in front of the lift; and the lift would come down if he pressed the button.

He knew he mustn't, that it was forbidden, that his father would be angry if he did; yet he reached up and pressed it.

But nothing happened, the lift didn't come, and why? Because some careless person had forgotten to shut the gates—'monkeying with the lift', his father called it. Perhaps the workmen had forgotten, in their hurry to get home. There was only one thing to do—find out on which floor the gates had been left open, and then shut them.

On their own floor it was, and in his dream it didn't seem strange to Peter that the lift wasn't there, blocking the black hole of the lift-shaft, though he daren't look down it. The gates clicked to. Triumph possessed him, triumph lent him wings; he was back on the ground floor, with his finger on the button. A thrill of power such as he had never known ran through him when the machinery answered to his touch.

But what was this? The lift was coming up from below, not down from above, and there was something wrong with its roof—a jagged hole that let the light through. But the figure was there in its accustomed corner, and this time it hadn't disappeared, it was still there, he could see it through the mazy criss-cross of the bars, a figure in a red robe with white fur edges, and wearing a red cowl on its head: his father, Father Christmas, Daddy in the lift. But why didn't he look at Peter, and why was his white beard streaked with red?

The two grilles folded back when Peter pushed them. Toys were lying at his father's feet, but he couldn't touch them for they too were red, red and wet as the floor of the lift, red as the jag of lightning that tore through his brain. . . .

THE FACE

EDWARD POSTGATE was a one-woman man. Or perhaps it would be true to say, he was a man to whom one facial type appealed. He wasn't singular in this, for most men have their favourite type. But he was singular in the fact that no other type, or even variation of his own type, seemed to attract him at all. Long before he married Mary Elmhirst, this type was enshrined in his consciousness and most of his friends knew what it was. Not because he told them; he was reserved about such matters, and his marriage, when it came, was a surprise. But the girl's face was not a surprise, for anyone who had done examinations with him or played bridge with him, or sat with him at a committee or a board meeting, could not help knowing it. He was an inveterate dood-ler. Sometimes he covered the margin with abstract designs; sometimes with plumes and feathers (he was especially fond of drawing ostrich feathers), but most often it was a face, and it was always the same face, recognizably the same, from whatever angle he drew it. The back view was particularly characteristic, for the girl of his dreams, unlike girls in real life, always did her hair the same way—in a knob low down on her neck. Edward was enough of a draughtsman to be able to show that her hair was dark and shining, her eyes violet blue, her colouring red and white—almost a deep red on the high cheek-bones. Parted in the middle her hair swept round a broad forehead, and was drawn back, but not pulled back, to emphasize the slightly concave line that led from her cheek-bones to her small round chin. However many curves he gave her mouth, it was always a wide one, otherwise her nose, whose low arch made a curve that didn't vary, might have looked too large.

'There's that girl again!' we sometimes said, and hardier spirits even said to Edward: 'Why don't you try another type for a change?' Where-at he would smile and sometimes scrunch the paper up. Many of us thought that he was in love with an ideal, a Dulcinea who, unlike Don Quixote's, never had and never would exist in real life: she was an alibi for feelings that he only had on paper. Not that he avoided women's society—he was attached to several, and they to him; but in his relations with them there was a marked absence of the obsessiveness that showed so clearly in the drawings; he scarcely seemed to prefer one to another, nor did any of them resemble, even remotely, the face he loved to contemplate.

Edward was a well-built, fair-skinned man, with pale-green hair and amber eyes—at least they said so, I couldn't quite see it. To me he was self-coloured—not in the sense of being an egotist, he was anything but that—but he had no light and shade: he presented a uniform hue, the neutral hue of a good fellow. One didn't have to like him first to find him likeable; he was likeable at once. Many a hostess finding herself a man short used to say, 'Can't we get hold of that miserable Edward?'— only to find that another hostess had got hold of him. In company he always seemed to be holding himself back, as if he had something he didn't want to part with; it was the energy, I suppose, that he needed for his paper-mistress—his drawing-mistress, as we sometimes called her.

So his marriage, at the age of twenty-eight, came as a great surprise. Mary Elmhirst didn't belong to any of the circles he frequented, he ran into her at some seaside town, and they were married almost at once. The match was suitable in every way; she was a doctor's daughter, at once gay and serious-minded; he worked in the City. As a bachelor he had been a social asset and in continuous demand at parties. As a married man he didn't exactly drop out, but he would go nowhere without his wife; he ceased being Edward, he became Edward and Mary, or per-haps Mary and Edward. In the social and every other sense he lived en-tirely for her, and it then became more than ever apparent how super-ficial his previous friendships had been. We accepted this with a smile and a shrug; a few tried, and one or two pretended to find, rifts in the Postgates' matrimonial lute, but these were so obviously unfounded that they passed into a joke, a joke against the gossips. Happy the couple that has no history, but also the less interesting: Mary and Edward, whether meaning one or both of them, ceased to be names that came up much in conversation, and where they did, it was chiefly as types of conjugal felicity. Nothing more would happen to them except a child, and this, strangely enough, they did not have, though they were going to have one when five years later Mary Postgate was killed in a motor accident.

It was like a looking-glass being broken—the picture was no longer there, nor did the fragments that remained present any coherent pattern. What had happened to Edward? What was happening? What would happen? It was anybody's guess, and meanwhile, after the letters of condolence sometimes easy to write but in this case next to impossible, we were in a state of suspense and bewilderment, unable when with Edward, or even apart from him, to decide whether 'yes' or 'no' was the more appropriate word. Did he prefer to see people, or not to see them? Was it better to refer to his loss, or not to refer to it? One felt that he, too, was dead, had died when all he stood for died; but he wasn't, he was up and going about; and if we could find some definite mode or pattern of thinking and feeling about him, it might help him to find one for himself. Perhaps he had found one, but if so he didn't disclose it. He withdrew further into his pre-marital reserve. That he was still attending to his business, and wasn't actively ill, at any rate physically, was all we knew with certainty about him. After a while he began to move about a little socially, he returned to circulation; but he didn't function as a person, he was like a clock that people still look at even though it has stopped.

Everyone of course was sorry for him, I not least, being one of his oldest friends, and a born bachelor, as he had seemed to be—though not with the facial attachment that he had. I would say to him: 'Edward, come in for a drink on Thursday—I'm having a few friends,' and as like as not he would accept, and yet he might as well have stayed away, for he didn't bring himself with him, not even the muted self we used to know. We were sorry for him, I repeat, but you can't feel the pang of sorrow indefinitely: the nerve gets overlaid and ceases to respond. He was still a charge on our feelings—'Poor Edward!'—but he was no longer news.

And then somebody remarked, who had been with him at a meeting, that he had started to draw the face again. All the years that he was married, and for some years after, he hadn't drawn it. Possessing it he hadn't needed to, and losing it he hadn't the heart to—at least this was the explanation generally given. The face, so my informant told me, and this was soon confirmed by others who had seen it in other versions, was still the same face, hadn't altered in any particular—it was even the same age it used to be. I felt a little sceptical about these rumours, but one evening, when I was playing cards with him, I saw it myself, decorating the bridge-marker. Time, as someone said of Dr. Johnson, had given him a younger wife. But was she still his old wife, Mary, or a potential new wife? Or just his obsession with his ideal?

Nothing happened for a long time, and then a mutual friend called
Thomas Henry told me that at a café in Restbourne where he was having tea he had been served by a waitress, whose face was the facsimile of
Edward's model, the spitting image, he said. Thomas Henry was a fussy
little man, twice married, and as meddlesome as a woman; he was fond
of starting hares, especially matrimonial hares, for other people to follow
up. Now he was all agog. 'But what can we do about it?' I asked him.

'Well, bring them together.'

'But how?'

'Tell him to go down to the café and see for himself.'

I deprecated this—it seemed too crude.

'We don't know how he feels,' I said. 'It might upset him terribly—
you can't monkey about with people's emotions in that way.'

'All the same,' said Thomas Henry, 'it might be the saving of him and
bring him back to life, and think how nice for her!' That aspect of the
case hadn't occurred to me, nor, I must say, did it appeal to me. A waitress in a café! Without being a snob I thought it most unsuitable, and
said so. 'Why,' said Thomas Henry, 'you old diehard, we live in a class-
less society, or soon shall, and all he cares about is the Face. He doesn't
care about anything else.'

'Oh, nonsense,' I said, 'he's an idealist through and through. It wasn't
just chance that Mary was as nice as she was nice-looking. The Face is
the face of a lady—Besides, it may not be his face—the face he thinks
about—at all. We've only your word for it.'

'Well, go and see for yourself,' he said.

It happened to be very inconvenient for me to do this, and besides,
I didn't want to spend the day going to Restbourne, just to have tea and
come back. And what a wild-goose chase! I was Edward's age, nearly
forty, and doing things I didn't like was becoming increasingly hard
for me. Self-discipline is all right for the young, but for those of riper
years it is just another brake on the already overclogged machinery of
living. All the same, for the sake of my old friendship with Edward I
decided to go to Restbourne and inspect the waitress.

I saw her the moment I got inside the Krazie Café, and seeing her I
saw what Thomas Henry meant. I hovered, looking for a table at which
she would be serving; luckily she came up to me and showed me one. I
scrutinized her as she stood waiting for my order. Yes—the resemblance
was most striking—even to the deeper colour on the high cheek-bones
—though that, perhaps, owed something to art, for she was more made-
up than Mary had been. Her voice was made up too; it had an obvious

overlay of gentility but Edward didn't draw voices. I called her back to ask her for some jam; the hands that brought it were innocent of a wedding-ring: they were larger than Mary's, and not so pretty, but Edward didn't draw hands. What was she like in herself? Like Mary? How could I tell? She didn't chat much to the other customers, and they paid her no special attention. How tantalizing it was! Before I left I must say something to her—something to draw her out. But I was hopeless at that sort of thing: I hadn't the right touch: least of all the light touch. I couldn't leave it to the moment of settling the bill; at the risk of being a nuisance I must again ask for something. But how could I, when the table was groaning with food and I never ate tea anyway? Distaste for my mission increased: I longed to get it over. Never a chatterbox myself, the waitress seemed the last person in the world I wished to talk to. I must; but not at the cost of eating my way through all those viands. Hastily pouring all the hot water into the teapot, I caught her eye.

'Some more hot water, please,' I said, forbiddingly.

When she brought it she said: 'Why, you are thirsty!'

I didn't like her familiarity but it broke the ice.

'Do you know,' I said, 'you remind me of someone I used to know.'

'Somebody nice?' she asked.

'Er . . . very nice.'

'And were you thinking I might do instead?'

It was what I was thinking, but not in the sense that she meant. Instantly I decided that she would not do, but that I ought to give her another chance. Besides, there was something else I wanted her to tell me.

Ignoring her question I said: 'She might have been your twin, she was so like you. . . . Her name was Mary Elmhirst.'

'I have a twin sister as it happens,' she said, 'and she's very like me, except she dresses differently, more of a mouse, you know, and doesn't wear much make-up. Otherwise people couldn't tell us apart, we're always being mistaken for each other—it's quite inconvenient at times. I'm Doris—Doris Blackmore—no relation to your friend, I'm afraid. I hope you're not disappointed.'

I answered at random: 'No, of course not. But it gave me a slight shock, I mean the likeness did.'

'Someone you were fond of?'

'The wife of a friend of mine.'

'Oh, I'm sorry.'

Whatever she meant by that, I liked her better for saying it.

'Well,' I said, 'I must be off.'

'But you haven't drunk your hot water. I don't believe you really wanted it. You just wanted to——'

'You don't make an extra charge for hot water, do you?' I interrupted.

She laughed.

'I make an extra charge for talking. I don't talk to many of our customers.'

'No?'

'No. They want to start something funny with me, the men do. I thought that you——'

'No,' I assured her. 'It was just the likeness.'

She looked disappointed.

'Oh well, then, if you don't——'

'But I've enjoyed it,' I said firmly, 'all the same.'

'A bit lonely, are you?'

'I suppose we all are, at times. Look, there's somebody wants you.'

She turned her head. 'I see that you don't,' she said, walking away with exaggerated slowness.

I thought, 'You impudent hussy,' but I didn't feel as annoyed as I'd expected to. When she had attended to the other customer she came back.

'I suppose you want your bill.'

'Yes, please.'

She made it out and handed it to me.

'Do you generally talk that way to girls?'

'Oh no,' I said, fumbling in my pocket, 'I'm like you, I hardly talk to anyone.'

'Pay at the desk, please,' she said, looking sullen.

I laid a shilling on the table.

'All right, but that's for you.'

'I don't know that I want to take it,' she said. 'You haven't much respect for a girl's feelings, have you?'

Angry tears stood in her dark-blue eyes. I was amazed and jumped up from the table. The bill paid, I walked past her to say good-bye, but she took no notice of me.

'I saw what you meant,' I said to Thomas Henry for the third time. (I had edited the story, leaving out the last part.) 'It's an unbelievable likeness. But she wouldn't do at all. She's utterly unsuitable.' I had said this three times too.

'All the same, I think we ought to tell him.'

'But why? Nothing would come of it, at any rate, nothing but harm.'

'I think we owe it to him.'

'An item for his experience account? No, really, Thomas Henry. Besides, how could we bring the subject up? I've never heard him mention Mary since she died, and I've never dared to mention her to him. The wound went much too deep. You never know what's going on in people's minds. The idea of another woman looking like her might upset him terribly, and destroy whatever compromise he's been able to make with himself and life about her. We know he's made one, because he still functions like an ordinary person. This might upset the balance and then God knows what would happen.'

'He still draws the Face.'

'Yes, but we don't know why. It's probably just to keep Mary's image in his mind. It would be tasteless and tactless beyond belief to suggest to him that he might be interested in another woman, and above all that woman.'

'You yourself didn't seem to dislike her all that much.'

'I? My dear fellow, I was amused by the whole episode, but only because there was a time limit to it. If I'd had to spend another five minutes in her company I should have died.'

'You never liked the company of women very much.'

'Well, not women of that type.'

'That's for him to decide. The point is, we must give him the chance. With Mary he was blissfully happy. He fulfilled himself in her. He lives for one person; the rest of us are shadows. Now he's emotionally mutilated—paralysed. If you could see the emptiness of his life——'

'I can't, and nor can you.'

'—you'd realize that anything is better than the void, le néant. You've never been attached to anyone——'

'How do you know?'

'Isn't it obvious? You're quite self-sufficient. Whereas he——'

'Well, I'm not going to tell him.'

'Then I shall. But first let me get it right. She works in Restbourne, at the Krazie Café, and her name is——'

'I've forgotten.'

'But you knew it a moment ago.'

'Well, I've forgotten now. And I beg you, Thomas Henry, not to tell him anything about her. I beseech you——'

'All right, I won't bring you into it——'

'For God's sake don't.'

'And I'll take all the blame and all the credit, too, if it comes off.'

'If what comes off?'

'Well, if the Face fits.'

When I next saw Thomas Henry, some days later, it was in the company of other people, and we hardly spoke. I knew I was avoiding him, and I thought he was avoiding me: but why? Edward I did see to pass the time of day with: and to my surprise I found myself asking him to lunch with me.

'What about next Saturday?'

'Let me get my little book,' he said. 'I'm afraid I'm engaged on Saturday.'

'Well, the following Saturday?' He turned the leaves.

'I'm engaged then, too. Silly, isn't it?'

'I know you can't get away easily in the middle of the week,' I said, 'but what about Wednesday?'

'I'm not quite sure about Wednesday,' he hedged. 'I'll let you know.'

'Don't let me be a nuisance,' I said, 'but it would be nice to see you. You lunch out sometimes, Edward, don't you?'

'Oh yes,' he said with his polite air that kept one at a distance, 'but just at this moment I seem to have more engagements than usual. I'll tell you about Wednesday.'

A day or two later he telephoned that he couldn't manage it. I was unaccountably disappointed, for much as I liked Edward I had never set great store on seeing him.

The next time I met Thomas Henry was at a cocktail party, and this time I didn't let him escape me. 'What about Edward?' I asked. 'Did you tell him about our friends at Restbourne?' I used the plural as a precaution: friends sounded less compromising than friend. But he looked round apprehensively and said, 'Not here, I think. Stone walls——'

'No one else can hear you,' I said, shouting above the din. 'I can hardly hear you myself.' When he still wouldn't be drawn I pinned him down to dinner the next day.

A strange tale he told me. He was unhappy about it, as he should have been, and very much on the defensive.

'I couldn't have guessed what would happen,' he said. 'I acted for the best.'

'No one does so much harm as those who go about doing good,' I said, quoting Bishop Creighton.

'You never run that risk,' he retorted tartly.

'Well, not on this occasion, perhaps,' I answered, 'and I warned you not to.' Realizing we were on the verge of a quarrel, and I might get no more out of him, I succeeded in pacifying him: few things make one angrier with other people than being angry with oneself.

He had been playing bridge with Edward and seen the face appearing on the bridge-marker. He made no comment at the time, but when Edward was giving him a lift home he plucked up courage and said he had seen a girl whose face reminded him of the face Edward had been drawing — he didn't say it reminded him of Mary, and now I come to think of it, I don't believe any of Edward's friends had ever remarked to him on the resemblance, though they often spoke of it to each other. Edward asked him where he had seen her, and Thomas Henry told him, but couldn't tell him her name because I had forgotten it.

'You didn't tell him that?' I asked.

'Oh, no. I left you out of it, as I promised to.'

Then Thomas Henry asked if he would be interested in seeing her, and Edward said he wasn't sure; he said the drawings were a vice which he had given up when he was married. He said this in quite an ordinary tone and changed the subject. But when he next saw Thomas Henry he told him he had been down to Restbourne.

'Oh!' I said.

'Yes, but the bird had flown. There was no one in the café in the least resembling her. He went to Restbourne three Saturdays running, and twice in the middle of the week, making some excuse of going on business — five times altogether, but he never saw her.'

'She might have been away on holiday,' I said, 'on those three Saturdays. It's August.'

'I suggested that,' said Thomas Henry, 'and he's going to try again. He would have asked about her, but he couldn't, not knowing her name.'

'Did he seem upset?' I asked.

'He certainly couldn't talk of anything else.'

'Look what you've done, Thomas Henry! You can't say you weren't warned.'

'No, but it may have given him an object in life. He was much more animated than he used to be.'

The next time we met, Thomas Henry was less optimistic. 'He's been down there again,' he said, without bothering to explain who 'he' was, 'and she isn't there. He told me he thought I'd made a mistake, because he wasn't a good draughtsman, and what he drew corresponded to something inside him, not outside (he didn't mention Mary). He said that each line had a special meaning for him, and any deviation from it, in a human face, made that face quite unlike the face of his conception. And yet he couldn't help thinking that I might be right, and that one day she might come back, and he would find her. "She may be ill," he said, "or one of her relations may be ill. In the working-classes, some relation or other is nearly always ill" — you know the way he talks about the working-classes, as if they were another type of human being.'

'They are,' I said.

'Oh, nonsense. But I do think we should do something for him — he can't go on like this, commuting between here and Restbourne like a . . . like a . . .'

'Shuttle on a loom,' I said. 'Well, you do something, Thomas Henry, it's your pigeon. Vous l'avez voulu, Georges Dandin.'

'Yes, I felt for him more than you did. I saw a fellow creature suffering, and wanted to relieve him. Whereas you——'

'Passed by on the other side.'

'It's nothing to be proud of. But now you can do something to rid him of his obsession. You can go down to Restbourne, Ernest, and find out what's happened to her.'

'Why not you? I'm not specially keen on the south coast in August.'

'Because you talked to her, and made yourself conspicuous, as no doubt they all remember in the café. You might even pose as a relation.'

'Thank you,' I said. 'One of the sick ones, perhaps.'

'Oh, do go, Ernest. You're a man of independent means. It's much easier for you. You don't have to be in any special place at any special time, so why not go to Restbourne?'

'Restbourne is the last place I want to go to,' I replied. But in the end I went.

The appalling vulgarity of that town! Nowhere has the proletarianization of the English race gone so fast, or so far, as it has at Restbourne. It is the apotheosis of the synthetic. I dreaded it, and when I got there it was worse than I remembered — an exhibition of what was, to my middle-class mind, a substitute for every form of pleasure. Not that it was not expensive, for it was; everyone seemed to have money to burn. But how joyless that sometimes gay proceeding made them! How they trailed about on the sea-front, well fed, well dressed (so far as they were dressed), well tanned, well oiled (sometimes in both senses of the word), but among the lot not one whom a photographer, still less a biographer, would ever want to make his subject.

It was a relief to sit down in the Krazie Café, for a chair is a chair, and tiredness is tiredness, whatever a mass-produced consciousness may have done to take the reality out of most objects and sensations. She wasn't there, Doris Blackmore wasn't there: I saw that at a glance; and the full weight of five hours thrown away, and five pounds thrown away on railway-trains and taxis, fell on me so crushingly that I groaned aloud. And sharpening my general disappointment was a particular one which I couldn't or wouldn't account for then. Deep down in me I had hoped to see the waitress. Why? To bandy words with her? To let her know where she got off, or didn't get off? I couldn't tell. But my sense of grievance was so overwhelming and acute that I did what, coming down in the train, I hadn't thought possible—for me, at any rate. With a clear conscience, which for some reason mine wasn't, it should have been quite easy; just a few words, casually uttered, as if the inquiry was the most natural in the world, and the thing would have been done. But in the train, however often I rehearsed them, whatever accent of indifference I gave them, they would not pass my lips. Now I knew they would, and when I had paid my bill I went up to the woman who seemed to be in charge and said:

'Can you tell me what's become of the waitress, Doris Blackmore I think her name was, who used to be here?'

At that the woman's face stiffened and she said shortly:

'I'm afraid I can't. She left us at a few days' notice. Naturally, we did not pay her her week's wages.'

'How long ago was that?'

'Over a month, I think. She said she was fed up, and she was earning good money, too. They're all alike—you can't rely on them. A whim, a fancied slight, a boy, you never know what it is, and then they're off.'

'A pity,' I said. 'She seemed to be a nice girl.'

The manageress pursed her lips and shrugged.

'No nicer than the rest. They're spoilt, if you ask me.'

'And you don't know where she's gone?'

'I'm sorry, but I can't help you.'

Well, that was that. My next step was to tell Thomas Henry (who was going to pretend that he had made the journey down to Restbourne) to tell Edward that the Face had been, well, effaced. Useless to look for it; better forget about it. And this he did, assuring Edward, who didn't want to be convinced, that any further raids on Restbourne would be fruitless. Fruitless for me, too, I reflected. The incident rankled like a sore place that hurts and is desired, as Cleopatra said, not only for its own sake but for the contrast with the healthy tissues round it.

At that time I had a flat in Knightsbridge overlooking Hyde Park and it was my nightly custom, for the sake of my health, to take a brisk constitutional in the Park before retiring. Between Hyde Park Corner and Wellington Barracks was my usual beat, but it was not only my beat, I shared it with a great many others who were not there for their health. Some sat, some stood, some walked, some drove up or drove away in motor-cars that seemed to hug the kerbstone in a peculiarly intimate manner and in some way—perhaps by exuding a moral cloud—to darken the surrounding air. I won't say anything against them for fear I should offend the live-and-let-live spirit of high-minded persons; but walking by them I had to run a gauntlet of hullos, dearies, darlings, and other forms of affectionate solicitation, and I got very tired of it. Indeed, but for a certain obstinacy, and the feeling that the Park was mine as well as theirs, I should have bent my steps another way.

When accosted I had not, as some men have, a polite formula of refusal ready: I swerved or dodged or walked straight on. But one evening I couldn't, for my solicitrix, who had risen from a seat a few yards farther on, planted herself in front of me and blocked my way.

'Hello, darling,' she said.

If her face hadn't been almost touching mine I should have recognized her sooner. If I had been less put out I should have recognized her sooner.

'Doris Blackmore!' I said at last.

'The same,' she answered. 'I've seen you several times doing your nightly dozen, or whatever you were here for, so I thought, "Why not me as well as one of the others?" '

'I don't come here to pick up women,' I said.

'I thought not, but one can't be sure, I haven't had much experience you see. Even the older ones can't always tell.'

'They can't, indeed,' I said.

'No need to be snooty. You might be wanting something—other men do.'

I made no answer.

'Do you know,' she said, 'yours is the first face I've recognized since I've been on the game.'

'On the game?'

'Well, on the batter, hustling, there are lots of names for it.'

'I could say the same,' I said. 'Yours is the first face that I've recognized among your crowd.'

'You're one of the lucky ones,' she told me, without rancour. 'You can pick and choose, whereas we – Well, so long. Nice to have seen you.'

She was strutting off, with that peculiar stiff gait they all affect, when I caught her up.

'Why on earth are you doing this?' I asked.

'Oh, I dunno. It's a break, at any rate. I got browned off at Restbourne. After you came——'

'Yes?' I said.

'Well, I just felt I wanted to do something else. That's all there is to it.'

'You'll get browned off doing this.'

'There's more variety and much more money, too. Some of us make forty pounds a week. I'd sooner go the whole way with somebody than natter with them at a tea-table. Some men think they're men just because they've been accosted. Some just come to look at us. We're not all so bad. I've heard of a Tom who blew a policeman's whistle for him when he'd been kicked in the groin and couldn't move.'

'I wasn't criticizing you,' I said, 'or them.'

'It's not a bad life. Most men are all mouth and trousers – well, I like the trousers best, if you see what I mean.'

'You mean without the trousers.'

'Yes, I suppose I do. Well, bye-bye, Mr. So-and-so. You didn't tell me your name. London's such a big place. It's nice to think we're neighbours.'

'Look here,' I said.

'I can't afford to waste another minute. Big Harry will be after me.'

'Are you here every night?'

'Yes, till they send me somewhere else.'

'Good-bye, good luck,' I said, and shook her hand. 'Perhaps I shall be seeing you.'

As a rule, on my nightly rambles, my thoughts follow their own course. But this time they wouldn't, they kept returning to the problem of Doris and Edward, digging straight lines from me to them, making an angle which, when I came into it, assumed the dignity and completeness of a triangle.

But I didn't come into it much. The wave of tenderness I had felt for

Doris the waitress didn't reach to Doris the whore; I could only see her as a member of her profession, for which I felt no sentiment at all. An uneasiness, a twinge of guilt I did feel, wondering if my visit to Restbourne, and the kindness I hadn't meant to show her, had been the last straw which broke the back of her virtue—if she was virtuous then.

But Edward, that unknown quantity, would he mind what her calling was, if she had the face he dreamed about? Like most of his circle, Edward was well off. It was taken for granted that any of us had unlimited supplies of gin and vermouth, or whatever drink was in favour at the moment. He had dropped some money over his marriage, for the settlement he had made on Mary came back to him at her death much reduced, when the Inland Revenue had had their whack. More than once, in expansive moments, he had praised the wisdom of parting with one's money in one's lifetime—at which some people pricked up their ears. 'But,' he said, 'most of my friends are my own age, and better off than I am, so where would be the point? I must give some of myself with the gift, or it's no fun; and nearly everyone I know has much more personality than I have—they couldn't do with more.' So it became a sort of game to find for Edward a possible legatee, and many very odd ones were suggested, though not, of course, to him. He was right about his lack of personality; he was more real when he was being talked about than when he was present. He used to say his friends invented him. But the current of his being flowed in a secret channel invisible to us.

Of all the suggested recipients of his bounty none was quite so fantastic as Doris Blackmore. Yet was she really so unsuitable? Besides having the Face, hadn't she almost all the qualifications, including lack of personality? Having been all things to all men, she might find it the less difficult to be one thing to one.

'Edward,' I said, one evening when we were together, 'excuse the question, but have you ever been with a prostitute?'

He frowned, and fixed his amber eyes on me.

'Why, no,' he said.

'Does the thought of them repel you?'

'I've never given them much thought.'

'Nor had I until a night or two ago when one accosted me in the Park, and do you know, she rather took my fancy.'

'Did you get off with her?' asked Edward.

'Well, no, it isn't in my line. But I talked to her and found her interesting and sympathetic. Does that shock you?'

'Not in the least,' said Edward. 'I'm not shocked by sexual irregularities or even' — he smiled — 'by sexual regularity.'

'Would you care to meet her?'

'Not in the street, perhaps.'

'No, at some restaurant. She wouldn't look different from other girls — I'd see to that.'

'Very well,' he said. 'But can she get away? I mean, their bosses keep them pretty hard at work.'

'I'd give her something she could show for herself.'

'Well, let me in on that. What do you think — a fiver?'

But when I told her that a friend was going to join us, she seemed disappointed.

'I thought it was only you,' she said.

'Only me? You're not flattering,' I said. 'But yes, you are. Still, this friend of mine, he's a nice fellow, and of course I need a chaperon.'

'I should have thought you were old and ugly enough to look after yourself.'

'That's where you're wrong. At my age I can't afford to take risks.'

'I suppose you want me to get off with him?'

'Good lord!' I said. 'But if I did, would you object?'

'Object?' she repeated. 'Girls like me can't afford to object to anything.'

'Oh, come,' I rallied her. 'Your life is one long record of objections — all that I know of it, which isn't much. You objected to the Krazie Café; you objected to being talked to, you objected to not being talked to——'

'Only because you were so inconsiderate.'

'Inconsiderate?'

'All right,' she said, 'I'll come.'

Doris's conversation wasn't dull — at least not dull to me — but it was limited. She liked it to be a sparring match; she also peppered it with catch-words of the day — euphemisms and verbal subterfuges. 'Fair enough' for something that wasn't quite fair; 'Jolly good' to make something sound jollier and better than it was; and 'All right' with an interrogative inflexion to cover something that was not quite all right.

But we were both handicapped. We waited and waited, she and I, churning out gobbets of small talk. Conversation always becomes difficult between two people who are waiting for a third who doesn't come. The flow of communication is held up by the mere fact that at any moment it may be broken; and a kind of suspense starts which paralyses the tongue. I seized the opportunity to sing Edward's praises: he was the most amiable of men and the soul of punctuality. This sounded a little hollow in view of his manifest unpunctuality, and Doris, who was looking very pretty and anything but tartish, said:

'I suppose he doesn't want to meet somebody like me. Fair enough.'

'Oh, no,' I said. 'He was most anxious to meet you. He's not a man with silly prejudices and besides——' my voice trailed away under the accusing eye of the clock, which said eight-thirty. An invitation to dinner—eight-thirty for eight! One could tease him about that.

'I don't think much of a man who says he'll dine out with a prostitute,' said Doris unexpectedly. 'No nice man would.'

'What about me?'

'Oh, you're different. He's thought better of it, you can bet your life, and I don't blame him.'

'It's not like him to be late.'

'So you keep saying. I expect it's not like him to be dining with somebody like me.'

'Don't keep saying that—you're not like anyone except yourself.'

'All he wants is to go to bed with me.'

'A moment ago you were saying that he wouldn't come because you were a——'

'That's right, try to make me contradict myself.'

'Mr. Lenthall, please, Mr. Lenthall, please,' intoned a page-boy in a high-pitched nasal sing-song, threading his way between the tables, fixing each guest in turn with a speculative, hopeful stare. 'A telephone call for Mr. Lenthall, please. Mr. Lenthall, please.'

It was only when he had called my name for the fourth time that I realized he meant me.

'Excuse me,' I said, rising.

'Is that your name? You never told me. You never tell me anything.'

I didn't like to leave her to herself—I had a vague idea that the other diners might rise and drum her out—but I was glad to get away. As a companion, the telephone made less demands than Doris.

'Is that Ernest?'

'Yes, you old devil. Why aren't you here? Where are you?'

'At Restbourne.'

'Where?'

'At Restbourne.'

The story he told me didn't to me make sense. I had to believe it because Edward was nothing if not truthful, but believing it I also had to doubt my sanity. The telephone-box became a cage, a padded cell.

'You can't mean that.'

'But I do mean it. I'm terribly sorry, but you do understand, don't you? Make what excuses for me you can.'

'I don't understand a single thing, so how can I make excuses for you?'

'Tell her what I've told you.'

'I can't explain why now, but she won't believe it any more than I do — not so much. She'll have a special reason for not believing it. She'll scratch my eyes out — you don't know what women of that sort can do.'

'Tell her it was love at first sight. She must be used to that.'

'To lust no doubt, but not to love. You are a brute, letting me down like this. And I don't believe you're in Restbourne at all, you're here, in the next room.'

Edward laughed. His happiness had made him pachydermatous. He kept saying he was sorry, but not a trace of shame showed in his voice. It was so full of triumph and personal elation that I hardly recognized it.

'Are you spending the night at Restbourne?'

'Yes, and perhaps to-morrow night. I must ring off now — she's waiting for me.'

'Well,' said Doris. 'What did your boy-friend say? You were so long he must have told you the whole story of his life——'

'He did, in a way. But now let's order dinner.'

Steak was one of the things she asked for, and stout to wash it down, but I persuaded her to have champagne. 'You'll need it,' I said, 'and so shall I.'

'I don't suppose you could tell me anything that would surprise me.'

'I think I can.' Then suddenly I had a doubt — for what's in a name? Had I jumped to some idiotic conclusion? Was it a damp squib after all?

'I'm waiting,' Doris warned me.

'Well, he's at Restbourne. There, I knew you'd be surprised.'

She recovered herself quickly.

'So are about eighty thousand other people. What's odd in that?'

'It would take too long to tell you.'

'Everything's taken long to-night.'

'Well, here's your steak at any rate, and my grilled sole.'

I asked the waiter to pour out the champagne. Doris attacked her steak.

'I'm still waiting,' she said. 'All you've told me so far is that your friend's at Restbourne. Is that stop-press news?'

'Well——' I began.

'I wish you wouldn't go on saying "well". What's the use of a well without any water?'

'It's who he's with.'

'Who *is* he with? A woman, I suppose. Probably a woman like me. Restbourne is stiff with them.'

I stared at her. I had so often seen the Face coming to life under Edward's pencil that it had something legendary and hypnotic about it, something of the immortality of art that made it more memorable than the living model. If Mona Lisa had sat beside her portrait, it would have overshadowed her.

'I don't know if she was like you,' I said, 'but she had the same name, Blackmore.'

That shook her a little, but only for a moment.

'It's a common name—not that we were brought up common. There are loads of Blackmores.'

'Perhaps. But not at the Krazie Café.'

Then I got my effect—the same effect that Edward's announcement had had on me, but more so.

'You don't say so!' she said, and a mist, perhaps the expression of her inner bewilderment, clouded her dark-blue eyes. 'A Blackmore at the Krazie Café! It doesn't make sense.'

'It didn't to me,' I said.

'I left there five weeks ago—how could I still be there?'

'That's what I asked myself.'

'Sounds dotty, doesn't it?' she said. 'Was he kidding you?'

'He's not that sort of man.'

'What took him to the Krazie Café anyway? What took you, for that matter?'

'Ah, thereby hangs a tale,' I said. 'Some day I'll tell you.' But I didn't think that we should meet again.

'You keep stirring your drink with that long mushroom thing,' she said. 'What good does it do?'

'It takes the effervescence out.'

'You've taken the effervescence out of me. You've knocked me side-ways. Well, you're here, and I'm here, so what do we care——'

'You're too young to remember that song.'

'My father used to sing it. "Well", as you're so fond of saying, your friend is at Restbourne with Miss Blackmore – not at the Krazie Café, it shut long ago, and not with me, because I'm here with you. It's amazing, isn't it?'

'It is.'

'You asked him to meet Miss Blackmore in London – I don't know what you meant by it – and he's with another Miss Blackmore at Restbourne. Perhaps he thought we were the same.'

'That's a question for metaphysics.'

'I don't understand your long words. But it is odd. But don't let's let it spoil our evening. . . . He didn't tell you what her other name was?'

'No. But I have just one clue. She must look exactly like you.'

'Like me?'

'Yes, or else he wouldn't be with her.'

Doris frowned, then suddenly her eyebrows lifted and her whole face shone with understanding.

'Why, it's my sister!'

'Your sister?'

'You don't remember much, do you? The twin sister I told you about. The quiet one.'

'I do remember something.'

'I don't keep up with my family much, especially now. I was never any good at writing letters. . . . But it must be her. The sly-boots! She didn't like her job, and always had a hankering for the Krazie. Yes, Gladys, that's who it is. It might almost be me, for she's the dead image of me.'

'The living image.'

'Yes, you're right. She always was a close one. But why should she bother to tell me? I didn't tell her when I went to London. Why write a letter, if you aren't going to get anything out of it? But she's a good girl, if you know what I mean, and I hope he'll be good to her.'

'I'm sure he will.'

'What a chance! It might easily have been me, she's exactly like me, though not so pretty as I am, some people say. Still, good luck to her.'

The full magnitude of her loss was becoming clear to Doris, and the Pêche Melba lay untasted on her plate.

'It may be just a passing fancy for both of them,' I said, but I didn't believe it.

'I wish I was in her shoes. Some people have all the luck.'

Our conversation languished. I thought wonderingly of Edward.

What must have been the pressure on his feelings, to take him back to Restbourne, when he had been assured the bird had flown! And his blind faith had been rewarded: I felt sure that as long as Gladys lived, the Face would vanish from his doodlings.

It was getting late. We bandied words for a bit, but there was little zest behind her thrusts and parries. 'If you knew how I felt about you, you wouldn't look so pleased with yourself' was the best she could do.

'It makes you feel old, doesn't it?' she said suddenly.

'What does?'

'Oh, I dunno, the whole thing—seeing your sister get married before you do. You think he'll marry her?'

'I'm sure of it.'

'Jolly good. I never wanted to marry—I've seen too many people part—and I don't expect you do.'

'Well, not at the moment,' I said ungraciously.

She sighed musically.

'Too comfortable, I suppose. Well, I don't blame you. I should like to write to Gladdy, though. We call her Gladdy, or Glad—though she never was glad so as you'd notice. Perhaps she'll be gladder now. I needn't tell her what I'm doing here—she doesn't know, none of them do. But I should like her to know I wish her well. Or do you think I'd better wait until she's hooked him?'

'I think I should.'

'They might not tell me—but he'll tell you, won't he?'

I saw the implication of this, and said rather unwillingly:

'Yes, of course.'

'So if I don't hear, you'll find a way to pass it on. All right? I wonder if they'll invite me to their wedding.'

'I've no doubt they will.'

'The more fools they—I shouldn't, in their place. I suppose it will be ever such a smart wedding—bang on and whizzo. The real McCoy. Heigh ho!' She gave her musical sigh, and looked up at the clock. 'Good lord, I must be off. But I must powder my nose first.'

'Look here,' I said, when she came back, refurbished, 'I've wasted a lot of your time, and it hasn't turned out as I thought it would. If you are disappointed, so am I. Now what about a little remembrance?'

I didn't have to fumble, I had the notes ready in my pocket.

'I've told you before,' she said, rising, 'and I don't mind telling you again, you've got no respect for a girl's feelings. You can keep your blasted money! I shall tell Uncle Harry I was ill, and so I am—you've made me ill, and I wouldn't go back with you, not even if you asked me!'

She glared at me through unshed tears and for a moment the impression of the Face was so intense that I could hardly see hers for it.

'That's O.K. by me,' I said. 'I don't like these transports so soon after dinner. They give me indigestion.'

At that she laughed, and by the time we reached the pavement—now her haunt—we were friends again. Only a few steps to the kerbstone, but how the tap-tapping of her heels betrayed her! And then a passing taxi bore her off.

THE CORNER CUPBOARD

IT was the first September of the Second War, and Philip Holroyd had decided to leave his flat in London and settle in the country out of the way of the bombs. The place he hit upon was in the West of England, about four miles from a middle-sized market town which he did not think would interest the enemy. Being a bachelor, and as helpless as bachelors generally are, and also a writer, as helpless as writers generally are, he knew he could not fend for himself: he must have a cook and a daily woman. The house, like many other houses, was called the 'Old Rectory', and was, of course, much too large for Philip; perhaps he would not have taken it but for the urgency of his desire to get away from London. In September 1939 travelling by train was difficult: he paid the house a brief visit, and when he heard that several other people were after it he took it on the nail, being easily influenced by threats. The pride of the well-worn Victorian furniture was a magnificent doll's house, but there were some good pieces of an older date, which, occurring haphazard with the rest, and not given any special prominence, gave the place a kind of dignity and unself-consciousness. These included, in the room Philip had marked out for his bedroom, since among other advantages it had the inestimable one of being nearest to the bathroom, an old mahogany bow-fronted corner cupboard, which, unlike some of the cupboards and chests of drawers, was empty of the owner's possessions. It will do for my medicines, thought Philip, who was something of a hypochondriac.

To find a cook was his most urgent problem. The woman who had looked after him in London, being cockney-born, refused to leave it. He dreaded the thought of having to get used to a new person; he was too timid to give orders with conviction, but at the same time liked things done his way. Having lived for many years alone, he was not at all adaptable and was prone to make mountains out of molehills. Although in London he had plenty of friends his experience with each had become taped: they neither gave nor took from him anything new. The unpredictable was his bugbear. Unconsciously he had withdrawn into himself and grown a shell, albeit a soft one.

Days passed with no news from the Registry Office in Shuttleworth; and when at last they wrote that they had found someone who they thought would suit him it was too late for him to go to interview her; the man in the Foreign Office who had taken his London flat was on the point of moving in. So he engaged Mrs. Weaver without seeing her, but not (as might have happened nowadays) without a reference. 'She is a woman', wrote her late employer, with whom she had stayed a year, 'who needs a good deal of special attention and sympathy which, in our rather large and busy family, she has not always been able to find. She is honest and clean and within her limitations a good cook. Where there is only one in family she would, I think, feel more at home. She responds quickly to encouragement and appreciation. The loss of her husband in the First World War seems to have unsettled her in some ways.'

In her own letter Mrs. Weaver gave her age as forty-six—which happened to be Philip's own age—and said that she hoped to be able to oblige him in every possible way. All this predisposed him in her favour; the need for sympathy and attention was one that, in spite of being an egotist, he was quite ready to meet; indeed, he rather fancied himself as a consoler. When he arrived at the Old Rectory she was already installed.

For the first day or two, in spite of his resolution to ladle out sympathy and appreciation, he didn't see much of Mrs. Weaver. He was busy trying to assimilate the strangeness of his new surroundings. All those outhouses and stables, which the old rectors had no doubt been able to find a suitable use for; couldn't, indeed, have done without! That weedy courtyard with its central drain, through which the water (it had been raining plentifully) took so long to run away! And the garden with its towering trees, traversed by a sullen but romantic rivulet, how much too large it was for the gardener who was said to come three times a week! And the emptiness and silence, after London! A car coming by (the house faced the village street) was quite an event; one listened to its entire progress, from the first throb of the engine to the last. And soon, if petrol-rationing really became a fact, these irruptions into the silence would be fewer, almost non-existent! Already he could hear his own footsteps, the footsteps of a single man, walking alone. Isolation made Philip Holroyd busy with his thoughts as never before; they had the intensity of sensations. Then suddenly he remembered Mrs. Weaver and her need for sympathy.

'Excuse me,' he said, going into the kitchen. Flanked by a larder and a pantry and a second kitchen, and having a back-stairs defended by a door opening out of it, it was a room where meals for twenty people might have been prepared. 'Excuse me,' he repeated, for he was a man who liked to err on the side of politeness, 'but I wanted to tell you how very much I enjoyed the supper you gave me last night. The cheese soufflé was a dream, and it is such a test of cooking.'

Mrs. Weaver looked up at him from the deal table where she was making pastry. Her hands were floury. Her face was round and pink, framed by soft brown hair that was going grey. She parted it in the middle; it was thin and straggled a little, but not untidily. Her figure was short and compact. She had a pleasant, almost sweet expression, which didn't change much when she spoke.

'I'm glad you liked it,' she said. 'I always say that men are easier to cook for than women.'

'Oh, do you think so?'

'Yes, they have better appetites for one thing. My husband——'She stopped.

'Yes?'

'He had a very good appetite. He was a guardsman, you know—in the Grenadiers. He was a fine big man. You remind me of him, sir.'

Philip was slightly above middle height. A sedentary life had thickened his figure, and doubled his chin, but he couldn't help being pleased at being compared to a guardsman.

'And for all he was so big,' went on Mrs. Weaver, 'he was like a child in some ways. He went on playing with soldiers to the end—he was that proud of his regiment. He hated the Coldstream Guards and wouldn't hear them mentioned. I nursed him all through his last illness, when the hospital threw him out, saying they could do nothing more for him. I washed him and shaved him and did everything for him. If you were to fall ill, sir——'

'Oh, I hope I shan't,' said Philip hastily. 'But it's nice to think——' he didn't finish the sentence. 'By the way,' he said, 'is there anything you want? Anything I can do for you to make you more comfortable? I'm afraid your room isn't very comfortable.'

'Oh, no, sir, I'm very happy with you. But there's just one thing——'

'What is it?' asked Philip, when she hesitated.

'Well, sir, it sounds so silly.'

'Never mind, I'm often silly myself.'

'I hardly like to tell you.'

'Out with it.'

'It's the small tortoiseshell butterfly, sir. I can't bear the sight of it. There was one fluttering about the room when my husband was dying. When I see one I go——'

Philip took a hasty glance round the darkening kitchen.

'I don't know much about the habits of small tortoiseshell butterflies,' he said, 'but I fancy they only breed once a year, in the summer. If you happen to see a stray one, call me and I'll get rid of it. I'm quite handy with a butterfly-net.' He made a mental note to buy one.

'Thank you,' she answered, without smiling. 'And I don't like anything that's made of tortoiseshell, either. It makes me want to . . .'

'I'll see there isn't any,' said Philip firmly. 'I'll go along now and round up every bit I find. There's a cigarette-box in my sitting-room— But I'm afraid you must be lonely, as well as having too much to do. Mrs. Featherstone is coming in to-morrow, the daily woman, you know. She lives in the village. She'll be company for you.'

Mrs. Weaver didn't seem to welcome this idea.

'At any rate she'll only be here in the mornings,' she said.

Philip bowed himself out and made straight for the cigarette-box. It was a useful object and a nice one, with *Cigarettes* scribbled across the lid in silver, and silver mountings at the corners. A wedding-present perhaps. But it must go, and so must the buhl clock on the chimney-piece. How bare the room looked without them! What else? Philip ranged the house for the dark, seductive gleam of tortoiseshell, suddenly developing an attachment for the substance that he had never had before; the sense of so many unoccupied rooms all round him gave him an odd feeling; but his search went unrewarded until he came to his own bed-room where, on the dressing-table, lay his comb. He could easily do without it for a day or two; its job was almost a sinecure, he had so little hair. But where to put the culprits so that they shouldn't offend Mrs. Weaver's vision and make her do— whatever they did make her do? In the corner cupboard, of course. There she would never see them.

He opened the two rounded doors, and stood and stared. Unpacking, he had heaped his pharmacopœia (almost his first thought was for it) on to the two lower shelves of the corner cupboard. He had never counted the separate items but there must be nearly thirty. He hadn't bothered to set them straight or even to stand all of them up: that was to be for another day, the day until which Philip postponed so many things. And now they were all arranged and tidy.

Philip's first reaction was one of gratitude to Mrs. Weaver, who had taken so much trouble for him. His second was more complex. On the middle shelf the medicines had been put in the way that any tidy-minded person might have put them. But on the lowest shelf they had been arranged in a certain order that betrayed intention and design. They had been *drawn up* in a kind of formation, the tallest bottles lining the cupboard wall, the medium-sized ones in front of them, and at the feet, so to speak, of these, a third row of smaller vessels, jars and tubes and such-like. The two formations faced each other at right angles, and in between was an empty triangular space like a stage, which seemed to be waiting for something to happen.

Clearly it all meant something: but what did it mean?

Then the meaning flashed on Philip. The bottles were soldiers, two sides drawn up for combat: and the space between them was a battle-field.

He smiled at this odd fantasy of Mrs. Weaver's; it was some kind of psychological legacy from her guardsman-husband, who in his last ill-ness used to play at soldiers. And yet mingling with his amusement was a faint uneasiness; there was too much tension, too much implied enmity in the little scene for it to have been set for comedy. Philip was sensitive to the influence of objects; he responded not only to their aesthetic but to their personal appeal. Among the bits and pieces that he had brought from London was a silk Heriz rug. He liked all Eastern carpets but the silk rugs of Heriz had a special fascination for him, parti-cularly this one. Framing a brick-red ground its border had a scrolling pattern in crimson; and the crimson reappeared in figures on the ground itself together with other colours, palest buff and turquoise blue. But it was the wooing of the two reds that most delighted him. In favoured moments he could get an ecstasy from contemplating it that amounted to a minor mystical experience. The best moment was when he was called; then, tea-cup in hand, he would fix his eyes on the rug beside his bed and await ravishment.

Here was another kind of symbolism and Philip didn't altogether like it. . . . But the top shelf was still unoccupied. Into it he put the little clock, the cigarette-box and the comb, all the gleanings of his tortoise-shell harvest. He thrust them to the back, without any regard to military formation, and in front of them erected a barricade of miscellaneous objects — a long roll of cotton-wool in a blue wrapper, some packets of paper handkerchiefs, and other things of vaguely medical use, which effectually obscured them.

Putting the matter out of his mind he was turning to go when a thought struck him: Why not lock the medicine-cupboard? He went back. The cupboard had a lock, and it had a key; but the key didn't turn in the lock, and the tongue of the lock had no slot to fit into — the slot had been torn out. Philip frowned. The vandalism of these days! The deception, so characteristic of them, of fitting a sham lock which didn't do its job! The eyewash! Then he smiled at himself and almost blushed. What had induced him to think of locking the cupboard, as if it was some sort of Bluebeard's chamber, as if it harboured a threat! It was too silly, and might offend Mrs. Weaver, whose only fault was that she had been kind enough to tidy up for him. Besides, she would have no reason to go to the cupboard again; it would be the daily woman's job to 'do' his bedroom; Mrs. Weaver wasn't even under contract to 'do' his sitting-room — the 'lounge' as she called it.

At eight o'clock next day Mrs. Weaver brought him his early morning tea. Bethinking himself, he said, 'How kind of you to put my medicine-cupboard straight. It was in an awful mess.' She gave him a surprised, uncomprehending look, so he repeated what he had said, with additional expressions of gratitude. Still getting no reply he asked her to give him his bed-jacket. This she did, at once, helping him into it with affectionate concern.

Presently he began to hear the whirr of the carpet-sweeper, the swish of dustpan and brush, the creak and thump of moving furniture, noises which sound so sweetly in the ear of the lie-abed. Mrs. Featherstone, of course! He must remember to have a word with her. At last his staff problem was solved: everything was under control.

There remained the orders — the kitchen orders — for the day. At half-past ten Mrs. Weaver came into his sitting-room with a preoccupied air, but without the writing-pad she usually carried. She came to a stand in front of him, her hands clasped across her body. Philip rose.

'I'm afraid I can't stay with you any longer,' she said. 'You see, I've become too fond of you.'

Philip was utterly taken aback. His first impulse was to resent this intrusion on his feelings which he had guarded from assault for so many years. Dismay succeeded resentment as he saw his domestic edifice crumbling.

'You see, I've become too fond of you,' Mrs. Weaver repeated inexorably.

Philip had to say something.

'You'll . . . you'll get over that,' he faltered. 'These things . . . do happen, but . . . they soon wear off. You . . . you will find someone else.' Not too soon, I hope, he added mentally.

'I was very fond of my husband,' said Mrs. Weaver, 'but it was nothing to what I feel for you.'

Philip longed to say, 'Oh, don't be silly!' but he was a kind-hearted though a far from passionate man, and felt he must meet her on a human plane. But how? He had never received a declaration of love before.

'Don't you think you could give it a trial?' he coaxed. 'I mean, to stay here and see how you felt in a few days' time? You might see another side of me, you might even'—his voice rose hopefully—'come to dislike me!'

Bursting into tears Mrs. Weaver left the room.

Philip paced up and down it, breathing out noisy sighs. How clumsy he had been! Yet could he have done better? Had she mistaken the expressions of sympathy and appreciation which her previous employer had enjoined on him, for signs of love? Utterly at a loss, half rueful, half angry, he wandered into the passage where he met Mrs. Featherstone, sweeping the stairs. At the sight of him she straightened up; a tallish woman, painfully thin, with a high complexion, bleached blue eyes, and frizzy hair dyed almost red. Longing to talk to someone, he engaged her in conversation, and so much did he appreciate her tart and salty remarks, in which no hint of a tender emotion was discernible, that he chattered far more freely, and more intimately, than he meant to, and was only deterred from taking her into his confidence about Mrs. Weaver by noticing that the kitchen door, a short way down the passage, was half-open, like a listening ear.

'Oh,' he broke off, 'you must be wanting your elevenses. See you to-morrow, shan't I?'

Mrs. Weaver did not return to the topic of her affection; she neither withdrew her notice nor renewed it, and Philip began to hope that she was thinking better of it. Try as he would, he couldn't meet her on the old cordial terms; his voice, he knew, was distant and formal, his enunciation too distinct, and his good-night cold. Shutting his bedroom door he vaguely felt he was shutting something out. Perhaps he needed a tranquillizer, a dose of bromide. He went to the corner cupboard.

At first he didn't take in what he saw, he only realized there was a change. The stage which had been empty was now occupied—but by what? At the back a small broken bottle reared its jagged edges, its base strewn with splintered glass; and in front of it lay a white object made of cotton-wool, roughly shaped to form a female figure. But it wasn't white all over, for covering the middle of the body was the blood-red petal of a rose. Beside the prostrate figure, pointing at its vitals, was the unsheathed blade of Philip's pocket-knife.

Otherwise there was no change: the serried ranks of bottles looked on, unmoved in any sense.

Philip backed away, severely shaken. He tried to tell himself that it was all an accident—well, not an accident, his pen-knife couldn't have got there by accident, nor could the cotton-wool, but somebody rummaging in the medicine-cupboard, not meaning anything special, perhaps trying to get a bottle out (some servants didn't think that taking their employer's medicine was stealing), might have produced these odd, surrealist effects. For a moment he thought of calling Mrs. Weaver and confronting her with it; but how did he know she had done it? The daily woman might have.

Somehow he felt he couldn't go to sleep with that thing in the room; it had the air of being dynamic, not static; the intention that created it was still at work. He couldn't lock his bedroom door, it had no key. He would have liked to move into another room; but would the bed be aired? Better the ju-ju concoction in the corner cupboard than a damp bed. But he would need something stronger than bromide now; one of those small red sausages from the phial that seemed to kneel so gloatingly beside the . . . well, the corpse. Overcoming his distaste he gingerly detached the phial from its rank, and opening it swallowed two capsules.

'Good morning, Mrs. Weaver,' he said, as she placed the tray by his bedside. Feeling muzzy, he was slow to come to himself. 'Would you mind giving me my bed-jacket?' When she did not appear to hear, a resentment against her mounted in him, and he said with anger in his voice, 'Would you be good enough to give me my bed-jacket?' Said in that imperious way the request sounded silly, and his resentment mounted. 'Can't you give me that jacket?' he almost shouted, and then she handed it to him, holding it away from her as though it was something that needed decontamination. 'Look here,' he said. 'When I give you an order, I expect you to obey it, do you hear?' She didn't answer, and her silence seemed to give her an advantage over him. 'And there's another thing,' he said. 'Are you responsible for the tomfoolery in the medicine-cupboard?' And when again she didn't answer he jumped out of bed and, taking her roughly by the arm, pushed her towards the cupboard and opened the doors. 'Look at that filthy mess,' he said. 'Did you do it, or didn't you?'

At last she found her tongue. 'I didn't do it,' she said with some dignity. 'I know nothing about it.'

'All right,' fumed Philip, 'I shall ask Mrs. Featherstone to clean it up.'

'Ask her by all means,' Mrs. Weaver said.

After breakfast Philip Holroyd felt bitterly ashamed of his outburst. It was unlike him to lose his temper, and for such a trivial reason, too. He blamed the sleeping-draught, which sometimes made him irritable, and more mortifyingly, a kind of sex-resentment which Mrs. Weaver's declaration of the morning before had kindled in him. Poor woman, she had every right to fall in love with him, preposterous as it seemed; and had not Goethe said, 'That I should love you is no concern of yours'? When she came in to take the orders he would apologize to her, but meanwhile a mess was a mess, and he must ask Mrs. Featherstone to clean out the medicine-cupboard — ask her guardedly, of course, because in view of Mrs. Weaver's denial, she might have done it herself; after all, his bedroom was her province. But he didn't think she had. What dire offence from amorous causes springs! Unless he kept watch on his tongue he might lose both his retainers. Perhaps he had better take the blame himself.

Could he have done it himself? Writers were notoriously absent-minded. The thought was disquieting but it was also too fantastic, and going to look for Mrs. Featherstone he dismissed it from his mind.

He could not find her, nor could he hear anywhere the indefinable but unmistakable sounds of her presence. The house was silent. Returning to his sitting-room he saw, what astonishingly had before escaped his notice, that the room had not been touched since yesterday. It looked stale, tired and untidy. Explanations chased each other across his mind. Cleaning-women were notoriously fickle. Perhaps Mrs. Featherstone had taken a dislike to him; perhaps she had interpreted his too forthcoming manner yesterday as a sign of deeper feeling, just as Mrs. Weaver had. Perhaps——

Before he went into the kitchen he found himself knocking at the door. Mrs. Weaver's manner was neutral; she showed neither pleasure nor displeasure at his entrance. Had she seen Mrs. Featherstone? No. Had she any idea why Mrs. Featherstone hadn't come? No, she wasn't

interested in Mrs. Featherstone's affairs. These daily women——
'Then I had better go and see her,' Philip said. 'Meanwhile, for lunch
I might have—, and for dinner—. The omelette last night was
delicious. What a good cook you are, Mrs. Weaver!'

How pleasant to be away from the house and in the open air! Philip
quite enjoyed his ramble down the broad, straggling village street,
liberally besprinkled with cowpats, pleasantly aglow with September
sunshine. But when he reached Mrs. Featherstone's white-washed cottage with its porch of trellis-work, her daughter told him she was ill in
bed. 'Mum's none too good,' she said. 'The doctor calls it a haemor-
rhage. All to do with those ulcers. She's always been too thin, he says.'
    Walking back, Philip didn't notice the sunshine, or the country sights
and sounds. He went straight up to his bedroom and peeped inside the
medicine-cupboard. Not seeing very well he opened the doors wide. It
had been swept and garnished. Once more the serried ranks of soldier-
bottles guarded an empty stage.
    So several days went by without more manifestations, and Philip
began to put the whole thing at the back of his mind. He was punctual
in inquiring about Mrs. Featherstone, however. She had been taken to
hospital, and every day her condition was said to be 'unchanged'.
Philip's efforts to replace her were unsuccessful. Two women came to
see him; he showed them over the house, making light of its size, and
introduced them to Mrs. Weaver, who though not affable was not ungracious; but neither wanted the job, and when they went away gave
him the impression that they had come out of curiosity.
    Without more manifestations . . . But Philip had cheated. He had
made a rule not to look inside the corner cupboard unless he really required some medicine. This seemed sensible. What was less sensible was
that more than once, when he did need some, for minor ailments brought
on by the chalky water, he refrained. Why? Because, he told himself,
he had got into the habit of taking too much medicine. The real reason,
which he didn't acknowledge, was a reluctance to open the medicine-
cupboard door.
    Oh, but this fibrositis, which a single application of liniment would
charm away! 'Mrs. Weaver!' he called down the passage. 'Have you
any oil of wintergreen?'
    'What for, sir?'
    'To rub on my stiff neck.'
    'I'm afraid I haven't, sir.'

'Then would you be an angel and fetch me a bottle out of my medicine-cupboard? A smallish bottle, on the left side, I think.'

Mrs. Weaver, the catspaw!

In she came, bearing the bottle.

'Shall I give your neck a rub, sir?'

'Oh, no, thank you. I can do it quite easily myself.'

'I often used to rub my husband's neck, sir.'

'Did he have fibrositis too?'

'Yes, and not only in his neck, sir. He had it all over him. I could give you a rub, sir.'

'I'm sure you could, but I think I can manage.'

'It's easier for someone else to do it, sir.'

'But it's such a sticky business.'

'Not if you only use the tips of the fingers. I always use my finger-tips. They are much more sensitive.'

'I'll remember to use mine,' Philip said.

'Excuse me, sir, but have you any objection to my rubbing you? It always did my husband so much good.'

Now don't lose your head, Philip told himself, but impatience got the upper hand.

'If you think I'm your husband——'

'I don't, sir, my husband was a guardsman and a gentleman, not an Oxford undergraduate and a cad.'

'I'm sure he was,' said Philip, far too angry to relish being called an undergraduate. 'I'm sure he was, but did he never tell you——'

'Tell me what, sir?'

'Well, to leave him alone?'

Aghast at the cruelty of these words, Philip closed his eyes. When he opened them Mrs. Weaver had gone.

He put off rubbing his stiff neck until he went to bed. To do so suited his habit of procrastination—just another half-hour before I start rubbing! Also it would be more prudent, as well as pleasanter, to get straight into bed after the operation: less likelihood of catching a chill. Also, if he did it on his way to bed one wash and one undressing would take the place of two, for he would have to take some clothes off to get at his neck. And he would not dirty his vest and shirt as well as his pyjamas. But the chief cause of the postponement was a different one. After Mrs. Weaver's exit he had had the usual revulsion of feeling about her. He had behaved abominably to her and he ought to apologize. The best way of apologizing would be to call her in and ask her to rub his neck after all. 'I'm so sorry I was irritable, Mrs. Weaver. Please forget about it, if you can, and give my neck a rub. Just wait a minute while I take my shirt off.' He rehearsed these sentences and others like them, but somehow couldn't bring himself to act upon them. Since the incident he had only seen Mrs. Weaver's face beyond the hatch when she put the food through, and it told him nothing. At what time did she retire for the night? At about half-past nine, he thought, and kept involuntarily looking at the clock, his neck protesting sharply as he did so. But the clock wasn't on the chimney-piece, it was in the corner cupboard, and probably not going, since he had omitted to wind it up. How silly: he had his wrist-watch, of course, and it said ten o'clock. If he called her now she would probably be in bed, and come down in her nightgown or her pyjamas, or whatever slumberwear she favoured, and that would never do.

He felt an unaccountable unwillingness to go to bed, and lingered on watching the dying fire. A fire made work; he oughtn't to have it, really, now that he was without a daily woman: to-morrow he would tell Mrs. Weaver not to light it.

At last he dragged himself upstairs, but when he reached his bedroom he realized he had forgotten the oil of wintergreen. He must turn the lights on and go back and fetch it. Down he went through the quiet house. It was on the sideboard where Mrs. Weaver had left it, and even at a distance exhaled a strong whiff of her presence. Its own smell, when he took the cork out, was much more reassuring.

Remember the finger-tips . . . He rubbed gently along his neck, and as far round to the back as he could reach; Mrs. Weaver was right: it was easier for someone else to do it, but that someone had to be the right one, which she was not. He lengthened out the process, turning up the bottle, taking little nips, as if he was a wintergreen addict.

Now there was no excuse for these delaying tactics: he must get into bed. But before getting into bed, he must put back the bottle—put it back into the corner cupboard.

But why? Why not leave it on his dressing-table till the morning, when somebody else—Mrs. Weaver in fact—would put it back? He wasn't mad about the corner cupboard and she was, or seemed to be: if he put it back he would deprive her of a pleasure. But he saw through his own cowardice, for cowardice it was; he mustn't let it grow on him, mustn't let neurosis grow on him, or soon he wouldn't be able to do the simplest thing, not cross the street, perhaps, which was far more dangerous, even in the country, than putting a medicine-bottle back into its place.

When he was only a few feet from the cupboard he heard the sound of something dripping. Was it the tap from his wash-basin? But no, the tap was turned off. Back he came and saw, couldn't help seeing, a dark pool like an inky sunburst on the bare boards below the cupboard. He stooped to touch it; his upturned finger came back red, not black.

A quotation, or perhaps a misquotation, from Landor stole into his mind: 'Dost thou hear the blood drip, Dashka?'

The curtains were flung back, the stage appeared: rather the same scene as last time, but there were differences. Another bottle faced him, its neck broken and cracked down all its length. Through the crack the red cough-mixture oozed. The cotton-wool corpse, white dabbled with red, was not a woman's but a man's; elementary as the modelling was, the figure was faintly obscene. And the blade of the pocket-knife, instead of pointing at the vitals of the victim, was plunged into its neck. There was something else too, the explanation of which didn't dawn on Philip at the time: a sliver of coarse yellowish paper, cut out of a telegram: SEVERELY WOUNDED, it said.

Rage struggled with terror in Philip's breast, but for the moment rage prevailed. Magic, indeed! He'd show her! He'd give her magic! But what, and how? His mind had never worked along those lines before. He looked up. On the top shelf lay the fat roll of cotton-wool in its flimsy wrapping of blue paper which he had intended as a barricade against the evil influences of the tortoiseshell. Had Mrs. Weaver, prying in the cupboard, moved it, and had the sight of what lay behind it touched her off? . . . She had plucked it like a goose: feathers of cotton-wool were everywhere, mingled with thin shreds of blue paper. Philip followed suit, and soon had fashioned from the yielding medium the grotesque likeness of a female form. But what to do with it? Exactly what harm did he intend her? What kind of death were those implacable soldier-bottles to witness?

The doll's house on the landing just outside his door possessed a kitchen, and the kitchen had a stove, a big old-fashioned thing with an oven-door that opened. He took the stove out and suddenly his evil purpose seemed to animate it, giving it the cold fascination of a lethal instrument. But he must clean the cupboard first, for no blood was to flow. He must shift the scene so that no competing image should weaken its effect. He worked with nailbrush, soap and towel—Mrs. Weaver kept her kitchen very clean. How much verisimilitude should he aim at? He wanted his tableau to be death-like, not life-like. Softly he closed the oven-door on the plump neck; the head was well inside; the arms and legs and trunk sprawled outwards. His horror of himself increased almost to faintness; through the salutary odours of the medicine-cupboard he thought he could detect a whiff of gas. And there must be one, there must be. He turned his bedroom gas-fire on, and listened to the exciting continuous susurration of escaping gas. Death could breathe out without ever breathing in. But *he* could not, and it was to escape himself and his own fate, not to hasten Mrs. Weaver's that he turned the tap off and lurched out of the room.

In which of the outhouses he spent the night he never knew. But it gave him a sense of security so profound that under it he slept and slept and slept. Only by degrees, as he was crossing the courtyard in the broad daylight, did memory of the night before return to him, and then only as shapes and colours of feeling, not as facts. But by the time he reached his door he had more or less reconstructed the story. It horrified him; the future yawned at his feet.

Hardly had he got into bed and kicked out his cold hot-water bottle when there came a knock at the door and Mrs. Weaver entered, bringing his morning tea. She drew the curtains and, without being asked, handed him his bed-jacket.

'How is your neck this morning, sir?' she inquired.

Philip turned his head. It hurt him very much, which was strange, for he had felt nothing of it for ten hours.

'Not much better, I'm afraid,' he said.

'You should have let me rub it, sir. My husband——'

'Ah, how good you were to him,' said Philip. 'And yet he died in the end, poor fellow.'

She made no answer but sniffed the air and said,

'There's a slight smell of gas in here. Shall I open the window wider?'

'Do.'

'I always think gas is dangerous,' she went on. 'And so I'm afraid I must give in my notice.'

'Oh, Mrs. Weaver!'

'Yes, I must leave to-day, and I'll forgo my wages. I had a dreadful dream.'

'Oh, what?'

'That I was being gassed. That I had put my head in a gas-oven. What could have made me dream that?'

'What indeed? But dreams go by contraries, you know,' said Philip.

'I'm not so sure,' said Mrs. Weaver, pensively. 'I'm not so sure. I've ordered the taxi for ten o'clock. I will cook your breakfast.'

On an impulse Philip jumped out of bed. His foot struck against something hard—it was a skewer, a meat skewer.

'Mrs. Weaver,' he called after her, 'you've forgotten something.'

When she came back he handed her the skewer.

'A skewer?' she said. 'However did that get here?' It dropped from her fingers and lay between them, pointing, he was glad to see, in her direction. She stooped to pick it up.

'No, leave it,' he said. 'I'll see to it. And there are two things you can do for me.'

'Yes, sir.'

'First, would you telephone to Shuttleworth Hospital and ask how Mrs. Featherstone is?'

She came back with her neutral face, and said that Mrs. Featherstone had taken a turn for the better.

'And now would you kindly put the bottle of wintergreen back into the medicine-cupboard?'

From the bed he watched her open the bow-fronted doors. One glance showed him that all his magic apparatus of the night had been dismantled.

'Tell me one thing,' he said. 'Do you know who tidied up the medicine-cupboard?'

'No, sir,' she said, and closed the door behind her. Fingering the meat skewer, which was long, thin, sharp and crowned by the traditional crook, Philip almost, but not quite, believed her.

Below him on the blue rep carpet, the Heriz rug, which had lain un-regarded for the past few days, suddenly caught his eye. At first to his bewildered mind it seemed a rug like any other; then slowly it began to assert itself and declare its wordless message. Who had woven it, he wondered, who had coloured it with his thoughts? What passions had gone into it, at the confluence of the pale red and the dark? He could not tell nor did it matter; indeed nothing seemed to matter when once the silken spell began to work.

THE WAITS

CHRISTMAS Eve had been for all the Marriners, except Mr. Marriner, a most exhausting day. The head of the house usually got off lightly at the festive season, lightly that is as far as personal effort went. Financially, no; Mr. Marriner knew that financially quite a heavy drain was being made on his resources. And later in the evening when he got out his cheque-book to give his customary presents to his family, his relations and the staff, the drain would be heavier. But he could afford it, he could afford it better this Christmas than at any other Christmas in the history of his steadily increasing fortune. And he didn't have to think, he didn't have to choose; he only had to consult a list and add one or two names, and cross off one or two. There was quite a big item to cross off, quite a big item, though it didn't figure on the list or on the counterfoil of his cheque-book. If he saw fit he would add the sum so saved to his children's cheques. Jeremy and Anne would then think him even more generous than he was, and if his wife made any comment, which she wouldn't, being a tactful woman, he would laugh and call it a Capital Distribution — 'capital in every sense, my dear!'

But this could wait till after dinner.

So of the quartet who sat down to the meal, he was the only one who hadn't spent a laborious day. His wife and Anne had both worked hard decorating the house and making arrangements for the party on Boxing Day. They hadn't spent the time in getting presents, they hadn't had to. Anne, who was two years older than Jeremy, inherited her mother's gift for present-giving and had made her selections weeks ago; she had a sixth sense for knowing what people wanted. But Jeremy had left it all to the last moment. His method was the reverse of Anne's and much less successful; he thought of the present first and the recipient afterwards. Who would this little box do for? Who would this other little

518

box do for? Who should be the fortunate possessor of this third little box? In present-giving his mind followed a one-way track; and this year it was little boxes. They were expensive and undiscriminating presents and he was secretly ashamed of them. Now it was too late to do anything more: but when he thought of the three or four friends who would remain un-boxed his conscience smote him.

Silent and self-reproachful, he was the first to hear the singing outside the window.

'Listen, there's some carol-singers!' His voice, which was breaking, plunged and croaked.

The others all stopped talking and smiles spread over their faces.

'Quite good, aren't they?'

'The first we've had this year,' said Mrs. Marriner.

'Well, not the first, my dear; they started coming days ago, but I sent them away and said that waits must wait till Christmas Eve.'

'How many of them are there?'

'Two, I think,' said Jeremy.

'A man and a woman?'

Jeremy got up and drew the curtain. Pierced only by a single distant street-lamp, the darkness in the garden pressed against the window-pane.

'I can't quite see,' he said, coming back. 'But I think it's a man and a boy.'

'A man and a boy?' said Mr. Marriner. 'That's rather unusual.'

'Perhaps they're choristers, Daddy. They do sing awfully well.'

At that moment the front-door bell rang. To preserve the character of the house, which was an old one, they had retained the original brass bell-pull. When it was pulled the whole house seemed to shudder audibly, with a strangely searching sound, as if its heart-strings had been plucked, while the bell itself gave out a high yell that split into a paroxysm of jangling. The Marriners were used to this phenomenon, and smiled when it made strangers jump: to-night it made them jump themselves. They listened for the sound of footsteps crossing the stone flags of the hall, but there was none.

'Mrs. Parfitt doesn't come till washing-up time,' said Mrs. Marriner. 'Who'll go and give them something?'

'I will,' Anne said, jumping up. 'What shall I give them, Daddy?'

'Oh, give them a bob,' said Mr. Marriner, producing the coin from his pocket. However complicated the sum required he always had it.

Anne set off with the light step and glowing face of an eager benefactor; she came back after a minute or two at a much slower pace and looking puzzled and rather frightened. She didn't sit down but stood over her place with her hands on the chair-back.

'He said it wasn't enough,' she said.

'Wasn't enough?' her father repeated. 'Did he really say that?'

Anne nodded.

'Well, I like his cheek,' Even to his family Mr. Marriner's moods were unforeseeable; by some chance the man's impudence had touched a sympathetic chord in him. 'Go back and say that if they sing another carol they shall have another bob.'

But Anne didn't move.

'If you don't mind, Daddy, I'd rather not.'

They all three raised questioning faces to hers.

'You'd rather not? Why?'

'I didn't like his manner.'

'Whose, the man's?'

'Yes. The boy—you were right, Jeremy, it is a boy, quite a small boy—didn't say anything.'

'What was wrong with the man's manner?' Mr. Marriner, still genial, asked.

'Oh, I don't know!' Anne began to breathe quickly and her fingers tightened on the chair-back. 'And it wasn't only his manner.'

'Henry, I shouldn't——' began Mrs. Marriner warningly, when suddenly Jeremy jumped up. He saw the chance to redeem himself in his own eyes from his ineffectiveness over the Christmas shopping—from the general ineffectiveness that he was conscious of whenever he compared himself with Anne.

'Here's the shilling,' Anne said, holding it out. 'He wouldn't take it.'

'This will make it two,' their father said, suiting the action to the word. 'But only if they sing again, mind you.'

While Jeremy was away, they all fell silent, Anne still trying to compose her features, Mr. Marriner tapping on the table, his wife studying her rings. At last she said:

'They're all so class-conscious nowadays.'

'It wasn't that,' said Anne.

'What was it?'

Before she had time to answer—if she would have answered—the door opened and Jeremy came in, flushed and excited but also triumphant, with the triumph he had won over himself. He didn't go to his place but stood away from the table looking at his father.

'He wouldn't take it,' he said. 'He said it wasn't enough. He said you would know why.'

'I should know why?' Mr. Marriner's frown was an effort to remember something. 'What sort of man is he, Jeremy?'

'Tall and thin, with a pulled-in face.'

'And the boy?'

'He looked about seven. He was crying.'

'Is it anyone you know, Henry?' asked. his wife.

'I was trying to think. Yes, no, well, yes, I might have known him.' Mr. Marriner's agitation was now visible to them all, and even more felt than seen. 'What did you say, Jeremy?'

Jeremy's breast swelled.

'I told him to go away.'

'And has he gone?'

As though in answer the bell pealed again.

'I'll go this time,' said Mrs. Marriner. 'Perhaps I can do something for the child.'

And she was gone before her husband's outstretched arm could stop her.

Again the trio sat in silence, the children less concerned with themselves than with the gleam that kept coming and going in their father's eyes like a dipping headlight.

Mrs. Marriner came back much more self-possessed than either of her children had.

'I don't think he means any harm,' she said, 'he's a little cracked, that's all. We'd better humour him. He said he wanted to see you, Henry, but I told him you were out. He said that what we offered wasn't enough and that he wanted what you gave him last year, whatever that means. So I suggest we give him something that isn't money. Perhaps you could spare him one of your boxes, Jeremy. A Christmas box is quite a good idea.'

'He won't take it,' said Anne, before Jeremy could speak.

'Why not?'

'Because he can't,' said Anne.

'Can't? What do you mean?' Anne shook her head. Her mother didn't press her.

'Well, you are a funny girl,' she said. 'Anyhow, we can but try. Oh, and he said they'd sing us one more carol.'

They set themselves to listen, and in a moment the strains of 'God rest you merry, gentlemen' began.

Jeremy got up from the table.

'I don't believe they're singing the words right,' he said. He went to the window and opened it, letting in a puff of icy air.

'Oh, do shut it!'

'Just a moment. I want to make sure.'

They all listened, and this is what they heard:

'God blast the master of this house,
Likewise the mistress too,
And all the little children
That round the table go.'

Jeremy shut the window. 'Did you hear?' he croaked.

'I thought I did,' said Mrs. Marriner. 'But it might have been "bless", the words sound so much alike. Henry, dear, don't look so serious.'

The door-bell rang for the third time. Before the jangling died down, Mr. Marriner rose shakily.

'No, no, Henry,' said his wife. 'Don't go, it'll only encourage them. Besides, I said you were out.' He looked at her doubtfully, and the bell rang again, louder than before. 'They'll soon get tired of it,' she said, 'if no one comes. Henry, I beg you not to go.' And when he still stared at her with groping eyes, she added:

'You can't remember how much you gave him last year?' Her husband made an impatient gesture with his hand.

'But if you go take one of Jeremy's boxes.'

'It isn't a box they want,' he said, 'it's a bullet.'

He went to the sideboard and brought out a pistol. It was an old-fashioned saloon pistol, a relic from the days when Henry's father, in common with others of his generation, had practised pistol-shooting, and it had lain at the back of a drawer in the sideboard longer than any of them could remember.

'No, Henry, no! You mustn't get excited! And think of the child!'

She was on her feet now; they all were.

'Stay where you are!' he snarled.

'Anne! Jeremy! Tell him not to! Try to stop him.' But his children could not in a moment shake off the obedience of a lifetime, and helplessly they watched him go.

'But it isn't any good, it isn't any good!' Anne kept repeating.

'What isn't any good, darling?'

'The pistol. You see, I've seen through him!'

'How do you mean, seen through him? Do you mean he's an imposter?'

'No, no. I've really seen through him,' Anne's voice sank to a whisper. 'I saw the street lamp shining through a hole in his head.'

'Darling, darling!'

'Yes, and the boy, too——'

'Will you be quiet, Anne?' cried Jeremy from behind the window curtain. 'Will you be quiet? They're saying something. Now Daddy's pointing the gun at him—he's got him covered! His finger's on the trigger, he's going to shoot! No, he isn't. The man's come nearer—he's come right up to Daddy! Now he's showing him something, something on his forehead—oh, if I had a torch—and Daddy's dropped it, he's dropped the gun!'

As he spoke they heard the clatter; it was like the sound that gives confirmation to a wireless commentator's words. Jeremy's voice broke out again:

'He's going off with them—he's going off with them! They're leading him away!'

Before she or any of them could reach the door, Mrs. Marriner had fainted.

The police didn't take long to come. On the grass near the garden gate they found the body. There were signs of a struggle—a slither, like a skid-mark, on the gravel, heel-marks dug deep into the turf. Later it was learnt that Mr. Marriner had died of coronary thrombosis. Of his assailants not a trace was found. But the motive couldn't have been robbery, for all the money he had had in his pockets, and all the notes out of his wallet (a large sum), were scattered around him, as if he had made a last attempt to buy his captors off, but couldn't give them enough.

THE PAMPAS CLUMP

'But what is it you don't like about the pampas clump?' I asked.

'Well, it's untidy for one thing,' Thomas said. 'It doesn't grow evenly and always seems to need a haircut. A shrub should be symmetrical.'

'It isn't exactly a shrub.'

'No, it isn't. A shrub would be more self-controlled. It's a sort of grass — and grass needs cutting. Besides, it's all ages at once, some of it's green, some sere, and some dead. And then its leaves break and dangle depressingly.'

'But aren't we all like that?'

'Not so obviously. We are more of a piece. Anyone would know that you were forty-one, Fergus, and I was thirty-eight.'

I flattered myself that I looked younger than Thomas; there was a deep line between his brows and his eyes behind his spectacles were tired and restless.

'How old is the pampas?'

'Oh, any age. It was here, you may remember, when I bought the house. I've often thought of getting rid of it. It's so suburban. It doesn't fit into an old garden, like this one is supposed to be.'

'But if it's old itself?'

'It must be, or it wouldn't have grown to such a size. But that doesn't make it any the less suburban. People live to a great age in surburbia, and sometimes grow to a great size. . . . And besides being untidy, it makes the grass round it untidy too, it sheds itself.'

'A plant has to live according to its habit,' I argued.

'Yes, but I don't like its habit, or its habits. It offends my sense of fitness. Besides, it's dangerous.'

'Dangerous?'

'Yes. It looks fragile and wispy, but its leaves are like razors, they cut you to the bone. It's treacherous and dishonest.'

'Oh, do you think of it as a person?'

Thomas fidgeted.

'No, of course not, except in so far as something you don't like takes on a personality for you.'

'What sort of personality has it?'

'A semi-transparent one. It blocks the view from the french window, but if you look hard you can see through it—or you think you can. I'm always wondering if there isn't someone the other side of it who can see me though I can't see him or her.'

'Oh, Thomas, how fanciful you are!'

'Well, you try.'

Obediently I screwed my eyes up. The library had two windows, and from the french window, the one nearest to the fireplace, by which we were sitting, the pampas clump did indeed block the view. It cut the line of the hills across the valley. In the early October twilight it looked quite enormous; its cone-shaped plumes, stirred by a gentle breeze, swept the dusky sky, soaring above its downward-curving foliage as a many-jetted fountain soars above the water fanning outwards from its basin. And like a fountain, it was, as Thomas had said, half-transparent. You thought you could see what was behind it, but you couldn't be sure. That didn't worry me; I rather liked the idea of the mystery, the *terra incognita* behind the pampas. And Thomas should have liked it, too. No one ever called him Tom: at Oxford he was nicknamed Didymus, he was so much in doubt. Did he dislike the pampas because, in some way, it reminded him of himself, and his own weaknesses? I strained my eyes again, trying to see what lay beyond the soaring feathers and the looped, drooping, reed-like leaves. Perhaps . . . Perhaps . . . What did Thomas *want* me to say?

'There *could* be somebody,' I ventured.

'That's what I mean.'

'But he . . . she . . . they couldn't see you because . . .'

'Because why?'

'Because when a shrub . . . or something of that sort is near to you, it's more opaque than when it's at a distance. But if you don't like it, why don't you burn it?'

Thomas shuffled in his chair, and answered irritably, 'I don't like destroying things. Besides, it would only rise from its ashes like the phoenix.'

'But if it annoys you——'

'It doesn't annoy me all that much. Besides . . .' he stopped.

'Besides what?' I prompted.

'You'll think me silly if I tell you.'

'I find all your objections to the pampas frivolous,' I said, 'but tell me.'

'Well, I have a sneaking wish to find out if there *is* someone on the other side of it.'

I didn't laugh because I realized that what he had said meant something to him, something that had been in his mind for a long time. Was it an obsession that he wanted to get rid of, or was he really clinging to it? A ghost that worried him, but one he didn't want to lay? I had an idea.

'When the others come——'

He glanced up. It was half-past six by the French clock on the chimney-piece.

'Are you getting bored?' he asked. 'Julia and Hilary will be here any time now.'

'I didn't mean that,' I said. 'I'm glad to have this chance of talking to you alone. It's so long . . . I meant, couldn't we arrange a sort of *test?*'

'Of what?'

'Well, of whether there *is* someone behind the pampas clump or not.'

He seemed to ponder deeply. 'I don't know . . . I don't know. What had you in mind?'

'A sort of procession.'

'A procession? What sort of procession?'

'I hadn't worked out the details.'

Thomas shook his head, fretfully.

'I don't like the idea of a procession. Too many people, and it straggles.'

'Oh, this would be a small, select one.'

'I don't know what you mean,' said Thomas. 'I'm not with you.' There was a sound outside the house, scrunchings and small earth-tremors, and then a silence that indicated arrival. 'Here they are!' said Thomas, getting up and making for the door. 'Guests never seem to arrive at exactly the right time.'

'Have I your permission?——' I called out after him, but I don't think he heard.

Julia I knew quite well; she was fair and round and buxom and in her middle thirties. She had lost her husband in the war; and curiously enough as a widow she was twice the person she had been as a wife. As a wife she had taken on her husband's personality; as a widow she had recovered her own without losing his. Protectiveness was her strong point, and it was clear she had now extended it to Hilary. While her husband was alive she said 'we' more often than she said 'I': she said 'we' still, meaning herself and Hilary.

Hilary I knew much less well. She was tall and dark and slender and could look beautiful, but her beauty was ambiguous like the rest of her. I could not make her out, and the more I saw of her the less I understood her. A sphinx without a secret, perhaps. But a sphinx that has, I thought, its attractions for Thomas, for he tried on her many kinds of conversational approach, which she either evaded or answered in a way that he didn't quite expect.

'Are you going abroad, Hilary?'

'Well, as a matter of fact I've just been.'

'Of course, I knew that. You wrote to me from Venice.'

'Did I? I wrote so many letters.'

'We were always writing letters,' Julia put in 'when we weren't sightseeing. Hilary writes such good letters.'

'Do I? I often think they're all about myself, or nothing.'

'Yourself or nothing? Perhaps they are the same,' said Thomas with so much feeling in his voice that it cancelled out the rudeness. 'It's yourself we want to know about. But perhaps you have several selves. Julia's Hilary may be different from mine, and Fergus's different again.'

He raised an eyebrow at me. I thought he carried his probings further than politeness warranted. She didn't seem to resent them but they embarrassed her; she said the word 'I' non-committally and without conviction as if she was not quite sure to what it referred. I didn't want to be drawn but I had to say something — if possible something that would smooth the path for Thomas, who was so obviously taken by her.

'Walt Whitman said you ought to "publish yourself of a personality,"' I remarked.

'That I ought to?'

We laughed.

'No, that everyone ought to.'

Hilary looked troubled.

'That's what I find so difficult!'

'It's one of our problems,' Julia said, smiling, though it was certainly not a problem for her.

'But *are* you going abroad in the winter?' Thomas persisted.

'What do you think, Julia?'

Thomas shook his head in mock despair and before Julia could answer burst out, 'There you go again! Or rather, you don't go—and when you stay——' He spread his hands out, as though to indicate how inconclusive her staying was.

'We will go now,' said Julia huffily, 'and leave you to your port.'

She rose and we rose with her. Hilary was nearly as tall as Thomas; her full, flared skirt swung as she moved. Her charm showed in her movements; they told one something about her that her tongue could not tell.

'Now I like that dress of yours,' said Thomas, 'I like those thin Regency stripes, they are so definite—and the neat rows of forget-me-nots in between. As if we could forget you! It's almost a crinoline, isn't it? Who can tell where it ends and you begin?'

She coloured, and I said to cover her confusion, 'She's like the pampas clump.'

That was how we got back to it again.

It was too dark to do anything now, we decided; to-morrow between tea and dinner, Thomas said, should be the time for our experiment.

'But why so late?' I asked. 'Wouldn't it be better in the full sunlight?'

'How do you mean, better?'

'Well, a better test. In the twilight you might think you were seeing things.'

'We want to see things, don't we?'

'I thought you wanted to make sure, Didymus, that there was nothing . . . or something. As soon as the light begins to go——'

'Doesn't it seem more sporting,' he interrupted, 'to give the mystery a chance? I don't know how I should feel, after all this time, faced by complete certitude.'

'But I thought you wanted it,' I repeated, 'both as regards the pampas clump and . . . and . . .'

'And Hilary? Yes, I suppose I do. I want to be sure about her. But shall I be—about either of them—after the experiment? You called me fanciful, a moment ago.'

'Whatever happens,' I pronounced, 'or doesn't happen, it will change the direction of your thoughts. You won't be able to feel quite the same about . . . either of them again.'

We began to discuss the ways and means, and then Thomas said, 'I think it's time we joined the girls.'

Sunday dragged unbearably: I have seldom been so conscious of the passage of time. The house was liberally provided with clocks, most of them the French Empire type — ladies reclining, children holding baskets of fruits and flowers, all leading a timeless, leisured life. There was hardly one I didn't consult, but the clock in my bedroom was my favourite, because it lagged behind the others and gave me a respite. From what? I didn't really think that anything would come of the experiment, but its increasing nearness provoked a sense of crisis. Ridiculous! It couldn't fail to be a flop — although how much of a flop only Thomas and I should know — for we were not going to take the girls into our confidence — or, of course, the pampas clump itself. More than once during the morning, before Julia and Hilary had made their appearance, and while Thomas was still in church, I went out and studied it. It was a great big thing, the size of a small haystack; it dwarfed the lawn, which was large enough in all conscience, as if it had been a round of beef on a dessert-plate. Like other oversize objects it excited in me, at any rate, mixed feelings of wonder and resentment. Denser in some places than in others, it looked densest when I took my stand outside the french window in the library. Which, for the success of the experiment, ought it to be, transparent or opaque? If transparent, how easy it would be to cheat a little, force one's way into its reedy heart with a pair of secateurs, and thin it out! No one would be the wiser. But wouldn't they? Might not someone see me from a window? Besides, those leaves like razor-blades! I should come back criss-crossed with scratches, or perhaps cut to the bone and pouring blood! 'Why, Fergus, what on earth have you been doing to get into that state?' 'Well, Thomas, I tripped and took a header into the pampas clump, and it savaged me, just as you said it would.'

Giving the plant a wide berth I circled round it, feeling I was being watched. If only I could divide myself in two: become the subject and the object, as one can in thought, then I could make my *alter ego* face me across the pampas. How exciting to see, if I did see him, another Fergus, not a reflection but a real one, perhaps more real than I was! The essential me, in visible form! I had almost transferred Thomas's problem to myself when I looked up and there he was, only a few feet away from me. I had been too much preoccupied to see or hear him coming.

'Spying out the land?' he asked.

I started.

'Yes, I suppose I was.'

He said carelessly:

'You know, I've been thinking it over, perhaps in the light of the Christian faith, which you don't seem to hold——'

'I ought to have gone to church with you, I know.'

'Don't mention it. What I wanted to say was, perhaps we are not meant to see more clearly than we do—through a pampas clump darkly, and all that, and we'd better drop this scheme of ours. What do you think, Fergus?'

'I should be disappointed. What harm can it do? We should just pass by——'

'Oh, it's the principle of the thing. The idea is all right—quite poetical. But if you tried to *live* poetry——'

'Yes?'

'Well, you might come a cropper. . . . Hullo, here are the girls.'

Hilary was walking a little behind Julia, but Thomas addressed himself to her. 'Good morning, good morning, but it isn't morning, it's afternoon. What have you been doing with yourselves all this time? What have you been doing, Hilary?'

'Nothing much.'

'Nothing much? Couldn't you elaborate that a little?'

'We wrote some letters,' Julia said.

'You're always writing letters, Hilary! Always on paper, never in the flesh! Did you say you were staying here?'

'I used your writing-paper.'

Thomas tried a more direct approach.

'Did you say what fun you were having?'

'I said how nice it was, of course.'

'Did you say anything nice about me?'

Hilary reddened and said with difficulty, 'What else could I say?'

Thomas had to be content with that.

As the dead-line drew near, my heart began to beat uncomfortably. Between six o'clock and dinner is always an awkward time: tea is a thing of the past, drinks are still some way off. Remembering my cue I said:

'What shall we do now?'

To my astonishment Thomas answered, 'Isn't it rather nice sitting here?' ·

Was he really going to rat on me?

'Very nice,' I said, 'but oughtn't we to do something—something for Hilary to write home about?'

'We've written home,' said Julia, and Hilary stretched her hands towards the newly lit fire.

'You see,' said Thomas, 'she wants to sit among the cinders, warming her pretty little toes, and I should like to sit with her.'

'I have another plan for her,' I said.

'Drop it, Fergus. Forget it.'

I trained an Ancient Mariner's eye on him.

'All day,' I said, 'you've been asking Hilary questions which, if I'm not mistaken, she hasn't always wanted to answer.' I paused to let this sink in. Thomas's face remained expressionless, Julia nodded in approval, Hilary looked as if she wished I hadn't spoken. 'If I carry out my plan,' I went on, with all the impressiveness I could muster, 'Hilary may feel more inclined to answer questions, or Thomas less inclined to ask them.'

'What do you propose, then?' asked Thomas, disingenuously, for he well knew.

I saw that he was weakening.

'Just to go for a walk.'

'Go by all means,' said Thomas, 'but I shan't go with you. I shall stay behind and write letters, like Hilary. Remember, I went to church.'

'If we go for a walk we must change our shoes,' said Julia.

'Need you change yours, Hilary?' Thomas teased her.

She gave him a half-pleading look and got up to go.

'Let's meet in the hall,' I said. 'Mind, no shirking.'

The evening was warm with a slight mist rising from the grass.

'Which way?' asked Julia.

'Round by the silo. I'll show you. I'll go first.' I spoke with authority, as one who leads an expedition.

Julia automatically fell in behind me, and Hilary as automatically brought up the rear, and we were moving off when Hilary said, suddenly,

'Need we walk in single file?'

'Only for a minute, until we get our bearings,' and I headed for the far side of the pampas clump, the side away from the house. Reaching it I slowed down, and the little procession, like a cortège, well spaced out, trailed past the clump at a snail's pace.

We went on in this formation for a minute or two: and then Hilary called out: 'Can't we join up now? It's lonely being the cow's tail.'

'Of course,' I said, and stopped. As we were regrouping ourselves,

Julia said to Hilary, 'Why, darling, we're looking quite pale—I mean you are. Is anything the matter?'

'I'm all right now,' said Hilary, breathing rather fast. 'Just for a moment something seemed to come over me—a sort of goose-flesh—you seemed so far away, I couldn't reach you! I'm all right now,' she repeated.

'A touch of agoraphobia, perhaps,' I said. 'Let's go arm in arm.' I linked their arms in mine, and so we proceeded until our stumbles brought to an end this always risky method of progression.

'There's the silo,' I told them, as we disengaged ourselves.

'What a horrible object!' cried Julia. 'Why did you choose it for our *but du promenade?*'

'It looks prettier as you get nearer.'

'Oh, nonsense! You must be a surrealist.'

'What do you think, Hilary?' For even I felt impelled to try to drag an opinion out of her.

She answered with unexpected vehemence:

'I hate it—it looks so sinister—it's so black and thick and frightening.'

'Why, it's only a granary!'

'I know that, but let's go another way!'

I suggested the village. 'But,' I warned them, 'we shall lose altitude, we shall have to *climb* back.'

'Oh, Fergus,' cried Julia, 'what a slave-driver you are! Isn't he, Hilary?'

She didn't answer. I pleaded the need of exercise, for me and them; but I didn't explain, as we tramped through the village, and beyond it, that I felt an unaccountable reluctance to go back to the house. What effect would the experiment have had on Thomas? None, I felt sure, but even a negative result would be disappointing. So nearly an hour had passed, and it was growing dark, when weary and footsore (as Julia complained that she and Hilary were) we trudged up the slope to Hill House.

'What's that?'

We were approaching the house from the village, not the garden, side and there was a sort of glare behind it, that outlined the steep roof against the sky and couldn't have been an effect of the sunset, for it waxed and waned.

'What's that?' repeated Julia. 'Is the house on fire?'

'Or a chimney?' said Hilary, for once offering a suggestion. 'The sparks might be——' she stopped.

Sparks there certainly were, but they didn't come out of a chimney-pot; they were being whirled about the sky like fire-flies.

'Take your time,' I said. 'I'll hurry on.'

The pungent smell of burning met me in the hall. 'Thomas!' I called, 'Thomas!' and getting no answer went straight into the library. Here the smell was stronger and the glare fiercer; it lit up the room, lit it up so brightly that I saw at once on the round leather-covered table an envelope with my name scrawled on it. I tore it open.

'Dear Fergus,' I read,

'I saw two figures quite distinctly, yours and Julia's, but not a third, and I'm driven to think that Hilary doesn't exist—at least for me. I only exist for her—so why go on? I don't blame you for wanting me to make sure—I am sure now. You'll find me like Polly Flinders.

Love, Thomas.'

I ran to the window, where the glare came from, but it was not so much the glare that filled my eyes as the huge gap, black and ominous, like a cauldron hung over a furnace, where the pampas clump had been. Beneath it the flames still ran and leapt and spurted on their glowing bed of ashes. Outside the french window I felt their scorching breath upon my face and was soon beaten back. It was not until later, a good deal later, that I and one or two others found the charred remains and near by the twisted shard of the burst pistol which was still too hot to touch.

WON BY A FALL

'HAVE you ever tried to live a story?' I once asked a friend of mine. I hadn't seen him for a good many years, and in the meanwhile he had made his name as a novelist.

'Well,' said he, 'I try to live my stories while I'm writing them.'

'I didn't quite mean that. I meant, have you ever read or been told a story which took your fancy so much that you tried to translate it into real life, your own life?'

'You mean a sort of day-dreaming?'

'No, something more definite. I mean a deliberate attempt to make certain events which you've heard about come true, and happen to yourself.'

He thought for a bit.

'I can't say that I have,' he said. 'But if *you* have, tell me. There might be something in it for me.'

After this slender encouragement I began.

'Well, this is the story. It was told me by someone who had read it — I didn't read it myself. There was a man, a big, strong fellow——'

'Like you,' my friend said.

'Yes, to some extent. I couldn't have put myself in his shoes — identified myself with him, or whatever you call it — if he hadn't been. And he was about my age — I was twenty-eight at the time——'

'How long ago was it?'

'About six years. Like me, he was an athlete in a sort of way, and we had other things in common. I worked for a firm in the City, as I daresay you remember——'

'Yes, I think I do.'

'And they used to let me off for Rugger matches, even in the middle of the week. I think they felt I gave them some prestige—

though God knows how. The fellow in the story was a policeman——'

'You look rather like a policeman,' said my friend.

'Yes, I've been told so. He went in for wrestling, and sometimes he was excused duty, to take part in a scrap on the mat. Well, this policeman was in love with a girl, but she didn't care for him—I mean she quite liked him, but she was in love with another fellow, a violinist in an orchestra he was, with spectacles and hair falling over his eyes—not the sort of man you'd think a girl would take to.'

I regretted having said this, for my friend was no oil-painting. He was undersized and he wore spectacles. But he was so well known in his own walk of life that I didn't think his appearance mattered to him.

'Did the policeman and the violinist ever meet?' he asked me.

'No, but she used to tell the policeman about him when she was explaining why she couldn't marry him.'

'Oh, they were on those terms?'

'They walked out together quite a lot. She explained that she felt protective towards the violinist, which she couldn't towards a policeman, and this policeman was a particularly protective type, besides being a grappler.'

'And you?' my friend said.

'I was courting too, and the girl had a boy-friend, but she was different—she was cagey about him and never let on who he was. But she did say she felt protective towards him. "It's a man's job to protect a woman," I used to tell her, but she couldn't see it that way. In the end I got thoroughly fed up.'

'You're telling your own story now.'

'Only to show the similarities and the differences. I was on a spot just like the policeman was. His mat-work suffered, he lost his appetite, and when he was on the beat he started imagining things—a man with a sack on his shoulder who went into a cul-de-sac (no pun intended) and disappeared—I can't remember the details. And something about seeing an old illuminated manuscript in an ash-can, and when he went back for it, it wasn't there. He thought he was going potty, and all because of this girl.'

'What was she like?' my friend asked.

'I think she was slight and dark and not specially pretty, but she had it for him. Well, one morning about nine o'clock he was strolling along some London street in a dazed sort of way, not having slept—they didn't use sleeping-pills so much in those days—and he slipped on a piece of banana-skin and fell down and couldn't get up. Of course he knew about

First Aid and those things, and he knew that something must be wrong.
So he just lay there. As it happened there weren't many people about,
but presently a girl came up to him, and it was——'

'You needn't tell me,' my friend said. 'It was the girl he was in love
with. Talk of coincidences!'

'But they happen, don't they? And many people's lives turn on them.
Well, she saw him lying there, looking very pale, with his helmet in the
gutter and his leg twisted under him, and in spite of that she recognized
him and called for help, and they got him into an ambulance and took
him to hospital, and it turned out that his knee-cap was fractured, pretty
badly. The surgeon made a mess of setting it, so in the end not only did
he have to give up wrestling, he had to leave the police and get a job as
a doorman. But——'

'The girl married him,' my friend said.

'How did you guess? She was sorry for him, you see. She thought
she could give him something that he needed.'

'And they lived happily ever after?'

'No, not quite. He took to drink, as doormen often do; they work
such long hours, they often drop in for a quick one—and the glow of
self-sacrifice got a bit dim and sometimes she wished she hadn't made
it. That's life, of course.'

My friend agreed. 'But where do you come in?'

'Well,' I said, and somehow it wasn't easy to go on. 'I kept thinking
about the story and the more I thought about it the more I got into the
policeman's state of mind—half-desperate, you know. I hadn't minded
so much before I heard it. I had other girls in my life but the policeman's
story seemed to pin-point this one.'

'What was her name?'

'Rosemary.'

My friend made no comment, and I went on, 'Then it occurred to
me, Why don't I do what the policeman did? And then I laughed because of what you were saying, was it likely I should slip on a banana-
skin just as Rosemary happened to pass by? The chances were too much
against it. All the same, the thought kept nagging me, and one evening
when she told me she had almost made up her mind to marry this chap
—whoever he was—are you married, by the way?'

'No,' my friend said.

'Take my advice, and don't be. Well, that piece of news jolted my
imagination and gave me an idea. Why shouldn't I stage an accident
like the policeman's? Not a serious one like his, of course, though I

should make it look so—I should hobble away, leaning on her arm—
and not just anywhere, I wasn't too far gone to see how silly that would
be. But I knew of course where Rosemary worked—she was secretary
to some sort of executive in a street off Knightsbridge. I used to wonder
if he was the man, typists so often fall for their employers. And I knew
what time she had to clock in by—nine-thirty in the morning. We used
to save up things to tell each other—I more than her. I had learned her
daily schedule by heart—or all of it that mattered to me—so that whenever I thought about her, I should know what she was doing, at any
given time. She took the bus along Knightsbridge and then walked
down this side-street.'

'And you relied on finding a convenient banana-skin?'

'Ah, there I was clever. But to go back. I worked, as I told you, in the
City, practically the same hours as she did, and the City is a long way
from Knightsbridge. How could I be there when she was? One afternoon I told my boss I wasn't feeling well and could I have to-morrow
off? I'd never gone sick before. I remember his reply, he said: "Yes, of
course, Parminter. We've got to keep you fit, haven't we, for the match
on Saturday." So the next morning I was there in Wilton Place, walking up and down and——'

'Looking for a banana-skin?' my friend asked.

'No! Even in those days manners had changed, as you must have
noticed, and street manners especially. I was *eating* a banana. Between
bites I looked up and at last I saw her hurrying along, a little late, towards me. I dropped the banana-skin on the pavement, I put my foot
on it, and down I went.'

'Poor Parminter!'

'Well, yes, you're right. I was heavy then—I'm a good deal heavier
now—and I came a terrific cropper. My head hit the pavement and I
didn't know where I was for a moment. Then I saw Rosemary bending
over me.

' "Good God!" she said. "It's Gerald! Are you hurt?" '

I moaned, and tried to stir but couldn't.

' "Darling," she said—it was the first time she had ever called me
"darling"—"I know I mustn't try to move you, but I can kiss you,"
and she did. Then she said, "I'll get an ambulance." I was still feeling
groggy when the ambulance drove up, and it's a blur what happened
next, but they let her go with me. At the hospital they X-rayed me, in
case I had broken any bones or cracked my skull (you may think it was
cracked already!). I hadn't, but they said they must detain me for the

night for observation and I was put into a ward with several other cases — orthopaedic, it was called. Rosemary said she would go back to my flat and fetch the things I needed for the night. "Pyjamas? Toothbrush? Toothpaste? Hair-brush? Sponge? Razor? Shaving-brush? Shaving-cream? Bedroom-slippers, dressing-gown?" I had no idea she knew so much about a man's requirements and it all sounded so intimate, as if I'd spent the night with her, which of course I never had — she was too keen on the other fellow. She was back within an hour, but they wouldn't let her see me, because by that time I was suffering from shock — uncontrollable shivers was the form it took. They gave me strong sweet tea and put hot-water bottles round me, I remember. Oh, what a fool I felt, and frightened too: I thought I might have injured myself for life. And what was so mortifying, I had had scores of tumbles playing football, and thought I had learned how to fall. After a time the shivering wore off and then they told me that during the lunch-hour the young lady had telephoned about me twice; she sounded upset, the nurse said, but very sweet. Then a bunch of roses was brought in — roses in February, think of the expense! I took them with me when I left next morning — my bed was needed for another patient. But I could still hardly move: I had a bruise right from my ankle to my hip, and had to be helped into the ambulance and upstairs to my flat. I couldn't get about for several days, and might have starved if Rosemary hadn't come to my rescue. Of course, I missed the match.'

'But not the other match?' my friend said.

'Oh no, I married her.' While I was trying to think what to say next, he said:

'But wasn't that what you wanted?'

'Yes, but it didn't last.'

'Why not?'

'I'll tell you. One day — it was the third anniversary of our wedding day — we had a celebration. It was a slap-up affair, for I'd been doing well, and when we got home, I, being a bit tiddly told her the whole story, how I had faked the fall, and all that. I thought it would amuse her, but it didn't. She burst into tears and said, "You deceived me — I need never have married you." I was as upset as she was. I tried to make her understand that what I did, I did for love of her. But she wouldn't listen. She kept saying I had played a trick on her emotions. "You didn't need me you only wanted me. You've never had anything the matter with you from that day to this! You're the most self-sufficient man I know — you always fall on your feet!"

' "Well, I didn't that time", I couldn't help saying. '

' "Nor this time either," she sobbed, angrier than ever, and the next morning she left me.'

I couldn't have said those words so calmly once; but it was three years ago.

My friend got up and walked about the room.

'And so you lived the story,' he said, 'or part of it.'

'There isn't any more,' I said. 'She went off with another man – the man she'd always been fond of, I suspect – and asked me to divorce her, but I wouldn't.'

'Why not?' my friend asked.

'Oh, I dunno. I still loved her, I am still in love with her, I suppose. She might come back to me.'

'Would you divorce her now?' my friend said.

'I don't think so.'

'Not even if I asked you?'

'If *you* asked me?'

'You see,' he said, 'I was the other man and I wrote the story, little knowing . . . You were right about coincidences. I didn't have to fabricate a fall: I was always down and out, until she came. Perhaps my need is greater than thine, as Sir Philip Sidney didn't say. Without her, I should be——'

I got up. 'I'll think it over,' I said, 'I'll think it over.' I turned away blindly and in turning my foot caught in the fold of a rug and I went headlong. He helped me to my feet.

'Are you all right?'

'Yes, quite all right,' I gasped. 'But take care, and if she's anywhere about, don't tell her that I've had a real fall.'

A VERY PRESENT HELP

DEIRDRE O'FARRELL (it wasn't her real name, though she was Irish) had been George Lambert's mistress for three years. She would have been his wife if he had had his way; but her position with regard to husbands, past, present and to come, was dubious. 'It's quite impossible,' she would say when he urged marriage on her: 'don't ask me why.' He didn't ask her; he accepted her and everything about her without question, and those elements in her make-up that were mysterious and unexplained had a particular glamour for him. Like a retriever carrying a handbag, he was proud of being the bearer of her secrets.

A younger man would have been more exacting. A more experienced man would have looked askance at Deirdre. He would have seen what there was to be seen: a very pretty face, rather chocolate-box, and eyes so blue that they seemed to create a bluish mist between them and the beholder. Through this mist her eyes shone with so much innocence that (to use a vulgarism) it wasn't true. But to George it was true. What gave life and character to her face was a kind of determination to make good. She was, in fact, a calculating little minx, a sexual tease and sometimes a sexual cheat. Every now and then she would withhold her favours, saying, 'Oh, no, I'm not in the mood'; or she would find some pretext for breaking an engagement at the last moment, leaving George with an evening to himself; sometimes she would even hint at other attachments which might be going to supersede his. This policy, however, she used with the utmost caution; she had almost a genius for knowing how far she could go.

During the first two years of their relationship, however, she could have gone any length and George would not have noticed. The idea that he was being made a fool of never entered his head, and wouldn't have influenced him if it had. There was a difference of eighteen years between them; he was forty-one when they met, and she, she said, was twenty-three. He was so much in love with her that his one desire was to satisfy her every whim. Indeed, her caprices only served to make him love her more, for they gave him unlimited opportunities for self-escape, which was, for him, his natural form of self-expression. On her he threw himself away with both hands. No neophyte in love with the love of God, and resolved above all else to do His will, could have got more satisfaction from self-sacrifice than George got.

His education in love had been a late development for two reasons, one psychological, the other material. By nature he was timid with women, and, though he wasn't aware of it, an aesthetic idealist, a connoisseur of looks. Plain women did not attract him, and pretty women whom, from some feeling of inadequacy, he associated with the fashionable beauties of the glossy papers, he felt to be utterly beyond his sphere. As well might a working-man think of going into the Ritz and ordering a cocktail, as George could think of being within arm's length of a beautiful woman. The working-man could do it, no one would prevent him, supposing he had the money and a decent suit of clothes, but equally nothing could persuade him to. The act was not impossible, but it was impossible for him. And so with George. The nimbus of glory that surrounded a pretty woman, added to the sundering effect of class, made her to him as unattainable as is the summit of Mount Everest to the average pedestrian. George knew that other men had scaled it, but knew that he could not.

The nearest he got to his divinities was to cut their pictures out and pin them to the wall—where he gazed at them with awe and reverence, and desire, but oh! how distantly.

Otherwise, he had not had much to do with women, for the second, the material factor in his late development was lack of funds. An only child, he had never mixed much with other children. His parents, who were dead, had scraped together enough money to send him to a small public school, but not enough to leave him any. He had a black-coated job in the City, and being conscientious, over-conscientious, as well as fearful for the future, his work came first with him. Too much so, in a way; for his preoccupation with doing it well made him miss opportunities for advancement which other men, with a keener eye to their own interests, and a wider range of vision, would certainly have seized.

So the legacy, the very substantial legacy from a distant relation which came to him at the age of thirty-nine, found him totally unprepared, socially, emotionally and mentally. Morally he was not so unprepared; his strong sense of obligation found immediate outlets: all sorts of people, and causes, could be benefited. The material aspect of his new position took him longer to realize: in fact he had to be told that with the money at his disposal he could buy himself a partnership in the firm — a proposal which, when it came, the firm welcomed with enthusiasm, for not only were they glad to have the money, they were glad to have him too, a modest, loyal, trust-worthy, hard-working man who had given them good service and no trouble. It could be truly said that no one grudged him his good fortune or the privileges that went with it — one of which was much more leisure, and another a widening range of social contacts.

It was not surprising that he found himself accepted in circles hitherto unknown to him. He was well-mannered, passably good-looking and undeniably eligible; and if he could not always tune in to the wavelength of the people he was with, didn't quite speak their language or understand its nuances, these social shortcomings were readily forgiven him; indeed they were rather welcome than otherwise, for they made him into a kind of pet, a well-meaning animal that has not quite been trained. Several women, one of whom had incidentally been his pin-up girl, undertook to train him and were tireless in trying to raise him in his own esteem. In this they were not altogether disinterested; for they realized that unless a man had a fairly good opinion of himself, he could not be what they would have him be. But the harder they tried, the more deeply they involved him in their silken webs, the more they increased his sense of obligation and apartness. What could he do in return for all this enveloping kindness? Little presents he gave them, flowers and trinkets, presents which were sometimes misunderstood; but rapturously as these tokens were received, they left him with a haunting sense of falling short. They were not enough! They were not enough! Mrs. de Sole, for instance, 'Délice' to her friends; after an evening in her drawing-room, with all its amenities of relaxation, conversation, and near-love, he felt he ought to carry her heavy luggage for her, 'or miles and miles and miles.

Actually he didn't find it easy to spend money; the penurious habits of his early life clung to him; he didn't think he ought to live beyond his income, the idea of spending capital appalled him. Gradually he reached a more realistic view of his financial position, and moved from his small house in the suburbs to a comfortable flat in South Kensington; but it was weeks before he felt he could afford it and months before he dared to give a party.

The party, however, was a success, for all those present were determined that it should be; and when the last guest left, George was left feeling that at last he had done something for somebody.

His men friends did not take the same view of George's potentialities that his women friends took. Their attitude might be described as coarser. They did not, of course, take the same trouble with him, but none the less they had their eye on him — the dark horse, the unknown quantity. Needless to say they didn't want to get him tied up in married life, but women came into their calculations. They thought of love in terms of money, not money in terms of love. At least, some of them did. Most of George's new friends were men who talked of money, and with whom money talked; they had chosen him, not he them; he didn't know his way about in this new world, and was both surprised and flattered when anybody showed an interest in him. The women he gravitated towards were of a gentler and more sensitive type than their husbands, they found George a pleasant change. But the men, being more objective and detached, summed up his position in some ways more accurately than they did.

'What you want, George, is a dog,' said one well-wisher, more discerning than the others.

'A dog?'

'Yes, something that would wag its tail when you come in, and lick your face.'

George thought about this.

'But I should have to take it out for walks.'

'Not all the time. You are such a glutton for responsibility. Sometimes it would look at you with huge pleading eyes, and then you could rub its ears and fondle it. A dog will absorb far more affection than a human being.'

'Do you think I'm affectionate?' asked George.

'In a frustrated way, yes, very. These women you go about with aren't much good to you, you're half-afraid of them. I'm not saying anything against them, mind, in their way they're tops, but not for you. They are too complex, you need something simpler, and more natural. A dog——'

'Yes?'

'Well, it would fawn on you and you could beat it.'

'What a horrible idea.'

'Or you could fawn on it and it would bite you.'

'Isn't there anything between the two?'

'Not for you, there isn't. No, you need a dog, with a strong emotional current uniting you. Not the sort of friendship you have with Mrs. Hake, or Halibut, or whatever her name is. She must freeze the pants off you.'

'I don't know who you mean.'

'That middle-aged harpy who gets you on a sofa and twangs your heart-strings with her varnished nails.'

'Oh, Délice de Sole! She's an angel.'

'That's what I mean. You need someone more fleshly, who would let her hair down, and help you to let down yours. We must arrange a party for you.'

That was how George met Deirdre. At the party were two other girls rather like her, and decidedly unlike the women that George was in the habit of consorting with. An atmosphere of good-fellowship prevailed. Champagne loosened tongues and George's feelings. As well as talking to him they talked at him and about him—the industrious apprentice who had made good and come into a fortune, the man who had the ball at his feet, the lucky chap whose name had got into the papers. Much of what they said was quite untrue but all of it was flattering, and even more intoxicating than the wine: under the admiring glances flashed at him, George began to feel the hell of a fellow.

Presently one of the other couples rose and the man, apologizing, said they had a date. 'We don't want to break up the party,' he added. 'That's all right,' their host said; 'Annette and I have a date too, at that new place, the Late Session; and it will be pretty late before we're back. But there's plenty more to drink; why don't you and Deirdre, George, stay on, and make an evening of it? It's only eleven o'clock. That is, if neither of you has a date?'

George and Deirdre exchanged glances. 'What do you think, Deirdre?' he asked. He didn't know her other name.

'I'm all for staying here,' she said.

'Well,' said their host, rising and taking Annette's hand, 'we couldn't be more sorry—it's too bad that it's turned out like this. But you will make yourselves at home, won't you? You know the geography of the house'—he waved his hand to indicate it—'at any rate Deirdre does. Good-bye, my children, don't get into mischief,' and he was gone, with his companion, almost before they had time to thank him for their lovely evening.

It was the first of several such evenings, some organized by George, to whom spending money was now becoming easy, even exhilarating.

But he grudged sharing Deirdre's company; after the party he could have her to himself. Himself—his very self, only attainable in Deirdre's arms.

But no, it was attainable in other ways. Everything he did for her, every present, every treat he gave her, every wish of hers, expressed by her or anticipated by him, that he fulfilled, gave him, in a lesser degree, the same sense of wholeness and integration. He felt, and even looked, proud of being a man, and walked down Piccadilly with his hands in his pockets, looking as if he owned it. Even thinking of her, he was twice the man he had been. Only she could give him this freedom; with other women, the women he had known, he was still shy and diffident, anxious to please and sometimes succeeding, but always being acted on, not acting. Gradually he frequented them less and less; the silken threads by which they held him were a frail tie compared to the hawser which fastened him to Deirdre.

So for two years he was entirely happy. She could do no wrong for him. Her moods and caprices, the small slights and snubs, rebuffs and disappointments, by which she sought to make herself more precious to him, all seemed part of her; he scarcely distinguished between her melting and her stony moods. But then something in him became sensitized and if she was unkind to him it began to hurt. Now there were two Deirdres instead of one; and the second made him suffer. In vain he told himself that she had always been like that; it was unreasonable that something he had always taken for granted and not minded should suddenly become a grievance. He blamed himself more than her for his resentment, and was miserable until, at whatever cost to his pride and sense of fairness, he had made it up with her. He tried to make these tiffs and reconciliations into a habit, part of his emotional routine; an item on his experience account; but it didn't work out so. His feelings, instead of toughening, grew more tender; his eyes had a hurt, anxious look, which his other women friends, on the few occasions when he saw them, remarked upon. How quick they were to notice changes in him! He couldn't conceal from himself that he was unhappy; the joys of reconciliation and forgiveness (forgiveness of himself rather than her) became of shorter duration; soon, as an anodyne, they hardly counted. He was forced into making a distinction, which he had never made before, between her acts and her: Deirdre was one thing, what she did was another, so he told himself; but try as he would he couldn't keep them apart. It wasn't only the smart of the disappointments, which she was so expert in inflicting, that made him miserable; it was the nature that prompted them, his sense of which was like a smell that persisted even

through her most fragrant and most yielding moments, and had something frightening about it: the smell of cruelty.

One evening at a party, a rather smart party that he had taken her to
at her request, though not quite sure she would fit in, he suddenly felt
ill—food poisoning or gastric flu—he didn't know what it was. He
caught sight of his face in a looking-glass, and it more than confirmed
what he was feeling. It wasn't easy to detach Deirdre from the young
man she was talking to, but at last he did, and told her of his plight as
well as he could, for by now the room was spinning round.

'I don't want to go now,' she said, 'I'm having a good time. You'll
be all right. Get a hot-water bottle and go to bed.'

'Oh, do come back with me,' he begged her. 'I feel so odd, I don't
know if I shall be able to get home.'

'Don't be silly,' she said. 'You know what an old fusspot you are.
I'll look in and see you on my way back, if it isn't too late.'

He lay awake shivering and sweating, with his bedroom door open,
hoping to hear her key turn in the lock, but he hadn't heard it when,
towards three o'clock, he fell asleep.

His daily help was busy in the room when George woke up. He had
had a dreadful night with bouts of vomiting and diarrhoea, sometimes
alternating, sometimes simultaneous; and the blackness before his eyes,
as he plunged across the passage to relieve them! Once he had to crawl.
He didn't always get there in time, as his bedclothes bore witness.

'Never mind,' said the daily help, 'I'll change them for you. Don't
try to get out of bed—I'll change them with you in it.'

He rolled from one side to the other, and somehow the distasteful
task was done.

He could have had a servant living in, but most of his spare cash went
to Deirdre, to keep her flat and her; for he had persuaded her, as much
for his sake as for hers, to give up her secretarial work. With this she
sometimes taxed him. 'You've taken away my livelihood,' she said.

She said, she said . . . Something that Deirdre had once said, and
which he couldn't remember, was vexing George's throbbing brain
when the telephone bell rang.

'Perhaps you'd rather I went away?' the daily woman suggested. 'It
may be something private.' He nodded weakly.

'Hullo, is that George? I didn't recognize your voice, you disguised it.'

'I'm laid up in bed.'

'Speak a little louder, can you?'

George repeated it.

'Oh, I'm sorry. I'll come round and see you. I couldn't come last night—it went on too late.'

'When will you come?'

'In half an hour or so.'

The morning passed; the daily help, who usually left at twelve o'clock, went out to buy some fish for his lunch—'I'll boil it for you,' she said.

George protested that he couldn't eat it.

'You must get something inside you,' she said, 'after all that vomiting.'

How kind she is, he thought, but the thought made him uneasy—she was doing something for him, meeting what she believed to be a wish of his—she was putting him in her debt, making him dependent on her. Receiving a favour, he felt uncomfortable. But Deirdre would be here any minute now, and for her he could do something—but could he, bedridden? He heard the click of the key turning—Deirdre at last! But no, it was the daily help again, for sounds came from the kitchen. At last the telephone bell rang.

'Darling, how are you feeling?'

'A bit better, thank you, but not much. When will you be round?'

'Isn't it too bad, I've been asked out to lunch, I may not get to you till tea-time. I'll make you some tea, but you'll have to tell me where you keep it.'

'I'm not sure if I know myself.'

'Oh, well, I'll find it. I must dash now.'

Presently the daily help came in, bringing the boiled fish on a tray, laid out very neatly. 'And I thought you might like some peas and potatoes.' His mouth watered at the sight of the food, but his stomach warned him, and he put the forkful down, while he tried to decide how serious the warning was. 'Hadn't you better have the doctor?' she asked. 'You don't look any too good.'

'Oh, I don't think so, you see my temperature is normal.'

'Well, try to eat a bit, and then have a nap and I'll come in and give you your tea.'

'It's very kind of you,' he said, 'Mrs. Buswell'—suddenly remembering her name. 'But Miss O'Farrell's coming in to do that. By the way, where is the tea kept?'

She always left the tea-tray ready when she went away.

'In the cupboard beside the fridge, on the second shelf. Well, bye-bye for now, sir, and I'll come later on and give you your supper.'

'How good of you,' he said. . . . But he didn't feel quite happy about the arrangement. He ought to have been giving her her supper.

Struggling with nausea he swallowed down some fish, picked at the peas, nibbled the potatoes; after an initial revolt, his stomach seemed to tolerate it, and, as often happens after eating, he felt better—well enough, in fact, to take the nap that Mrs. Buswell had recommended. (Was she taking one? He hoped so.) But when he woke he felt feverish and his sense of touch was out of order. Warm things felt cold; cold things felt colder; getting out of bed, wondering whether to be sick or not, he shivered in the August warmth. No matter, it was past four o'clock. Deirdre would soon be here.

Just at the moment when expectation had reached its peak, the telephone bell rang.

'Darling, it's me. I hate to disappoint you—if you are disappointed—but I've gone down to the country—it is so heavenly now, we're going to have a bathe—so I shan't be there to give you your tea. And I was so looking forward to it. But you'll be able to get it for yourself, won't you? And I'll come round in the evening.'

'What time?' George asked.

'Oh, any old time, but well before your bedtime. So long, my dear. Think of me taking a header. Ugh!'

She rang off.

George wrestled with his disappointment, but again and again it reared itself and struck at him, thriving on successive decapitations like a hydra. Even more than his body, his mind was troubling him, and if he tried to play off one against the other they united and made common cause against him.

He took his temperature. It was 101. He derived some comfort from the thought that his body was showing fight against the poison; but all the same he wished his temperature had been normal. Perhaps he had better call in the doctor. He dialled the number, only to be told that his doctor was away on holiday. Another doctor was attending his patients: would Mr. Lambert like to call him? In a frenzy of frustration George said no, then wished he hadn't, and sheepishly rang up again to ask the other doctor's number. Again his energy petered out; he couldn't bring himself to summon a strange doctor. He worked himself up quite a lot over this, then lay back and tried to relax and think it was another person suffering, not he—a device that succeeds, if at all, only when one is feeling nearly well. He tried various forms of mental consolation—that he wasn't bankrupt, that he was in bed, the proper place, not exposed in the desert being slowly devoured by ants, that he had friends who would be sorry for him if they knew. But would they be, when he had so shamefully neglected them?

This brought him back to Deirdre, who did know but didn't seem to be specially sorry. 'That's Deirdre all over!' How often had he used this phrase in her defence, in the days when what she was made anything she did seem unimportant. But now it didn't help.

If only she would come! The outside door opened and shut. Someone had come. 'Deirdre!' he called, as if by calling her name he could ensure that it was she; she must be Deirdre, if he said so. But it was Mrs. Buswell who came in, and with the slightly resentful air of someone who has been called by the wrong name, a name, too, dearer than her own. Would he like some soup, she asked, and then a nice poached egg? George said he would; but wasn't it giving her a lot of trouble? Mrs. Buswell seemed a little put out, then smiled and said it was a pleasure to look after him. Slow as usual at taking in the idea that anyone could want to, George murmured excessive thanks. 'It doesn't do to be always giving,' she said cryptically. 'People impose on you. You should take as well as give.'

'Oh, but I take a lot!' said George. 'Not in the way I mean,' said Mrs. Buswell. 'And it doesn't do them any good, either.'

Wondering if it was what the doctor would have ordered, George ate his supper. He lingered over it, partly from loss of appetite, partly to eke out the interval before Deirdre came. Those long waits, with nothing but his thoughts to feed on! His thoughts were sicker than his stomach, or whatever part of him it was that had turned against him. Guiltily he remembered Mrs. Buswell. She would not go away, he was convinced, until he had eaten the last morsel. The last morsel took a great deal of getting down, but by swallowing it he felt he had done something for her, a little redressed the balance of mutual benefit. The look of satisfaction on her face rewarded him.

Swish, swish. Now she was washing up, and all for him. What a good creature she was! But he hoped she wouldn't still be there when Deirdre came.

She wasn't. She came in to bid him goodnight.

'I should take one of those red pills if I was you,' she said. He was surprised that she knew what they were for, and that she took so much interest in his belongings.

'Would you give me the bottle?' he asked, for he did not keep the tablets by his bed, for fear he should forget how many he had taken.

She brought them, and he shook out two, and handed her the bottle, which she replaced.

'I hope you'll have a good night,' she said, 'I shall be back again at seven o'clock.'

Seven o'clock! He hadn't realized she came so early; she lived in a distant suburb, and must get up at six. What a sacrifice, and all for him! He made an effort to accept the sacrifice as something due to him; but it didn't go down much more easily than his supper had.

He would take the pills, but when? He didn't want to be asleep when Deirdre came. Nine o'clock, ten o'clock, still she hadn't come, but then she kept late hours, and she slept late, too. He often had to wake her. It was one of the things he most looked forward to, her moment of returning consciousness. She was so young, it took her a long time to come to herself—and him.

How long should he give her? Till midnight, he decided; but when midnight came and he had taken the pills he didn't get off for a long time, for his unconscious mind, of which she had possession, kept nagging at him like a watch-dog.

Asleep at last, he dreamed, and dreamed of Deirdre, whom he had never dreamed about before; he had often wished he could. Having her he didn't need to dream of her; perhaps that explained it. He was back at the party where he had been taken ill. It was very like the original party, except that the lights were brighter and between the rugs the parquet floor was shinier. He was still asking her to go back with him, and the young man still waited impatiently and possessively at her elbow. 'Can't you see I'm busy?' she said. 'I'm trying to make a date with Rupert and you keep barging in.' Suddenly the floor tilted up, almost level with his eye, and he clutched at her to steady himself. 'Oh, do take care,' she said, 'you'll spoil my dress,' and he saw it was an oyster-coloured silk dress that he had given her, but not the one she had gone to the party in. 'Give him your arm, Rupert, I think he must be drunk.' The young man put out a helping hand but George shook it off. 'He's nothing to do with you,' he said to Deirdre, 'it's me you should be thinking of.' 'Can't you leave me alone one single minute?' Deirdre asked. 'I was just beginning to enjoy myself.' The room dipped and swayed, but somehow George managed to keep his feet. 'But you ought to come with me,' he said. 'You would come with me if you loved me.' At that both she and the young man laughed. 'Love you?' she said. 'I've never loved you, and now I almost hate you.' 'Never loved me?' said George, aghast. 'You mean to say you've never loved me, all this time?'

'No, of course not.' 'But I always thought you did.' 'What made you
think so?' George became confused. 'Because . . . because . . . because I
loved you, I suppose.' 'Yes, that's just it. You were so intent on loving
me that you never asked yourself if I loved you. You never thought of
my side of it, I never came into it except as somebody you were in love
with. If you'd asked me whether I loved you, I should have told you
no. It's the first question most men ask, but you didn't ask it because
you didn't mind. You were in love with love, not me. If I'd existed for
you as a person it might have been different, but I didn't. If you'd asked
me to do something for you, except just one thing, it might have been
different. But as it is——'

George reeled and crashed to the floor, and when he came to himself
he was in fact on the floor, having fallen out of bed for the first time
since he was a child.

He woke to a sense that something terrible had happened, but couldn't
imagine what, for he himself felt better. But the thing would not let
him enjoy his convalescence; it kept demanding to be known and recognized, and at last through a barbituric mist it forced its way.

Deirdre didn't love him, she had never loved him. She had appeared
to him in a dream to tell him so, and the message was far more real and
convincing than if she had spoken with her own voice, for it was the
pure essence of experience, with no admixture of circumstance to dilute
it. It was her spirit speaking straight to his — yes, straight, for she had
told him straight.

It explained why she hadn't come back with him from the party, why
she hadn't looked him up during the day, it explained everything that
had puzzled him in her behaviour since first her behaviour began to
puzzle him.

He felt he could not survive the blow, and the fact that he felt better
physically made him better able to suffer mentally. He scarcely knew
how to think, for all his thoughts that counted with him began and
ended in Deirdre. Now they had nowhere to begin or end.

What time was it? It must be past seven, for through the square of glass
over the door the light was shining, which meant that Mrs. Buswell had
come back. He could not hear her, though. She must be taking great
pains not to wake him. He called her and she came in, still on tiptoe.

'I was just going to bring you your tea,' she said. 'It's eight o'clock.
Did you have a good night?'

George told her what had happened in the night.

'You fell out of bed! Poor Mr. Lambert! I might have known, the bedclothes are in such a mess. I meant to make your bed again last night, but thought you were too tired. Now when you've drunk this tea, see if you can get up and I'll make it for you. Or I'll make it with you in it. I do like to see a man look comfortable.'

'How kind you are.'

George found that he could stand without his head going round. While he was sitting in his dressing-gown the telephone bell rang. Mrs. Buswell, who was nearest, answered it. 'It's Miss O'Farrell,' she said, and a shadow crossed her face.

'Ask her to ring up later, Mrs. Buswell.' No sooner were the words out than he wished he could recall them.

'Mr. Lambert doesn't find it convenient to speak to you, Miss O'Farrell.'

What a way of putting it!

Expostulatory sounds came through the telephone.

'In about half an hour, he isn't well,' said Mrs. Buswell.

Torn between misery and a slight sense of relief at the reprieve, George watched Mrs. Buswell making the bed. The feeling that he ought to be making it for her, not she for him, was less pronounced than he expected. But soon another thought came.

'Why, it's Sunday! You ought not to be here on Sunday!'

'I came because you weren't well,' said Mrs. Buswell, 'and you were all alone.'

What a wonderful woman! George began to speculate about her. What was she really like? What had her life been like? He had never asked her. He had always taken her and her services for granted; he had never shown, or felt, any curiosity about her. He paid her, and that was all, unaware of the treasure hidden in her.

Back in bed he took his temperature. It was still a hundred, but health does not depend on the thermometer, and he felt definitely better.

The telephone bell rang.

'Good morning, darling. Who was that rude old thing who answered the telephone just now? She seemed to hate my guts.'

'The daily woman,' said George, stiffening.

'But aren't I your daily woman? I always used to be. But what I wanted to say was, How are you, darling?'

'Not very well.'

'You don't sound well, your voice sounds different. When can I come and see you?'

This was the crucial moment. George heard himself say:

'I don't think you'd better come. It may be something catching.'

'Some dreadful germ? Then perhaps I'd better not come. Oh, dear, and I do want to see you. Perhaps it's a good thing I didn't come last night. It was too late anyhow. We had such fun, though. I wish you had been there.'

'I was in bed.'

'I know, I know. Poor George! What luck you didn't give it to me, whatever it was. You can't have, or it would have come out by now, wouldn't it? Well, so long, darling. Let me know the first moment you're out of quarantine.'

George spent a miserable day. Why had he committed this ridiculous act of self-sacrifice and deprived himself of Deirdre's presence? It wasn't for her sake, or her health's sake, that he knew quite well; it was because——

Oh, hell!

A hundred times he made up his mind to ring her, and tell her he knew he wasn't infectious; a hundred times, prompted by the dream, he unmade it. He wondered if he was going mad.

He tried to distract himself by reading, but since he met Deirdre he had almost given up reading; she was his book, into which he had dipped deeper and deeper until, to change the metaphor, he was nearly drowned. How could a book, a mere commentary on life, give him what Deirdre gave him, which was life itself? Listlessly he turned the pages. What was paper as an interest, compared to flesh? What appeal to the heart had the printed word, compared to the voice that came from Deirdre's lips?

His loneliness increased, and with it the bitter self-reproach of having brought it on himself. He tried to attend to business; that was quickly done: at the office they begged him not to come back until he was quite well. Business: it had become automatic to him, second nature: he kept it in a compartment to itself, sealed off from his feelings. Sentiment in business: there was such a thing, but it was not the sentiment he needed.

Well, then, he had his friends, quite a number of them, for hadn't the catastrophe itself happened at a party where he knew almost everyone, though Deirdre didn't? Why not ring them up, and ask for sympathy?

One after another he went through their names; he even got out his address-book, in case he should have overlooked someone. Once these names had meant a great deal to him: they had meant the warmth of greeting, the exchange of ideas, the interplay of slight but real emotions The reassurance of goodbye-to-meet-again, the sense, when it was over, that something had been added to the value of life. The value of life! But what did the value of life mean, in this tormented and bewildered age, when every value was being called in question? How did life benefit, or its values, if he and Mrs. Plastosell, of whom he was secretly a little afraid, she was so fashionable and so sophisticated, played an intricate game of cats-cradle on a sofa, gossamer webs spun out of airy nothings that involved some flattery on her side and a good deal of self-complacency on his? She condescended to him, and he lapped up her condescension: but he wasn't himself with her, not his true self: he played a part, half self-effacing, half self-advertising: she didn't liberate him, as Deirdre did. With Deirdre he could be absolutely himself and more: George plus, plus, plus, plus. With Mrs. Plastosell he was George minus, if he was anything.

He took up the telephone to dial her number: but when he had got half-way he put the receiver back.

'You ought to have the telly,' Mrs. Buswell said. 'Not all the time, like some people do, they're potty, to my way of thinking. But just for times like this, when you haven't anything to amuse you. It *gives* you something, that's the point.'

'I could have one,' George said.

'Well, it would take your mind off. And there are some quite good programmes. When my second husband died, and when my eldest daughter died, and when my son-in-law — that's the husband of my youngest daughter, or was, died — I don't know what I should have done without the telly. You see I depended on them, in a way. Not for money, of course. The telly made up for some of it.'

'I see,' said George, whom this catalogue of catastrophes had made a little ashamed of his own sorrow.

'Yes, it gives you something, if you see what I mean, it's like a present. Not that I'm against giving, far from it. I'll give with anyone, so far as I can afford it. But there comes a time when giving doesn't satisfy — you have to have something in return, if you take my meaning.'

'I think I do.'

'It isn't fair, and it's just as bad to be unfair to yourself as it is to be unfair to other people. You don't get anything out of being unfair to yourself.'

'No.'

'And they misunderstand and take advantage. They impose on you. It's happened to me, before now, poor as I am. Not with my relations, though, I will say that.'

'I'm imposing on you now,' said George. 'I'm taking advantage of your good nature.'

'No, you're not. I'm glad to work for you.'

'But what do I give you in return?'

That's stumped her, George thought.

'Oh, I dunno. I suppose I like seeing you around and then we have a chat together sometimes. And then you pay my wages.'

'That isn't much,' said George.

'And then I'm sorry for you.'

'Because I'm ill?'

'That, and other things.'

What did she mean? She knew about his relationship with Deirdre, of course; she couldn't help knowing. But she couldn't know about his dream and how it had upset him.

'For everything you've done for me,' he said, 'I'm more than grateful. Tell me something I can do for you and I'll gladly do it.'

'You just lie still and get better,' she said. 'Then you'll have done something for me. And take a tip from me, sir, though it's not for me to give it. You'd be happier without that Miss O'Farrell hanging round.'

During the next few days the telephone bell rang many times and each time George answered it in a different spirit. Desire, despair, grief, anger — anger lasted a long time: how dared she not love him when he loved her, and had done so much for her — given her the life she never could have had without him? Now he was like a nut whose kernel has been eaten by a worm; he could almost hear himself rattle. The emptiness, the dryness! No current could recharge him; the battery was worn out. He could never go through all this with another person, the expense of spirit had been too great. The expense of spirit in a waste of shame: had it been that? Were the moralists right to warn you against the sins of the flesh? Most of his friends believed, and he too had believed, that the senses fed the mind and nourished the affections; without their co-operation the spirit withered, but if so, why was he in this plight — mentally, emotionally and spiritually bankrupt? With no friends, no interests, no hopes, just an abyss, a void, where Deirdre had once been?

Then came revenge. Ah, he would show her! Hate was a stimulant as well as love; he would get the same satisfaction from hating her that he had once got from loving her, the same delight from thwarting her wishes that he had once got from granting them.

'Darling, I didn't recognize your voice.'

'You say that every time you ring me up.'

'But every time it's true.'

It probably was true, for every time they spoke on the telephone he had a different feeling for her: now it was hatred, and hatred speaks with a different voice from love.

'But darling, you can't *still* be infectious! It's four days now.'

'But you're so frightened of infection.'

'Yes, but I could put my head in through the door.'

'I shouldn't like to think I'd given you something.'

'But you've given me so many things! I shouldn't mind one little tiny germ.'

'Let's put it off another day. It would be safer.'

'Darling, it must be as you wish.'

In spite of the joys of hatred, he suffered agonies each time he said he would not see her. And hatred disagreed with his digestion. All his life he had been delicate, suffered from headaches, bronchial asthma and attacks of fibrositis; during the three years he had been in love with her all these had disappeared; he had a clean bill of health. But now no longer. The symptoms of food poisoning, or whatever it was, had gone, but he still didn't feel himself. All his processes, mental and physical, were disorganized. He flourished on agreement. The spirit of opposition, denying his deepest impulses their outlet, was making a sick man of him. He forgot little things, was constantly mislaying his belongings — sometimes he couldn't see them when they were staring him in the face, a sort of amnesia of the eye — and his daily routine, the order in which he did things, got hopelessly confused. He cleaned his teeth with shaving-soap and tried to shave with tooth-paste. What would happen at the office, where he was due back on Monday?

'Take her back! Take her back!' said the voice within him that always pleaded for her; 'take her back, and let things go on as they used to! She is no different now from what she was; she was always like this, only you didn't know it! Can't you re-establish the relationship on the basis of truth? Truth is antiseptic, it will cleanse and heal the wound, and then when she behaves in character you won't be angry, because you know what makes her tick! You were in love with a false Deirdre, created by your imagination; aren't you man enough to love the real

one, now that you know her faults? She loved you, knowing yours —
women are more realistic than men——'

'But she didn't and doesn't love me, that's just it.'

'How do you know?'

'Because she told me so in a dream.'

'A dream! What sort of evidence is a dream?'

Then followed a part of the record that George was altogether too
familiar with — the pros and cons of the dream. But hadn't her subsequent behaviour verified it, hadn't Mrs. Buswell's hints and ultimate
outspokenness confirmed it?

Without Mrs. Buswell he would have given in, for every time that he
forgave Deirdre (and in his heart he forgave her seventy times seven) he
felt so much better physically and mentally, so nearly restored and inte-
grated, that sometimes he would snatch up the receiver and start to dial
her number. 'Darling, I'm quite all right: do come round now!' Mrs.
Buswell was never present when he committed these extravagances, but
her invisible presence restrained him from fulfilling his intention.
Regretfully he put the receiver back.

It was the vision she had given him of reciprocal affection dominat-
ing, softening, yes, and even sweetening, physical love. Physical love,
she must know all about it, a working woman who had had two husbands. But she insisted on reciprocity: she didn't think that love was
healthy without it. 'But surely, Mrs. Buswell' (so he argued with her
shade), 'unselfish, unrequited love is the noblest of all emotions? The
love that religion itself enjoins on us — the love that expects no return?'
But she wouldn't have it. 'God himself,' she said (in these imaginary
conversations), 'wouldn't expect us to love Him unless He first loved us.'

On Saturday the telephone didn't ring; the morning passed and still
it didn't ring. At lunch-time when people are most likely to be in,
George rang Deirdre.

'Welcome 9191.'

'Hullo, darling, does that sound more like me?'

A pause, some readjustment at the other end, he couldn't tell what.

'Yes, it does, it does sound more like you.'

'Well, what about coming round to see me? I'm not catching now.
You could even kiss me if you wanted to.'

'Of course I want to, but . . .'

'But what?'

'Well, I'm engaged this afternoon.'

'Then come at drink-time.'

'Yes, if I can manage it.'

He had brought himself to the point of not expecting her when Deirdre came.

'Darling, of course I'm glad you're better but I should be gladder still if you hadn't been so cruel to me.'

'Cruel to you?' George repeated, when, after some hygienic holding back their kiss was over. But his conscience smote him: he had been cruel, or had meant to be.

'You said you were too ill to see me, but I think you were shamming.'

'If you had come to see me you would have known I wasn't.'

'To begin with, perhaps. Then you said you didn't find it *convenient* to speak to me—such a nasty way of putting it.'

'Mrs. Buswell said that.'

'I don't care who said it—it came through your mouthpiece, and all the time I was in agonies, wondering what was happening to you.'

'You were having a bathe when I was worst.'

'You couldn't expect me to stay indoors all day, George dear, just because you had a tummy upset. And you've always said you wanted me to enjoy myself.'

'Oh, don't let's bicker,' George said. 'You're here now, that's the great thing.'

'Yes, in the end you sent for me, just as if I was some sort of call-girl.'

'Oh, what nonsense you talk.'

'It isn't nonsense at all—you've changed towards me. You don't love me any more.'

'What?' said George, and his heart missed a beat.

'You don't love me any more, that's why I've done what I've done.'

'What have you done?' asked George, and a nameless terror clutched him.

'First tell me you're truly sorry, and then I might not do it.'

'But you said you had done it.'

'Well, I have and I haven't. If you said you were sorry and were really nice to me——'

George took her in his arms.

'—then I might change my mind. But I don't think I shall, because, you see, I know that you don't love me.'

'I do love you, I do love you!'

'No, or you wouldn't have played me up like you did. That's why I decided——'

'What did you decide?'

'I oughtn't to tell you because it has to do with someone else.'

'Who?'

'Now you're asking.'

Sounds came from the kitchen—it was Mrs. Buswell, his ally, come to cook his supper.

Something stiffened in him.

'Of course I'm asking, and I wish you wouldn't treat me like a child.'

'It was only because I didn't want to hurt you.'

'Hurt away,' said George. 'You can't hurt me more than you have hurt me these last few days.'

'Don't you think I can?'

'Just try.'

'Well, darling, since you must know, though you can't say I haven't warned you, it's Rupert.'

'That man at the party?'

'Don't call him that man, darling, he's very well off and very nice to me. He said he'd like to——'

'Well?'

'See a lot more of me. Don't misunderstand me—we're just great, great friends, that's all.'

Mrs. Buswell, in the kitchen, was making quite a clatter. George released Deirdre and got up shakily.

'Then go to him,' he said.

Deirdre turned her large eyes on him, those eyes that stained with blue the intervening air, and suddenly he saw the fear behind them. 'You don't mean that, treasure, do you? You don't really want me to go to Rupert?'

'You can go to hell for all I care.'

'Oh, but sweetie-pie, you wouldn't like that, would you? You wouldn't like to hear me sizzling, because you would be there, too, because in a way, you know, you seduced me—it wasn't nice of you. And I've been with you all these years, as everybody knows. If you send me to Rupert——'

'I'm not sending you.'

'If you let Rupert have me——'

'It was your idea, not mine.'

'Well, you'll be lonely, won't you? You won't find another girl to make things as easy for you as I have. You're shy, you know—you haven't much self-confidence with a girl when it comes to the point.'

George said nothing.

'And you know you've messed my life up — the best years of my life. You've trailed me around and put a stigma on me — Rupert won't like that.'

'But you said he wanted you to go to him.'

'Yes, darling, he does, but I don't want to — not very much, that is. Of course he loves me and I could get to love him——'

'Well, why not?'

'Because I love you better, oh, much better.'

What a racket Mrs. Buswell was making in the kitchen!

'You don't love me,' George said. 'You told me so yourself.'

'I told you so? I never. You must have dreamed it.'

'Well, if I did, it's true, and you must go now.'

'Go? Go where?'

'Out of this flat.' And taking her arm George began to propel Deirdre to the door.

'Oh, but how can you be so cruel? I haven't anywhere to go to— only my own rooms, that you pay for. Oh, what shall I do? It wasn't true what I told you about Rupert — he doesn't want me, and I don't want him. I only said it because you were so unkind to me.'

'Get out of here, get out!'

'How can you turn me away like this, when you've been so fond of me and done so much for me? You've always been so good and generous——'

'Get out — get out!'

The door shut out the sound of Deirdre's sobbing. George sat for what seemed a long time, looking at his knees, then round the room, then at his knees again. Like everyone who has taken violent action he was unable to comment on it.

There was a knock at the door.

'Come in,' he said, hardly knowing whom he was going to see.

'She's gone,' said Mrs. Buswell.

'I thought she went half an hour ago.'

'No, she didn't, she stayed on the landing, outside the door. She rang once or twice but you didn't hear and I wouldn't let her in — I said you were resting. Of course she didn't dare to use her key. I should get it back from her, if I was you. You never know. She's gone now.'

'Oh, dear, Mrs. Buswell.' The 'dear' might have been for her, or part of the exclamation. 'What do you think about it all?' Somehow he took it for granted that she knew what had been happening.

'I say good riddance to bad rubbish.' She looked with compassion at his working face. 'Don't take on, sir, she's not worth it.'

George wasn't so sure; he didn't know how to feel, and it seemed incongruous, disproportionate, almost incredible that the emotional experience of three years could be ended by one small act of violence, lasting only a minute.

Much later in the evening, after Mrs. Buswell had gone, he went to the telephone and dialled a number.

'Can I speak to Mrs. de Sole?'

'Speaking. But who is that?'

'George Lambert, Délice.'

'*George?* I didn't recognize your voice.' Would his voice never be the same again? 'You *are* a stranger. Well, when can we meet?'

'Could I come round and see you now, or is it too late?'

'It's never too late to mend. I'm not clairvoyante, but I suspect you want to tell me something.'

'Don't be hard on me, will you? I've just been rather hard.'

'On yourself, no doubt.'

'No, on someone else.'

'Well done, I congratulate you. But you won't find me hard—I shall be softer than silk, snow, swansdown, anything you can think of.'

A HIGH DIVE

THE circus-manager was worried. Attendances had been falling off and such people as did come — children they were, mostly — sat about list-lessly, munching sweets or sucking ices, sometimes talking to each other without so much as glancing at the show. Only the young or little girls, who came to see the ponies, betrayed any real interest. The clowns' jokes fell flat, for they were the kind of jokes that used to raise a laugh before 1939, after which critical date people's sense of humour seemed to have changed, along with many other things about them. The circus-manager had heard the word 'corny' flung about and didn't like it. What did they want? Something that was, in his opinion, sillier and more pointless than the old jokes; not a bull's-eye on the target of humour, but an outer or even a near-miss — something that brought in the element of futility and that could be laughed at as well as with: an unintentional joke against the joker. The clowns were quick enough with their patter but it just didn't go down: there was too much sense in their nonsense for an up-to-date audience, too much articulateness. They would do better to talk gibberish, perhaps. Now they must change their style, and find out what really did make people laugh, if people could be made to; but he, the manager, was over fifty and never good himself at making jokes, even the old-fashioned kind. What was this word that everyone was using — 'sophisticated'? The audiences were too sophisticated, even the children were: they seemed to have seen and heard all this before, even when they were too young to have seen and heard it.

'What shall we do?' he asked his wife. They were standing under the Big Top, which had just been put up, and wondering how many of the empty seats would still be empty when they gave their first perform-ance. 'We shall have to do something, or it's a bad look-out.'

'I don't see what we can do about the comic side,' she said. 'It may

come right by itself. Fashions change, all sorts of old things have returned
to favour, like old-time dances. But there's something we could do.'

'What's that?'

'Put on an act that's dangerous, really dangerous. Audiences are
never bored by that. I know you don't like it, and no more do I, but
when we had the Wall of Death——'

Her husband's big chest-muscles twitched under his thin shirt.

'You know what happened then.'

'Yes, but it wasn't our fault, we were in the clear.'

He shook his head.

'Those things upset everyone. I know the public came after it happened — they came in shoals, they came to see the place where someone
had been killed. But our people got the needle and didn't give a good
performance for I don't know how long. If you're proposing another
Wall of Death I wouldn't stand for it — besides, where will you find a
man to do it? — especially with a lion on his bike, which is the great
attraction.'

'But other turns are dangerous too, as well as dangerous-looking.
It's *being* dangerous that is the draw.'

'Then what do you suggest?'

Before she had time to answer a man came up to them.

'I hope I don't butt in,' he said, 'but there's a man outside who wants
to speak to you.'

'What about?'

'I think he's looking for a job.'

'Bring him in,' said the manager.

The man appeared, led by his escort, who then went away. He was a
tall, sandy-haired fellow with tawny leonine eyes and a straggling
moustache. It wasn't easy to tell his age — he might have been about
thirty-five. He pulled off his old brown corduroy cap and waited.

'I hear you want to take a job with us,' the manager said, while his
wife tried to size up the newcomer. 'We're pretty full up, you know.
We don't take on strangers as a rule. Have you any references?'

'No, sir.'

'Then I'm afraid we can't help you. But just for form's sake, what
can you do?'

As if measuring its height the man cast up his eyes to the point where
one of the two poles of the Big Top was embedded in the canvas.

'I can dive sixty feet into a tank eight foot long by four foot wide by
four foot deep.'

The manager stared at him.

'Can you now?' he said. 'If so, you're the very man we want. Are you prepared to let us see you do it?'

'Yes,' the man said.

'And would you do it with petrol burning on the water?'

'Yes.'

'But have we got a tank?' the manager's wife asked.

'There's the old Mermaid's tank. It's just the thing. Get somebody to fetch it.'

While the tank was being brought the stranger looked about him.

'Thinking better of it?' said the manager.

'No, sir,' the man replied. 'I was thinking I should want some bathing-trunks.'

'We can soon fix you up with those,' the manager said. 'I'll show you where to change.'

Leaving the stranger somewhere out of sight, he came back to his wife.

'Do you think we ought to let him do it?' she asked.

'Well, it's his funeral. You wanted us to have a dangerous act, and now we've got it.'

'Yes, I know, but——' The rest was drowned by the rattle of the trolley bringing in the tank—a hollow, double cube like a sarcophagus. Mermaids in low relief sported on its leaden flanks. Grunting and muttering to each other the men slid it into position, a few feet from the pole. Then a length of hosepipe was fastened to a faucet, and soon they heard the sound of water swishing and gurgling in the tank.

'He's a long time changing,' said the manager's wife.

'Perhaps he's looking for a place to hide his money,' laughed her husband, and added, 'I think we'll give the petrol a miss.'

At length the man emerged from behind a screen, and slowly walked towards them. How tall he was, lanky and muscular. The hair on his body stuck out as if it had been combed. Hands on hips he stood beside them, his skin pimpled by goose-flesh. A fit of yawning overtook him.

'How do I get up?' he asked.

The manager was surprised, and pointed to the ladder. 'Unless you'd rather climb up, or be hauled up! You'll find a platform just below the top, to give you a foot-hold.'

He had started to go up the chromium-plated ladder when the manager's wife called after him: 'Are you still sure you want to do it?'

'Quite sure, madam.'

He was too tall to stand upright on the platform, the awning brushed his head. Crouching and swaying forty feet above them he swung his arms as though to test the air's resistance. Then he pitched forward into space, unseen by the manager's wife who looked the other way until she heard a splash and saw a thin sheet of bright water shooting up.

The man was standing breast-high in the tank. He swung himself over the edge and crossed the ring towards them, his body dripping, his wet feet caked with sawdust, his tawny eyes a little bloodshot.

'Bravo!' said the manager, taking his shiny hand. 'It's a first-rate act, that, and will put money in our pockets. What do you want for it, fifteen quid a week?'

The man shook his head. The water trickled from his matted hair on to his shoulders, oozed from his borrowed bathing-suit and made runnels down his sinewy thighs. A fine figure of a man: the women would like him.

'Well, twenty then.'

Still the man shook his head.

'Let's make it twenty-five. That's the most we give anyone.'

Except for the slow shaking of his head the man might not have heard. The circus-manager and his wife exchanged a rapid glance.

'Look here,' he said. 'Taking into account the draw your act is likely to be, we're going to make you a special offer — thirty pounds a week. All right?'

Had the man understood? He put his finger in his mouth and went on shaking his head slowly, more to himself than at them, and seemingly unconscious of the bargain that was being held out to him. When he still didn't answer, the knot of tension broke, and the manager said, in his ordinary, brisk voice,

'Then I'm afraid we can't do business. But just as a matter of interest, tell us why you turned down our excellent offer.'

The man drew a long breath and breaking his long silence said, 'It's the first time I done it and I didn't like it.'

With that he turned on his heel and straddling his long legs walked off unsteadily in the direction of the dressing-room.

The circus-manager and his wife stared at each other.

'It was the first time he'd done it,' she muttered. 'The first time.' Not knowing what to say to him, whether to praise, blame, scold or sympathize, they waited for him to come back, but he didn't come.

'I'll go and see if he's all right,' the circus-manager said. But in two minutes he was back again. 'He's not there,' he said. 'He must have slipped out the other way, the crack-brained fellow!'

THE CROSSWAYS

ONCE upon a time there were two children, called Olga and Peter, and they lived on the edge of a huge forest. Olga was nine and Peter was seven. Their father was a woodman and very poor. Their mother's name was Lucindra. She came from another country; their father had met her in the wars. She was beautiful and had fine golden hair. Though she was sometimes dreamy and absent-minded and would suddenly speak to them in her own language, which they didn't understand, she was very fond of them and they loved her.

But Michael their father was a stern man and they were both a little afraid of him. Even Lucindra was afraid of him, for when he was angry he would scold her and sometimes tell her he wished he had never married her. And when this happened she wished she had never married him, but she did not dare to say so; besides he was strong and handsome and could be kind and loving when his fits of bad temper were over.

One thing he had always told his children, they must never on any account go farther into the forest than where they could still see the sunlight shining through the edges. The trees were so thick and the paths so few and hard to follow that even the foresters themselves sometimes lost their way. And there were dangerous animals as well, wolves and bears and wild boars. Michael still carried a scar from a gash that a bear had given him; it ran all the way from his elbow to his shoulder, making a bluish groove in his skin which you could feel with your finger. When he wanted to impress on them the danger of going too far into the forest he would show them the scar. Olga used to try not to look at it but Peter said he would like to have one like it.

Michael would not let even Lucindra wander about in the forest alone though sometimes he took her with him when he went out with his horse and cart. Then they would eat their dinner together under the trees, and she looked forward to that. But he usually went on foot, for the road soon came to an end and branched off into footpaths which lost themselves among the trees. So she did not know much more about the forest than the children did. But like them she wanted to know more, for their cottage was miles away from any town, and sometimes weeks passed without her seeing anyone.

One afternoon, however, when Michael was away at work, a stranger called. He was a young man, slight and slim, with hair as fair and eyes as blue as hers, which was not surprising for he came from her own country and had heard of people whom she knew. He was a pedlar who sold bead necklaces and brooches and bracelets and ribbons. These did not interest Peter very much but he also had pocket-knives and scissors and many other things. He brought them all out of his bag and laid them on the table in the kitchen which was their living-room; they shone and glittered and suddenly the whole place seemed much more cheerful, though Lucindra kept shaking her head and saying she was much too poor to buy anything. The young man said he didn't expect her to, but he went on bringing more and more things out of his bag, even after it looked to be empty, and he was so gay that soon they were all laughing, Lucindra most of all; the children had never seen her laugh like that. And finally she went out of the room and came back with some money, and bought a bracelet for Olga and a pocket-knife for Peter and a necklace for herself. Then she told the young man he must be getting on his way, otherwise it would be dark; and he laughed and said he was in no hurry, because he knew the forest quite well. But greatly to the children's disappointment she would not let him stay. So, telling her how unkind she was, he began to gather together his bits and pieces and put them back into the bag. The children could not take their eyes off him as one by one he packed the treasures away; and every now and then, if something was specially pretty, he would raise his eyebrows as though inviting them to buy it; but each time Lucindra shook her head. 'You must go, you must go,' she kept saying. 'All in good time,' he answered and looked slyly at the children, who knew that he was delaying his departure on purpose. But at last he got up and swung his sack over his shoulder and they followed him to the door where his horse was nibbling the grass; and he fixed the sack on a sort of pannier on its back and jumped into the saddle and wished them good-bye.

'Which way are you going?' Lucindra asked.

'To the Crossways,' he answered, smiling down at them.

'Where's that?'

'Don't you know?' They didn't, and then he told them that in the heart of the forest there was an open space where many roads met; 'and one of those roads,' he said, 'leads to the land of your heart's desire.'

'But how would anyone find the place?' Lucindra asked.

'Easily,' said the pedlar. 'Just follow the full moon until you come to it.' He pointed upwards and there was the full moon hanging low over the forest.

'But how do people know which road to take?' Lucindra asked.

'Oh, it's marked with a signpost,' said the pedlar. He laughed again and rode off, and they went back into the house, which seemed very dull and empty.

Soon after that their father came in and the children at once began to tell him about the pedlar. They were still very excited and could think of nothing else, for they had never had such an adventure in their lives before. 'Did you see him in the forest?' they asked. 'I saw no pedlar,' he answered frowning. 'I believe you dreamed the whole thing.'

'Oh, no, we didn't. Look, look, look.' And disregarding their mother's warning glance they showed him the bracelet and the pen-knife, and made Lucindra go and fetch her necklace, for she had already put it away. When he saw the necklace he grew still more angry and upbraided her bitterly for spending so much money. 'We're hard up as it is,' he said, 'and you must needs go buying things from this smooth-tongued scoundrel. Never let me see you wearing them.' Peter and Olga began to cry, and their mother let the necklace slip through her fingers on to the floor. 'If ever I catch him I shall know what to do with him,' Michael said. So they never told him the rest of the story or spoke of the pedlar any more.

It was a hard winter and it set in early, but in spite of that people did not seem to want wood as they used to, and Michael grew more and more morose and sour. Often when he came home he would not speak to them at all, and sat apart brooding, or went out again mysteriously and did not come back till after midnight. There was no pleasing him. If they sat quiet as mice he would complain of their silence; if they talked he would tell them to shut up. This was not so bad for the child-ren as it was for their mother, for they now went to the village school and so had company. It was a long way to walk but they enjoyed it; they felt free the moment they got out of the house, and rather dreaded coming back, to find their mother drooping and listless, and their father, if he was at home, not lifting his head when they came in. Sometimes they lingered and talked to their friends, but they never spoke of the state of things at home, because they had promised their mother not to.

One evening they had stayed away later than usual and were beginning to feel hungry and look forward to the hot, steaming supper their mother always prepared for them; so in spite of everything they found themselves longing for the moment in their homeward walk when they could first see the light shining through the windows. But there was no light and when they got into the house it was empty. They called and called but nobody answered, so they began to feel rather frightened and went out of doors again. It was much lighter out of doors because there was a moon.

'It's a full moon,' whispered Peter to Olga, 'like that evening the pedlar came.'

They went back into the house and found some matches and lit the lamp, and felt a little more cheerful, for it showed them their supper keeping warm on the hearth. They did not go to bed when they had eaten their supper; they sat in chairs like grown-up people. But Peter had gone to sleep before their father came in.

'Where's Cindra?' he said in a thick voice. (He called her Cindra sometimes.) 'I asked you, where's Cindra?' Peter woke up and began to cry. They told him all they knew. 'But she can't be gone,' said Michael disbelievingly. 'She wouldn't leave us.' He got up and went into the bedroom and stayed there a long time. When he came back his hand shook and he was so pale that his hair looked quite black. 'It's true,' he said, 'she has gone. I found a letter. She says I'm not to try to follow her. She's gone where her heart calls her. What shall we do? What shall we do?'

When Olga saw that he was frightened she suddenly felt sorry for him and much less frightened herself.

'Don't worry,' she said. 'We know where she's gone to, don't we, Peter?'

'Where, where?' their father asked, his eyes darting at them.

'To the Crossways.'

'Nonsense,' he snapped. 'There is no such place.'

'Yes, there is,' said Olga patiently, 'in the middle of the forest. You can find it by following the full moon.'

'The full moon!' he echoed scornfully. 'I know every inch of the forest and I tell you there isn't any Crossways.'

'Please, please don't be angry,' Olga begged him. 'Let Peter and me go, if you don't believe us.'

'Let you go,' he said, 'and lose you too? Haven't I told you that the forest is dangerous? Do you want to send me mad? Sit still and don't stir from here till I come back.'

He went out and they heard him calling 'Cindra! Cindra!' until his voice died away.

'There's only one thing to do,' said Olga. 'We must find her and bring her back.'

'But what about the bears and the wild boars?' said Peter.

'Oh, I shouldn't worry about them,' said Olga. 'I'd much rather you went with me, of course, but if you're afraid I'll go alone.'

This made Peter feel much braver and they started off. They met with no difficulty in finding the way, for the moon made a pathway through the leafless trees; and at first they were not at all frightened, for when they looked back they could still see the light in the cottage windows. They walked hand in hand and their feet made a pleasant rustling on the fallen leaves.

'Will she be pleased to see us?' Peter asked.

'Of course she will, we're her children,' Olga answered.

'But suppose we don't find her at the Crossways?'

'Then we must go on until we do find her. The signpost will say which way she went.'

Whiter and whiter grew the moon as it swung into the heavens, and colder grew the air.

'I don't think I can go on much longer, Olga,' Peter said.

'You can if you try.'

It was then that they saw the bear. It was walking on all fours when they saw it, but when it saw them it stood up.

'Oh, it's going to hug us!' Peter cried.

'Nonsense,' said Olga, but her voice trembled. 'Perhaps it'll give you a scar like the one Daddy has,' she added, hoping to encourage him.

'I don't want a scar now,' sobbed Peter.

'All right,' said Olga. 'I shall just tell it why we've come.'

She went up to the bear and explained that they were looking for their mother, and the bear seemed satisfied, for after swaying a little on its feet and shaking its head, it got on to all fours again and shambled off.

After this escape they both felt very much better, and as if nothing could now go wrong. And suddenly they found that they were not walking on a path any longer, but on a road, a smooth straight road that led right out of the forest. On either side the trees seemed to fall back, and they were standing on the edge of a great circular plain which the moon overhead made almost as bright as day.

'Now we shall soon see her,' Olga said. But it wasn't quite so easy as she thought, for the plain was dotted with small, dark bushes any one of which might have been a human being; and Peter kept calling out, 'Look, there she is!' until Olga grew impatient.

They saw the Crossways long before they came to it. It was shaped like a star-fish, only a star-fish with fifty points instead of five; and the place where they met was like white sand that has been kicked up by the feet of many horses.

But their mother was not there and they walked slowly round the centre, looking at each signpost in turn to see which led to the Land of Heart's Desire. But not one gave any direction; they were all blank, and presently the children found themselves back at the signpost they had started from.

Then in the silence they heard a little sound like a moan, and looking round they saw their mother, lying in a hollow beside the road. They ran to her and she sat up and stretched her arms out and kissed them many times.

'We've come to fetch you back,' they said.

She smiled at them sadly. 'I can't come back,' she said. 'You see, I've hurt my foot. Look how swollen it is. I've had to take my shoe off.' They saw how swollen her foot was, and it was bleeding too. 'You'd better go home, my darlings,' she said, 'and leave me here.' 'But we can't leave you,' they both cried. And Peter said, 'Look, there are some people coming. They will help us.'

He ran towards them crying, 'Please help us', but they paid no heed and did not seem to see him. One after another they found the signpost they were looking for, and went the way it pointed, laughing and singing.

'They can't see us,' Lucindra said, 'because they are going to the Land of their Heart's Desire, and we don't belong to it.'

Then both the children felt cold and frightened, much more frightened than when they had met the bear.

'Couldn't you walk if you leaned on both of us?' Peter asked. She shook her head. 'And how should we find the way?' she said. 'The moon won't help us to go back.'

They lay down beside her, clasping her in their arms, and tried to keep awake, for the cold was making them drowsy. Just as they were dropping off they heard a footstep coming down the road; they did not pay much attention for they knew they would be invisible to whoever came. But Olga roused herself. 'I'm going to try again,' she said, and standing up she saw a long shadow like a steeple, and in front of it a man, walking very fast.

'Oh, Daddy, Daddy!' she cried. But his eyes were wild and staring, and bright with the empty shining of the moon. Terrified lest he too should not recognize them, she seized his hand. He stopped so suddenly that he nearly fell over.

'Where is your mother?' he cried.

'Here! She is here!'

She pulled at his hand, but he shrank back when he saw them, and without looking at their mother he said, 'Cindra, I came to say good-bye.'

'But it isn't good-bye,' cried Olga. 'We want you to take us home.'

He shook his head. 'No, no,' he said. 'I have been unkind to her. I am not worthy of her. She must go where she wants to go.'

'But you must take her, you must!' Olga besought him. 'Look at her, she has hurt her foot and can't walk.'

For the first time he brought himself to look at her, and went up to her and wonderingly touched her foot.

'Do you really want to come with me?' he asked.

'Yes, yes,' she murmured. 'But do you know the way?'

'I know the way all right,' he said with a touch of his old arrogance, and stooping down he lifted her in his arms.

Suddenly they saw written on the signpost, which had been blank before, 'The Land of Heart's Desire'.

It pointed straight back the way they came. And the moment their feet were turned towards home they began to laugh and sing, just as the others had.

PER FAR L'AMORE

THAT August in Venice, an August between the wars, the mosquitoes were particularly poisonous and voracious. Even the Venetians, who are usually immune, being inoculated against these pests, sometimes appeared with reddened wrists and swollen faces. Nor did the insects abide by their own rules; they did not wait for twilight to begin their feasts; they bit by day as well as by night. Hotel proprietors and their staffs, even while covertly scratching themselves, would not admit that there was anything abnormal in the visitation; 'E la stagione,' they would observe philosophically: 'It is the season.' Most Italians take comfort in the thought that manifestations, however unpleasant, are following a natural order, and are apt to say they are, even when they are not. But the visitors to Venice, waking with puffy eyelids and twisted bumpy lips, after perhaps many an hour spent crouching or kneeling under their mosquito-nets, trying to make their bedside lamps shine into the dark folds where the mosquitoes lurked, were not so easily satisfied, and many of them took wing like their tormentors, and flew to mountain resorts, which were said to be above the mosquito line. The only section of the community who profited from the outbreak were the chemists, who did a roaring trade in oil of citronella, small coloured candles guaranteed to suffocate mosquitoes, and other forms of insect-bane; it was before the days of Flit and DDT. But their triumph was short-lived for they were soon sold out—not only of preventives against the bites but even of remedies for them, and were reduced to fobbing off their customers with sunburn lotions and beauty preparations which, so they declared, would have the same effect as antiseptics.

To add to this misfortune a heat-wave of almost unexampled virulence struck the city. Indeed, it struck the whole Italian peninsula. Every day the local paper, the *Gazzettino*, and the national papers, the *Corriere*

573

della Sera and the *Stampa*, published a list showing the maximum and minimum temperatures of all the large towns in Italy, including Benghazi which then formed part of the Italian empire. Benghazi was always top with upwards of 40 degrees Centigrade; but whereas of the others, Rome, Milan, Naples, Florence and Bologna always had a maximum temperature higher than that of Venice, which never rose above 35, Venice always had the highest minimum temperature, for it never fell below 26. Shallow and tepid, the lagoon, which had no chance to cool off, embraced the city like a permanent and inescapable hot-water bottle. Sometimes the more mathematically minded of the English and American tourists, those who were still capable of making the effort, might be seen at some café table, pencil in hand, making the complicated calculation that reduces Centrigrade to Fahrenheit. 'Ninety-four today,' they would lament, 'one degree lower than yesterday, but the humidity is greater—eighty-nine per cent, only two degrees less than in New York.'

The nights seemed hotter than the days. In the afternoon the wind would veer from north to south, from the borino to the scirocco, and by six o'clock—the one tolerable moment of the day—it would be blowing lustily: the visitors snuffed it up, auguring each other a cool night: but by eight o'clock the breeze would have died down, and then the baking pavements and lukewarm canals gave off all the heat they had stored up during the hours of sunshine. Later the full moon would show its rim, fiery as a conflagration, behind the island of San Giorgio Maggiore, and slowly mount until the whole of its great disc, blood-red, and swollen as if it too had been mosquito-bitten, would rise above the roof-tops. Clouds surrounded it and sometimes streaked it, indigo clouds edged with rose, like the clouds in Tintoretto's pictures, making the hopeful think a storm was brewing; but they were only harbingers of heat, and presently the moon swung clear of them and climbed into the dark vault of the night, losing as it went its ruddy hue, changing from copper to amber, and at last to shining white, a waxen death-mask pitted with blue shadows.

Dining late on the terrace of his hotel, against which the ripples of the Grand Canal lapped softly, Mr. Henry Elkington watched it, while he waited for his wife and daughter who, however late the hour, were always later. The terrace was the coolest place, as cool as any spot in Venice, he imagined; yet he felt the sweat collecting on his forehead and saw it glistening on the backs of his hands. Every now and then it would trickle stealthily down his chest and he knew, though he could not feel it, that it was also coursing down his back, for when he leant against the upholstered chair and then leant forward, the chair stuck to his white linen coat. A dark patch must have formed there, an unsightly mark and one that would leave a stain; but at fifty-odd he didn't mind that as he would have minded twenty years ago. He minded the discomfort more, however, and grudged the physical effort of flipping at the mosquitoes. Guided to him unerringly by the red-shaded table-lamp, as by a beacon, they announced themselves with a venomous ping — where were they exactly? His face and head and hands he could to some extent defend with whirlwind gyrations like those of a demented windmill; but his calves and ankles, which were their happiest hunting-ground, those he could not protect. And, tired by sleepless nights, his mind kept telling his sense of self-preservation that it would be better to give up the struggle, adopt a policy of appeasement and let the little creatures have their fling.

Apart from all this he wasn't feeling well; he had some psychosomatic disorder that made his flesh creep even when the mosquitoes were not stinging it. He felt as though his skin didn't quite fit him, it was loose in some places and tight in others; and much as, in one way, he welcomed every breath that blew, another part of his sensorium shrank from it. He was hot and cold by turns; perhaps he had a fever.

Hope stirred in him, however, for his wife, before she went to dress, had promised she would ring up Countess Bembo and say that after all they were afraid they would not be able to stay on for her party, two days hence. He, Henry, was not well, that was to be the excuse: the mosquitoes and the heat had got him down, and the three of them were departing on the morrow for the Dolomites. The Dolomites! The mere word, with its suggestion of fresh mountain air, mosquito-free, breathed new life into him and he called the waiter for another dry martini.

He had had the greatest difficulty in persuading Maureen to take this step. Not that she was, normally, indifferent to the needs and even the whims of a husband who had given her almost everything she asked of life, except romance. She knew what was due to such a husband, and she did not grudge it him. But this was a special case. Countess Bembo was an important Venetian hostess, perhaps the most important, and her party was to be one of the highlights, perhaps the highlight, of the season. It would be a thousand pities to miss it. For herself she, Maureen, would not mind; but Annette would be so terribly disappointed. Annette was only twenty and it was her first visit to Venice. Venice had gone to her head; she could find no flaw in it. She wasn't worried by the heat and the mosquitoes, she thought them rather fun – part of the tremendous fun she was having at the endless parties to which she was invited. Young men buzzed round her – Henry could not keep count of the Nino's and Nini's and Gigio's and Gigi's, or tell them apart, they were as like each other as mosquitoes; but he had to admit that they were good-looking and had excellent manners, and Annette obviously found them far more interesting and exciting than the young men she knew in England. Sailing, bathing, playing tennis, dancing, she went off with them for hours at a time. Henry was slightly worried by these absences, but Maureen seemed to know exactly how far her daughter should be chaperoned, and would draw the line, or not draw it, in circumstances that to Henry's thinking were precisely similar. One thing had always been clear: no conjunction of circumstances whatever must be allowed to prevent Annette's attendance at the Bembos' party.

This was the first time for days that they had dined alone. Annette was her father's darling as she was her mother's and Henry would not have dreamed of depriving her of a pleasure if he had not felt that his health was at stake. Those newspaper paragraphs grew every day more frequent: 'Colto da malore', struck down by sudden illness, this or that middle-aged man (they all seemed to be in the decade between fifty and sixty) had fallen down in the street and been taken to hospital, where he had either instantly expired or been adjudged curable in (at the least) twenty days. Sudden death or three weeks' confinement, three weeks' grilling in a Venetian hospital! Henry, who was of a full habit, trembled at the thought. Now, looking out at the Venetian night, at the gondolas passing below him, dipping and prancing, at the whole medley of small and large craft, hung with lanterns, some silent, some with solitary singers, some with concert parties thrumming mandolins, he tried to recapture the fascination, the sense of heady joy, that the scene had once held for him. But now it spoke to him of nothing but the wish to get away and slake his suffering, sweltering body in the cool air of the mountains.

There was a touch on his shoulder, light as a mosquito settling, and he looked up into Annette's radiant face. 'Mummy's just coming,' she said.

This was not quite true. Maureen appeared about ten minutes later. Henry could not tell from her expression what the verdict was to be: Maureen seldom introduced an important topic until the conversation had turned on other matters. Then unobtrusively she would slip it in. While they confidently munched their scampi and Henry was toying with his grilled sole, Maureen remarked:

'I didn't forget to telephone to Loredana Bembo, Henry dear.'

Hope surged up in him.

'Oh, and what did she say?'

'She couldn't have been sweeter about it. First she said she was fright-fully sorry you were feeling the heat—she sent you all sorts of affec-tionate messages.'

Henry's heart sank.

'And she said she entirely understood your wanting to go away. She wished she could herself. But Henry, she *implored* us not to fail her. She said that so many people had chucked—because of the heat, you know, and the mosquitoes—that it would hardly be a party at all—about thirty people for dinner at the most. She said that except for us there wasn't a cat in Venice.'

'I'm not sure that I like that,' said Henry with a feeble attempt at jocularity.

'Well, you know what she meant. And it is hard on her, isn't it, when she's made so many preparations. And she said the nicest things about Annette. I really don't think we could let her down now—do you, darling?'

'Perhaps not,' said Henry doubtfully.

'And oh, Henry—I nearly forgot—she said you needn't be afraid of the mosquitoes because there wouldn't be any. She's thought of the most amusing way of keeping them out. She thought of it entirely for you, she said. It's to be a secret until the evening of the party.'

Henry realized that there was nothing for it but to give way with a good grace.

Somehow or other he managed to survive the next two days, but not unscathed, however. Taking his morning stroll to the flower-shop in San Stefano (he had to renew the flowers in their sitting-room every day, for after twenty-four hours they had wilted from the heat) he suddenly felt dizzy: the sun seemed to strike right through him, like a sword, as if the proper defences of his body had ceased to operate. 'Colto da malore'! In a panic he looked about for shade but there was none: the sun stood right over the long, acorn-shaped campo. Then he espied an awning and staggered to it. Standing in its exiguous shadow he felt as a shipwrecked man might feel on a rock, with the ocean raging round him. But where next? Frightened though he was, he didn't want to risk the moral defeat of going back without the flowers: besides, Maureen would be so disappointed. Half-way to the shop a projecting doorway lent a modicum of shade. He gained it, and gaining it retained some of his lost confidence. It was all nerves! But no, it wasn't, for scanning the campo he saw other pedestrians pursuing the same policy as his; avoiding the torrid centre where the statue was, they were slinking round the circumference, hurrying from one island of shade to the next. Still, none of them dropped down dead, and soon he plucked up courage, and almost swaggered into the flower-shop, where the flowers were being sprayed with jets of water and the sudden coolness was unbelievably delicious.

But he didn't go out again that day till after sundown, and the next day, the day of the party, which dawned as hot as noon, he gave the flowers a miss and didn't go out at all until their gondola drew up to the brass-railed landing-raft and Maureen said to the gondoliers, 'Palazzo Bembo, sa!' as if, on that evening, there could only be one destination.

Casa, Maureen should have said; house, not palace. In some ways the Bembos were old-fashioned, and affected the nomenclature of an earlier day than that in which the houses of patrician Venetian families came to be styled palazzos. Theirs was one of the few ancestral homes in Venice inhabited entirely by the family who built it, and kept up in appropriate state. This evening that state had been much augmented. If there was not a powdered footman on every step of the grand staircase, there were a formidable number, all the same; and if they were not professional footmen, but farm-workers imported from the Bembos' country estate and put into livery, the effect was none the less magnificent. Passing them on the staircase, and vaguely noting their white-gloved hands and red, perspiring faces, Henry felt that afflatus of the spirit which earthly glory sometimes brings. Other Venetians gave parties that were like parties everywhere; but the Bembos' party had its special cachet.

Light-headed but heavy-footed he stumbled, and clutched at the plaited rope of crimson silk that, threaded through stylized hands of polished brass, hung in festoons against the wall. Good luck! said somebody. A step or two ahead of and above him were Maureen and Annette: what energy was displayed in their sprightly, springy tread! His ankles were swollen under his black socks, and the slight exertion of climbing the staircase was bringing the sweat out on his back.

In an ante-room off the *sala* stood Loredana Bembo, an imposing figure, splendid in jewels, and by her side her husband, a short, thickset, baldish man, but with an unmistakable air of authority about him. 'It was so good of you to come,' she said to Henry. 'And I promise you a hundred lire for every mosquito-bite you get to-night.' A hundred lire was something in those days; it will pay me to get a bite or two, thought Henry, and waited for the buzz, but it didn't come, and when at last they all sat down to dinner, he saw why; the windows were defended by thin metal grilles, of mesh so fine that even a mosquito couldn't find its way through. He had seen them before, of course; his own sitting-room in the hotel was fitted with them. They couldn't be the secret Countess Bembo had spoken of.

He wasn't sitting next to her, an ambassador and a man of title occupied these coveted positions. Of his two neighbours, one was an Italian, one an Englishwoman who always came to Venice at this time.

'What is Countess Bembo's secret?' he asked her. 'Or haven't you heard of it?'

'There is something,' she said.

'Do you know what?'

She shook her head. 'Loredana always has something up her sleeve,' she said. 'Let's hope it won't be too peculiar.'

A member of one aristocratic Venetian family, married into another, Loredana Bembo was a law unto herself. Conventional when she chose to be, if the fit took her she would flout convention. At such times a reckless look would come into her eyes. 'E originale,' her friends said of her, 'she is an eccentric,' and if they sometimes criticized her they were also proud of her and a little afraid. What she said went, what she did got by.

The champagne flowed, and as fast as Henry drank it his labouring, overheated skin discharged it. He dabbed his neck, his face, his hands. Perhaps it would have been wiser not to drink, but he could not forgo the momentary relief each swallow brought him – the immediate physical relief, and the deliverance from his nervous premonitions. All nerves they were: to-morrow this time he would be at Merano breathing freely. Drinking freely he could better imagine that paradise. The faces opposite him were a blur, but one was Maureen's, and another, farther to the left, between a Nino and a Gigi who were both talking to her at once, was Annette's.

At last the chairs scraped on the smooth *terrazza* and they left the dining-room, in Continental fashion, the men and women together, a little group of white shirt-fronts and bare shoulders. Up they went, up-stairs into the second *sala*, for the Palazzo Bembo had two, two great galleries that ran the whole length of the building. Breasting the ascent, however, they stopped, as a crowd stops, automatically, almost barging

into each other: and little cries broke out and circled over Henry's head.
'Ah, che bello!' As they moved on and up, these exclamations, and
others like them, screams and trills and chirrups of delight, went on,
and Henry, reaching the top, saw what it was that had provoked them,
though for a moment he didn't quite take in what it meant. He blinked
and looked again: what was it, this array of snowy surfaces, booths,
tents, tabernacles, this ghostly encampment under the great chandelier?
Then, drawing nearer, he saw: it *was* an encampment, an encampment
of mosquito-nets. Following the others' lead, Henry began to circulate
among them. They were of all shapes and sizes, some square, some
domed and circular, some tapering to a peak like army tents. To one
and all gaily coloured pennons were attached, indicating their purpose.
Under the chandelier, where the light was brightest, was pitched a
cluster of square tents meant for bridge, as their label, 'Per far una
partita', testified. Beyond them, farther from the light, round and square
forms alternating, were other tents reserved for conversation: 'Per far
la conversazione' was the device they bore. Beyond them, where the
light was fainter, was ranged another group, only big enough to hold
two armchairs apiece: 'Per far l'amore' was the legend that these tempt-
ingly displayed. A gasp went up; had Loredana gone too far this time?
And beyond these again, one in each corner of the room flanking the
tall gothic windows, where the light from the chandelier hardly reached
them, almost out of sight, were two much smaller refuges. These at
once aroused the curiosity of the guests: what could their purpose be?
They peered and peered at the labels, which were not coloured or cut
into fantastic shapes, but sober rectangles of white cardboard, with plain
black lettering on them. Then there was a chuckle, which sooner or later
was taken up by everyone: 'Per i misantropi', they read, and soon the
words were on every lip.

The first tents to be occupied were the bridge tents: the impatient
players made straight for them, and within a minute or two the cards
were being dealt. If some of the guests were too slow off the mark, and
lost their places at the bridge-tables, they concealed their disappointment and joined the conversationalists. One or two paired off, and
somewhat sheepishly and defiantly made for the tents of love: cries of
encouragement followed after them. As far as Henry could make out,
no man or woman chose to be self-proclaimed a misanthrope: the two
lone tents remained unoccupied. But he had scarcely time to see, for it
was like a game of musical chairs – one had to find one's seat or be left
standing, and the idea of standing was much less bearable to Henry even

than the idea of talking. 'Per far la conversazione!' There was a vacancy: in he went and sank down in a chair. There were iced drinks in misted glasses on the table, and round it three people whom he knew quite well: it might have been much worse.

He it was who drew together the tent-flaps and tied them with gay bows of scarlet ribbon: if the tents were not mosquito-proof, as he suspected, they looked as if they were, which was a great thing: he could relax, he needn't flap and flip, and screw his face up, or make other uncivilized gestures of the mosquito-ridden. Outside, no doubt, the creatures hummed, they must, for at both ends of the *sala* the windows stood wide open, and with two glittering chandeliers to guide them they couldn't miss their way. No, it wasn't too bad. The muslin kept out some of the air, of course, but how clever of Loredana to have thought of it all! She had turned those twin plagues, the heat and the mosquitoes, neither of which was funny in itself, into a joke. She had converted them into a social asset, she had countered them with a creation that was beautiful and strange. The party would be long remembered.

Fuddled though he was, and ready to accept unreality, Henry began to wonder where, in what muslin arbours, Annette and Maureen had taken shelter. The first question was quickly answered. Faintly, from below, came the strains of a dance-band.

'You didn't know?' said someone. 'They're coming in after dinner to dance, a whole crowd of them. It's we old-stagers who are sitting up here.' He was an Italian and *vecchietti* was the word he used: 'a little old', such a nice word, there was no equivalent for it in English, we were less considerate to old age. Henry didn't mind being a *vecchietto*. So Annette was accounted for: she would be downstairs dancing with a Nino, or a Nini, a Gigio or a Gigi. She would be sure to be enjoying herself.

But Maureen? He looked about him. Even here where the light from the chandelier was fairly strong, you couldn't very well see through the muslin; you could see the shadowy shapes of other tents, but you couldn't tell who was inside them; in the case of those farther away, nearer the windows, you couldn't tell if anyone was inside them. Maureen was so efficient, so practised socially; she would have found her niche—not with the bridge-players, for she wasn't one, not—he smiled to himself—in one of the *temples d'amour*, for that didn't interest her—she would be taking part in another conversation-piece, perhaps next door to his. While with the surface of his mind he gossiped with his fellow guests his inner ear was alert for the inflexions of Maureen's voice; and so intent was he on listening that he didn't see the figure that more than once passed by his curtain wall, stopping and peering in and circling round; and it was one of the others who first saw her and said, 'Guardi, Enrico, isn't that your wife who goes in search of you?' At once Henry jumped up and excusing himself untied the ribbons and let himself out into the air.

'What is it?' he said, moving with her into a space between the tents that was out of earshot. 'Anything I can do?'

'Darling, I've got a splitting headache,' she answered. 'I really think I must go back. It came on suddenly—it's the heat, I suppose. But I don't want to spoil Annette's fun, she's having the time of her life, and I don't want Loredana to know, she has so much on her hands already. So I'll just slip out—she'll never notice—and Luigi and Emilio can take me back to the hotel.'

'I'll go with you,' Henry said.

'No, darling, don't do that. What I should like you to do, if you don't mind, is to wait for Annette and bring her home. When you go you can explain to Loredana and make my apologies. I know it's a frightful bore and you're not feeling well either—but just this once! It really wouldn't do to let Annette go back alone, we know she can be trusted but people would talk about it. I hate to ask you to, but it won't be for long—what time is it?'

'Just twelve,' said Henry. 'There's the Marangona.'

They listened, and above the hubbub of voices and dance music they heard the solemn sound of the great bell tolling midnight.

'I won't tell Annette that I'm going,' Maureen said, 'and don't you tell her either; it might spoil her fun. I'll send the gondoliers straight back and tell them to wait for you. Now we mustn't be seen talking together any more or it will look odd.' Before Henry could speak she had turned away, and with slight inclinations of her head to left and right was making for the staircase.

Henry made a movement to follow her and then turned back. She knew her own mind, no one better. But what should he do? Irresolutely he looked towards the tent he had left—but was it the same tent? He couldn't be sure, and anyhow another man had taken his place, leaving the flap open. Several of the tents had their flaps open, the occupants preferring air and light to freedom from mosquitoes. He picked his way among the tents. Which one should he invade? They all seemed full. Even the bowers of love, which were more opaque than the others, had darker shadows in them. He was shut out! For a moment he felt as a wandering Arab might, whose tribe had exiled him. But he mustn't stand there moping: he would go down and watch the dancers.

Plenty of other guests were doing the same: on gilt chairs and settees they lined the walls; behind them the crimson brocade stretched upwards to the ceiling of painted beams; pictures and mirrors hung above them. His tired mind could not synthesize the scene. Better try to find Annette — ah, here she was, on the arm, or in the arms, of a young man. Her face was rapt and expressionless: she passed within a foot of Henry without seeing him. She was in another world, a world of youth into which he could not penetrate — a world which jealously guarded its own feelings, especially from lonely wallflower fathers. The music whined and groaned and thumped and stammered. Where was she now? There were other rooms, rooms for sitting out in, that led off the *sala*. He mustn't seem curious about her, he mustn't feel curious about her, she didn't belong to him, she belonged to all those young men, the Nino's, Nini's, Gigio's and Gigi's, and the emotions they aroused in her: emotions which sometimes made her youthful face look stern.

Here she was again, on another arm, this time; and this time her face was not so much rapt as set, and in the lines of her body there was the tautness of strain, such as you see in a plant that is being forced to grow in a shape it doesn't like. Was she a captive? He thought her eyes met his: he longed to say, 'Oh, please come here and talk to me a moment!' But he must not; if she had been in another continent she could not have been farther from him.

At most times she could see a joke as well as anyone, indeed she often laughed when he saw nothing to laugh at. But where her young men were concerned she was, it seemed to him, as impervious both to humour and to reason as her mother was in matters of social etiquette and observance. She took it all with deadly seriousness, even when she was laughing and flirting with her swains; and she resented any comment on her conduct, however sympathetic and well meant.

'Does she really know what she is doing?' he had once asked her mother. 'She seems to think that love to-day is different from love at any other time.'

'Oh, Annette's all right,' Maureen replied. 'Besides, there's safety in numbers. We mustn't interfere, we must let her find her feet. If she was really serious about anyone, I should know.'

'Yes, but this isn't England,' Henry said. '*Autres pays, autres mœurs.*'

Maureen shook her head. 'We mustn't spoil her fun,' she said. It had become a slogan.

Henry did not like watching people dance, it pricked him with nostalgia and a sense of guilt that he, too, was not dancing; so after a while he went upstairs again. This time he spied a breach in one of the muslin fortresses: it widened, a head emerged and a voice urged him to come in. He obeyed. The flap was folded to, the bows were tied, the outside world withdrew. But it was only a brief respite. The other man of the trio looked at his watch: 'Why, it's two o'clock,' he said. 'Dobbiamo filare — we must be off!' The warmth and graciousness of their farewells made Henry feel more lonely than before. Again he descended to the ballroom, this time he would risk Annette's displeasure, beard the Nino's and the Gigio's and beg her to come back. 'Your mother isn't well!' — that should be his plea. But this time he couldn't see her in the milling throng; she had vanished: face after beautiful face looked blankly down at his. Perhaps Loredana knows where she is, he thought, and diffidently approached his hostess where, fresh and animated as five hours ago, she sat, magnetizing the men on either side of her: but just out of range of her conscious glance he stopped. With a hundred or more guests about her, how could she know where Annette was? And it would be a clumsy, tactless question anyway; how Annette would hate the notion of a search-party, of being run to earth! And he might have to explain, prematurely, about Maureen, too. So he waved to his hostess as gaily as he could, and she shouted something out to him: Venetians always shouted at you — in ballrooms as well as from bridges — something he couldn't catch: was it good night? Did she think he was taking his leave? Making it as inconspicuous as possible? He couldn't tell, and slowly, availing himself of the silken rope, he climbed to the upper gallery.

It was in semi-darkness; in the splendid chandeliers only a few lights sparkled. Had all the non-dancing guests, the *vecchietti*, departed? The encampment hadn't been dismantled; nothing had been put straight: the servants had left the task of tidying till the morning. Peering in, he saw the cards scattered on the card-tables. The more distant tents, the bowers of love, he could hardly see, still less tell whether they were tenanted. He passed by them towards the windows and saw, with a sudden rush of longing, the two tents set apart for the misanthropes. Either would be a refuge. He chose the farther one, in the darker corner; once inside, he felt rather than saw that he was its first occupant. Draw the flaps and make them fast; let the mosquitoes sing outside! Dimly the thud and whine of the music reached him; it had no power to disturb him now: it was a lullaby. Soon he fell asleep.

He dreamed and in his dream he was still looking for someone, but it wasn't here, it was in the bright sunshine among the bathing-huts and cabins of the Lido. The search was most embarrassing, for all the cabins had their blinds drawn down, and every time he knocked an angry voice said, 'Who's that? You can't come in.' 'I'm looking for my daugher, Annette,' he explained. 'She's a tall girl, dark, and rather pretty. I want to take her home. Have you seen her?' 'We have seen her,' the voice replied, 'but she doesn't want to go home, and she'll be angry if you try to find her. Nino and Nini and Gigio and Gigi are looking after her. She has her own life to live, you know.' 'Yes,' said Henry, 'but her mother is anxious about her. She doesn't want her to go home alone — it wouldn't do. People would talk about her. Please tell me where she is.' 'She's somewhere here,' the voice said grudgingly, 'but you won't be able to get in because the door's locked. This is a *temple d'amour*, so please leave us in peace.'

Oddly enough Henry knew at once which door the speaker meant and went straight to it. But now he was carrying some flowers, flowers he had bought in the Campo San Stefano that morning, and he was glad of this because they gave him an excuse. He knocked and said very humbly, 'Please let me in, Annette, and don't be angry with me: I've only come to give you these flowers — you can wear them in your hair or anywhere you like, but you needn't wear them at all if you don't want to. Not everyone likes flowers.' But though he knew she was inside she didn't answer, and he saw that the flowers were withering in his hands.

He wasn't really asleep, he was only dozing, and the dream kept repeating itself in other sets of circumstances which were much less clear than they had been in the first one, until at last the visual aspects of the dream grew indistinct and only the sense of frustrated search remained.

When he awoke he thought he was in bed, his own bed with the mosquito-curtains round him. Gradually he remembered, and his first sensation was one of relief: he had outwitted Time and all those boring hours of waiting, they had slipped past his tired consciousness and now Annette would be ready and perhaps waiting to be taken home — and not best pleased at being kept waiting. He must go to her at once. For a moment that seemed as easy as it would have in a dream: then full awareness of his situation dawned on him. He was here in the Palazzo Bembo and it was quite dark: too dark to see his wrist-watch. He struck a match: it showed a quarter to five. He let himself out into the open, and as his eyes got used to the darkness saw around him the ghostly forms of the encampment, looking strangely large and solid. No sound came from any part of the building. He had been forgotten, that was it. The ball was over and in the general concourse of good-byes his absence had been overlooked. Someone would have taken Annette back; it only remained for him to go back too.

All this was something to be thankful for. But when he began to think about his situation, it didn't seem so simple. To begin with, how was he to get out of the house? And how, if discovered, would he explain himself? Would he be mistaken for a burglar? And how would he get home? Annette would have taken the gondola. He would have to walk, and he wasn't sure he knew the way.

He went to the window and leaned out. It looked on to a garden, a square garden, quite large, one of the few gardens in Venice. Dawn was not far away: he could see the Renaissance pavilion at the end, the shadows of night still dark between its columns. Nothing stirred, though he could hear the plash of the fountain in the centre. Would he have to go through the garden to get out? He had never approached the Palazzo Bembo on foot. Somewhere, he supposed, there must be a narrow *calle*, an alleyway that led to the main street. But where?'

Baffled, he turned away from the window and, treading cautiously between the tents—afraid of catching his foot in one and tearing it down—he made his way to the other end of the great *sala*. Light met him as he went, the accumulated radiance of the lamps of the Grand Canal. He leaned out of the window, and drank in the familiar scene. How beautiful it was—Venice asleep! Perhaps this was the only hour out of the twenty-four when no one was abroad.

His roving, loving eye at last looked downwards. Moored to the blue *pali*, which looked curiously foreshortened from above, was a gondola. The gondoliers, in their white ducks and blue sashes, were asleep: one curled up on the poop, the other stretched out in the hold: each was using his curved arm as a pillow. Whose gondola could it be? Why, it was his—his gondola, with Luigi and Emilio in it. But why were they there, why hadn't they gone home to bed?

A solution occurred to him. If they had taken Annette to the hotel, as they must have, probably accompanied by some cavalier—Annette's young men always accepted a lift—she might have sent them back to fetch her father. She would have looked for him, no doubt, before she left. But would she? Assuming she had remembered him at all, would she not have concluded that he had left the party earlier, with her mother, and dismissed the gondola when she reached the hotel? Or could it be that the party wasn't really over and she was still somewhere about?

He stole downstairs into the lower *sala*. All was in darkness there, but he sensed its disarray—the debris of the party without the party spirit. His flesh creeping as if from contact with something dirty, he returned to the upper *sala*, and on an impulse shouted down the palace wall, as loudly as any Venetian could have:

'Luigi!'

When he had repeated it a few times there was a movement in the boat, and with sighs of escaping sleep, almost as loud as steam, the gondoliers rose to their feet and looked incredulously upwards.

'Have you seen the signorina?' he shouted in Italian.

'Nossignore.'

'Didn't you take her home?'

'Nossignore.'

'How did she go home then?'

'She must have gone on foot.'

She might have done, but was it likely? Telling the gondoliers to wait—for waiting, even more than rowing, was their métier—he tried to work it out. She might have thought it fun to walk, but would she have forgotten the gondola? Except where her boy-friends were concerned, Annette wasn't inconsiderate. It would have been very inconsiderate to leave Emilio and Luigi out all night.

His musing steps had brought him back to the encampment. Unwillingly he re-entered its precincts. How alien it was. Like something conjured up by an enchanter—purposeless, yet with a potent personality of its own, and not a pleasant one: a personality that recalled the lawless deeds of desert warfare. He was careful not to brush against the muslin fabrics. Each tent had its flap ajar—all the birds had flown. But no, one tent was shut. As though by compulsion he approached it. It was shut, and there were two other odd things about it. The tent was laced as tightly as a shoe, but the scarlet bows were tied on the outside, not the inside; and its pennon had been torn off, torn roughly off, for where the join had been a dark rent showed, and if he peeped through it——

He didn't peep but stood at gaze obsessed more deeply every moment, by a sense of momentousness that was totally devoid of meaning. If, as he felt it might, the secret, the solution, lay inside the tent——

It did lie inside, sprawled over the two chairs, but he would not let himself believe, and here the darkness helped him; for it wasn't growing lighter with the opening day, it was going back to night. Needing air and a moment to confirm his unbelief he staggered to the window, the one that overlooked the garden, and there he saw the massy thunder-cloud piled high against the light and heard without heeding it the rumble of the storm that was to end the heat-wave. The lightning flashed and flashed again; the mirrors on the walls reflected it; a sudden gust blew in — a solid wall of wind that struck the tents and bent them all one way, like spectres fleeing. A flash lit up the whole length of the *sala*. He could not shirk his duty any longer, his duty as a man and as a father. Something might still be done to help, to reanimate, to bring back—— But nothing could be done; around the darkening neck the scarlet fork-tailed pennon had been tied too tight. Another flash told him no more than he knew already: but the next lit up the legend on the noose. Two words were missing, hidden by the strangler's knot, but the operative word was there, the last one, and his memory supplied the rest: *Per far l'amore*, to make love.

INTERFERENCE

AFTER his tenants had left, Cyril didn't try to replace them: let their rooms stand empty for a while, he thought.

They had never been unoccupied before, or not for long, since Cyril bought the house twelve years ago. Then the Gooches had them, the couple who kept house for him; it was only when they left to better themselves that the rooms fell vacant. Cyril couldn't afford another couple; the ministrations of the daily woman, helped out occasionally by the gardener, Mr. Snow, who had his own flat at the top of the house, must suffice his needs. But the housing shortage pricked Cyril's conscience; the empty rooms, that echoed to his tread, were to his spirit like a cold hot-water bottle on his flesh; they chilled it. Hence the tenants, who had no service obligations and who paid Cyril instead of being paid by him.

Five rooms they had, two bedrooms, a bathroom, a sitting-room and a kitchen. Awkwardly placed, they didn't constitute a flat or a maisonette or any sort of dwelling you could give a name to. The kitchen and the sitting-room were self-contained and had their own entrance, a green door giving on the garden, invisible from Cyril's part of the house. One went downstairs to them, as if to a basement, but it wasn't really a basement: their windows looked out on the garden, not on an area wall, for the house, being perched on a steep slope, had an extra storey on the garden side, making four in all.

What a strange house it was. Built on to at different times, it had no plan or method. Few of the eighteen rooms were on the same floor-level as the others; a step up or a step down led to them. The architects, it must be admitted, hadn't wasted any space on passages or landings; door followed door with a suddenness that confused strangers. In the days when Cyril had visitors to stay they often lost their way—indeed it was some time before Cyril could find his. Some of the rooms were roughly pentagonal in shape, with the doorway in the short fifth wall: should the door happen to be open, you got an oblique view of the room—you took it by surprise—walls meeting, pieces of furniture sidling up to each other—all most irregular.

The tenants' bedrooms and bathrooms were also self-contained, behind a door that shut them off from Cyril's domain. But between them and the sitting-room was a tract of common ground—a section of the staircase that, winding its way up from below, made a brief halt outside the tenants' door. Only eight steps impaired their privacy, but sometimes Cyril met the Trimbles on them. 'Unlucky to cross on the stairs,' he would say gaily, and it always seemed to amuse them.

Mr. Snow hadn't been in favour of letting the rooms off. He could look after the house perfectly well, he said, when Cyril was away. Tenants—well, you never knew who they were, or what they might be up to.

As far as the Trimbles were concerned, Mr. Snow turned out to be right. Cyril did know something about them, of course. They were Midlanders who had come south from Birmingham and bought a tobacconists' and newsagents' business in the large town near which Cyril lived: they had been in lodgings till they answered his advertisement. Others had answered it too, there had been quite a number of applicants for Cyril's five rooms. But they all had something against them—children, dogs, unreasonable requirements—whereas the Trimbles had nothing against them. They were a sober, serious couple who minded their own business and gave no trouble: Mr. Snow admitted that. He even made friends with them, came down from his eyrie to sit with them, and accompanied them to the village local, where, so report said, they were making headway in the (for a foreigner) never easy task of making friends.

And how well Cyril had got on with them! When they met on the staircase, which was almost the only occasion when they did meet—what smiles and hand-shakings there were, what solicitous inquiries into each other's health and comfort! How often Cyril would ask if everything was to their liking, and how invariably they would answer that they couldn't possibly be better off than they were! Mr. Trimble was tall and thin and sallow; he wasn't prepossessing but had a nice smile that flickered across his face. She was fair and stout and dumpy, with big blue eyes that smiled continually, and a faint foreign accent: she might have been an Austrian Jewess.

For several months, then, all went well, and Cyril was so used to its going well, and to his own automatic reactions to the Trimbles' unfailing amiability when they met on the stairs, that he began to take not only their amiability but their presence for granted. So what was his amazement when one day, happening to mention them to Mr. Snow, he received the chilling answer:

'I haven't seen much of them lately.'

'Not seen much of them? I thought you saw a good deal of them.'

'At the start I did,' said Mr. Snow. 'But it often happens that things don't go on as they began——'

Cyril's heart sank.

'I hadn't noticed anything——'

'You will, sir, you can take my word for it.'

'Do you know what's wrong?' Cyril asked.

'I have an idea, sir, a very shrewd idea, but I shouldn't dream of telling you.'

'Oh, do tell me,' Cyril begged.

'No, sir, those things are best left in the minds of those who invented them.'

Cyril was not left long in doubt, however. When next he met the Trimbles on the stairs they did not return his greeting. Disappearing behind their door of partition they shut it none too gently. But the time after that they stood their ground, and Mr. Trimble said:

'I'd like a word with you, Mr. Hutchinson.'

Cyril noticed that contrary to custom, he was smiling but his wife was not. Resenting the man's tone, he said:

'I'm rather busy now. Will another time do?'

'I'm afraid it won't, Mr. Hutchinson. You see we're not standing for it.'

'I didn't ask you to stand,' said Cyril.

'Mr. Hutchinson, you're trying to evade the issue. I said we're not standing for it, we are giving notice. But first we want an explanation.'

'Yes, we want an explanation,' repeated his wife, with a set face.

'An explanation of what?' Cyril asked, mortified to feel that he was trembling.

'Don't try to evade the issue, Mr. Hutchinson,' put in Mrs. Trimble. 'We want an explanation of the interference.'

'The interference?' repeated Cyril. 'What sort of interference? Do you mean electrical interference? Are you speaking of your television set? I know the reception here is none too good.'

'Mr. Hutchinson, bluffing won't get you anywhere. We want your explanation before we report the matter to the police.'

'The police? What on earth do you mean?'

'Come, come, Mr. Hutchinson, you know quite well what we mean.'

The reiteration of his name infuriated Cyril.

'Unless you stop annoying me, Mr. Trimble *and* Mrs. Trimble,' he shouted, '*I'll* call the police and give you in charge for insulting language and behaviour. Now for the last time, what is this interference you complain of?'

Mr. Trimble's smile at last left his face, and he said sullenly:

'The interference with our things.'

'Interference with your things?' Like many mild men, when he lost his temper Cyril lost it thoroughly. 'Are you accusing me of some act of indecency? I wouldn't interfere with your things . . . not with a barge pole.'

He saw his anger had cowed them.

'All we know is,' the man said, 'someone has been in our apartments, moving things about, reading our letters, prying and spying. And who can it be but you? You've got the duplicate keys.'

Cyril drew a long breath.

'That settles it,' he said. 'I'll call the police.'

They both protested that this was the last thing they wanted; they even denied having mentioned the police at all. But Cyril was adamant. They had appealed to the police and they should have the police. Crest-fallen, the couple shut the door on themselves, and Cyril retired to his study, fuming and shaking. Any declared enmity made him feel ill.

The village copper was an old friend of Cyril's and predisposed in his favour. All the same, he conducted his inquiry in an impartial manner. Mr. Snow was summoned, and the daily woman. Mr. Snow said that he had been in the Trimbles' sitting-room a few times, at their express invitation; he suggested he had never wanted to go. Asked if he had ever moved any of their things, he did not at first answer; then he said temperately, 'No, why should I? I've got my own things to look after.' The daily help was still more nonchalant. Yes, she had heard of the Trimbles and knew they occupied part of Mr. Hutchinson's house; when pressed she admitted she had passed the time of day with them, but that was all: she was a woman who kept herself to herself. 'It's the only way,' she added darkly. She didn't look at the Trimbles while she was speaking; she gave the impression that they were not there. Cyril could not emulate his retainers' lofty unconcern, but repeated his denials of any sort of interference in the Trimbles' quarters. He laughed nervously after saying this, it seemed so absurd that the ambiguities of language should again betray him into an impropriety; but the policeman did not notice. Asked if they had missed anything as a result of the interferences, the Trimbles admitted that they hadn't. The policeman shrugged his shoulders. Could he see the room where the alleged interferences occurred? They trooped down into the sitting-room, which was long, low and oval at the garden end. Furniture had been moved, said Mr. Trimble; this chair, for instance, had been there; and these letters—he pointed to them but didn't hand them round—had been taken from this drawer and put in that one. Ornaments had been moved and a table-lamp knocked over; but no damage had been done and nothing was missing. In that case, the policeman said, he could take no action; he hoped there would be no recurrence of the interferences; but if anything was stolen or damaged they must let him know.

Nothing was; and after the Trimbles had gone, taking their belongings with them, Mr. Snow gave it as his opinion that the whole thing had been a frame-up on their part, staged to cover the fact that they had found a better job elsewhere, and wanted to break their lease. The other possibility, that Mrs. Trimble had reached an age when women were liable to imagine interferences of various kinds, he discounted; besides, it was the man who brought the matter up. 'In my opinion, sir, you're well rid of them,' he said. 'I never did hold with having them here—it was different with the Gooches—at least they worked for you. And they never complained of interferences. You may be sure it was a put-up job.'

Cyril wasn't so sure. He felt he had been too hasty. The question of the interferences was not brought up again. After a period of cutting each other on the stairs, the Trimbles and he resumed relations—distant relations it is true, but such as permitted him to say good-bye to them with some show of goodwill. And he got the impression that they were sorry to go. But the whole episode left a bad taste in his mouth, of which the always unpleasant experience of having to dislike someone you have previously liked was only part.

So the five rooms were left tenantless, swept but not garnished. Cyril occasionally inspected them. A sort of compulsion, tingling with expectancy and dread, drew him towards them. Their very emptiness contained a sort of personality; he was aware of it the moment he unlocked the door: he felt he ought to apologize for intruding. The habit grew on him; the day seemed incomplete unless he had paid the rooms a visit. Sometimes he put this off until the evening when the summer twilight softened the impact of the glare from the bright curtainless windows on bare walls and uncarpeted floors; sometimes he left the inspection until bedtime, when he had to use a torch, for the Trimbles had taken with them all the detachable electric bulbs. Sneaking about on tiptoe he felt he was up to no good; passers-by, seeing the light flash from his torch, might think mischief was afoot and report it. The Dong with the Luminous Nose! But no, they wouldn't, for there were no passers-by: that side of the house was bounded by the river and the trees that bordered it: even the policeman couldn't see him. As time went on, one daily or nightly visit did not seem enough: he felt he must repeat his tour of inspection and maybe repeat it more than once, perhaps in his pyjamas, in case some aspect of the emptiness had escaped him. At such times he felt a heightened sense of being, as if he was in communication with something, and he would come away sweating and exhausted, as though from some nameless spiritual effort.

One day Mr. Snow said to him, 'Why don't you let me look round those empty rooms, sir, instead of you? I can do it last thing, when I lock up.' Cyril was startled: he had no idea that Mr. Snow had caught him at his little games. He thought quickly. Might this be a way out of his obsession—for such he recognized it to be? Would his subconscious mind, that throve on sacrifice, accept Mr. Snow's sacrifice of time and trouble as a substitute for his? At least let him try. 'Yes,' he said, 'that would be very kind of you, Mr. Snow. And would you come and tell me before you go to bed that everything's in order?'

Soon after eleven o'clock a knock came at his study door, and after the interval that elapsed before anyone entering the room could circumvent the screen that shielded his armchair from draughts, or other forms of surprise, the gardener stood before him. 'I have to report, sir, that all is present and correct,' he said, reminding Cyril that he had served in the army in the First World War—and with a little salute he was gone, almost before Cyril had had time to thank him.

Cyril struggled with himself, or rather with the part of him, the inward trouble-maker, that was so intent on upsetting his peace of mind. Was this the solution? How could he be sure that Mr. Snow had seen— all there was to see? Would he feel obliged to check up on the gardener's nocturnal investigations, which would almost certainly have been less thorough than his own? Would Mr. Snow have known exactly *what* to look for? The fact that Cyril himself did not know made the question no less urgent. And there was another question—ought he to let Mr. Snow take the *risk*?

His mind's unconscious use of italics brought Cyril to the verge of realizing how absurd was his neurotic dilemma—a realization which had before now exorcized his sick fancies. It was all too silly! Of course there was no risk. Mr. Snow might be a year or two nearer seventy than he, Cyril, was; but he was hale and hearty, a match for any tenant, any imaginary tenant he might encounter in those empty rooms. Besides, he had volunteered for this night-service; Cyril hadn't asked him to take it on.

Gradually the urgent sense of something left undone that would haunt his sleepless hours—perhaps make them sleepless—faded, and on that night, and for many subsequent nights, Cyril went to bed without misgivings. 'All present and correct!' *What* was present? It didn't matter, if what was present was correct.

Rarely did Cyril feel sleepy after dinner, but sometimes he did, and this was one of those times. It didn't mean he would sleep well at night, rather the opposite, so he tried to fight it off. Do what he would his head kept nodding and if he let it loll on the chair-back a host of scenes and impressions, unrelated to each other or to his present situation, flooded into it. Once or twice Mr. Snow, returning from his nightly round, had found him asleep, a thing Cyril much disliked—he hated being taken at a disadvantage, with an unprepared expression on his face that might reveal who knew what about his private thoughts. And this danger was real and imminent for eleven o'clock was drawing on; at any moment now he might expect the knock that heralded Mr. Snow's appearance.

At last it came, louder, he thought, than usual. Thankful for his wakefulness, he called out, 'Come in!' To his surprise, nothing happened. It was most unusual for Mr. Snow to need telling twice. 'Come in,' he called again and then he heard the door open, and footsteps behind the screen, and put on the smile of welcome he kept for Mr. Snow.

But it wasn't Mr. Snow who stood towering over him—it was a stranger, a huge man with a red, pear-shaped face, and eyes as black as the moustache which mounted guard over his unseen mouth. After a moment's silence, 'Good evening,' said the stranger. 'Good evening,' said Cyril, and rose uncertainly to his feet. 'You said come in, so I came in,' said the man. 'I hope I don't intrude?'

'Of course not,' Cyril answered. 'But . . . but . . .' He didn't know how to go on and added, 'Please sit down.' The stranger seated himself in the farthest away of the three chairs and Cyril sank back into his.

'I came to look for something, that's why I'm here,' the man said, 'and I thought perhaps you could help me to find it. I see the birds have flown.'

'If you mean the Trimbles——' began Cyril.

'I do mean them,' the stranger said. 'In their rooms was something of mine that I want back.'

'What is it?' Cyril asked.

'I'm not at liberty to say,' the stranger said.

'Then I'm afraid I can't help you,' Cyril said. 'They left some weeks ago and took all they had with them.'

The stranger nodded.

'But it may still be here,' he said. 'Don't you ever feel there's something here, waiting to be found?'

'If you would tell me what it was——'

'No, that I can't do,' said the man. 'But I'll tell you what I can do—I can take these rooms of yours that are standing empty, and then I may come across it. You let the rooms, don't you?'

'No,' said Cyril.

'You let them to the Trimbles.'

'Yes, and I wish I hadn't.'

'You'd find me a quiet tenant, Mr. . . . .'

'Hutchinson is the name.'

'You'd find me a quiet tenant, Mr. Hutchinson. You wouldn't hear me much or see me much. You'd know what I was doing—you wouldn't have to keep tabs on me——'

'I tell you I don't want to let the rooms,' said Cyril.

But the man steam-rollered on as if he hadn't spoken.

'There are the others, of course.'

'The others?'

'Yes, there are seven of us, but we could all squeeze in.'

'Haven't I told you I don't want to let the rooms?' cried Cyril in mounting exasperation.

'Yes, but hadn't you better think again, and take us in, since you can't keep us out?'

'Can't keep you out?' repeated Cyril, staring at him. 'You'll see if I can't keep you out!'

He jumped to his feet. The man rose too, huge, powerful, immovable, the heaviest single object in the room. But when Cyril threw himself on him he wasn't there—he had dissolved into a black mist, impalpable to Cyril's groping hands. When Cyril came to himself he was back in his chair, his mind awhirl with conflicting speculations. Who was he? Where was he? Had he fainted? Had he been asleep?

He glanced at the clock. Nearly half-past eleven. Why didn't Mr. Snow come? Had something happened to him? Ought Cyril to go in search of him? 'Mr. Snow! Mr. Snow!' No good calling him; whether he was upstairs, in his own rooms, or downstairs, in those other rooms, he could never hear, so many doors and staircases intervened.

If anything had happened to Mr. Snow it would be Cyril's fault for letting him take the risk, an elderly man armed only with a torch. Supposing he wasn't in the house at all, supposing he had seen something that upset him, and had wandered into the streets? Then Cyril would be quite alone in the house, at anybody's mercy.

So when the knock came, he didn't at once answer it, not knowing who the visitor might be. And when it turned out to be Mr. Snow, with his thin Vandyck face and steady eyes, Cyril could hardly refrain from some demonstration of joy—shaking hands with him or even kissing him. Back to normal! Normal might be a dull-sounding word, but how blessed it was when applied to the temperature or the spirits! Down to normal, up to normal, dead normal.

'I didn't come before, sir,' Mr. Snow apologized, 'because I heard that you had company.'

'Company, Mr. Snow?'

'Yes, sir, I heard you talking to someone.'

Cyril was silent; then he said:

'You heard me talking to someone, but did you hear anyone talking to me?'

'I couldn't say, sir.' Mr. Snow's tone registered a slight affront. 'I heard your voice, sir, and then of course I didn't listen any longer. I thought someone had dropped in to call on you.'

'But wasn't the street door locked?'

'No, sir, nor the door downstairs, because I hadn't done my round yet. Actually, I came in from the garden through "their" door, you know.' The Trimbles were always 'they' to Mr. Snow.

'Did you see anyone in the garden?'

'Well, sir, I might have seen someone, some unauthorized person, I won't say that I didn't, but you know how dark it is, I couldn't be sure. I switched my torch on, because you can't be too careful, but I didn't see what you could call a person. Were you thinking it might have been your visitor, sir?'

'Yes—no—I——'

'Anyhow,' said Mr. Snow firmly, 'I'm glad to be able to report that all is now present and correct. Good night, sir.' Giving his little salute, Mr. Snow withdrew.

All absent and correct, yes; all present and incorrect, yes; but present and correct, no: the two ideas were mutually exclusive. Conscientious as Mr. Snow undoubtedly was, sharp as his old eyes might be, certain things were outside his range of vision, if not beyond his hearing. He might not see what there was to see, and it wouldn't be fair, in future, to let him take the risk. Cyril waited till he was out of earshot, then took the torch he had left on the hall table, and with stealthy tread began to grope his way downstairs—an anonymous, questing figure, invisible behind his torch, his whereabouts unknown.

Was *he* the something his visitor had come to look for? Was he? Was he? He felt lost now: what would it feel like to be found?

NOUGHTS AND CROSSES

FREDERICK CROSS had lost his diary and without it he was, in the face of the future, helpless. He relied on it absolutely. The mere act of writing in it left as little impression in his memory as if his memory had been the sands of the seashore. He had to have the book itself. 'Bring me my tablets!'

But no one in Smith's Hotel, where he was staying, could bring them, and retribution had come swiftly, for this very evening he was expecting some people to dinner and he didn't know who they were. He didn't know their names and wouldn't recognize their faces. He just remembered he had asked them for to-night.

It would have been very much worse, of course, if it had been the other way round—if he had been dining with them. That would have been a real settler. The only hope was that they would ring him up to confirm the engagement—a very slender hope. They still might, though it was now half-past seven, and dinner was at eight.

He remembered how the invitation had come about: it had come about, as invitations often do, at a cocktail-party. His host had led him up to Mr. Blank and said: 'I am sure you will have a lot to talk to each other about, Fred. Mr. Blank has just started as a publisher, and he is very much interested in the Jacobean Dramatists.'

Fred had written a book on the Jacobean Dramatists which no publisher had seen fit to take. With almost indecent haste he had invited Mr. Blank to dinner, and for good measure had included his wife in the invitation. Hardly had he got the words out, and given the publisher his address and the time for meeting ,when they were swept away from each other. He had had no time to take in his interlocutor's appearance; not a single feature remained in his memory, and as for the wife, he never saw her, though he understood she was at the party.

However, in a few minutes the mystery would be solved. He had nothing to do but wait, and the hotel porter would announce his guests. To ensure that this should happen he lingered in his bedroom; the porter would then have to ring him up and notify him of the guests' arrival.

Punctually at eight o'clock the telephone bell rang and the porter's voice said: 'A lady and gentleman to see you, sir.' 'What is their name?' Fred asked, but disappointingly the porter had rung off.

The couple were standing in the lounge, the middle lounge, for there were three: one across the passage, one divided from the middle lounge by a wall of glass. Fred Cross went up to greet his guests.

'This is my wife, Mr. Cross,' the man said, introducing a rather florid-looking lady, whose face broke into a smile with many lateral wrinkles. The man was tall and dark and clean-shaven, it wasn't easy to place him; he didn't look especially like a publisher, but then what publisher does? He didn't look like anyone whom Fred remembered; but there was nothing remarkable in that: the party had been a blur of faces.

When they had sat down with their inevitable dry martinis and had exchanged a few platitudes about the weather (it was a coldish night in November) the man said:

'We are particularly pleased to see you, Mr. Cross, because there is a matter in which I think we could help each other. I daresay you know what it is.'

Fred was, on the whole, a man of direct speech and inclined to come to the point straightaway; but he was used to the oblique approach of business men, and ready to adopt it.

'Well, yes,' he said, 'I rather think I do.' In his mind's eye he saw the typescript of his work on the Jacobean Dramatists, which the hands of many publishers' readers had dog-eared. At the risk of sounding facetious he added, with a smile:

'It's to do with something that happened a good while ago.'

'Yes, it is,' the man said. He did not smile, but his wife smiled brilliantly, showing her teeth.

'When we have talked it over,' said the man, 'perhaps you wouldn't mind coming round to our place, where you may find one or two more who are interested. Joe Cossage, for instance.' He looked at Fred Cross rather closely.

The name Joe Cossage conveyed nothing to Fred, but the field of Jacobean studies was a wide one, and he couldn't be expected to have heard of all the gleaners in it.

'I should be delighted,' he said, trying to conceal his eagerness. 'But shouldn't we have dinner first?'

'Dinner?' said the man, and if Fred hadn't been so engrossed in thinking about his book, he would have noticed the question mark and the time-lag before his guest said: 'Dinner would be a very good idea.'

'Of course, I haven't got the book with me,' Fred remarked.

'We didn't suppose you would have, did we, Wendy?' the man said to his wife who flashed her smile at his unsmiling face. 'But we should like to have a look at it, I can tell you, and so would Joe.'

'I mean, I haven't got it here,' said Fred, blushing for himself and his over-eagerness to sell his wares. 'As it happens——' he tried to make his voice sound casual — 'as it happens I've got it upstairs.'

'Whew!' said the man, and something that might have been his soul, if he had one, seemed to appear in his face, so intense was his expression. 'Can we wait till after dinner, Wendy?'

'If Mr. Cross wants us to, I'm sure we can,' his wife said.

'Oh, yes, let's wait till afterwards,' said Fred, lightly. He regretted his unbusiness-like precipitancy, now that he saw that the others were anxious to see the book as he was to show it to them.

'As long as you don't change your mind about it,' said the man. 'We weren't sure you'd want us to see it, were we, Wendy?'

'Joe thought he'd come across with it,' his wife said, smiling.

'Well, a lot hangs on it, you see,' the man said, 'a lot hangs on it. That's why we weren't sure——'

'And a lot hangs on it for me, too,' Fred Cross interrupted.

The man glanced at him quickly. 'Yes, I suppose it does,' he said. 'That's why we thought persuasion might be necessary.'

Fred felt immensely flattered. Persuasion, indeed! If they only knew how he was longing to part with his treasure! But he mustn't let them know. He had already shown his hand too plainly.

'I won't be too unreasonable,' he said. 'I'll meet you as far as I can.'

The man seemed to notice his change of tone, for he said:

'We don't want just to look at it, you know. We want to *have* it.'

'Of course, of course,' Fred Cross said soothingly. 'After dinner we can talk about terms.'

'We'd better do that at our place,' the man said.

'Just as you like,' said Fred Cross, rather grandly. 'Now what about another round of drinks?'

They agreed. As Fred was going to the bar to give his order the porter came up to him and said: 'A lady and gentleman have just come and asked for you, sir.'

'Another lady and gentleman?'

'Yes, sir, there they are. They came a second ago, sir. I was just going to tell you.'

Fred followed the porter's eye. The couple were standing in the next lounge, with their backs to him, looking about them with the relaxed curiosity of people whose minds are comfortably on their dinners.

Oh, that damned diary! Here was another muddle. What was he to do? Five was an awkward number. How did he know the two couples would mix? And how could he introduce them to each other when he didn't know either of their names? Perhaps the porter could enlighten him.

'They didn't give a name, sir,' the porter said. 'They simply asked for you.'

Just as he feared! What an embarrassment to have to ask the two couples to introduce themselves to each other, and also to him! And who were the second couple, anyway? From a back view he didn't seem to know them, either. But better not look. He would have to act quickly. It would be a disaster, he now saw, if the second couple stayed, just as he was on the point of concluding a deal with these new publishers. For politeness' sake they would all have to talk about other things, and the opportunity might slip through his fingers, never to return. He *must* get rid of them.

To give himself a breathing space, he said to the porter:

'Perhaps another time you would ask visitors to give their names?' — but even while he saw the man's face stiffening under the rebuke he remembered that he might need his co-operation, that in fact he needed it now, and added quickly:

'Charlie, would you do this for me? Tell the lady and gentleman that I'm terribly sorry, but I've been taken ill, in fact I am in bed, and I can't give them dinner to-night. I shall be in the bar — just tell me if it's O.K.'

He crossed the bar (ill-omened phrase) and in a minute or two the porter informed him that the couple had gone. 'They said they were very sorry to hear you were ill, sir,' the man concluded, not altogether without malice.

'Oh, well,' Fred Cross sighed with relief, but he felt uncomfortable. He didn't like telling lies or getting other people to tell them for him; and he was superstitious enough to wonder whether saying he was ill might not make him ill, or bring him bad luck in some way.

When he rejoined his guests he seemed to have been away for hours, though in fact it was only a few minutes. The arrival of the drinks coincided with his apologies and smoothed over the interruption; but the conversational thread had snapped and it was only when dinner had been some time under way that they picked it up again. His guests seemed to fight shy of it, and Fred wondered if this was a policy they had agreed on between themselves, while he was out of hearing, with a view to lowering the advance they were prepared to pay on the book, or the royalty, or both.

'There are so many Smith's Hotels in London,' the woman was saying, with her bright automatic smile, 'almost as many as there are Smith's bookshops. We weren't quite sure which yours was.'

'Joe told us it would be this one,' said her husband, glancing at Fred.

Again Fred wondered who this Joe might be, who seemed so conversant with his whereabouts. But it wasn't by any means the first time that a stranger to him had furnished a third party with his address. More people know Tom Fool than Tom Fool knows. But he had every reason to be grateful to Joe, whoever he was.

'Yes, there are a lot of Smith's Hotels,' he agreed. 'But,' he added humorously, 'I think this is the chief one. And for that matter' – the thought struck him suddenly – 'there are quite a lot of Frederick Crosses. It's a common name. I know another myself.'

'Yes, Joe thought there might be another,' said the man, 'but as it turned out he was wrong.'

'I'm glad he was,' said Fred. 'I can't think of another Fred Cross who has to do with books. And this hotel is quite a haunt of literary men.'

'Of men with books to sell?' said his guest, lowering one eyelid into what, if it had been more mirthful, might have been a wink.

'Yes, men with books to sell,' said Fred, delighted to have got back to books at last. 'And men who have sold them too, of course. Now as for mine——'

'We want to see the book first, you know, we want to know what's in it, don't we, Wendy?'

'Oh, well, you shall,' said Fred, cautious now in his turn, 'that is if you're really interested, as you seem to be.' If they were on their guard, so would he be on his. He would whet their curiosity with hints. 'I could give you a bit——'

'All in good time,' the man said hurriedly. 'All in good time, but a list is what we want.'

'A list of names, I mean,' Fred went on, 'my authorities – my colleagues, I suppose I could call them since I'm a bit of an authority myself

—a bibliography, you know. And I've done quite a lot of research, too. I've dug about in all sorts of places that most people don't know about, besides London and Oxford and Cambridge. Oh, I've unearthed some interesting facts—facts, let me tell you, not just hypotheses. You'd be surprised how much I've learnt.'

The husband and wife listened in silence; then the man said, sipping his wine, 'It's facts we're chiefly interested in, facts and names. You said you went to Cambridge?'

'Oh, yes, I did quite a lot of work in Cambridge. In Cambridge it's comparatively simple—people are ready to tell you what they know.'

'Did you come across Ben Jonson in Cambridge?' the man asked, lowering his voice.

Fred Cross laughed.

'Oh, yes, of course I did.'

'And Jack Webster?'

'I expect you mean John Webster,' Fred corrected him.

'I daresay he's called John sometimes,' said the man.

'Of course I know him,' Fred said. 'He's my favourite. But I didn't find out much about him.'

'Your favourite, is he?' the man said, disagreeably. 'Well, there's no accounting for tastes. And who else did you dig up? Did you dig up Dick Skipton?'

This name was strange to Fred. Was Dick Skipton a dramatist, or a critic, or a scholar—someone he ought to have heard of? He didn't want to admit a gap in his omniscience, they would think the worse of him if he did, so he said casually, taking a chance, and hoping that Dick Skipton wasn't dead, 'If I didn't meet him I heard a lot about him.'

'You seem to be well in with the whole bunch,' observed he man in a neutral voice, and his wife gave her quick smile, which seemed at the moment oddly out of place.

'Well, it's my job to be,' said Fred Cross, modestly. 'I've spent several years, you know, trailing them, tracking them down. I flatter myself that I know as much about them as anyone does. I believe that you are interested in them, too. If you care to ask me a question about any of them, sir, I should be only too glad to answer it if I can.'

Rather to Fred's surprise, his guest didn't take up the challenge. Instead he said, yawning into his wife's smile:

'I'm ready to take your word for it.'

Fred thought that this was carrying the pose of indifference rather far. 'It's been a labour of love, you know,' he said. And when they looked rather rudely incredulous, he added: 'It may be morbid of me, but I like the company of all those thugs and assassins.'

'You're welcome to them,' the man said rather grimly. 'But the main thing is, you've got their dossiers.'

'Oh yes, I have,' Fred said. 'But I'm sorry you don't like them. They did things so picturesquely. "Enter executioners with coffin, cords and a bell." The killers of to-day are . . . well . . . more prosaic.'

'I'll say they are,' said his guest, with a sudden lapse into Americanese. 'I'll say they are. Now, Wendy, we must go and make up our faces, and then we'll take Mr. Cross on to our place. It's not too early for you, is it, Mr. Cross? We've got the car outside.'

'No, indeed,' said Fred. He felt the meal was being terminated rather abruptly; but he was as anxious as his guests seemed to be to get down to business.

Left alone, he sat for a moment at the table, thinking. No doubt the pair, besides powdering their noses, wanted to say a word to each other in private about terms. While they were doing that he would go up-stairs and fetch the book. Even his rather shabby bedroom wore a cheer-ful air, such was his elation, and when he took the typescript out of his suitcase, instead of greeting him with the leaden look of a child that has never managed to make good – the look that only an oft-rejected type-script can give – it seemed to say: 'Your faith in me has been justified after all.' I'll wrap it up, he thought, handling it affectionately; it won't matter if I keep them waiting, it'll make them the more eager. How often had he done up this selfsame parcel; even the brown paper had been used before. But this would be its last outward journey until it returned to him with his proofs.

The book under his arm, he walked downstairs, scorning the lift. As he was crossing the middle lounge – always some Rubicon for a Cross to cross – he heard his name called. Not a good sign had the voice been imaginary, but this time it was real, as real at any rate as the loud-speaker's voice, which penetrated to the very nerve-centres. 'Mr. Whis-ton, please. A telephone call for Mr. Whiston, please. Mr. Fred Cross would like to speak to Mr. Whiston, Mr. Fred Cross calling Mr. Whiston, please.'

The hotel seemed to echo with it. Of all the coincidences on this evening of coincidences, this was the one that surprised Fred Cross the least. Experience had taught him that there were other Fred Crosses in the world besides himself. It was a lesson in humility which he had thoroughly learnt. Sometimes it vaguely depressed him that he had to

share his name with so many other men but to-night he was proof
against depression; he was morally certain that his 'Jacobean Dramatists' was in the bag (what bag? whose bag? A bag unknown to Brewer's
Phrase and Fable).

As the message was being repeated, the porter said to him:

'Your guests are waiting for you in the car, sir.'

He sat on the back seat with the publisher's wife, and didn't notice much
where they were going, so occupied was he in trying to keep up a conversation with her invisible but (he felt sure) existent smile. True to his
resolution, he gave away as little as he could, and she was just as un-
forthcoming. Their conversation, like an iceberg, trailed unmeasured
depths beneath it. Childishly, Fred found this mystification rather fun.

London spreads out a long way in all directions; when at last Fred felt
he could take a rest from social effort and look about him he didn't
know where he was, but the street lamps were fewer than they had
been, and the houses farther apart. A minute or two later the man said:
'This is us,' and drew up at the kerb.

The 'place' he had been taken to was much less grand than the size of
the car suggested that it would be: it was in fact a bed-sitting-room in a
semi-detached house. Many people lived like that nowadays, but they
generally made the bed, or got it made, before the evening. As though
aware of this thought the woman said:

'Sorry the room's in such a mess, but we had to make an early start
this morning. What about some whisky, Bill?'

'In there,' the man said briefly, indicating a small cupboard which,
when opened, was seen to house a surprising number of objects meant
for a variety of uses: but drinking was one of them.

When the gas-fire had been lit the room seemed more habitable, as
well as warmer. Fred and his hostess occupied the armchairs on each
side of it; the man cleared a space among the bedclothes and sat down
on the bed.

'Joe's not here,' he said.

'He may be on some job,' said Wendy.

'Well, good luck to him and good luck to the book,' he said.

'To the book!' he said, and raised his glass. They all drank to it and
Fred was suddenly aware of the parcel under his arm. Self-consciously
but proudly he began to fumble with the string. This was his moment.

'Some book!' the man said, watching him.

Fred agreed. 'It took me——' he broke off, remembering he had told them before how long the book had taken him to write — remembering, too, that publishers are not necessarily impressed by the extent of an author's industry. 'Well, you know how long it took me,' he substituted. 'Time wasn't an object: accuracy was what I aimed at.'

They both nodded, and out the typescript came. It had at once, for his eyes, the too bulky, too ponderous look of a literary work, however slender, that has always missed its market. Printed in the middle was the title, its worn, faded ink almost indecipherable against the pale blue of the folder, and in the bottom right-hand corner Fred's name, and his address, which seemed at the moment very far away.

The man took the book from him. 'I wasn't expecting a big book like this,' he said, 'I must put on my glasses.' The horn-rimmed spectacles transformed his face and for the first time he looked like a man who might be interested in books. He turned the pages. 'Middleton, Marston, haven't heard of them. Oh, here's Ben Jonson. Where's the list you spoke of?'

'You'll find it at the end,' said Fred.

The man began to read the names out, and then stopped. 'Strikes me there's some mistake here,' he said. 'Somebody's been having a game,' he repeated giving the innocent phrase an unpleasant sound. 'A game with us, it looks like. Somebody has. What do you make of it, Wendy?'

He handed his wife, if wife she was, the book: the pages turned rapidly under her reddened nails.

'I can't make head or tail of it,' she said. 'It might be somebody's idea of a joke. . . . Perhaps this gentleman will explain.'

Fred cleared his throat.

'It's my book,' he said, with such dignity as he could muster, but with a fluttering at his midriff. 'My book on the Jacobean Dramatists. I thought you were interested in it. . . . I was told you were.'

'Who told you?' the man asked.

It was only when he couldn't remember his informant's name — a name he knew as well as his own — that Fred realized he was frightened.

'But you are publishers, aren't you?' he asked.

For a moment it seemed just rude that neither of them answered; then it seemed strange, with the strangeness of their faces, the strangeness of the room, and the strangeness of his being there at all.

'I thought——' he began.

'You thought a good deal, didn't you?' said the man. 'It's our turn to think now. Someone, as the poet said, has blundered. Someone will be for it, I suppose.'

The repetition of the word 'someone' began to get on Fred Cross's nerves.

'If you're not interested,' he said, half-rising, 'I'll take the book away.'

'Sit down, sit down,' the man said, patting the air above Fred's head. 'We *are* interested, and we don't want you to go away, not yet. We haven't quite done with you, as the saying is. Now as for this book——'

'It's quite simple,' said Fred, trembling. 'I see you're not interested in it. I'll take it away.'

'It isn't so simple as that,' the man said. 'Someone has found out something that someone has got to forget—or there may be trouble, and we don't want any trouble, do we?'

'No,' said Fred mechanically.

'I'm not mentioning names,' the man went on, 'it's better not to mention names, we haven't mentioned names, have we?'

'You know my name,' Fred said.

'Yes, but we're not interested in your name. It's our names that matter. She's Wendy and I'm Bill—those are our names. You can call us by them, if you like.'

Fred Cross had never felt less inclined to be on Christian-name terms with anyone.

'And you might want to write to us,' Bill went on. 'You might want to send us a Christmas card, for instance.'

'I don't think I shall,' Fred said.

'You never know,' Bill said. 'Now here's an envelope.' He fetched one, slightly soiled, from a heap of litter on the table. 'Have you a pen?'

Using the typescript as a desk, Fred set himself to write; his hand was shaking.

'Mr. and Mrs.——' he wrote, and stopped. Then he remembered: Whiston, of course. 'Mr. Whiston, please. A telephone call for Mr. Whiston, please.' But his hand was shaking too much. To gain time he raised it from the envelope and said:

'But you haven't told me your name.'

'Didn't we tell you?' the man asked. 'It was very careless of us. Are you sure we didn't?'

'Quite sure,' said Fred.

'What an extraordinary thing. We didn't tell you our name, or our address, or anything?'

'Nothing at all,' said Fred.

'Could you find your way here, if you wanted to pay us another visit?'

Suddenly Fred wondered if he could frighten them, and rashly said: 'I think I could.'

'Oh, you think you could? Well, just to make it easier for you, here's our name and the address,' Bill said, standing behind him. 'Take it down.'

Fred bent his head and set himself to write.

'Allbright,' said the dictating voice.

'Mr. and Mrs. Allbright, Flat C, 19 Lavender Avenue, S.W.17. Got that?'

Fred did get it, but he couldn't say so, for his head was lying on the typescript, and he was unconscious. When he came to he was in hospital. A policeman had found him stretched on the pavement in a deserted street. Almost his first inquiry was for his precious typescript, and almost the first action when he left the hospital was to get in touch with the man whom he had turned so inhospitably from the door. All the newspapers had reported his misadventure, and none of them failed to observe that the typescript had bloodstains on it. At last it was in the news, and this may have turned the scale in Fred's favour; at any rate the publisher accepted it.

Yet more publicity followed. The name of Allbright conveyed nothing to the police, but the name Whiston did.

'You were lucky you didn't let on you knew it,' the police told Fred, 'or you would have got a bigger bashing than the one you did get.' They had more serious charges against William Whiston than the assault upon Fred Cross, but that was one charge. Another Fred Cross soon figured in the proceedings, a much more sensational one; but he did not altogether steal the limelight from our hero, for the newspapers dared not mention him and his black doings without making it quite clear that he must not be confused with another Fred Cross, the well-known author, whose long-awaited work on the Jacobean Dramatists was soon to be given to the world. But one important piece of evidence in the case, a small black notebook containing a list of the names of a gang against whom William Whiston had a grudge, was never submitted to a publisher.

THE PYLON

The trees sloping inwards, and the hedge bounding the field beyond, made a triangle of green in which the pylon stood. Beyond it, fields again and then the railway embankment. Beyond the embankment more hedges making transverse lines, and then the roofs of houses bowered in trees, sloping up to the wooded hill-crest, outlined against the sky. But that was a mile, perhaps, two miles away; whereas the pylon——

There was general rejoicing when the pylon disappeared: Mummy was glad, Daddy was glad, Victor was glad and Susan was glad. The morning when it happened they all crowded to the window as if they had never seen the view before. Nor had they—the view without the pylon. Ever since they came to the house ten years ago it had been there —an eyesore, a grievance. 'It would be such a lovely view,' they used to say to visitors, 'if it wasn't for the pylon!'

The pylon used to stand between two trees, a fir-tree and a copper beech, directly in front of the window, just beyond the garden. Instead of concealing it, they framed it. Every so often Victor, the optimist, now sixteen, would say, 'Daddy, I'm sure those branches are coming closer together! Next year, you'll see, they'll hide it!' And his father would reply, as like as not, 'They're not growing any nearer—they're growing farther apart! Fir-trees and beech-trees don't agree, you know!'

There it stood, between the trees, rearing its slender tapering height against the wooded hillside, the line of which it maddeningly broke, topping with its incongruous yard-arm the ancient earth-work that crowned the hill.

Now it was gone, and in its place they saw the trees that it had hidden and, more especially, two Lombardy poplars growing so close together that if you walked a little distance, either way, they looked like one.

And Laurie, the youngest of the family, too, was glad at first, or thought he was. When he heard his parents saying to visitors, 'Isn't it wonderful, the pylon's gone!' he would echo, in a grown-up manner ill-suited to his eleven years, 'Yes, isn't it wonderful?' Not that he disliked the pylon on aesthetic grounds, but he thought it was the proper thing to say.

But whereas their grievance against the pylon had been vocal for many years, their gratitude for its departure was comparatively short-lived. They would still say, 'How marvellous without the pylon!' but they didn't really feel it, and after a month or two they didn't even say it, taking their deliverance for granted, just as when an aching tooth is pulled out, one soon ceases to bless the painless cavity.

With Laurie, however, it was otherwise. Being outwardly a conformer — indeed a rather zealous conformer — he had joined in the delight his elders showed over the pylon's downfall. He tried to gloat over the square patch of concrete, marking its site, which the demolition squad hadn't bothered to clear away. But when he stood in front of the window, whichever window it might be — for having a southern aspect, most of the windows of the house had once looked on the pylon — and set himself to gloat, sometimes he would find his eyes straying, even shying away from, the remnant of its ruin. To the others the pylon had been an eyesore and a grievance; to him it was a landmark and a friend. How tall and proud it used to be — one hundred and seventeen feet high — the tallest object in the neighbourhood — taller than the hill itself, he liked to think, though his mind told him that its superior height was only a trick of the perspective.

From surveying the pylon-less gap with a lack-lustre eye it was a short step to trying to imagine it with the pylon there. And then Laurie realized that something had gone out of his life — some standard, was it, by which he had measured himself? No, not exactly that, nor only that. The pylon had symbolized his coming stature, his ambitions for himself as an adult. One day his short, plump body would shoot upwards, tall and straight as the pylon was; one day his mind, that was so dense in some ways, and so full of darkness, would fine down to an aery structure that let the light in everywhere and hardly cast a shadow. He would be the bearer of an electric current, thousands of volts strong, bringing light and power to countless homes.

The pylon, then, had served him as a symbol of angelic strength. But in other moods it stood for something different, this grey-white skeleton. In meaner moods, rebellious moods, destructive moods, he had but to look at it to realize how remote it was from everything that grew, that took its nourishment from the earth and was conditioned by this common limitation. It was self-sufficient, it owed nothing to anyone. The pylon stood four-square upon the ground, but did not draw its sustenance from the ground. It was apart from Nature; the wind might blow on it, the rain might beat on it, the snow might fall on it, frost might bite it, drought might try to parch it, but it was immune, proof against the elements: even lightning could not touch it, for was it not itself in league with lightning?

And so he, Laurie, in those moods when nothing favoured him, when everyone's hand was against him and his hand against theirs, insulated by the flawless circle of himself, he, too, enjoyed the pylon's immunity, its power to be itself. Whatever stresses might be brought to bear on it, it didn't care, nor, looking at it, did he, Laurie, care.

All that was over now; his companion was gone; and Laurie-the-pylon was no more.

Deprived of his second self he shrank, his imaginative life dwindled, and with it his other budding interests. An east-wind blight descended on his mind, dulling his vision, delaying his reactions. If he was spoken to, he didn't always hear, and if he heard he didn't always answer. 'But you don't *listen*!' Susan would chide him, in exasperation, and his brother, who went to the same day-school, would defend him: 'You see, he's so tiny, his ears haven't grown yet! They're really little baby's ears!' Then Laurie would lunge out at him, and in the scuffle regain the sense of immediate contact with reality that he had lost.

His mother and father, oddly enough, took longer to notice the change in him, for he had always been more talked against than talking. In fact they might never have noticed it but for his end-of-term reports. These made them think, and one, from Laurie's form-master, made them quite indignant.

'I wonder what's come over the boy,' his father said, knitting his heavy brows and tapping his finger-tips against his teeth. 'He used to be the clever one. Not quick and sharp like Victor, but thoughtful and original.'

'I expect he's going through a phase,' his wife said, placidly.

'Phase, indeed! He isn't old enough for phases.'

'You'd better speak to him, but if you do, be careful, darling. You know how sensitive he is.'

'Sensitive my foot! I'm much more sensitive than he is. You ought to warn *him* to be careful.'

'I only meant we don't want anything to do with Oedipus,' his wife said.

'You shouldn't spoil him, then. You should be much nastier to him than you are. I've more reason to worry about Oedipus than you have. Laurie might marry you, O.K., but he would murder me. It's *I* who am to be pitied. No one ever pities fathers. No one ever pities Oedipus's father, whom Oedipus bumped off. I think I shall expose Laurie on Mount Cithaeron, having first struck the toasting-fork through his toes.'

All the same, he put off 'speaking' to Laurie as long as he could, and when the time came he approached the subject warily.

'Well, old man,' he said, when he had got Laurie alone, 'take a pew and tell me how you fared last term.'

Deliberately he seated himself at some distance, for fear the nearness of his large strong body might arouse the wrong kind of response and inflict a Freudian bruise.

'Well,' echoed Laurie, heavily, 'I didn't do very well, I'm afraid.'

'You're growing too fast, that's the trouble,' said his father. 'It takes it out of you.'

'I only grew an eighth of an inch last term. They measured me,' Laurie added, almost as mournfully as if the measuring had been for his coffin.

Drat the boy, his father thought. He won't use the loop-holes that I offer him.

He pulled at his moustache which, unlike the bronze hair greying on his head, had kept its golden colour. Proud of its ability to keep its ends up unaided, he wore it rather long, a golden bow arched across his mouth and reaching to the wrinkles where his smile began. Tugging it was a counter-irritant to emotional unease. But was such an adult masculine gesture quite suitable in front of a small boy?

'How do you account for it, then?' he asked, at last.

'Account for what, Daddy?' But Laurie knew.

'Well, for your reports not being so good as they sometimes are.'

Laurie's face fell.

'Oh, weren't they good?'

'Not all that good. Mr. Sheepshanks——' he stopped.

'What did he say?' The question seemed to be forced out of Laurie.

Mr. Sheepshanks had said that Laurie's work was 'disappointing'. How mitigate that adjective to a sensitive ear?

'He said you hadn't quite come up to scratch.'

'I never was much good at maths,' said Laurie, as though he had had a lifetime's experience of them.

'No, they were never your strong suit . . . And Mr. Smallbones——'
Laurie clasped his hands and waited.

Mr. Smallbones had said, 'Seems to have lost his wish to learn.' Well,
so have I, his father thought, but I shouldn't want to be told so.

'He said . . . well, that Latin didn't come easily to you. It didn't to me,
for that matter.'

'It's the irregular verbs.'

'I know, they are the devil. Why should anyone want to learn what
is irregular? Most people don't need to learn it.' He smiled experimen-
tally at Laurie, who didn't smile back. He unclasped his hands and
asked wretchedly, but with a slight lift of hopefulness in his voice:

'What did Mr. Armstrong say?'

Mr. Armstrong was Laurie's form-master, and it was his cruel verdict
that had rankled most with Laurie's parents. It couldn't be true! It had
seemed a reflection on them too, a slur on their powers of parenthood,
a genetic smear, a bad report on *them*. And it was indignation at this
personal affront, as well as despair of finding further euphemisms, that
made him blurt out Mr. Armstrong's words.

'He said you were dull but deserving.'

Laurie's head wobbled on his too-plump neck and his face began to
crinkle. Appalled, his father ran across to him and touched him on the
shoulder, pressing harder than he knew with his big hand. 'Don't worry,
old chap,' he said, 'don't worry. When I was your age I had terrible
reports, much worse than yours are. You've spoilt us, that's what it is,
by always having had such smashing ones. But now I've got some good
news for you, so cheer up!'

Laurie raised his tear-stained face open-eyed to his father's and set
himself to listen. His father moved away from him and, drawing himself up to give the fullest effect to his announcement, said:

'It doesn't matter so much what these under-masters say, it's what
the *Head*master says that counts. Now the *Head*master says——'

Suddenly he forgot what the Headmaster had said, although he remembered that some parts of the report had best not be repeated.
Reluctantly, for he meant to keep the incriminating document hidden,
and believed he had its contents by heart, he pulled it out of his breast-
pocket, ran his eyes over it, and began rather lamely:

'Mr. Stackpole says, hm . . . hm . . . hm — just a few general remarks,
and then: "Conduct excellent". "Conduct excellent",' he repeated.
'You've never had that said of you before. It's worth all the others put
together. I can't tell you how pleased and proud I am.'

He paused for the electrifying effect, but it didn't come. Instead, Lauire's face again began to pucker. For a moment he was speechless, fighting with his sobs; then he burst out miserably:

'But *anyone* can be good!'

Trying to comfort him, his father assured him that this wasn't true: very, very few people could be good, even he, Laurie's own father, couldn't, and those who could were worth their weight in gold. After a time he thought that he was making headway: Laurie's sobs ceased, he seemed to be listening and at last he said:

'Daddy, do you think they'll ever build the pylon up again?'

His father stared.

'Good lord, I hope not! Why, do you want them to?'

Laurie shook his head as if he meant to shake it off.

'Oh, no, no, no. Of course not. It's an eyesore. But I just thought they might.'

That night Laurie dreamed that he had got his wish. There stood the pylon: much as he remembered it, but bigger and taller. At least that was his impression, but as it was night in his dream he couldn't see very well. But he knew that he had regained his interest in life, and knew what he must do to prove it to himself and others. If he did this, a good report was waiting for him. But first he must get out of bed and put on his dressing-gown which lay across the chair, and go down-stairs, silently of course, for if they were about they would hear and stop him. Sometimes, when he was sleepless, he would go out on to the landing and lean over the banisters and call out: 'I can't get to sleep!' and then they would put him to sleep in the spare-room bed, where later his father would join him. But long before his father came up he would be asleep, asleep as soon as his head touched the pillow, such an assurance of security did the promise of his father's presence bring.

And now if they heard him moving about he would just say that he couldn't get to sleep, and put off his visit to the pylon to another night. Oh, how clever he was! It was the return of the pylon into his life that made him clever.

Nobody heard him; they had gone to bed. The house was in darkness, but if he was a burglar he wouldn't mind about that: he would be glad; and Laurie-the-burglar was glad, too, as he tiptoed downstairs in his felt-soled slippers.

But the door – could he unlock it? Yes, the catch yielded to his touch as it would have to a real burglar's, and he remembered not to shut it, for he must be able to get in again.

He went round to the front of the house. Now the pylon was in full view: its tapering criss-cross shape indistinct against the hill-side, as if someone had drawn it in ink on carbon paper with a ruler; but where it rose above the hill — and it soared much higher than it used to — it was so clear against the sky that you could see every detail — including the exciting cross-piece, just below the summit, that Laurie used to think of as its moustache.

With beating heart and tingling nerves he hastened towards it, through the garden gate and out into the field, feeling it impending over him long before he reached it, before he could even properly see where its four great legs were clamped into the concrete. Now he was almost under it, and what was this? Something grinning at him just above his head, with underneath the words: 'Danger de Mort'. Abroad all pylons had them. He hadn't needed to ask his father what the skull and crossbones meant; he hadn't needed to ask what 'danger de mort' meant: 'Your French is coming on!' his father said. In England pylons didn't bear this warning; the English were cleverer than the French — they knew without being told. In England pylons were not dangerous: could this be a French one?

It was a warm night but Laurie shivered and drew his dressing-gown more closely round him. But if there was danger of death, all the more reason to go on, to go up, to be one with the steel girders and the airs that played around them. But not in a dressing-gown, not in bedroom slippers, not in pyjamas, even! Not only because you couldn't climb in them, but because in them you couldn't feel the cold touch of the steel upon the flesh. It would be a kind of cheating: you wouldn't win the good report, perhaps, which depended, didn't it? on doing things the hardest way.

Lest anyone should steal his night attire Laurie hid it under a low bush close by the monster's base. Clever Laurie, up to every dodge! English pylons had steps — iron bolts like teeth sticking out six inches from two of the four great supporting girders, and reaching to the top, making the climb easy. But this one hadn't, so it must be a French pylon. He would have to climb the face of it, clinging to the spars as best he could, for the pylon was an empty shell until almost the top, where a network of struts and stays, like a bird's nest in a chimney, would give a better foot-hold.

When he had started he dared not look down to see if his clothes were still there, because climbers mustn't look down, it might make them giddy. Look up! Look up! The climbing wasn't as difficult as he thought it would be, because at the point where the girders met, to form an X like a gigantic kiss in steel, there was a horizontal crossbar on which he could stand and get his breath before the next attempt. All the same, it hurt; it hurt straddling the girders and it hurt holding them, for they were square, not rounded as he thought they would be, and sometimes they cut into him.

That was one thing he hadn't reckoned with; another was the cold. Down on the ground it had been quite warm; even the grass felt warm when he took his slippers off. But now the cold was like a pain: sometimes it seemed a separate pain, sometimes it mingled with the pain from his grazed and aching limbs.

How much farther had he to go? He looked up — always he must look up — and saw the pylon stretching funnel-wise above him, tapering, tapering, until, when he reached the bird's nest, it would scrape against his sides. Then he might not be able to go on; he might get wedged between the narrowing girders, like a sheep that has stuck its head through a fence and can't move either way.

And if he reached the top and clung to the yard-arm, which was his aim, what then? What proof would he have to show them he had made the ascent? When his schoolfellows did a daring climb, they left something behind to show they had; the one who climbed the church-spire, clinging to the crockets, had left his cap on the weathercock; it had been there for days and people craned their necks at it. Laurie had nothing to leave.

And what had happened to him, this boy? What sort of report did he get? He had been expelled — that was the report he got. It had all happened many years ago, long before Laurie was born: but people still talked of it, the schoolboy's feat, and said it was a shame he'd been expelled. He should have been applauded as a hero, and the school given a whole holiday. Perhaps it was just as well for Laurie that he had nothing to leave, except some of his blood — for he was bleeding now — which wouldn't be visible from below. But they would believe him, wouldn't they, when he told them he had scaled the pylon? They would believe him, and make out his report accordingly? Would they say, 'Jenkins minor has proved himself a brave boy, he has shown conspicuous gallantry and devotion to duty, in that he has climbed the pylon which no boy of his age has ever climbed before, and in commemoration of this feat the school will be granted a whole holiday'?

Or would they say: 'Jenkins minor has been a very naughty boy. By climbing the pylon he has disgraced himself and the whole school. He will be publicly expelled in the school yard, and the school will forfeit all half-holidays for the rest of term'?

Well, let them say that if they wouldn't say the other! At any rate he would have made his mark.

Soon he was too tired to argue with himself: too tired and too frightened. For the pylon had begun to sway. He had expected this, of course. Being elastic the pylon would have to sway, and be all the safer because it swayed. But it shouldn't sway as much as this, leaning over first to one side, then to the other, then dipping in a kind of circle, so that instead of seeing its central point when he looked up, the point where all its spars converged, the point where his desires converged, the point which meant fulfilment, he saw reeling stretches of the sky, stars flashing past him, the earth itself rushing up to meet him. . . .

He woke and as he woke, before he had time to put a hand out, he was violently sick.

'I can't think what it can be,' his mother said. 'He can't have eaten anything that disagreed with him; he ate the same as we did. You didn't *say* anything to upset him, did you, Roger?'

'I told him about the reports,' her husband said. 'You asked me to, you know. I did it as tactfully as I could. I couldn't exactly congratulate him on them, except on his good conduct, which he didn't seem to like. Yes, I remember now, he *was* upset: I did my best to calm him down and thought I'd succeeded. I hope the poor boy isn't going crackers — we've never had anything like that in *my* family.'

'He's highly-strung, that's all, and your presence, Roger, is a bit overpowering. I know you don't mean it to be, but if I was a little boy——'

'Thank goodness you aren't.'

'I might be frightened of you.'

'How can he be frightened of me, when he wants to sleep with me?'

'I'm often frightened of you,' said his wife, 'but still I want to sleep with you.'

'This is getting us into deep waters,' Roger said, stretching himself luxuriously. 'But you won't be able to sleep with me to-night, my dear, because you've arranged for me to sleep with Laurie.'

'Yes, he's in the spare-room bed.'

'He'll never find another father as accommodating as I am.'

'Oh, I don't know.'

'At any rate I hope there won't be any repetition of the incident — the upshot, the fall-out, or whatever you call it.'

'I'm sure not, he was fast asleep when I left him. But you know, Roger, he *was* a bit light-headed — he kept muttering something about the pylon, very fast in that indistinct way children talk when they're ill and half-asleep——'

'I hope he doesn't take *me* for the pylon.'

'Oh dear, how silly you are. But what I mean is, if he wakes up and mentions the wretched thing, because it seems to be on his mind, just say——'

'What shall I say?'

'Say that it's dead and buried, or cremated, or on the scrapheap, or whatever happens to pylons that have outlived their usefulness. Say that it's nothing to be afraid of, because it *doesn't exist*, and if it did——'

'Well?'

'If it did, which it doesn't, it's still nothing to be afraid of, because men made it and men have taken it down, taken it to pieces. It's not like Nature, there whether we want it or not; it's like the things he makes with his Meccano. From what I gathered he seemed to think it could have a kind of independent existence, go on existing like a ghost and somehow hurt him. He reads this science fiction and doesn't distinguish very well between fiction and fact — children don't.'

'All right, all right,' said Roger. 'Don't worry, Anne. I shall have the situation well in hand. I shall say, if he wakes up, which please God he won't, "Now, Laurie, just pretend the pylon is me" — or I, to be grammatical. That will re-route his one-track mind, and turn it in a different direction.'

Anne thought a moment.

'I'm not sure that I should say that,' she said. 'If he asks you, hold on to the pylon being *artificial*, something that man has made and can unmake, and that's all there is to it.'

'Very well, dear wife,' said Roger, and they parted for the night.

Laurie was lying, cheeks flushed and breathing quickly, on the extreme edge of the bed, as he always did to give his father room. Gingerly Roger stole in beside him, and laid his long, heavy body between the sheets. Lights out! He slept late, for his wife wouldn't have them called, and woke up wondering if Laurie was awake.

He wasn't; his face was much less flushed and his breathing normal.

I'll stay in bed till he wakes up, his father thought. He may have something to say to me.

At length the boy began to stir; consciousness returned to him by slow stages, and deliciously, as it does in youth, down gladsome glades of physical well-being. Sighs, grunts and other inarticulate sounds escaped from him, and then he flung his arm out and hit his father full across the mouth.

'Hi, there, I'm not a punching-bag!'

Laurie woke up and gave his father a rueful, sheepish smile.

'Well, say good morning to me.'

'Good morning, Daddy.'

'Now I've got to get up. You, lazybones, can stay in bed if you like.'

'Why, Daddy?'

'Because you weren't too well last night. Your mother gave a poor report of you.' He paused, regretting the word, and added hastily, 'That's why you're here.'

Laurie's face changed, and all the happiness went out of it.

'Because I had a bad report?'

'No, silly, because you weren't well. You were sick, don't you remember? In other words, you vomited.'

Laurie's face lay rigid on the pillow: the shadow of fear appeared behind his eyes.

'Yes, I do remember. I had a dream, oh, such a nasty dream. I dreamed the pylon had . . . had come back again. It couldn't, Daddy, could it?'

'No, of course not.'

'Will you have a look, to make quite sure?'

'All right,' his father said. 'Anything for a quiet life.'

There followed a convulsion in the bedclothes, gusts of cool air rushed in. The room grew darker. Standing in front of the low casement window, Roger's tall figure blotted out the daylight. The outline of his arms down to his elbows, his shield-shaped back and straddled legs showed through the thin stuff of his pyjamas; his head, that looked small on his broad shoulders, seemed to overtop the window – but this was an optical illusion, as Laurie knew. Pulling the bedclothes round him he breathed hard, waiting for the verdict.

His father didn't speak at once. It'll do the boy good to get a bit worked up, he thought; strengthen the reaction when it comes. At length he said:

'Seems to be a lot going on over there.'

'A lot going on, Daddy?'

'Yes, men working, and so on.'

'What are they working at?'

'Can't you hear something?' his father asked, still without turning round.

Laurie strained his ears. Now he could hear it quite distinctly borne in through the open window — the thudding and clanging of the workmen's hammers.

'What are they doing, Daddy?'

'Well, what do you think?'

Laurie's mind went blank. Often it happened that when his father asked him something, a shadow seemed to fall across his mind.

'Is it anything to do with the pylon?'

'You're getting warm now.'

'Are they — are they——?'

'Yes, they are. They're working on the concrete platform where the pylon used to stand.'

'They're not building it up again, are they, Daddy?'

'I couldn't tell you, old chap, but I wouldn't put it past them.'

Laurie's face fell. If only his father would turn round! His imploring glances made no impression on that broad straight back.

'But if they are, Daddy, I couldn't go on living here.'

'I'm afraid you'll have to, son, it's our home, you see. You'll get used to the new pylon, just as you got used to the old one.'

'I shan't, I shan't!' wailed Laurie, hungering more and more for the sight of his father's face. 'Can't you tell them not to do it, Daddy? Can't you *order* them?'

'I'm afraid not. They wouldn't pay any attention to me, Laurie.'

At the sound of his Christian name, which his father only used for grave occasions, and at the idea that there existed people for whom his father's word was not law, the bottom seemed to drop out of Laurie's world, and he began to whimper.

Then his father did turn round and looked down at his hapless offspring, from whom all stiffening of pride and self-control had melted, huddled in the bedclothes. He stifled his distaste and said what all along he had been meaning to say but had put off saying until the last of his son's defences should be down.

'Don't worry. I was only having you on. They're not building a new pylon. They're just breaking up the old one's concrete base. And high time, too. I can't think why they didn't do it before.'

As he turned away from the window the sunshine which his body had displaced followed him back, filling the room with light. He sat down at the foot of the bed.

The effect of his long-delayed announcement had been magical: it surpassed his wildest hopes. Laurie was radiant, on top of his world, another creature from the abject object of a moment since. He tried to put his relief and gratitude into words, but could only smile and smile, in a defenceless almost idiotic way. To break the silence his father asked:

'What made you frightened of the pylon? Had it done you any harm?'

'Oh, yes,' said Laurie, recollection contracting his smile into a frown, 'it *had*.'

'What kind of harm?'

Laurie considered. How could he make the pylon's mischief plain to his father?

'Well, it made me sick for one thing.'

'Oh, that was just something you ate,' said Roger, well remembering it was not. 'We all eat things that disagree with us.'

'It wasn't only that. It . . . it *hurt* me.'

'How do you mean, hurt you?'

'In my dream it did.'

'In your dream? You'll have to tell me about your dream. But make it snappy — I've only got five minutes.'

'Yes . . . perhaps, sometime . . . You see, in my dream it was much stronger than I was, and I couldn't get to the top.'

'Why did you want to get to the top?'

'Well, I *had* to, because of the report, and to see what sort of report they would give me if I did get to the top.'

'I know what,' his father said. 'When you're a big chap, bigger than me, perhaps, you'd better be a pylon-builder. Do you know how much they earn?'

Pure numbers had an attraction for Laurie, though he wasn't good at maths.

'No, tell me.'

'Ten shillings an hour when they're on the ground, and a pound an hour when they're in the air . . . You'd soon be a rich man, much richer than me. You'd like that, wouldn't you?'

'I don't want to be rich!' moaned Laurie. 'I want——' he stopped.

'Well, what do you want?'

'I want to be *safe*, and I shouldn't be if the pylon was there.'

'What nonsense!' said his father, at last losing patience. 'It's nothing to be afraid of.' He remembered his wife's words. 'It's only something men have made, and men can unmake. You could make one yourself with your Meccano – I'll show you how. It's only a few bits of metal – that's all it is.'

'But that's all the atom bomb is,' cried Laurie, 'just a few bits of metal, and everyone's afraid of it, even you are, Daddy!'

Roger felt the tables had been turned.

'You're right,' he said, 'I *am* afraid of it. But——' he tried to think of a way out – 'I never *dream* about it.'

As always, his father's presence gave Laurie a feeling of helplessness; it was as if his thoughts could get no further than the figure turned towards him on the bed, whose pyjama-jacket, open to the morning airs, disclosed a hairy, muscular chest.

'But I can't help what I dream, can I?' he said.

His father agreed, and added, 'But you *can* help being frightened – frightened afterwards, I mean. You've only to think——'

'But I do think, Daddy. That's the worst of it.'

'I mean, think how absurd it is. If you were to dream about me——'

'Oh, but I have, ever so often.'

His father was taken aback, and tugged at his moustache.

'And were you frightened?'

It took Laurie some time to answer this. He sat up, wriggled his toes, on which his father's hand was resting, and said:

'Not *exactly* frightened.'

'Well,' said Roger, smiling, 'what effect, *exactly*, did I have on you?'

Laurie shook his head.

'I couldn't quite explain. Of course, in my dream you were different.'

'Nicer or nastier?'

'Well, not nastier – you couldn't be.'

Now it was Roger's turn to feel embarrassed. He stared at Laurie, and all at once Laurie's face turned scarlet.

'Oh, I didn't mean that, you *know* I didn't,' he pleaded. His hands traced circles on the rumpled bedclothes and his head oscillated with them. 'I said not nastier, because you never *are* nasty, so you couldn't be nastier, if you see what I mean.'

'I think I do,' his father said, mollified and more relieved than he was prepared to show, 'although I am nasty sometimes, I admit. But how was I different, in your dream?'

'That's just it, you weren't so nice.'

Roger didn't like the idea of being thought less nice, even in some-one's dream. But he had to say something—he wouldn't let Laurie see he had been hurt.

'What was I like?' he asked, with assumed jauntiness.

'Oh, you were like yourself, to look at, I mean—not really like of course, because people never are, in dreams. But I always knew it was you.'

Less and less did Roger relish the idea of his dream personality being made known to him. Would it be cowardly to change the subject?

'Don't you ever dream about your mother?' he asked hopefully.

'Oh, no, *never*, nor about Susie or Victor. Only about you.'

There seemed to be no escape. Roger grasped the nettle.

'When you dream about me,' he asked, 'what do I *do*?'

'Oh, you don't *do* much, nothing to speak of. You're just *there*, you see.'

'I do see,' said Roger grimly, though he didn't really. 'And you don't like me being there?'

Laurie wriggled; his plump hands left off making circles on the sheet and clasped the front of his pyjama-jacket.

'No, I'm glad you're there, because I always feel safer when you are, but——'

'But what?' Let's get to the bottom of it now, thought Roger.

'Well, you make me think I've been doing something wrong.'

Roger's heart sank. It was too bad. Hadn't he always, throughout his parenthood, tried to give his children just the opposite impression—make them feel that what they did was *right*? Not so much with Victor and Susie, perhaps; he did tick them off sometimes, he really had to. But he had never succeeded in making them feel guilty; whereas with Laurie——

'Now listen,' he said. 'Stop fidgeting with your pyjamas or you'll be pulling off the buttons and then you *will* have done something wrong.' Switching himself round still farther on the bed he stretched his arms out towards Laurie and firmly imprisoned the boy's restless hands in his. 'Now listen,' he repeated, propelling Laurie gently to and fro, making the boy feel he was on a rocking-horse, 'dreams go by con-traries, you know.'

'What does that mean, Daddy?'

'It means that when you dream something, you dream what is the opposite of the truth. Do you understand?'

'Yes, I think so.'

'So, if you dream about me and I seem nasty, or about the pylon and it seems nasty, it really means——' he stopped.

'Yes, go on, Daddy,' said Laurie, sleepily. He was enjoying the rocking motion — so different from the pylon's sickening lurches — and didn't want it to stop. 'Please go on,' he begged.

'It means that we're both — the pylon and me too, well, rather nice.'

Before Roger had time to see whether this thought was sinking in, there came a thunderous knocking at the door. Releasing Laurie's hands he pulled his pyjama-jacket round him and called out, 'Come in!'

There was a stampede into the room, a racket and a hubbub like a mob bursting in, and Susan and Victor, fully clothed, were standing by the bed.

'Oh, you *are* lazy,' Susan cried. 'You haven't even begun to dress, either of you, and you haven't heard the news.'

'What news?' Roger asked.

'Awful news, dreadful news, the worst. Isn't it, Victor?'

'It's simply frightful. It's the *end*,' Victor said. 'You'll never guess.'

Their faces beamed with happiness.

'Well, why are you so cheerful about it then?' their father asked.

'Oh, just because it is so horrible,' said Susan, and their faces glowed afresh. 'You'll never guess, and so we'll tell you.' She caught Victor's eye to give him his cue, and at the tops of their voices they chanted in unison:

'The pylon's coming back!'

Dead silence followed; even the impression of noise, which had been as strong as or stronger than the noise itself, was banished.

'You don't *say* anything,' said Susan, disappointed. 'We hoped you'd be . . . you'd be . . . just as upset as we are, and there you sit in your pyjamas . . . like . . . like . . .'

Her voice died away into the silence which had returned with double force, and seemed to occupy the room even more completely than the uproar had.

Roger's voice broke it.

'But you're wrong,' he said. 'They're not making a new pylon, they're only breaking up the platform of the old one.'

'No, no,' said Susie, dancing to and fro. 'It's you who are wrong, Daddy. You aren't *always* right, you know. You see we've been across and talked to the men themselves, and they say they are building a new pylon taller than the last——'

'A hundred and thirty-seven feet high,' put in Victor.

'Oh, yes, a huge great thing. We were so horrified we couldn't wait to tell you. It's true, Mummy, isn't it?'

She appealed to Anne who, hitherto unnoticed, was standing by the door.

'Yes, I'm afraid it is,' Anne said.

'There, we told you! And now the view will be spoilt again for ever!'

Stung in his masculine pride, shorn of his mantle of infallibility, Roger lost his temper. These wretched children! Ill-mannered brats, why had he spoilt them so? 'Now you clear out!' he thundered, adding, 'I don't mean you, Anne.' But his wife had already gone.

Laurie remained, but where? He had slipped down between the bed-clothes, out of sight and almost out of mind. Now he came to the surface and let his stricken face be seen.

'Oh, Daddy!' he exclaimed. 'Oh, Daddy!' But what he meant by it he could not have told, so violent and discordant were the emotions that surged up in him. Indeed, they seemed to sound inside his head, drowning another noise that punctuated but did not break the silence: the hammerstrokes from which would rise a bigger and better pylon.

'I'm here, Laurie, I'm here!' his father said, but remembering the effect his presence had in Laurie's dreams he doubted whether it would be much consolation now; for was not Laurie always in a dream?

MRS. CARTERET RECEIVES

Mrs. Carteret Receives *was first published*
in Great Britain in 1971

MRS. CARTERET RECEIVES

From the social angle, as Proust might have seen it, the great cities of Italy have no counterpart in England. In England there were hierarchies still at the turn of the century and later, as long as each town, large or small, was an entity in itself only to be approached from outside by a long, laborious and possibly hazardous journey in a horse-and-trap or wagonette.

In such towns there were ranks, conditions and degrees; and a newcomer, be he doctor, solicitor, farmer, or someone not actively engaged in 'trade', was carefully vetted before he was admitted into the social club, the tennis club, the cricket club, the Masons', the Foresters', or any of the many clubs where men congregate to keep each other in, and outsiders out.

All this sounds very snobbish, but it was really not so; for certainly in the smaller towns everyone knew everyone else and was hail-fellow-well-met with him; there were no Trades Unions; the carpenter was satisfied with being a carpenter, and had no feeling of inferiority or envy when he talked to a white-clad member of the tennis club (perhaps lately elected) swinging his racquet. There was a kind of democracy based on neighbourliness and familiarity. Enter the motor-car, with its money-borne social distinctions and its capacity to move its owner and his family from a dull town to a gayer one, and this democracy of place and local habitations began to wane.

Not so in the great cities and even the smaller towns of Italy. There the bourgeoisie had, and no doubt still have, their social rivalries, their jockeying for place, their intrigues, their equivalents for keeping up with the Joneses (though it must be said that most Latin countries, if not so democratically governed, are socially more democratically-minded, than we are, and this is true of all ranks of society). They have not a

629

common parlance, a *lingua franca*, indeed they have not, least of all in Venice where only a few of the aristocracy can speak the dialect of the *popolo*, which is almost a separate language. At the same time a duchess could talk more freely to a window-cleaner (if such exists in Venice), and with less sense of the barriers of class than she could here. The Venetian *popolo* has very little sense of social or intellectual inferiority; a cat can look at a king, and address him too. But they have a very strong sense of pecuniary inequality. 'Questa Duchessa ha molti millioni' (This Duchess has many millions) and of this discrepancy they take what advantage they can, as their employers, should they be private or public, well know.

But what I wanted to say was that the social system of Italy in its upper reaches such as would have appealed to Proust, differed from ours in being predominantly urban, not rural. The great families, the Colonna, the Orsini, the Caetanis, the Medicis, the Sforzas, the Estes, the Gonzagas, the Contarinis and Mocenigos, had and no doubt still have, great estates in the country, but the centre of their lives, their *point d'appui*, was urban, in the city to which they belonged and over which they ruled.

In England, noble families are seldom denizens of the towns or counties from which they take their titles. The Duke of Norfolk doesn't live in Norfolk; the Duke of Devonshire doesn't live in Devonshire; the Duke of Bedford doesn't live in Bedford; the Duke of Northumberland does live in Northumberland, but Northumberland is a large county, and many people would not know that his home town was Alnwick, where his castle is.

At the time of which I write, bridging perhaps half a century between 1890 and 1940, English people, emigrants or semi-emigrants, had established a hold, based on affinity, in many cities of Italy, chiefly Rome, Florence and Venice. Others went further afield; but the lure of Italy, for many English people, especially those with aesthetic tastes, was irresistible.

'Open my heart, and you will see graved inside of it, Italy,' wrote Robert Browning; and how many of his compatriots have re-echoed those sentiments. The Italians, great and small, seemed to re-echo them too. There was a genuine feeling of affection, based on more than mutual advantage, between the two nations. I remember my gondolier saying to me when the troublous relationships between our two countries began over Sanctions, 'There was a time when an Englishman was a king in Venice.'

But that was much later.

Going back to earlier years and adopting (as far as one can!) a Proustian outlook of the upper ranks of 'Society', and how they comported themselves, one heard of the Anglo-American colony in Venice, residents with beautiful houses. They were completely different from and slightly aghast at the rash of moneyed visitors who invaded Venice after the First World War, a cosmopolitan crowd who thronged the Lido, behaved anyhow in the Piazza, and at a given date—dictated by fashion —departed one and all to an hotel on Lake Como. These rather noisy immigrants were called by the Italians 'The Settembrini', and various odd and irregular modes of behaviour were attributed to them.

As it happened this post-war violation of Venice coincided with, though it did not cause, the exit from the city of the older and stabler foreign colony. Some died; some just went away, and these included several distinguished ladies, titled and untitled, who had made Venice their second home, and had there entertained many eminent literary figures, some from foreign countries including Henry James, and also including (last and least) Baron Corvo, who bit the hand that fed and lent him money.

It cannot be supposed that the Italians, to whom Venice belonged, were socially inactive during this time; but they had no tradition of hospitality except possibly between themselves; they accepted hospitality from guest-hungry *forestieri*, but they didn't always return it. They had indeed a queen, a social sovereign, who, besides being a famous beauty, and the favourite, it was said, of a King, enjoyed playing bridge more than entertaining the bridge-players to dinner.

The Anglo-American colony, though now sadly diminished in strength and numbers and money, closed their ranks and were still the only section of the Venetian community who said to their friends— Venetians or foreign—'Will you come and have tea with me?'

Now Mr. and Mrs. Carteret, in their narrow and narrowing orbit, reigned supreme.

They had come to Venice in the last decade of the nineteenth century. Why they had taken this step of expatriation I do not know.

He was an American from New England, whose original name was Carter; she was a Jewess called Hannah Filkenstein from New York, whose family (they were bankers) was, it was said—and this was confirmed by many people who didn't like her—the first Jewish family to be received in the best New York society. She was one of the 400; 'I should not be here,' she said once, 'if it wasn't from having some holes and corners in New York.'

How James Carteret and Hannah Filkenstein ever met was never explained, still less why they married. It was said, of course, that he married her for her money; but he had money of his own. He was a small, rather chétif-looking man with a moustache (his wife once said to me 'No man can afford to be without a moustache'); he had a nervous manner and a high-pitched laugh. 'Oh don't, don't, don't, don't, don't,' he used to say, after any remark made by him or anyone else which had the faintest element of humour in it—as though the effort to laugh was more than he could bear.

He was a *petit maître*, literally and figuratively. He had exquisite taste and a talent as a painter in the style of Sargent. This he abandoned when he married. If his friends reproached him he would say, 'I gave up painting when I began to mingle with the rich and great.'

His wife had not his talents, but she was a very cultivated woman who spoke French and Italian (and probably German) rather slowly, as she always spoke, but quite correctly, and who read a great deal, though she would not always admit to this.

Together they occupied the Palazzo Contarini dal Molo; not a typical Venetian palazzo, but with the most beautiful view in Venice, and perhaps in the world; for being on the north side it overlooked the inward curve of the Fondamenta Nuove, on the Laguna Morta; and further to the left on the cemetery of San Michele (too beautiful to be thought of as a cemetery) and then towards Murano and Burrano. Those who had eyes to see could see what Guardi, one of whose favourite subjects it was, had seen.

But the view was not the only beauty of the Palazzo Contarini dal Molo. It had its garden. There are few gardens in Venice and this had a rival on the Giudecca; but it is, or was, the most beautiful. It was designed by Palladio or Sansovino, I forget which, and ran down a couple of hundred yards, with the lagoon lapping it, until it was outflanked by a dusty-red building on the right-hand corner. 'The Casino degli Spiriti' it was called. It was said to be haunted, hence the name; it was also said to have been Titian's studio, but no one was ever asked to go inside it. Some said it was empty and there was nothing to see.

But the greatest of the many beauties which emanated from the palace and to which, so to speak, it held the key, the enchantments over which it waved its wand, was the palace itself. Not outside; it was not a typical Venetian palace, towering upwards within a riot of ornament and embellishment; outside it was low and plain and unadorned, and might have been mistaken for a warehouse or even a workhouse. Oh, how different now from its former aspect! 'C'erano tante famiglie, tante, tante,' my gondolier used to say, occupying the palace before Mr. Carteret came and turned them out. Seeing its possibilities he took it over and transformed it into the vision of beauty it afterwards became.

My gondolier was obviously in sympathy with the 'tantissime famiglie' who had been evicted by the Carterets; but nothing succeeds like success, and many Italians, high and low, cannot resist its allure. The Carterets had made their will prevail, and others less fortunate than they (such is Fate, and the Italians have a great regard for Fate) must fend for themselves.

And so it came about that the Palazzo Contarini dal Molo, which had been occupied by tantissime famiglie, in indescribable squalor, was now occupied by two persons with a suitable number of retainers, in great grandeur. The moment one was admitted by the butler (who was also the Carterets' first gondolier, but so transformed by his black clothes that no one who didn't know would have recognized him) everything changed. He might have been admitting the guest into a church, so solemn and reverential was his demeanour as he walked rather slowly up the unimpressive staircase, keeping to the right, and treading softly as though on holy ground.

But when the door of the ante-room was opened, what a change! What a vision of beauty, subdued, protected from the vulgar encroachments of the sunshine by ruched honey-coloured blinds, drawn half-way down. And from the midst of this luminous twilight would appear Mrs. Carteret wearing, as often as not, the broad-brimmed straw hat which cast a shadow over the upper part of her face.

'Oh, it is you!' she would exclaim, with a faint air of surprise. 'I hardly expected you, but here you are!' (The element of surprise was never quite absent from her manner.) 'I was afraid some other engagement might have kept you, as it did once before, do you remember?' The embarrassed guest tried to remember an occasion when he had let down Mrs. Carteret, but couldn't, and at that moment Mr. Carteret, who had been somewhere in the shadows eclipsed by the ample form and wide-spreading hat of Mrs. Carteret, came to his rescue.

'We are so glad to see you,' he said, with the beginnings of a titter that seldom left his lips. 'Venice is quite a desert now since the dear Hohenlohes, and Lady Malcolm and Mrs. Frontisham died or went away—so we have found no one to meet you, alas!' And in the minutes following five more guests were ushered in, all with the most resounding names.

They looked about them—it was impossible not to, so great was the prestige with which the Carterets had contrived to invest their house—and then they followed Mrs. Carteret and her pale-blue silk fichu (meant for the cold or the heat?) into the dining-room, but not before aperitifs had been offered. These, though exiguous, were quite delicious, and I once asked Mr. Carteret what was the recipe. He hesitated long enough for me to feel I had made a *gaffe*, and then said, 'Please don't mind, but I think people might . . . might talk if two Englishmen in Venice served the same cocktail. Oh don't, don't, don't, don't, don't!'

With that and the cocktail I had to be content, although Mr. Carteret was only a recent Englishman, having changed his nationality for reasons best known to him, and his wife had followed suit.

All the rooms in the house were low by Venetian standards but the Carterets' dining-room had a ceiling by Tiepolo which one could not help looking at, so near was it to one's head. It depicted the glorification of someone—perhaps a prevision of Mrs. Carteret?—with angels, saints and *putti* assisting at the apotheosis.

Mrs. Carteret did not like the ceiling to be remarked on, but equally she did not like it not to be remarked on. With her, it was always difficult to get things right.

Course followed course; the cooking was excellent, the service beyond praise. At the end Mrs. Carteret might say, 'I'm afraid we have had a rather frugal meal—the cook is ill, as she sometimes is—so tiresome—so we have to rely on the kitchen-maid.'

No, it may have been a perhaps perverted and unrealizable wish on the part of Anna (née Hannah) to keep up standards, of whatever sort, that made her look so critically on the outside world. From her ivory tower she could afford, in every sense of the word, to do so. So-and-so was common (a word she was not afraid to use), so-and-so was stupid, so-and-so was ugly, so-and-so could not speak French and above all, so-and-so had no introduction to her.

Anathema! Away with them, and leave the world clearer for Carteret standards to prevail. In the provincial city of Venice (though she did not regard it as such) it was easier to make her considerable weight felt than in the capitals of Europe. So when a well-known couple, whose relationship was irregular, but who had a letter of introduction to her, asked what day would be convenient to call, she replied 'No day would be convenient.'

Snubs to you, and snubs all round, except to a few individuals who satisfied Mrs. Carteret's exacting conception of what is *comme il faut*, and even they were liable to fall from grace. I remember an instance. A friend who had every qualification for enjoying Mrs. Carteret's esteem appeared at dinner in a slightly décolleté dress (it wouldn't have seemed so now) and Mrs. Carteret, a storm on the rugged terrain of her features, rose and asked the guest to put on a shawl. She was not received again, even if she had wanted to be.

Receive, receive!

She herself had been received first into the Jewish Church, then into the Anglican Church, then into the Roman Catholic Church. What a number of receptions, each inflating her ego. No more receptions were in sight, except from the Pope.

Meanwhile her rôle was to make reception, as far as she was concerned, a stumbling-block.

'*Procul O procul este, profani!*'

The profane vulgar must be kept away, they would never climb the heights, or go through the initiations, that she had.

＊

She rose to her feet, a rather formidable escalation, very unlike Venus rising from the waves, and supported by her husband's fragile arm, said, 'We will have coffee in the drawing-room.'

The drawing-room was well worth waiting for; it was the most beautiful room in the house and some might have said the most beautiful room in Venice. It stretched the whole breadth of the building and looked out, on one side, on the long crescent curve of the Fondamenta Nuove, with the slender campanile of San Francesco della Vigna dividing it; and on the other side, the Laguna Morta, with the sad but exquisite cemetery of San Michele, and Murano and Burrano somewhere behind it.

'You mustn't let your coffee get cold,' Mrs. Carteret would say as her guests pressed their noses against the windows.

Thereupon they turned back into the room itself, which was painted or stuccoed in an indescribable shade of blue, at once dark and light, the changeful blue of the Italian skies, a perfect background for the tapestries and Chinese screens on the walls.

Sometimes Mrs. Carteret would say, when coffee and liqueurs were over, 'Would you like to take a stroll in the garden?' much as God might have said it of Eden, and the guests, already bemused by the heady qualities of the house, would follow her down the few steps that led to the garden, Mrs. Carteret preceding them, with careful footsteps. Dressed in beige, or some light colour with a tinge of pink in it (for in spite of her bulk she preferred light colours) she would lead the way, and someone said of her, a quotation I have never been able to trace, 'She hath a monstrous beauty, like the hind-quarters of an elephant.'

When we reached the fountain (Sansovino? Palladio?) which was the centre of the garden, she might say,

'I don't expect you want to go any further. Further on you can see the usual mixture of sandole and bragozze, fishermen plying their trade. I don't think they're very interesting.' And sometimes she would add, 'We have a gardener, but there aren't many flowers in the garden. Italians are not flower-minded. If you point to a rose and ask them what it is, they will say "*È un fiore*"—"it's a flower"—but they don't get any further than that.'

By then it was clearly time to go, although luncheon in Italy, with its aftermath, drags on for at least two hours before it is polite to leave.

*

How the Carterets acquired the Palazzo Contarini dal Molo I never knew. It must have been at some time when houses in Venice were cheaper than they are now. Also, it was far off the beaten track; from where I stayed, on the other side of Venice, the sunny side, it needed half an hour on foot or in gondola to get there.

James Carteret, I am sure, espied its possibilities; his was the artist's eye; and its connection with the Contarini family, to whom it had once belonged, no doubt endeared it to him. The Contarinis, after having seven Doges to their name, against the Mocenigos' six, were now extinct. Their last surviving member, at a party, claimed the privilege of going in last. 'All Venice,' he said, 'is my house.'

The Carterets were nothing if not snobs—he a genealogical snob, and she a social one. His name had originally been Carter, of an esteemed New England family. He did not think it imposing enough and when he came to Venice he added the 'et' that turned it to Carteret, the name of a distinguished English statesman. As time passed he persuaded himself and tried to persuade others that he was collaterally descended from the Carterets, and had only omitted the 'et' in deference to New England democratic feeling. The Anglo-American colony, or what remained of it, and some of the Italians, who were in touch with it, made jokes about this—'Carter-et-, et quoi?' or 'Carter-et cetera, et cetera.' His wife, who had been Hannah Filkenstein, followed suit by changing her first name to Anna. This too aroused ribald jokes in the select circles of Venice.

'My dear, have you taken to dropping your h's? You mean Hannah, not Anna.'

But none of these pinpricks pierced the Carterets, who were far too secure with their money and the beauty that they had bought and made for themselves, and that lay within and around them, and with the visitors to Venice who came with introductions and were received by Anna Carteret with varying degrees of welcome. I should never have been received in those hallowed precincts, but for my travelling companion, who had an introduction to her and who bore a well-known name, as a result of which a visiting-card inscribed in the most beautiful copper-plate, 'Mr. James Carteret', invited us both in an almost illegible handwriting, to lunch. We seemed to pass the test, at least he did, and when after some years he ceased to be a frequent visitor to Venice, Mrs. Carteret did not withdraw her favour (not her favours) from me, except on certain occasions.

I had formed the habit of lunching in my gondola in the lagoon—a picnic lunch—but it was delightful, and being young then, or comparatively young, I hated to forgo it. Mrs. Carteret, being old or comparatively old, much preferred having guests to lunch than to dinner. 'A mon âge,' she used to say, for the French language had then the chic which ours has not, 'I would rather lunch than dine,' and it is still a grief to me that I would not always fall in with her wishes. What did it matter, sacrificing a lunch on the lagoon by some dreary uninhabited island, when I could have had it with her and her guests ('no one to speak of') to the music of the plashing of the Palladio fountain? For she, like me, was fond of lunching out-of-doors, and the food appeared as though by magic still hot from the inside of the house.

But I did not always refuse these invitations to lunch, which were after all most acceptable and accompanied by amenities of company, food and service that I could never have provided for myself. But still I was unwilling to forgo my daily stint on the lagoon, on which I imagined my physical and mental health depended. During these exertions I worked up a tremendous sweat, and having been warned by my mother that it was dangerous to sit (possibly in a draught) in sweat-soaked clothes—when I was bidden to lunch with Mrs. Carteret I used to take a supply of dry garments, and ask if I might change in the gondoliers' room.

'But what do you *do* there?' she would ask, having given me permission. 'Wouldn't you rather go upstairs and be more comfortable in a bathroom?'

It was a pertinent question, for nothing could be less like the inside of the palazzo, designed for show, than the gondoliers' room, designed (if designed at all) for use. My plan was really easier and in the end she gave way to it.

In one corner there was a small wash-basin which did not admit hot water, where the two gondoliers presumably refreshed their bodies after their labours at the oar, before they presented themselves as model men-servants in the chambers above. A slight smell of what? of unwashed bodies—lingered around, for the gondoliers, and who could blame them?—did not always have the time or the inclination to transform themselves, skin-high, from their aquatic to their domestic rôles. Some guests (of whom I was not one) remarked maliciously of an effluvium of perspiration; but then Venice is so full of smells.

The gondoliers' room was not meant to be seen by the guests at the Palazzo Contarini dal Molo. Indeed it is doubtful if Mr. and Mrs. Carteret had ever seen it. It was, as far as it was anything, severely utilitarian. There were some ash-trays here and there, perhaps with the name of the hotel they came from on them, and some coat-hangers ditto, on which the gondoliers hung their walking-out clothes. There were a couple of stiff-backed chairs, not affording much relaxation to a tired man, a table or two and the remains of a carpet, which may have been in the palazzo before the Carterets bought it.

It wasn't a small room, for few rooms in Venice are small; and it had an unshaded light-bulb hanging from the ceiling, leaving the corners in a mysterious gloom, relieved, or unrelieved, by dim forms that one didn't want to see, and that I seldom saw because I usually came by daylight.

The gondoliers didn't seem to realize the squalor of their surroundings, they were invariably pleasant and invariably brought me a clean towel, and I, 'à mon âge', as Mrs. Carteret would have said, didn't mind the cold water, it was rather refreshing after the ardours and endurances of the lagoon.

Sometimes my gondolier would come and chat to the other two (for all the gondoliers know each other, even if they don't always like each other) in their dialect which I couldn't understand, though the word 'soldi, soldi' ('money, money') kept recurring. Beyond giving me a clean towel and the vest and shirt my gondolier had brought with him,

they paid no attention to me, and chattered to each other, almost
regardless of my presence. Then suddenly Antonio would get up, put
on his black suit and say, almost reproachfully, 'La signora lei aspetta,'
('Madam is expecting you') and usher me to the upper regions.
  Oh, what a change was there!

                                    *

As the years passed Mr. and Mrs. Carteret became ever more conscious
of their social position. They relaxed it in the case of certain people with
high-sounding names, 'Those poor *realis* of—' she said, referring to
certain royal personages visiting Venice who had not a very good name.
And when a woman of rank and title came to Venice and stayed with
some Lido-loungers of whom Mrs. Carteret did not approve, she said,
'When a woman of her position, or the position she once had, goes to
France and becomes *déclassée*, and then comes to Venice and stays with
riff-raff—I don't call that very interesting.'
  Interesting it was—but Mrs. Carteret could not equate 'interesting'
with what was not *comme il faut*. At least in certain moods she couldn't,
or wouldn't. But it was hard to tell what she was thinking, for her eyes
were enigmatic under the shadow of that broad-brimmed hat; and when
the 'riff-raff' who had taken for the season one of the largest palaces on
the Grand Canal invited the Carterets to meet their distinguished guest
the Carterets accepted, and I remember meeting 'Anna' as I had come
to call her (though I don't think she liked the familiarity) at the top of
the grand staircase, beneath the loudest clap of thunder I ever heard.
  Afterwards she asked the guest who had demeaned herself by staying
with the 'riff-raff' to dinner, but she did not ask them.
  No fry was too small or too great to be exempt from Mrs. Carteret's
liberal disapproval. Whether her attitude came from some long-hidden
inferiority complex who can say? There was no need for it; the
Filkensteins were the first Jewish family to be received into New York
society; and Carter was a well-known and respected name in New
England, before he added 'et' to it.
  Whatever the reason, Anna Carteret enjoyed putting people in their
place. It was said that her husband, with his high-pitched laugh and his
slight figure, half the size of hers, had his way in matters that were really
important; perhaps it was he who bought the palazzo, as it was he who
decorated it. She had the intelligence and the personality and the culture
but he had the taste and the talent and perhaps the will-power under that
fragile exterior, ornamented by an over-large grey moustache. 'No man

can afford to do without a moustache.' Perhaps it was a secret symbol of authority.

But to the onlooker, it was Mrs. Carteret who ruled the roost, and above all she who decided who should be received or not received.

'Received' was a word that loomed large with her. It implied a moral as well as a social standard, though she relaxed it in the case of certain eminent persons, not only 'the poor *realis* of—' but even of celebrities such as D'Annunzio. 'He's like a spider,' she said with a shudder, as far as that massive frame could shudder, and turned up her nose as far as she could, but she received him all the same.

Others were less fortunate. She had an old friend who had a house in Venice, to which he sometimes repaired, and whose social status was impeccable in England and in Venice, indeed it was by genealogical standards much higher than hers. But they had a tiff—about what I don't remember—but I expect it was a trifle, and they were for a time estranged. When he, who was as elderly as she, wanted to bring this misunderstanding to an end he wrote and asked if on a certain day he might come and call on her. To which she replied, that most unfortunately, on the day he suggested she was 'giving' a children's party, and there were no more chairs. It was unlikely that she had ever spoken to a child, much less entertained one.

This, to Sir Ronald, who knew the house well, and who knew that Mrs. Carteret would never give a children's party as she knew no children, and that even if she did there would still be at least a hundred unoccupied chairs in the palazzo, was an offence. But he gave way, as most people did, to Mrs. Carteret for she had the whip-hand. I am glad to say their quarrel was afterwards patched up.

Then I, after several years of happy relationships with Mrs. Carteret, fell foul of her. It was my fault, I should have known. My parents came to stay with me in Venice, and I thought they should be shown one of its less known but more beautiful sights, the Palazzo Contarini dal Molo.

I should have known that my parents could be of no possible interest to Mr. and Mrs. Carteret socially, genealogically, or publicly.

Mrs. Carteret was most gracious, she asked us to lunch, and she and James even came to lunch with us, in our palazzino. My parents stayed for three weeks, and towards the end of their visit I thought it only civil to ask Madame Carteret if we could pay her a farewell visit, not a *visite de digestion*, but just an acknowledgement of her kindness in having received us.

I suggested a day a week or more ahead, but a telephone message came

rom Mrs. Carteret saying she was very sorry but she could not receive
s as the garden was too wet.

Would it have been too wet in a week's time? Or would its humidity
ave interfered with our call, which had no connection with the
garden?

(A propos, Mrs. Carteret sometimes complained that her guests came
o see her only because they wanted to see the garden; or, alternatively,
hat when they came they never cast an eye on the garden (Palladio?
Sansovino?), which was one of the treasures of Venice.)

I was offended by her refusal to see my parents again on such a feeble,
pseudo-meteorological excuse, but I realized that I had mistaken her
nature, and it was my fault, more than hers.

No, it may have been a perhaps perverted and unrealizable wish on the
part of Anna (Hannah) to keep up standards, of whatever sort, that made
her look so critically on the outside world. From her ivory tower she
could afford to, in every sense of the word.

Another episode occurs to me. An old friend of mine and an old
acquaintance of Mrs. Carteret's, came to stay with me. In her beautiful
house in Chelsea she kept a salon to which the old, and even more the
young, were only too glad to be invited.

When I asked Mrs. Carteret if I might bring my old friend (and hers)
to call, her brow furrowed. 'This Boadicea of the South,' she said, 'cannot possibly receive this Messalina of the North—' and she added in a
lower tone, and with a slight closing of the eyelids, 'You know how
quickly news travels in Venice. When I told my dear Maria that the
daughter of an eminent Bishop might be coming to lunch, she replied,
"But Signora, how can a Bishop possibly have a daughter?".'

'She is not staying here,' said Mrs. Carteret, to make the position
perfectly plain, 'she is staying with a friend whom you know.' (She
didn't mention my name.) 'It is not for us to judge. Of course, heretics
have different ideas from ours, but many of them are good people
according to their lights, and so on Friday (no, not on Friday, which is a
fast day for us) we will have—' and a long list of comestibles permitted
by the Church followed.

But it must not be supposed that Mr. and Mrs. Carteret satisfied their
romantic longings by receiving the more important visitors to Venice or
(by what gave them perhaps greater pleasure) refusing to receive those
who were less important. Their romanticism went further than the
bounds of snobbery and super-snobbery in which to some extent it
fulfilled itself.

Mr. Carteret had his pictures on the walls of the ante-room. He had no reason to be ashamed of them and when visitors praised them and asked him why he had given up painting—'Oh don't, don't, don't don't!'—he would exclaim, and make his usual excuse for having stopped painting when he began to mingle with the rich and great.

Mrs. Carteret owed no apologies to anyone. She did not feel the need to exhibit her rather laborious knowledge of foreign languages, accurate and impressive as it was, and acquired—who knows how?—in holes and corners of New York, or her considerable knowledge of art and literature which she perhaps felt was beneath her, to any so-and-so who had been admitted to her presence.

In her case, as in his, this was a kind of negative romanticism, the rich, cultured, high-born American keeping the profane, vulgar, at bay.

Yet true romanticism demands more than negation and disapproval: it demands a positive gesture, something creative, something to hand down to the ages.

It happened before my time, and how it happened I never knew, but rumour told me it happened this wise. Mr. and Mrs. Carteret gave an evening party after dinner in the height of summer, to which everyone who was anyone was invited.

Refreshments no doubt were served, perhaps under the light of gondola lanterns, antique and modern: I can imagine their ghostly glimmering.

As the warm evening drew to its close, and the mosquitoes began to make their unwelcome attentions, there was a sudden movement, and there emerged from among the bushes, towards and around the fountain, a rush, a displacement of air quite indescribable—and there, said the guests, who could none of them afterwards agree, were a nymph and a shepherd, representing Mrs. and Mr. Carteret. For two or three minutes, hand in hand and foot by foot, they encircled the dim sub-aqueous shimmer of the fountain, frolicking and kicking their heels. Then other lights were turned on, fairy-lights away in the garden, and Mr. and Mrs. Carteret in a guise that was never agreed upon, ushered their guests out.

So no one ever knew for certain, though speculations were rife, what costumes Mr. and Mrs. Carteret had worn for their middle-aged pastoral idyll. Some went so far as to say they had worn nothing; while others said the whole thing was a hoax and the figures clothed or unclothed, that issued from the bushes and danced round the fountain had been hired by Mr. and Mrs. Carteret to give the impression of an old-time Venetian *bal masqué*.

Was this extraordinary exhibition the object of the party—to show Mr. and Mrs. Carteret in their primeval youth?

The guests never knew; they made their farewells and their exits not knowing what to say, and leaving the shepherd and the shepherdess in the darkness.

The incident was often referred to by their friends, but not by Mr. and Mrs. Carteret. They lived out, and outlived, their innate earlier romanticism and did not repeat the experiment. There were no more shepherds and shepherdesses in the garden (Palladio? Sansovino?). Only properly attired fashionable guests (with *one* exception) were entertained there.

*

Among the yearly visitors to the Palazzo Contarini dal Molo, was one who always escaped Mrs. Carteret's lively censure. This was Princess X, who came from a distant mid-European country, but who sometimes deigned to set foot in Venice. For Mrs. Carteret, Princess X could do no wrong. In the early autumn I used to be warned, 'Someone interesting is coming to stay with us. I hope you will be here.' The 'someone' was never mentioned by name, but I knew who she was. Her sojourns at the Palazzo Contarini dal Molo were brief, but they were much prepared for and looked forward to. When the princess finally arrived after adequate arrangements had been made, she did something which Mrs. Carteret would not have tolerated in anyone else. She was at least half an hour late for every meal. Lateness was something Mrs. Carteret bitterly resented: as she sometimes said to a belated guest, 'Better never than late.' But not to Princess X, whose late appearances were designed to make an impression. Wearing her famous emeralds, and her fading beauty, she would walk into the ante-room, looking vaguely around her, as if time was of no consequence, and Mrs. Carteret would rise laboriously to her feet and her husband more agilely to his, to greet her.

'Dear Princess!'

This was in the middle and late thirties, before the Abyssinian War, and Sanctions, which made relationships between our two countries increasingly difficult. Mr. and Mrs. Carteret, besides being by birth Americans, were old enough to be above the battle; they did not much care what happened so long as it did not happen to them in their secure peninsula of beauty. They were, if anything, for Mussolini who protected what they stood and reclined for. But the other Anglo-American inhabitants of Venice were not in such a happy case, and as the fatal year drew on, they also withdrew, as I did.

Exactly what happened to the Carterets when war was declared I never
knew. Rumours I did hear, many years later, when I came back to
Venice. Mr. Carteret had retired to the South of France, where he died
leaving the Allied cause a large sum of money. Anna had predeceased
him, perhaps in the first year of the war, perhaps before. We corresponded with each other until letters no longer reached their destination
Our fragile friendship was overwhelmed in the universal cataclysm.

When I went back after the war there were many changes: the Palazzo
Contarini dal Molo had passed into other hands, hands as unlike those of
its previous owners as could well be imagined. The *suore* (the nuns of
Santa Chiara, that noble and austere sisterhood) had bought it, and could
there be anything more unlike its present situation and meaning to the
world outside than it had in the days of Mr. and Mrs. Carteret? The
worldly and the other-worldly could not have been more violently contrasted. The only resemblance between its present and its former owners
was the extreme difficulty of being *received*. The nuns, by rules ordained
by their illustrious foundress, could not receive people from the outside
world. Those who wanted admission had to have special reasons,
religious passports so to speak, before they could be let in. In the
Carterets' day it had been just as difficult to obtain admittance; but how
different were the obstacles then! Then they were purely social; now
they were purely spiritual.

But, thought I, the *revenant*, as I walked along the extreme northern
fondamenta of Venice, past the Madonna dell' Orto with its wonderful
Tintoretto, past the Sacco della Misericordia—hated by the gondoliers in
bad weather—and looked down on the long curve of the Fondamenta
Nuove—so beautiful, so sunless—and then up at the closed and shuttered
windows of the palazzo—is it fair to think that Anna and James Carteret
would have minded so much the idea of their cherished and lovely house
being occupied by nuns?

Was it quite true that they stood for everything the nuns did not stand
for?—for material and snobbish values, and above and beyond them, the
values of art and literature, the aesthetic values which they never ceased
to uphold and to proclaim?

Looking up at the dull, uninteresting façade of the place, I thought
that never, never again even if the *suore* would receive me, would I
venture into those rooms, where beauty had once reigned and which
were now dormitories, refectories, toilets, and so on.

Anna Carteret, née Filkenstein, was a Jewess; when she came to
Venice she became an Anglican Protestant; after a while she was

eceived into the Roman Catholic Church. Her husband followed at a
hort distance—*non lungo intervallo*—these religious mutations of hers. It
was a grief to the Anglican Church in Venice, to which the Carterets had
presented a fine pair of bronze doors, when the Carterets left them and
went over to Rome.

These Vicar-of-Bray-like proceedings did, of course, excite hostile
comment not only from the faithful Protestants but also from the
Italians, who from afar and not much concerned took a cynical view of
their tergiversations and said 'I signori Carteret will adopt whatever
religion suits them best at the moment.' The Anglican Chaplain felt
especially bitter because when the Carterets removed their patronage
the Church had to close down.

Well, it was a rather shabby story and yet I could not help feeling that
Anna and James had, besides religious snobbery, some better reason for
turning their coats so often. Would any one as secure as they were in their
social position have changed the forms of their religious faith so often if
they hadn't been really interested in religion? They lost face with many
people, Protestants and Catholics alike, by doing so. They did not mind
such criticism for as Belloc said (*mutatis mutandis*)

> The trouble is that we have got
> The maxim gun, and you have not.

The maxim gun was in their case, of course, money and social prestige.
But I couldn't help feeling there was more in their changes of front than
that; money and social prestige they could have retained if they had been
Jews, Protestants, or anything else. I preferred to think that their changes
of mind had been genuine movements of the spirit. But was I right?

Gradually, when I went back to Venice, I began to hear stories—they
were not altogether rumours for I knew their gondolier, Antonio, and
I knew their doctor, and I knew Anna's faithful maid and confidante
Maria. Their accounts as to what happened to Anna Carteret in her last
hours did not always tally, but neither do the Gospels (no levity intended)
in their accounts of what happened in the life and death of Jesus Christ,
such a different character except in being an outstanding one, and critical
of human behaviour—from Mrs. Carteret.

She had seldom been ill, but now, in her late seventies, she was ill, and
she knew she was. Her doctor, greatly daring, told her she must stay
in bed.

'Is it serious?' asked her husband, who was going to Rome on a
mission to the Pope. 'Ought I to stay here?'

'I don't think so,' said the doctor. 'Signora Carteret has a very strong constitution and besides that, she is especially anxious that you should keep this appointment in Rome. I think it would do her more harm if you stayed than if you went. Signora Carteret—'

'I know what you are going to say,' her husband said.

'She doesn't like to be crossed. Speaking as a psychologist, I should say it would be bad for her if you cancelled your visit to Rome. In an illness of this sort,' the doctor didn't give it a name or he was not quite sure what it was, 'as in many other illnesses,' he added hastily, 'it is essential to keep up the patient's interest in life. Mrs. Carteret is, of course, deeply religious and she has set her heart on your being received by His Holiness. Your account of the interview will give her a stronger hold on life than any of my medicines. Equally, disappointment in a matter that means so much to her, would have the opposite effect. She has several times said to me, "I look forward so much to my husband being received by the Pope. It means almost as much to me as if the Holy Father were to receive me myself. My great fear is lest, knowing how concerned James is about my health, he may cancel his appointment and miss this golden opportunity".'

Mr. Carteret thought for a while.

'I shall pray for her as I always have. But would it be correct for me to ask the Holy Father to make intercession for her?'

'Why not?'

'He must have so many requests of that kind.'

'What if he has?' said the doctor. 'It is part of his business—*il suo mistiere*—to pray for others, and you and your signora have been generous benefactors to the Church.'

'So you think I should go?'

'I do, most decidedly.'

Mr. Carteret went.

*

What happened afterwards is confused and not wholly credible, especially as the evidence of the two eye-witnesses, if such they were, sometimes disagree. If only Dr. Bevilacqua (well-named for he was an ardent teetotaller and could have been relied on to give an accurate account of what happened) had not been called away to another bedside! Antonio, the Carterets' butler and first gondolier, and Maria, Anna

Carteret's personal and confidential maid, were still alive. I sought them out and they remembered me, not I think without affection, as a one-time habitué of the Palazzo Contarini dal Molo.

Their accounts differed in detail but essentially they were the same. Maria and Antonio, the two most favoured servants, may have been jealous or envious of each other. They were not malicious about Mrs. Carteret in spite of her arrogant ways, for she and her husband had left them well provided for.

According to Antonio, the doorbell rang at about 10 p.m., by which time (he said) he would have been in bed but for his concern for the signora. It was a stormy night in November; the north wind, the *bora*, was almost a hurricane. The Carterets' palace received its full force; hardly any gondolier or any sandolier, rowing a working-man's sea-worthy boat, would venture down the Sacco della Misericordia, where the wind collected and swept down as in a funnel. The only way to reach the palace on such a dirty night (*una notte cosi cattiva*) was on foot; and who would want to come then, unless it was the doctor?

Antonio opened the door cautiously and with difficulty, for the wind almost swept it off its hinges and him off his feet; and before he had time to ask who and why, a stranger had slipped in. He was wearing a flimsy raincoat and the red cap that sailors and fishermen sometimes wear; but he was obviously soaked to the skin, and even while he stood a puddle was forming at his feet.

'*Cosa vuole?*' asked Antonio. 'What do you want?'

The man, with water still streaming down his face, said, 'I want to see the signora.'

'I'm afraid you can't,' said Antonio, who was a big burly fellow. '*E impossibile. La signora is ill—è molto ammalata*—and she can see nobody.'

'All the same,' said the man who had stopped shivering, 'I think she will see me.'

Antonio glanced at the grotesque looking creature from whose meagre garments the rain was still oozing, and like most Italians, he was not devoid of sympathy for anyone in distress. But what to do for or with this man? A thought occurred to him. '*Rimanga qui*' he said, indicating the gondolier's room where I had so often changed my clothes to make myself presentable to Mrs. Carteret after sweaty expeditions in the lagoon, 'stay here, and I will lend you some dry clothes, and dry yours,' he added, 'and you can spend the night here and no one need know anything about it.' He pushed the man into the gondolier's room. '*Rimanga qui*,' he repeated, 'but I shall have to lock you in.'

But the man said, 'No, I want to see the signora. I have an appointment with her.'

'An appointment?' said Antonio, 'but the signora sees nobody, she is much too ill. And *in ogni caso*—in any case—she receives no one without a written introduction. Do you know her?' he asked, suddenly wondering if this sodden creature might be an old friend of the signora's (for do not many of us come down in the world?) and he, Antonio, might get into trouble for turning him away. 'Do you know her?' he repeated. 'Have you ever met her? What is your name?'

'My name,' said the man. '*Non importa*—it doesn't matter— but she will know me when she sees me.'

Quite what happened then I couldn't make out. Apparently Antonio pushed the interloper into the gondolier's room, locked the door on him, and went upstairs to consult Maria, whose bedroom had been moved next to Mrs. Carteret's and who was sitting up more or less all night during her illness.

He explained the situation to Maria.

'*Ma è brutto, sporco, e tutto bagnato,*' he said. 'He is ugly, dirty, and wet through.'

'*Non si può,*' agreed Maria. 'She cannot. But if she gets to hear—and she hears everything—that someone has called to see her and been turned away, ill as she is, she may be very angry.'

The sound of coughing was heard from the next-door room.

'She is awake,' said Maria. 'I will go in and see her—*é il mio dovere*— it is my duty, and say that this person has called.'

She knocked and went into the bedroom, a splendid state-bedroom, where lay under a magnificent four-poster, the ample, but slightly diminished by illness, form of Mrs. Carteret.

'*Cosa vuole?*' she said, with the irritability of a sick person, though she was very fond of Maria. 'What do you want? I was just dropping off to sleep. I was thinking of the signore—not the bon Dieu,' she corrected herself, shaking her head on the pillows, for the 'Signore' was another name for God, 'but Signor Giacomo, who has gone to Rome to be received by the Pope.'

Maria explained, as best she could, why she had butted in.

'What is his name?'

'He would not give it. He told Antonio you would know him when you saw him.'

'Has he a letter of introduction?' asked Mrs. Carteret, whose mind was going back to earlier, happier days.

'No, signora, *è proprio un lazzarone*—a real layabout—and you wouldn't want to see him.'

'Have you seen him, Maria?'

'No, signora, Antonio has locked him up in the gondoliers' room.'

'Tell him, Maria, whoever he is, that I can't possibly receive him. I am much too ill.'

She turned her tired head on the ample pillows and closed her eyes. How unlike the Mrs. Carteret of former days, a travesty of her, a cartoonist's caricature.

*

Maria brought her message, it seems, back to Antonio.

'She cannot receive him,' she said.

'Well, of course not,' said Antonio robustly. 'But we had to ask her—she's so touchy about these things, and he might have been an old boyfriend, *chissà?*—Who knows? And he might be a thief. Anyhow, he was in a bad way, and I gave him some dry clothes and locked him up. I'll let him out in the morning.'

Hardly had he said this when the door—actually there was no door, only curtains of consummate beauty that separated Mrs. Carteret's apartment from the meaner sides of the house (Mr. Carteret had his quarters elsewhere) opened and the stranger, still ugly, still dirty, still dripping, stood before them, an apparition as startling to their thoughts as if they had not been thinking of him, and they turned to each other, dismayed.

'I want to see the signora,' he said.

Antonio was the first to recover himself.

'You can't,' he said. 'La signora is much too ill to see anyone. Go back to where you came from.'

And he took the stranger by the shoulders to push him out. That was his version of the story. Maria was too frightened to remember; but she thought that Antonio's hand closed on something that recoiled, without giving way, and vanished behind the closed door of Mrs. Carteret's bedroom.

*

What next? Presence of mind is a rare quality and Antonio and Maria had spent whatever they had. They leaned their ears against the door and this is what they heard.

'*Chizzè?*'—the Venetian patois for 'Who is it?' The listeners were astonished, they had no idea that Mrs. Carteret knew the Venetian dialect, for though she knew many languages, they did not think that she knew theirs.

It was a deep voice, unlike hers; was she asking him, or he asking her?

The next sentence settled this. 'Who are you? Have you a letter of introduction? I am ill, and I cannot receive anyone without that. My husband is away—he is being received by the Holy Father—and I cannot imagine why my *domestici* let you in. Please go away at once, before I have you turned out.' Her voice, which had been unexpectedly strong, suddenly weakened, 'Who are you, anyway?'

The two outside the door waited for an answer.

A voice in no accent that they knew replied, 'I need no introduction, Signora. I am a common man, *un uomo del popolo*, a man of the people, but sooner or later I get to know everyone. In the end everyone has to receive me, and so must you.'

'Must? I don't understand that word—*non conosco quella parola*—I receive whom I want to receive, and I don't want to receive you.' Her voice grew fainter, but they heard her say 'What is your name?'

They could not hear his answer because he whispered it, perhaps he bent down and whispered it, and a cry pierced the silence, too thin to be called a scream.

Hearing this, Antonio put his shoulder to the door which was unaccountably locked, and went in. The electric light had recovered from the storm and was painfully brilliant; there was no sign of the stranger, but Mrs. Carteret's head had fallen back on the pillow. Was she asleep, or was she—?

They crossed themselves, and Maria closed her eyes. Leaving the bedside Maria noticed the dirty, wet footprints on the floor. 'I'll clean those up,' she said. 'La signora wouldn't have liked them. *Vadi giù*,' she added, 'go down into the gondolier's room and see if the man is still there.'

Key in hand and still looking frightened, Antonio went down to the room which had so often witnessed my post-lagoon ablutions. Coming back he said, 'No, *non c'è nessuno*.' 'There is no-one.'

THE SILVER CLOCK

Nerina Willoughby (so named because her parents, now dead, had liked the flower) had inherited their large house, as was right and proper, for she was their only child. Perhaps on that account she had never married; and was used to being, if not the idol of two people, at least their main object, the centre of their thoughts, and although she had had more than one offer of marriage, she had refused them. She was now thirty-one. Better be an old man's darling than a young man's slave, so ran the proverb; Nerina was good-looking, in a rather austere way, and well-off; her suitors were much younger than she, as perhaps Penelope's suitors were. So far, no middle-aged or elderly *prétendant* had presented himself, and lacking this rather doubtful incentive to matrimony—for though she was sure she didn't want to be a young man's slave—she wasn't quite sure she wanted to be an old man's darling. Her parents had doted on her, their ewe-lamb, much as a middle-aged husband might. But their devotion, in season and out of season, fretted her and demanded of her an obligation of gratitude to which she couldn't always respond and which gave her a feeling of guilt.

Independence, independence! Independence from human ties which are often, as they say, a bind. Better be by oneself, if sometimes lonely, than attached to another human being, probably more selfish than oneself, whose every move of oncoming or withdrawal, and the emotional strain and re-adjustment they entailed, must be met by a corresponding reaction on her part.

And so Nerina, who was far from wanting in affection, in fact too sensitive to its demands and too little inclined to impose her own, took to dog-breeding.

With dogs you knew to some extent where you were. They had their tricks and their manners, as the doll's dressmaker said; no dog was like another, each had to be studied; each had to be cherished; they gave what they had or withheld what they had; but they were, for Nerina, at any rate, objects of devotion on whom she could spend her care and affection without feeling that, sometime or other, they would try to get the upper hand of her. Difficult they often were; but they depended on her, as much as she on them; she never had to say (for at heart she was a disciplinarian) 'I must give way to Rex' (or whatever his name was) as so often women had to, with their husbands.

So Nerina was absorbed in the dogs; they were her interest, her occupation, almost her religion. In this she did not differ from many people who find in animals something they miss in human beings. A sort of *rapprochement*, not always to be relied on, for animals have their moods, as well as we, and sometimes more so, and the discipline, or self-discipline, which we try to impose on them, doesn't always work. An old friend, an animal-lover, once said to her, 'Cats don't see why they should do what you want them to do.' She was not averse to cats, and she recognized and accepted their independence of attitude.

But a dog, it is unnecessary to say, is not like a cat, it is essentially a dependent creature, and needs a great deal of attention paid to it, for which, as a rule, it repays a great deal of attention in return. The relationship is reciprocal but the onus of responsibility lies on the dog's owner. A dog cannot take itself for a walk, or if it does, it is liable to get lost or run over. At stated hours, therefore, it has to be taken out for exercise or to relieve nature which, for some reason, dogs seem to find a more pressing, as well as a more satisfying outlet for their feelings than do other animals.

Nerina's dogs, large shaggy creatures, though not the subject, I hope, for a 'shaggy dog' story, were almost a whole-time job; for besides the daily demands of each adult, for food, exercise, and so on, there were births, marriages and deaths. There were also illnesses; for dogs, perhaps owing to their long association with human beings, were subject to all kinds of epidemics; classic distemper was the most frequent and the worst, but there were always new ones cropping up—hard-pad, for instance—and happily dying down, almost as suddenly as they appeared. Nerina had to be always on the watch, by day and night, for some outbreak of ill-health in the kennels; and so did the vet, for although by this time she had almost as much experience of dog-ailments as he had, she relied on his trained opinion, and, to some extent, on the remedies he prescribed.

This was a bad day in the kennels, for some of the dogs, fifteen of them in all, old, middle-aged, young, and newly-born, had developed symptoms for which she couldn't account and they were clearly spreading. She had, as so often before, summoned the vet, for even if she knew as much about their ailments as he did, it was always better to be on the safe side. However, he couldn't come; he had been called out by the R.S.P.C.A. to separate some fighting swans, or rather to attend to the needs of one who seemed to be dying from the encounter. He didn't want to let down Nerina, who was a good client of his, still less to offend her, for there were other vets besides him, but, as he told her on the telephone, 'you wouldn't believe how often I am called out to deal with fighting swans, especially at this season, when they are mating. I daresay that if they weren't monogamous, they wouldn't get so excited, but they know that if they have set their hearts on a certain female to be their partner for life—their very long life—they say to themselves, "It's either him or me." You would hardly believe how savage they can be—no holds barred. It's twenty miles away, and I shall probably arrive too late, but I may be in time to give the loser an injection, if he'll let me, and the winner a good kick. I don't know why people are so fond of swans— they wouldn't be if they had to assist at their matrimonial proceedings. I'll come on to you directly afterwards, but it may be an hour or two. Meanwhile, from what you say, some salicylate of bismuth might allay the symptoms.'

Nerina had already administered this medicament, and was walking up and down the kennels, which were at a short distance from the garden, which itself was a long distance from the road, to see how effective it had been in staunching the alarming flow from the poor animals' insides, when she looked up and saw five or six youths, between seventeen and nineteen, who were following her movements with eyes that were cold and hard under their long hair.

They were trespassing, of course; but Nerina was too much absorbed in the plight of the dogs to pay much heed to them. She thought of offering them, sarcastically, a dose of salicylate of bismuth, but they appeared not to need it (though her kennel-ground *had* been used, in the past, by interlopers who had been 'taken short'); and she tried to dismiss them from her mind.

But they didn't go away; on the contrary, they came nearer, and as though by a pre-conceived plan, kept pace with her, almost step by step, and only a few yards away, on her sentry-go as she looked into the various kennels to see if the dogs were responding to treatment.

However, after a time this double perambulation, which had the air of an ill-natured mimicry, began to get on her nerves, and deflect her attention from the welfare of the dogs, which was her chief concern.

It was half-past seven in the morning. When she had the dogs to see to, she was oblivious of time; it might have been half-past five. The kennel-maid was away ill; the household, such as it was, was not yet astir; the gardener wasn't due until nine o'clock. Nerina was completely alone.

Meanwhile, the five youths drew still closer, and their attitude, as displayed in their faces and the looks which every now and then they interchanged—sideways and backwards—if not exactly threatening, were anything but friendly.

As a dog-breeder, and a dog-shower, Nerina had seen a good deal of the world and was acquainted with its seamier side, and when the dual patrol had gone on for half an hour—the little gang marching and whistling alongside, until they were almost rubbing shoulders with her—she felt it was time to do something. They all looked rather alike, black-avised with dark, dangling, dirty locks to match, but she turned to the one who seemed to be the leader, and said, 'Come in here, there's something I want to say to you.'

She led the way from the kennels to her sitting-room, her library, only a few yards distant, a limb of the main body of the house.

They followed her in and stood around her, with the same look, between half-closed eyes, suggesting something they would like to do, if they could decide on it.

Nerina didn't ask them to sit down; she stood in their midst, and looked up at them.

'Now,' she said, as briskly as she could, 'There's something I want to ask you. Why are you here? What is all this about?'

A shuffling of feet; an exchange of interrogative looks; and their spokesman said,

'It's the spirit of adventure, I suppose.'

'You call it the spirit of adventure,' said Nerina. '*I* should call it something else.'

And for several minutes she told them, looking up from one face to another, for they were all big boys, what *she* would call it.

When she had finished her tirade she nodded a dismissal, and the little gang, rather sheepishly, filed out, no more to be seen.

*

Not long afterwards the vet turned up. 'I'm sorry, Miss Willoughby,' he said, 'but those damned birds took longer than I thought. And it was

just as I expected—one of the cobs had done the other in—he was lying
down on the grass with his neck and his head stretched out and his eyes
glazing. I gave him an injection as quick as I could, but I'm afraid it was
too late—I didn't hear any swan-song—and I gave the other a boot,
which I hope he will remember. The lady in the case was standing by,
looking more coy than you can believe, so I gave her a boot too, just to
teach her. I suppose they can't help the way they behave, but it is
annoying, to be called out as early as that—just for swans, because they
are, or some of them are, said to be, the Queen's birds. And they are
nearly the only birds, besides cocks and fighting-cocks, and birds of
prey, which set out to kill each other. Sparrows have their squabbles but
they are soon over, and I wouldn't get out of bed to separate *them*. Now
what can I do for you, Miss Willoughby?'

Nerina explained, and together they inspected the suffering occupants
of the kennels. No need to tell—it was abundantly evident on the floor
of their well-kept abodes—what was the matter with them. But was it
a symptom or a cause?

'I'm sure you've done right,' the vet said. 'It's one of those unexplained
epidemics that dogs, even more than human beings, are liable to. But
you might also give them these,' and he brought out from his bag a
bottle of pills. He frowned. 'One never knows, in this kind of thing, if it's
better to let Nature take its course. Don't hesitate to call me if they aren't
improving. I hope that by tomorrow *all* the swans in England will be
dead.'

He waved and drove away.

*

Having administered his pills to the afflicted animals, some of whom were
willing to swallow them and some not, Nerina went back to her library
sitting-room, and sat down to answer some letters that had been too
long unanswered.

It was now eleven o'clock; the traditional hour of respite and relaxation. She might well have felt tired but she didn't, for work was more
of a stimulus to her than leisure, or pleasure.

Presently, while her fingers were still busy on the writing-paper, a
daily help came in with a tray, on which was some of the household
silver, that was cleaned once a week.

'May I have your clock, Miss Nerina?'

'Yes, of course,' said Nerina, nodding towards the chimney-piece where it stood, and the clock went away with the salt-cellars, pepper-pots, spoons and the rest of the silver-ware which Nerina, who was not much interested in such matters, thought it necessary to keep bright and shining.

The clock—the little, silver travelling-clock, had been a present, and she was fond of it. It was engraved, on the margin, 'For Nerina, from a friend.' It didn't say who the friend was, which made Nerina all the more aware of who it was.

She went on writing, always with an ear for sounds from the kennels, and didn't notice the passing of time, until she was suddenly startled by the pealing of the front-door bell, which, clanging in the kitchen, also resounded through the house.

Was there anyone to answer it, apart from the cook, who never answered the door if she could help it? Yes, there was Hilda, the silver-polisher, who didn't leave till after lunch.

Nerina settled down to her correspondence, but was disturbed by another, louder peal.

'Oh dear, must I go?' she asked herself, for she was more tired than she knew.

A third peal, and then silence, silence for what seemed quite a long time.

Nerina was licking the last envelope, and preparing to go out to see how the dogs were getting on, when Hilda came in.

'Excuse me, Miss Nerina,' she said, 'but something has happened.'

'Oh, what?' asked Nerina. She was not specially observant, and was obsessed by the thought of what might be happening in the kennels, but she saw that Hilda had a white face.

'It's the clock, Miss Nerina, your little clock.'

'What about it?'

'It's disappeared.'

Nerina got up from her desk. How many times, during the day, had her thoughts been violently switched from one subject to another.

'Disappeared?'

'Yes, Miss Nerina, I had it on the tray, ready to clean, and the door-bell rang, twice, no three times, when I was having my elevenses, and a boy was at the front door with a parcel. I told him where to put the parcel—groceries or something—in the pantry, and went back to the kitchen, to finish my cup of tea, and when I went back to the pantry, it was gone.'

'The clock, you mean?'

'Yes, Miss Nerina. None of us would have taken it, as you well know.'

Nerina did know. For a few minutes the loss of the clock, that symbol of an ancient friendship, which had faithfully told her the time of day in many places, and for many years, brought tears to her eyes.

'Never mind, Hilda,' she said, 'We shall get over it. Worse things happen at sea,' and she went out to look at the dogs, who were ill—which the clock, whatever might have been its fate, was not.

*

The next morning the dogs were clearly on the mend. Nerina and the kennel-maid, who was now recovered, between them cleaned out the grosser relics of the dogs' indisposition. Nerina was not usually time-conscious, but when she went back, after washing, to her sitting-room—a spy-hole on the dogs—the clock wasn't there, and the claims of human, as distinct from canine friendship, began to assert themselves.

When she had looked round for the tenth time, to see what hour it was, Hilda appeared.

'There's a young gentleman to see you, Miss Nerina.'

'A young gentleman? Who is he?'

'I couldn't catch his name, Miss Nerina. He speaks that rough.'

'Where is he?'

'In the hall, the outer hall. I didn't want him to come any nearer, because I think he's the same young man as came in yesterday, when you lost your clock.'

Nerina got up and went through another room into the hall.

There was a young man, who looked so like the other members of the group of youths who had (so to speak) dogged her footsteps yesterday, that she couldn't tell whether he was one of them or not.

'What do you want?' she asked him, rather curtly.

'It's like this, madam,' he said, and produced from his pocket her little silver clock. 'I found this on the drive leading to your house, and as it has your name on it, and your birthday,' he added, giving it another look, 'I thought you might value it, so I brought it back.'

She took the clock from his outstretched palm, which remained outstretched, as though for a reward; and slightly shook her head.

'I'm glad you brought it back,' she said. 'It makes things better for everyone, doesn't it?'

He didn't answer, and at once took his leave.

FALL IN AT THE DOUBLE

PHILIP OSGOOD had bought his house in the West Country soon after the Second World War, in the year 1946 to be exact. It had the great merit, for him, of being on the river—a usually slow-flowing stream, but deep, and liable to sudden sensational rises in height, eight feet in as many hours, which flooded the garden but could not reach the house. The house was fairly large, mainly Regency, with earlier and later additions; it had encountered the floods of many years without being washed away; so when he saw the water invading the garden, submerging the garden wall and even overflowing the lawn (on which swans sometimes floated), he didn't feel unduly worried, for the house stood on a hillock which was outside flood-range.

Philip had always liked the house, chiefly because of its situation, its long view over the meadows, and because it had, in one corner of the garden, a boat-house, and rowing was his favourite pastime. He sometimes asked his visitors, who were not many (for who can entertain guests nowadays?) to go out with him in the boat, a cockly affair, known technically as a 'sculling gig', with a sliding seat. It could take one passenger, but this passenger had to sit absolutely still—not a foot this way or that, hardly a headshake—or the boat would tip over.

Moreover, besides its natural instability, it took in water at an alarming rate, so that the passenger—he or she—found himself ankle-deep in water, though doing his best to look as if he were enjoying it. The landscape through which the river ambled, or flowed, or hastened, was perfectly beautiful, and this was Philip's excuse (besides mere selfishness) for beguiling his friends into the boat.

The day came when this treacherous vessel (happily with no other occupant in it) overturned, and Philip found himself in the water. Being a practised, though not a good swimmer, he was not unduly disturbed.

Although it was March and the water was cold—and he was wearing his leather jacket and the rest of his polar outfit—he thought: 'I will get hold of the boat and tow it back to the boat-house.'

Alas, he had reckoned without the current, swollen by recent rains, and he found that far from his towing the boat back to the boat-house, it was towing him down-river to the weir, where who knew what might not happen?

He at once relinquished the boat to its fate and after a struggle—for he was too old for this sort of thing—he reached the boat-house, the only possible landing-place, for everywhere else the banks were too high and steep, and he went dripping up to his bedroom.

It so happened that this very day he had engaged a new factotum, who was to cook and drive for him. His job with Philip was his first job of this kind—he had had others—and it was his first night in Philip's house. His room faced Philip's, an arrangement Philip was glad of, for being an elderly hypochondriac, he liked to have someone within call.

Nothing came of the river-episode—no pneumonia, no bronchitis—not at least for the moment—but who could tell? And suddenly he wondered if the house, which had seemed so welcoming and friendly over twenty years, had something against him?

*

The next morning, when the new factotum called him at eight o'clock with a pot of tea, he asked, just as a routine inquiry.

'How did you sleep last night, Alfred?'

'Oh,' said Alfred who, like so many gentlemen's gentlemen, when they still exist, had been in the Services, 'I didn't sleep a wink, sir.' He sounded quite cheerful.

Philip, who himself suffered from insomnia, was distressed.

'I hope your bed was comfortable?'

'Oh yes, sir, couldn't have been more comfortable.'

'I'm glad of that. But perhaps you are one of the people—I am one myself—who don't sleep well in a strange bed?'

'Oh no, sir, I sleep like a log. I could sleep anywhere, on a clothes-line with a marlin-spike for a pillow.'

Philip didn't know what a marlin-spike was, but as an aid to rest it didn't sound very helpful.

'I'm so sorry,' he said, baffled. 'Then what was it that kept you awake?'

'It was the noises, sir.'

Philip sat up in bed and automatically began to listen for noises but there were none. One side of the house faced the main road where there was plenty of noise by day, and some by night; the other side, on which his bedroom lay, overlooked the long broad meadow, skirted, at no great distance, by the main railway line from London. Philip, in his sleepless hours, was used to the passing of nocturnal trains: indeed they soothed him rather than otherwise. There was the one-fifty, the two-twenty, and the three-forty-five; he didn't resent them, he rather welcomed them, as establishing his identity with the outside world.

Alfred was standing by his bed, tea-pot in hand.

'Shall I pour out for you, sir?'

'Yes, please, Alfred. But what did you mean by noises?'

Alfred began to pour the tea into his cup.

'Oh, just noises, sir, just noises.'

Alfred (Alf to his friends) handed Philip his bed-jacket.

'But what sort of noises?'

'Oh, I couldn't quite describe, sir. First there was a pattering of feet on the staircase, really quite loud, and then I heard a voice say, like a sergeant-major's—very autocratic, if you know what I mean—"Fall in at the double, fall in at the double, fall in at the double."

'And what happened then?'

'Nothing much happened. The footsteps stopped, and a sort of smell—a weedy sort of smell—came into the room. I didn't pay much attention to it, and then I went to sleep.'

*

Thinking this over, Philip was puzzled. Could Alfred, or Alf, have possibly known that the house had been occupied by the Army during the war—the Second World War? There were people who could have told him—the gardener and his wife who lived upstairs could have told him, supposing they knew; but would they have had time to tell him, in the few short hours since his arrival?

But there it was—the tramping of footsteps down the uncarpeted staircase (for it would have been uncarpeted during the Army's occupation), the thrice-repeated command, 'Fall in at the double'—what did it mean?

And then this weedy smell?

*

Philip couldn't sleep the next night, and expected to be told that Alfred couldn't sleep either; but when Alfred called him with a bright morning face, and Philip asked him if he had had a good night or a better night, he answered promptly, and as if surprised: 'Oh yes, sir, I slept like a log.'

Philip was glad to hear this, but something—a suggestion, a muttering from his subconscious mind—still irked him. He knew that certain people—people in the village and outside—had certain reservations about his house. What they were he didn't know, and naturally, they didn't tell him; only a faint accent of doubt—as if referring to some rather shady acquaintance—coloured their voices when they spoke of it. But when he asked a friend of his who owned a much larger and grander house, if he thought his riverside abode might be haunted, his friend replied, 'Oh Philip, but is it *old* enough?'

Philip was slightly offended. It was a vulgar error to think a ghost needed a long pedigree. His house was quite old enough to be haunted; and this recent visitation, if it was one, had nothing to do with the house's age as a resort for ghosts.

He was not unduly superstitious but there was a nerve in him that vibrated to supernatural fears, and though he tried to calm them during the following days, by the reflection that he had lived in the house for over twenty years without any trouble other than the normal troubles—burst pipes, gas escapes, failures of electricity and so on, that are the lot of many old and decaying houses—he didn't feel so comfortable, so at home with his home, with his thoughts as he used to be.

Supposing?

But was there anything, abstract or concrete, spiritual or material, to suppose?

Alfred professed to be psychic, and familiar with poltergeists and other familiars (Philip laughed to himself, rather half-heartedly, at this mental joke), otherwise he wouldn't have taken the manifestations on the staircase so lightly; but that didn't explain why they had such an obvious bearing on the recent history of the house.

Forget about it, forget about it, and Philip had almost forgotten about it when, a few nights later, he was awakened by a thunderous knock on his bedroom door, three times repeated. It was the loudest sound he had ever heard; the footsteps of the Commendatore coming up the staircase in *Don Giovanni*, were nothing like as loud.

'Come in!' he shouted, unaware of the time, and almost unaware, having taken a sleeping pill, where he himself was. 'Come in!' he shouted again, thinking that perhaps it was Alfred with his early morning tea.

But no one came; and it couldn't have been Alfred, for when he looked at his watch, it was five o'clock in the morning.

Turning over in bed, he tried to go to sleep; but his subconscious mind had taken alarm and wouldn't let him; and he lay awake listening for another summons until three hours later, when a much gentler, hardly audible knock, that didn't even expect an answer, announced Alfred with Philip's early morning tea.

Philip turned a tired, sleep–deprived face towards him.

'Did you have a good night, Alfred?'

'Oh yes, sir, pretty good. A few noises, you know.'

'You didn't hear a terrific hammering on my door' (Alfred's bedroom door was only an arm's length from Philip's) 'about five o'clock this morning?'

'Oh no, sir, nothing like that. A few scurrying noises, could have been rats.'

Philip, with lack-lustre eyes, sipped his tea. Could he have *imagined* the knocking? No, it was much too loud. But could it have been a sound heard in a dream—the tail-end of a dream? Philip hadn't had many dreams of late years. Sleeping-pills inhibited them; that was one of their side-effects, and a bad one, for dreams were an outlet for the subconscious mind, and if denied this outlet, it took its revenge in other ways. In madness, perhaps? One *saw* things in dreams of course and one was aware of conversations; but were these conversations conveyed by sound, or by the illusion of the dream? As far as his recollections went, communication in dreams went by sight, and by some telepathic process, and not by sound—certainly not by such sounds as the four tremendous thumps which had awakened him.

So convinced was he of their material reality that while he was dressing he opened his bedroom door, and examined its other side, fully expecting to see marks on it which might have been made by a sledge-hammer. There were none; the off-white paint was as smooth and un-dented as it had always been. To make assurance doubly sure, he held the door open, where the light could catch it at different angles; and then he saw something which in all his twenty-odd years of opening the door, he had never seen.

Beneath its coating of thick paint, something was written, printed rather. White over white, very hard to decipher, but at last he made it out:

PRIVATE

LIEUT.-COLONEL ALEXANDER McCREETH

Well, that explained itself. Lieut.-Col. McCreeth had occupied Philip's bedroom.

Sometime during the war years he may have used it as an orderly-room, a sitting-room, or a bedroom, but when using it he didn't want to be disturbed. Was the repeated rat-tat-tat meant to disturb his privacy, perhaps for military reasons? The previous owners of the house, who had occupied it for a year or two after the Army left, had redecorated it, and tried to wipe out all trace of their military predecessors. They must have spent a lot of money on it, and then gone away, quite ready to go, apparently, for they had sold it to Philip at a reasonable price. No haggling. Why?

It was years since he had seen the vendors and he didn't even know their whereabouts. And if he had, what could he ask them?

He began to entertain absurd fancies, such as that it was he who had been ordered to fall in at the double and the mysterious knocking was meant to awaken him to the urgency of some military exercise, for which he would otherwise be late. Perhaps the safety of the country depended on it. Perhaps an invasion was imminent?

Not now, of course, but then.

Gradually these fancies began to wear off, and only showed themselves in an almost invincible reluctance, on Philip's part, to ask Alfred if he had had any more psychic experience. At last, when all seemed set fair, he put the question.

'Oh yes, sir, often. But I didn't want to tell you, because I thought it might bother you.'

Philip's heart sank.

'What sort of things?'

'Well, nothing that I've heard myself, except those noises I've told you about, and the voice saying "Fall in at the double!" But anything may happen in an old house like this.'

'But you haven't heard anything else?'

'As a matter of fact I have, sir, but it's only gossip, things they natter about at the local. Places like this, so far from civilization, they haven't much to talk about.'

'Tell me what it was.'

'May I sit down, sir?'

Alfred sat down, bent forward to get his shirt-cuffs into the correct position, leaned back and said:

'Well, it was about this Colonel.'

'You mean Colonel McCreeth?'

'Yes, Colonel McCreeth. They couldn't pronounce his name properly —they're uneducated here. But they said he was unpopular with the other men who were living here, in this house I mean, at the time. He was a dictatorial type, like some of them are, and they had it in for him. He used to get them up from bed when it wasn't a bit necessary, just to look at the moon, so to say, pretending there was an air raid, when there wasn't. And so they got fed up.'

'I don't wonder. And then?'

'Well, he picked on a certain bloke who had said or done something out of turn and gave him C.B.—this house counted as a barracks, I believe—and this bloke, and three or four others, slept in my room— you may remember how it was in the Army, sir, they didn't always pay much attention to the comfort of the men.'

'Yes, I do remember,' Philip said.

'Well, this fellow was a sort of trouble-maker, and he had it in for the Colonel, who wasn't liked by any of them, and he got their sergeant, who didn't like him either, to make a sort of plot. Very wrong of them, of course, and against discipline, but you can't try people, even soldiers, beyond a certain point.'

'Of course not.'

'So, as I was saying, they put their heads together, and ran downstairs, saying "Fall in at the double", and the sergeant knocked at the Colonel's door—your door, sir—and he came out in his pyjamas—and said, "What the hell is this?" And the Sergeant said, "It's someone down by the river, sir. He's acting very suspicious. We think he may be a German spy." The Colonel cursed, but he got into his coat and trousers—it was a cold night—and went with them—about three dozen of them— down to the river bank. And what happened afterwards no one seemed to know. You know what men are like when they get angry and excited. It spreads from one to another—a dozen men would do what one man wouldn't—and the Colonel was a heavy drinker—but anyhow the upshot was he fell into the river, and was found drowned at the weir below your house. The river was low, so he wasn't carried over it.'

'Dear me,' said Philip, though a stronger expression would have suited his feelings better. 'Do you think any of this is true?'

Alfred smiled and shrugged his shoulders. 'They're that uneducated in these parts.'

*

A few nights later at the same hour as before, five o'clock, Philip was awakened by a knocking at his door. 'Come in!' he shouted, still fuddled with sleep, and still unaware if he was awake or dreaming, 'Come in!'

he repeated, and it was then he heard the thrice-given order, 'Fall in at the double, fall in at the double, fall in at the double,' followed by the clatter of heavy footsteps on the bare boards of the staircase.

So intent was he on listening to this that he didn't see his bedroom door open—it may have opened of itself as it sometimes did when not securely latched—but at any rate it was open, as he could tell from the moonlight from the hall window, above the staircase, struggling into the densely curtained room. Faint as it was, the moonlight showed him that someone had come in when the door opened, for he could dimly descry the head and the back of a tall man, edging his way round Philip's bed, apparently looking for something. It was more like a presence than a person, a movement than a man, the footsteps made no sound on the thick carpet, but it seemed to stop in front of the wardrobe, and fumble there.

A burglar? If it was a burglar, and if all he wanted was a few clothes, well and good; he might be armed, and Philip was in no state to resist an armed man. Some said—the police even said—that in certain cases, in this age of violence, it was safer not to 'have a go' at a man who might be desperate.

The telephone was at his left hand, the switch of the bedside lamp at his right: yet he dared not use either, he dared not even stir, lest the intruder should realize he was awake.

After what seemed an unconscionable time, he heard or thought he heard, sounds of groping in the recesses of the wardrobe. This activity, whatever it was, ceased and a silence followed which Philip took to mean that the burglar (for who else could he be?) had finished his search and was taking himself off. Philip pressed the back of his head against the pillow and shut his eyes, for the man was now coming towards him, face forwards. But Philip's pretence of sleep hadn't deceived him; he stopped and peered down at him. Philip's eyes opened: they couldn't help themselves, and he saw the stranger's face. Mask-like, the indistinct features kept their own secret, but their colour was the colour of the moonlight on them. Drawing nearer, stooping closer, outside the moonlight's ray, they were invisible; but a voice which must have come through the unseen lips, though the whole body seemed to utter it, said:

'Fall in and follow me. At the double, mind you, at the double,' and a shadow, momentarily blotting out the moonbeams, slid through the doorway.

Seized by an irresistible inner compulsion, Philip jumped out of bed and without waiting to put a coat over his pyjamas, or slippers on his feet, followed the visitant downstairs in a direction he knew as well as if it had been directed to him by a radar beam.

On the wall that separated the garden from the river he saw first of all a line of heads, he couldn't tell how many, wearing Army caps, turning this way and that, bobbing and nudging, and heard an angry buzz of talk, as of bees, whose hive is threatened. At the sign of his precursor, only a few yards ahead of him, silence fell, and they drew apart, leaving a gap between them in the shallow river-wall. But they were still leaning towards each other, some of their faces and silhouettes moonstruck, the rest in darkness.

'Now, boys, what is all this?' asked their Colonel, for he it must have been, in a cheerful, would-be rallying tone. 'Why have you got me up at this time of night? There isn't an air raid.' And his moonlit face, revolving slowly in its lunar circuit, scanned the night sky.

'No sir, you know what it is,' said a voice, a low, level voice charged with menace. 'We're fed up with you, that what it is.'

They were beginning to close in on him, their hands were already round his legs, when he called out, 'You've done this before. Take him, he's my double!' And he pointed to Philip, shivering behind him on the lawn.

'Shall we, Jack? Shall we, Bill? He's one of them, we might as well.'

Their strong hands were round him and Philip, hardly struggling, felt himself being hoisted over the garden wall, to where, a few feet below, he could see his own face mirrored in the water.

'Let's get rid of the bastard!'

*

The next thing Philip knew was a hand on his shoulder, and he heard another voice, saying:

'Good God, sir, what are you doing here? You might catch your death of cold.'

He couldn't speak while Alfred was helping him over the wall.

'Thank you, thank you,' he gasped, when he had got his breath back. 'I might have been drowned if it hadn't been for you. But where are the others?'

He looked back at the depopulated garden wall, no dark heads bobbing and whispering, neck to neck, no limbs bracing themselves for violence; only the moon shining as innocently as that de-virginated satellite can shine.

'But how did you *know*?'

'I have my ways of finding out', said Alfred darkly. 'A hot bath, a hot bottle, a whisky perhaps, and then bed for you, sir. And don't pay any attention to that lot, they're up to no good.'

THE PRAYER

ANTHONY EASTERFIELD was not really religious, unless the word 'religious' is capable of the widest and vaguest interpretation, but he was religious to the extent of not being a materialist. He was sure he was not a materialist, and if the word was mentioned in his presence, or if he came across it in a book, or if it occurred to his mind unbidden (as words will), he at once chased it away. Materialist indeed! Perish the thought! The human race was dying of materialism. Better a drunkard's death which did at any rate result from some form of spirit.

At the same time he was aware that many of the phenomena of which he specially disapproved, 'the worship of the motor-car', for instance, had a relish of spirit, if not of salvation in it, besides the petrol to which motorists were addicted, for in one sense they were alcoholics all.

He himself had a car, and a man to drive it—for Anthony couldn't drive, and he knew, from mortifying efforts to pass the driving test, that it was much better for himself and everybody else that he shouldn't try to.

The car was a convenience to him, but to his driver it was much more than a convenience, it was an emblem of religion. His driver was not satisfied with it, or with its performance in many, if not in all, directions —as many people are dissatisfied with their religions (if any), feeling that their religions have let them down. Anthony's car had often let Copperthwaite down, and it was anything but the status-symbol that he coveted; at the same time the creed of automobilism was in his blood, and nothing could eradicate it.

'What you really want, sir,' (on a special occasion he would deign to call Anthony 'Sir' though he would more willingly have addressed the car as such) 'is a car with a prestige value.'

(The fact that Anthony did not and never would 'want' such a car never penetrated Copperthwaite's car-intoxicated consciousness.)

'Now the Roland-Rex 1967,' he went on, trying to make the arcana of automobilism clear to Anthony's non-mechanical mind, 'with over-drive, under-drive, self-drive, automatic gears, et cetera, is just the car for you. It is a splendid car. I could tell you more about its performance, only you wouldn't be interested, but its prestige value is enormous. I doubt if even a Rolls-Royce—'

Anthony Easterfield was indifferent, or nearly indifferent, to the prestige value of a Roland-Rex, but he knew that Copperthwaite's interest in it, besides being mechanical, was also snobbish, and snobbism implies a sense of values that is not simply materialistic, even if it could scarcely be called spiritual.

To make people stare! To watch them gather round the Roland-Rex, wide-eyed with admiration, exclaiming to each other, patting and stroking it if they dared—venerating it as an object of excellence. To surpass, to excel! Not to keep up with the Joneses but to leave them behind, scattering and gaping. The *deus ex machina*! The God in the car!

Copperthwaite spent hours, literally hours, on Anthony's common-place little car, making it shine so that you could see your face in it; and when its lower quarters went wrong, as they often did, he would be under it with outstretched legs, and his face, if it were visible, which it seldom was, wearing a beatific expression, as if at last he had found true happiness. And if Anthony called him to come out of his dark grimy, oily hiding-place into the light of day, he would look disappointed, and almost cross, as if his orisons had been interrupted.

Laborare est orare. Copperthwaite's happy (although to Anthony), his unenviable labours, were a form of prayer to the *deus ex machina*, the god in the car. If only he could save up enough to buy a Roland-Rex! Then Copperthwaite's dream would come true, and if his labours were doubled, so would his prayers be. To be prostrate under the chassis of a Roland-Rex! To feel its oil dripping gently on his face! To be in close touch with its genitals (excuse the phrase) what bliss! What more could a man want? To labour for, and by so doing, to pray to the embodied principle of mechanical engineering! To communicate with it (no levity intended) by the oil dripping from it—to be at one with it! Anthony envied Copperthwaite his instinctive identification with the object of his devotion, his conviction that it was more important than he was, and that in its service was perfect freedom.

Anthony had learned to recognize a Roland-Rex, for when they passed, or, as seldom happened, overtook one, Copperthwaite would draw his attention to it. 'Now that's what we ought to have, sir.'

Anthony, who wanted Copperthwaite to be happy, would groan inwardly and think about his bank-balance.

He realized that Copperthwaite's passion for cars was of a religious nature, and respected him for it, for he too, was religious after a fashion, although it was a different fashion from Copperthwaite's.

Laborare est orare. To work is to pray. Yes; but is the converse true? *Orare est laborare?*—to pray is to work? It may be; many people besides the Saints had wrestled in prayer. Sweat had poured off their foreheads, tears had run down their cheeks; they had thrown their bodies this way and that; they had been taken up unconscious for dead. All this due to the physical effort of prayer. Labour! Could anyone labour more than that? Copperthwaite certainly laboured in his unuttered prayer to Anthony's car; he withdrew himself from the light of day, he put himself into the most uncomfortable positions the body could assume, while studying and communing with the object of his adoration—albeit with its baser parts. His communication with it was immediate and instinctive, and needed no effort on his part; he required no confirmation from the car to assure him that he was completely *en rapport* with it, and it with him. Labour thrown away! No fear; even if he couldn't find out what was wrong, the attempt to do so was its own reward. Another time, another hour or two, with his back on the cement and his eyes on a jungle of pipes (what he actually saw that so captivated him, Anthony, who was totally devoid of mechanical sense, never knew), he would find out, and his loving identification with the car would be closer than ever.

As for being brought out unconscious! Copperthwaite never looked more alive and kicking (for he had more or less to kick himself out) than when he emerged from under the car, patted its bonnet and gave it a grateful and a loving look.

Anthony's orisons were physically much less laborious, for they only involved kneeling and sometimes wriggling and pressing his forehead against the bed, or the chair, or the pew, or wherever he happened to find convenient for his devotions. He didn't go to church much; he knew, or had known, the order of the service so well that he listened to it with only half an ear; he preferred private to public worship. Following its majestic sequence did not give him time to slip in his own petitions. These needed an effort of memory which he could not compass while the clergyman, the choir, or the congregation, were all shouting or muttering against it. His prayers needed constant modification; this or that person had to be left out, this or that person put in. The task of selection and discrimination was difficult; and to perform it, Anthony felt he must be alone with God, undisturbed by the traffic noises, and the traffic signals, red, yellow, and green, on the Road to Heaven.

But did he really believe in the efficacy of his prayers? Did he really believe they would be answered? Did he believe in God, as implicitly and explicitly, as Copperthwaite believed in his car? Or was it all a superstition on his part, a sort of insurance against some calamity that might befall his friends or himself? or, having forgotten to mention this or that desired benefit, to have deprived them, and him, of some happiness?

He put his friends first, because he had had doubts about the propriety of praying for himself; perhaps for oneself one could only ask God to forgive one's sins? To ask him to forgive other people's sins was an impertinence, an almost blasphemous prompting of God's Will, that Anthony would never be guilty of. Some of his friends were quite bad, and urgently in need of divine, moral and spiritual aid, so Anthony never presumed to mention who they were or how they could be improved.

His prayers, however, did include a long string of names of friends for whom he made a general, and sometimes an individual petition. They were divided mainly into two groups: friends who were still living, and relations of friends who had died. Anthony never counted them up (he had a Biblical distrust of counting the numbers of people) but together they must have come to forty at least. As he murmured the name, its owner for a moment came back to him, each one, living or dead, a link in the chain of his life, a link of love, a continuation of his own personality, a proof of identity, his and theirs.

But there are always snags, even in prayers. Anthony did not offer prayers for the dead. Not for doctrinal reasons, but because he thought he could do nothing for them; they were in the hands of God. But he prayed for the comfort and consolation of their relations, and friends, even when he knew that their relations and friends were quite glad to see the last of them.

The list of these relations and friends grew longer and longer, as, one after another, from love's shining circle the gems dropped away. A queue formed; and Anthony, in self-defence, had to omit certain names in order to make room for others, just as, in the cemetery of San Michele in Venice, the bodies of the dead are only allowed a few years of earthly habitation before they are turned out. Without having to accuse himself of favouritism, Anthony had to decide whose relations were in the greater need of his prayers, who should stay and who should go.

There was another thing. Some of Anthony's friends whom, living, he had prayed for, had before they died and passed out of the land of the living, changed their names, owing to divorce, re-marriage, titles for themselves or their husbands. Would God know the original 'Mary' of his prayers for the living, for the Mrs. X, or the Lady X, for whose bereaved relations Anthony asked God for sympathy? Anthony knew how absurd this question was. God was no student of Who's Who or Debrett; he would know who Mary was; but just as in ordinary conversation one has to explain who 'Mary' may be, so, in Anthony's appeals to the Deity, he felt he ought to explain who this 'Mary' was. God was no respecter of persons; but Anthony felt he should take the trouble to differentiate this Mary from the other Marys, one of whom had been the mother of Christ.

Another thing that made praying laborious was that in this long list of names he might have left out someone. Every religion has its ritual which must be strictly observed; a small fault, a casual omission, may invalidate the whole proceedings. Anthony knew his prayers by heart, and wasn't ashamed of rattling them off at high speed so long as he gave a flick of affection to each name, alive or dead, for whom he prayed. But sometimes he had the feeling that one name—just one—had escaped him. And then he must start all over again, and sometimes twice, to make sure that no one had been omitted. Apart from the effort of repetition, he didn't like doing this; he felt it smacked of conscience, not of devotion, but all the same, he had to.

His prayers for the living, who had not been bereaved, but were perhaps sad, and ill, and unfortunate, were easier, because he felt that for them his intercessions were the living word of encouragement, and not the dead word of condolence. For them he did not have to pray for the negative blessings, if negative they were, of consolation and comfort; he could pray for their future happiness (if not, of course, based on some improper relationship), the success of their undertakings, their personal, general and material welfare. There was nothing wrong in this. The Old Testament had condemned many, indeed most things, but not the ideal of prosperity. Prosperity had been taken from Job: it was indeed the *gravamen* of his spiritual suffering. But in the end it had been restored to him ten-fold.

So Anthony did not feel it was irreligious to wish for his friends, not too much burdened and borne down by sorrow, the desire of their hearts, even in the material sphere. Did not devout Roman Catholics pray to St. Anthony, his namesake, for the recovery of some unimportant object, a wrist-watch, for instance, which they had lost? One could not, oneself, pray to God for the recovery of a wrist-watch; in relation to God it would be outside one's terms of reference; and, as a Protestant, one did not pray to the Saints. But on behalf of someone else, one might, and that was how Anthony came to pray that Copperthwaite, to whom he was much attached, might be granted the gift of a Roland-Rex motor-car. He did not think of himself as concerned in the gift: he only wanted it for Copperthwaite.

*

Rising stiffly from his knees, after an unusually long and laborious session of intercession, he felt he *might* have done someone a good turn. It is difficult to know what a friend really wants; and what will be good for him if he wants it. Copperthwaite wanted a Roland-Rex.

*

A few days later Copperthwaite came to him with a rather stiff face and said,

'I'm afraid, sir, I shall have to ask for my cards.'

Copperthwaite had been with Anthony for a good many years, and the phrase was unfamiliar to him.

'Your cards, what cards, Copperthwaite?' He thought they might be some sort of playing cards.

'My cards, sir, my stamps and my P.A.Y.E., same as you have always paid for.'

'You can have them, of course,' said Anthony, bewildered. 'That is, if I can find them. But what do you want them for?'

Copperthwaite's face stiffened yet more: Anthony could hardly recognize him.

'Because I've been offered a better job sir, if you'll excuse me saying so. I've been happy with you, sir, and you mustn't think I don't appreciate what you have done for me. But a man in my position has to look after himself—you might not understand that, sir, being a gentleman.'

'I don't understand,' said Anthony, still bewildered.

Copperthwaite's face grew stiffer.

'An American gentleman—no offence to you, sir—has asked me to go to him. The porter in this block of flats told him about me. He pays very good money.'

'I can raise your salary, if you like,' said Anthony, his own face beginning to stiffen.

'Oh no, sir, I couldn't ask you to do that, I'm not a gold-digger, and besides—'

'Besides what?' asked Anthony crossly.

'Besides, he has a Roland-Rex car, and it's always been my ambition to drive one, as you know, sir.'

'When do you want to go?' asked Anthony.

'A week next Saturday. That will give you time to find another man.'

'I'm not sure it will,' said Anthony. 'But meanwhile I'll look for your cards.'

*

The week passed, and Anthony tried in vain to find a replacement for Copperthwaite. In answer to his advertisement, several candidates for the job presented themselves and interviews were arranged. He was on his best behaviour, and they were on their best behaviour; who could tell? 'There is no art,' as Shakespeare, or his spokesman, truly said, 'to find the mind's construction in the face.' As for references, so his friends assured him, they were often written by the applicants themselves. 'Mr. Anthony Bragshaw' (surprising how many of them were called by his own name) 'is honest, sober, and trustworthy: a good driver, and an excellent plain cook. I have no hesitation whatever in recommending him for the situation he is applying for.'

Two or three of these replies were written on the writing-paper, and contained the telephone number of the applicant's employer: but when he rang up the number, he did not get a reply.

Anthony himself could not cook, nor could he drive: pushing up the seventies, he needed outside help. Meals were not so difficult; he could go out for food. And as for transport, there were buses, and tubes and taxis, if one could find a taxi at the right moment. It was ridiculous to complain of things which, as Sir Thomas Browne said, 'all the world doth suffer from' (including death).

He didn't know what to do with his car, so he left it in the communal garage, where it had a place, 5A. Sometimes, when he engaged one of the porters, or a casual man to drive it, it was neither found in 5A, nor returned to 5A. Someone else had been taking it for a ride.

Copperthwaite himself Anthony saw, from time to time, for his employer lived on the opposite side of the Square, in one of the few houses that hadn't been 'converted' into flats. Anthony didn't always recognize him, for Copperthwaite had been so smartened up. He wore the conventional chauffeur's uniform, blue suit, black tie, peak cap—

and he looked straight ahead of him, as if other cars were in the way
(as they often were).

He and Anthony used sometimes to exchange distant greetings in
which the condescension (if there is a condescension in greetings) was
always on Copperthwaite's side. And indeed the Roland-Rex was a
sight to dream of, not to tell. At least Anthony, with his ignorance of all
that made one car superior to another, couldn't have told! But he did
at least realize that here was a car that from its sheer bulk, more noticeable
behind than before, as if it wore a bustle, took up half the street.

Copperthwaite did not always recognize Anthony when Anthony on
foot, and Copperthwaite, eyes half closed, installed in his Roland-Rex
fortress, met each other. The smugness on Copperthwaite's dozing face
was sometimes more than Anthony could stand.

He consoled himself with the thought that Copperthwaite was (to
misquote Mrs. Hemans) a creature of inferior blood, a proud but child-
like form.

All the more was he surprised when one morning he received a letter
with no stamp on it, brought by hand.

Dear Sir, (it said)

I wish to inform you that I have now terminated my engagement
with my present employer, Mr. Almeric Duke. It is not on account of
any disagreement with Mr. Duke, who has been both generous and
understanding, but I am not happy with the conditions of my service,
especially as regards the car. From what I am told, I understand you
have not found another man, sir, to drive your car and minister to your
comforts, and if you will consider my application to take me back into
the position in which I was always happy, I shall be much obliged.

I am, sir,

Yours respectfully,

J. Copperthwaite.

Anthony studied this missive with mixed feelings. Copperthwaite
had not treated him well. His daily help, who had been with him a good
many years, and had known one or two of Copperthwaite's quickly
changing predecessors, once said to him, 'You're too easy-going with
them, Mr. Easterfield, that's what it is.' She did not mean it as a compliment. All very well and good; but if Anthony wasn't easy-going with
them, indeed if he criticised them—their cooking, their driving, the
friends of both sexes, or any sex, that they brought into the flat from
time to time, their unwarrantable absences or their sometimes more
disturbing presences—at the faintest hint of criticism they departed,

almost before the offending words were out of his mouth. 'Easy-going' on his part meant easy-going on theirs; but if he had adopted a policy of 'hard-going', he trembled to think what the results might have been.

It was the recollection of these fugitive characters that made Anthony think more kindly of Copperthwaite. Copperthwaite had treated him badly but he had at any rate given him a week's notice; he hadn't just 'slung his hook' (to use an old-fashioned expression), leaving the keys of the flat and the car-keys on the table with a pencilled note to say he was 'fed up'.

No, during the years that he and Copperthwaite had been together they had got on very well—not a 'misword' between them. His daily help, who was nothing if not censorious, may have thought that Anthony was too easy-going with Copperthwaite; but there was no occasion for hard feelings.

Never take a servant back again was the advice of our forebears. The word 'servant' was now out of date, it was archaic; it could never be used in polite or impolite society. A 'servant' was 'staff': even one 'servant' was 'staff'. One envisaged a bundle of staves, of fasces (infamous word) once used as a symbol of their office by Roman Lictors, and then by Mussolini.

Copperthwaite a staff? The staff of life? Thinking of the dreary days and weeks that had passed since his departure, thinking of his forerunners, so much less helpful and hopeful than he, looking to the future, which seemed to hold in store nothing more alluring than an Old People's Home, Anthony began to think more favourably of Copperthwaite's return.

In spite of his elders' advice not to take back a 'servant', what harm could Copperthwaite do if he came back? He could become more 'bossy', Anthony supposed; he had always been a bit bossy, he used to decide for Anthony many small problems of food, wine, and so on, that Anthony had been too tired, or too old, or too uninterested, to decide for himself.

The worst he could do was to leave, as he had just done; and Anthony had survived that, and no doubt would survive it again.

*

But why did Copperthwaite want to give up this much better-paid, much more glamorous job, with the American gentleman on the other side of the Square, with the Roland-Rex to give it added prestige value?

Dear Copperthwaite, (he wrote)

If you would like to come back here, please do. I have made some tentative enquiries for other Staff, but I haven't fixed up anything, so if you want to come back you are at liberty to, and of course I shall be pleased to see you.

My car is still in the garage. It hasn't been used much since you went away, and I expect various things will have gone wrong with it, the battery will have run down and the tyres will need pumping up, and the *oil!*—but you will know about this better than I do.

Please let me know when you are ready to return, so that I can answer the answers to my advertisements for another Staff.

       Yours sincerely,

             Anthony Easterfield.

Copperthwaite's reply came promptly.

'Will be with you on Monday, Sir.'

So he must have given in his notice to the American gentleman before he got Anthony's answer. Rather mortifying to know that Copperthwaite took it for granted he would be welcome back: but what a relief to know that the rhythm and routine of his life so dismally interrupted would be resumed.

Say nothing to begin with; make no comment; express no curiosity.

Such were some of Anthony's resolutions on the Saturday before Copperthwaite was due back on Monday morning. But, when the bell of the flat-door pealed at 8 a.m. on Sunday, he was taken by surprise. Who was this? What was this? The porter, telling him he had left a tap dripping, flooding the flat below? An urgent letter on Her Majesty's Service, demanding Income Tax? The postman—but the postman never rang the bell unless he was carrying some object (usually of evil import) too bulky to pass through the letter-box—and besides, the post didn't come on Sunday.

So pessimistic was Anthony's imagination that he could not think of any summons at eight o'clock in the morning that did not presage disaster or even doom. A mere burglar, with a sawn-off shot-gun or a blunt instrument would have been a relief compared with the horrors Anthony had begun to envisage.

Copperthwaite said, 'I came a bit early, sir, because I know that eight o'clock is about the time you like your tea.'

'Well, yes, I do,' said Anthony, putting all his previous thoughts into reverse. 'And I expect you want some tea too.'

'All in good time, sir, all in good time,' said Copperthwaite, 'but meanwhile may I dispose of these bits and pieces?'

The bits and pieces were two very heavy and expensive suit-cases, made of white leather. Anthony admired them and wondered how Copperthwaite had come by them: the American gentleman, no doubt. He even envied them although when full—when bulging, as they now were—he couldn't have carried them a yard.

'Well, you know where to go,' he said, laughing rather feebly, 'the first on the right. You won't find it changed—no one has had it since you were there. All the same,' he added suddenly, 'I think the bed—the mattress—ought to be aired. The bed-clothes—the sheets and blankets are all right. They're in the airing-cupboard.'

'Don't worry, sir,' said Copperthwaite, bending down to pick up his suit-cases, 'aired or not aired, it's the same to me.'

Strong as Copperthwaite was, forty-three, forty-five?—his features showed the strain as he stooped to lift the suit-cases.

Anthony went back to bed, with various emotions, of which relief was uppermost. It was against his routine to say prayers in the morning, but he made a short act of thanksgiving for the mercy just received. A few minutes later appeared Copperthwaite, tea-tray in hand. Wearing his service-jacket he looked so like his old self—his slightly Red-Indian self—that Anthony could hardly believe that he had been away three, four, how many weeks?

'A steak for lunch, sir?'

'No, Copperthwaite, not a steak. My teeth, my remaining teeth, aren't equal to a steak. A cutlet, perhaps.'

'Yes, sir, a nice, tender cutlet. And for this evening a nice bit of fish, a Dover sole, perhaps.'

'No, I think a lemon sole. They don't sit so heavily on one's tummy, and they're cheaper, too.'

'I meant a lemon sole,' said Copperthwaite.

'Did he?' thought Anthony, with his eyes bent on Copperthwaite's broad retreating back, and his blue-black hair, which he kept short and trim, army-fashion. Does he remember my requirements automatically, or has he been thinking them up?

The sound of voices disturbed his cogitations. His daily help had arrived. 'So you're back?' he heard her say, 'like the bad penny, who always turns up.' Anthony jumped out of bed and shut the door which Copperthwaite had left ajar, so he didn't catch Copperthwaite's *riposte* which was something about some bad pennies being there all the time.

Later, when Anthony emerged at breakfast time, they seemed to be billing and cooing.

Soon afterwards, when Copperthwaite was in his room, presumably unpacking his impressive suit-cases, Anthony said to Olive,

'Copperthwaite has come back.'

'So I see, Mr. Easterfield,' she answered drily, and giving him a poke, or, as some would say, a back-lash, with the carpet-sweeper. 'So I see,' she repeated, 'and how long for?'

'Oh, I don't know,' said Anthony carelessly. 'I've no idea what his plans are, or if he has any. You may know better than I do.'

'I have nothing against Mr. Copperthwaite,' said Olive, drawing herself up and reclining, so far as one can recline, on the pole of a carpet-sweeper.

'I've nothing against him,' she repeated, 'but this I know, he'll go *when* it's his interest to go, and *where*,' she added dwelling on the words, 'it's his interest to go.'

'Then why,' said Anthony, taking her up, 'did he leave this much better job with the millionaire across the Square, and come back here, where he doesn't get half as much money or half as much time off?'

This will be a facer for her, he thought. But it wasn't.

'I wouldn't know,' she said, starting off again with the carpet-sweeper, 'I wouldn't know what goes on in a man's mind. It might be that this American—and not only Americans either,' she added, giving Anthony a straight look, 'was one of those who—well, I needn't explain. Mind you, I'm not saying anything against Copperthwaite, but he may have felt the game wasn't worth the candle.'

'The candle?'

'You know what I mean, sir.'

'I don't,' said Anthony, although a faint flicker of enlightenment played across his mind—'but if he didn't do whatever . . . whatever they wanted him to do—isn't that a good mark for him?'

'I'm not saying it is or it isn't,' said Olive darkly. 'With those sort of people you never know. Keep away from them, I say.'

'But that's just what he has done,' said Anthony, rashly.

'Time will show,' said Olive, who was apt to repeat her more gnomic utterances. 'Time will show.'

Anthony's curiosity, never very keen, was whetted by Olive's insinuations, and the temptation increased to ask Copperthwaite why he had left a job so much better than the one he had come back to. 'Better not,' he told himself, falling into Olive's habit of repeating herself, 'better not. All in good time, all in good time.'

The thunderous sounds of Copperthwaite's unpacking suddenly ceased, and he himself appeared at the door of Anthony's sitting-room. At least it must be he, this radiant figure dressed in the smartest chauffeur's uniform, peaked cap in hand.

'Would you be wanting me to drive you anywhere, sir?' (Sir, now, not Mr. Easterfield, as of yore.)

'Well, no, Copperthwaite,' Anthony said, rising from his chair to greet this splendid apparition, 'I've nowhere to go, and I'm not sure if the car' (he hardly liked to mention this ignoble vehicle) 'will be—well, will be in going order. You see, it hasn't been used . . .' He stopped, feeling that tactlessness must go no further.

'I see, sir,' said Copperthwaite, as if envisaging a great number of things. 'Leave it to me. But first I will put on my working clothes.' He sketched a salute to go.

'There is lunch,' said Anthony humbly.

'Oh yes, sir, I've arranged for that, and Olive has been quite helpful.'

He disappeared, and Anthony began to write some letters. What a relief to have Copperthwaite back! But when he thought of that magnificent uniform, and its probable cost, he began to feel uneasy. Ought not Copperthwaite, or he, Anthony, to return it to Copperthwaite's late employers? No doubt the Americans could well afford it; but the cynical saying 'Soak the rich,' began to reverberate unpleasantly in his mental ear.

Should he say something to Copperthwaite? Should he suggest that the uniform ought to be returned? When Copperthwaite was in his employ, he had expressly wished not to wear a uniform; he inferred it would be a badge of servitude, and in any case too posh, too ostentatious for Anthony's humdrum purposes. Anthony himself could imagine his friends saying, if they came to the door to see him off, as they sometimes did, and saw his second-hand, second-rate car waiting at the kerb, with a uniformed chauffeur—uniformed, and how!—'We are *impressed*, Anthony, we really *are* impressed!'

No sound in the flat, but Anthony was restless, he went out and took a turn round the Square (if a square can be circled). His footsteps came slow, clogged by his thoughts. Shall I turn back? he asked himself, seeking for some sort of compromise between himself and the Moral Law. Shall I go up to Ramoth Gilead, or shall I forbear? Shall I tell Copperthwaite to return his ill-gotten gains to the Americans, or shall I leave it?

At the opposite side of the Square stood the Roland-Rex (by now he knew its contours only too well), drawn up outside the owner's door. Sitting at the wheel, indeed asleep at the wheel, was a chauffeur, immaculate in a uniform similar to Copperthwaite's. He looked like part of the car's furniture, indeed like part of the car; he was the same colour, his figure might have been an extension, as a reproduction of its lines; his immobility a parallel of its own. Function for function, what difference was there between them?

Anthony completed the circuit.

No car outside his own flat; but he pressed the button; the garage-door swung open, revealing a set of loose boxes, so to speak, in which some of the tenants kept their cars. He remembered the number of his: 5A.

At first he saw nothing except his car, then, sticking out from under its bonnet, a pair of feet and leggings.

'Copperthwaite!' he called, hardly expecting an answer.

But after much wriggling, Copperthwaite came into view, so dirty in his overalls, so changed from his glorious appearance of an hour ago, that the transformation was hardly credible.

He struggled to his feet.

'Yes, sir?'

'I just wondered', said Anthony, 'how you were getting on?'

'Very well, sir,' said Copperthwaite, composing his face to disguise the slight irritation he felt at being disturbed at his work; 'Very well, sir. But I'm afraid the car needs a good deal of attention. It's been neglected, sir.'

Anthony said nothing.

'Yes, sir, it's been neglected, and of course a car doesn't like being neglected.'

Anthony couldn't resist saying,

'Like human beings, I suppose.'

'Yes, like human beings,' said Copperthwaite, mopping his brow with a sweaty handkerchief, and without taking, or appearing to take, Anthony's point. 'But human beings can fend for themselves.'

He gave the car an over-all look, in which compassion, interest, and adoration—yes, adoration—were blended.

The sudden impulse that makes one ask a question that one would never, in ordinary circumstances and after due consideration, ask, made Anthony say,

'Why did you leave that excellent job with the American gentleman

on the other side of the Square? I thought—in fact you told me yourself
—it was your ambition to look after a Roland-Rex.'

'So it was, sir,' said Copperthwaite promptly, his eyes switching to
Anthony's battered car. 'And shall I tell you why—why I didn't go on
there. I mean, because the money was good and the boss gave me all I
wanted, including the uniform, which I didn't want. It was because—'

'Because of what?'

'The Roland-Rex was a perfect car, no complaints.'

'Then why?'

Copperthwaite gave Anthony a look that pitied such lack of understanding.

'Because there was nothing I could do for it. Nothing ever went
wrong with it, it didn't need me, I couldn't—I couldn't mix myself with
it—it was a stranger, if you know what I mean. I sat there like a stuffed
dummy—the car could have looked after itself, and almost driven itself,
without me—'

He stopped, and gave another look at Anthony's shabby old roadster.

'Your car isn't a Roland-Rex, sir, but as long as you are in it you will
be driving with me as well as in it.'

Anthony found this remark obscure.

'Well, of course I shall be driving with you, because I can't drive
myself, but what do you mean by, I shall be driving with you, as well as
with it?'

'Because I *am* the car, sir.'

*

Anthony tried to fathom this out.

'Does the car mean all that to you?' he asked incredulously.

'It does, sir. It means a great deal to me, as you do, though not in the
same way—begging your pardon, sir.'

Anthony heard the church bells ringing.

'Good gracious, it's Sunday!' he exclaimed. 'I'm all out in my dates—
I wasn't expecting you till Monday.'

'Yes, but one day doesn't make much difference, does it?'

'Of course not.' Anthony wondered where Copperthwaite had spent
Saturday night. 'But when I was walking round the Square I noticed
that your . . . your late employer had another chauffeur.'

Copperthwaite shrugged his shoulders.

'Oh yes, Mr. Duke doesn't let the grass grow under his feet, and there are plenty of blokes who will give up their weekends if they see a good job in prospect, and a uniform too.'

The bells sounded louder. Eleven o'clock could not be far away.

'Well, I must be off,' said Anthony to Copperthwaite's retreating form, which was edging itself, feet first this time, as if some octopus power, stronger than himself, was sucking him into the tentacles of the car's dark underneath.

Rapture began to glow on Copperthwaite's upturned face.

'If you are going to church, sir,' he said, wriggling from shoulder to shoulder, 'say a prayer for me.'

'Yes, of course,' said Anthony, 'but what would it be?'

'Oh, I don't know, sir, you know more about prayers than I do, just a little prayer for me, and a big prayer for the car.'

'But isn't it past praying for?'

'No, sir, not as long as I'm here,' and with that Copperthwaite's tired, dirty, but jubilant face disappeared under the bonnet.

An answer to prayer, perhaps?

PARADISE PADDOCK

MARCUS FOSTER acquired his house, Paradise Paddock, with the maximum of discouragement from his friends. 'We looked at ninety-eight,' one of them said. 'We spent the best part of a year house-hunting, and every single one of them had something hopelessly against it. Either it faced the wrong way, or it had a cellar full of water which would have to be pumped out, or it had no water at all, no electricity and no gas, or it was so far from anywhere that such important things as food could never be delivered, and staff, supposing one could find them, would never consent to stay, and anyhow there were no suitable quarters for them to stay in, and—well, at last, when we were quite desperate, we found Wrightswell, which was so much too big that we had to pull half of it down.'

Marcus was utterly at a loss, for he felt that where his practical or comparatively practical friends, the Larkins, had failed, he was most unlikely to succeed. When he surveyed the length and breadth of England, sometimes with a map, sometimes relying on his imagination, he didn't know which way to turn.

But turn he must, for the people who had let him their house, for the period of the war, now wanted it back.

Where could he go? He was a bachelor and an orphan, aged fifty, by no means rich but not too badly off. The thought of all England lying before him, studded with houses, each of which had some vital drawback, appalled him. And what of Henry and Muriel, the couple who had served him well for so many years, in spite of Muriel's chronic melancholia and Henry's occasional outbursts of temper, where would *they* go?

Marcus was not without friends, and he decided, with an unconscious foresight, that he had better try to find a house that was near to some of them. In the town of Baswick, in the west country, he had several good friends. Baswick must be his first house-hunting ground.

How to start about it? Marcus found the name of a house-agent in Baswick, and applied to him.

Marcus's quest had at the same time, vis-à-vis the vast area of England, a limitation which might be a hindrance but also might be a help. He wanted a house by the river, where he could row his boat. Boating was his favourite pastime—boating of a relaxed, unskilful, unprofessional kind, just plodding along a river, in a skiff with a sliding seat, thoughtless, mindless. But something from the movement and from the rustle, heard or unheard, of Nature around him, gave him a peace of mind which he couldn't give himself.

Baswick was on a river.

The house-agent, a red-faced beefy-looking man, said, 'I think we've got just the place for you. It's called Paradise Paddock. It was occupied by the Army, and perhaps still is, but we'll go and see.'

Marcus, certain that the expedition would be a wash-out, jumped into the car, and in a quarter of an hour they were there.

It was a mill-house, the river dammed up on one side and flowing freely, but not too freely, on the other. So much Marcus took in, before, crossing a little bridge, they stood in front of a paint-blistered front-door, and the agent rang the bell.

A lady answered it, dressed in the casual clothes of an artist, as in fact she turned out to be.

'Yes?' she said.

The agent advanced a step or two.

'I understand this house is for sale,' he said.

'Well, I'm the owner of it,' she replied, 'and I can assure you it isn't.'

The agent was by no means taken aback.

'I'm sorry, Madam,' he said, 'I must have been mistaken.'

'Not to worry,' said the lady. 'Since you've come out here, perhaps you would like to see over the house.'

It had been built at different times, and on different levels; not a room that had not a step up to it, or a step down. Not only that, they seldom faced each other squarely, they eyed each other widdershins. But Marcus liked them all.

He told the owner so. 'I'm so sorry you don't want to part with the house,' he said, when the tour was over, 'but I quite understand.'

'I didn't say I didn't want to part with it,' the woman answered, 'I only said I was the owner of it—I and my husband—and that it was

not for sale. But we might change our minds, given a suitable induce-
ment.'

'Well, perhaps you will let me know,' said Marcus, with a caution that
was usual with him, for he hated decisions, and could only make them
on the spur of the moment, or not at all.

'I can let you know now,' the woman said. 'We *are* prepared to sell
it, if you will name a sum.'

Marcus glanced at the agent, whose porphyry-coloured face became
for a moment mask-like, before he said, 'I think £5,000 would be a
fair price.'

'Oh, surely,' the woman protested.

'The house isn't everyone's choice, as perhaps you know,' said the
agent, giving her a look. 'I don't say it's damp, but it well may be, since
there is water all round it. I doubt if you would get a higher offer.'

'I must ask my husband,' she said, showing them the door.

It hadn't occurred to the innocent Marcus that she was meaning to
sell it all the time.

When he took possession, he brought with him the furniture and
objets d'art that he had been collecting during the war years. At first they
made the house, or some of it, look habitable. Later, when he had been
toying with them and moving them this way and that, it looked less
so. One thing that he couldn't find a suitable place for was a turquoise-
coloured beetle—obviously meant to be Egyptian for it had a cartouche
on its back, but too large, he thought, to be a real scarab. He had bought
it at an antique shop for a few shillings.

A friend, who had travelled much in the Near East, took a different
view.

'One never knows,' he said. 'I don't like the look of it and I should
get rid of it, if I were you.'

Marcus, who was superficially superstitious, and hated to see a single
magpie, or the new moon through glass, or to spill the salt, or break a
looking-glass (which, happily, he had never done) was fundamentally
anti-superstitious, and thought one shouldn't give way to it. . . .

'How have things been going here?' his friend asked.

'Oh, quite all right,' said Marcus, with an assurance that his expression
belied. 'One or two people have had troubles. A friend of mine fell
downstairs and broke a bone in her hand, and the gardener fell down
some steps which were rather greasy—it rains so much here—and had to
have some stitches put into his elbow. But these things happen in the
best-regulated establishments.'

'But *you* have suffered no inconvenience?' asked his friend, surveying the curious little object, with its rudimentary antennae, which looked as if they might wave.

'None,' said Marcus.

'All the same,' said his friend, 'I should get rid of the creature, if I were you. It isn't a creature, of course, but it looks rather like one.'

Months passed that were not uneventful, and his friend again came to stay.

'Well, how goes it?' he asked.

'What do you mean?'

'Well, domestically and otherwise.'

'Oh,' said Marcus, 'nothing much. My cook fell into the river, one night, looking for her cat. She dotes on it. The cat I hardly need say, was quite safe in some outhouse, and would never have dreamed of plunging into the river, especially in this cold weather. Happily, Mrs. Landslide's husband was at hand, and he hauled her out, wet through, but none the worse for her ducking. There was something else,' he added, unwillingly, 'but it happened only a fortnight ago, and I don't much want to talk about it.'

'Tell me, all the same.'

'Well—but not well—the gardener's young daughter, Christine, was riding her bicycle on the main road, coming away from school, and a lorry hit her, and well—she died. Not very nice, was it?' said Marcus, with a tremor in his voice. 'They haven't got over it, of course, and I don't suppose they ever will. They don't blame me, I'm glad to say; it was no fault of mine, though I had given the bicycle to Christine as a birthday present.'

His friend considered this.

'Have you still got that scarab?'

'Yes.'

'Well, if I were you I should get rid of it.'

'But how? It wouldn't be enough to sell it, or give it to somebody I disliked. I don't know much about black magic, but I am sure it involves some kind of ritual.'

'You're right,' said his friend, 'it does, but there are ways and means.'

'Such as?'

'Some method that combines secrecy with publicity. For instance, if you were in a railway carriage—only it must be *crowded*—'

'Yes?'

'And you threw the scarab out of the window without anyone

seeing—without anyone seeing—' he repeated—'then you might break its spell. I know it sounds quite silly and there are other ways. You didn't steal it, did you?'

'No, I bought it over the counter, as I told you,' said Marcus huffily.

'What a pity. But if you could make someone *else* steal it—stealing is very important in these matters—that might do as well. Where do you keep it?'

'Locked up in a drawer. To tell you the truth, I almost never look at it. I'd rather not.'

'Well, take it out of the drawer, and put it in some prominent place— on the chimney-piece, perhaps—and see what happens.'

Marcus pondered the alternatives. He was even more loath to touch the object than he was to look at it; and what made matters worse, he despised himself for entertaining such ridiculous fancies. However, a seed sown in the subconscious mind is hard to eradicate. Events seemed to have confirmed his friend's warnings. He unlocked the drawer and, hunching his shoulders with distaste, took the 'creature' out. Its embryo whiskers, its wings, if wings they were, folded sleekly and closely on its back, disgusted him; its sinister expression alarmed him; and he went so far as to get a pair of tongs to convey it to the chimney-piece in his study.

No one will want to steal it, he told himself; I only wish they would.

Mrs. Crumble, his daily help, had been several months in his employ. She cleaned and dusted and, if, as rarely happened, she broke something, she nearly always told him—rather as if it were his fault. 'You leave so many things lying about,' she complained, 'it's a wonder they don't all get broken.'

'Never mind about breaking them,' he said, 'so long as you keep the pieces. Then we can patch them together, if they're worth it.'

This she always did, but one morning he noticed a gap on the chimney-piece (for his eyes were trained towards the scarab) and a few minutes later Mrs. Crumble came in with a long face.

'I'm afraid I've broken that insect, sir,' she said. 'I was only flicking it with the duster, and it fell off the ledge and broke.'

'Never mind,' said Marcus, hardly concealing his relief, and added automatically, 'Did you keep the pieces?'

'No, sir, I didn't. It was that broken that no one could have mended it, so I threw the pieces out. I hope it wasn't valuable?'

'Not at all,' said Marcus.

He was just rearranging the objects on the chimney-piece when

Henry, his factotum, came in.

'I don't want to tell any tales, sir,' he said, 'but I happened to see Mrs. Crumble slip that big beetle into her bag. I only say so because I don't want you to suspect that I or my wife took it. We would never do such a thing, but I thought it was only fair to us to let you know.'

'Quite right, Henry,' said Marcus.

Three days later Mrs. Crumble's daughter, a child of twelve, came in and said importantly, 'Mum isn't coming today. She's been took bad. The doctor thinks it's appendicitis.'

It turned out to be something worse than that, and within a few days Mrs. Crumble was dead.

Marcus was very much upset, and his conscience smote him, for hadn't he deliberately exposed the scarab as a bait for somebody's cupidity? Yet he couldn't help being relieved that the 'insect', the 'beetle', the 'creature', had been safely disposed of, and out of the house. Imagine, therefore, his consternation when, a few days after the funeral, the doorbell rang, with a particularly piercing buzz, and when he opened the door, there was Mrs. Crumble's daughter standing on the threshold. She was carrying, linked to her finger, a small parcel wrapped in brown paper.

'Oh, Mr. Foster,' she said, and stopped. Her eyes became moist, and tears fell from them. 'Mum told me, when she knew she had to go, to give you this. It's that beetle creature you had on your mantlepiece, she said. She said she took a fancy to it, and told you that she had broken it, but it wasn't true, and she did not want to die with a lie on her lips. Almost the last thing she did, before she was taken from us, was to wrap it up. So here it is,' said the girl, holding out the parcel for Marcus to take.

For once Marcus was able to make up his mind quickly. Never, never would he accept, above all from a dead woman's hand, a gift which had given his subconscious mind, however misguided it might be, so much anxiety.

'It was too kind of her to have thought of it,' he said, handing the parcel back, 'and too kind of you to have brought it to me. But please, *please*, keep it. It may be worth something, my dear child, I don't know; but if it is, or if it isn't, I shall be more than thankful for you to have it, in memory of your dear mother's kindness to me.'

The daughter sniffed a little, and reached for the parcel.

'It's quite pretty,' she said, doubtfully, 'but since you would like us to keep it—'

'I *should* like you to keep it,' said Marcus firmly, 'and I hope it will bring you good luck.'

Marcus again asked his superstitious friend to stay with him for a weekend. To Marcus's surprise, for his friend was punctilious in such matters, many days passed before he received an answer. The friend excused himself; he was in Rome, but would be back in a few days. 'I met several friends of yours,' he said, 'and we talked about you.' He didn't say he hoped that Marcus would renew the invitation, as he well might have, for they were old friends, but Marcus did at once renew it. At one time he had spent several winters in Rome, and apart from wanting to see his friend, he wanted to gossip about his Roman friends. So he suggested another weekend, in fact two other weekends.

'You needn't worry about the scarab,' he added, 'I have disposed of it, I'll tell you how, and the house is now exorcised and purified.'

His friend replied that he was delighted to hear this, but he could only stay over one night, as he had to be back in London on Sunday evening.

Marcus was slightly hurt by this, but reminded himself of the danger of getting touchy as one grew older.

They talked of many things, of their Roman acquaintances, who seemed to have grown more vivid to Marcus with the passing years; then, inevitably, of the 'occurrences' at Paradise Paddock.

'What have you done with that scarab?' his friend asked.

'Oh,' said Marcus negligently, 'my daily help stole it.'

'What happened then?'

'Oh, then she died. It was very, very sad. But she needn't have stolen it, need she? I didn't ask her to.' He still felt guilty.

'I think you have been lucky,' said his friend, looking round him and sniffing the air. 'I think—I *think* so, Marcus.'

The open door of the study gaped, at an acute angle, on the open door of the dining-room.

'It's strange how right you have been,' said Marcus. 'I must confess, I didn't really believe you about the scarab, but then I was brought up in a sceptical atmosphere. My father—' he paused—'well, he was a rationalist. You half convinced me—but only half. Calamities happen in every house—this isn't the only one. You know that local people call it The House of Death?'

'I didn't know.'

'Well, they do and the reason may be that for two hundred years it has been called Paradise Paddock—the association between Death and Paradise is rather encouraging and beautiful, I think. Out of one, into the other.'

His friend fixed his eye on the open doorway.

'Should we go for a little walk, do you think? I sleep badly, as you know, and they say, "After dinner, walk a mile".'

'A mile is rather a long way,' said Marcus, 'but let us take a turn, by all means. Only it will have to be mostly on the pavement—the road, with all this traffic, is really dangerous.'

'I *would* like a breath of fresh air,' his friend said.

They started off, following the pavement. Under the street lamps the traffic roared beside them.

'Shall we go back now?' Marcus asked.

His friend turned his head in the direction in which Paradise Paddock presumably lay.

A little onwards lend thy guiding hand
To these dark steps—a little further on,

he quoted, obviously unwilling to return.

They proceeded, and it was then that Marcus's friend, catching his foot on the kerb, fell headlong. To Marcus's consternation he didn't pick himself up, but lay on his back, one leg tucked under him, the other stretched out at an unnatural angle.

Marcus tried to help him to his feet, but he resisted.

Writhing a little, he turned his screwed face towards the street-lamp overhead, which invested it with a yellowish pallor and gasped, between broken breaths, 'Thank you for only breaking my leg—you might have killed me. Did no one ever tell you you had the Evil Eye?'

ROMAN CHARITY

IN some day and age which I won't try to identify—it might be now—
Rudolph Campion was sent to prison. Campion wasn't his real name;
it was a name he had assumed partly because some of his forebears were
English, which was then, and still sometimes is, a recommendation,
something to put on a passport, or what served him as a passport, for he
had more than one. Rudolph Campion, Englishman. He himself could
hardly remember what his real name was. It certainly wasn't English;
but then, as now, it was a disadvantage to be stateless, especially for
someone who travelled about the world as much as Rudolph Campion
did.

Living such a nomadic life, it was surprising that Rudolph was
married, and not so much that he was married, as that he still had married
ties. His wife had left him, bored with his itinerant life, in one of the
countries that he from time to time frequented; she wanted to settle
down, she said, and not always be a camp-follower, often living under
canvas, whatever the weather. So at some point in his wanderings, not too
far from a capital city where such civilization as recent wars had left, still
remained, she told him she had had enough, and would seek her fortune
in this city; she did not say how.

In her late thirties, she was almost as good-looking as he was; in fact if
it hadn't been for his good looks—bearded, moustachioed, with thinning
hair, unkempt and shaggy—a man of today he might have been—
she wouldn't have stuck to him as long as she did. But there were other
men with equal physical attractions, who liked a settled life, and a
home, and she didn't despair of finding one.

It took her some time to come to this decision, for had they not been
married twenty years? and she, like many women in this and other
ways more far-sighted than men, valued a stable personal relationship.

This she had enjoyed with Rudolph (Rudy to her, though never rude). He might have strayed; he probably had; but she was not upset by the suspicion of his possible infidelities, when he was out of sight (as he so often was) but not out of mind. He always came back to her, and was as loving as he was loved; and though she didn't really know, and didn't much want to know, what his actual business was, although she did know that an element of danger attended it, when they pitched their moving tent a day's march nearer a destination in this country or in that, his friends, for he had friends or accomplices in many countries, knew that she came first with him. The news of their relationship seemed to precede them: she never had to explain who she was; she was accepted, in whatever society, as belonging to him and he to her; a good-looking and above all, an inseparable couple. The personal vanity, the sense of being esteemed for their own sake, which many people and most women have, was amply satisfied for Trudi by her Rudy—a joke which his friends, who were seldom hers, often made. Never could she remember a time when, however little she had to do with the business in hand, Rudy had pressed her to make herself agreeable to some hard-faced little man, on whose favour, or favours, success depended. She might have yielded, for Rudy left her much alone, and as the Italian proverb says, 'One gets tired of home-made bread.'

No, in their twenty years together he had never, so to speak, pushed her into a corner, never made her feel that she was just an adjunct, a useful business-asset, but otherwise rather a drag. Perhaps he hardly could have, for she couldn't enter a room without making her beauty felt.

All this she realized; but as the rain dripped through the canvas of the tent—they didn't always live in a tent, but between times they had to when they were on the run—she said to her daughter who shared two-thirds of the tent with her, the other third being curtained off for sleeping-quarters, and other masculine requirements. Rudy didn't seem to mind the dripping rain.

'Angela, I think I shall have to make a change. I'm very proud of your father, but this sort of life doesn't suit me. It may be all right for a man, but I'm getting too old for it. And now that you're engaged to be married—'

'I was married yesterday, Mother, but you were so busy with one thing and another, I didn't like to tell you.'

The mother and daughter turned to each other on their dampening beds.

'You didn't like to tell me?'

'No, I thought it was kinder not to.'

'Speak lower, he might hear you,' Trudi began to whisper.

'Oh no, he sleeps like a log. But I know I'm a responsibility to you in the odd life he makes you lead, so when Jacko asked me to marry him—'

'Jacko?'

'Yes, you've seen him several times. Well, I said yes.'

'Jacko?'

'Yes, he's got a job as a courier, and we like each other. I mightn't have done it, but I knew it was a strain for you, living with Father, in these conditions, and with me in tow. I didn't know that you were going to take the step of leaving him—but I would have married Jacko even if I had known you had—.'

'Jacko?'

'Yes, he's a nice fellow, a reliable sort.'

'You're sure?'

'Oh yes, quite sure. He's not a substitute for Father, whom I've always loved, just as you have, and shall always love. But I can't *do* anything for him, any more than you can. He's a lone wolf, and picks up his living wherever he can find it. I don't think we need feel sorry for him—he'll always fall on his feet. But I shall always keep in touch with him, as no doubt you will, and if ever he gets into a jam—'

'I shall hear what he says, I shall hear what he says,' said her mother. 'At any rate he will have you to fall back on.'

'Yes, always.'

'Jacko or no Jacko?'

'Yes, Father will always mean more to me than anyone. And to you, Mother?'

'I'm not quite so sure. Twenty years is a long time. I'll tell him to-morrow.'

They listened to the dropping of the rain, a soothing sound, before they too dropped off.

So next day Rudy learned that in a very short time he was to be wife-less and daughter-less.

In those days, as in these, political prisoners were not always well-treated and if they fell into the wrong hands—and there were a good many wrong hands to fall into, no matter whom they might be working for—their lot was not likely to be a happy one. It was a risk of Rudy's trade—his international trade—and he was prepared to accept it, just as any man who engages in one of the many sports and occupations which involve risk to life and limb, is prepared to accept it. Indeed, it was no doubt the risk attached to his present job, whatever it was, that made him choose it; he wouldn't have been happy in a humdrum occupation where no danger lurked. No thrill, no wondering if he would just turn the corner, no spice of life.

And so far it had worked quite well. There had been anxious moments when he was glad to have his car outside; moments when his command of languages (he had been brought up to know three) suddenly failed him; moments when some suspicious looking stranger followed him to the door, and asked for his address. He would give an address, an imaginary address, and within an hour or two he and Trudi would be far away, pitching their tent; and Angela would be with them. The tent was in the boot of the car, and they had brought pitching it to a fine art; in half an hour or so it would be ready and soon afterwards a delicious meal would be ready, too; for Rudy was a big man and a hungry and a thirsty man; leading the life he did, with much strain on his nervous and physical constitution, he couldn't go without sustenance for long. Both his wife and his daughter enjoyed seeing him tuck into his food and swallowing down a bottle of wine. There was another bottle for them, too, if his mission had been successful. What matter if they were on the run? Being on the run brings appetite and thirst.

But now things were different, and in more ways than one. No longer was Rudy able to make his entrée into an assemblage, perhaps unfamiliar to him, and unfamiliar with him, as a family man with a beautiful wife, and a hardly less beautiful daughter, moving slowly and gracefully maturing, through her adolescence. No longer could he divert the attention of the company from him to them, while he had a quiet talk with someone he wanted to have a word with, and who might want to have a word with him. He didn't exactly take refuge behind them; but they were his cards of identity; while they were around, engaging the others in conversation, he didn't have to wonder much if people were looking at him.

Now all this was changed. The semi-social life on which so much of his success as an agent (an agent for whom? for what?) depended, had lost its context.

*

Rudy was a man of action, and action, such as it was, and wherever it was, involved a good deal of danger. This he not only accepted, he welcomed it for he was made that way; but being a professional, he didn't go in search of it; to avoid it was as much a matter of self-training and self-discipline as to confront it when it came.

These two complementary qualities had helped him to get out of a number of tight places. His wife and his daughter had helped him, too, not physically, for he never wanted them to run unnecessary risks; but by their mere presence, which gave him an air of respectability and solidity which deceived a good many people.

How far he valued them for themselves, and not just as adjuncts to his appearance and personality—his image—he himself would have found it hard to say. While they were with him it was a question he did not even ask himself: he took their presence, and what they did for him, and what he did for them, for granted. They were reciprocal services in a good cause. The cause of what? Freedom perhaps, though freedom is such an elastic term; and some of his co-adjutors wondered which side he was on. But business is business, and as someone has said, a lie in business is not a lie. Rudy had availed himself, cautiously of course, of this precept.

Now he had to explain himself. It wasn't difficult to explain that his wife was tired of travelling, which was true, and was now living in Warsaw, which was not true. For his sake, as well as Trudi's and Angela's, he did not want their whereabouts to be known. He also explained, which was true, that Angela was married and expecting a baby—he did not say where, for who knew where, or where not, a baby might be born?

This freedom from family ties gave him as a man who was still attractive to women, a good many opportunities which he was not slow to take; not only from the amorous angle, whatever that might be, but from the information sometimes supplied. He knew that information was double-edged, but he relied on getting more than he gave.

But he was not heartless, and though not yet forty, he sometimes thought rather wistfully in the loneliness of his leaking tent, pitched between somewhere and somewhere, or between nowhere and nowhere, eating his viands, on which he relied so much, out of a tin, or tins, in his solitary confinement, of the domestic amenity and seeming security he had once enjoyed. Those softer moments! When he came back tired and hungry from some mission, and smelt from afar the smell of a delicious dish that was cooking for him on the little oil stove, and heard, from nearer to, the gentle muffled swish and a rustle, so different from a man's direct and decisive movements—loudly proclaiming their object

instead of trying to conceal it—of the participants who were preparing
his evening meal! Mouth-watering prospect! And more than living
up to its promise. While he was eating he didn't talk much; just a word
here and there escaped the otherwise inarticulate smacking of his lips.
But afterwards, full-fed, finishing the bottle of wine or spirits, if they
were in funds, for he could drink at a sitting a bottle of brandy or
sligovitz, or vodka, or grappa, or calvados or whatever might be the
spirituous tipple of the country; then he became expansive, and told
them a little, but not (for their own sakes) too much of what he had been
doing during the day—the contacts he had made, the possible development, and their probable next destination. To all this they listened
eagerly, even avidly, and fondly watched his face as (unknown to him)
its taut features slowly relaxed to reveal a husband and a father.

And afterwards, when the dividing curtain was drawn he could hear
their lowered voices (whispers meant not to disturb him rather than to
prevent him hearing what they said), after which he dropped off in a
genial alcoholic haze, with a sense of protective influences round him,
and replete in every sense, he slept like the proverbial log, till dawn, or
until the clock in his subconscious mind (as reliable and less noisy than
an alarum clock) told him it was time to get up. Even if he had possessed
an alarum clock he would not have used it, for it would have disturbed
the slumbers beyond the curtain (not the Iron Curtain) and sometimes
he was off before day-break.

Comfort! Comfort! He might not have admitted it to himself, but it
was comfort that he missed, and business, however much it may sharpen
the other faculties, does not always warm the heart.

He had had many surprises in his life, his life as an international spy,
but the greatest and the most unforeseen was when almost simultaneously
his wife and his daughter decided to leave him. He had always been
ready, as indeed he had to be, to accept facts—but he could hardly credit
this one. Leave him, after twenty years of wifehood, and perhaps longer
still of daughterhood? He couldn't and didn't blame them; blame didn't
come into his code of behaviour, in which success and failure were his
only criteria. He knew he hadn't been a good husband and father, but
there were many worse; he might have treated them as camp-followers
but they were willing to be so treated; he had shared his good times as
well as his bad times with them, and set aside some money for them,
which was no doubt one reason why they had left him. He had counted
on their loyalty, not on their love; love was a thing he didn't take into
account, except in the crudest way, as leading to someone or something.

All the same, in those lonely nights in the tent, when he heard no whispering of women's voices, and smelt no smell of the creature comforts they were preparing for him, he knew he was missing something. It never entered his mind that they might be missing something too.

He didn't often sleep now, as aforetime he used to, in the comfort of a luxury hotel; but sometimes he did, and it was there that the unexpected happened. In the middle of dinner, with a bottle of wine half empty on the table, two men touched him on the shoulder and before he had time to pay his bill, or anyone had time to pay it for him, he was marched away and bundled into a waiting car, not his car, which was outside in the car-park. 'Can't I get my things?' he asked in the language of the country. 'No, we've got all your things that matter,' was the reply, and no more was said until he found himself, handcuffed, in a small cell, seven feet by five with a grated window at the top, admitting the air, and a grated window in the door, admitting a dim light from the passage. An unshaded bulb hanging from the ceiling showed him a straw mattress in the corner, and one or two pieces of furniture which might have been made out of the same substance as the cell.

Here they left him; but presently a warder came in with a small bundle of clothes which he recognized as his. 'This is all you'll want,' he said, 'we've got the rest. I'll show you where the place is,' and unlocking the door he indicated where Rudy could relieve himself. 'But you'll have to knock on the door—there's always me or one of us in the passage. Lights out at ten o'clock. Breakfast at six. These handcuffs are a bit tight, I'll give you some second-grade ones, and you can stretch your arms a bit. No fooling about, mind. Good-night.'

The new handcuffs did indeed give Rudy more freedom of movement. Instead of being clamped together, with only an interval of a few inches between, hardly enough, not enough, to enable him to satisfy the most rudimentary needs of Nature, his hands now stretched to his hips; he could feel parts of his body that before had been beyond their scope; he could have picked things up from the dirty stone floor, had there been anything worth picking up. He could even embrace himself, or part of himself, had he felt so inclined. This freedom! But compared with the earlier restriction it seemed like liberty. Now he could sleep again; he had always been a good sleeper, but with his hands tied so tight in front of or (according to the gaoler's whim) behind him, he had been unable to sleep, and his breakfast of bread and water, or whatever insubstantial substance took its place, found him more tired than he had been at ten o'clock lights out.

But now, folding and unfolding his arms so as to give him as little discomfort, not to say pain, as might be, he awoke, not refreshed, but with the blessed sense of having slept.

Gradually he adjusted himself, as best he could, to his new life. Small reliefs, that in the old days he would have taken for granted or not noticed—the cleansing of his cell from certain noxious insects—seemed like a gift from Heaven. And what a blessing it was to go out into the light of common day and join the other prisoners in their half-hour's exercise inside the high-walled courtyard. Here they were allowed to speak to each other, those who had the necessary gift of speech, for they were of many nations and languages. Some had known each other recently, some from long ago; but the majority, of whom Rudy was one, were too low-spirited to want to talk much. What was there to talk about, between those flat, encircling walls, outside which life went on, with its incentives and excitements, whereas inside all was static and uneventful, without hope, promise, or future? Only death; and for death he sometimes longed. He couldn't understand why he hadn't been executed before; 'they' had plenty against him, a whole dossier, and from time to time they made him stand up in his cell while they questioned him. Sometimes he was too weak to stand up, and asked permission to sit down on his straw bed. He answered, or parried the questions as well as he could, and as well as his tired mind would let him. He had to keep a constant watch on his tongue, for he didn't want to involve other people more than he could help—it was an occupational obligation to keep his mouth, as far as might be, shut.

He wasn't subjected to any physical or bodily torture, in these inter-rogations, except a very hard strong light from an electrical instrument they brought with them, shining on his eyes. It dazzled and distressed him, and drove almost every thought from his head; to keep his head, or what remained of it, was his chief concern.

They are trying to wear me down, he thought, they are trying to wear me down, and perhaps one day they will, and perhaps I shall tell them everything—what is true as well as untrue—for he knew only too well, that for some psychological reason, physical or even emotional pressure will induce a man to tell the truth, instead of the lies to which spies are accustomed and which they have already carefully prepared.

They are waiting for me to break down, he thought, they are waiting for me to break down, and he who had always been proud of his strength, felt this as an almost personal affront to his image of himself.

Meanwhile his fears for his health were being too well justified.

Needless to say, there was no looking glass in his cell—why should a prisoner want to look at himself? much better not. They had taken away his razor, as no doubt they do, and always have done, in many prisons, and for obvious reasons: but they had left him his little pocket mirror, in which, in better days, he used to study his face to see if it looked like what he wanted it to look like at the moment.

And now, what a picture did it present! He had usually been clean-shaven; he had sometimes, when the occasion seemed to demand it, been bearded; but beards need a good deal of attention and in the absence of scissors, his face, as he saw it reflected, was almost unrecognisable, and also shaming, for he had always been proud of his looks which had taken him a long way on his uneven road to temporary prosperity.

And now another thing, another physical thing, connected with the conditions in which he lived. The chain of his handcuffs had been considerably lengthened, so that he could now scratch himself (an almost necessary activity) in places where before he could not; but owing to his hands and wrists being of extra size, they chafed him, bringing to those parts sores and inflammation which took away what little physical comfort he had left. His gaoler, who was by no means un-sympathetic, for a gaoler, reported this to the prison doctor, and the doctor, seeing Rudy's swollen and suppurating hands, recommended handcuffs at least an inch wider, to help circulation and enable the blood to flow. This was a great relief to Rudy, whose robust constitution responded to any mitigation allowed it, and by degrees, the swelling died down, leaving behind them hollows where the flesh and muscles used to be.

Being technically stateless, though he had (or had had, before his belongings were confiscated), more than one passport he could not appeal to any country for aid, and even if he could have, the country he appealed to would certainly not have recognized him. Now that spying was an almost organized occupation, he had hoped that he might be exchanged for some opposite number (he could think of several); but it hadn't happened—for how could he get in touch with some country to whom he had been of service? It didn't seem likely to happen. In fact he had no one in authority to appeal to; and meanwhile he grew thinner, and less and less, physically and mentally, his old self.

For it was his misfortune that the country which had caught up with him and detected him was a poor country, and overrun by refugees; they had no food to spare for themselves or for the refugees, political sympathisers, who swarmed over them; and those who came last on the list, for physical sustenance, were political prisoners, of whom, for one reason and another, they had a surfeit.

Rudy's diet was hardly enough to keep body and soul together; looking at himself, when he was allowed to have a bath, as sometimes the prisoners were, he hardly recognized the fine figure of a man he used to know.

*

Occasionally, but only occasionally, and under the strictest supervision, the prisoners were allowed to receive visitors. Such visitors, of course, had to be carefully 'screened', and more often than not, they were turned away at the gateway of the prison. So what was Rudy's surprise, when his gaoler told him, almost as if it was a command not a concession, that a lady wanted to see him. 'She says she is your daughter. I don't know if you know about her. But sometimes we let in relations.'

'Just a moment, please,' said Rudy, who was lying on his bed, half naked, owing to the intense heat. 'Just a moment.' He tried to collect his thoughts, if any, but the sound of running water in the lavatory at the end of the passage gave him, as it gives many men, an uncontrollable desire to pee. 'Take me down there, will you?' he said, waving towards the sound, for without the gaoler's permission, and presence, he couldn't relieve the needs of Nature.

'All right, but hurry up,' the gaoler said, 'Ten minutes is the most you'll be allowed.'

'I shan't need ten minutes here,' answered Rudy, on the threshold of the *pissoir*.

Natural needs, as so often they do, brought him to a sense of his general situation. Who was it who wanted to see him? For weeks, months, it seemed, he had been cut off from contact with the outside world. He had given up hope of ever seeing it again. He hardly even wanted to see it, so inured had he become not only to the privations but to the utter lack of personal incentive, the desire to make himself known and felt, which is the almost inevitable consequence of even a short spell in prison.

'Hurry up,' repeated the warder, just behind him. 'You've only got ten minutes.'

Rudy followed him back, and in a few moments the door of his cell re-opened.

'Father!' she exclaimed, but she recognized him before he recognized her, this glorious young creature, dressed in what he imagined was the height of fashion, pearls, bracelets, even a little tippet of fur in case the broiling evening should turn cold.

They embraced and embraced, her beautifully attired body to his half-naked one. But it was the body of her father.

When her tears began to dry she said,

'But you're so *thin!*'

'They don't give us much to eat here,' he said, as casually as he could.

His daughter had of course seen him in 'his prime', how many months ago? when the shield of partition between his sleeping-quarters and theirs, opened to reveal a half-clad figure, asking for something—probably a drink—disappearing almost as soon as it appeared—leaving behind a scent of unwashed masculinity, soon to be washed, for Rudy was particular about that and always had his white-enamelled basin, and his soap, and his washing flannel ready—for anything that might occur. Now he had none of these, he couldn't even wash, except under supervision.

This question of personal cleanliness was uppermost in his thoughts when he drew away from his daughter and said,

'You must find me very changed.' She mistook his meaning and said, 'Of course you're not changed, dear Father, except for those nasty handcuffs, and because you look so *thin*. What can we do about that?'

'Nothing,' said Rudy, 'so far as I know. This miserable country can't afford to give its subjects let alone its refugees, let alone its prisoners, a decent meal, so why should I be favoured?'

His daughter didn't answer for a moment; she knew their time together was getting short; she could see the gaoler pacing up and down the passage, with an eye on his watch for he was soon to be off duty, and a look through the grille inside to see how things were going on. Darkly his helmet gleamed.

With the sudden impulse of a woman Angela said, 'There's something I *can* do. If you agree to it, Father. Only we have to be quick.'

Smiling at him with the intensity of affection she had always felt for him, she raised her right hand to her black velvet bodice; her left hand, lovely-fingered, played around her waist in a vague semi-circle, as if awaiting a cue from the other. Her head bent forward; her smile grew more inviting as if it was the very messenger of love.

He was sitting on his straw bed, she on the hard chair opposite. He looked at her with incomprehension, alarm, almost hostility.

'What do you mean?'

The beautiful hand drew down her black velvet bodice, and exposed her breasts. 'I have a wet nurse,' she said, 'should I need one, but I have plenty of this to spare.'

For a moment Rudy could say nothing. He, who had relied so much on eating and drinking, had spent many weeks almost deprived of both. He fixed his altered face, so pale and shrunken within its covering of untutored hair, on his daughter's, beautiful in itself, still more beautified by art.

'What do you mean, Angela?'

She said nothing, but with a still warmer smile, leaned, full-bosomed, towards him.

Then he took the meaning, and wracked by thirst and hunger, took, like a child, what she offered him; nor did he desist until the shadow of the warder, passing the grille, warned him that the feast must be finished.

He wiped his mouth.

'Another time, another time?' he murmured.

'Yes,' she said, but before they had time to say more, the warder was in the cell.

'Now you must go, Madam,' he said.

*

His daughter's visit, and her gift of fresh milk, so different from the milk he was used to, so long in bottle and so often sour, completely changed Rudy's whole outlook. He was not forgotten! He was still in contact with the world outside! And with his own family! Until now he hadn't realised how much they meant to him; at the thought of them his whole being seemed to revive. He hadn't time to ask Angela how, or where, her mother was; he hadn't time to ask her how she had tracked him down; he hadn't time to ask the hundred questions he wanted to ask. He had been, quite literally, like a baby at the breast, whose one desire is to slake its thirst and its hunger and can only utter inarticulate sucking sounds meanwhile. In the process he lost all sense of shame; he didn't feel that he, a grown man, should not be finding this kind of sustenance from anyone, least of all his daughter; he didn't care that the warder, passing and re-passing his cell, could see through the small iron grille just what was happening; his physical need was so great that it quite over-came all civilized feelings. He was a starving animal, and nothing more.

When she had gone his mood began to change. The renascence which her presence, and her present, brought him didn't at once fade; the first sustained his spirit, and the second his body. It was surprising how much better he felt for both—united to the world, not only the outside world which he could only dimly perceive through the grating in his cell, or a little more amply, over the shoulders of the surrounding walls—but to the world of the flesh which, in the days of his triumphant health, he had always taken for granted. The idea of being *ill* was too ridiculous!

But since his daughter's visit he realised how far he had gone downhill (down-ill, he thought, for he had English in his blood and was still capable of a play on words). Not only was he unattractive to look at, as his little mirror showed him, but his invincible health was failing him. Angela with the benison of her breast, had for a day or two restored it; but when, if ever, could he expect to see her again?

He knew, and had always accepted the conditions of the kind of life he led; but foresight, and experience are very different things.

If only she would come again! It wasn't only his thirsty mouth that asked this question and his whole physical system, deprived of all the dainties that used to succour it; it was the longing for *home*, not that he had ever had since he could remember a real home, but somewhere, however transient it might be, where he could *expand*, take his shoes off, throw his clothes down, asking nobody's permission, and then expect a good hot meal; and later, if he wasn't too tired, but he was never tired, the dividing curtain would come down, and Angela would take his place outside and he her place inside, as the case might be.

How far away it seemed from his present life, if life it could be called. Angela's visit had brought back a whiff of it which recalled the happy past; but as it faded, it left a feeling of unbearable desolation. She would never come again, she would never come again! It would have been better if she had never come at all.

*

She did come, however. The gaoler, with a faint smirk, said, 'There's a lady to see you. The same one as last time. Shall I let her in?'

'Of course,' said Rudy, hardly believing his ears. But he had to believe his eyes.

She looked too ravishing! Among the prison visitors who could have looked like her?

When the gaoler ushered her in he warned, 'Fifteen minutes, mind, and no larking about.'

An extra five minutes was something. After their embracements, which lasted longer than before, and longer than they ever had in the days of Rudy's prosperity when the life of action had seemed so much more important than domestic felicity, her right hand, her white hand, moved as before to the black velvet of her *corsage*, the invitation in her eyes and lips was overwhelming; her left hand, just as white with its slender, curling fingers, lay as it were on guard, in case, in case—of what? Rudy did not ask himself; he stared at his daughter with greedy, staring, incredulous eyes, and eyebrows raised so high that their ridges made semi-circles reaching far up his forehead.

While he was slaking his hunger and his thirst he was oblivious, as he had been before, to what was going on outside; he did not hear the warder's wary footsteps crossing and re-crossing the door of his cell, or see the helmeted head as it peered inwards.

After a while he drew away like a breast-fed child that has had its fill; and then became aware of the reality round him, his own semi-nakedness which, in spite of its emaciation, still preserved and perhaps emphasized the beauty of his body, contrasting with and yet recalling her fullness and healthiness of form, and the facial likeness between them, as she drew her velvet mantle round her.

'Aren't you rather hot in that?' he asked idly, with a father's instinctive privilege to criticize, and wiping the sweat off his chest with the weekly handkerchief the prison laundry allowed him.

'Oh no, darling, it's much colder outside than it is in here. And besides—'

'Besides?'

'Well, I have to be in the fashion. I should be wearing this even if I was on the equator.'

The time was running short. Rudy tried desperately to think of things he wanted to ask his daughter; questions he could ask without risk, and which could be answered without risk, for he didn't know whether his cell was wired for listening in.

'How is Trudi?'

'Very well, I see her quite often. She has people looking after her, I think she's all right.'

'And you, Angela?'

'Yes, I'm all right too. Jacko is a nice fellow'—and she indicated her bracelets and her necklace.

'And he doesn't mind you coming here?' asked Rudy, aware almost for the first time of the claims of personal relationships, as distinct from those of business.

'He doesn't know, and if he did, he wouldn't mind.'

'You're sure he wouldn't?'

Angela made a wide gesture with her arms, her beautiful arms, a very feminine version of her father's, which had nothing left but the bones and muscles.

'And you will be able to come and see me again?'

She smiled.

'Why not?'

The grating of the opening door, the warder's face, dark under his helmet.

'It's time, please,' he said, though the words were a command, not a request.

Angela rose and kissed her father, and then, bestowing a grateful smile on the grim-faced warder, she departed.

Where has she gone? thought Rudy. In his job it was safer not to ask people their destinations, and still safer not to reveal his own. Safer not to disclose his own locality, little as it mattered, for it wasn't a destination—if only it had been!—and perhaps he was safer here than anywhere else. He hadn't been subjected to a formal interrogation or tortured, except by the glare of the electric torch, from which his eyes still sometimes ached and smarted, it could have been much, much worse. Deep within himself, he didn't think he would escape alive. He was stateless, or rather he had too many states, too many passports, to appeal to any single one: they would all disown him, and none of those he had worked for, as he had so often reminded himself, would want to exchange him for another spy. He awaited his fate.

And yet, since Angela's second visit, his fate seemed less gloomy than before. Not less settled, not less determined; but somehow less lonely, less beyond the scope and reach and sympathy of ordinary mortals, who lived square vegetable lives, hail-brother-well-met characters, with no problems other than domestic or financial—nothing to compare with the aspect of a firing squad, or whatever agent of death awaited him.

And yet, apart from the physical stimulus, greater than the ordinarily well-fed businessman or working-man could conceive, coming from his daughter's breast, was something more emotional and more spirited —something that might have been experienced by a baby, who was not old enough to have had any other experience. A feeling of security, of not having to depend on others outside his ken, still less on himself, for his livelihood—in both senses of the word—returned to him. It didn't convince his mind; his mind still knew he was under sentence of death; but it did release, in his subconscious mind, a feeling of hope.

If Angela had twice come to see him, might she not come a third time, bringing with her the inestimable benefit of her breast and the different but equally inestimable benefit of her presence?

She did come again, quite soon, within a week; and in the joy of their reunion it didn't occur to Rudy that this was odd, considering, as he knew, that the prisoners were only allowed visitors once a fortnight.

'Don't tell Trudi where I am,' he whispered, as his daughter was letting fall her dress, silk this time, for even she had come to feel that comfort was preferable to fashion, but black still, because it suited her and showed off her white skin and her lovely hands. 'I'd rather she didn't know where I was, just tell her I'm alive.'

Angela nodded. She was now wearing her hair in a new style, piled up on the back of her head: it suited her nose which (like Cleopatra's?) was a shade too long; and the coronal of hair, into which she had introduced fragmentary gleams of shining metal, perhaps silver, balanced it.

Of this Rudy, intent upon his meal, was no more aware than a baby would have been.

Afterwards she lingered with him, talking about the outside world, which had become almost an illusion to Rudy, so distant was it from his personal experience. And then he heard her say—an interpolation in a quite different context—'I know the way out.'

He nodded in answer, for words might be overheard, and soon after, the door opened to its minimal extent, and the warder said, glancing at Angela, 'I'm afraid you must go now, Madam.'

Rudy kissed his daughter; after all that was allowed; and surrendered her to the warder. For some reason for which he couldn't rationally account, he put his ear to the grille which gave him little vision of what was going on in the passage, but did allow him to listen to their retreating footsteps.

Angela's third visit had renewed his interest in existence: he thought of himself as potentially alive, not as dead. Is it always a blessing to exchange resignation for hope? Rudy couldn't tell, but he knew that hope was stirring in him. 'I know the way out,' Angela wouldn't have said that inadvertently. 'The way out' of what? There were so many predicaments to know, or not know, the way out of, with many of which Rudy was familiar; emotional situations, financial situations, all sorts of situations. Did she mean the way out of prison?

Lying on his palliasse, under his blanket, more heavy than warm (sometimes he threw it off because of the heat) he tried to make sure what Angela meant. As a rule a good sleeper, and still a good sleeper now that he had accommodated himself to his chains, he tossed and turned, and suddenly one of his hands came free from its manacles. He could hardly believe it, but so it was; his right hand was loose, it could do whatever it wanted, or he wanted it to do, scratch him, stroke him, anything. Amazing! And suddenly it came to him why, and how this had happened. Several weeks—months?—of semi-starvation had so reduced his physical frame that his hands and wrists, which used to be larger, as well as stronger, than most men's had shrivelled, had shrunk to under-handcuff size. He hadn't freed himself; his captors had freed him, to a certain very limited extent, simply by not giving him enough to eat.

Cautiously, because he still couldn't believe it, he tried with his left hand. A little wriggling, and out it came from its iron clasp. His arms were free!

He lay in or on his bed, moving them about, touching parts of himself that had long been out of touch, his feet, his legs, his chest, his chin, his head, the small of his back, all the anatomy of himself which for so many weeks, so many months, had been as unreal, as meaningless, as a map of the world—his world—long out of date.

Leaving the gyves and the chain which connected them under the diseased blanket, he got up and walked about his cell, exulting in his freedom. But only for a moment; although it was dark it wasn't safe; he could hear the gaoler's footsteps, perambulating outside; and although the gaoler must have heard many a sleepless prisoner pacing his cell, it wouldn't do to awake suspicion. Rudy went back to bed (if the phrase is not too misleading) and after some effort, fixed on his handcuffs again. He waited for a while, to enjoy his sense of freedom; but when he realised that without his familiar bandages he wouldn't sleep (let alone the danger of being found without them in the morning) he put them on again. How blessed can confinement be, once one is used to it!

Rudy had been used to it, at any rate resigned to it, until these irruptions of his daughter's presence renewed his taste, not only for the taste of her bosom, of which, much as he relished it and felt the better for it, he was secretly ashamed, as for the free world outside these walls, where he could express himself as a man should and even order his own food!

Meanwhile he dared not take off his manacles, except in the privacy (the only privacy he had) of his bed, and didn't know what to do with his new-found freedom.

The next time Angela came she was dressed to kill. Even Rudy who

ike many men (and many women, for that matter) could hardly believe
that a relation so close to him as a child, could be outstandingly beautiful.
Trudi was a good-looking woman; Rudy as he had cause to know, was
or had been, a fine figure of a man. But that between them they should
have begotten this wonderful-looking creature! For almost the first
time in his life Rudy had a sense of physical inferiority. Other kinds of
inferiority he had often felt: social inferiority, financial inferiority,
mental inferiority; but physical inferiority, no. With his clothes on, or
without them, he had always been as good as, or better than, the next
man.

And then to have sired this worshipful creature!

'A poor thing, but mine own.' Rudy didn't know the quotation, but
he had the humility to feel, just as an equal, perhaps greater, number of
people have not, that a home-made product is less to be esteemed in the
eyes of the world than a shop-made product which has had the advantage
of advertisement and public acclaim. Angela had neither: she was just
the daughter of him and Trudi, and the idea that she had looks to attract
general attention, such as a film-star might have, had never occurred to
him.

Yet why had the gaoler given her and him these special privileges, for
today no time-limit had been set on their intercourse?

Something moved in Rudy's mind, and when their lunch(?), tea(?),
dinner (?) was over, he wiped his mouth with his weekly handkerchief,
and said, and meant it, 'I am so grateful to you, darling.' He stopped,
shocked and astonished at this verbal expression of emotion, which he
had perhaps remembered from some film. 'What I mean is,' he amended,
'it is good of you to come and see your old dad, who isn't like what he
used to be.'

He glanced at himself, as much as he could see; the famous muscles
were there, especially the bunch of deltoid like a cricketball on his right
shoulder, of which he used to be proud, and which was the more in
evidence now that his flesh had receded from it. 'You've been kind to me,
Angela,' he ended lamely, 'and so has Trudi, though I don't want her to
know, as I told you, where I am. I don't know how you found out, for
that matter.'

He didn't expect an answer, but he suddenly felt a slip of paper in his
hand, and a flood of light dawned on him.

'Eat it, and when he fetches me, hit him as hard as you can.'

They looked at each other. Rudy swallowed the paper and realised
what a woman, whose beauty was taken for granted by him and many

others, might mean to a sex-starved prison-warder.

It explained a lot; it explained why Angela had been admitted to his cell, more often than other visitors would have been. It explained why their times together had been prolonged beyond the statutory limit. It explained—

Rudy put on his jacket to cover his nakedness, or semi-nakedness, for he still had his trousers, and his shoes, the white gymshoes he wore for exercise.

'Do I look all right?' he asked, buttoning up his jacket.

It was then he remembered his handcuffs. He was still wearing them, the chain between them sagged over his thighs. Many times since he had learned how to unloose them he had practised the art, and the art remained. With his hands on his knees, the chain between them, he looked like a prisoner in irons, but he could release himself at any moment.

'Do I look all right?' he repeated.

'Of course, dear Father, you always look all right.'

As the sound of the warder's footsteps, between their five minutes' interval, died away, he gave his daughter a meaning look and twitched his shrunken wrists and claw-thin fingers which the handcuffs no longer held.

Their eyes met: she understood what he meant.

Rudy pulled down the sleeves of his worn-out jacket; he thought of the days when it had served him in awkward moments; reinforced by his daughter's physical help, his being knew what to do in case of a fight. He had had many fights in his day; he knew where to plant the blows, he knew where the pressure-points were—under the elbow, behind the shoulders, in the groin, and he memorised them, while he and Angela were talking.

'Time for you to go, Madam,' said the gaoler, opening the door.

Rudy didn't wait. At the sound of the gaoler's footsteps nearing stealthily, he had unleashed his hands, and the gaoler, taken utterly by surprise, was lying sprawled, his face hidden by his crash-helmet, motionless, his eyes adrift, on the stone floor.

'Follow me,' said Angela.

Rudy followed her through devious ways where no one challenged them, for every prison has its times off, to a small door beyond which stood a car. Angela's car. They got in and drove away.

Rudy fell asleep; but waking up he asked, not knowing where, or even who he was,

'How did you know the way?'

'Don't ask me,' she said accelerating. 'I've been that way before, more than once.'

Her tone told him something, but not everything; and trying to solve the puzzle, he dropped off to sleep again.

For most of the time Rudy was asleep; he woke up when he saw lights flashing, then he dropped off again.

*

After a few hours they stopped abruptly, and Rudy, waking from his half-dream, said 'Where are we?'

'At the frontier,' Angela replied. 'It's quite all right, Father, I've got your passport, the bearded one,' she laughed, 'which looks quite like you, at least as you used to be.'

Rudy could hardly take in what she was saying, but the customs official seemed satisfied. Rudy, lurching, opening and closing his eyes, couldn't take in what was happening.

Then they were off again, for an hour or more, and it was dark before they arrived.

Angela had to help him out of the car for he wasn't steady on his feet, and didn't know which door to get out of, hers or his, or how to open it.

'Where are we?' he asked.

'Oh, a long way away,' she answered, still carefully lending him her arm. 'They won't find us here. Besides, it's another country. Don't you remember the customs?'

Dimly he did, but though his eyes kept closing, he still remembered, subconsciously, the dangers attaching to a life like his, and the dangers they might involve for other people.

'Is this your house?' he asked, still accepting her aid towards the unlighted windows.

'And will your husband—I can't remember his name—mind? And you have the baby—' He spoke as if the baby might mind, too.

'Oh no, the baby is quite happy. He's asleep now, at least I hope so. And Jacko knows all about it (now). He isn't here at the moment, but he's in sympathy with you, otherwise I couldn't have done—well, what I did do.'

Still, Rudy wasn't quite convinced, and the seven devils who enter in when one has been expelled, began to raise their heads.

'Shall I sleep in the garage? I shall be quite comfortable there, or in that hut in the garden—' Tired as he was he had an instinct for the precautions he ought to take.

Angela opened the front door.

'I shall be bitterly offended,' she said, 'if you sleep anywhere but in the house. And so will Jacko. Your bed is aired—everything is laid on. Now what would you like for supper—a mixed grill, an omelette? or what?—An appetiser of course to start with. There are plenty of them,'—she waved towards the sideboard, where the bottles gleamed, whisky, gin, vodka, each with its special appeal, its message of encouragement to the weary human race. 'Or would you like something else, another sort of cocktail?'

'I would like you,' he said, and before she had time to assent or dissent he had clasped her in his arms. Gently she released herself, and bared her bosom to him for the last time.

PAINS AND PLEASURES

THERE is always room for improvement, but there is not always time for it. Henry Kitson had reached and over-reached the allotted span. In his youth he had been something of a teleologist. An immense and varied field of ambition lay open to him. He would become one with his desires; he would achieve an important and worthwhile aim in which his whole self, all the contents of his personality, such as they were, would be completely and forever expressed.

These aims took different forms. He would climb the Matterhorn (in those days a considerable feat) and, if he had known about it, he would have wanted to climb the North face of the Eiger. He would also play the 'Moonlight Sonata' quite perfectly: the last movement would have no terrors for him. Adding to these achievements he would learn to read, and to speak, at least five languages; his Aunt Patsy, his father's eldest sister, had done so, so why not he? He would reduce his handicap at golf which was 12, to scratch or even to plus something. He would write a book (he couldn't decide on what subject) that would be a classic, immortal: the name of Henry Kitson would resound down the ages.

And he had other ambitions.

Alas, none of them had materialised, and here he was, in the early seventies, with nothing to show for them. He was comfortably off, with a pension from the firm in the City who had employed him for nearly half a century, and with the money he had saved up—for he had not, mentally, grown old with the years; he was not, and could not be, 'his age'; he still regarded himself as the impecunious, ambitious young man he was at twenty-five.

Apart from the tendency which often overtakes elderly men to regard himself as penniless, his situation was most fortunate. He had, as general factotum, a retired policeman, who cleaned his cottage, cooked his meals and drove his car. Wilson ('Bill' to Henry Kitson) was perfect:

he did everything he should, and nothing he shouldn't. In this he was very different from some of his predecessors, who had done everything they shouldn't, and nothing that they should.

Coming at the tail-end of this procession of mainly unsatisfactory characters ('character' was a word used in the old days, but in a different sense, when a prospective employer was asking for a reference) Bill had, of course, for Henry, an overwhelming advantage. After many years of domestic darkness, Bill was the light. Whenever Henry thought of him he gave (if he could remember to) thanksgiving to Heaven for Bill.

At the same time it was a great temptation, as it always is if the opportunity arises, to flog the willing horse. Bill, like Barkis, was willing; and Henry sometimes asked him to do jobs that he would never have dared to ask of any of Bill's less amenable forerunners.

With the advent of Bill, 'a soundless calm', in Emily Brontë's words, descended on Henry. Domestic troubles were over; nothing to resent; nothing to fight against; no sense of Sisyphus bearing an unbearable weight uphill. No grievance at all. Had he lived by his grievances, was a question that Henry sometimes asked himself. Had his resistance to them, his instinct to fight back and assert himself and show what he was made of, somehow strengthened his hold on life, and prolonged it?

Now he had nothing to resist. What Bill did with his spare time—if he occupied it, as Henry suspected, at the pub and the betting-shop, was no business of his. As far as he was concerned, Bill could do no wrong.

But just as someone who has always carried a weight on his shoulders, or on his mind or on his heart and who is suddenly relieved of it, feels in himself a void, an incentive to living suddenly taken away, even so Henry, lacking this incentive, found his life empty, almost purposeless.

Gratitude to Bill was his major preoccupation, but how to express it? Bill was by no means indifferent to money—he liked it and he knew more about it than Henry, with a lifetime's experience of business, did.

Little presents, Bill was not averse to them; but they didn't represent to Henry even a small part of his indebtedness to Bill. Perhaps a bonus of ten per cent for honesty?

Undoubtedly, Henry Kitson's retired and retiring life was the happier for Bill's presence, and for his presents to Bill, but it was also the emptier, now that his grievance had been taken away. Most people need something to live against, and if this objective, positive or negative, is removed, they suffer for it. Henry had friends in the neighbourhood whom he saw as often as he could; but they did not supply him with that extra-personal incentive.

'Live with one aim, but let that aim be high'—or low—which he had had when X, and Y, and Z were ill-treating him, and whose malfeasances, he felt, must be resisted to the ultimate extent of his emotional if not his personal prowess.

With Bill in charge of his domestic affairs, there was nothing at all to be resisted, nothing to aim at—for Bill was a placid, self-contained character, who had seen a lot of the ups and downs of life, and had little to learn from it which Henry, with the best will in the world, could supply.

So this life stratified itself into a routine, pleasant but nearly featureless. There were, however, two features in his day which had an emotional content and significance, and to which he clung, for they represented what he liked, and what he disliked: as long as he stuck to them and could look forward to or dread them, he knew he was keeping the advance of senility at bay.

One was concerned with Bill. Bill in common with many other men, rich and poor, criminal and honest, liked a drink: and Henry saw to it that Bill's 'elevenses' should be a tot of whisky. With all the variations of vocal expression at his command, he would ask Bill if he would like a drink; and Bill, with all the variations of expression at his command, would say 'Yes'. From the time when he was called, at 8 o'clock, Henry looked forward to this little episode. At the word 'drink' Bill's dark eyes would glow, like coals that had suddenly been set alight. 'Good health!' he would say, before he took his glass into the kitchen. Henry never failed to get pleasure from his simple interchange of amenities, just as he never failed to get pain from the other cardinal event of his day, and unfortunately he had longer to anticipate it. This was to put out his cat, Ginger, at bed time. He was fond of Ginger, but Ginger was old and set in his ways, and did not like being put out. Being a neuter, he did not have the same motive that many cats have for prowling about at night, growling and yowling and keeping everyone within earshot awake. He wanted to be warm and comfortable; and although there was a shed and an outhouse in the garden which he must have known about, he preferred Henry's fireside, and when Henry opened the garden door to put him out he would streak past through Henry's legs and sit down in front of the fire, purring loudly and triumphantly.

Henry found this daily or rather nightly ejection of Ginger very painful; but it was inevitable, for with age he had lost whatever housetraining he ever had, and misbehaved accordingly. It fell to Bill's lot to deal with these misdemeanours, which always happened in a certain place, on some stone flags by the cellar-door. Perhaps Ginger thought that his oblations would be more acceptable there than anywhere else; and as someone said, 'it is impossible to make a cat understand that it should do what you want it to do.'

When bed-time approached, Henry picked Ginger up and carried him towards the garden-door, the fatal exit. Then Ginger would purr ingratiatingly, as though to say, 'You can't have the heart to do this.' Sometimes, in rebellious moods, he would struggle and claw and scratch: but the end was always the same; he made a desperate dash to get back into the house. Often the hateful process had to be repeated more than once and Henry peering through the glass door (which he couldn't resist doing) would see Ginger's amber eyes fixed on him with a look of heart-rending reproach.

Henry knew what the correct solution was: *he* should clean up the mess that Ginger made, and not leave it to Bill. But how tempting it is to flog the willing horse! And if ever he yielded to Ginger's protests, whether in the form of purr or scratch, and let him stay indoors, he refrained from asking Bill what had happened outside the cellar-door.

Not that Bill ever complained. When Henry surreptitiously went down to the cellar-door and saw and smelt the unmistakeable traces (however carefully cleaned up) of Ginger's nightly defecations, not a word was said between them.

But as time passed, and the pension-supported Henry came to rely more and more on his daily routine of living, with nothing to jerk him out of it, the problem of pleasure and pain, as exemplified by Bill's whisky elevenses in the morning, and Ginger's compulsory expulsions at night, began to assume undue importance. Henry simply did not *want* his septuagenarian happiness to depend on these two absurd poles of emotional comfort and discomfort.

What *could* he do? Human beings were (so it was generally thought), more valuable and more important than dumb animals (a ridiculous expression, for many animals including Ginger were far from dumb). Certainly Bill was much more valuable to him than Ginger was: Bill was an asset of the highest order whereas Ginger (except for Henry's affection for him) was merely a debit. He was very greedy; he did nothing to earn his keep; he could not, and did not try, to catch the most unsophisticated mouse; he was just a liability and a parasite.

Bill, though such a mild-mannered man, must in his time have been a tough character, and used to dealing with tough characters, criminals, murderers and such, as policeman have to be.

'I wish I knew what to do about Ginger,' Henry said. 'He makes such a fuss when I turn him out at night. But you know better than I do, I'm sorry to say,' (and Henry was genuinely sorry) 'what happens when he stays indoors. It's not his fault, he doesn't mean it, he can't help it, but well, there it is.'

'I know what you refer to, sir,' said the ex-policeman with an instinctive delicacy of utterance, 'and I think I know the solution. Indeed, I have been turning it over in my mind for some time. It's really quite simple.'

'You mean it would be simple to have Ginger put down?'

'Oh no, sir,' said Bill, horrified. 'Nothing as drastic as that. Ginger is a good old cat, he wouldn't hurt a mouse.' (This was only too true.) 'I am attached to him, just as you are, and when I said the solution is quite simple, it *is* quite simple, if you know what I mean.'

'I'm not sure that I do. What *is* the solution?'

'Just this, sir. Give him a box with sawdust in it, and put it where he usually—where he usually does his business, if you know what I mean—and I'll show it to him and then if he doesn't understand at *once*—but he *will*, all cats do. I'll put his paw in it, and he will soon know what it's for—and, and act accordingly.'

'What an excellent idea,' said Henry, a little patronisingly. 'I wonder that I never thought of it. There is an empty seed-box in the greenhouse, I think, that would be just right for the purpose. And sawdust I suppose is quite easy to get hold of.'

'Well, not all that easy, sir,' said Bill. 'But having in mind the ash-tree that fell down, which I am cutting up for firewood, it shouldn't be difficult, in fact I've got nearly enough already.'

'Thank you very much, Bill.'

Ginger was duly introduced to the box, and his paw gently embedded in the sawdust. This he took very well, purring all the time; but when the ceremony of initiation was over, he did not use the box for its intended cloacal purpose, but settled down in it, with his fore-paws tucked under him, and his tail neatly curled round his flank, and went to sleep.

Next day he was discovered still asleep in the sawdust box, but alas, only a few inches away were the extremely malodorous vestiges of Ginger's digestion or indigestion, which the box had been intended to absorb.

'Never mind,' said Bill, 'he'll learn in time.'

But Ginger didn't learn. He spent many hours, sometimes all day, slumbering on his sawdust mattress, purring to himself, no doubt, instead of sitting in front of Henry's comfortable fireplace purring to *him*.

'I'm afraid Ginger isn't going to learn, Bill,' said Henry.

'It looks like not,' said Bill. 'You can't teach an old cat new tricks.' He laughed at this sally. 'But we can give him a few days' grace.'

*

The few days passed, but Ginger did not learn. He still regarded the sawdust box as his bed; and like a well-conducted person, he did not wish to pollute it. It was woundingly evident that he still preferred it to Henry's fireside and that his adjacent loo was very convenient to him.

Henry knew that he himself ought to undo what Ginger had done; but somehow he couldn't bring himself to. 'I am over seventy,' he reasoned, 'and why should I sacrifice myself to the selfish whims of a cat, especially when it has been given every opportunity to satisfy the needs of Nature in other ways?' All the same, he didn't relish the nightly ordeal of turning Ginger out.

'I'm afraid our experiment with Ginger hasn't been successful,' he said to Bill. 'He goes on making a nuisance of himself. I wonder if *you* would mind putting him out at night? He doesn't like it, he claws and clutches at me, but I dare say that with you he would be more—more sensible. Would you mind?'

'Of course not, Mr. Kitson,' replied Bill, who when he remembered, preferred to call Henry 'Mr. Kitson' rather than 'sir'.

*

Days passed; Henry saw little of Ginger, so content was he on his sawdust bed that he didn't bother to visit Henry in the sittingroom. Henry caught fleeting glimpses of him in the garden, tail-twitching, intent on birds which he was far too old to catch. 'Blast him!' thought Henry. 'Ungrateful beast!'

One day there was a knock at his study door. 'Come in!' said Henry, who had always asked people not to knock. 'Come in! Who is it?'

'Oh, *Bill!*' he exclaimed, instantly welcoming. 'What can I do for you?'

He hadn't noticed how upset and how unlike himself Bill looked.

'It's like this, sir,' Bill began and stopped.

'Like what, Bill?' asked Henry, and his heart turned over with a presage of disaster.

'It's like this,' Bill paused, and repeated more slowly and with a note of authority in his voice that reminded Henry that he had once been a policeman, 'It's like this.'

'Like what?' Henry asked again.

'It's like this,' Bill said, and he looked taller under the toplight of Henry's study, and almost as if he was wearing uniform, 'I want to give in my notice. I want to ask for my stamps.'

'But *why*, Bill?' Henry asked, aghast.

'Well, Mr. Kitson, you may think it silly of me, but it's because of Ginger.'

'Because of Ginger?' Again Henry's heart smote him. 'You mean because of the messes he still makes?'

'Oh no, Mr. Kitson. I don't mind them at all. They're all in the day's work, if you know what I mean.'

'Then what *do* you mind?'

'I mind putting him out at night, sir. He claws and clutches and scratches me—you wouldn't believe it. Not that I'd mind with a human being, I've had plenty of people to deal with much worse than he is—after all, he's only got his claws, and I think he's lost most of his teeth, but all the same, I don't like it, sir, and that's why I'm giving in my notice and asking for my cards.'

Henry was not too distraught to ignore the dignity of Bill's resignation.

'What will you do now, Bill?' he asked.

'Oh, well, sir, I shall find something. There are jobs waiting for a single man. I'm not a single man, really, I'm a widower, which is the nearest thing, and I have no ties. I haven't put an advert in the paper yet, but I shall find a job you may be sure.'

Henry, too, was sure he would find another job; but where would he find another Bill? It was all too wretched, but he knew men of Bill's type and they didn't change their minds easily once they were made up.

'Listen!' he said loudly, as if Bill was deaf. 'I don't mind cleaning up the mess that Ginger leaves and I don't mind putting him out at night. I know the way he claws and scratches, but I thought that with you who feeds him, he would behave better than he does with me. It seems that he hasn't, and I am very sorry, Bill, but I shall be only too glad to take him on, eating, sleeping, and whatever else he wants to do—and relieve you of the responsibility.' (Just as Ginger relieves *himself*, he thought but did not say.)

'I couldn't ask you to do that, sir. You have been very good to me, but I shall find a job where there aren't any animals to work for.'

At this rather ungracious remark Henry Kitson groaned again.

'I know I ought not to have left the dirty work to you, Bill,' he said, with the belated contrition that most people feel at one time or another. 'I know I shouldn't have, and if you agree to stay I'll be responsible for everything to do with Ginger, by day or by night.'

'Oh no, sir, I couldn't let you do that, a gentleman in your position. And in any case, it isn't *that* that I mind.'

Henry groaned again. He was utterly at a loss.

'Then what *do* you mind, Bill?'

'I mind putting him out at night, Mr. Kitson. He creates so, you wouldn't believe it, but yes, you would, you've had it so often yourself. It isn't his scratching and mauling I mind, it's when he purrs and tries to pretend I'm doing him a kindness. I'm not that tender-hearted, but I know what it's like to spend a night in the open,' the ex-policeman added.

Henry's eyes grew moist.

'Well, I'll put him out tonight.'

'Oh no, Mr. Kitson, I'll see to him.'

But Henry displayed unexpected firmness.

'No, no, let's leave him indoors. And if anything happens, I'll take care of it.'

'Very good, sir,' said Bill, smartly. 'Good night, sir,' he added, on a note of finality that echoed through the room when he was gone.

*

Ginger was lying in front of the fire, on one of his rare visits to Henry's study since he had yielded to the superior attractions of the sawdust box. He purred, as he always did when Henry so much as looked at him. Every now and then he stretched out his paw, as though trying to make himself more comfortable than he already was. Every now and then he half opened his eyes and looked at Henry with what Henry called his 'beatific' expression, suggesting his mysterious but not unkindly insight into the past, the present, and the future.

'I won't disturb him,' Henry thought, turning out the light, 'let him stay here if he wants to; and if he prefers the cellar-door he knows the way.'

At eight o'clock the next morning Bill appeared as usual, bringing Henry's early-morning tea. He drew the curtains.

'There it is!' he said.

Henry had heard this aubade before, but he was always foxed by it.

'Where is what?' he asked.

'The day,' said Bill.

Henry, nursing again his discomfiture at not having foreseen this obvious answer, sat up and looked out of the window. It was a dreary November day, but Bill didn't seem uncheerful.

'I'm afraid I've some bad news for you,' he said.

Henry tried to collect his waking thoughts. A pall enveloped them. How could Bill be so unkind?

'I suppose you mean that you are leaving?' he said, stretching out his hand for the teapot.

'Oh no, Mr. Kitson, it's much worse than that.'

'What can be worse?' thought Henry miserably, and uttered his thought out loud. 'What can be worse, Bill?'

'It's much worse,' said Bill.

Eight o'clock in the morning is not the best time to receive bad news, and especially if one doesn't know what it is. Henry relinquished the teapot and sank back on the pillow.

'Tell me,' he said.

'Well, Mr. Kitson,' said Bill, with his back to the light, while he was arranging Henry's clothes on a chair, 'to tell you the truth—'

'Oh, do tell me, Bill.'

'To tell you the *truth*,' Bill repeated, as if one sort of truth was more valuable than another, 'Ginger is dead.'

'Good God,' said Henry, who had envisaged some cosmic nuclear disturbance especially aimed at him. 'Good God!' he repeated, with intense relief. And then he remembered Ginger last night, sitting on the hearth-rug and purring loudly whenever Henry vouchsafed a look at him. 'Poor Ginger!' he said.

'Yes, sir, and I feel very sorry about him too. Ginger was a good old cat. Would you like to see him, Mr. Kitson?'

'What, now?'

'Now, or any time. He's there, he isn't far away.'

Henry got out of bed. He put on his dressing-gown and followed Bill downstairs.

'The usual place,' said Bill.

It was dark down there, so they turned on the light. Ginger was lying in his sawdust box, looking quite comfortable and life-like, except that his head seemed to be twisted over.

Henry stooped down and stroked his cold fur and half listened for the purr that didn't come; then he led the way upstairs.

'He seemed so well last night,' he said to Bill.

'Oh yes, sir, but animals are like that, just like human beings, if you know what I mean. Here today and gone tomorrow.'

Henry felt the bitter sensation of loss that we are all bound to feel at one time or another.

'But he seemed so well last night,' he repeated.

'Yes', replied Bill, 'but he was very old. We all have to go sometime.'

An unworthy suspicion stirred in Henry's mind, but he stifled it.

'And now I've got to lose you, too, Bill,' he said.

'Oh no, sir,' said Bill, promptly, 'I've thought it over, and I don't want to go, that is, unless you want me to.'

A wave of relief—there was no other word for it—swept over Henry.

'Please stay,' he said, 'please stay, Bill.'

'Yes, I will, Mr. Kitson,' Bill answered and there was a surge and an uplift in his voice. 'We've got cutlets for lunch—will that be all right?'

His pronunciation was rather odd, and he made it sound like 'catlets'.

*

'Would you like a drink now, Bill?' Henry asked. 'Or is it too early?'

'I won't say no,' said Bill, and the light began to glow behind his coal-black eyes.

PLEASE DO NOT TOUCH

VIVIAN VOSPER was a bachelor who lived alone in a very small mews house in a burglarious part of London. All parts of London are burglarious to some extent, but this one was particularly so. Twice his house had been burgled, and the second time he had been beaten up and tied up by some masked men and had only managed to wriggle himself free from his bonds after an hour or more of skin-abrasive effort and a great deal of physical and nervous discomfort. The police, when he was able to summon them, were very kind and helpful as they always are; they asked him if he was suffering from shock, and he said No, but he was wrong, for no sooner had they left, promising to do their best to find the culprits, than he was seized by uncontrollable shivers, and felt obliged to call in his doctor in the early hours of the morning, a thing he had never done before.

He survived, however, and he hadn't lost much of value for he hadn't much of value to lose; chiefly the drinks he kept on the sideboard, to which the thieves had liberally helped themselves, before relieving themselves, as in the habit of burglars, all over his sitting room floor. With the help of his daily help, who came at eight o'clock in the morning, he cleared up the mess; but the material stink of it, no less than the indescribable smell of violation that any burglary brings, remained with him for several days.

Then there was all the bother of applying to the insurance company for the value of the articles he had lost, not only the bottles of drink, so expensive nowadays—but silver, and vases, and trinkets.

But though he hadn't much minded the first burglary—indeed he was in bed and asleep when it happened and didn't know about it until the morning—he did mind the second, with its violence and its sequel of nervous shock, not to mention the loss of objects that he treasured; and

723

like the hero of Poe's story, 'The Cask of Amontillado', he vowed revenge.

It was the story that gave him his idea, for though he had no cask of Amontillado and no cellar to wall up the miscreants, or the 'villains' as the police sometimes called them—such a quaint old-fashioned word— supposing he had been able to; he had a few bottles of Amontillado sherry which would serve as a bait. He would doctor them; but how, and with what?

As a butterfly-collector many years ago (he was now over sixty) he still had a small phial of cyanide of potassium to refresh (if that was the word) the evaporating supply in the white plaster-of-Paris basis of his killing-bottle. In those far-off days you could obtain the stuff simply by signing the chemist's poison-book; but there was enough of it left to account for several gangs of burglars.

It was so long since he had given up butterfly-collecting and moth-collecting. For some reason he preferred moths to butterflies. Not only because there were so many more of them—two or three thousand compared with a mere seventy species of butterflies. True, some of the moths were very dreary; there was the Wainscot family, the Footman family, each member of those two families being almost indistinguish-able from the other and only of interest in their slightly varied drabness to experts of whom Vivian had never professed to be one.

On the other hand, some of the moths were very exciting. The Oak Eggar, for instance, with its strange capacity (radar-inspired no doubt) for attracting a husband or a wife from many miles away; there were the tiger-moths, so decorative; there was the lappet moth (lasciocampa quercifolia) which Vivian had never succeeded in capturing. And the puss-moths, dear creatures, with their green caterpillars, aggressive and hostile in demeanour, but with their soft silken tongues making impene-trable chrysalis little fortresses out of the hard bark of a poplar tree.

And the hawk-moths of course, all the hawk-moths. More than once it had been Vivian's good fortune to capture the Convolvulus Hawk Moth (sphinx convulvuli), that rare visitant; but never, in spite of diligent study of the potato fields had he ever discovered either the larva or the imago (as they called the perfect insect) of the Death's Head (acherontia atropos) both of which were said to squeak, if disturbed.

Looking at the little poison-bottle, so long disused, he thought of these creatures (now, thanks to chemicals, much rarer than they used to be) which he had loved and yet had doomed to an untimely death, stretched out on a setting-board, the wings that had borne them so freely through the air pinned down at an unnatural angle, and when released from the bondage of the stretching-board transferred to another more elegant mausoleum.

They had died painlessly, of that he was sure; a slight fluttering of wings over the poison-drenched plaster, and all was over. When at one time he had sealed their fate with an infusion, an exhalation of chopped-up laurel leaves, it had been more lingering.

They had done him no harm, no harm at all, and as he thought of their poor bodies slowly decaying under glass-covered shelves in a cabinet which neither he nor any one else looked at, he did not feel happy with himself.

But the burglars *had* done him harm; they had not only robbed him and beaten him up and pinioned him as if he was a moth on a stretching-board, they had callously left him to get free as best he could, or to die if he couldn't. 'Ye are of more importance than many sparrows' Christ had said; and Vivian persuaded himself that he was of more importance than many moths.

He uncorked the little bottle, and cautiously, very cautiously, sniffed its contents. Yes, there it was, that almond-breathing, aromatic, but lethal smell. He snatched his nose away. Better be on the safe side. The moths and butterflies, poor creatures, hadn't been able to snatch their noses or probosces away; they had the stopper of the bottle clamped down on them.

Vivian's mind went over these old memories, from the time when he thought it was almost a personal triumph to insert a crimson-underwing, its helpless wings held tightly between his fingers, into the lethal chamber, a miniature forecast of the gas-chambers employed by Hitler.

'Why am I doing this?' he asked himself as, with the cyanide safely stoppered, he advanced towards the elegant, festive, festive, cheer-inducing bottle of Amontillado. 'Why am I doing it? Is it like me to do it? I have never wanted to hurt anyone before—except a few insects, and I never thought I was *hurting* them, only *collecting* them, as so many naturalists have. Has my nature changed? Have I become a different person just because a few bandits from whom half the people I know, people with far more precious things to lose, have suffered more than I have? Would it not be better,' he asked himself, still with the half empty little bottle in his hand, as he approached the big brim-full bottle of Amontillado, 'to forget all about it? If it is true, as they now say, that violence is inherent in human nature, who am I to resent being its victim? I mean'—he hastily corrected himself—'to resent suffering from it at the hands of other people? Of course if I'—and he looked down at the innocent-looking poison—'were to *retaliate*, it wouldn't be *violence*, it would just illustrate the well-known law that every action has an equal and consequent reaction.'

He took the bottle of sherry and uncorked it. Better drink a glass, he thought, that way it will look more natural. He enjoyed the drink; what a pity (for now his sense of behaving unlike himself was taking the upper hand) to spoil such good wine. Yet spoilt it must be or else—he couldn't finish the sentence even to himself. He took the little bottle—how small it was compared with the big one—and decanted from it into its large neighbour a fragrant tablespoonful, then corked both bottles up.

It's all nonsense, he told himself, it's just a joke. In the morning I shall feel quite different and empty both the bottles down the drain; but in the meanwhile it would be safer to take precautions.

Having written on a stick-on label, in the largest capital letters, 'PLEASE DO NOT TOUCH' he affixed it to the sherry bottle, which he placed in a prominent position on his drink-table so that neither by day nor night could its warning notice be ignored.

He went to bed but not to sleep, for his nervous constitution being unaccustomed to the idea of such a violent emotion as vengeance, avenged itself on him with an attack of acute indigestion, so acute that he wondered if he might not in some moment of misadventure—perhaps when he was decanting the cyanide into the sherry-bottle—have touched the fatal fluid with his finger and 'despatched his finger travelling to his nob,' as Meredith once said—meaning, he touched his head. And from his head it was only a matter of inches to his mouth, and then—

Two or three times during the night he got up and went downstairs into his sitting-room, where he kept the drinks, just to make sure that the bottle was in place, that no mouse, for instance, had nibbled at its cork, for since his butterfly collecting days Vivian had become almost a Buddhist in his dislike of taking life. No, it was untouched and apparently unfingered, though it had begun to assert its presence as if it were the only object in the room. At length, after a dangerously large dose of barbiturates, he went to sleep.

Next morning he woke with the usual sense of presentiment and inability to face the day. As a rule this wore off when he was up and about; but today it lingered. He must offer some explanation of this bottle to his daily help.

'Ethel,' he said, 'have there been any more rats here just lately?'

'Yes, sir,' she answered promptly, 'there was quite a big one in the kitchen and it scared me stiff. These old houses, they breed rats. Ever since I've been with you, sir, these rats have been about, and in my opinion they breed here, down in the basement, where we never go, for it's a darksome place and not nice to go into. If I wasn't that attached to you, sir, I should have given in my notice long ago, for if there's anything I hate, it's rats. And most people feel as I do.'

'I don't like them myself,' said Vivian, looking nervously round the room. 'They give you the creeps, don't they? And they are so artful, almost like burglars.'

'Yes, sir, and as I've often said before, you ought to put down some poison for them. I know it isn't a nice thing to do, but they aren't nice, either. In my flat, which is a modern flat, not like this old place, which may be picturesque but isn't healthy, we don't have rats. If we did, I doubt if any of the tenants who value cleanliness would stay.'

Vivian saw an opening here.

'Well, as a matter of fact, Ethel, I've been thinking over what you said and I had an idea. I've had some poison in my medicine cupboard for many years.' He explained why. 'Now I've put some of it in this bottle of sherry'—he held the bottle up for her to see—'because I believe rats are very partial to sherry.'

'I've never heard that, sir, but they'll eat or drink anything that a human being wouldn't touch.'

Again he held the bottle up for her inspection.

'I've labelled it "Please don't touch." Rats wouldn't understand that'—he gave a little laugh—'but sometimes when we're both out of the house people do come in, window-cleaners, electricians, and such-like—Mr. Stanforth, a few doors away, has the keys, and I trust him absolutely. You know him, don't you?'

'Oh yes, sir, he's an old friend. It was through him I came to you.'

'I'm grateful to him for that, and for many other kindnesses. But what I wanted to say was someone might come into the house with the best of intentions, and seeing this bottle they might be tempted—one shouldn't put temptation into people's way—to have a swig. So I labelled it, "Please don't touch".'

'I'm not sure if that would stop them, sir.'

Vivian saw the point of this.

'There are other bottles'—he waved to four or five—'that they could dip into. Meanwhile, shall we lay a trap for the rats? And if so, where?'

'In the kitchen, I think. That's where they like to come to pick up what they can—not that I ever leave any food lying about. But they have a nose for whatever isn't meant for them.'

'A saucer, do you think? Anything as long as it doesn't poison you or me.'

'I know exactly what, sir. That little Chinese bowl, it won't spill over, however hard they try.'

'Well, take the bottle, Ethel, and we'll see what happens. But be very careful. Hold your breath while you're putting the stuff in.'

She smiled at his scrupulosity, and presently returned with the bottle, its contents diminished by an eighth.

*

Vivian couldn't cook for himself, except a breakfast egg which Ethel generally cooked for him. For his main meals he went out to his club, to which he invited friends, if he had not been lucky enough to be invited by them. Otherwise he lunched or dined alone, in solitary state.

Sometimes, however, he went into the kitchen in case there was some tit-bit that Ethel had bought for him which didn't need cooking. He rather enjoyed these exploratory visits to the fridge. But today— the day of the rat-hunt—having been asked out to dinner, he lunched at his club and didn't go into the kitchen.

The next morning, after a better night than the last, he was greeted by Ethel with a radiant face.

'Do you know what's happened, sir?'

Vivian was mystified.

'No.'

'Would you like to see?'

Vivian, having no idea what he was going to see, said 'Yes, of course.'

After a short interval the door opened and Ethel appeared, with glowing face, holding by its tail an enormous rat, cat-like in size.

'I found it this morning, sir, close by the bowl. It must have been thirsty, because the bowl was half empty, but it couldn't get any further because the poison had done its work. It didn't suffer at all, so you needn't think about that. I'm going to show it to the man what collects the garbage and ask him if he's ever seen such a big one. But I think we ought to put some more sherry in the bowl, in case another comes along.'

The next morning another rodent sherry-addict did come along, and suffered the same fate as its predecessor; it wasn't quite so large, but suspended by its tail it made a considerable impression on Vivian, reclining on his bed.

For two or three days there were no more rodent casualties, and then appeared another larger than the other two.

'They're the talk of the whole mews,' Ethel said. 'Everyone here has rats in one way or another, and they all want to know how you get rid of them. I told them you had a secret, but I wouldn't tell them what it was, sir, even if I knew, without your permission. It's something he puts into a bottle, I said. I wouldn't be surprised if Mr. Stanforth himself came round and asked you—he's that plagued by rats. I didn't say you would be prepared to tell him, sir, because it's a trade secret, as you might say, and you're no professional rat-catcher. But he was most insistent.'

Mr. Stanforth had a flat in one of the mews houses, and was a very useful and valued member of the little street, because most of his neighbours entrusted their door-keys to him, so that if they lost them, as sometimes happened, he was prepared to let them in, at any hour, or if a tradesman called with goods to deliver, or the postman with a parcel when there was no one at home to receive it, Mr. Stanforth took charge and in due course restored the errant object to its owner.

Having been there twenty years he was known to nearly all the residents, most of whom availed themselves of his services, for which he charged no fee but received enough in tips handsomely to augment his pension.

And not only did he know the residents, he knew by name or by sight many of the visitors, many of the tradesmen who served them, and all their daily helps, if they had any. He was in fact a mine of information; he knew far more about everyone in the street than they knew about each other; and being an ex-policeman he had a keen eye for any stranger, especially any suspicious-looking stranger, who invaded its precincts. At the same time he was no night-watchman, and since many burglars, though by no means all, operate by night, he had not been able to detect who were the miscreants who had twice broken into Vivian's house. He did, however, tell Vivian, with whom he was on friendly terms, that he had a clue and was following it up, 'It could have been somebody who knew your house,' he said rather darkly, 'because after they had trussed you up they seemed to know where to look for everything, they got away that quick, or so you told me, Mr. Vosper.'

'You are quite right,' said Vivian, remembering with renewed bitterness the long silence that had followed while he was trying, sometimes hopefully, sometimes despairingly—to release himself from his bonds. 'But I haven't any friends who are burglars.'

'You never know nowadays,' said Mr. Stanforth, 'you never know. Now what was it you wanted to see me about?'

Vivian had almost forgotten why he had telephoned to Mr. Stanforth, asking him to look in if he had a moment to spare.

He looked round his sitting-room, hoping to be reminded.

'Oh, it was this,' he said, taking the sherry-bottle, and holding it up for Mr. Stanforth's inspection. 'It contains some stuff I use to poison the rats.'

Mr. Stanforth's eyes brightened as he took the bottle from Vivian's outstretched hand.

'Of course I've heard about it, sir,' he said excitedly. 'We've all heard about it, and how you've used it to get rid of a dozen rats.'

'Well, not a dozen, but five or six.'

Mr. Stanforth looked disappointed at this reduced number of casualties. 'They're a perfect pest in these old-time dwellings. I suffer from them myself, so I know.' With his hand on the cork he asked, 'Can I take a sniff, sir?'

'Yes,' said Vivian, 'but careful, careful, it's rather dangerous, so I put this on it'—and he pointed to the label, PLEASE DO NOT TOUCH,—'in case someone should come in while I'm out, and be tempted to take a swig. You mustn't put temptation into people's way. You Mr. Stanforth know who can be trusted and who can't, but present company excepted, we all fall into temptation sometimes, especially working-men who get thirsty delivering goods—'

'Oh yes, Mr. Vosper, I know what you mean.'

'You keep tabs on them, as far as you can, but you can't be answerable for everyone, so I thought I'd just tell you.'

'Quite right, sir, and I'll drop a hint where I think it might be useful.' He paused. 'You haven't got the recipe, sir? There are quite a lot of our neighbours, not to mention me, who are plagued with rats, and I'm sometimes asked, "How does Mr. Vosper get rid of his?".'

Vivian hesitated before he explained. 'But the cyanide is hard to get hold of in these days. It happened I had some by me from when I was a butterfly-collector. Chemists are pretty strict about it now. But there's no harm in trying.'

'I'll remember that, sir. You don't mind if I mention this to some of the others who are plagued by rats?'

Oh no, Mr. Stanforth, but just warn them that the stuff is dangerous.'

*

Days passed and nothing happened to disturb the harmony of Rateable House (as Vivian's dwelling was bitterly called). No more rats; doubtless being the most intelligent of animals, with an instinct for survival which we have lost, they had informed their fellows that Rateable House was a place to be avoided. No more scratching and scurrying behind the wainscot; no more wondering if it was a rat or a mouse, or something less tangible but more horrid.

The disappearance of the rats had one effect which Vivian didn't know whether to regret or not: it had taken away Ethel's one subject of conversation. Sometimes she forgot and began, 'If it wasn't for those awful rats—' and then, remembering they no longer existed, fell into an offended silence, as if their absence was an even greater grievance than their presence. 'Those rats,' she once said enigmatically, 'did help to keep burglars away.'

'How do you mean, Ethel?'

'Well, most burglars are frightened of rats, just as you and I are.'

'So they may be, but they can't tell from outside if there are rats inside.'

'They have their own ways of finding out. Rats and burglars are much the same, as you should know, sir. They're both thieves, and they pass on information to each other, we don't know how.'

Soon she discovered new causes of complaint, irregularities in what she felt should be Vivian's fixed routine—clothes omitted from the laundry basket, objects mislaid which had cost her much time, and much waste of time, to track down. But these were only ruffles on the smooth surface of their relationship, protests, demonstrations against his taking her services too much for granted. And more than once she said, 'I will say this, Mr. Vivian, you got rid of those rats, which is more than most of us can do.'

Vivian thought the matter over, and the further away the two burglaries were the less they seemed to matter, and the less likely to recur. A fire may happen twice in the same house, but it won't happen a third time; the principles of probability, though so wayward in their action, for misfortunes seldom come singly, were against it. Vivian increased as far as he could, his antiburglar precautions; he lined his front-door and his two ground-floor windows with wreaths of protective and ornamental iron, as the Venetians, more practical in such measures than we, have always done, and he hoped for the best.

He realized, of course, that in a 'permissive' society, it was the victim, if so he could be called, who was in the wrong. He should have redoubled his efforts to safeguard his property against the very natural and, according to some psychiatrists, the almost laudable efforts of thieves to take it from him. When he came home, after dining with a friend, he surveyed with some satisfaction the intricate ironwork with which he had sought to thwart the thieves in their natural, praiseworthy impulse to get hold of him and his belongings. Permissiveness was the pass-word to today's society; and little as he agreed with it he felt slightly guilty for trying to stand in its way.

On the sideboard in his sitting-room still stood, among the other aperitifs, the bottle labelled 'Please do not touch'. No one had touched it except the rats and they were long ago extinct. When Vivian looked at it and saw the liquid was still half-way below the P of 'Please', he felt relieved and also (why?) a little disappointed.

Then came the night, for it was night about 3 a.m. by his watch, when, the unexpected happened.

From his bedroom which was directly above his sitting-room, he heard noises difficult to describe; stealthy shufflings, furniture creaking, and occasionally a whispered word. What to do now? He crept out of bed, locked his bedroom door, fastened the window as quietly as he could, and returned to bed though not, of course, to sleep. The telephone was by his hand; should he ring the police? No; the intruders would hear and either make off with the swag or break through his bedroom door, enter (breaking and entering!), cosh him and tie him up. The police themselves said that in cases such as these, where dangerous criminals were about, discretion was the better part of valour. Pulling the bedclothes over his head he feigned sleep and only hoped that the tell-tale ticking of his heart would not be heard by those below.

Thus camouflaged from sight and insulated from outside sounds he himself could not hear at all distinctly. But, cautiously shifting the bedclothes, it seemed to him that the sounds underneath had ceased. No doubt the burglars had made off, taking with them what their predecessors had left them to take. Yes, the silence was complete. No use shutting the stable-door after the horse has gone; but Vivian felt that without danger to life and limb he could now dial 999. He explained what had happened; and the police officer said they would be round in a quarter of an hour.

These tidings gave Vivian a sudden burst of confidence, and not only confidence but curiosity. He would like to see what the thieves had actually taken; what they had left would be plain from the cloacal smell when the sitting-room door opened. Holding his nose against that, he gently pushed the door open.

But before he had time to shut it and flee upstairs he had taken in the whole scene, or some of it, the two masked figures bending over a third whose mask had fallen off, and who was lying on the floor with his arms spread out as if crucified, and his legs knotted together, crossed like a Crusader's so that they looked like one. The back of his head was towards the door, his chin tilted upwards. He looked like a butterfly on a stretching-board, and as motionless.

The two men who were bending over him jumped up. 'We'll leave him to you, governor,' said one of them, and before Vivian could answer they pushed him aside, made a dash for the front door which they had presumably forced open, despite its chevaux-de-frise defences, and the next thing he heard, for there was no sound in the room, was the whirr of their car starting up and fading away down the quiet street.

Vivian had little experience of death and didn't know whether the chin-tilted figure on the floor was dead or alive. Alive, he thought, for sometimes it twitched as a butterfly may twitch on the setting-board, long after it is dead. A sort of reflex action. But ought he not to find out? A revulsion seized him; why had this ill-meaning stranger chosen to come and die on him, if dying he was, and not already dead. Standing by the door, rooted to the spot where he had been pushed since he opened it and felt the rush of bodily-displaced air left by the accomplices, he felt an almost invincible reluctance to go further, to investigate further a region of experience as unknown to him as it was distasteful, and forced upon him by events. Yet it was not unknown; not many weeks ago he himself had lain on the self-same stretch of the self-same floor, struggling to free himself from his bonds, and growing feebler with every effort. It was an age of violence; but now it was not he but someone else who was demonstrating it.

Who?

A knock which Vivian didn't hear, and two policemen were in the room. The scene seemed so natural, so usual to them that their expressions hardly altered.

Fortified by their presence Vivian, who had been lingering in the doorway as a means of escape (upstairs? out into the street?), went into the middle of the room, and for the first time looked the burglar full in his upturned face. Distorted as it was, it was the face of a man he knew quite well; not a friend or an enemy, but an acquaintance whom he had sometimes met and exchanged a few words with at cocktail parties. The revelation came as a terrific shock, altering the whole current of his thoughts, and he clutched the table to steady himself.

The sergeant who was bending down with his ear to the burglar's heart, straightened himself.

'I'm afraid he's a goner,' he said, 'but we'll have to call an ambulance. May we use your telephone Mr. Vosper?'

'Of course,' said Vivian, surprised that the sergeant knew his name.

'They'll be here in a few minutes,' said the sergeant, putting down the receiver, 'but meanwhile may I ask you one or two questions?'

'Of course,' replied Vivian, automatically.

'I must tell you that anything you say may be used in evidence.'

'Of course.'

'This man was a burglar, there's his mask to prove it.'

'Yes,' said Vivian, looking down with a distaste that amounted to horror at the frail black object. 'There were two other men with him, also masked, but they made off when they saw me.'

'You were lucky,' the sergeant said. 'And now, Mr. Vosper, can you tell us anything more?'

Vivian suddenly felt faint.

There was whisky on the sideboard and another glass.

'Will you join me in a drink? But for God's sake don't take that one.'

He pointed to the half empty bottle, and the half empty glass, on the table.

'It's against regulations,' said the sergeant, 'but we won't say no,' and the three of them drank their whisky straight.

'Cheers!'

'I take it there's poison in that bottle,' said the sergeant, with his glass to his lips. 'Why?'

'Oh, for the rats. I've had a lot of trouble with rats, everyone in this street has. I've got rid of them all now.'

'All your rats?'

'Yes. Eight of them. Nearly all my neighbours have wanted to know my recipe, but they can't get the proper ingredients.'

'Why? Sherry is easy to come by.'

'Because chemists are more particular now than they used to be.'

For a few moments the three men sipped their drinks in silence. Then the sergeant said to his colleague with a grin,

'Tastes all right, Fred, doesn't it?'

Fred nodded assent.

'But if we both drop down dead,' said the sergeant playfully to Vivian, 'you'll be responsible, you know.'

'Oh no,' said Vivian, trying to fall in with his mood, 'because it isn't against regulations for *me* to drink.'

The sergeant smiled, and still with the smile on his face, looked down at the body crucified on the floor.

'You don't know who it is?' he asked suddenly.

Better not try to deceive the police. 'Yes, I do, he was a man I used to meet at parties, and who came here once or twice.'

'So he knew his way about?'

'I suppose so,' said Vivian. 'But there isn't much to know,' and with an inward-turning gesture he indicated the cramped proportions of his house.

'You didn't let him in, by any chance?' asked the sergeant, looking down speculatively at the body, one of whose outstretched hands, tight-fingered, might have been clutching the sergeant's chair-leg. 'He's a good-looking chap, or might have been once.'

'I don't know what you mean,' said Vivian. 'Between them they forced the door open while I was asleep in bed. That's all I know.'

'Forget it,' said the sergeant soothingly. 'No offence meant, but we have to ask these questions. You'd be surprised, Mr. Vosper, if you knew how many men living alone as you do, complain of burglars who aren't really burglars, but burglars by invitation, so to speak.'

'Then how do you account for the mask?' asked Vivian, looking at the fragile object which a draught from the two open doors was turning backwards and forwards.

'You never know what they'll be up to,' said the sergeant. 'A mask doesn't always mean what it seems to mean. I could be wearing this uniform'—he touched the medals on his tunic—'and not be a policeman at all.'

Vivian stared at him incredulously.

'Yes, it is so, Mr. Vosper, and that's why we can't leave any stone unturned. I'll take this'—and without any appearance of distaste, he stooped to pick up the frail object, which seemed all the frailer between his thick fingers. 'You can't tell me his name, by any chance?'

'I can,' said Vivian, and told him.

'I thought it might be,' said the sergeant, 'I thought it might be. We've had our eye on him for some time.'

'Shall I hear any more from you?' asked Vivian.

'You may—you may. But it won't be serious. You go to bed, Mr. Vosper,' said the sergeant, gently.

'What about the front door?'

'We'll fix it, and have a man on the watch.' He looked at Vivian again. 'You don't remember me,' he said, 'but I came here the other time you were burgled and beaten up and tied up. You were in a pretty bad shape, if I may say so.'

'I don't remember,' said Vivian, 'I don't remember much of what happened after they set about me.'

'I wasn't a sergeant then,' said the policeman, reminiscently, glancing down not without complacency at the three stripes on his sleeve. 'And I hope I shall be a Chief-Inspector before you have to call me in again, Mr. Vosper.'

The bell rang, unnecessarily, since the street door and the sitting-room door were open, and the sergeant's colleague let in two men who from their appearance might have been murderers.

'Just take him up,' said the sergeant, 'I don't think there's any need to be extra careful with him.'

The men bent down and their practised hands lifted the corpse, with as little expression on their faces as if they had been furniture-removers.

All the same, for Vivian, something went out of the room into the clear night air that wasn't a bit of furniture.

'There's nothing more, I think,' said the sergeant. 'You've got rid of the eight rats, or did you say nine?'

'Eight,' said Vivian.

'Well, I hope you won't have any more, Mr. Vosper. But just to make things straight, do you mind if I lock the door of your sitting-room to keep you safe and to let our forensic expert have a look at it? Just a matter of routine. He'll come early in the morning, before you are up, or down, perhaps.'

'By all means,' said Vivian, rising as the sergeant rose. They stood together in the passage, while the sergeant locked the sitting-room door and put the key in his pocket.

'Eight rats are better than nine, aren't they?' he said. 'Goodnight, Mr. Vosper.'

'Vengeance is mine, I will repay, saith the Lord.' Vivian brooded on those words as he went upstairs to take his sleeping tablets. They didn't contain cyanide of potassium, but they were poison, all the same.

Revenge, revenge. It was an emotion as old as jealousy, from which it so often sprang. It was a classic emotion, coeval with the human race, and to profess oneself to be free of it was as de-humanizing, almost as much, and perhaps more, as if one professed oneself to be free of love—of which, as of jealousy, it was an offspring.

How many stories of the past, how many actions of the present, were founded in revenge. Vivian could hardly think of one that wasn't. Even the New Testament, that idealistic vision of the better world, wasn't free from it, or why should Christ have cursed the barren fig-tree? 'Revenge is sweet, and flavours all my dealings,' said, or sang, a character in one of Gilbert and Sullivan's operas, with playful irony, no doubt, but with a substratum of truth.

Vivian had got even with his tormentors, and the guilty had suffered for the guilty. *Ruat coelum, fiat justitia!* Justice had been done, and he, Vivian, had been its instrument.

Was it something to be pleased about, something to be proud of? He didn't know, just as he didn't know if the police-sergeant had accepted his story about the rats. He wasn't afraid of that. His daily help who, unexpectedly sadistic, had cut off and preserved the end of their tails, tail after tail on a string, because she said, and perhaps she was right, that rats didn't need telling twice, still less eight times, that a place wasn't healthy for them. She would confirm it; Mr. Stanforth, the porter, would confirm it; Vivian's rat-infested neighbours who had tried in vain to get his recipe for rat-bane, would confirm it. So the sergeant's suspicions, if he had them, could easily be allayed.

Would the human rats, the burglars who frequented the mews dwellings, be equally perceptive? Vivian asked himself. He couldn't hang up their tails because, as far as he knew, they hadn't any; but they had their bush-telegraph, just as the rats had, and the word would go round.

Vivian rubbed his shoulders and several other parts of his anatomy which still ached and perhaps would always ache from the attentions of the other gang of bandits, how many weeks ago! Well, if one bandit had paid the penalty and was now beyond feeling any ache or pain, so much the better for him. How and why had he fallen into this bad company? Why had he told them—mistakenly—since it had already been looted—that there was something in Vivian's house worth pinching? When he had come there once or twice for a drink, he must have noted an object or two that caught his connoisseur's eye. They weren't there now, nor was his connoisseur's eye, closed for ever in the mortuary.

In his medicine-cupboard, half concealed behind ranks of innocent medicines, was the half-empty bottle of cyanide which the police-sergeant had forgotten to impound.

On an impulse Vivian went downstairs. His sitting-room was locked against him but in the basement he found another bottle of Amontillado.

Corkscrew in hand he carried it up to his bathroom, opened the door and the window and set the tap running. Then with a trembling hand he poured out a measure of sherry into the washbasin and replaced it with one of cyanide.

Who was this? Who was he? A Vivian he did not know. But as he stuck on to the sherry-bottle a label (in red ink this time) PLEASE DO NOT TOUCH, and cautiously sniffed the almond-breathing perfume, he had a sensation of ineffable, blissful sweetness.

HOME, SWEET HOME

IT was his old home all right, as he knew the moment he was inside the door, although who opened it to him he couldn't remember, for in those days of long ago who could remember who opened the door to him? It must have been one of his parents' servants who were often changing, and he himself wasn't a frequent visitor, he had been about the world so much; but the feeling, the sense of the house, as apart from its visible structure—the front hall, the inner hall—were as clear to him as they ever had been: as vivid as a scent, and not exactly a scent but a combination of thoughts, feelings, experiences, an exhalation of the past, which was as vivid to him now, and as much a part of him, as it had ever been.

He didn't ask himself why he was here—it seemed so natural that he should be—and then he remembered that he was expecting a guest—a guest for dinner, a guest for the week-end, a close friend of his, whom his parents didn't know, though they knew about her, and were expecting her, and looking forward to seeing her.

What time of year was it? What time of day? Dinner-time, certainly, for the light that filtered through the big north window was a diluted twilight when it reached the hall, revealing not so much the outlines as the vague, shadowy almost insubstantial shapes of the pieces of furniture he knew so well. And yet his inner mind recognized them as intimately as if they had been floodlit—perhaps more intimately, since they were of the same substance as his memory.

But while he was still under the spell of their rather ghostly impact on his consciousness, his awareness of himself as expressed in them, another thought, more practical and more immediate, penetrated it—where was Helen Furthermore, for she was the object of the exercise, and the reason why he had returned so unexpectedly to his old home? She needed looking after, and it was his job to look after her, for she did not know the rest of the party, who he somehow divined, were his relations, mostly older than himself, but he couldn't be sure, for he hadn't seen them— but they must be somewhere about—nor did they know her.

She might be late, of course, but she wasn't often late; she prided herself on not being late, but perhaps the taxi they had ordered for her— they must have ordered one—hadn't recognized her at the station, and she was wandering to and fro outside its precincts, with the desolate feeling that the non-met visitor has—what to do next, where to go next—for there wouldn't be another taxi at that wayside station. He could almost see her passing and repassing her little pile of luggage— not so little, for she never travelled light—growing more indistinct with each encounter in the growing gloom and more indistinct to herself, also, as the question of how to reach her destination grew more and more pressing until it began to occupy her whole being.

And then, quite suddenly, there she was—not in front of him, but behind him and round about him, a presence rather than a person. Someone must have let her in, as he had been let in, he couldn't quite remember how, because the front door opened on a little hall divided by a pair of glass doors from the middle hall where he was standing.

But it was she all right. He turned and recognized her not so much by her face, for it was covered by the dark veil she sometimes wore, but by the unmistakeable shape that was as much a part of her personality as she herself was.

'Valentine!'

'Helen!'

They must have exchanged those salutations and no doubt others, in a medium for him and perhaps her, of uncontrollable relief as if some terrible disaster had been providentially averted. He didn't see how, but he had the impression, that her impedimenta had been suitably removed; and the next thing was a compulsive necessity—for his mind could only harbour one idea at a time—to introduce her to her fellow-guests.

Why should they be in the dining-room and not the drawing-room? He didn't know; but he took it for granted that they were, and he was right, for when he opened the door for Lady Furthermore, he saw them all under the bright light of the chandelier, six or seven of them, seated round the dining-table, which was not laid for dinner, but rather like a board-room table surrounded by directors (bored indeed, for goodness knew how long they had been sitting there).

They all looked up and Valentine, who felt he must make an apology for himself as well as an excuse for her, said 'Here we are, late I'm afraid. This is Helen Furthermore,' and he was retreating behind her to let her make the effect which she always made, when the lights went out and the room was filled with darkness.

What to do now? Valentine's social conscience was still in the ascendant; come what might, he must introduce Helen to her fellow-guests. But how, when they were invisible even to him? No doubt the light would come on again. But it didn't, and meanwhile there was a slight muttering round the table which boded no good, as though Valentine himself had fused the lights.

It did not seem to surprise Helen to be ushered into an almost pitch-dark room, with in the middle a vague impression of heads and forms ranged round an oblong table. But she was noted for her social tact which had served her on many occasions more important, if less surprising than this; and Valentine, taking courage from her acceptance of it, with the additional encouragement of her hand in his, which no-body could see, began a tour of the table.

'Who are you?' he asked, bending over the first head that presented itself, if presented be the word, in the gloom.

'I'm your Uncle Eustace.'

'Uncle Eustace, this is Lady Furthermore,' (he hadn't meant to give her her title, but the situation seemed to demand it) 'who has come to spend the weekend with us, as I'm sure you know. May I introduce you to her?'

The head turned round, showing a pallid cheek, that certainly recalled Uncle Eustace.

'Of course, my dear boy, I am very happy to meet Lady Furthermore. I hope she will forgive me for not getting up, but in this darkness I feel I am safer sitting down.'

His voice quavered. How old could Uncle Eustace be?

'Please don't move,' said Lady Furthermore. 'I look forward so much to seeing you when . . . when the lights let me.'

Always groping, she and Valentine advanced a step or two. Then Valentine bent forward over a bowed head.

'Who are you? Please forgive me asking, but it's so dark I can't see my hand before my face—or your face,' he added, hoping it sounded like a joke.

'I'm your Aunt Agatha.'

It was rather annoying that 'they' should recognize him and not he them. But voices change; hers sounded very old.

'Dear Aunt Agatha. I am so glad to see you—at least I should be, if I *could* see you!' The joke, as he knew, fell rather flat. 'But I want to introduce you to a great friend of mine, Lady Furthermore, who has come to spend the weekend with us.'

'Lady Furthermore? I seem to know that name.'

'Yes, I'm sure you do.'

'She was a child when I—'

'I've always been a child,' interposed Helen, 'and I know that when we really see each other—'

'Yes? Yes?' said the old lady, who was obviously a little deaf.

'You will realize that you have weathered the storm better than I have.'

'Oh nonsense,' the old lady said. 'I can't see much, I couldn't, even if it wasn't dark—but I've never seen a picture of you since I don't know when that didn't look like what you have always looked like.'

'Thank you,' Helen said, more moved than she cared to show, but what matter since it couldn't be shown.

Together the two went on, addressing and being addressed, till they came to the chair at what must be the head of the table.

'Forgive me,' said Valentine, 'but who are you, if I may ask?'

'I'm your father.'

It took Valentine several moments to recover himself. He wondered if Helen had heard. 'Dear Daddy,' he began, 'this is a great friend of mine, Lady Furthermore. You've often heard me speak of her—'

At this moment there was an extraordinary noise between a crash and an explosion, and lights broke out, where it was impossible to say. Yet they were not lights in the sense that they banished the darkness: they were blue flares, wedge-shaped like arrows, piercing the room from end to end. And Valentine said to himself, 'Of course, it's the gas!' For many years ago, when the lighting of the house had been changed, much against his father's wish, from gas to electricity—'gas gives a much better light,' he used to say—he had a gas-bracket left in every room in case the electricity broke down, as he rather hoped it would. And now the gas—not like ordinary gas, but like flares at an old-time fair—was penetrating the room from every angle, blue arrows that like lightning flashes revealed nothing except themselves, and a sickly sheen of terror on the faces round the table.

Valentine grasped Helen's arm. 'Let's get out of here!' he said, and in a moment they were safe in the hall without apparently opening the dining-room door or shutting it.

Out of sight, out of mind. Valentine's memories of what had just taken place, perhaps from the excitement of the moment which often obliterates the details of a sensational happening, perhaps from some other cause, were already growing dim; they hadn't quite passed away, they had left a residue—of feeling? of sensation? of subconscious conviction?—that still lingered. The house didn't belong to him as he now realized, for there were other claimants. But he never suspected that it still belonged to his father. And this added very much to his new and growing preoccupation. Whoever might own the house, Helen was his guest as they all knew; and so far she had been treated very scurvily. She had not been shown her room: where was it? Upstairs, of course, but which room, the East Room? the South Room? When he tried to think of the bedroom accommodation and its access to bathrooms his mind became confused. All this should have been arranged by whoever the house belonged to, his father presumably, for his mother was long since dead—or was she? She was not at the table with him, at least he didn't think so, for he had not had time to complete his tour of introductions round the table before the gas fireworks began. Somebody would know, of course; but where was somebody? Where was anybody? He had an invincible reluctance to re-enter the dining-room with its shafts of blue light (*those* he *could* remember) playing on the upturned, frightened faces of his elderly relations and perhaps setting the house on fire despite his father's faith in the innocuousness of gas.

The residue of these happenings in his sub-memory affected his new preoccupation. Helen had not been treated in a guest-like manner, and above all she had not been offered a drink. A long cross-country journey and she had not been offered a drink! She must need one terribly, just as he wanted one terribly; her throat must be parched as his was, and with more reason for (so his mental map told him) she had travelled much further than he.

But what sort of drink would she like? That was one besetting question. A gin and vermouth, a dry martini, his mind kept repeating. But how could he ask her when he didn't know where the drinks, if any, were kept? And would a dry martini be specially welcome to someone whose system, like his own, was already on the dry side? Vaguely, incoherently, came back to him the memory of his visits to her, when drinks of all sorts were immediately offered, and every provision for his comfort had been arranged beforehand. And now this. He couldn't quite remember what happened after her arrival; he didn't want to, it was too mortifying, too humiliating. Could inhospitality have gone further?

Where was she now? If she had vanished into the comparatively hospitable night, small blame to her; but no, she was somewhere about, though he couldn't always locate her: sometimes at his back, sometimes on his left side, sometimes on his right, never in front, because in front of him was the large brass bowl? urn? container? which housed, as it always housed, the King Fern (*Osmunda Regalis*)—such a beautiful name, and it did not suit her. If only she would stop flitting and fluttering and let him have more than a side-glimpse of her! If only she would be more *stable*—for in ordinary life she was as stable as an anchor. At last she settled, like a butterfly; like a butterfly she was captive under his net.

'Helen,' he said, trying to see her expression under her veil, 'I feel so distressed about your visit, but I really couldn't have foreseen what was going to happen' ('and I can't now,' he might have added). 'But what particularly worries me is that you haven't had a *drink*. You must need one after your long journey, and I *want* one,' (this sentence had been repeating itself in his mind). 'But how, and where are they—the drinks I mean? The people are somewhere in the dining-room.'

He understood Helen to say she didn't care if she had a drink or not; but he didn't think this was true, and he himself was assailed by an appalling thirst.

Suddenly he had an idea which seemed like an inspiration flooding his whole being. The drawing-room, of course! Why hadn't he thought of the drawing-room? Before, it had appeared quite natural that Helen and he should have been received (welcomed was not the word) at a bare board in the dining-room; now it did seem strange when the drawing-room, the traditional place for hosts whoever they might be to greet their guests, was still available. And a vision of the drawing-room at once crossed his mind, with its cheerful yellow wallpaper counteracting its cold northern aspect, *and*, most important of all, in the right-hand corner facing the door, a gate-legged table bearing a tray of glasses and drinks, most of them non-alcoholic, for his father belonged to a generation which had not heard of dry martinis, but had heard of whisky and sherry. Better whisky or sherry than nothing. The drawing-room was, for the moment, the only solution.

'Helen,' he repeated to the face under the veil, 'let's go into the drawing-room. We might find something there, something to drink I mean. And at any rate we shall be by ourselves.'

He thought her slight inclination of the head signified assent and so he led the way, up four steps and then to the right, to the drawing-room door with its pseudo linen-fold panels which were difficult to see because his father, economical in most ways, was especially economical about the use of artificial light.

Imagine their surprise, therefore, when the door opened to reveal a blaze of light—no fuse here—illuminating every part of the room from corner to corner and from cornice to cornice, and not least the crossbeams in the ceiling which an Italian craftsman, early in the last century, had concealed beneath intricate designs in stucco. But before Valentine had time to do more than realize that the gate-legged table in the corner was still there, his eyes were astonished by another sight. So far, being of an acceptant nature, he had taken everything that happened for granted, but now—!

There were six or seven little beds in the room, arranged side by side or end to end; and in each was a child, of indeterminate age and sex, asleep. Asleep when he and Helen came in; but when the light shone on their eyes they began to rub them, and having rubbed them, to set up a pitiful wail, each child taking it up from the next.

Beneath her veil which was so thick that even the brilliant light could not penetrate it, Helen's face was unreadable. I must get her out of this, he thought; this is worse than the dining-room. 'Please sit here,' he said, indicating a stiff-backed armchair which besides being the only chair in the room, commanded a view of the various beds, 'and I'll sit here,' and he sat down on the edge of the bed of a squalling child.

But before he and Helen had time to consult each other, or take in more than a tossing sea of bedclothes, a figure entered the room. It was a hospital nurse, dressed as such.

'What on earth are you doing here?' she asked.

Valentine, for the first time in many years, lost his temper.

'And what on earth are *you* doing here? What right have *you* to be here? This may not be my house, but it is the house of my family, the Walkovers, have you ever heard of them?'

The Sister touched her forehead, a gesture that might have meant anything.

'Yes, I have heard of them. Many years ago the Corporation—'

'The Corporation? *What* Corporation?'

'The Corporation. They bought this house from a family called Walkover, for a home for disturbed children.'

'Disturbed children?'

'Yes, here are some of them. And I can tell you that your unwarranted presence here is disturbing them more.'

Wails and screams gave credence to her words, but they only exasperated Valentine.

'I don't believe you for a moment,' he said. 'My relations are downstairs, and I'll fetch them up to tell you you are trespassing. Trespassing, do you hear?'

Having to make this scene in front of Helen aggravated his indignation. 'I'll order you to get out,' he shouted, 'and leave this place to whom it belongs. I came in here to get a drink for my friend Lady Furthermore—'

He wouldn't subject Helen to the indignity of introducing her to the Sister.

'There is some milk on the table in the corner,' the Sister said, 'and you are welcome to it, if you don't make too much noise.'

Valentine went to the table, seized a bottle of milk and hurled it at the Sister. A whitish streak, half fluid, half powder, such as might have been exuded by a bomber in the intense cold of the stratosphere—a sort of Milky Way—followed, until the missile struck the chandelier, and for the second time that night, darkness prevailed.

Helen was still with him; how they got out of the room he didn't know; how they got out of the house he didn't know; but he did know, or thought he knew, that he had put her on a train to somewhere.

'Where am I?' he thought, and then a sense of his proper environment—his bed—came back to him. 'But why am I so thirsty?' for he was longing, as never before, for a dry martini. 'Oh for a dry martini!'

The experience must have been real, from its mere physical aftermath; for never before had he woken up at night pining for a drink. He sat up in bed; where were the ingredients? They were downstairs behind a locked door; and the only thirst-quencher at hand was a long-opened bottle of sherry. He turned over and gradually his throat and tongue resumed their normal functions. 'I must have imagined it all,' he thought, 'and I hope that Helen has imagined it, too.'

With a vision of her stranded on some wayside railway platform, drinkless, even milk-less, it took him a long time to go to sleep.

'Anyhow,' he thought, 'she is well rid of Castlewick House.' He hadn't remembered the name of his old home until now.

THE SHADOW ON THE WALL

MILDRED FANSHAWE was a bachelor woman in her early forties. She was an interior decorator, and valued as such by quite a wide circle of customers and friends. But she was better known, to most of them, by her neuroses. Of these she pretended to make fun, just as they, without pretending, made fun of them to her. 'Have you seen a single magpie lately, Mildred? I mean a magpie without a mate?' 'Have you seen the new moon through glass?' 'Have you broken a looking-glass?'—'You must have, because looking-glasses are part of your stock-in-trade,' and so on.

If such enquiries were half teasing, they were also meant to be therapeutic, a way out for Mildred from the tyranny of her superstitions—if tyranny it was. Her friends were too fond of her to think she was making them up, much as they laughed at them. Laughter, even unkind laughter, they thought, is one way of curing an obstinate obsession.

But much as friends may laugh at you and much as you may laugh at yourself, it isn't an inevitable cure for something—difficult to define, more difficult to avow—which has got well below the surface.

Naturally in the course of business Mildred was asked to spend half-days or days or weekends with her clients or would-be clients. The day-by-day visits she didn't mind, indeed looked forward to them; but she rather dreaded the weekends, because when she was left to herself, especially in a strange house, her irrational fears were liable to get the better of her.

Her friends knew of this peculiarity and were tolerant and sympathetic, even while they smiled at it. 'We must have the house exorcised before we ask Mildred to stay!'

Joanna Bostock was a good customer and a good friend. Mildred had worked for her and knew her house well—that is to say, she knew parts of it well. The entrance hall was supported on each side by two honey-coloured columns that divided the main structure of the ground floor. To the right was the large dining-room with two long windows balancing the façade of the house; to the left was the main staircase, with its stained-glass windows, of Victorian date, and to the left of the staircase, a library and a drawing-room from whose doors, sometimes shut and sometimes open, Mrs. Bostock and her guests, when she had any, parted for the night, slowly going upstairs, politely making way for each other—'No, you, please'—until the hall was left unoccupied and Mrs. Bostock, or her butler, if she had one, turned out the light.

Mildred had been to Craventhorpe many times in the exercise of her profession, and knew its outside well. Around an oval patch of lawn crowned by a fountain said to be by Bernini, which was supposed to play but never did, a gravel sweep led to the front door. Long, low, and built of the most beautiful pink-red brick, this was the aspect of the house which was meant to catch the beholder's eye. Leaving her car, Mildred, who was by nature over-punctual, would sometimes walk to the left, where the west wing of the house, no less beautiful than the front, overlooked the garden and the tulip-tree, a truly monumental arboreal adornment which many people (for the house was sometimes open to the public) came from far to see. How it soared into the air! How its blossoms, not very like tulips, but near enough, gave it an exotic, an almost fabulous appeal! It was said to be the tallest tulip tree in England. Be that as it might, Mildred could never look at it without awe.

Generally, at this point, where the garden sloped down to a duck-pond, where the ducks were said to drown their redundant offspring, Mildred would turn back to the front door to announce her arrival.

But sometimes she made a circuit of the house. Its northern and its eastern aspects were very different—they were its *back* parts, they were almost slums! Joanna had never asked Mildred what to do with these outside excrescences, botched up at such or such a date and, architecturally, not fit to be seen. It was not true, as some people said of seventeenth- and eighteenth-century builders, that they couldn't go wrong. They built for show, for outside or for inside effect. And if it didn't show, they couldn't care less.

Craventhorpe was built in the shape of a hollow E; and the hollow, over which the architects had taken no trouble, was an eyesore to Joanna Bostock. What to do with it? Make it a sanctuary for wild birds? But they had the pond to disport themselves on or in and indulge their instincts. (She was fond of animals of all sorts.) Or grass it over? Or make it a miniature maze with an occasional garden statue, naked except for being bearded, leering over the edge of the hedge at the visitors laughing, but half frightened, by their efforts to find their way out?

Joanna hadn't consulted Mildred about this outside job, which didn't need curtains or carpets or colours for the walls; nor had she consulted her about the east wing, one side of which looked down on the empty space, and was seldom used except for children and grandchildren. (Joanna was a widow whose husband, dying young, had left her the house and the children to go with it.)

*

Afraid of arriving too late, afraid of arriving too early, Mildred was the first guest to be announced. (For some reason she was relieved that Joanna had found a temporary butler.)

After the usual embracements, 'Darling,' Joanna said, 'I am *so* glad you came before the others. Now come and have a drink, I am sure you need one.'

She led the way to the library where the drinks stood on a glass tray with gilt handles, a glittering array.

'Now what?' she asked. 'Which?' She had a way of making invitation seem still more inviting.

'Oh, a very little for me,' said Mildred. 'Just some Dubonnet, perhaps.' Joanna poured it out for her, and whisky on the rocks for herself.

'Darling,' she said, 'I'm very glad you came early—you could never come *too* early—' She paused and added, 'You've never stayed here before, have you? I wonder why?'

'Perhaps because you never asked me,' said Mildred, sipping her drink.

Her hostess frowned. 'Oh no, I'm sure I've asked you scores of times. But you're always so much in demand.' She paused again, and poured out another tot of whisky. 'Isn't it awful how this grows on you? Not on you, dear Mildred, who dread nothing,' she laughed, a little tipsily. 'Not even a *mill*, and we haven't one round here, not to speak of, unless you dread a *thousand* things?' She laughed. 'Now what was I going to say?' She seemed to rack her memory. 'Oh, yes, our other weekend guests. I won't say who they are, even if I could remember, but you know most of them, and they will be overjoyed to see you, even if you—'

She stopped, and Mildred remembered Joanna's reputation for forgetfulness.

'So we *should* be eight for dinner, and I hope we shall be, but there's a man I can't rely on—he has some sort of job, half international, I suppose—you wouldn't know him, Mildred. He's called Count Olmütz—'

'No, I don't remember that name.'

'Well, he's an old friend of the family if I can call myself a family.'

'Oh, Joanna.'

'Yes, I mean it. But what was I going to say?'

'I've no idea.'

'Well, this man Olmütz should be coming in time for dinner'—Joanna glanced at the clock, which said 6.30—'if it's only to make the numbers even. We can have general conversation, of course, and you are so good at it, dear Mildred, but eight is a better number than seven, more cosy—and he has a lot to say, too much perhaps. But what was *I* going to say?'

'I've no idea.'

'Oh, now I remember,' Joanna said. 'I know you don't much like staying away from home.'

She stopped and gave Mildred a piercing look. 'But what I wanted to say was, you needn't feel nervous in *this* house. You have done *so* much for it, you know it so well. Indoors it's your creation, except for that eyesore that looks down on the courtyard—'

'I've seen it, of course,' said Mildred. 'I know the rest of the house much better.'

Voices could be heard in the hall.

'Well, what I wanted to say,' said Joanna hastily, 'before the immigrants break in, was, that in case you should be nervous in that long, rather lonely passage, I've put Count Olmütz in the room next yours, to keep you company, so to speak.'

'Oh,' said Mildred smiling, 'then I ought to lock my door?'

'Oh *no*,' said her hostess, apparently shocked. 'He's not at all that kind of man. I put him there well, as a sort of background, background music. He doesn't sing, but I'm afraid he might *snore*.'

'I remember the passage,' said Mildred, drawing her wrap round her, for the house, like many country houses, wasn't overwarm. 'You never asked me to do it up—perhaps you didn't want it done up?'

'Oh, I think it must look after itself,' said Joanna carelessly. 'A house is a hungry beast, and the more its appetite can be kept at bay the better. But there was something I wanted to say to you—can you remember what it was?'

'I've no idea.'

'Oh, now it comes back to me. This old friend of mine, Count Olmütz, is—what shall I say?—a man of irregular habits. Now, don't look alarmed, Mildred—not irregular in *that* sense, or I shouldn't dream of putting him within ... within striking distance of you. No; I mean he's irregular in relation to the time-factor. I never quite know when he is coming, and I don't think he knows himself.' She heard a sound and looked round. 'Could that be a car driving up? Well, it might be him, coming back from one of his errands, his missions as he calls them. I hope he will be here for dinner because he's so amusing and will make our numbers even, but if he isn't, *tant pis*! He drives himself and may arrive at *any* time. We have that arrangement—*c'est entendu*—and the front door is always left open for him.'

'What, always, every night?' asked Mildred. 'Aren't you afraid of burglars?'

'Oh no, just at weekends, when he's able to get away. But he never knows when he can, and sometimes he arrives in the small hours. He's not in the least like a burglar. But if you happen to hear a noise in the night it will just be him, turning in, so to speak.'

Mildred thought this over.

'By turning in, you mean—'

'Oh, just dossing down for the night.'

'But won't he be rather disappointed,' asked Mildred, faintly malicious and slightly apprehensive, 'to find himself relegated, exiled to the eastern side? I mean,' she said boldly, for in these days one could say anything, 'wouldn't he rather be nearer *you* than act as the *preux chevalier* of an unknown female, in a remote quarter of the house?'

'No,' said her hostess, 'decidedly not. There are a good many reasons why not. I needn't go into them, but I can assure you that for everyone concerned, *for everyone concerned*,' she repeated firmly, 'it is the best arrangement. Listen,' she added suddenly, 'didn't you hear something?'

'You asked me that before,' said Mildred. 'There are so many sounds.'

At that moment the door opened and the butler said,

'Mr. and Mrs. Matewell, Madam,'

Joanna hastened towards them.

'Oh, darlings, I hope you didn't have too bad a journey?'

'Oh not bad at all,' said Mr. Matewell, a burly figure with a roundish squarish head to match, and dark hair growing sparser. 'Not bad at all except for a slight incident on the M4 which I'll tell you about.'

'Thank goodness it was no worse,' said Joanna, fatuously. 'Now here is Mildred, you all know each other.'

'Of course, of course. The maker of the home beautiful!' Mildred smiled at this pleasantry as best she could.

'And before we have drinks,' said Joanna, 'which I'm sure you must both be pining for'—and she led them towards the drink-tray—'shall I tell you who else is coming?'

'Please do!'

'The MacArthurs, that makes us six, Peter Pearson, such an invaluable man, seven, and . . . and—'

'Who is the eighth?' asked Mrs. Matewell, noting her hostess's hesitation.

'Oh, an old and great friend of mine, Count Olmütz. I don't think you know him.'

'No, but we've heard of him, haven't we, George?' said Mrs. Matewell, appealing to her husband, who seemed slightly at a loss. 'And we're longing to meet him, aren't we? He sounds such a romantic character. Didn't he own the house before you had it, Joanna?'

'No, he didn't own it,' said Joanna, shaking her head vigorously, 'he didn't own it, but he had something to do with it, I don't quite know what. I've sometimes asked him, but he's rather reticent. He may be here any minute and then perhaps he'll tell us. Ah, that may be him.'

It turned out, however, to be the MacArthurs, with the invaluable Peter Pearson. 'Weren't we lucky?' Mrs. MacArthur said. 'Peter phoned us this afternoon and asked us if we were coming to you. I don't know how he guessed, but Peter knows everything.' Peter looked somewhat abashed but Mrs. MacArthur said 'We were only too glad to give Peter a lift.'

They settled down to their drinks and Peter turned out to be the life and soul of the party. 'I wish I could be two men,' he said, 'instead of half a man' (this shameless admission only evoked a giggle), 'because you're expecting another man, aren't you, Joanna, a real tough man.' He shuddered, albeit selfconsciously.

'I don't think we'll wait for Franz,' said Joanna. 'He's so unpredictable.' She tried to keep the irritation out of her voice. 'Don't change unless you want to, but let's have our baths—if we want to. Dinner about eight.'

*

Dinner was a pleasant meal and no one worried unduly about the absent Franz—indeed, none of them except Joanna knew who he was. They had only heard tell of him, and if Joanna worried about him she didn't show it. Once, when his name came up, 'He's a law unto himself,' she said. About eleven o'clock they all retired for the night. 'You know your way?' said Joanna to Mildred.

'Oh yes, it's along the main passage, and then to the left.'

'I'll come with you,' said Joanna. 'Your name's on the door—I keep that old-fashioned custom—but you might not see it in this poor light. I hope your room won't be *too* uncomfortable—the bathroom is just opposite.'

They stopped where a sort of visiting card stuck to the door, 'Miss Mildred Fanshawe', made clear whose bedroom it was. 'And Franz is next to you,' she added, indicating his name-card, 'Count Olmütz'. 'Don't worry if you hear noises in the night. He sometimes comes in late. I'll leave the light on in the passage to guide him on his way—if it's turned out, you'll know he's arrived. Here is the switch if you want it, but I hope you won't. Goodnight.' and Mildred found herself alone in her bedroom.

It was a comfortable room, with a wash-basin and mid-Victorian water-colours on the walls, but to Mildred's expert eye it sadly needed doing up—it was 'tatty'. Suddenly she had an almost irresistible impulse to look at the room of Count Olmütz, her next-door neighbour.

She would know if he had materialized because if he had, the passage would be in darkness. But would it be? Might he not have forgotten to turn the light off? So unpredictable . . . . Just one little peep behind the scenes . . .

But not now. It could wait. She must get ready for bed, a long ritual which included a bath. She always took a bath last thing, because it was said to be good for insomnia, and she had her face to do up. All this made bedtime a moment of crisis, a culmination of instead of a calm from the day's worries, which good sleepers have never known.

When she opened her door the darkness was almost blinding. She switched on the passage light and saw, outside her stablemate's door, a pair of large muddy suede shoes. So the Count had arrived and she must restrain her curiosity. In English houses, thought Mildred, visitors don't leave their shoes outside the door, as they do in hotels—it's a sort of *nuance* that a foreigner might not know. The shoes were so muddy they needed cleaning, and no doubt the butler—the temporary butler—would see to that.

Why hadn't she noticed the shoes before? Mildred asked herself. And then she remembered that soon after she retired to her room, the lights in the passage had been turned off. Now they were on again—of course, she herself had turned them on.

What a fool I am, she thought, what a fool! But it wasn't the prospect of his over-large shoes which deterred her from knocking at his door, it was just his name on the plain card, fastened between four tiny triangles of brass, that made her hesitate.

She went back to her adjoining room, relieved as everyone is from the danger of self-exposure. She went through her customary bedtime ritual—with her a long process—but she knew she wouldn't sleep if she didn't. 'I'll have a bath first,' she thought, 'and then a sleeping pill.' Insomnia was her bugbear.

The water was still hot—in some country houses it cooled down after midnight—and she lay with her eyes half-closed and she herself half asleep, in a bath of chemically-enriched foam. 'Oh to die like this!' she thought, though she didn't mean it. Some of her neuroses she had managed to overcome—the claustrophobia of travelling in a crowded train, for instance—and some she hadn't. A friend of hers had died in her bath of a heart attack. There was a bell over the bath (as used to be the custom) but when help came it was too late.

There was no bell over this bath, supposing there had been anyone to answer it, but Mildred had long made a principle of leaving her bath-room door ajar. If someone came in—*tant pis*—she would shout, and the intruder, man or woman, would of course recoil.

It was well known that a hot bath was good for the nerves—so useful to have medical authority for something one *wanted* to do!

Mildred was luxuriating under the aromatic pine-green water, her limbs indistinct but still pale pink, when a shadow appeared on the shiny white wall facing her. It might have been someone she knew, but who can recognize a shadow?

It was Mildred's habit—unlike most people's—to have her bath with her head to the taps—and the shadow opposite on the gleaming wall, grew larger and darker.

'What do you want?' she asked, feeling a certain physical security under her opaque covering of foam.

'I want *you*,' the shadow answered.

But had he really spoken? Or was it a voice in a dream? There was no sound, no other sign, only the impress of the face on the wall, which every moment grew more vivid until its lips suddenly, like the gills of a fish, sprang open towards its snout.

Nobody knows how they will behave in a crisis. Mildred jumped out of the bath shouting. 'Get the hell out of here!' And for the first time in many years she locked the bathroom door.

That would settle him!

But it hadn't, for when she came back from her physical and mental encounter with the key and looked round her with the ineffable relief of having done something that was hard to do, she saw the shadow, perhaps not so distinct as it had been, but with the upturning fish-like gills clearer than it was before.

So her way of escape was blocked: she was a prisoner now.

But what to do?

She got back into the cooling bath and turned on the tap—but no doubt in response to thermostatic control, the hot water was cooling too. Cold when she got out of it, she was colder than when she got in. Meanwhile, those thin, fishy lips gnawed at something she could not see.

Courage begets courage. 'I won't stand for this,' thought Mildred. 'I won't spend the night in this freezing bathroom' (actually it wasn't cold, but it felt cold to her). 'Take this, you beast!' and she flung her sponge at the shadow. For a moment its profile, which was all she had seen of it, was disturbed until the thin lips resumed their yawning movement.

What next? She hadn't brought her dressing-gown into the bathroom, it hadn't seemed necessary: she wrapped her bathtowel around her, unlocked the door, and plunged into the passage. The light was on; had it been on when she crossed the passage to the bathroom, half an hour, or an hour, ago? She thought not, but she couldn't remember; time was no longer a measure of experience to her, as it was after breakfast, with recognizable stopping-places—so long for letters, so long for her job, so long before lunch—if there was time for lunch. Nearly everyone divides their days into fixed periods of routine. Now these temporal landmarks had gone; she was alone in the passage, not knowing what hour it was.

But as a good guest she must turn the lights off. Had she left them on in the bathroom? She felt sure she hadn't, but she must make *quite* sure. With extreme reluctance she opened the bathroom door just far enough to peep in.

It was, as she knew it would be, in darkness; but she could still see on the wall facing the bath the last of the lingering image, lit up by its own faint radiance, its phosphorescence, but hardly resembling a face.

Had it been smouldering there all the time, or had it been relit when she opened the door?

What a relief to be back in the passage, under the protection of Count Olmütz, whose presence or whose proximity was to have saved her from these irrational fears! She had had them all her life, but never before had they taken shape, as it were, to her visual eye as they had to Belshazzar's.

When had he arrived? She had seen his shoes, his outsize shoes, when she first ventured on to the landing—prospecting bathwards. Then his door was shut, she could have sworn it; now it was ajar; but under the influence of any strong emotion, especially fear, time ceases to be a timetable.

She almost laughed when she remembered that she had asked Joanna whether she should lock her bedroom door! Some women locked theirs even when there was no threat of a nightly visitant, burglar, marauder, raper, or such-like.

She locked hers, too; but she couldn't lock out the sound from the next room—a sound hard to define—something between a snore, a gurgle, a croak and a gasp. She knew how throaty and bronchial men were, often coughing and clearing their throats and advertising their other physical ailments—a thing which women never did. She had always thought that a snoring husband would be better grounds for divorce than infidelity or desertion or cruelty—though was not snoring itself a form of cruelty?

How ironical that she should have to protect herself from her protector!

Happily she had brought her 'mufflers' with her (being a bad sleeper she dreaded casual or continual noises in the night). She stuffed them into her ears. But they didn't muffle the noise from next door; and suddenly Mildred thought, on her way from her dressing-table to her bed, 'Supposing he should be *ill*?' One thought of a protector as invulnerable to anything, especially to illness; but why should he be? He might have got 'flu or bronchitis or even pneumonia. Perhaps her hostess had put them side by side to protect each other, in that forsaken wing of the house!

However unconventional it was to beard a stranger in his bedroom, she felt she really *must* find out. Conscientiousness was part of her nature. Over-conscientiousness was the cause, together with guilt, of many of her neurotic fears.

Putting on her dressing-gown she went back into the passage. It was again in darkness, but she knew where the switch was.

What should she say to him? How should she explain herself? 'I am sorry to burst in like this, Count, but I heard a noise, and I wondered if you were quite well? Forgive me, I hope I haven't woken you up.' (This would be rather disingenuous, for the only deterrent to an inveterate snorer is to wake him up.) 'Oh, you *are* all right? There's nothing I can do for you? I am *so* glad, goodnight Count Olmütz, goodnight.'

She rehearsed these words, or something like them, under the bright unshadowed bulb in the passage; she made that movement of bodily tension known as 'pulling oneself together' that one often makes before doing something one dislikes. And then she stretched her hand out to push open the door which had been ajar; but it wasn't, it was locked, and no amount of rattling the handle (as if one wanted to break into a lavatory) would open it.

She could have sworn the door had been open, yawning, agape, the last time she crossed the passage; but how often had she crossed it? Fatigue and fear confused her memory; moreover, they confused as such things will her idea of what to do next, or what to do at all. But the stertorous sound, rising and falling as if a body was arguing with itself, came through the locked door plainer than ever.

Back in her bedroom she tried to reason it out. What should she do? Was it any business of hers if her next-door neighbour suffered from bronchial catarrh? Many people, many men at any rate, subside into wheezings when they lie down in bed. It was a sign of age—perhaps Count Olmütz wasn't very young? There was a bell in her room— there were two in fact—close by her bed, one of which said 'Up' and the other 'Down'. 'Up' would be the one to ring: presumably the household staff would be 'up' and not 'down'. But would they be 'up', in another sense of the word, at one o'clock in the morning, and would anyone answer if she did ring? And if some flustered housemaid—supposing there was one—appeared, what would Mildred say? 'The gentleman next door is snoring rather loudly. Can you do anything about it?' It would be too silly.

'Leave it till the morning, leave it till the morning.' She had done her best, and if Count Olmütz chose to lock his door, it was no concern of hers. Perhaps he had decided to lock it against her, as she had once thought of locking it against him.

She got into bed, but insomnia is a relentless watchdog and would not let her sleep. The sounds were growing fainter—the donkey's bray seemed to be petering out, when suddenly it took a new tone—a combination of gurgle, gasp, and choke, which made her jump out of bed. It was then that she saw—and wondered how she could ever have forgotten—the door of partition, the door that divided her room from his.

She switched on her bedside lamp. She had her electric torch with her and she switched it on too. 'More light!' as Goethe said. The key turned in the lock, but was the door locked on the other side too? No, it wasn't; whatever his motives for secrecy, Count Olmütz had forgotten to lock the door on his side.

'I mustn't startle him,' she thought, putting her small hand over the torch's beam; so it was only gradually that she saw, piecemeal, what she afterwards thought she saw—the arm hanging limply down from the bed, the hand trailing the floor, the averted head and the familiar shadow on the wall behind—but with this difference that the gash, or gape, between nose and throat was wider than the fish's gape that she had seen before.

There was no sound. The silence was absolute, until she pierced it with a scream. For the head—the nearly severed head—was not the head of Count Olmütz, whoever he was; it was the head of a man she knew quite well, and whom Joanna knew quite well, in former days. There were all sorts of stories about him, some of which she knew; but she had not heard or thought of him, still less seen him, for a long, long time: not until tonight in fact.

But was it him? Could she be sure, she asked herself as with hands trembling with haste she began to pack her suitcase. A distorted face, with a gash under it, need it be somebody she knew? Recognition isn't an easy problem; on an identification parade could she have picked out a man, with his head thrown back and something blackish trickling down him, as somebody she knew?

No; but she dared not go back to confirm it or deny it.

She seized a sheet of writing-paper from the table at the foot of her bed.

'Darling, I have had to go. A sudden indisposition, 'flu I think, but I don't want to be ill on you, especially as I know you are going abroad next week. Lovely visit.' She hesitated a moment. 'Make my apologies to Count Olmütz.'

Like many women, she travelled light and packed quickly: then looked round to see if she had left anything behind. 'Why, I'm still in my pyjamas!' The discovery made her laugh hysterically. She slipped them off, put on her travelling attire, took a glance at herself in the mirror to see if she was properly arrayed for a long drive in the small hours.

Yes, she would pass; but *was* there anything she had left behind? The torch, the torch! She must have dropped it in her flight from 'the Count's' bedroom and she would need it to find her way through the dark passages, into the hall, out through the front door, on to the drive—left, right? right, left?—to the garage yard.

She couldn't go through these complicated manoeuvres without the torch, feeble as its ray was, and she must have dropped it out of reach behind the door of partition.

Sometimes clutching her suitcase, sometimes letting it drop on to the floor, she debated her next move, until dawn—like a picture frame—peeped behind the edges of the window curtains.

'Oh, damn it,' she said, and unlocked the dividing door.

There was a switch on his side as there was on hers, a device convenient no doubt for clandestine couples. Her fingers found it at once and light broke out, almost exploded from the central chandelier. What would it show? She only wanted to see one thing—her little torch. There it lay, almost at her feet.

She grabbed it, but in spite of herself she couldn't help looking round the room, dreading what she might see. But she saw nothing: nothing to alarm her, only an ordinary bed with the sheet turned back, so bravely, oh! not a crease, not a stain on it, still less a man under it.

'What a fool I am,' she thought, retreating to her room, but not forgetting to re-lock the intervening door or the door into the passage. The house was well supplied with keys. Just as, after a thunderstorm, one feels the weather will be settled for ever, she unpacked again, took out her pyjamas, made the necessary adjustments to her face, and slept peacefully.

The maid who brought her breakfast brought a note with it.

'Dearest Mildred, Do forgive me, but I can't say goodbye for I have to go away early—such a bore. Please ask for anything you want. Love, Joanna.'

*

Mildred called the maid back.

'You don't happen to know where Mrs. Bostock has gone?'

'No, Madam, she doesn't always tell us. I haven't seen her—she just left this note. Shall I draw the curtains, Madam?'

'Yes, please.'

How brave one is by daylight! Finishing her toast and marmalade, thinking how absurd even for someone who professed to be psychic, had been her visions of the night, she got out of bed, didn't bother to put on her dressing-gown, and unlocked the communicating door.

Night flooded in, hitting her in the face; but of course it would be dark for the curtains had not been drawn as hers had; no doubt the housemaid had been told not to call Count Olmütz, who arrived so late and slept so late. It was strange, after the cheerful radiance of her room, to be plunged into darkness again; strange and disquieting.

'Oh, why should I bother?' Mildred asked herself, with an eye on her dismantled suitcase, 'it's no business of mine.'

Curiosity killed the cat. It didn't kill Mildred, although what she saw seemed to have killed two people, if what they had given to each other was the blood that united them in a tangled coil, blood almost as dark and solid as to be snake-like.

Darkness gave way to daylight, and all was in readiness for Mildred's flight. Gratuity in hand, she muttered some words to the butler who had come to fetch her suitcase, words of thanks and words of warning, as casual as she could make them, and as hasty. 'The police, my lady?' asked the butler, wide-eyed. She had no time to disclaim the title but said, 'Well, there is something *dripping* in the room next door; it may be a plumber's job.'

'Very good, my lady, but in my experience, the police come quicker than the plumbers.'

*

'Will the police find anything,' Mildred wondered, 'that I have found or haven't found?'